# PSYCHOHISTORICAL CRISIS

# PSYCHOHISTORICAL CRISIS

## DONALD KINGSBURY

TOR®

A TOM DOHERTY ASSOCIATES BOOK
NEW YORK

PSYCHOHISTORICAL CRISIS

Design by Heidi Eriksen
Edited by David G. Hartwell

A Tor Book
Published by Tom Doherty Associates, LLC
175 Fifth Avenue
New York, NY 10010

www.tor.com

Tor® is a registered trademark of Tom Doherty Associates, LLC.

Library of Congress Cataloging-in-Publication Data

Kingsbury, Donald.
    Psychohistorical crisis / Donald Kingsbury.—1st ed.
        p. cm.
    "A Tom Doherty Associates book."
    ISBN 0-312-86102-8 (acid-free paper)
    1. Memory disorders—Fiction.   2. Brain damage—Fiction.   I. Title.

    PR9199.3.K44226 P77 2001
    813'.54—dc21

                                                    2001041540

First Edition: December 2001

Printed in the United States of America

0   9   8   7   6   5   4   3   2   1

To Viola
who dropped into my life like a song from the stars.

# Acknowledgments

A. E. van Vogt, Isaac Asimov, and Poul Anderson opened up the avid mind of a teenager to the vast reaches of Galactic Empire. Jim Lambek taught me enough mathematics to think about the problems that psychohistory posed. David Hartwell collared me at Readercon and convinced me to take this story off the shelf where it had been moldering. Gregory Benford had useful suggestions for the short version that appeared in his *Far Futures* anthology. While I wrote this longer version David's insights into the craft of novel writing proved invaluable. He also induced me into feeding his cats at Pleasantville, where I might write undistracted—except for his vast collection of books. Moshe Feder took on the hard job of keeping my slow hand moving with comments and suggestions as he watched over my shoulder via e-mail. And bless the unsung heroes in the Tor production group who gracefully taught me the grammar rules my rebellious teenage mind had refused to learn and who managed to find a way to display an impossibly long title. And Tom Doherty for being there and making books like mine possible.

# PSYCHOHISTORICAL CRISIS

# PROLOG

*In all of the more than seven hundred centuries of mankind's recorded inter-stellar wanderings and the more than six hundred centuries since the discovery of the first crude hyperdrives, there have been many regional stellar interreg-nums. But there has been only one galaxy-wide disintegration which leaves us in awe of its breadth and scope. No part of the Galactic Ecumen escaped.*

*The Dark Interregnum between the First and Second Galactic Empires—be-ginning with the Nacreome Revolt in the 12,116th year of the Galactic Era and ending with the Pax Pscholaris of 13,157 GE—is often referred to as the Dismal Intellectual Age but, in fact, was a period of renascent, even unexpected, scien-tific achievement . . . Many centers of . . . notably on the Periphery world of Faraway . . .*

*Introduced by exiled Imperial scientists, the walnut-size atomic power pod revolutionized . . . Faraway's transmutator was a fundamentally new . . . The levitator . . .*

*But the dynamism of Faraway was not the only source of innovation. Dur-ing the last three centuries of the disastrous decline of Splendid Wisdom's twelve millennia of Empire, the list of scientific inventions of non-Imperial and supposedly barbarous . . .*

*. . . the Warlords of sybaritic Lakgan, making an abrupt entrance onto the galactic stage in the fourth century of the Dark Interregnum, disturbed the smooth flow of history . . . while reuniting more than three million stellar sys-tems. It is little realized that the overextended conquests of the False Revival were driven by the achievements of the secluded Crafters of the Thousand Suns Beyond the Helmar Rift who, for centuries, had held a Lakgan contract to dabble in the science of pleasure-center stimulation. Their totally unforeseen develop-ment of a tuned form of the psychic probe, allowing a high-bandwidth linkage*

between the human brain and an exterior transducer, caused a major perturbation in our Founder's Great Plan of Galactic Revival by moving human behavior, en masse, outside of the original parameters of human psychology.

During the early centuries of its debut, the tuned probe's major utility was unappreciated—it was used mainly as a method to control the emotions of one's opponents, notably by the brilliant Warlord Citizen of Lakgan, Cloun-the-Stubborn, who unleashed upon the Galaxy a cadre of minstrels adept at playing a visi-harmonar instrument that controlled and set human motivation. Only gradually did the tuned probe come into use as a tool to access a portable quantum-state device that has come to be known to us as the personal familiar. Today such a linkage with a "fam" seems obvious; a modern man can hardly understand how, for eighty millennia, the unaided mind . . .

Hidden from the tumultuous politics of the Interregnum, a covert group of psychohistorians, whom the Founder left to monitor his work in secret, spent the greater part of the two centuries that followed the Deviation exploring the limits of the tuned probe and integrating its effects into the mathematics of a Revised Plan. This work by the Founder's elite Pscholars eventually became the basis of the Second Empire, which . . .

—From the Interregnum Exhibit at the Bureau of Historical Sciences

# THE 87TH OF CLOVES, 14,810 GE

*In the Long Ago and Far Away, when the first of our mystically inspired ances-
tors rose from their animalhood to grope after civilization, our priests declared
that the Highest Moral Authority commands a man to refrain from murderering
another man. And yet . . . since those misty times, as mankind scattered its
seed among the stars, seeking enlightenment, that very priesthood has always
taken upon itself the onerous task of redefining murder to exclude whatever current methods are being used by the peerage-of-the-moment to kill their fellow
men.*

> —Emperor Ojaisun-the-Adroit, 3231–3245 GE, prior to his execu-
> tion for depraved malthanatostomy by an ambitious daughter, after
> being defeated at Lalaw II

*Eron Osa?* He should at least—at least—be certain of his own name. He spoke the
mental sound. "Eron Osa." He listened carefully to its echo. EErroonn OOssaa.
Until it faded away on a whisper. Eron Osaaaaa . . . He couldn't be sure. The resonance was familiar only in a distant way, as if it was an identity he had used as a
child. Then who was he *now*? He was damned if he was going to ask the robed men
on the podium.

A helmeted court crier announced that it was the 87th watch of the month of
Cloves of the 14,810th year of the Galactic Era, sixteen centuries and fifty-three
years after the establishment of the Second Empire. A court formality.

Such linear facts, unlike his identity, were water-clear in his mind. Physically
he was inside the dermis of invincible Splendid Wisdom, a place he had feared and
sought all his life though he couldn't remember why now that he was here in this
teeming vortex of power whose people were so introverted upon themselves that
they were hardly conscious of their planet's rotation around a sun. The 14,810th

*year*? On Splendid Wisdom the year was merely the time it took for light to travel one league, and a league saw no dawn or sunset and passed through no seasons. For an unreachable moment Eron was a child staring up at the slow rotation of stars through trees somewhere else in the Galaxy. A league was only the cold 16th power of the meter, another unit so ancient that most scholars believed it had been created by the almost mythical Eta Cumingans—though Eron's mindless-mind suspected that it was even more primordial than that and in doing so gave him a stabbing hint of a place he had been—in a fully adult body. But the image was gone before he could resolve it.

All these thoughts were comically inappropriate for a man who was on trial for his life, whose mind was locked up in custody and destined for destruction. Why? For what? It was puzzling. Without his mind, he didn't even understand the charges.

Disorientation was evoking a mad mixture of base fear and astonished awe. He was a dumb animal thrust into captivity. Essentials about the nature of his plight were continually eluding his consciousness while trivial physical details received by his senses struck him in unnaturally splendid ways that distracted from some vital quest. Though he recognized *this* marvelous interior as the revered star chamber of the psychohistorian's Lyceum—maddeningly, he was never able to recall *what* failing had brought him here to judgment—if what was going on *was* a judgment ritual. He was certain that the nobly dressed men in front of him *were* powerful psychohistorians even while their identities were as hard to bethink as his own.

His accusers—yes, they were accusing him—had forcibly sundered him from his quantronic "familiar"—and its absence from the back of his neck left vertiginous gaps in his past that staggered him when he tried to perform mentally—the abilities of his "fam" had been part of his mind ever since he had learned how to hug his father's knees. Did he even remember it being taken? Yet, in spite of mysteries confounding his past, even his recent past, the present remained vivid. The *meaning* of many things eluded him, but the immediacy of color and shape filled the void, astounding his senses.

Baroque balcony-stalls, inlaid with carved wood, bridged the plasteel pillars. The pillars rose up, level after level, until they branched into transverse arches and buttresses that blossomed around stained luminescent splendor. In a planet like Splendid Wisdom, crusted over with city, architecture had gone wild with its interior decor. He recognized the famous Cross of the Arkhein, an artifact of Splendid Wisdom predating the Empire by eighteen millennia. Why should he remember so well those hardy settlers who had carved it but remember little else from more recent history?

Richly surrounded, his famlessness anguished him. When he asked himself simple questions like who had conceived this vast architectural magnificence, his mind received no answer—had the construction predated the Great Sack of Splendid Wisdom? . . . but what *was* this intrusive idea of a devastating Sack? . . . something to do with the Interregnum? . . . but just how long ago had this Interregnum blighted the Galaxy? . . . a century? . . . a millennium? . . . ten millennia? . . . the numbers, the details, wouldn't come. No matter. The chamber was beautiful. Why did he think that those brilliant transparencies up there glowed so unnaturally?

No, no. Avoid these glorious distractions. Focus on the rostrum. Not easy. Though he was *sure* he was understanding most of the words, the *strings* of words themselves seemed to meld into gibberish. Half his thoughts could not be completed because large domains of his mind remained unresponsive. Still, some intents formed clearly. When he concentrated, he could follow the emotional tone of the trial well enough to sense that things were proceeding in an ominous way which he was in no position to control. The strategic mistakes he seemed to have made were evidently lethal. He was at the mercy . . .

On the carved dais sat an ancient machine, quaint, scuffed, now elevated to ceremonial tasks. It had once hummed unobtrusively in a corner of the Founder's office, a nondescript disintegrator for debonding unwanted desktop trivia into constituent atoms. The frustratingly anonymous rulers of this court floated above the rostrum in aerochairs, respectfully girding their machine. Did it serve as their holy executioner?

He felt strongly that he should be able to attach names to the faces of his accusers. He was certain that he had once known them, every one, powerful psychohistorians all. Every face was familiar. But each face—*almost* with a name—flickered beyond the reach of his scrutiny. Were they . . . ?

Probing the past, trying to give it meaning, became too much of a strain and his attention was drawn, in fascination, to the court's formal robes—viridian and safranine silken chasubles embroidered with carnelian symbols. Unexpectedly those symbols reminded him that he was a mathematician—but the mathematics itself was tantalizingly out of reach. It occurred to him that it must be the loss of the *mathematics* that he was regretting with such pain.

A stately Pscholar of the psychohistorians left his chair to stand solemnly beside the Founder's ancient atomizer. He seemed to be the court's spokesman, there to announce the collective will. But when he spoke, it was with the voice of a man who made his decisions independently of counsel. "The matter is settled. Eron Osa . . ."

The defendant went into alert. So Eron Osa *was* his name! It annoyed him that the court knew his name well enough to condemn him but that he did not know theirs to condemn them. Still, it was exciting to hear his name verified. It took away one question mark.

". . . is to be executed by disintegrator—his Doom to be carried out immediately." Evidently this superannuated god liked bare decisions better than any pretty verbal frills of justification that might be attached to them—the old master had no more to say. With a flick of two fingers he called in the bailiffs from the shadows of the balconies and then waited, wearing a long face as he did so. Somehow it was distasteful for him to be personally involved in . . . murder? But his face showed that he was not thinking of it as murder. As . . . cleansing?

The boot-clack of the bailiffs came up behind Eron. A lesser Pscholar on the far end of the rostrum raised his aerochair above the others. He was old, too. He seemed frustrated by the bluntness of the sentence—perhaps preferring a more flowery prelude to execution. "Jars . . ." he began his plea. But the spokesman-judge lifted his hand in a staying motion and the protest went silent. The offending chair sank back to the common level.

Three bailiffs took their prisoner from behind, their arms replacing the damping-field which had been keeping Eron viscously in place.

*Jars.* The thrust of a second recognition elated Eron. It seemed more important to be able to attach a name to this face than to have been sentenced to death. Jars *Hanis,* of course. A First Ranking psychohistorian. Rector. Had he remembered more than the name? How could a final appeal be made to this man? And in a hurry!

The name had the confusing ring of solid friend and mentor—but lately . . . did enemy fit? How could old Jars be his enemy? Struggle as Eron might, the name brought up no real memories of conflict, no rationale for the present situation, only bewilderment. Another damn hole in his mind, information he must once have off-loaded into his fam. Or accessed via a fam index.

When he tried to compose an appeal, no coherent statement formed in his mind.

The bailiffs stripped him of his robes and advanced him up the stairs onto the elaborately carved podium. He offered no resistance. They were armed with neuronic whips; he could go willingly or go paralyzed. He stared implacably at his scourger, with half an eye on the disintegrator. A young Pscholar was supposed to die with dignity, but, at the moment, Eron Osa couldn't even remember what dignity meant.

First Rank psychohistorian Jars Hanis met his gaze with the expressive face of the very experienced who did his duty no matter how great the pain. Eron was not able to read the expression—disdain? fury? triumph? fear of the unknown? It could have been any of these things. Eron's attention was compellingly turned to the leathery fam that Jars had produced in his hand, Eron's fam, the mental wealth of one short lifetime, stolen, still whole. He stared at it, coveting all the precious experiences he no longer remembered.

The First Ranker spoke. "By an infamous act you have violated the conditions of the covenant, Eron Osa, and our duty to mankind calls for us to deal with that offense quickly." Jars' hand flicked through a code-gesture, probably the same one that the Founder had used when in a mood to clear his desk. The ancient disintegrator activated, petals opening. Centered within its bronze maw was a light hardly brighter than the ambient illumination, but moving slowly in chaotic turbulence.

How did one defend oneself against such a machine? Bits of odd information came to Eron's organic mind from the Order of Zenoli Warriors. There was an attack move—kai-un—he could make right now that would *sweep* his leathery fam from Jars' hands (breaking them) while propelling his body into a swinging thrust that would take out the three bailiffs before they could even think about using their neuronic whips. It would be over in half a jiff.

Except . . . even his muddled mind knew that the zenoli reflexes were no longer there, that his muscles were out of training, that zenoli skills required the intercession of a fam. It was weird to be so certain of this; he had no idea when he had last trained or what it meant to be zenoli.

He stood at a moment of entropic no return. All that he valued was about to cease. His wishes did not count . . . yet still, at this last moment, he couldn't resign; he willed time to freeze . . . futilely. The fingers of Jars Hanis continued to move forward, as if holding garbage, then slacked their grip. Eron's eyes attached to his fam as it went spinning down into the maw of the disintegrator. The opal turbulence there erupted into a flash of coruscations—which sank away immediately. In the finality of that flash the resolving capacity of Eron's conscious mind had been degraded by a factor of a hundred. He would *never* be able to awaken from his haze. Never . . .

The petaled maw closed. A whole life's work—uncountable skills, his offloaded memories, the nuances of an active life—all lost to oblivion. And those secret love poems . . . *I'm dead,* thought Eron in shock. They had confined him inside the mind of an animal! *What foolish thing did I do to come to this?* Gone was his vast hoard of associated data, far larger than any organic brain could hold, gone were his quantronic agents, his research staff, his reminders, his organizers. He no longer knew even enough about what he had done to repent for his sins. He couldn't release his eyes from the machine of his death.

Anger, uncontrolled by his fam, was surprising him with its intensity. He needed distracting. While slow tears leaked from the pressure vessel of a monumental rage, he glanced upward again at the glory of a distant ceiling. At least his senses were alive! Other than the rage, his organic mind seemed to be working well, what sluggish little there was of it. Is this what a dog felt like in a viceroy's palace?

He was escorted by the bailiffs through the labyrinthine Lyceum to an obscure room among the laboratories and given plebeian clothes. The room was entirely white. The white was so soft that even corners seemed to blend into the whiteness. A narrow mirror showed a man in his early thirties, and that was the first time he had been able to calibrate his age. The bailiffs withdrew, leaving him with a slight woman in white whom he was tempted to flee—but he noticed the discreet presence of bulbous damping-field generators which she could probably arm faster than he could think. Or else they were built-in roboguards ready to interfere if his actions went beyond certain parameters. The bailiffs had only been for show. The lethal mechanical controls were hidden.

Then he noticed the *tentacled machine*. He had almost missed the calibration and training apparatus—which was also all white; the technician who stood beside the calibrator was unwrapping a fam! Great Space! His judges weren't intending to leave him as a famless cripple? It was a wildly exhilarating hope! A man reduced to the state of an unbalanced landlubber cartwheeling around his arse aboard a buffeted ship in microgravity is grateful for *any* offer that promises him familiar stability. And if it wasn't *his* fam, it was a fam!

The technician seated him in her calibration chair and left him to undergo a spinal scan. When she returned she began to instruct him brightly in the use of this common-issue fam, while checking her holos and asking questions as she made adjustments to the fit. *This* fam contained none of his memories or his hard-earned abilities—but it did hold useful behaviors to guide him within the planetopolis maze; it could provide him with info about government regulations, manage his new pension, or act as an extensive reference library. The library seemed to include a repertoire of behaviors that he surmised wryly might be appropriate for a reformed criminal. A government-issue soul for the executed. It was far from optimal, but it would have to do. Would he be able to upgrade its mathematical abilities?

The room's entrance shutter, behind Eron, silently admitted a second man. Eron remained unaware of the arrival until fingers at his neck were removing his newly adjusted fam. He turned, ready to grab it back. One of the judges. What now? Hope given and hope withdrawn? With a curt phrase the old Pscholar dismissed the technician. He did not elaborate beyond his dismissal, his eyes fixed on the woman until she was out of sight behind the wall's sound barrier. Even then he waited. He turned to Eron. It was a sluggish moment before Eron identified the judge who had made the feeble protest attempt on the rostrum.

"Well, boy, are you able to recognize me? I have to make this visit a quick one. We won't have time to get reacquainted."

"Your face is very familiar. I'm sure we've met."

The grizzled Pscholar snorted. "You were a student of mine when you were in your arrogant twenties—and a good one. You probably can't even remember why you should be sorry you left my protection. I regret that I have been in no position to help you. Even my heaviest guns don't have that kind of range. Let me introduce myself. Hahukum Konn."

The name, and the fierce expression, triggered organic memories that he hadn't been able to access without the mediation of his quantronic fam. "The Admiral-Engineer?" It was a weird memory that *couldn't* be real but one so vivid he couldn't let it go. It was a dream from the dawn of science. Konn wore the blue uniform and thirteen-starred tricorn of an Admiral of Ultimate Sam's Amazing Air Fangs—mercenary fighters of ancient Rith? "I remember—maybe a dream—together we were flying over Girmani in a roaring winged battleship of our own make. You were grinning like a maniac all the way. I can still hear the roar—it went on for hours. When we landed there were cheering crowds of ugly sapiens waving swastikas. I remember the dancing."

"You remember that, do you?" Silently he took out of his pockets some flat photos, shuffled through them, and handed Eron a picture of the two of them beside a preposterous but half-familiar riveted battleship. "Do you remember yourself calling me the Crazy Admiral, not to my face, of course?"

"You had a cook. Magda. She died here on Splendid Wisdom. I remember you reading poetry to your cook."

The Pscholar snorted again. "I sincerely hope you are never going to be able to remember all the stories you used to know about me!" he exclaimed while glancing around to check, again, that they were alone. He opened his robe to poke with his finger at a spy beam suppressor on his belt. "I want no record of our chat. In the meantime are you able to understand me?"

"I admit to a bad case of . . ." Eron searched for the right word. ". . . disorientation."

"Indeed we may have trouble conversing. Ninety-five percent of your vocabulary is gone. However, what's left of it probably covers ninety-five percent of the words used in ordinary speech. If anything I say draws a blank, speak up." Then he put a hand over the utility fam, which he had returned to its position upon the white table. "A warning. This bit of diabolical machinery is *poison*. Accept it gracefully to avoid suspicion—but don't use it!" Konn paused, then repeated himself for emphasis. "Don't use it!"

"I'm supposed to spend the rest of my death famless?"

Eron's obtuse recalcitrance annoyed the old psychohistorian. "You were once a very impetuous young man and had little respect for my excellent advice—mainly because you didn't have the experience to understand it. I *needed* you and you failed me. You aren't in any position to understand my advice now—but *take* it! There are standard memories in that government-issue fam. It holds behaviors that will aid you in building a new life for yourself on Splendid Wisdom. But they'll lead you along a comfortable trail that the old Eron Osa would *not* have wanted you to take."

"I've *got* to have a fam, even if it is standard issue."

"Stubborn to the core! You only *need* one because you are addicted to a test rating in the thousands. Why are you so sure you can't function without? Because everyone else has one? Because you've never been smart enough to disconnect from your fam and exercise your naked brain to keep it animal-sharp? Do you need a fam? It depends upon *where* you have to function. If you travel in space, you need a spacesuit—but your body can stay alive quite nicely without a spacesuit if you confine yourself to the surface of a habitable planet. That late model of body you inhabit has almost two hundred thousand years of testing built into it; your organic *parts* have been tested to destruction billions of times and refined for millions of years, many for hundreds of millions of years.

"Now look at this fam *thing*. It was only invented, in its first crude form, during the Dark Interregnum. Men *just as incompetent and as confused as you are right now* were able to build the First Galactic Empire over a period of ten millennia and, for another two, hold it together under a government that spanned the spiral arms. What makes you think you've *got* to have a fam?"

"I'm a psychohistorian," Eron whispered.

A flicker between pity and anger crossed Hahukum's eyes. "Eron Osa. *Under-*

*stand this.* You are *through* as a psychohistorian. *Through.* Build a new career. As artist. As street clown. Your genius was part of the fam you grew attached to as a child. It was a symbiosis. It's *gone.* Your organic brain is probably one of the finest mathematical talents in the Galaxy—certainly the equal of our Founder's—but, *famless,* it probably has only three to five percent of the capacity it wielded only a few watches ago. And yes, the Founder *was* a famless psychohistorian," Konn added, enjoying his backhanded putdown of a man they all revered. It was Konn's pointed way of emphasizing how far psychohistory had come since its pauper beginnings.

Eron wasn't ready to let another fam get out of his grasp; his arm almost twitched as he prepared to sneak it to a less visible place. Hahukum noticed and gripped Eron's hand, easing it away from temptation. "Don't even think about it, boy. All fams aren't the same. Would you marry your parole officer? Bide your time. A *good* fam is worth waiting for. Meanwhile search out some of the old mental disciplines. You need a bout of mental calisthenics. From what I can deduce of your past month's performance, your organic brain has gone shockingly flabby—or you would never have permitted yourself this mess."

"What was my crime?" asked Eron, desperate to know.

Again the Admiral ripped out his snort. "*I'll* never tell you. I'm just as afraid as Hanis that you'll do it all over again—even minus your quantronic thumbs. Information in a fam-neural system is distributed in some ways like a hologram, and so an enormous amount of that which was stored in your fam will have degraded representations in your organic brain. You'll regain pieces of it—and tantalizing hints of the rest. My certainty is that you'll never be able to re-create all that you were. Too much is missing . . . I hope."

It was infuriating to be condemned yet not allowed the knowledge to repent! What had he done! Again rage staggered Eron, even as he knew rage was unlike his normal self. "Kill me then! Kill me like you killed my fam!"

The blast of emotion caused the Admiral's defenses to trigger his personal force-shield; he had to smile while deactivating it. "But killing you wouldn't help"— he sighed—"any more than vaporizing your *fam* has helped. Jars Hanis is as wrong as a man can be. Psychohistorical crises aren't precipitated by the actions of one man. *This* historical crisis began in the quiet of the interstellar night *long* before you were born. It does not depend upon you to proceed. Jars is a creature of the suns. My nightly vision sees the ghosts of future events centuries beyond his range." Scorn. "If you'd worked with me, you would have been part of the solution." Regret. "You wanted to be part of the problem." Anger. "It's too late now for either. You're out of the game." Resignation. "And damn it, I could have used you. In my futile fantasies I travel back in time and discover you when you were a twelve-year-old hothead and offer you a fabulous scholarship—under *my* guidance."

"Did you know me back then?" asked Eron with an eager curiosity.

"When you were unspoiled and empty-headed? No," said Konn wryly. "I tested a few ideas in the Ulmat Constellation during your youth and so chance might have put us together then—but it didn't. It's a big Galaxy. Maybe even *I* couldn't have saved you."

"I can save myself." From where his defiance came, he did not know. It seemed to be an integral part of his personality. "I'm going to reestablish myself as a psychohistorian."

"No." The negative wasn't a refusal; it was just sadness and a sigh. "No, you're not. Forget it!"

"Were you my friend?"

"More than you ever knew."

Overwhelming grief. "Help me. I have to start somewhere." Eron was suddenly bawling and it shocked him, to be shaking like that, real tears running down a convulsing face. He had expected his fam to modulate his grief, and again his fam wasn't there. How *weird* to be an animal. "There must . . ." he said between sobs ". . . be something . . ." he took a breath ". . . I can do."

Hahukum didn't have the heart to discourage the boy with more good advice. He didn't know what to do or say. He pulled out a small printed book that he often carried with him.

"Try this. You were fond of books when I knew you. I often read this one when I'm fam-disconnected. Exercise for the raw brain. Makes it work. Takes me back to my animal roots. Dissociation is not popular but my belief has always been that disconnecting from one's fam is healthy once in a while. I do it regularly." He grinned. "Of course, maybe I'm just getting ready to survive the time when Hanis gets to do to me what he did to you." Eron did not take the book and so Konn pressed it into his hands. "I'm serious. Read it."

"With my eyes?" The tears were gone as quickly as they had come. He had gone from grief to being appalled.

"You're expecting to download?" asked Hahukum sarcastically.

Eron stared at the slim book. He was used to scanning them in with his fam; it was hundreds of times faster that way. The book wore a gold title in an obsolete typeface. *Selected Essays by the Founder.* Eron was shocked by how difficult it was to read even that much.

"People quote the Master a lot," said Konn wryly. "They talk about him in grand terms—but they never read him. Obsolete. But I like his stuff." He waited until he had caught Eron's direct gaze. "I've always been impressed by how much our Founder did with so little. Pretty good stuff for a mere famless mind." He held Eron's gaze commandingly. It was his way of giving Eron hope, though he had none himself. The Founder, famless, *had* taught himself psychohistory.

"Thanks. I wish I could remember having worked with you."

"My mother gave me the book a long, long time ago. Down in the nether worlds." He pointed at his feet, referring to the lower depths of Splendid Wisdom. "She was barely making grade as a tax clerk. She wanted *me* to be somebody. Mothers are like that." He smiled wistfully. "Fathers, too."

## 2

# IN THE LAIR OF THE ADMIRAL,
# 14,790 GE

*"Death haunts an Emperor as he grows wise in mind and feeble in body. Haunted he seeks a kingly son out among this starry expanse of suns—where there are no sons."*

> —Soliloquy of the Emperor Maximoy-the-Polite, from Act 3 of Valodian's last play, *The Twilight of an Emperor.* Valodian is credited with reviving the tradition of the Lament as it was perfected in the 98th century GE.

When Eron Osa was twelve years old and the Founder had been dead for more than twenty-seven centuries, "Admiral" Hahukum Konn was already a feisty eighty-three. For decades he had been trolling the ocean of galactic space in search of the Second Empire's mysterious adversary whose shadow self skulked through his ocean of numbers. This year he had a first nibble, but wasn't sure the fish (or the flotsam) was still hooked. The Ulmat Constellation seemed to be the first of the anomalous regions to have reacted to one of his discrete probes.

He paced patiently to and fro across the shining floor of "Hahukum's Bridge" waiting for his then most valuable student to arrive—Nejirt Kambu was brilliant, a possible successor, often late for appointments. But the "Admiral" never waited or paced with an idle mind; now his attention bided the time by focusing itself on the needs of his wounded battleship.

Behind sleeping forcefield spires, the colossal warship brooded in defiance of its terrible dismemberment, a black and skinless superstructure of spars and ribs and breakup-bulkheads—still breathing—as if being stripped, exposed, and flayed had not yet brought defeat, only the readiness to strike out with one last deadly flash at anyone from the stars who dared to attack.

Beyond was the panorama of a mottled planet under siege.

The Horezkor was a major warship of the Middle Empire period, produced in minor quantities, the first one being commissioned in the year 5517 GE. Almost three thousand were built during that century, many serving well beyond normal retirement age.

"The Mad Admiral" had been working with pleasure on this unfinished model of the ancient Imperial dreadnought. The Horezkor dominated the ebony hover-space above the bridge's workshop table. So formidable was this vast war-machine that it cast upon Konn an unreal aura, as if he were a giant placed among the stars. One might hardly notice that both ship and man were embedded in a vast scholarly maze deep inside the Lyceum metropolis where students were apprenticed to the psychohistorians of Splendid Wisdom's Second Empire, a Lyceum itself embedded in a planetary city that regulated the commerce and life of the Galaxy.

Konn's imposing title was the awesome one of Second Rank Pscholar in a commanding meritocracy that defined only one higher level. "Second" rankled him, and, from dread of his displeasure, he was more often called "Admiral" than "Second"—even though he had never held a military commission at any time in his long life. Only his enemies called him "Second." He loved his hobby because it rested him from the deadly game of galactic sleuth. The history of military vehicles was so much simpler than tracking down a coming psychohistorical crisis.

He wore simple naval uniforms—but deliberately chose them from a selection several eons out of date to fend off complaints by backbone-stiff naval regulars who felt in their staid hearts that the impersonation of a naval officer ought to be a capital crime. His skull was shaved in curious planter-rows of tuft and skin-shine, the legendary style of Kambal-the-First whose cabal of renegade ships had first conquered this planet of the central galactic glitter when it had been a minor world of farmers and tradesmen quietly innocent of their strategic location and meritorious climate. The gulfs of space had once been a moat that protected the castle planets of civilization. By Kambal's time, the central galactic bulge was swarming with shipwise nomadic "barbarians" hungering for a better place to live than the desolate homeworlds settled by their unfortunate ancestors. Kambal was the archetype of an admiral.

After a lifetime of looking, Konn had been able to collect only a few mementos of the Horezkor might of the sixth millennium, notably several precious photos of the warcraft's immense interior by the warrior-mistress of Emperor Daigin-the-Jaw. The relevant design files for the ship had vanished from naval archives somewhen in the last nine millennia, perhaps destroyed during the Great Sack of Splendid Wisdom in the dark years, perhaps the victim of housecleaning.

But now he had everything he needed for a full reconstruction. It had happened suddenly after years of frustration. To the delight of Hahukum Konn, his protégé, Nejirt, had reported back to Splendid Wisdom from his evaluation assignment in the obscure Ulmat Constellation with a grin on his face and (in his diplomatic pouch) working assembly virtuals evidently used to refurbish at least two of the legendary Horezkor dreadnoughts during the warlord period of the Interregnum. Of course it didn't really matter if they ever got the model put together or not.

What really mattered, and Hahukum knew it, was the stability of the Second Empire in an era of subtle cultural complexification which made the old equations work slightly differently than they had in the past. The future was always branching, branching, branching—and there were more branches in this golden age than there had ever been before, some of them dangerous. Hahukum's thoughts of the past mingled with his thoughts of present concerns. He could trust Nejirt to find for him the plans of an old battleship, but how far could he trust Nejirt to pick those futures for mankind that would keep the soul of the race alive?

There was an unfortunate conservatism in this twenty-five-year-old boy. Rigidity? It was a worry. He always had potatoes with whatever he ate. He listened only to music that had a beat. Not that Konn wasn't a conservative himself. The trick was in what you conserved. All successful radicals built their careers on a very carefully chosen foundation. The mathematical system of the Founder wasn't a public info-machine that automatically answered questions it already had on file; psychohistory was an instrument that had to be strummed by a musician.

One had to listen for, and pick out, futures as well as predict them.

A good psychohistorian was as much a composer as he was a seer. Rigid musicians made bad music. Could Nejirt tell the difference between the traditions that actually buttressed the foundations of society and the thousands of trivial traditions, mere baroque decorations? Would he listen to beatless music and hear nonmusic?

While the Admiral worked on his battleship model, his mind played with subversive scenarios of galactic politics. About trouble. About longings for action. It wasn't enough to be intuitively sensitive to the subtle susurrous of dark hints unnoticed by ordinary ears like those of Jars Hanis. It wasn't enough to be able to hear the rustle of armed malefactors somewhere out there in the jungle of stars. The kind of impalpable sensitivity that Konn was so proud of in himself was certainly the mark of genius—but, as his enemies were quick to point out, it was also the mark of the superstitious fool and the mark of the wacky paranoid. He needed evidence more confrontable than subversion masquerading in the open as background noise.

Damn it, he needed to be on the bridge of a modern Horzekor fighting an enemy he could get his teeth into.

There was much to be said for sitting at a comfortable desk within a handwave of the most powerful simulators in the Galaxy while statistically filtering the data arriving via Splendid Wisdom's pervasive stellar bureaucracy—but *seeing* a villain emerge as an unexpected pattern in false color overlays and *slashing* such a villain in the flesh were two different things; in the end there would be no escaping the plunge into that tenebrous galactic maelstrom out there and returning with his culprits on a sling.

But he needed bodies, plots, the location of bases. He needed his hands on an enemy agent who could be questioned at length. He needed loyal soldiers brilliant enough to do his dirty work.

Not easy. Konn had long ago learned that to get results he often had to act without authorization. That made his work more difficult. He had no allies. The others—that grandiose Hanis—were all tramping down the path of greatest probability—the easy way to go that led who knew where. The most probable of futures could suddenly branch into a thousand pathways flying by too swiftly for deliberate mathematical choice. For twenty-seven centuries the psychohistorians had ruled, and they all seemed to think this had earned them an eternal ride.

The whole of the Pscholarly collective adamantly believed there were *no* mysterious adversaries; they denied Konn's analysis, unable to believe that the foundation of a crisis was already under construction—shouldn't the Founder's mathematics be predicting it?

The Admiral cursed as he attached a part to his model and it fell off. Every generation had to relearn that its map of the universe was only a map, that no map contains all the details. For years, Konn was turning up contradictions that the Founder's model couldn't account for—bizarre tiny effects drowned by the brilliance of the main model of psychohistory. The anomalies were so slim that even Konn had his doubts. Doubt didn't deter him. To follow the course of rightness one has to be willing to be wrong. Those who were most certain of their rightness had the highest probability of being wrong.

Would he dare deputize Nejirt for an unauthorized and dangerous ferreting mission? That was the question he was mulling at the back of his mind. Damn, but that boy was late. He picked up the fallen part with his microwaldo and repositioned it.

The Horezkor warship was an astonishing joy to rebuild. There were distinct advantages to being a powerful psychohistorian with spiderlike access to any part of the governed Galaxy! He could, even without majority consent, send out talented boys, anywhere, to carry out his desires. If he put these boys to serving the interests of his hobby, well, he could always say that he was "giving them valuable research experience." With alert students like Nejirt pandering shamelessly for him, life lost part of its deadly seriousness, sometimes even becoming amusing. Power was always limited, but earned power was still *power*. From the very earliest months of his rule-confined youth, deep down in Splendid's bedrock warrens, Hahukum had known how to use and abuse power without crossing the fatal line of self-destruction.

He admired the half-completed dreadnought smugly. Nejirt *had* been indispensable. If this youth could be so brilliant at espionage when success didn't matter, perhaps he *was* the ferret Konn could trust for the big job.

This ship was such a find! Manipulators inserted a tiny bulkhead hatch. What a story! Dark Age brigands had plundered two colossal Horezkors from an abandoned Imperial Space Museum of an earlier age. The pirates had acted on commission from the warlords of a vanished kingdom called the Thrall of the Mighty. Priceless loot! Such ingenious scavengers, those Interregnum cutthroats! There seemed to be no record of the final fate of the two dreadnoughts—lost in the internecine battles of a violent age—but a third hull, ransacked for spare parts and thereby crippled, stoically rode on display at the Ulmat's central hyperspace terminal in the Mowist System in the Ulmat, the last remains of a naval memorial to a fearsome emperor.

The model's savaged bridge was exposed to the depredations of Konn's tweezers. Piping hung loose as if teased aside by a robosurgeon's expert scalpel. From the workbench Konn stared at his creation, contemplating his next addition. He sat relaxed in a frozen pose with a cup of mint tea in one hand and a miniature hyperatomic motor in the other, his fingers doodling with its brilliant red and silver surface. The goggles of the microwaldo manipulator perched above his eyebrows. Skintight control gloves for the waldo, yellow, lay flopped across the weapons rigging.

This was the mock-up of a warship so vast that even scaled to the length of two tall men, it had to be toured by miniature camera. Konn was deciding whether a virtual diagram would help him during the next stage of the restoration. Any tridim or cutaway or exploded view that he might need could be evoked from the wall emitters by the mnemonifiers.

How could he best use Nejirt Kambu while hiding his purpose from Jars? He put that extraneous thought aside to concentrate on an immediate assembly problem.

Though intended for psychohistorical inquiry, the workshop's mnemonifiers had been blatantly loaded with arcane files of naval architectonics. It was another misuse of power, but a powerful psychohistorian was allowed his harmless foibles. His interest went as far back into the mists of time as hand could reach, to the confusing ocean, air, and space vessels of the prehyperflight cultures of the Sirius Sector who seemed to have enviously adopted and mixed each other's histories in order to claim the role as the original forebears of galactic mankind.

When the workshop walls weren't in use to display the inner guts of eighty millennia of warcraft, they played fanfare to the Admiral's spirits by championing the deeds and valor of the recent but bygone Empire. Konn enjoyed this chance to exhibit the masterpieces from his hoard of military art. All his life he had been culling through the long tradition of a bureaucracy that had obsessively commissioned panoramic spectacles to glorify the exploits of Imperial Grandeur. Some of it had survived the Sack.

Behind the model Horezkor, to complete the illusion of awesome might, a surround screen radiated with the somber depths of an ancient artist's vision: larger than life, a Middle Empire fleet—each ship emblazoned with the feared Stars&Ship—was palpably engrossed in its patrol over a pastel planet unruffled by signs of the fury which mankind's fiercest navy had been able to drop upon it. The artist was a master of the kind of double-meanings that can be slipped past an arrogant Emperor. In his ironic vision, the Imperial Navy had been shrunk down to a mere swarm of insectoids whose annoying bites on the vast world below could be discerned only by a viewer's most careful scrutiny.

Nejirt arrived late, stepping through the workshop's airseal shutter, but not uncomfortably late, and Konn showed off the newest details of the miniature dreadnought to his student, without whom the reconstruction would be nowhere. The meeting began with polite conversation. "I have the bridge well blocked out and accurately, too, I think—it should even stand up to a zoomscan—but I'm going to have trouble with armament. The Thrall of the Mighty wasn't able to arm the Horezkors to more than a fifth of normal weaponry, so I have some blanks to fill in. Otherwise I'm in shipyard paradise."

Nejirt seemed glad to postpone what he knew was going to turn into an intellectual sparring match of major proportions. He noticed in Konn's hand the red and silver replica of the ship's huge hyperatomic motor. "Nice motor. You're sure of those? The hulk at Mowist that I saw has long been stripped of its motors. They have pretty fakes installed, but ones I wouldn't trust for authenticity."

"Ah, but remember that I multisource my data! Look at this!" The larger-than-life panorama of the planetary siege winked out. It was replaced by a virtual training demo from the Middle Empire period. A guild technician's inspection tour now rolled tridimensionally across the wall, zooming in for close-ups of every possible repair of a bulky hyperfield generator, a behemoth when compared with the elegant designs that had begun to appear during the Interregnum.

Discussing ancient warships wasn't the real business on the agenda. Hahukum Konn began to search for a way to break off his fun and get on with the serious tasks. He put his tools aside and washed his hands in the sprayer while he continued the irrelevant small talk.

The students of the Lyceum knew him as a queer soul, and he suspected that he was not always liked—they looked askance at the political wars he waged within the Fellowship—First Rank Jars Hanis was constantly at loggerheads with him—but he had earned his Second Rank status honestly via an uncanny ability to extract significant morsels out of almost noise-level data. His sifting skill with raw input had earned him subtle immunities, and he used immunity to violate custom whenever he damn well felt like it. He knew Nejirt was in awe of him. He was quite willing to exploit that awe.

What to do?

Decisions! He was faced with a promising acolyte who had spent a year knocking about the Ulmat and whose maturity required careful assessment before he could be considered for any more critical assignment. Konn was not a man who trusted, on faith, a student fresh out of the Lyceum's top institute, not even one who came with the highest recommendations, not even one who brought him delightful gifts—*especially* not when a henchman of Jars Hanis had been on his examination board. Nejirt was still only a promise in spite of all the formidable course work he had done. It was a delicate matter. There was grilling to be done.

Perhaps he should delay. He could soften Nejirt by inviting him for this evening's dog hunt through the wilderness tunnels—but the dogs would be a distraction. There seemed to be no avoiding an arena duel across a stage of high-powered analytical tools.

Konn finished washing his hands only after his meditations had taken the suds all the way up to the elbows. "Glad you came at my call. I've famfed your report." He meant that he had scanned the boy's report directly into his familiar, bypassing his eyes. "I've had time to think about it." By which he meant that his quantronically sentient fam had done most of the work of assimilating the contents for his dual-brain. "We need to review some points together. I've set up a room for us."

"Yes, sir."

The young Pscholar followed his older mentor out onto a mezzanine looking down on the Lyceum's great yard, which was sometimes used for rallies but more often used to stage spectacular displays. Its four-story-tall illusions were controlled by a hundred million computers, awesome when the lights were dimmed and, say, the whole galactic spiral was on display. At the moment, they had no need for that kind of tool. They disappeared down a ramp into the maze of the operations complex, Konn's territory, his hub, his neuron with its dendritic reach out into the stellar cortex of the civilization of man.

It was a short walk from there to an augmented sanctum off one of the neutral corridors. The two psychohistorians took a moment to tune their fams into a slice of the Lyceum's main computer mind. Konn called up the relevant reports into a virtual carousel for easy access. "Grab a seat," he said over his shoulder while selecting the equipment he wanted. Five chairs surrounded a small amphitheater, and the Seventh Rank youth slipped into the nearest. Illumination faded to dark.

The emplacement had the tense feel of a battle station; Hahukum Konn was, himself, fond of fantasizing this tiny arena into the fantasy turret of an imaginary Second Empire warship—one with magical hypersight that could zoom anywhere and weapons whose persuasive range was galactic—but he kept his silly whimsy to himself. He activated the projector. Above the central bowl appeared a holo summary of the Ulmat operation. Either of them had the option of superimposing their comments as a fam-generated overlay.

In the lull that followed the holo bloom, Konn watched Nejirt cautiously analyze what had been done to his numbers. There was a strongly implied criticism of his work buried in Hahukum Konn's compact summary. The young psychohistorian settled into a solid defensive posture and waited patiently for Konn to initiate the first sortie. When the Admiral waited him out, the boy spoke, apparently only to break the silence, for his voice was bland, hardly listening to what he was saying, mind focused on the display, storing up answers for the debate to come. "It was a lively field study you handed me, far more fascinating than any of those stereotypical cases we slaved over in sim."

"The Ulmat Constellation may be a mere field study to you," Konn began gently, "but *I* see it as a brewing disaster in a kettle. The site needs attention—even attack—now, *long* before it goes critical. I'll tell you what's bothering me. I'm not clear about your inference on the resonant pumping. You don't seem to take the buildup toward crisis seriously. I've seen similar patterns of crisis in many different places. Please explain."

Konn was referring to the odd psychosocial interactions he had long detected between the Ulmat worlds, deadly pushes and pulls that were feeding on each other and seemed to lead with a high probability to what the Pscholars called a topozone crossing. In layman's language that meant a region where the time-constant for reliable prediction became short—the Ulmat was moving into prophecy-shadow, a flash of historical turbulence that would temporarily blind psychohistory's prescient eye.

Nejirt was unperturbed, even amused by Konn's concern. He spoke politely. "I made extensive use of the Hasef-Im test. The resonance has passed its maximum and has even been decoupled." He communicated some mathematics directly through fam interchange, all of it too compact and modern for an old hand like Konn to grasp. "Consequently it isn't liable to recur for centuries. The disturbance seems to have moved into a damped phase." The tense young Pscholar accented his words by adding dashes of color to the holograph that hovered between them. Irrelevant—but pleasant formatting. Second Raters loved their formatting.

*He's trying to snow me,* grumbled Konn to himself, wishing that these freshmen would at least attempt to talk less like pendants. The Admiral had never heard of the Hasef-Im test. Another damn thing he was going to have to blot up to keep abreast of these damn kids! He wasn't rattled; the test was probably one of those arty-smarty things that saved students from boiling their own coffee so that they'd have more time for drinking. More power to them. What he did notice was that Nejirt was wary of him and not willing to talk outside of his orthodox report. Not good. It spoke of a mind unable to explore beyond the safety of preestablished umbilicals.

Konn was blunt. "Damping? It doesn't look like brakes to me. Maybe, but I'd be damn careful before I believed it. I check and double-check *everything* that has a bad consequence. I picked up the Ulmat effect ten years ago when no one else saw it. And we only began to apply decoupling efforts three years ago, my shot. I'd prefer to *clobber* a perturbation that dangerous when its snorkel is just peeking above the noise level, but standard operations call for countermeasures with minimal visibility. I'm outvoted and I agree that's probably for the best. But here you are seriously suggesting that these *gentle* countermeasures have been effective *already*? All we've done so far in the Ulmat is start a five-man news group and an aggressive local cut-rate hypertrip service—it should be another decade before we can even *measure* our tampering!"

"I haven't claimed that the countermeasures have been effective at all—I agree, not enough time—I think the damping is a normal chaos intrusion. The Ulmat perturbation just fizzled. That's normal. Most perturbations do fizzle."

"I'm not sure we even know what's been *driving* the perturbation," grumbled Konn.

Nejirt Kambu tried to hide a smile. "You suspect a conspiracy?"

"We do not *need* a conspiracy to account for the disturbance." The "Crazy Admiral" was used to needling and never lost his temper. Konn was chided widely for his conspiracy theories. Jars Hanis and his crowd even made a regular issue of it. "There's an old saying that if you kiss a girl on Ixno you can start a chain of events that leads to violent revolution on Splendid Wisdom—it would be easy to assume that the whole Ulmat perturbation began with something as innocent as a kiss. Then the situation is not dangerous at all." Konn couldn't resist a note of sarcasm. "Then even a *novice* like you could handle it." He paused for emphasis. "But if it *were* a conspiracy . . ."

"Highly improbable," said Nejirt indulgently. What he meant was *impossible*. "You know that."

*I do, do I?* What Konn hadn't told Nejirt Kambu was that the recently conceived Ulmat correctives were *designed* on the assumption that there *was* a conspiracy. A bluff, of course, but sometimes, when one took a shot in the dark at the sound of a twig snapping, one was rewarded with the discreetly muffled flight of surprised feet. That was, in itself, more information than could ever be deduced from the mere snapping of a twig. "Just for the sake of argument suppose someone *was* deliberately trying to move the Ulmat beyond the sight of all Pscholars in order to create a staging area for a major revolt."

Nejirt's polite amusement remained. "That someone would be so ineffective that we wouldn't even notice. The deviation from normal fluctuation wouldn't be measurable."

"Oh? Because . . . ?"

"Sir, you are trying to force me to say that the interference *could* be measurable because your conspirator *could* be utilizing some crude form of psychohistorical manipulation?"

"Indulge me."

The boy backstepped. No traps for him. "The Founder set up Faraway so that as it developed politically the Pscholars could . . ."

". . . could do what we have done," rumbled an annoyed Konn. "Set up a stable political climate in which the leadership of Splendid Wisdom is accepted because it is effective. We predict disasters and prevent them. I admit we are good at it, especially me. List me some disasters."

Nejirt laughed at an obviously rhetorical request.

The Admiral ground on. "Let's skip over mundane calamities and the ones we handle after the fact by managing their consequences. Let's talk about a real upheaval—somebody confronting us with our own mathematics. Do you really expect that our methods will *never* be duplicated? Knowing what *we* expect to happen, they could counter us."

"But if they were *that* good, they would come to the same conclusions we do and implement the same solutions. Converging technology. After seventy thousand years don't all aircraft have the same optimal forms? There would be a period of discord, then the two groups would merge."

Konn was furious but did not challenge; he nodded in concession. It was not agreement he felt. What he was concluding pained him—his mind had filled with an abrupt decision *not* to work with this brilliant young man in whom he had placed so much hope. He was bitterly disappointed. *He is not my son.* How many well-trained blind conservatives could the Lyceum graduate in one year? Too damn many.

Still, Hahukum Konn *couldn't* have forced the discussion further even had he wanted to. The Admiral was an intuitive thinker, not a verbal one. The boy he disagreed with was right by all the symbolic arguments known to Konn. They had been through the same school and forged from the same curriculum, and, aside from a different level of maturity, they thought with the same words. Certainly the Founder had established the central result rather definitively.

The overwhelming probability was that any infant group trying to duplicate the modus operandi of psychohistory would be subsumed by the parent body, the amalgamation being driven by self-interest. If two organizations were practicing psychohistory independently, their forecasts would countermand each other and thus become useless. What could be the incentive for mastering a very difficult subject only to choose to use it in a way that made it ineffective?

If everyone were free to choose a different future for mankind, the tug-of-war would ensure the realization of *nobody's* future—all freedom would be lost in gridlock and all men would become the slaves of chaos. Total freedom creates the ultimate dungeon. Whenever a man decides to expand his degrees of freedom by doing something really sassy, like taking up residence in a sunspot, he is soon locked into a situation in which he has no degrees of freedom at all. There are *always* boundaries to freedom.

The Founder had chosen to pursue a political system that defined near-optimal boundaries. Then he had gone on to create a society that maximized general freedoms by eliminating foolish futures. He had never pretended that this was to be done by fatalizing the lives of individual men—any more than an engineer would try to force a deterministic path on each atom passing through an optimized heat engine.

The Founder's proof that only a single psychohistory would evolve (as a single physics had long ago evolved) was lengthy and tortured, but it had been refined by twenty-seven centuries of polishing. Konn of the Second Rank had been over the proof personally and whatever flaw it might contain, he was not the mathematician to find it—he was no theoretician; his talent was a nose that quivered when data smelled slightly different than theory tasted.

Long ago Konn had accepted the whole thesis that within the political system created by the Founder, it was impossible for any group out there among the stars to duplicate psychohistory. He would have said that the work of the Pscholars during the Interregnum had *made* it impossible. Even now his best logic yielded the Founder's scenario. But such traditional reasoning no longer moved him. Hahukum Konn had worked his way up from Splendid's bedrock to Second Rank by never taking *anything* for granted. His eighty-three years had taught him to be a man of iron principle. He never, never finagled data to fit theory. And the data . . .

The data contradicted the Founder!

What disturbed Konn was that the Ulmat wasn't the only anomaly. There were many more. There were fully *thirty-seven* perturbations he couldn't account for to his liking. In a Galaxy of a hundred quadrillion humans, it was hardly surprising that some locations resisted the long-term direction of the Pscholars' Fellowship. Yes, chance alone *could* be responsible. But psychohistory, a gambler who owned the house, had ages ago mastered the herding of chance. (Even the weather on Splendid Wisdom was managed by the deft application of manageable forces: evaporation towers, control of atmospheric perfluorocarbons, etc.) That made these thirty-seven trouble spots peculiar; for more than a century they had been maverick. It was as if the weather had developed its own goals and cunning. Meteorologists have no equations for intelligent weather.

Mindless and unminded chaos will lunge out of its masking cover at unpredictable times to wipe out the finest forecast of man and computer, creating vast regions of turbulent history requiring the finest of the Pscholars' resources to calm. The Second Empire depended upon the vigilance and eye of men like Hahukum Konn for its very survival; he was one of those patient predators who scanned the Cimmerian borders of predictability with a cat's green eye. And he was afraid that they were now facing a chaos which had evolved enough intelligence to oppose psychohistory. That was a chilling thought. Evil is no ally of morality. Evil would be willing to destroy the whole of the stability that the Founder had achieved.

Konn found that he was recording Nejirt's measured speeches but was no longer listening to them.

The seriousness of the circumstances demanded that the Admiral choose his hunting dogs prudently. His standards were not going to permit Nejirt to become his trusted aide. Despair! Nejirt was the *fifth* promising student he'd had to reject. Whom could he rely on? Who was there to use in the field?

Perhaps he'd have to go outside of the Lyceum. Catch them young, like the navy did. There were a thousand academies out among the reaches, pretraining aspiring psychohistorians. Take some youths, early, and shape their outlook years before the conservatives got to them. An Admiral's cadre! He grumbled at the unlikeliness of it. Maybe. Desperate times brought desperate measures.

Nejirt was a little upset, beginning to repeat himself in the way people will when they feel they no longer have an audience. Konn was a kind man; it was no use berating an acolyte for failing to meet high expectations. Use him for what he did well and let it go. Konn refocused. "Well, we've sharpened our wits on each other to the point where I'm very hungry. I know a place where we can sharpen our knives on roast pig. You haven't said a word about your girlfriend yet. Last time you couldn't stop talking about her. And when my belly is full you can clue me in on this Hasef-Im newfangle about which I know nothing."

It was Nejirt's sleep-watch and so he went home to bed after a pleasant dinner and stroll on the Balasante Concourse with his mentor, but it was prime-watch for Konn—he was only beginning his "day." He chose the rigor of the hunt to cool down his brain but never really stopped thinking about his student. During the yapping of the dogs through his Club's meticulously groomed hydroponic wilderness he took the time to think up a promising dead-end job for his protégé—a job that needed to be executed with great competence but one that did not require more talent than Nejirt possessed. The *thirty million* star systems to be monitored had plenty of places for boys like Nejirt.

Thirty million was a comforting number. Those thirty million systems surely contained at least *one boy* who could be molded into a master sleuth.

Konn's favorite dog, big-eared and black-spotted, trotted up and rose to his haunches, two succulent gessem in his jaw, one with a broken wing. Using his long gengineered fingers he handed the fat, bald cave-flyers to his human before settling back on his knuckles. Konn bagged the birds, patting his assistant on the head, "Atta boy, Rhaver!" and began to unholster the beast's stun gun. "ICanDoItMyself," grumbled the dog in a throaty dog accent that only dog lovers can understand. Konn smiled. The dog understood the smile as permission to take over the unstrapping of his weapon. He struck a pose of importance.

It wasn't impossible that someday Konn might hunt down a boy instead of cave-flying gessem. He would train the boy to be his prize hunter, as he had trained Rhaver. How could he let the Lyceum continue to deliver him mere wolves? "Does hunting please you, Rhaver?" Rhaver thumped his tail against the ground and licked the bejeweled rings on his tree-climbing fingers before swirling around to try to catch the itch on his tail.

*Ah,* thought the psychohistorian, *if only dogs had been bred for brains as well as for hunting prowess!*

# 3

## THE TWELVE-YEAR-OLD SON
## OF THE ADJUDICATOR, 14,790 GE

*Agander developed in a difficult location nested between the roils of a messy nebular cloud and positioned off the natural interstellar trade routes. Socially it might have evolved into an eremitic world disjoint from the neighboring Ulmat stars, but its moderate climate and abundance of water formed an attractive haven that counterbalanced its isolation. For the first twenty-two thousand years after colonization Agander remained a free state, sure of its immunity from the flaws of the universe. As a paradise it was able to seduce the loyalty and lust and envy of the distant Ulmat peoples who claimed Agander as one of their own; as an island it was able to remain aloof from the "local" politics.*

*Nine millennia ago, abrupt change swept the Ulmat Constellation. In 5643 GE . . .*

*All our mathematical studies of Ganderian society have shown a stable Esfo-Naifin Quandary-Chain installed at the time of Agander's unexpected and forced subjugation to the First Empire, characterized by a violated sense of invulnerability and expressed as an unwillingness to be vulnerable.*

*If we choose to exploit this Quandary-Chain, we can expect that within a century . . .*

—Oversee Probe Searchcode Report Orange-4: Possible Sites for a
Forced Theac-Chaos Event
Dated Version: 14,642y/08m/37w/7h/78i
Author: CronCom

Twelve-year-old Eron Osa, being the son of the Adjudicator to the Ulman of Agander, was allowed the run of the Ulman's summer Alcazar. He used his privilege to engage the unwary in charming conversation that always had an ulterior motive.

His spying he disguised with innocence. He wasn't malicious: just curious about the love lives of his elders, the political relationships of Ganderians to the stars of the night sky, and, most important, curious about who among his peers were going to get sent to the best schools. He had never met a school he liked and had been expelled from more than a few, which was why his father had hired a private tutor.

On this bright day he sat in the entertainment room forcing an animated chat with four Hasani moneysmiths, none of whom would have spoken to a child had he been one of their own people. But they were newly arrived by starship on business with the Ulman's Adjudicator and felt obliged to humor the man's son. To remind themselves that he was a mere child, they made allusions to events which they "knew" could mean nothing to Eron. By deliberately talking over his head they felt less demeaned to be caught with a child, unaware that Eron had already collected critical pieces of a puzzle that no one was supposed to be able to fit together. He understood all that they said.

Why had a cut-rate hyperspace transport line suddenly constructed new berths at Agander's hyperstation when Ganderian policy had *always* been to semi-isolate their planet from the rest of the Ulmat and *especially* from the interstellar commerce that connected the Ulmat with the heartbeat of the Empire? For reasons of location, the operation couldn't possibly be profitable. Eron Osa's young mind had noted this curiosity long before he had connected it to his father.

He had been spying on his father for years, partly because his father was taciturnly unreadable, partly out of anger. He kept track of the old satyr's love life but carefully never informed his mother because *then* his patriarch would find out about his spying and that would precipitate *doomsday*. He'd probably be packed up and sent off to Star's End without an allowance.

Once, directly in the eye of Eron's spy beam, his father had fought bitterly with Melinesa, his mistress, about sins a grown man should have outgrown, all to Eron's hidden fascination, especially because she was nude. But when the father then stalked boorishly from her rooms, his uncontrolled anger had appalled Eron: he who carried a gun had no need of anger! Worse, his father's stupid "honor" had not even allowed the man to grace himself with an apology. What a klutz! Without bothering to ask permission, Eron gleefully forged an eloquent plea for forgiveness in his father's stead and delivered it at the darkest moonset, dropping the missive in between two buds of a strategically placed star-rosebush where Melinesa would be sure to find it on her morning's walk. Then he skedaddled away on fast, silent feet. He had an adult (and very secret) flare for the romantic idiom.

From his voyeur's viewpoint, Eron had fallen dizzily in love with the elegant Melinesa. She had once kissed him on the forehead during one of their rare meetings in the flesh (a state occasion), smiling into his eyes without even knowing that he *knew*. From such infatuation it was only a small step to forging his father's "unforgeable" electrosignature to a youth's heartfelt blathering—thus earning for his father an undeserved night of reconciled passion. It was the duty of a son to see that his father conformed to the highest standards of behavior with women. Eron believed in poetic exculpation for churlishness; honor be damned.

Still, it astonished Eron—shook him even—to discover from these mere Hasani that his *father* was taking bribes. A Ganderian taking *bribes* from the Empire! It was unthinkable. Osa Junior bowed his excuses to the moneysmiths, exited through the slit in the drapes, and allowed himself to wander aimlessly through the maze of the Alcazar's curtained corridors, dancing from slither belt to slither belt, careful to stay four paces behind any other traveler so as not to offend them.

The long walk gave him time to think—with his fam set at accelerated assimilation. He was faced with a complicated matter of family honor. A full watch passed before he could decide upon his stern moral duty. Then it was another stint out on the Field of the Athletes, marching up and down the field to his inner drums to find the courage to do it. Back inside the Alcazar he touched his personal "kick" in its hidden holster—the sidearm his father had trained him to use as a five-year-old. No male of Agander felt dressed without his sidearm and his underwear, neither of which it was polite to expose in company. When he was alone in a corridor, he checked the charge because it was unmannerly to check one's charge in public. Eron was now set to face down his father with the truth.

A swift bit of sidestepping took him off the belts and to his final destination, a huge bootharium where the Alcazar's staff sustained ultrawave communication with the stars. A steward led him to a tier of small alcoves, then waited politely as he chose one. It did not matter that Eron was the Adjudicator's son, he was never allowed to wander around the critical core of the palace without an escort; such were the subtle protocols of Agander, masked as the privilege of honors.

The alcove was decorated by a flying flight of frothy-headed messenger birds, a furred avian imported by Agander's original settlers. A replica of the messenger bird stood at the center of the alcove on one long chromium leg, ready to lay a gleaming Personal Capsule. But it was not interstellar distances Eron had to span—he only wanted access to his father in the tower-office above the bootharium. At a gesture the replica shifted weight to its other leg, revealing a visiplate. "My dad," he stated in answer to the implied question. The visiplate needed no further codes or information. It had recognized him and was able to deduce his purpose.

The elder Osa showed displeasure at the disturbance. "Eron, Eron . . . I told you we will have an answer by tomorrow. The school will reply and they will accept you—your tutor, bless him, has seen to that. And why aren't you with him now?"

"I'm on assignment."

"And playing hooky, as usual?"

"I'm finished. I have to see you now."

"Eron, I'm preparing for a very important meeting. No."

Eron paused, assessing his father's many vulnerabilities. Which one could he activate that was good enough to get him admitted to his father's office? "Sir, I've been investigating Vanhosen. It's not a good school. I don't like it. I want something better. I won't go!"

His father froze. "You will! That's nonsense. You and your school games! You get up here this inamin! I haven't got time for this!"

The steward who had escorted him into the vast bootharium was already receiving his new instructions when Eron emerged from the alcove; Osa's disobedient son now had no choice about where he was to go next—exactly where he had intended to go. Smiling, Eron followed his "custodian" to the levitation stage, preparing his confrontational speech while the verticule floated them gently up into the tower.

He had no intention to discuss his schooling. *Immediately* upon facing his father he proposed to catch his pater-felon unaware by directly launching into higher matters of honesty and bribery! His tutor had trained him to a keen edge. He was only twelve but he felt well prepared to outfox his father in *any* philosophical contest—especially when his father was positioned on such morally weak ground. A son had to let it be known that he was disgraced to have such a parent!

The senior Osa swiveled as they arrived. He had been pacing beside his desk. Before he finished his turn he was already moving forward, his glare dismissing the steward. He did not speak. His commanding authority demanded that no one speak until he, Adjudicator Osa, spoke first. Only then did he fire off his tirade about education and the necessity of attending a good school. It was futile to interrupt him. He did not spare in his description of the toothed demons who awaited little boys who neglected their studies. "It's Vanhosen! It's been arranged! I *could* send you here to school on *Agander*. And how would you like *that*?"

The elder Osa had guessed right; Eron shuddered at the threat even while he stood against his father's blast. He opened his mouth to reply . . .

But the father got there first. "I'm sending you to the best school on Mowist! Mowist is the central power of the Ulmat, the hub that joins us with Empire. Great Space, child, the mistakes you make now will be exacting payment from your hide for the rest of your life! Mistakes can kill or cripple you! If you don't get your education while you are still a suckling youth, you'll be wandering around like a famless beggar by the time you are manhigh!"

Eron was humiliated now, mainly angry because he had been unable to launch a thrust powerful enough to redirect his father's surprise attack. This man was so *frustrating*! "Vanhosen is a pimple on the Galaxy!" he half threatened, half whined. "If I go there I *will* have to pay! It'll give me hide-pimples for the rest of my life." He glared back into the blazing eyes of a daddy. How could he get off *this* subject and launch *his* attack?

But his silly pout had set his father to ranting and raving again. Eron ranted back, trying to hold his own but aware that he was losing every exchange. The ancient Imperial weaponry decorating the walls mocked him, for these were the weapons that had once vanquished Agander. He could still deliver his low blow—the details of the bribes his father had taken—but it began to seem less tactically wise to escalate this row about the mere details of a schooling into a war over treason. Something choked the words in his mouth—fear.

He intensified the contretemps in a safer way, mocking Vanhosen by comparing it to Kerkorian. His sudden left hook was a hit. Ah! Instantly he took advantage of his father's stagger by lauding Kerkorian's rival, Splendid Wisdom's Lyceum. A right hook. Another hit. That excited Eron into a rally of blows; he called upon his fam to supply the qualifications for a long list of schools far superior to the best that Mowist could offer, something Eron had researched assiduously. In a Galaxy of thirty million settled solar systems, that was easy. He was able to denigrate Vanhosen until it began to sound like a prefam nursery.

"All right, all right," said a calmer Osa Senior. He stared down quizzically at his son's slight figure. "So . . . you've been studying the scholastic scene? Serious study! What a change!" Sarcasm. "Yes, there are better schools than Vanhosen," he agreed with the grayness of ashes. "They are also *expensive*. Even getting you to Mowist is *expensive*. Do you realize how many people live and die on the planet of their birth simply because it is too *expensive* for them to leave it? You complain about your fam—you call it 'junk,' you arrogant little beast—and do you know what I had to *pay* to get my hands on one of such 'inferior' quality? And do you know how *expensive* it is to send you off to school so that . . . Oh, Space it! You *are* going to Vanhosen. And," he commanded, "you *are* going to do well. Or I will *wring* your neck. Now get out of here!"

It was during this speech that Eron understood *why* his father had been taking those bribes all these years. He was in need of money for his son! Sons were even more expensive than mistresses! The revelation shocked Eron speechless. Still, he couldn't abandon his defiance. "I'll *never* go to Vanhosen!" He was as close to tears as he could get without shaming himself. Later, he didn't remember leaving his father's office or dropping down the verticule or renting a flighter to retreat into the hills, for he didn't become conscious of his surroundings again until he was among the remnants of yesteryear's Agander.

The rented flighter he left somewhere down below. He drove his wilting body to keep on running. He ran atop a crumbling windwall, his hair wild in the steady wind. Nothing seemed reasonable at the present moment. The ruins overlooked a sun-drenched valley hundreds of kilometers across and . . . fifty meters straight down a talus slope. The wall that took the impact of his young feet had been struggling with twenty-six centuries of neglect and could hardly be considered safe. Pieces of it had been fainting into the waiting abyss for the past millennium.

His fam began to deliver to him probability-of-accident data in bright visual overlay, images of a gust-blown body inducing a rock-slide tumble. In days of yore, standing here, he would have been picked up by the wind and blown away; the eons of decay had ruined the windwall's ability to amplify mountain breezes up to gale strength. The ruin had once been the feeder of a power plant, Agander's way of coping with the now almost forgotten collapse of Empire. When fusion power is gone, there is always the wind and the water.

In a laggardly response to his fam's warning, the boy stopped running. But his energy wouldn't contain itself. He stayed in one place on the wall—dancing the jig, his shirt flapping in the wind. He stared out over the valley. The Alcazar was almost invisible in the green expanse of forest. Only bits of the spire that communicated with the stars were apparent through the haze. To the left he could see the eraser marks where an ancient city had once been laid out—before Time changed its mind. He was still determined to defy his father. It was a point of honor now *not* to go to Vanhosen.

He couldn't talk to his mother about his decision. And he could only dream about confiding to Melinesa his innermost needs. None of his friends would understand. There was only that strange alien farman he could trust. To trust his tutor upset the boy because no Ganderian really trusted *any* farman, but nevertheless Eron trusted him. It wasn't as if Murek was his friend. He didn't know *what* or *who* Murek was—except that his tutor was better than any school Eron had ever attended.

He didn't even know where Murek Kapor lived—somewhere in the True City that served the Ulman of the Alcazar discreetly from behind the hills—because he had never needed that information. But just the thought of going there tonight triggered his fam into supplying a map and pictures. Ah, Kapor owned an apartment by the Sacred Park. In a black tower. He could reach it shortly after nightfall.

# THE AGENT OF THE OVERSEE,
# 14,790 GE

*... surprising countermeasures used by the Second Empire Pscholars to resta-bilize the local long-range politics in the isolated stellar region of the Ulmat are not traditional and suggest that our interference has been detected ... unortho-dox mathematics ... Within sixty years there is a fifty percent probability of ... unless ... Recommend stealthy abandonment of the Ulmat Offensive ... Our lack of effective operatives on Splendid Wisdom can no longer be tolerated.*

—Overseer Inspectorate HiCode Report Red-75
Dated Version: 14,790y/02m/92w/3h/10i
Author: SeliCom

It was fatal for a seditionist to let his identity find its way into the data banks of Splendid Wisdom's Second Empire, and so Hiranimus Scogil guarded his true name behind aliases and his true biology behind genetic masks—not a particularly difficult task in a Galaxy of multitudes so vast that the roving proctors of the Empire chose to maintain order by ignoring individuals in favor of management by statistical aggregate. This slim youth of twenty-five did not even exist in any High database, not on Splendid Wisdom or in any Sector Central. But as Murek Kapor ...

Most people carried their fam at the base of the neck or as a collar or headpiece and thought of it simply as an auxiliary information source that communicated with their brain via tuned probe when they needed fast data or detailed graphics or heavy-duty analytical faculties. Scogil's was different. His unique "familiar" had been modified to hold a second personality.

After four years, Hiranimus Scogil half believed he *was* Murek Kapor, a star-wandering tutor who had found a comfortable position in the highlands of Agan-der's Great Island, teaching genteel mathematics to the precocious Osa boy. He chafed, not pleased that the Ulmat's Oversee Group had cursed him with a complacent cover persona more inclined to observation than action. *We become what we do.* He chafed as a mere *observer.* It wasn't enough to monitor a plan whose script had been computed a 150 years ago. A field agent also needed to be responsive. All successful plans are fine-tuned on the battlefield.

This Murek Kapor *thing* was annoyingly capable of overriding Scogil's more daring initiatives, if not his thoughts. Scogil could overwhelm this parasite in cases of dire emergency, even in cases of whim, but such an effort was far too exhausting to be carried out on a daily basis—it was easier to leave "him" in control. And Kapor was the kind of character who couldn't even imagine adding a faster spin to the Galaxy; he was a viewer of life, reluctant to commit to the hurly-burly, an earnest wretch whose seriousness extended no further than an interest in his afternoon walks.

What better place to stroll, today, than down a slope of ruins among the thrust of pyre-trees rooted in stones and rubble so rounded by age and redolent with ferns that no one any longer remembered their ancient purpose? Naturally, grumbled Hiranimus Scogil to himself, his damn Kapor identity was content to take his damn strolls *alone.*

He pushed his way under a carmine pyre-branch—and emerged into a spectacularly tranquil copse. Delightful. It surprised him. Sometimes Scogil had to admit to himself that he was beginning to enjoy these walks, too; *damn, damn, and Spacedamn,* it was becoming easier and easier to fall into Kapor's demoralizing habit of contentment.

This hallowed ground, in the middle of the True City, was thought to be too sacred to build upon. Few Ganderians could agree on the reasons. Kapor wasn't the type even to ask but Scogil liked to keep his mind busy by fitting every curious detail of this culture into its psychohistorical context. After all, he *was* a trained Smythosian even if he had been drafted for less demanding fieldwork because he hadn't qualified as a theoretician.

Over the years he must have walked through this park a hundred times but he had never been able to learn much about its antiquity. A surreptitious dig-and-dating had allowed him to place the catastrophe nine thousand years ago, at a time when the First Empire had already spread itself across half the Galaxy, a date in good agreement with the results of the Esfo-Naifin cultural analysis. Didn't that date place the Conquest near the great campaigns of Emperor Daigin-the-Jaw? Some drastic shock of confidence—*it can't happen here*—had been dealt to Agander's pride by their defeat.

By now normal dispersion and immigration should have weakened the reverberations to a whisper below the noise level, but not here. Agander's high isolation index seemed to dominate the important equations. Ganderian culture had been frozen in time at a moment of profound loss.

The associated tales of the trauma were conflicting, depending upon the source. Some of the stories couldn't be true or were bits and pieces of events that had happened thousands of years apart. Agander's historians cared little for the truth. Plot and drama and feeling were everything. After centuries of polishing and retelling, a rousing tale took on the patina of truth and was believed—even when the final story was obviously crafted out of boldly contradictory materials. Such mutable legends continuously found ways to garrison this culture's mental fortress with the archetypical recalcitrance that so served the ends of the Oversee.

Scogil had often vowed that starting early some prime-watch he would delve into more reliable sources for details of the old battles. Perhaps a scholar would have to journey to the very hub of the great galactic arms, there rooting among the archives in the catacombs of Splendid Wisdom. But had the relevant records survived the Great Sack? Splendid Wisdom was itself a cauldron of deceptive myth. Who could take seriously the wild stories that were told of *that* world?

Here the thunderous sagas of Agander spoke their poetry of an attacking swarm of Imperials . . . of heroic battles . . . of long sieges . . . of a rearguard suicidal stand . . . of defiant resistance to the interstellar armies of the First Empire . . . of ghosts who still whispered their valorous tales to children. The real story was probably simpler—a minor fleet carrying the insignia of the Stars&Ship dispatched against Agander as a local mop-up operation during the pacification of the Ulmat . . . a command center bombarded from space by a single battleship . . . perhaps fifty inamins of ferocity . . . massacre. Time had obliterated the facts.

Now—nine thousand years after—immortal ferns and tall pyre-trees reigned over just another one of mankind's lost graveyards. Sunbeams leaked through the mantle of leaves like swords of light dipped in respect to the gravestones. Irony. Who had been the winners? Even the First Empire was long dead, its ghost emperors raised to the godhood of myth.

On passing out of the bloom of the pyre-woods Hiranimus Scogil wandered downhill through tall grasses, attracted by a distant fast-paced melody. The music radiated from the park's sunken arena. Down there the ruins weren't associated with Empire—this was a more youthful site than the higher slopes—the tiered arena dated from the Interregnum when Agander, briefly, had answered to no Empire.

Scogil selected an upper perch atop the stone steps that served as seats, an audience of one, watching the young rousters practice their act. On Agander nearly everyone was a musician. They tended to insist on building their own harmony backpacks, or on molding their own string violers from resin recipes transmitted by family ritual, or on strumming some heirloom visi-harmonar. Even a distrusted farman was welcome to listen to their ancient music—from some outer echelon.

Ah, how natural it was, ears cocked to mellow sounds at twilight's approach. Tempting. A man of Kapor's disposition might, in fact, have chosen to settle here in this galactic noplace. Many had. Agander wasn't the most powerful world of the Ulmat Constellation—but it was the most pleasant. His tutor's salary was good; Squire Osa was a fair if distant patron; the weather (for an open atmosphere) was invigorating—and Agander's strange inbred ways held enough riches to fascinate a man for a whole lifetime. Even Hiranimus was fascinated.

But he didn't approve of the man he was becoming who wasted his time being mesmerized by musicians while the newer Second Empire slithered its lines of force around ever more distant stars. This time there were no armadas to oppose. The Pax Pscholaris was enforced by psychohistory, and to contravene its power one had to be a cleverly placed mathematician. Why had he allowed himself to opt for this damned slow-paced assignment? Why was he letting the languid persona of Kapor rot his soul? There were worlds to conquer!

Yet the music *was* good, and how gaily the musicians jigged while they played down there! Why was it that watching joy could make a man so sad and separate? He was too far above the stage for them to see his weepy eyes. How melancholy to be a soldier on the peaceful fringes of a roiling civilization. Could he really give up the battle that was developing beyond the star-clouds to settle in this quiet utopia? The Ganderians didn't really like farmen—that was the rub—and that in itself was a good enough reason *not* to make a home on Agander, a good enough reason to hate the place—if one valued a sense of belonging.

But, of course, *that* was why he *was* here.

The Ganderian cultural distinctness, by the laws of psychohistory, made this world a fertile breeding field for sedition. Its people, unique among the systems of the Ulmat, had always refused to *perceive* themselves as a part of any Imperium—while at the same time, for century after century of contradiction, producing far more than their normal share of galactic functionaries. To escape assimilation one may imitate the strongest group in sight while at the same time despising them. Fecund soil indeed. Any seed of sedition, drifting in from space, needed only to root and adopt the patience of a Kapor.

With twilight the mood turned—from playing, to rambunction and, from harmony, to the chatter of gossip. Hiranimus ambled down the steps and sauntered in among the performers while they packed their instruments. He was always willing to make affable conversation with these Ganderians even though they always seemed to change the subject when he intruded. It didn't matter. In time one got used to the way a Ganderian distanced himself. They might not be at ease with a farman but they were always polite. It was enough—if, like Kapor, one had been conditioned not to need friends.

The red-haired violist took the least trouble to fake her politeness. While she smiled thinly and joked with him about the weather, she touched the light weapon in her built-in jacket holster, a silent signal of contempt for a man she believed would not bear arms because he had already capitulated. Murek Kapor, well rehearsed, disarmed the hostility by not being offended. But Scogil, watching his own act, was surprised that he was actually feeling what this artifact, Murek, was designed to feel—aloofness. He really didn't care. The hostility really didn't matter. Space and Damnation, he wasn't even *acting* anymore!

Unable to attract a companion from the musicians, he broke off by himself, working his way farther down the slope. There the park abutted the city. He hopped on the slithering ridepath toward his tower. Four years was surely too long a time to live someone else's life. Kapor had been designed to wear the subtle persona of a loyal citizen of the Second Empire: would the erosion continue until Scogil woke up at the end of a nondescript sleep-watch, his loyalties reversed, worshiping in awe the distant oligarchy? Was he destined to *become* Murek Kapor, while the passionate rebel faded into an artificial existence? He smiled as the ridepath carried him along willy-nilly. A man forever without close company began to talk sophistry to himself!

During jagged moments when he felt alienated by his aloneness, he found it easy to blame his sour mood on the haughtiness of every Ganderian who had ever snubbed a farman; it was still too painful for a man as young as Scogil to concede that a secret life of sedition might create its own alienation.

He owned an apartment inside the walls of the Black Tower. To discourage unwanted visitors, there were neither corridors, nor lobby, nor levitator. At the receiver in the tower's gate, a sleek bodyform enveloped him, zipping him through passageways he never saw and then up into the patio of his studio habitat where it unfolded to release him, then vanished, leaving him to a farman's privacy.

He was expected—by the machines. Already his cuisinator had prepared him an excellent meal. He smelled the bay leaf that was said to be of old Rith though its tree seemed to be native to fourteen other worlds—a smell which meant stew. The fonepad was blinking with a call. When decoded by his fam, it turned out to be a frantic plea from his youthfully impetuous student who could never understand why he didn't just attach a phone to his fam so that he could be of service when he was needed. Father trouble again.

Scogil smiled as he ladled out meat and vegetables in thick brown sauce. These family crises of galactic proportions! Such was life! Scogil's duties often called for him to be an advisor and confidant as well as mathematician. No matter—that boy was the best part of his job, even if . . . He sighed. First, food for his stomach!

He ate while he assembled from his archives the next lesson for young Eron Osa. Hiranimus Scogil tended to make his students sweat intellectually before pandering to their lesser needs. With layered merges he constructed a trap—a mathematical problem that could be solved only painfully within Eron's range of knowledge—but could be solved quickly by means yet unknown to Eron. Would the boy plunge ahead, trying eagerly to conquer the morass of computation by brute force? Or was he ready to be wary of Scogil's traps? Think first, pounce later. It was never simple to teach reason to an energetic child who already "knew" the answer before he got there.

What was he to do about the boy's war with his father? Should he call now with soothing words or let the kid fry in his socket until morning? Thoughtfully Scogil carried his sherbet out onto the black marble balcony. There were several things he could try—but the unhurried personality of Murek Kapor took over his thoughts. He dabbled with the simple pleasure of small spoonfuls of the tasty ice and relaxed as the soft sun descended between mountain clefts in a splash of reds and yellows. Enjoy the sunset. Scogil tried to fret but Murek knew Eron would survive at least until dusk.

As he watched, the stars of the Ulmat began to appear in the sky along the eastern horizon, some sharp, some dimmed by the local interstellar clouds. The brightest constellation in the sky was the nebular blaze of eleven proto-suns whose disks provided the Ulmat with its wealth. Then, as the sky grew darker, the stars of the Second Empire began to overwhelm the heavens from the boundary of the clouds all the way up to the blazing zenith.

Few such sacred moments ever went uninterrupted . . .

With an unobtrusive whisper, the fam at the base of his neck began to alert him to a second message of far higher priority than the tantrums of a mere student: a Personal Capsule, coded for Murek Kapor, had just arrived for him back in his studio.

He sighed. The part of him that was Kapor was disinclined to move. It was a slow planet; he was content to let the message wait, at least until the last of the stars were out and the night breeze was drifting through the towers. But *Scogil* was restless. It could only be instructions from the stars. He was starved for contact. Scogil forcefully overrode his Kapor and set his sherbet glass under the chair. Deliberately he got up and took himself inside.

In the communication's alcove his hand fetched the iridescent sphere from the velvet robogrip of the transporter, holding it between four fingertips and thumb in front of his face. He was both excited to be receiving a Capsule and annoyed at the sender, not because a Capsule's contents might be intercepted, but because the reception of a Personal Capsule from beyond the Ulmat left a man of his station conspicuous—ripe for rumor in a culture pathologically willing to invent rumors about farmen. Why would a mere tutor of the son of a minor flunky of the Ulman of the Ulmat be conniving with who-knew-what? His role was to remain invisible.

The Capsule, by tasting his fingertips, checked the key gene sequences set into its address record—status: true. It took an infrared scan of the flow pattern of blood in his face—status: true. Was he alive?—status: true. It gave itself permission to deliver its coded message.

The communiqué was accepted directly by the fam leeched to the spinal cord at the base of Hiranimus Scogil's skull. It was decoded, then fed directly into Scogil's brain via a linked tuned probe. He stood there, stunned. First was a command sequence that released him from his Murek Kapor construct. He felt no immediate difference—but he was free, he was himself again. Second came a promotion in rank. Only then was he told that the whole offensive in the Ulmat Constellation was being terminated. One hundred and fifty years of effort aborted! His four years here had come to naught!

No reply to the Capsule was possible. It carried no source. It could have come from anywhere in the Galaxy—probably from a nearby ship that had since jumped to a new location. For a moment of desperation Scogil thought about what he could salvage of the operation—and his fam automatically began to review the whole of the works-in-progress. He canceled the scan. It was too late. The seditionist cells grafted into the fabric of the Ulmat by the Oversee were by now *already* scattered. Even the Agander contingent had lifted off-planet twenty watches ago—he was now the senior man of a rear guard. It galled him that the bulk of the departure had been completed without his knowledge—but that's the way it was in a covert operation. The less you knew that didn't concern you directly, the better.

But *why* such a sudden retreat now? Futile to ask himself; he wasn't going to be able to answer such a question; he had neither the relevant psychohistorical equations nor the input data-matrix. His duty was to act; later perhaps he could find answers to his questions.

Foremost, he had to arrange for a smooth departure of the remaining technical support groups. The Oversee couldn't instantly remove all units of its invisible army without creating discontinuities that might attract the attention of the Pscholars. What grew unobtrusively in place tended to go unnoticed—but the sudden vanishing of a large landmark might generate a curious ripple of transients. The ubiquitous agents of Splendid Wisdom had the minds of frogs: they weren't able to see a *sitting* fly, but they swiftly lapped up bugs dumb enough to *flit* across their visual background.

With the crumbling Capsule still in his hand he began to plot a course of action—and his fam took up the suggestions and began to flesh out the details and to compute psychohistorical probabilities on the alternatives. It was going to take him at least 120 to 140 watches before he could find his own excuse to leave Agander. In the meantime . . . He made a few calls. He set up the beginnings of a bankruptcy and sale. He canceled a publishing contract and accelerated the printing of another document to the public archives. He enjoyed being the swiftly decisive Scogil again. Kapor, thank Space, was now inactive—except as a passport name.

Still meditating, he muttered the call-words for the house genie to vanish the Capsule's ashes and went out to the balcony to retrieve his sherbet glass with its spoon now embedded in greenish sludge. It hit him then, under the stars, the meaning of the retreat. Splendid Wisdom had noticed them. The time of jockeying for position under a cloak of invisibility was over. An unpredictable era of open battles had begun. That was to Scogil's liking, but it was frightening, too. When one is weak, the optimal strategy is to strike from hiding so deftly that the enemy does not even realize he has been hit. Briefly he regretted that he was not theoretician enough to anticipate the Pscholars' next move. He was, by nature, a man of action, and he already knew his drive would take him to Splendid Wisdom itself. Whether he was ordered there or not, he would go—no matter how many years it took or how many roundabouts.

In his mind he was already there, at the blaze of the galactic center.

# HYPERLORD KIKAJU JAMA
# AS DETECTIVE, 14,790 GE

*. . . so much for business, my dear Kikaju. I'm not sure anything will ever come of it other than prison, but we can hope. I'm looking forward to my return to Splendid Wisdom and the mellow light of Imperialis which has shone for so many eons upon the heart of the Galaxy. For an archaeologist like myself, field trips are the blood of life—but civilization down in the warrens becomes wonderfully appealing after so many months of rough living with the winds of space a mere skin thickness away.*

*I'll close this letter with an anecdote which you may find amusing since it belies your favorite theory, which I have never subscribed to, that however domineering the Pscholars may be in their political actions, they are basically honest. I have never been impressed by their integrity. People who are so determined about their secrets always, always, always have deeds to hide. A man who needs his secrets is telling the universe that he is vulnerable.*

*Remember last year at Canarim's party when you were insisting that nowhere in the Archives of Splendid Wisdom was there evidence that Faraway, during the whole span of the Interregnum, had detected the existence of the monitoring Pscholars? Even you believe half of the Pscholars' lies. Canarim had made, I thought, a convincing case that Faraway had once detected a Pscholar's nest in their midst and destroyed it—about the time of the final Lakgan War, he surmised. You scoffed, claiming total lack of evidence and seeing only the mythological hand of rumor at work, laying its false trail. I had to remind you, rather rudely I'm afraid, that victors always rewrite history to conform to some self-important image of their merit. Secrecy, to the Pscholars, is a virtue. They do not want any of us to believe that anyone has ever penetrated their secrecy— or even that it can be penetrated.*

*But is that true? Isn't it poppycock to claim that Faraway's "faith" in the Founder's Plan was an essential ingredient of its success during the*

*Interregnum? Would Faraway's populace really have lost their nerve and drive had they known that Pscholars were monitoring and "adjusting" their history whenever they strayed from the Great Plan of Galactic Revival? To assume that Faraway's scientists—all familiar with the concepts of stability and feedback—would not have suspected the Founder of setting up an apparatus to monitor and stabilize his Plan has always seemed absurdly naive to me. Well, the scientists of Faraway DID suspect—and tremble!*

*The Pscholars' power is everywhere and Faraway is but a shadow of its former self. Who has a greater ability to slant the past in their favor and hide from us what they do not want us to know? But even the powerful cannot lie well enough to coordinate all the many bits and pieces of flotsam floating loosely around the universe. You will be interested in the enclosed copy of some flotsam which the Pscholars have not been able to "rewrite" since it was only recently found on a ghastly mummy-crewed Faraway shipwreck (deepspace), a disaster which the salvaged log places subsequent to the final Lakgan war (circa the first century after the Sack). I was serendipitously allowed to examine the ship's (damaged) memory module since I am one of the few experts on Faraway naval codes of that era.*

*Most of the fragments concern log entries or ship's manifest—supplies for an unnamed prison camp—dull—but one title that begins in the middle of a sentence hints at disciplinary action against a crewman. He seems to have given minor but unauthorized aid to a prisoner belonging to a group of "subversives" known as "the Fifty," identified openly as psychohistorians unmasked by a Faraway anti-espionage team. These "traitors" were evidently shipped in secrecy to a planet called Zurnl to be exiled or executed.*

*It is thus plain that the Faraway government of the time was aware of and very afraid of psychohistorical manipulations. The dates are . . . My star charts do not contain a planet or system under the Zurnl cognomen. Zurnl does not appear when I run correlations going back as far as the exploration of the Nacreome Periphery by the I.S.B. Strange! I will not be brave enough to publish the item, at least not until I find out why this piece of history has so conveniently "vanished" from our Splendid Archives. You may wish to pursue the matter discreetly—I know of your interest in such curiosities. I am attaching the relevant parts of the log, scanty though they be. If you ever locate the whereabouts of this "Zurnl" inform me.*

> *with a joyous "So there!" I am yours faithfully, Igar*

*P.S. As a "bribe" to insure my dedicated efforts on their behalf the salvagers included in my "pay" a bejeweled jade egg found with the captain's effects. It is of no use to me or to my line of research so I am sending it on by devious means since you seem to be able to profit from such baubles out of the past. It is not*

*necessary—but if you do manage to sell this stone, I could use the twenty per-
cent finder's commission. It is pretty and should be worth something to the sort
of clientele you serve.*

—Excerpt from a Capsule by Igar Comoras to Hyperlord Kikaju Jama

The Hyperlords of the First Empire had, since an Order of Council in 6654 GE,
been political procurators who controlled the military men of the navy for Imperialis. As comfortable in court as among the stellar intrigues of competing provinces,
they had been willing and able to deploy force, even battleships, against the enemies of the Court when reason and protocol failed. But Hyperlord Kikaju Jama
could no more imagine the open power that they had wielded than *they* could have
imagined the labyrinthine shadow schemings of his Second Empire mind.

Hyperlord Kikaju Jama was a Lord in name alone, anointed by a feverish
grandmother who was in love with old genealogical records. He lived invisibly
among the masses in a world orchestrated by a coterie of psychologists who ruled
the vastness of *their* empire not with battleships but with feathery leverings upon
mathematically determined critical events. Jama dreamed of power but spent most
of his life pretending to powers he did not have. He knew he was a blatherer, but
that amused him—who would suspect a pompous fop to wield real power? Super-
cilious fools never drew the kind of attention that was dangerous to life and limb!

He stood in front of the mirrored sanitor of his opulent dressing room, washing and perfuming his robo-illuminated genitals, while contemplating the difficulty
of obtaining spare parts for antiques, an issue that every antique dealer always had
to confront from time to time. An ordinary antique with an authenticated template
was never a problem—if it malfunctioned, junk it and manufacture a new one. But
those rare items of such delicate detail that they could not be duplicated in a manufacturum always posed a problem when they failed—such as, for instance, this
jade egg that his friend Comoras had so naively posted to him and that had only
arrived ten watches ago.

He had thought of nothing else for the last million jiffs ticked out by his antique clocks.

How could old meticulous Igar, an archaeologist specializing in the Interregnum, have mistaken it for mere polished, diamond-studded jade? But, alas,
there was *always* too much to know, and Igar, after all, was a bit-master whose expertise was documents rather than knowledge of artifacts. Even Jama, himself,
might not have recognized its true nature except that a customer had tried to buy
one from him years ago. His fam *never* forgot an item that people had actually
sought from him.

Since Igar's Personal Capsule of the month past, Jama had been frantically
racking his fam for ways to locate the purported Zurnl's coordinates. To be able to

catch the Pscholars in a lie of repression! Indeed, there was no trace of a Zurnl in the Splendid Stellar Archives—a prolonged trawl, carefully hidden within a round of routine "antique authentications," had come up empty.

Then, after abandoning this net of dead ends, came the ironical miracle right out of Space! Innocently he had opened up the package to examine the latest from his mad archaeologist friend, anticipating nothing, expecting only an amusing bauble, a jade egg of dubious value. After all, this was the man with whom he had conducted an irregular but profitable trade in contraband Interregnum items. Under the room's dutiful gaze-following eyelight, his fingers undid the delicate wrap of "smuggler's cloak," revealing an ovoid whose surface was intricately etched and seemed to be embedded with fine diamonds.

Great Founder!

The shock of instant recognition assaulted his eyes, the eyelight dimming as his pupils enlarged. He knew this item, legendary among a tiny group of specialized antique dealers. Only a few of them had ever appeared in the catalogs and almost none ever came up for sale at any price. Could the awesome computing power of a galactarium really be locked in a green stone so small? It looked like just another gewgaw that could be made at whim in any simple manufacturum. But he knew its innards remained too intricate to be recorded by even the best of template scanning technologies, an antique dealer's dream. A galactarium. A galactarium which had been on a ship that had actually orbited Zurnl. What treasure might its charts reveal?

Extracting stellar coordinates from the device proved not as easy as unwrapping Igar's stealthy package; it took him five wakeful watches to decipher the controls and then, alas, when activated, the ancient galactarium threw off a shower of stars, fizzed, and died. Perhaps the malfunction wasn't serious—he suspected that his ovoid needed only a replacement of its atomo-unit—the original Faraway atomos had a reputation for failing after as little as a decade of continuous operation. Such failures were unavoidable at their micro-operational temperature. This one had gone out in typical atomo failure mode. But the breakdown might be only the beginning of trouble. Was the rest of the circuitry still functioning? He dared to hope.

Sheltered as it had been inside a dead spaceship at deep-space temperatures for 2300-plus years, the prognosis was good. Cosmic ray damage couldn't have been that great considering the reputation of early Faraway engineers for six-dimensional connection-space redundancy—to say nothing of the reputation for quantum device self-repair agents active down to four degrees absolute. It was simple logic to check the atomics first—but finding a proper atomo replacement meant frustrating delays while rummaging at antique conventions and laboriously traveling through Splendid Wisdom's maze of prefectures just to get to the gatherings. This was a seriously obsolete part! No ordinary manufacturum was licensed (or precision coded) to build atomic power stations that could be cradled in the cup of a tablespoon!

Still, he was confident that the anticipated Zurnl data resided in this antique, since the galactarium had been in use by a Faraway trader of the 125th century GE–*before* Zurnl had achieved "special" status . . . and then (!) fortuitously lost to all possible after-the-fact historical revision. There was no way a Pscholar could have tampered with its database. It was only a toy with memory for a mere ten billion stars, but a Faraway toy of the right century would hardly neglect the coordinates of even trivial stars within Faraway's then sphere of influence.

Ah, the bother he was going to have to go through for a nonstandard atomo power thumb! As he rolled his eyes, the room's eyelight–tuned to illuminate whatever caught its master's attention–arced madly in sympathy. Before he could complete this gesture of exasperation the swinging eyelight caught a misplaced pink mopcap tossed up there on the outstretched arms of a blue-eyed doll. She was perched on her tiny balcony set into the high wall. That's what he would wear! The mopcap's fat scales of velvet were a perfect match for the rest of his intended outfit.

Off on the antique circuit again! There was no help for it. He selected his blatant clothes from the rotating wardrobe rack, slightly out of style as befitted an antique dealer, a jacket with bells along the seams and tight striped pants, then a proper light-purple wig with topknot and matching fingernails. The mopcap, of course. His most difficult decision was an ear perfume to match the fragrance of his genitals. Even when one went out among the masses in search of atomo-units, one had to be ready to make foil with the female sex.

The eyes of three of his antique dolls, each from a different millennium, each from its own petite balcony, followed the Hyperlord as he stepped out of his dressing room. He paused for stage effect, practicing on the dolls. Ever in synchrony with his gaze, the auroral eyelight lingered on his miniature garden, flew across angular and pearly walls, touched a desk, shot down a hall. For a moment its soft beam settled on the hand-size jade ovoid sitting in the golden-legged cup which the Hyperlord had chosen for its nest.

He took the object in his hand. Kikaju had no manual but he was an antique dealer used to making do without instructions. He fiddled and poked with a prior knowledge of Faraway's early Interregnum devices, and finally the little atomo-unit was revealed. Stuck, though. He whacked it out against the palm of his hand and peered at its shape in the eyelight. It was not of the same quality as the galactarium–different suppliers. The galactarium itself was an oddity–not the sort of practical thing one associated with the early generations of Faraway Traders. Perhaps it was a gift for a daughter or mistress, a one-of-a-kind crafted for a very rich trader. Who would ever know? The truth lay buried in the sedimentary layers of time. He held a fossil, preserved but stripped of its story.

PSYCHOHISTORICAL CRISIS

Where were all the stories? There was an old song, "Gone to flowers, every one!"

Mankind's potentates lay sandwiched within layers eighty thousand or more years thick: the Splendid Imperial Mausoleums set in the sedimentary crown, themselves perched atop rich layers of pre-imperial expansion that all but buried the sparse gravemounds of the first mysterious subluminal migrations in the Sirius Sector—silent potentates all the way down to the basement strata of tombs holding the mummified lives and riches of the post-simian despots of old Rith and Alphacen and Isua whose monuments were themselves raised upon the unmarked mass graves of luckless opponents. Who was left to tell the stories of the rings still wrapping those anonymous finger bones? Kikaju Jama liked to think of himself as an appreciative grave robber.

In the layers of history far above the Eta Cumingan invention of the hyperdrive, expatriate mercenaries, having lost their war and commander, elected a young Kambal to extract their remnants from disaster. He chose a safe refuge in an increasingly competitive galactic core without knowing that he was laying the foundation for the First Galactic Empire. He only knew he was seizing a pacifist—and undefended—Splendid Wisdom because it was weak. Jama owned a prize comb from that Kambal Dynasty court, but who knew its maker or its wearer? The piratical Frightfulpeople who followed the Kambals and built a planetopolis to rule their stellar suzerainty had themselves been crushed beneath their monolithic architecture and pipe-tunnel mazes by the teeming bureaucratic culture that rose to power on top of them. Another layer. Other titles.

Give the invincible Hyperlords a couple of meters in the landfill for their bones and their seals of power. Titles. Fossil titles cluttered the stratified detritus of the Imperialis tradition, each reflecting a single transient moment on the galactic stage, some still remembered by pretenders like Jama, others lost and forgotten. The Sack of Splendid Wisdom was the dividing layer between modern and ancient history. But even the formidable Faraway Traders of recent origin were gone, their stories with them. Who would ever know the stories that this miraculous ovoid might tell?

Kikaju Jama had a moment of glee. All that remained of the eighty millennia of humanity's grandeur was Jama's grubby little antique trade!

He gave his lofty ancestors only these most casual passing thoughts. The distant power of once-mighty Hyperlords was too remote for him to envy. Kikaju Jama was passionately nostalgic for a much later time in history when complacency had taken the whole of civilization into the darkness of the (by now only dimly remembered) Black Interregnum. What thrills! What glory!

From a quiet domination by avaricious men who swarmed around the star called Imperialis, the whole Galaxy had fallen into chaos, war, collapse, massive die-offs, extinction, defeasance—fertilizing, alas only temporarily, a wonderful era of anarchic inventiveness. Who else could have produced this exquisite ovoid of magical power? It had been a fabulous millennium! Kikaju dreamed of a new and better interregnum, the thirty thousand years of turbulence that the Founder had promised and taken away, chaos that might still drive mankind to new highs and new depths.

Who were these fifty Fellowship psychohistorians who had been transported to Zurnl in a Faraway ship that later vanished in deepspace? Why had they been written out of history by their own brothers, the Founder's sons who spent a millennium at lethal infighting over dominance of the Galaxy? Intrigue lay out there on the Periphery where once had shone the greatest power of the Galaxy's darkest night! A stab of thrill! He could sense another of his antique expeditions coming on. When the star-spanning Pscholars *lied,* wasn't Igar right? Weren't they exposing a weakness? In time, might not the sum of their weaknesses be used against them? It was a pointing compass! To the source!

And . . . if, while skulking about, he could scrounge up some articles for sale, so much the better for a poor working-class nobleman!

The mobile eyes of dolls farther along the hallway watched from their niches as Jama strutted up to the central drop-in with its recessed recliners and domed ceiling entrance. He finger-snapped. His telesphere bloomed dutifully in midair beside him, poised for service. He must get his galactarium repaired.

"Activate weasel," he told the telesphere. "Full security. Retrieval ability but no traceback. Repeat, no traceback." The absence of Zurnl in the archives was a sure clue that Zurnl was a delicate subject connected to who-knew-what conspiracy of silence.

The Hyperlord was paranoid enough about his activities to use an expensive commercial trolling utility with full security capabilities. Less security was quicker, but he never used such degraded "shorts." His probing weasel would be cleverly constructed. There would be no way to identify its source for its quantum nature was such that any attempt to follow a reply back to the source would erase the weasel before it was received.

"Touch active antique sites," he commanded in a subdued murmur. "Restrict to Splendid Wisdom." With that command he was supplying his weasel with an address list. He decided the list was broader than necessary. "Review."

Notices of current ateliers, fairs, conferences flashed inside the telesphere— fading if he showed indifference, expanding into graphical glory if he showed a flicker of heed. Of course, there were too many. With tiny gestures of his fingers he restricted the scan to cover the antiques of the Interregnum and then again, impatiently, gave priority to the most convenient of the locations within an easy eight-watch travel range. In case that wasn't enough, he supplied discretionary parameters so that the weasel might make its own decisions, even if it had to go off planet.

The weasel would touch and leave most sites without a trace. It had enough intelligence to match site to query, send back a scouting report if an item caught its attention, or wait for a reply, if appropriate, while continuing its search elsewhere.

The query was keyed to find people who repaired specific kinds of early Faraway antiques. To make the weasel's task less daunting, he gave it a date bracket to work within, covering the galactarium's probable active life span as well as other parameters that listed the galactarium's attributes.

"Send."

Then he left to see if the cuisinator could whop up an egg sandwich without soaking the bread. Damn machine. Perhaps he should try a new bread recipe. Such a bother. One of these months he was going to buy an *intelligent* cuisinator that made meals on time without being told what to prepare. Sit down and eat. That's the way Hyperlords used to do it!

When, munching his soggy sandwich, he returned to the telesphere, its surface was already flashing with a scout report, an advertisement. The address given was that of some culture-forsaken conurbation up north called the Kirin Sovereignty. The place seemed to have met all of his requirements.

FARAWAY MECHANICS
How did the Magicians of the Periphery do it?
Any Faraway device dissected, understood.
Study the laws of scaling.
Private workshop.

The trillion denizens of Splendid Wisdom were relegated to hundreds of thousands of arrondissements, precincts, domains, jurisdictions—scattered through the depths and beneath the leafy rooftops, taking in tunneled rock, winding through the towers that rose over drained seabeds, and gerrymandered across the choice locations of mountain ranges whose height gave the rich an awesome view of the parks atop their plastic-metal planet. No man had memory enough for it all. Kirin? Never heard of it. It wasn't even in his fam. But locationwise it was close enough.

His telesphere provided him with geopolitical and geographical overviews of the district. Jama deduced that Faraway Mechanics, full as it might be of enthusiasm, was probably not a wealthy group—the Kirin Sovereignty was constructed along the cleft of an old subduction zone and would therefore be a low-rent warren. He booked his rooms accordingly, in a monastery—he was, after all, not a wealthy antique dealer; he had to pay for his ostentation with discreet savings where he could.

In case Faraway Mechanics might fail him, he waited for his weasel to work up a series of secondary destinations. He picked and chose, ran a program to optimize travel time, storing the itinerary in his fam, then called up the tourmaps he might need. Without a tourmap to overlay labels, outlines, and directions upon one's vision, at demand, a traveler was lost.

Jama always traveled light. In a shake of jiffs he put together a codpiece containing his few necessities: templates for a set of clothes that he could have made at any public manufacturum, some tie pins, a lace neckpiece, spare rings, six shades of perfume, and a shapechanger's toolkit. Just in case, he included templates of best-selling antiques. The codpiece's bulkiest item—uncondensable as a template—was the defunct galactarium.

His fam automatically reminded him of nonpostponable duties. He grumbled. But he *did* have to go back to set his water system for overhaul—the cuisinator's last batch of wine carried a faint bouquet of piss. Further delay of repairs was not prudent. Probably his septic unit was due for replacement—an outrageous expense. These ancient abodes in questionably chic neighborhoods were never trouble-free! To think that there were planets in the Galaxy with real running water gurgling out of mountain streams! The trick was to wait for the unit's stuttering to subside before attempting an overhaul. The whole process was automated, but there always seemed to be final details left as an exercise for the user! Yes, like flushing that last batch of wine.

Even so, he couldn't resist a few sips while he did so—after all, it was *Hyperlord* piss. Before winking out, the telesphere confirmed that his local appointments had been rescheduled and that all was in houseguard mode. And his fam confirmed that the check list was now done. Voilà! He could leave. He kicked a heel and floated up the levitator through the drop-in dome, into the safety airlock, and out into the stale public air of his hive-corridor.

Humiliating to have to live in a hive even if there was a cachet to being first among the wave of redevelopers! One could almost see the pipes and conduits and narrow robot-runs along the bare tunnel, bare now for more than a millennium, almost sanctified by time in its bareness—there had been no attempt to hide gutty nastiness behind some artful facade, such was the haste of the builders who had reconstructed Splendid Wisdom after the Sack, builders dead now for sixtyne centuries. Beauty is temporary; haste persists. No matter, the bustle of the main thoroughfare was a short walk away.

The Concourse of the Balasante! How Hyperlord Kikaju Jama loved his strolls along this covered passageway of humanity. It stretched for a hundred kilometers. But he had no time now for a drink on the Plaza, or a leisurely promenade around the great airshaft that cut open the living layers of the city to dizzying wonder—if one had the stomach to look. His excuse was that he had a pod to catch. It would be almost two watches of cramped zooming through the transportation net before he could reach the Kirin Sovereignty—and then only if luck routed him around the tunnel maintenance crews. Flying was not an option for a poor nobleman.

Strapped into his too-narrow pod, jostled by the twists and turns of acceleration, he dreamed of an orange sun lost in some boondocks of the far periphery.

# FARMAN AND GANDERIAN BOY, 14,790 GE

*This particular Quandary-Chain of the Agander series, though in appearance highly stable, is susceptible to moderate Theac pumping. In Table-1 is a list of possible artificially generated Theac-Chaos Events that we can expect to bloom across time-ramps of . . . Riote's theorem demands that the Post-Events stemming from any of these Events cannot be predicted by any method to a reliability coefficient greater than 0.4. If we are undetected during setup . . . It should be possible to arrange the unpredictability zone to last from fifty years to two centuries before the advent of Kraniz restabilization. Such a psychohistorical time-shadow is more than adequate for our purpose.*

*. . . many examples of secondary links along the quandary-chain . . . for instance, it has become a ritual among Ganderians to always carry weapons which must never be used, a manifestation of the unresolved (second-order) trauma activated during the Interregnum when Agander's vulnerability again became acute.*

> —Oversee Probe Searchcode Report Orange-4: Possible Sites for a
> Forced Theac-Chaos Event
> Dated Version: 14,642y/08m/37w/7h/78i
> Author: CronCom

The night was well advanced. All traces of the spherical Personal Capsule were gone. The frenzy of activity at his release from the Kapor personality had subsided. A weary Hiranimus Scogil was ready for bed, and so he dimmed the walls and laid out a hand of cards from Agander's Royal Deck of Fate for a relaxing game of solitaire. The Ax of Mercy was the first card he drew.

And at that moment the pellucid form of the tower's Security Butler consolidated in his studio's small foyer and made a slight guttural rumble to attract attention. "Eron Osa is requesting entrance," the apparition said.

"He's *here?* At this time of night?"

"He's armed."

"The usual?" The public order brought about by the resurgent Second Empire had been unable to uproot a long local tradition of suspicion. Since Agander's murder rate remained a hundred times lower than galactic normal and violent crime was nearly nonexistent, the law had little incentive to make palm-size blasters illegal. Scogil had never been at ease with a kick in every shoulder holster, and never carried one himself, but that was only another thing that marked him as a peculiar farman. "Check the serial." By law all weapons radiated their identity.

"Registered." The butler provided diagrams and specifications—a children's model, nonlethal beyond a range of one meter. "A toy."

"Some toy." One did not spank students who all brought blasters to class. The only benefit was a student body which tended to reason among themselves very carefully. It was probably the foundation of Ganderian politeness.

The apparition waited. It had no precedent upon which to act; Eron had never before visited his tutor's home. When no instructions were forthcoming, it became impatient. "Shall I ask him to check his weapon?"

"Forget it. Let him in. Dismissed."

The butler vanished, and a transport bodyform popped through the pod-lock, unfurling to release a small boy—before it, too, vanished. "You didn't answer my call!" the boy accused.

"I was making up your next assignment," Hiranimus said affectionately, neglecting to mention all the other matters that had been occupying him. "Trouble with your father again?"

"We fought!"

"Did you blast him to smithereens?"

Eron looked up at him without comprehension. It wouldn't have occurred to him to use a weapon on his father even though he was a deadly shot. He carried his kick like normal children of the Galaxy wore pocket flaps on their jackets, a matter of style and posture. "He wants to send me to, ugh, Vanhosen!"

Now *that* was a much worse crime than murder. Scogil smiled. "Vanhosen! He wouldn't dare do that to a jolly fellow such as yourself!"

Eron Osa called upon the robowall to provide a layabout couch and threw himself down on it. "Oh, yes he would! My father is loathsomely nefarious!"

The conjured couch was a clashing purple and did not match Scogil's elegant taste in color or shape. He made a resolution to sit down tomorrow at his studio's console and drastically restrict the creative range of his appurtenancer. Perhaps he could teen-proof the device—but no use bothering with such trivialities now. He dimmed the lighting further to make the eyesore more palatable. "All right, Eron.

Let's get to the source of your horror. I don't understand the problem. Vanhosen is probably the most prestigious school in the Ulmat. Mowist is a vibrant world. I would have liked an assignment there myself."

Eron groaned.

"Your father is barely able to afford such a meritorious institution. Mowist isn't far away, but even transportation off Agander isn't cheap. He certainly won't be able to treat your siblings as well. You'll take your first interstellar trip. You'll see places you can't imagine. You'll be taught by some very great scholars."

"Yah, yah. And after five years I'll get to join the ranks of all the other billions of Imperial lackeys!"

That's what his father wanted for him, Scogil knew. He wanted a son in the Service of the Second Empire, a son who had made it, a son who might even work outside of the Ulmat. Eron was his most trying child, but far and away the most brilliant. "And you have other plans?"

"The toads at Vanhosen sit on their stools and croak to the sky! What can they teach me? They don't even know mathematics as well as a *dumbtop* like you!"

Scogil was properly amused at the boy's ferocity—and at the implied back-handed compliment. He called up an extension to the couch, black and shaped in better taste, before flopping out beside the boy. "And if you could have what *you* wanted?"

"The Academy at Kerkorian—or maybe"—the boy's voice became plaintive—"the Lyceum on Splendid Wisdom."

Scogil's heart chilled. Kerkorian was out of the question—Eron didn't even re-motely meet the academic requirements, nor could his father afford access to that kind of elite. As for Splendid Wisdom—there were many Lyceums on Splendid Wisdom, but Eron meant *the* Lyceum—well, his father could afford it because tu-ition and expenses were free, but there were *millions* of applicants for every opening. Not a chance. "You have high hopes for yourself," said Hiranimus soberly.

"You said—"

"I know I've told you that you were brilliant—part flattery, part truth. But bril-liance isn't all that counts." He paused. What was this kid trying to tell him? Both Kerkorian and the Lyceum were known for their psychohistory schools and little else. But Eron had never hinted before that he was interested in psychohistory. And Hiranimus, as the mathematician Murek Kapor, had studiously *avoided* men-tioning psychohistory as a mathematical discipline. Where had the boy picked up such an interest? Yet who didn't recognize that the Second Empire was run by the laws of psychohistory? No one had to know what it was to be impressed by its power! Every boy who had been trained to dream of power before he had learned to talk would dream himself the master of psychohistoric technique. Best to be di-rect. "Are you telling me that you want to become a psychohistorian?"

"Of course! Why else would anyone beat his brains out on math!"

Psychohistory, the highest pinnacle of mathematics. Eron wouldn't even know what that meant at his age, but his *ambition* would know. No wonder he and his father were locked in combat. His father would understand what an impossible goal his son had set himself. Eron would be too thick-headed to take such impossibilities seriously. The Pscholars guarded their secrets with an implacable fanaticism. "There are problems . . ." began Scogil tactfully.

". . . because my fam isn't good enough," completed Eron resentfully.

*That, you little monster, is the least of your worries.* "When you were born, young man, your father scoured the Ulmat for the very best fam that his sticks could buy. He paid a fortune for it, two years' income for him. You had full use of that fam by the time you were three and mastery of it by the time you were five. It might have been fabricated in some forsaken shop—but it was a fam designed on Faraway, don't forget."

The sullenness was suddenly gone from Eron. He became pragmatically impish. "But it's *still* not good enough. And Faraway *used* to have a reputation."

Faraway, on the galactic rim, had been the dominant civilizing force during the Interregnum, and its traders had reconquered three quarters of the domain of the old First Empire before its remote location had drained it of talent. Perhaps no other planet in all of human history had so revolutionized the physical sciences. But its technological leadership was long a thing of the past. "Sometimes a not-quite-good-enough fam can stimulate your wetware to perform above and beyond the call of duty," Hiranimus admonished.

The boy bristled. "I don't believe you *said* what I just *heard* slip off your vocals. You think like that mechanical book!" Eron had once been impressed by the reconstructed book in the historical alcove of the Ulman's Summer Alcazar with its seven hundred gears and cams and push-rods that looked up sage aphorisms by the Penniless Peasant after industrious whir and clack. "I know better. You don't get to be a psychohistorian with a second-rate fam like I'm stuck with! Why wasn't I born to a rich father! It's disheartening!"

Scogil was watching the golden highlights in Eron's brown hair, a reflection from the ceiling lamp, almost a halo effect as if his brilliance had to leak out electrically. Intelligence appeared early in a child; judgment did not. "You *were* born to a rich father."

"Not as rich as the Ulman. Not as rich as he *should* be if I'm to achieve anything in this dumb Galaxy. Not as rich as he *wants* to be." The sullenness was back.

Time for reassurance. "No man is rich enough to buy a fam that will make a psychohistorian out of his son. It's the synergism between fam and brain that makes the difference." Scogil was surprised at the rancor he felt. *His* fam had been crafted by the wizards of the Thousand Suns—and, in spite of that advantage, *he* had failed, at least as a theoretician. It was a marvelous conceit that this student of his might actually make it. Perhaps it could be arranged.

"Can a fam be upgraded?" asked the boy.

Scogil grinned. Most people never even asked that question—their enthusiasm for a fam upgrade was about equal to their ardor for a brain transplant. "It's been done. Expensive. It's not the sort of thing you fool around with lightly. A child's brain fine-tunes to its fam. It's a lifetime relationship, established early."

"How much of a boost of my analytical powers could I get that way?"

"You *could* end up a moron. Have you ever talked with a famless adult, or with someone who has been fam-damaged? To make an analogy: how willing are you to let a surgeon use knives to rebuild your wetware?"

"I know a kid at school who fell off a roof. His fam got pierced. He had it *repaired*."

"Was he any smarter afterward?"

A pause. "No." More time to consider. "He was dumber," conceded Eron before he changed the subject. "I can't just wait around until I'm an old man before I get into a good school. The brain deteriorates after ten. From then on, it's all downhill. At the school I go to I can already feel my mind turning to soup. I'm *twelve*."

"That's why your father hired me."

"He could have hired a *good* tutor!" Eron grumbled.

"Hey, I'm not that bad!"

"I'll bet you only went to *third-rate schools* or you wouldn't be working for a *second-rate* assistant accountant like my father!"

"*Adjudicator* to the Ulman, Eron; be fair. And how can you tell what my job really is? Can you be sure that I'm not the highest paid talent scout in this arm of the Galaxy? Really now, I *have* jumped around to a few marvelous worlds. I might even have pull at a few good schools. Perhaps it is possible to do something for you—but you'll have to study hard."

"I *do* study hard," fumed Eron.

No use arguing. Scogil materialized a wall screen and began to pop algorithms into its controller via fam command. How might he introduce psychohistory to this too-bright child without calling it that? Certainly he couldn't reveal his Smythosian connection. He skipped his prepared lesson, no longer inhibited by the Murek Kapor persona who never did anything dangerous. He decided to build an impromptu lesson around the Ganderian ritual that, in effect, placed a blaster in Eron's hidden holster every morning.

Symbols began to trace onto the screen. "That mess is an Esfo-Naifin Quandary-Chain. What would you do with it?"

"How would I know? I've never seen it before!"

"Hey, stay calm. This is not a test of what you know. I'm just probing to see how your mind works, if it works at all."

"Is this one of your traps?" asked Eron warily.

"No. Just *think*. You've seen dynamic equations before. What's going on here?"

Eron did not like this kind of open-ended test. Defensively he turned to comedy and began to flap his elbows. "Cluck, cluck. I see bird tracks!"

"Sure. But what do they say about the bird?"

Eron pondered for a long time while Scogil made not the slightest sound. Finally: "I don't know. You want me to guess? Along the time line it's got to generate a self-stabilizing run. But I don't know what the symbols mean. You've got to give me definitions before you give me equations. *You* told me that."

Hiranimus refused to utter a word of comment.

Eron couldn't stand the silence and strained for something more to say. "If you had a handle on the red parameter, you could tweak it into an unstable bloom up the time line."

Scogil was impressed. "Why the red parameter?"

"Your Esfo-Naifin Whatchamacallit isn't sensitive to the other params—and don't try to trick me! It *is* sensitive to the red, isn't it?" He didn't seem convinced and wanted confirmation. "I'm not familiar with crazy notations!"

"Quit telling me how stupid you are. You're right. Now what could you use it for?"

Eron shook his head. "Space only knows. My fam's lookup tables don't even list Esfo-Naifin Whatchamacallits by name or form!"

Hiranimus, manipulating the screen through his fam, filled in some initial conditions and expanded the projected expression. "What's that a description of?"

"How should I know? I'm only a twelve-year-old kid with pokey quantronics zived to my spinal."

"*Not* so pokey." He became the tutor again. "It's a description of the arms-carrying customs of Agander. It's a description of that little blaster there in your shoulder holster."

Eron looked down at his kick as if he had never seen it before. "You're sewing eyelids to my cheek. You can't describe *customs* with *mathematics*!" He was contemplating his mentor with disdain.

"And what in the Galaxy do you think psychohistory is all about?"

Eron glanced back in astonishment at the wall with its luminescent curlicues. He stared fixedly at the Esfo-Naifin Quandary-Chain, obviously computing with all fam and wetware resources. Then he grinned mischievously as his first answer came to him. "It's wrong," he said.

"Explain."

"Backtracking gives a source-point only two thousand five hundred years ago. That's wrong! We've *always* carried blasters."

"So says the fine poetry of Ganderian mythology, but if you want to become a passable psychohistorian, you'll have to be more careful with your history than a Ganderian troubadour. Two and a half millennia puts you back in the 124th century." Scogil replaced the equation with an Imperial History Skeleton—12,338 GE was the date of the sack of Splendid Wisdom. "Early 124th puts you thirty or forty years before the final collapse. The First Empire is disintegrating. We're in the Interregnum. *That's* when Ganderians first began to carry small arms. Not a trace of them in the whole of Ganderian records before that—and Ganderian history predates the

Empire by about 165 centuries. A psychohistorian doesn't *believe* myths; he *investigates* them." The Esfo-Naifin Quandary-Chain reappeared. "The question is why did such a habit as yours persist long after the *need* for personal arms?"

"To defend ourselves!"

"Great Plasma Tongues of Space, against what? I'm a farman. Who trusts a farman? Yet I could attack, unarmed, an octad of hostile Ganderians and not have to worry about their blasters. Using a blaster is taboo on Agander."

"No it's not! I know how to use one! I'm fast and accurate!"

"Yes. Nevertheless, you've never used one to kill a man and neither has your father—or anyone else you know."

"I *could.*"

"That's the myth. But look at the equation. The temporal stability of the weapon-carrying ritual is strong, has been strong over millennia, but that very stability demands nonuse. Widespread employment of small arms would produce a bloom—see the red parameter again." Scogil gave his student time to verify his statement. "I repeat, why did such a habit persist long after the *need* for personal arms? It takes energy to maintain such a habit—you've got to buy the weapon; you've got to keep it in working order; you've got to learn how to use it and keep your skill up to par. You've got to wear the damn thing all the time. But you can't *blast.* What's the utility?"

Eron was confused. "To defend myself!" he repeated with exasperation.

"No. The utility of the little kick sitting in your holster is to maintain the *illusion* that there is an enemy out there who must be kept at bay. A blaster is ineffective against an illusion—to try to use one *against* an illusion would only reveal one's impotence. A Ganderian *can't* use a weapon without proving to himself that he *is* defenseless, and the only reason he carries a weapon is to prove to himself that he *isn't* defenseless. It's called a *ridge,* something you *can't* use but *have* to own to feel secure. The old battleships carried planet-busters but I never heard of one being used."

"You're not making much sense," complained the boy.

"Take out your blaster and point it." A part of Scogil made sure that his body was now more than a meter distant from the "toy."

"No." Eron was uncomfortably defiant.

"That's an order!"

Eron slowly removed the tiny blaster from its shoulder holster and pointed it, the safety on, careful not to aim at his mentor. "This is silly."

"All right. Now tell me who the enemy is?"

"I don't see anything."

"In your mind's eye. It's in your bones; every Ganderian can see the enemy standing in front of him. Let your imagination do the work for you."

"An outsider?"

"Who might that outsider be?"

"The Second Empire?"

"The Second Empire is real time. You're targeting an illusion. What's the kick ready to take out?"

"I've got a bead on your cruddy wall!" exclaimed Eron angrily.

"Have you ever noticed that Ganderian stories, no matter how modern, are always retellings of the old mythology? Who is the enemy in the myths?"

Eron lowered his blaster. Carefully he slipped it back into the discreet holster that was part of his jacket. "The First Empire. The viceroys. The soldiers. The Emperor. That was a *long* time ago."

"The vitality of those myths suggests strongly that Agander never recovered from the trauma of being conquered by the First Empire. When you wakedream, do you ever pop off Imperial Marines as they drop from the sky in the funny armor they wore in that bygone era?"

Eron Osa stretched out on the couch, hands clasped behind his head as he pulled up visuals of his old time-wasting fantasies. Staring eyes glazed over with pleasure. "No, nothing as dumb as that. That wouldn't get you anywhere—too many of them," he scoffed. "I'm smarter." He grinned. "I secretly assassinate *viceroys*. Sometimes I take them prisoner and make ransom demands. It's a silly game. I'm always a zenoli supersoldier, but the zenoli mercenaries didn't appear until the Interregnum when all the viceroys were already dead. It's fun, though; fiction is fiction and you've always said that Ganderians have never been able to keep their history straight." Again Eron became the imp. "Your theory has a vast hole in it."

"Oh?"

"Your Esfo-Naifin Whatchamacallit has an origin 2,500 years ago. You said yourself that the First Empire was already dead by then—so how could little me carrying a blaster be a memory of a trauma that happened umpteen millennia earlier?"

Scogil was beginning to regret the enthusiasm with which he had launched into this conversation. If he didn't watch himself, he would blow his cover. "Let me answer with a lecture. Just sit. Don't fidget. Listen. Put your fam on record."

"Here we go again. Don't you ever run out of lectures?" Eron assumed a mock straitjacketed pose.

"Unresolved traumas reverberate. A *prime*-trauma can spin off new Esfo-Naifin ridges for thousands of years, a fresh branch every time the culture hits a restimulative bump. The Interregnum was a powerful restimulator of the original First Empire conquest—Agander was finally *free* again, but again it was being attacked from outside by forces it couldn't resist. For a culture like yours, with a remarkably low stability drift, sixty-seven centuries wasn't enough to erase the most frightening event in its history."

Eron raised his finger. "Point of information. You're telling me that Ganderians never carried weapons before the Interregnum?"

"Yes."

"I don't believe you—we were *never* wimps like you—but for the sake of argument, continue."

Scogil rose to his full height. "Stop thinking like a pompous Ganderian and think about *force!*" He was now looming over a surprised Eron. With one sudden motion he lifted the boy bodily into the air by the fabric of his jacket, simultaneously disarming him and kicking the blaster across the floor—all before Eron even began to react. The boy hung from his tutor's grip, stunned. "The Imperial Conquest wasn't a game!" Scogil roared. Eron began to try to resist. "It wasn't mythology!" continued Scogil relentlessly. "It was *force!*" He put one of Eron's resisting arms out of commission. "The army that attacked the Ulmat was probably greater in numbers than the total population of Agander." Scogil began to lock the boy in a death hold to counter his every struggle. "Do you think their occupying units would have tolerated personal blasters? Under the Imperium Ganderians *never* carried small arms because the viceroys wouldn't permit it; the offense carried the *death* penalty. If you dared to carry a small weapon you were summarily executed!"

He laughed and tossed the shaken Eron back onto his ugly couch and continued in a now-calm voice. "And as far as I've been able to delve into pre-Imperial times, Ganderians thought themselves above the use of *all* weapons. A peaceful people; a law-and-order sort of people, like you. They *thought* their superior kind of civilization rendered them invulnerable. They *thought* the interstellar reaches put them in an unassailably high castle." Scogil smiled with all of Kapor's charm. He could still command that. "*All* of you *still* think of yourselves so!"

Eron was sitting bug-eyed. "Don't ever do that again! You scared me witless." He glanced at his kick on the floor but didn't dare try to retrieve it.

"The *conquest* scared your *people* witless. It didn't fit Agander's gestalt of the universe. It was incomprehensible. It was alien to Ganderian experience. Different cultures handle traumas differently because they are built out of different collective experiences with different mathematical representations. Yours made the decision to hang on to the Ganderian assumption of invulnerability even though the Imperial occupation *forcibly* proved it false! To keep that illusion your ancestors had to lie outrageously to themselves to the point where they can no longer accurately remember their own history. They remember farmen as *wimps*. *Never* make that mistake! Your ancestors institutionalized the lie. A lie is a time-trap loop because it is an attempt to change an event that can't be changed. Tell a lie and the original event remains the same, and so one is forced to loop back and tell the lie again . . . and again . . . like a running child with his foot nailed to the floor."

Eron didn't know whether he was a terrified animal or a participant in a rational discussion. "Next time you threaten me with an illustrated lecture, warn me a shake of inamins in advance and I'll hyperjump out of here, maybe to some place safe like intergalactic space or the heart of a neutron star." He glanced as his blaster again, started to reach for it, and then withdrew. "Can I have my kick back?"

"Sure."

"I won't blast you."

Scogil grinned. "You aren't *fast* enough to blast me."

Then Eron's fear turned to anger. "You lied to me! You told me that you were a nonviolent civilized citizen of the Galaxy! I believed you!"

"Things aren't always what they seem. Now—are you going to lie to yourself and reconstruct that image of yourself as an invulnerable man who can take on the Galaxy with his toy? Go ahead, pick it up. It will make you invulnerable again."

Eron just sat there. Then the shaking began. Scogil said nothing, giving the boy all the time he needed to digest what had happened. Eron tried to pick up his weapon but couldn't make his body do so. He grinned sheepishly. "I'm scared," he said. Then he went down to the floor, made sure the safety was latched, then holstered his kick. "Your history lessons make me green at the gills. I *know* that was a demo. I *know* you're really a nice person. But that was *scary*."

"And Ganderians are *still* scared of the First Empire, nine thousand years after the fact. No matter how many times they relive the event, the First Empire still wins. And the old, unresolved fears keep coming back to shake them up. Every time that old fear of the old Empire is restimulated, Ganderians collectively make a *new* decision never to forget that they are invulnerable. Your useless toy is only one of a thousand harmonics of that fear. It can all be reduced to mathematical equations."

An intrigued Eron Osa took on the expression of a child who has scented a cunning speculation. "Tell me the truth, you dirty old ugly fanged rat. Are you a psychohistorian? Maybe a spy from Splendid Wisdom?"

Hiranimus liked the directness of this kid. Eron wasn't devious. He didn't like to keep his opinions under cover like those wretched Pscholars. "Well, son, I would have *liked* to have been a jet-hot psychohistorian." That much was true. He sighed before launching into his least favorite lie. "But I'm just an ordinary moon-run of a mathematician who is enthralled by the exotic practical uses of my trade. I don't have access to the *real* tools that allow psychohistorians to predict the gross aspects of our future. The Pscholars of Splendid Wisdom keep their secrets well. Pscholars believe that if everyone could predict the future, Pscholars would no longer be able to govern." *And we Smythosians, who have dabbled in the art of prediction, hope they are right.* "Let's just say I'm a sinner who delights in playing with morsels of forbidden knowledge. That's a theme from some of the older mythologies. I'm not very dangerous; I haven't yet even reached the stage where I can predict whether a planet's sun will rise tomorrow."

"Even *I* can predict that, you *dumbtop!*"

"I am now predicting that you will be in my guest bed within the inamin."

"What if I say no? Staying in the same house with you is going to give me nightmares."

"I can always play the viceroy and *make* my prediction come true."

Eron didn't protest. He was enjoying his rebellion against his family and looked forward to sleeping in a strange bed. When the boy stood, Scogil discreetly dismissed the awful couch. He saw to it that Eron was comfortably established in the back room, tucking him into a special comforter Hiranimus had brought from some distant stellar bazaar. Eron was fascinated by its lightness and crazy-quilt design—and couldn't believe that its warmth wasn't some exotic electronic trick; how could such a miracle derive from physics so simple that even a goose would understand?

"We'll discuss schools again in the morning after I've slumbered on it. Good sleep."

Eron gave a last adulating glance at his mentor standing in the hall's reflected light. "I feel like a traitor. I wish I had a farman for a father." The door vanished.

Hiranimus retreated to his study where he set up a silent comm link through his fam to the elder Osa at the Ulman's Alcazar. He was going to tell on his student and did not want to risk the kid's wrath—his walls were soundproof but not immune to a good fam's sensitive audio pickup. He made the call to his patron while setting the camera to show himself in the best possible light as he settled into his working chair in his most dignified pose. The screen acknowledged contact.

"Yes?" queried the Adjudicator.

"Osa, your son is here with me. I think it best that he stay here for the night." The words were transmitted from an electronic simulation of Scogil's voice box so there would be nothing for Eron to hear.

"So that's where he went! That's a relief. He left here in quite a huff—I wasn't sure what he was going to do. How we spoil our eldest sons—is it out of naïveté? He has talked to you?"

"We discussed his school plans."

The camera at the other end moved back for a long shot. The elder Osa was pacing in a large room with decorated mordants, prized relics of a grimmer age. "I thought I gave him very reasonable alternatives. I wasn't prepared for his upset."

"Vanhosen is an excellent choice. There are probably other places that would better match his peculiar talents."

"Ah, as usual, Murek, you are the consummate diplomat." A sober Osa sat down so that his camera could transmit a portrait shot. "You realize that I operate under financial constraints. Money matters don't seem to impress the younger generation, at least not my son who thinks that because I am an intimate of the Ulman, I have unlimited resources which he is all too willing to exploit."

"Perhaps I can suggest alternatives."

"Expensive ones," grumbled the Adjudicator.

"There are scholarships available. There are schools that pay highly to attract talent."

"He's too young and unseasoned. He's only *twelve*. At that age one's reasoning powers are rough and clumsy and lack judgment. There are huge gaps in his knowledge and maturity. I really don't understand why he is insisting on going to university at his age."

"I understand and I must agree with him. Mathematics is a young man's game and early high-level training is essential. The choice of school can be critical."

"So you think mathematics is his talent? You are not biased because *you* are a mathematician? It's true that he's been good with puzzles since he was a tike. I've always thought that was because of that damn jazzed-up fam I bought him."

"His bent astonishes me. And the fam you gifted him, out of the mad loyalty of a father who wishes the best for his son, is only a small part of it. I strongly suspect that he is the best math student I'll ever teach. I have no doubt that he's going to outclass me before he's twenty."

"He'll have to find work. We Ganderians don't believe in aristocratic laziness no matter how refined the indolence."

"I believe you want him prepared for the Empire's bureaucracy?"

"That's an ambition I've had for him that I've never advertised."

"The *Pscholars* are all mathematicians."

"I'm not fool enough to be *that* ambitious for my son."

"You should be. It is true that the probability of him becoming a psychohistorian is vanishingly small—but it is the *conditional* probability that counts. It is also *highly* improbable to find him in possession of talents which I discern in abundance. He has the caliber of a psychohistorian."

"I wish I trusted you, farman." The face on the screen was bleak with doubt and indecision, a father who wanted the best for his son but was unwilling to plunge the carrier of his genes into a disaster. "Eron was suggesting Kerkorian. You, too?" The expression was agony, a man desperately trying to find sacrifices he could make to afford such a luminous university.

Scogil called upon his most unctuous Kapor façade to quench the man's agony. "Kerkorian is so famous that it can afford to bankrupt its supplicants. But this is a vast galaxy. There are *better* schools out there with lesser reputations most anxious to recruit students with Eron's ability."

"And you think I can afford to send him gallivanting about the Galaxy in search of a wraith? At his age?"

"No need. Urgent family business is taking me to Faraway. I could chaperone your son on a small adventure—the idea delights me. And I'm certain that I could arrange an interview with the registrar of the Asinia Pedagogic. My mathematical credentials are impeccable, as you well know. Asinia you will not have heard of; I doubt that it exists in any archive on Agander. It is a school accredited by the Pscholars. I have contacts in a fund that will settle all of his expenses. If he does well at Asinia for four or five years, he will be picked up by the Pscholars for final training."

"Psychohistory at Faraway?" The father was incredulous. The Founder of the

Second Empire had established Faraway as the leverage force to recivilize a Galaxy fallen into chaos. The mathematics of psychohistory had been a tool *deliberately* left out of that psychohistorically created culture. And poor Faraway was no longer even a minor galactic power. It was the stuff of legend—like the lush landscapes that once covered the deserts of a badly used Rith. Faraway was a quaint place for tourists, for antiquarians who revel in the ruins of ancient glory.

Scogil, alias Murek Kapor, only smiled. "You've forgotten that Faraway once produced mathematicians who revolutionized the physical sciences. Half of the devices we use today owe something in themselves to principles invented on Faraway. Even your son's fam was designed and manufactured on Faraway. Those political skills that once illuminated the Galaxy have now dimmed to twentieth magnitude— but Faraway was *never* known for political sagacity; it was known for its physical science. You still can't find finer teachers of math than at Asinia. They just aren't rich anymore, and they have a hard time attracting worthy students. The Kerkorian staff are on the cutting edge of mathematics, but Asinia trains more qualified *students*. I assure you that the Pscholars pick over Asinia's best graduates. Your son couldn't be better placed."

"And how much will this escort and pampering service of yours cost me?"

While he was talking to Osa Senior, a mad plot began to hatch in Scogil's mind, and, thinking fast, he began to negotiate its framework before he had even blocked out the details to himself. "You don't understand, Honorable Osa. Circumstance forces me to leave your service. Honor obliges me to place a boy as endowed as your son in good hands. My hypership's cabin is already paid for," he lied. "It will cost me nothing to bring Eron with me."

They haggled for a while longer. They made a deal that the senior Osa couldn't afford to ignore. And a deal that presented intriguing possibilities to an ambitious Hiranimus Scogil.

When the connection was broken, he stayed in his aerochair without moving, examining those possibilities. The whole of his scheme was not yet well formed. Maybe he'd have to abort. But with a psychohistorian's ability to see the nodes that had to be touched in order to advance into a particular future, he began to sketch out the critical details to himself. Somewhere along their route he would have to alter Eron's fam in subtle ways. Even Splendid Wisdom was not privy to all that was known in the Thousand Suns about quantum-effect switching. Yes, it might work— and if it did work out, he would advance himself dramatically, and he would advance the cause of the Smythosian Oversee.

Scogil's imagined machination hinged on the off chance that eventually it could be useful for the Oversee to have a primed and innocent traitor at the very heart of the Pscholar's Fellowship—a long shot that might then propel a failed psychohistorian, who hadn't even made it to the bottom level of thinkers, into a plum assignment on Splendid Wisdom. Hadn't the Oversee already advertised that they didn't have enough operatives in the Imperialis system?

He laughed. At the moment it was all just wild plotting on overdrive, a kind of aftereffect of the release from his Murek Kapor restraints. Space, was it good to be free to think again!

*But what a rotten thing to do to a little kid,* he condemned himself. He was appalled that he fully intended to feed his fam-altered victim to the Pscholars, a child sacrifice to the gods. It was probable that the Fellowship would accept this genius. It was also probable that, in due time, Eron would find himself enrolled in the Lyceum at Splendid Wisdom. For what?

He liked Eron. *Poor little devil.* If things went awry—and they *would* go awry— Eron might find himself waylaid in some gruesome hell. He shuffled the cards he had left scattered on his desk. Ah, if only a hand dealt from Agander's Royal Deck of Fate, laid out in the mystical Matrix of Eight, might really be able to predict the boy's future and guard him! Not even psychohistory could do that. Psychohistory was silent on the future of any one man.

But for all his qualms as he sat motionless in his study, Scogil felt a bitter envy. Eron Osa would get the *real* training. Eron Osa would graduate from *the* Lyceum. It would be Eron Osa who would operate out of Splendid Wisdom. It would be Eron Osa who mastered the true line of psychohistorical thought, not some twisted perversion of the Founder's work built by madmen attempting to reconstruct psychohistory from inadequate data thousands of years old.

# RECOVERING FROM CAPITAL
# PUNISHMENT, 14,810 GE

*As psychohistorians we like to claim that our mathematical methods allow us to make predictions about the future when we start with a certain critical set of carefully measured initial conditions. Our detractors dispute this. Still others attack our philosophical stance. Is Thanelord Remendian correct when he portrays us as callous Determinists who view all men as automata performing the motions of some scripted fate? Thanelord Remendian, as self-appointed advocate of Total Freedom, sees quite the opposite: humanity as a noble collection of souls each applying Free Will to attain his own Special Destiny.*

*We need not answer Remendian, but we must have our philosophical position well thought out among ourselves. It is a gross mistake to believe that an accurate ability to predict implies determinism. It does not.*

—"The Eighth Speech" given by the Founder to the Group of Forty-six at the Imperial University, Splendid Wisdom, 12,061 GE

The first time Eron Osa opened Admiral Konn's copy of the *Founder's Selected Essays* after being executed, he never got past the initial two paragraphs. Some of the words he had to sound out before he could recognize them. Without fam access to the instant "gestalt-meanings" of a ten-million-word dictionary, his effort was leaden. Often Eron just gazed blankly at the open book in frustration—half expecting the ghost of his dead fam to imbibe the page all in one glance, to project vivid images based on the contents, to run simulations while exploring the mathematical ramifications, to traipse with him down byways of associated thought.

None of this happened. He was left bobbing in his aerochair in a dim room, staring at squiggles on thin cellomet in a typeface no one had used for two millennia. It was a book laid out with pride and craft, some pages wondrously illustrated with presspoint animation and active equations. The room's light glared harshly over his shoulder, having lost its baffles and half its lum-tiles. There were no fam-feed jacks in the archaic book. The actual reading of the manuscript seemed to be a one-word-at-a-time chore. Real drudgery! And he had to *think* about the words without any handy tools to think with. He would have given up but he still had the strong illusion that he was a psychohistorian and on the verge of understanding everything.

The concepts seemed familiar, but Eron wasn't sure if he had actually read any of the Founder's words in their original format. The baud rate of eyefeed was shockingly slow. He was used to a leisurely comprehension rate of something like 2,048 words per jiff by famfeed and vastly higher input for storage mode. Reading was horrible! He could live faster than he could read about it!

Unfortunately, large chunks of the information input during a famfeed—even the selected parts of it that was used by the organic brain—were cached in the fam. That, thought Eron sourly, was probably the reason his own brain was now so empty. He wondered how much storage space was actually available inside the human head. Not much, obviously! Neurons were gross macromachinery!

How was he going to learn without famfeed! Where was he going to store his thoughts—in his stomach? He glanced covetously at the government-issue fam tossed carelessly over the back of a chair. Not *that* one, but he was going to have to beg-borrow-steal a real fam somehow—and spend the painful years training it.

During his "rebirth" Eron's wardens had arranged for him a cheap hotel room on one of the lower levels of Splendid Wisdom near the Lyceum. The furniture morphed from the wall, stark white, old, used, cramped. The plumbing in the dispozoria needed replacing. The holographic projections made by the comm console were fading and didn't seem to adjust to a sharp definition. The picture wall didn't work.

All they had left him of his old life were his clothes and his little red metricator. He seemed to know what that was for. It was a physicist's pocket tool, small enough to be gripped inside a fist. It would measure almost anything: hardness, distance, spectra, acceleration. Maybe he couldn't recall all the things it could do. He had one vivid memory of sitting at a table eating a sandwich and using it to measure the local pull of gravity, but he couldn't remember which planet or why.

He needed to get out of this prison, take a walk maybe—not too far. Timidly he left the tiny apartment. Out in the city corridor he felt bolder and began a quick-paced exploration romp.

Eron spent the next terrifying interim trying to relocate his hotel. Had he gone *down* a level? *Up?* One clothing shop seemed familiar until he discovered that it was a common franchise in this neighborhood. He had completely lost his sense of orientation. The discreet signs seemed mostly to be of the fam-readable kind, where information was overlaid in tri-D on the visual cortex when needed—and he wore no fam. He asked directions and got answers in the off-planet dialect of some recent immigrant. Perhaps a fam could have deciphered the well-intentioned garble of sounds and gestures.

In the whole of this vertical neighborhood, there were no multilevel spaces that he could find, no reckless use of vegetation. Not everybody was working. Some residents were old and vacant and even sat in the corridors or the levitator lounges to watch the world flow by. Two tough youths assessed his wealth. Or maybe it only seemed that way because here was a class of people of whom he had been oblivious in his previous life. Maybe, just maybe, they were all right. Maybe they were dangerous only to strangers. Maybe they weren't dangerous at all. Still, he fled from them in a kind of childish panic that took him down corridors and zigzagging commercial alleys and well-lit levitators that lost him completely but miraculously delivered him "home" again. The surprise of finding himself in front of his hotel astonished him into a burst of tearful thanks.

After awakening from a restless sleep, he remembered—and chose safety over adventure, spending the next multiple watches alone in his apartment—doors sealed, averse even to a brief restocking excursion—while he continued to struggle with the Founder's first essay, polishing his painful reading skills. His troubles did not stem only from a lack of the utilities usually provided by a fam—he didn't even command all of his *organically* based faculties. His mind was used to the brain/fam dialog, and some critical areas of his wetware seemed to be accessible only by key stimulation via fam-cue. The mental paths leading into these sepulchers were effectively blocked by his famlessness—and, to find their barricaded treasures, he had to guess his way blindly through neural codes. Being a moron was hard labor. Well, back to his studies!

Determinism. And more determinism. He reread the opening of the Founder's "Eighth Speech" many times. Psychohistory was a science of prediction. Did an ability to predict imply determinism? In this Galaxy where an elite controlled the future in which the society was destined to live, people were apt to debate such philosophical points. Did it matter?

To distract himself from the reading, Eron sniffed the pages of this book that had been shaped into pocket size for carrying close to the heart by someone who loved to read. It smelled as if it had been printed a thousand years ago, and the title page said so. That spoke of a time well after the Founder had been reduced to a holographic glimmer in some vault and well past the farthest reach of that great man's primitive mathematical vision—yet still centuries before the birth of anyone presently alive.

Enough sniffing. *Keep the book open and try to read.* Eron did his best to imagine the ancient debate between Thanelord Remendian and the Founder. There would be flamboyant clothes, snuff, perfume, gestures, and admonitions—but without his fam's visualizers he saw only ghosts on a darkened stage. He plodded on.

The essay began its demolition of Thanelord Remendian's thesis by fielding a clear definition of determinism, one that struck Eron as weirdly familiar. At the same time, it startled him—the way things do that have been around for a long time, un-noticed. He concentrated. He was still enough of a mathematician to realize that defi-nitions are the framework of sound argument. They *must* be understood. He tried.

A deterministic universe requires One Future and One Past, immutable. It requires that every governing equation of motion have a Unique Solution whether worked forward or backward in time—even if we can only approximate that Solution in ever refinable steps. Choices become illusions. Determinism allows no branches, no random events, no errors, no noise. In such a universe even an omnipotent god is powerless to intervene. A universe cannot, by definition, be deterministic when man or god has choice, or if the guiding equations, given the same initial conditions, can be made to yield more than one result through branching, randomities, quantum superposition, error, or noise.

Remendian is mistaken to tar us as determinists. Psychohistory fails as a deterministic system simply because NONE of its probabilistic equations have unique solutions. This should not surprise us. After all, even the most rigorous equations of physics have long been framed in such a way that two identical initial states will not lead to exactly the same outcome. The neomystic philosopher Bohr . . .

At this point in his discourse the Founder went off into a technical discussion of the mathematical underpinnings that a deterministic *physics* would require. Eron had the comfortable illusion that he understood all the symbols and how the meanings were related, but when he actually got excited and tried to manipulate the dynamic symbols . . . he could do nothing. It was humiliating. Not to be able to follow the Founder when he was glossing over the easiest of the conundrums of primordial physics! Eron summarized the Founder's points for himself to get a grip on them, using the apartment's decrepit console as a doodle-pad.

All viable physical descriptions of our universe seem to require:
1] Time-symmetry. The physical equations determining state change are unaltered by the substitution of negative-t for t, where t is time. (The laws of our physics cannot be modified by a time reversal.)

Imposing determinism as an additional constraint then implies:
2] Reversibility. The physical equations determining state change cannot contain traps. (The system will not be determinable if it can dispatch information to conveniently inaccessible states like alternate worlds or black holes.)

The (perhaps apocryphal) father of physics, Newton, had been claimed by no less than eighteen worlds of the Sirius Sector. The great synthesis of the ancient newtonian theurgists was deterministic because it naïvely contained no information traps. Being that, newtonianism failed to derive entropy from first principles; thermodynamics *requires* a built-in mechanism for lossy information compression. Even after careful experimentation by the mystical heisenbergians had established the uncertainty of position/momentum, many of these dawn theurgists still clung to theological dogma that all information about the past was somehow retained in the positions and momenta of the current superposed states of the universe; nothing could be forgotten. The universe has mostly forgotten these men.

The Founder speculated that this stubborn conception of the universe as an all-remembering entity had been inherited from a then-common belief in an all-knowing God whose eye saw the whole of eternity. The tacit (and false) assumption that the underlying fabric of the universe was described by the artificial mathematical entity called a manifold fostered the illusion because a manifold has no upper limit on the amount of information that can be impressed upon it.

Gripped by a fit of industry, Eron confirmed the Founder's careful proof that a deterministic universe requires more info storage space than the physical nature of the universe allows—using a marker on the cleanable wall because his holopad was down. Neat. He left it there as wallpaper.

In the real world, information about past states is continually being lost—quantum wave-functions de-cohere, things fall into black holes—and so present initial conditions never contain enough information to reconstruct the past (except on a probabilistic basis). Because of time-symmetry, an inability to reconstruct the past is mirrored as an inability to predict the future (except on a probabilistic basis). The job of accumulating information about a future time is never complete until the moment when that future becomes the present.

Our "now" contains neither the whole of the past nor the whole of the future, or, to put it another way, "now" contains the roots of all possible pasts—but won't tell us which particular root is ours—and contains all possible futures in the branches of its tree—but won't tell us which of those limbs we are about to climb out on.

No psychohistorian, no matter what godlike powers he might acquire, can predict an absolute future—too much information about the future is missing in the initial conditions of the present; no historian, no matter how meticulous, can write the definitive history—too much information about the past has been irretrievably lost.

That established, the Founder went on to describe how mathematics could determine the maximum upper limit on the amount of information that the present held about the future. Once the limits were known, mathematical method was free to give its best estimates of which futures we faced and what variables controlled the probability attached to a future.

The Master began to play amusing games with his audience—"the Group of Forty-six," long dead, plus Eron, recently dead. They were asked to pretend that every Past Event was trying to encode itself in digital form to be transmitted through time to be filed by a harried Present in its bulging storage cabinets. He made it sound like he was chatting with the past over a wire. Eron grimaced. "Hello. This is the past. Get out your decrypter and I'll tell you what really happened back here—hope you have enough storage room."

As more and more messages accumulated, the physical size of the information "bits" has to shrink to be accommodated. Not a problem in the magical mathematical realm of a manifold, but in the real world—Eron could hear the Founder smiling—things got hairy when the Bureaucrats of Filing were eventually faced with the archival problem of finding space inside a cubic Planck-length for, say, the history of the Emperors. Yet how have bureaucrats everywhere always solved such an information overload problem? They condense the original into a brief memo, hide the memo inside the papers on their desktop, and hand the original report to an office boy with orders to lose it. Physicists have invented a fancy name for this bureaucratic procedure—they call it de-coherence.

Of course, by time-symmetry, the events of the future were also sending messages to be stored in the same bulging cabinets and getting the same treatment. "Hello. This is your future speaking. Have I got news for you. But please make room in your storage space for my message." Those famous branchings into alternate futures (the classical emperor-in-a-coffin conundrum) weren't branches into other worlds at all; each branch simply represented one question ("Is the emperor alive?") that was unanswerable because the procedures of the Bureaucrats of the Present didn't yet have a place to store the answer. A bit of information about the past must be erased to make room for every new bit of information about the future.

Definition: The information content of an event, in bits, is exactly the number of yes/no questions needed to differentiate it from all other possible events. Consequently, if information is never lost—a deterministic requirement—any message describing an event had to carry from the past to the present exactly the same number of bits as were in the original event. Was it possible for such a transmission to be lossless?

The Founder was making sport with the determinists, catching them, teasing them, tweeking their noses, and letting them go. How could Remendian ever have mistaken this cat for a mouse? The Founder waxed with exaggerated humor about the trials and tribulations of a deterministic universe in which information conservation was a fact: every event that had ever happened was still out there transmitting its own information load, clogging every possible transmission line of space-time in a simultaneous attempt to wash ashore onto the present.

Eron tried to comprehend the preposterous magnitude of such a load. A whimsical analogy crossed his mind. He imagined the communication network of Splendid Wisdom burdened with the continual lossless transmission of every message that had ever been generated on Splendid Wisdom for the last fourteen millennia! Somewhere in there would be a wandering packet carrying Thanelord Remendian's deathless order for breakfast on the morning of . . . consisting of three pig embryos in buttered thyme sauce on toast. He laughed, imagining the fate of a universe whose very survival depended upon the pristine maintenance of that message!

So much had been lost.

The universe was still here.

The Founder wrote out equations that illuminated the error.

Deduction: Determinism requires a transfinite channel capacity in order to maintain the transmission of all of its lossless messages. Space must be infinitely divisible.

At that point in his essay, the Founder took off his gloves. In a mere four lines he developed the formula for the real channel capacity of space. Prominent in the formula was the Planck length. The bandwidth of the universe wasn't great enough to deliver the past's messages losslessly to the present. Nor the future's messages losslessly to the past. The real universe seemed to be "printed" in an "ink" whose "particle size" could never be less than the Planck length.

The Founder proceeded to outline some of the ways in which the universe was known to lose information.

> 1] What drops into a black hole can't get out again, not even under time reversal. Black holes eat information permanently. Loss of information creates more uncertainty about the past, which is the same as saying that the information consumed by a black hole increases entropy.

> 2] Information is stored ambiguously at the quantum level to conserve bandwidth—for instance, data about position and momentum overwrite each other in the same "registers"—playing havoc with a physicist's ability to pin down past or future. To operate in the present the universe never needs to know a particle's position and momentum at the same time, so it doesn't store that information independently.

> 3] A physicist may predict the *pattern* of hits that an electron beam makes in passing through two slits, but he cannot predict where any *particular* electron will hit; that information involves processes that are not derivable from any initial condition. The universe minimizes its use of bandwidth with such a compression technique. A physicist can look at a particular "hit" after the fact but cannot then backtrack the path of the electron that made the hit.

> 4] A physicist can predict *how many* alpha particles will be ejected from a gram of uranium in the next jiff; but he cannot tell you when a *particular* uranium 238 atom will change state to thorium 234. Worse, the wave equations that describe uranium's radioactivity, by time-

symmetry, say that uranium has the same half-life whether it is moving forward or backward in time. But we know that the atoms in the uranium 238 sample we hold in our lab have been stable for the billions of years they have existed outside the supernova that created them! Quantum mechanics will not allow us to assume that, if we reverse time, these same uranium atoms will all *remain* stable for the billions of years it will take them to travel back to their mother nova. Bandwidth is limited. The universe eliminates inessential information. The uranium will not be able to return through time via the same path by which it arrived because the information that described that path no longer exists. A uranium atom's moment of death is independent of its history.

The Founder concluded his discussion of physics with an elegant proof that in a *deterministic* universe, since *nothing* can be uncertain, entropy, the measure of uncertainty, must always be zero and so cannot increase. In a world without information loss, thermodynamics is impossible. Constant entropy is another word for stasis. Very little of interest could exist under a deterministic regime.

Eron threw the book across the room and sat down cross-legged on the floor to sulk. It was a mighty sulk. If entropy increases and information is lost as we move into the future, then entropy must *decrease* while information *increases* as we trace events back into the past. That was only logical—but how could such an antisymmetric conclusion square with the time-symmetry of physical law? Eron cried himself to sleep. He couldn't understand the simplest things anymore. He was a moron, an animal!

But when Eron awoke, he *understood*. His sleeping mind had resolved the dilemma—a joyous miracle to Eron. It had produced a simple model within which even a famless mind could play. Its laws were time-symmetric. It was *not* deterministic because its future was only partially predictable and its past was only partially knowable. The model contained no arrow of time; entropy increased regardless of whether one took the model forward or backward in time.

He had dreamed a circular necklace of beads along a wire, the black and white beads stationary, the mobile blue beads always moving either clockwise or counterclockwise.

1] The black beads sometimes changed state from black to white—emitting a mobile blue bead as they did so with equal probability to right or left.

2] A blue bead passed through any black or blue bead it hit but was absorbed by contact with a white bead.

3] When a white bead absorbed a blue bead it changed state from white to black.

4] The black beads emitted their blue beads with a random frequency dependent upon how many blue beads had passed through them.

A simple universe.

At time zero, knowing which beads were black and which beads white, how could the future state of the necklace be predicted? What had been its past? Because of time-symmetry, both problems were the same. Because the system was nondeterministic, neither the future nor the past could be known with certainty, but the *probability* of any particular future or any particular past could be computed absolutely. From those probabilities one could compute the uncertainty—the entropy—of any future or past. Entropy *increased* as the model was stepped into the future, and yes, just as the Founder said, the entropy *increased* as the model was stepped back into the past.

In a *deterministic* universe where each action had its certain outcome, reversibility and time-symmetry were the same thing.

But in a *probabilistic* universe, reversibility and time-symmetry were very different concepts.

So much for Eron's wishful desire to go back and start all over again as a twelve-year-old; to time-travel back to his younger self he'd have to violate all the laws of thermodynamics. He laughed.

The equations of motion for smashing a goblet against the wall were exactly the same as the equations for assembling a goblet out of flying pieces of glass—but the probabilities were vastly different. The picture was beautifully time-symmetric. A process can be totally reversible—yet what is easy in one direction can be daunting in the other.

Eron felt reborn. It was exhilarating to find out that he could *think* without a fam—even if he did his best thinking while asleep. The feeling made him smile again and again. He picked the Founder's book off the floor and began again at the beginning. He *still* had to struggle with the words, pronounce them until they made sense, read and reread the sentences. He found the place where he had left off and smoothed the battered page. He was beginning to understand how an unaided brain functioned—a problem he hadn't faced since he was three.

The Founder continued:

> In our search for the future does a lack of deterministic equations cripple us? Not at all.
> Our psychohistorical tools CAN predict the critical branching points of our most probable social futures. Complexity has its own metalevel of simple modes. We can predict social structures to a high degree of ac-

curacy along a millennial time scale just as physics can predict the orbit of a given planet on a scale of thousands of years. We do not pretend to predict the life of a single individual just as the physicist doesn't pretend to be able to predict the path of a molecule in his given planet's atmosphere.

We compute many futures, not all with the same likelihood. It is not pleasant to see, dominating the timescape, a full 30,000-year galactic-wide interregnum, but our math has examined less severe, if much less probable, branches. One under current investigation promises a simpler dark age on a much-collapsed time scale. There are nudge-nodes where the probabilities can be drastically altered by small forces within our command.

Can there be a nonfatalistic role for individuals in our branching vision? Of course! Our large sample-size social model assumes that SOME humans will take advantage of ALL of the degrees of freedom permitted. Psychohistory shows us ways of constraining various degrees of freedom so that . . .

On the other hand, psychohistory does not allow us Thanelord Remendian's Total Freedom. Freedom unrestrained implies that every equation of action will contain an Infinity of Solutions—forcing the future to be totally unreadable. All prediction becomes impossible once every event is equally likely. Try speaking without being able to predict what your mouth will do. Try reaching for a glass of water when your fingers refuse to obey the constraints of any physical law. Without prediction, power cannot be applied rationally; even omnipotent power is helpless.

Psychohistory is neither deterministic nor licentious. It defines the constraints under which history must unfold and spotlights the low-effort choice points. Our model operates within a phase-space. The degrees of freedom allowed are far LESS than the dimensionality of the space of "total freedom" but far GREATER than the "deterministic" model which allows NO choices at all.

Gently Eron lowered the sacred book into his pocket. He wondered how much freedom *he* had left. Steady reading with little sleep had tired him, but he felt good. The exercise had pulled up fresh memories. One of the images was especially vivid, but he couldn't place it. He saw a public square in front of a hotel, yes, on a strange planet whose name escaped him. When was it? Well, it was the memory of a young boy. He was gripping his first book, bought much to the dismay of, yes, his *tutor*. A huge book about the Galaxy's ancient Emperors. And his tutor hadn't been pleased at the prospect of paying starfreight on a *book* whose content was more properly stored inside the head of a pin!

# YOUNG ERON BEGINS HIS ADVENTURE, 14,790 GE

*Emperor Daigin-the-Jaw*
*b: 5561 GE d: 5632 GE*
*reign: 5578 GE to 5632 GE*

*. . . during the midphase of Our Awesome Empire's inexorably patient sweep across the Galaxy, Daigin-the-Jaw ascended at seventeen . . . A charismatic mover, he sought to abandon Splendid Wisdom's centuries old policy of sly political assimilation for an impetuous strategy of rapid conquest. The Imperial bureaucracy, flushed with millennia of successful expansion, saw this youth as the embodiment of its ambition. They assembled and deployed for him the most formidable array of armies ever to swarm the human starways.*

*. . . only thirty-four when his strike forces numbered seven billion soldiers . . . exploits legendary. At forty-eight, personally in command of the Thirteenth Fleet . . .*

*. . . a stellar tide of rebellion marred his final victories, ending only with his death by perfidious ambush at the second battle of Blackamoor Cross . . . more than six thousand planned invasions put on hold . . .*

*—A Short History of Our Splendid Emperors*

In a weaker gravity than Agander's, Eron Osa bounded down the stairs of the narrow street with his newly acquired *Short History* gripped in both hands under one arm. He had been running all morning up and down the hillwalks and over the rideways of the Ulmat Constellation's capital metropolis, poking into stores and botanical gardens, even exploring the hallowed grounds of the Vanhosen Scholarium at a lickety-split pace that no registrar would be able to match. (Having narrowly escaped the fate of being forced to study at Vanhosen, he was in no mood to be trapped inside its halls for years by unhappy lackeys in the thrall of his father.)

He did stop once at a collegiate café to memorize the faces of the students he would never mix with long enough to know—silly girls with golden finger claws and arrogant boys with funny hats. Then he ran on. He had embraced as much strangeness as he could soak up before lunchtime. Down the stairs! Leap and fly!

Tutor Kapor sat, unsweating, at the appointed table in the little café in the square across from their hotel. Eron plunked his book on the tabletop. "I'm not late!" He sank down in his seat with relief.

"A book?" queried his mild tutor.

"I bought it at a used-data emporium. Chip displays, all upstaging each other! I was bogglefied! You'll never find such stuff trawling through an archive! It was enough to transmute the brain! I was staggering around the aisles dazed when I bumped into a *bookshelf* on the third terrace. Books are a lot quieter. What a relief!"

"You've never seen a book in your life!" admonished his tutor.

"I know!" Eron exclaimed happily. "That's why I bought one." He added defensively, "It's not on *your* money stick—it was *my* credit. It's all about the lives of emperors." He saw less than approval in the eyes of Murek so he added accusingly, "You told me to study history!"

Eron's elder companion nudged the volume. "I'm thinking about the freight charges. You didn't, by any lucky chance, pick up the book's template? With a piece of junk this massive, it's easier to manufax a new copy every time you want to read it than to lug it around with you between the stars."

"I can't keep it?" Eron was stricken.

Tutor Kapor spun the tome a half turn on the tabletop to read the title. *A Short History of Our Splendid Emperors: Kambal-the-First to Zankatal-the-Pious.* He hefted it to make a more scholarly assessment. "Ooof. My arm exercises for the morning," he added dryly. He examined the title page. "It's an old book." He sniffed it. "Cellomet. Old for sure. If I recall right, Zankatal-the-Noose predates our Founder by about a century." A tip of the head meant that Eron's tutor was about to elaborate on his comment. "'Noose' is not his official name, of course—it's just what Zankatal was called out here in the nether reaches of the Galaxy where he was not thought to be so pious."

He leaned back and slapped the heavy cover. "Sure, you can keep your book, Eron—as long as you learn what every young traveler has to learn: the freight to Faraway on this book is far more than the book will ever be worth. Since those charges *will* be on my stick, I'm going to ask a favor of you; you're going to have to *read* the damn book. And it's an *old* book—there's no famfeed; it's all eyefeed, page by page." He laughed. "That'll teach you to buy books!"

"It's not really a book!" sulked Eron. "It's automated!" He flipped out a fold-in back-cover flatplate. "It's got an index. Press a button and it flips open to the right pages in sequence. There aren't any pictures on the pages, but the flatplate will give you any picture you want." He produced the animated vizeo of some emperor who offered them a posed benediction against a Splendid palatial interior. "Hot zits!" he exclaimed while looking at the grand architecture, which dwarfed even the majestic furniture. "They lived like that?"

"Look at the *words,* the *words,*" admonished his tutor, who couldn't stop for a jiff being a teacher.

"*You* don't know what I've already read," replied the stung student. "*You* think it was Daigin-the-Jaw who conquered the Ulmat. You told me that. You're wrong. It was his son, Arum, in the reign of Daigin-the-Mild, who dropped in with his fleet and cut off our balls and then went home to Splendid Wisdom and cut off the Emperor's balls just to show the Galaxy who was boss. When I found that, that's when I bought the book. They don't put stuff like that in the archives on Agander! Here!" He opened the pages at the right section, just to prove that he had found out something his tutor did not know.

> Emperor Daigin-the-Mild
> b: 5597 GE d: 5671 GE
> reign: 5632 GE to 5641 GE
>
> ... born aboard the warship *Santaerno* to an unknown Imperial concubine during the full fury of his father's Persean-Cara Campaign. A music scholar and dilettante, the youngest and least favored son of Daigin-the-Jaw was raised to power—only watches after his father's suspicious death—by a war-weary court desperately ready to pursue a hasty policy of galactic reconciliation and consolidation.
>
> ... was probably unaware of the arrest and execution of six of his half brothers during the prefatory rituals before his coronation. The seventh and wiser brother, Arum, a popular commander in his father's armada, refused to return to Splendid Wisdom for the accession, pleading urgent military duties. Two years and three assassination attempts later, Arum answered the court's vile actions by ordering the Eighteenth Mobile Fleet out along the Persean Arm to a swift subjugation of the Ulmat Constellation. The flawlessly executed attack had no other purpose than as a warning to the bloodily pacifist court to mind its own business or suffer slit throats.
>
> Daigin-the-Mild ruled ineffectively with repeated attempts to reconcile with Arum until his impatient brother, weary of a game that required him to pretend loyalty to a brother he despised, returned to Splendid Wisdom at the head of his fleet, there to publically castrate the Emperor and send him off to exile, the flow of Empire now safely in his own hands.

Emperor Arum-the-Patient
b: 5591 GE d: 5662 GE
reign: 5641 GE to 5662 GE

As Emperor . . . maintained a fondness for his haven in the Ulmat.
He used the Ulmat Constellation as his major naval base and later established there an Orbital War Museum in honor of his father. His nostalgic poems, especially "Ode to Agander's Night," was very popular at
court until he was poisoned by his mother . . .

Eron stopped reading with a wistful smile on his face, still astonished that an Emperor had noticed his home planet. "Arum must have liked Agander. To have written a poem about us . . . but I couldn't find the poem. I looked! Everything should
be connected to everything else, so you can find things!"

A robotray brought the two intent scholars their lunch and waited patiently for
them to remove the book before it would set the table. Murek took a bite of
smoked fish, imported, probably Frisan; Mowist life had never evolved as far as
fish. "There are a hundred quadrillion people out there all writing their memoirs
and taking cubes of their newest baby, and you expect everything to be linked with
everything else, and instantaneously, all the way back to the cave paintings of Las-
caux? That a student's life should be so easy! The Galaxy is a vast place," he said
tritely.

"A biography of the Emperors ought at least to have a reference to an Emperor's poems!"

"I'll bet that if you let me teach you a few of the tricks of historical research,
you could find that poem within a year."

"I hate it when you make curiosity sound like work! I know something easier
to look for. As emperor, Arum set up a war museum out here in the Constellation
somewhere. Battleships and everything. To honor his father. What happened to it?
Did all that super blasting power go into orbital decay and burn up, or what?"

This was just an offhand question that Eron wanted his omnipotent tutor to
answer *at once,* but what he got for a reply made him wish he'd kept his mouth shut.
"That's a good question to practice one's wits on," said Murek in the voice he used
when outlining an assignment.

They had only ten watches on Mowist before they were to ship out of the Ulmat Constellation entirely, and Eron found himself trapped into long bouts of historical research about a *museum* that wasn't even there anymore! He was given a
whole list of things to do, not all of which made sense. Eron could understand a
few stints of frantic archival searching on the hotel's obsolete equipment, but . . .
interviewing people he didn't know? checking out naval hobby shops? famfeeding
museum management consultant brochures?

But he actually did find out what had happened to the Orbital War Museum.

Daigin-the-Jaw's surplus military artifacts, after millennia of preservation, had been pirated during the Interregnum and sold off to local warlords. This he reported glumly to his tutor. The man was not sympathetic, as was his dry nature. "What did you expect? An ancient Imperial dreadnought of the Horezkor class sitting out there waiting for you to inspect it?"

"Yeah," said Eron dreamily, "that would have been nice."

"Then why didn't you talk to the local tourist bureau?"

Eron looked up quickly. When he saw the twinkle in his mentor's eye, he knew instantly that he had been had and rushed off to the hotel's comm to check out all the tourist attractions. Yes, there was a Horezkor dreadnought on display, the only ship of Arum's Museum armada that had not been sold or stolen—lacking at the time any functioning hyperdrive motors or weapons. A few hundred years ago the restored hulk had been incorporated as a part of the Greater Station, which served the Ulmat's distant interstellar traffic.

Eron had missed it only because, from Agander, he and Kapor had hypered into Mowist's Lesser Station, which served the local Ulmat routes. Belatedly Eron checked their outbound reservations from the Greater Station, and much to his chagrin found a full-color advertisement for the "astonishing" Horezkor tour.

He thought about the enigma of his tutor, the young farman who was taking him, miraculously, on the adventure of his life from which he would probably never return. His father expected him to return, but once Eron had seen Agander from orbit—a blue-green wispy white ball against the spectacular clouds of space from which it had "recently" formed—he had made the conscious *decision* never to return. Was such a decision revokable?

He wandered back to their hotel room and found Kapor asleep, but he didn't care. Nefarious humor didn't deserve consideration. "Are we going to take the Horezkor tour before we board our ship?" he demanded in a loud voice. "It's two kilometers long. It's got everything! When it was built it had the largest hyper-atomic motors in the universe! Please."

A half-opened eye looked up at him. "Wouldn't miss it. It's on our itinerary."

"Why didn't you tell me? You rat!" Eron was angry enough now to shake his mentor fully awake—but he didn't.

"I'm dumping you at Faraway," said the sleepy voice from the bed. "You can't expect me to do your research for you forever. A lot of Pscholars think their math is so powerful that they can ignore the past when they predict the future—but they lose the kind of insight that makes for the elegant use of their tools. If you want to get as far as Splendid Wisdom and make your mark there, you've got to know a million years of history well enough to dream through the rise and fall of any civilization before breakfast."

"A million years! We haven't been around that long! The Empire is still a baby!"

"You don't think we were born in the sublight ships of the first expansion

DONALD KINGSBURY

wave, do you? Home is a cave, food consists of slugs that live under rocks, and the starry sky is a shining cave roof just out of reach. A lot between then and your own civilization. You'll have to know it all, and I'm not going to learn it for you. I'm going back to sleep. It's the middle of my sleep-watch! You're on your own." Then in the direction of the light he said, "Off!" before turning back to Eron. "Your next assignment," he continued in the darkness, "is to find out what was in the Ulmat before mankind arrived."

Eron reluctantly let his taskmaster sleep, but thought indignantly hurt thoughts nevertheless. He *already* knew the precolonization history of the Ulmat! Nothing! All the planets in the Ulmat Constellation were young, the oldest having coalesced no more than two billion years ago. Agander was the youngest of them all. Soup! That's what the colonists had found. Yeach, and soup that probably didn't even taste very good. Only Mowist had once supported multicellular life, little nondescript spiny things that had been a kind of a water pump. Rakal hadn't even had soup—no water. *Dumbtop Kapor thinks I don't know anything.*

But he soon forgot the slight and was, in his imagination, marching through the guts of a battleship in all the full-color glory that an active fam could provide to the mind's eye. He gave the orders on the bridge. He reviewed tier after tier of battle stations. *He* was the commander who had once conquered Agander!

# 9

# TWO MEN FIND EACH OTHER, 14,790 GE

*When atomic power was discovered by our feral ancestors seventy-four millen-nia ago, the apparatus was simple enough—but both monstrous and danger-ous. The fires were blocks of carbon alternated with uranium slugs, piping, and control rods. Naturally unstable isotopes were extracted as bomb ingredients. The first crude city-destroyers were carted to their targets by twelve men in huge aluminum flying fortresses powered by air-breathing engines. There are hints in the record that a whole continent was once made radioactive by the failure of a fission power generator . . . At the time of the original sublight star-ships, when isolated stellar cultures diverged over ten millennia for lack of power to maintain communications . . . a slow process of evolution was perfecting a mass-to-energy technology that could deliver both a high-energy density and a vanishing gamma emission rate . . . ushering in the era of expansion based on Eta Cuminga's hyperspace technology . . . After forty-eight millennia of ineffi-cient double-pole hyperdrive design, the engineers of Splendid Wisdom began building the first massive Oerstan hyperdrive motors that tapped into the paral-lel energy of the . . . probably the major factor giving Splendid Wisdom's navy an . . . At the other end of the scale, during the decline of Imperial . . . the magi-cians of Faraway mastered the process of local phased charge-flipping, using these hydrogen-fueled microannihilation devices to . . .*

—From the Interregnum Exhibit at the Bureau of Historical Sciences

Kargil Linmax was a big-boned man who hefted Kikaju Jama's galactarium in a six-fingered hand while he gave it a quick eyeball scrutiny in the doorway of his spacious workshop. "Looks like a gaudy fake to me!" he roared in the general di-rection of the Hyperlord with a voice that might have been calling up all five-fingered hands on a warship.

Jama moved his ears back a head-width. "I know an ancestral Faraway Trader who would be miffed at your lack of faith in his judgment," he said in defense of his property, slightly miffed himself. "I myself watched it project stars. I can guarantee that it was once owned by a Trader. The friend who procured it for me is very reliable."

"And it kifizzled right after you bought it? The best fakes do that. They kifizzle before you find out that they can't really do what they are supposed to do." He flipped his bug-eyed power-spectacles down over his nose and stared. "It doesn't look like any Faraway design I've ever seen, not remotely. Pretty little thing, though. Who knows? It's possible that it's authentic. By the fourth century"—he was implying Founder's Era, not Galactic Era—"there were some very rich traders and they contracted some of the damnedest of intricate art pieces. I've seen stranger. The artist wouldn't have been local to the Periphery, though. That's not a count against it. The oddest people hypered out of nowhere down onto the shores of Faraway in that era. Let's bounce your toy off the deck."

At the shocked look on Kikaju's face, Kargil's laughter boomed. "Just an expression. At the scholarium I was trained as a nanomechanic. We learned a very gentle touch, which I'm afraid we've always called 'bouncing'—in case you once again hear those dreaded words from my mouth."

"You are by profession a nanomechanic?" The Hyperlord was impressed and unconsciously took his mopcap in hand, looking for a rack upon which to hang it.

"The scholarium was eons ago; I never practiced. The navy took my contract and I spent my working life uselessly involved in the maintenance and perfection of secret naval ultrawave combat protocols. Faraway antiques are just a hobby of mine to keep me out of trouble in my old age. I've a nice shop, mostly naval surplus that I kidnapped from storage graveyards."

"An impressive set of equipment," the Hyperlord commented wryly as he stepped into the warehouse-spacious workshop. Some of the resident machines were so small that they hid themselves inside their own armored cleanboxes and could be visited only by electronic microscope. Some were mobile roboassistants of alien design and mobility. Some of the machines were enormous. "It looks like you raided a hidden First Empire cache."

Linmax laughed. "The fill-your-eyes bulk is mostly cut-rate earthquake mountings—an exchange of mass for finesse. You noticed on your way from the station, down those cockamamie stairs, that I live inside a canyon face and am staring into the homes of my neighbors across fifty meters of natural air shaft. A hundred years ago a fault line slipped right beneath your feet. Glad I wasn't born then." He grinned. "The sheared apartments were scrapped rather than rebuilt. Left a gap that makes for friendly yodeling contests. We still get our teeth rattled sporadically—nothing serious, mind you, but I take my little precautions."

"Great stars!" exclaimed an appalled Jama, fidgeting with the velvet scales of his cap. "Why would anyone live here!"

"Cheap rent." The big man grinned again and ran his six-fingered hand through white hair. "You don't think the pension of a retired naval officer is enough to keep a man alive, do you?"

He had extracted the dead atomo-unit from the galactarium ovoid and was clamping the tiny power supply inside a cleanbox for analysis. "And what is your interest in Faraway antiques?" But before Jama could reply, Kargil Linmax grimaced. "Bad news and good news. The atomo is a Farliquar, compact shape but shoddy design. A very small outfit that was in production less than three years before it failed: 374 to 377 FE. They made exorbitant promises and couldn't deliver. Some good stuff, but poor quality control. Screwed up on their war contracts. First Farliquar I've ever seen. So it's authentic—but you won't find a replacement." He read more numbers off his instruments. "Looks like an intermittent failure—the worst kind. Maybe jiggling it or banging it against your head would make it work. Except the repair might not last more than a few jiffs. Might melt your doodad. I wouldn't bet that your piece isn't a cheap knockoff cobbled out of war surplus and sold to a gullible Trader by some non-Faraway shyster. Where did your reliable friend find it—in some Trader's buried discard heap?"

"Then it's junk?" queried a stricken Hyperlord.

"Means nothing. The atomo might have been used because all the good ones were being sucked up by the war effort. But don't get your hopes up."

"I should tell you that it's been in space for a couple of millennia."

"Salvage? That could be good or bad. I'll look for cosmic ray damage. The really bad news is that I don't have any mating atomos in stock—and neither will anyone else. If you can spare the credit, I'll build you some. An octad is as cheap as one. The worst that can happen is that we blow up the workshop." He demonstrated with a wide fling of his hands. "When the zoning flunkies come after us, we'll blame it on the fault line. Us local types have learned how to blame *everything* on the quakes."

Jama had not found a place to hang his hat so he readjusted it to his head. Anxiously he watched a cheerful Kargil open up a larger cleanbox and insert the powerless jade artifact into its vicious-looking interior.

"We leave it there. I'm doing an outrageously slow analysis, but that way I get to use very soft fingers." He made some adjustments. "We now have time on our hands. We can chat on my balcony and yodel."

From across the shop floor, they were approached by a six-year-old girl with a breadroll stuffed with slaw and cheese, her attention on the wavering surface that brimmed atop the glass of juice she was bringing to Kargil. "Papa, you have to eat!" She turned to Jama. "And what would you like, sir?" The "sir" was added because of the elaborately important way their visitor was dressed.

"He starves, Sweet Toes," said Kargil, already munching on his roll. "If I can turn him into a paying customer, we'll keep him for dinner."

She saluted crisply and ran off. The military salute so startled the Hyperlord that he just stared at her retreating figure.

"Well, after all," explained Linmax gruffly, "I'm her commanding officer."

"You're her grandfather?"

"Space, no!"

Metal clanged under two pairs of feet. Jama turned and glanced back in the direction of the ruckus and saw a five-year-old boy being chased by a loudly protesting two-year-old along a second-floor gallery at the front of the workshop. A family! "My apologies." The Hyperlord bowed as he tried diplomacy to correct his gaff. "You must be the father of these youths, of course!"

"Not likely! The father of Sweet Toes," said Linmax sternly, "murdered her mother and then jumped to his death while trying to take with him both his daughter and the railing she was clenching for dear life. I happened to be there when she most needed kind attention—I know how to unweld fingers from metal. A home for her came as a bonus. No use burdening the social services with the shards of such a case. They are efficient but lack . . . well, you know what I mean." He sighed before continuing with his story.

"One unwise decision, of course, leads to another," he lamented. "The baby you saw chasing the boy was brought to me by a distraught neighbor—who labors under the misapprehension that I have a kind heart. I've been running an informal local government to handle events beyond the capacity of the bureaucracy. Baby Girl—we'll *have* to give her a name—was evidently abandoned. She has no birth certificate, at least her gene class doesn't match any of the trillion on planetary file. And she's no immigrant because she has no nanocertification stamp in her cells to tell us that she's been declared free of the horrors that plague our Galaxy. I checked that myself. About the boy, don't ask."

They were out on the balcony now, airseals hissing behind them, standing over a jumble of other balconies and unplanned stairs and arching breezeways that went up and up and down and down—and down. Carefully, very carefully, Hyperlord Kikaju Jama reached out and clenched the plasteel railing for dear life while settling himself into a plastic chair. He was pleased that it wasn't an aerochair. There was no doubt in Jama's mind that he was one of these Splendid Cowards who grew green around the gills when he saw something farther below him than the bottom of his feet. Kargil already had his shoes up on the railing while he waved at a neighbor who was beating the dust from her rug *into public air*. Amazingly antisocial! Such anarchy thrilled the Hyperlord. People like that could be led into revolution!

Kargil Linmax turned affably to his customer. "You were telling me about this interest of yours in Faraway antiques before I so rudely interrupted you."

"The artistic achievements of the anarchic governments of our last Dark Age fascinate me."

The old naval officer guffawed. "Governments? Dandies like you were out there during the Interregnum hacking up the planets for firewood because there *were* no governments."

"That is an unnecessarily extreme statement. There were many experiments in government at the time, many more than in today's lethargic Galaxy. I was thinking of the interesting experiment in self-rule that the scientists of Faraway set up when they were exiled to the Periphery."

"With all due respect, your Hyperlord, that was hardly an experiment. Democracy is as old as Rith of Sol, if we can believe mythology. It was invented by simian slave-holding homosexual misogynists who lived with their irascible gods up on Mount Olympus or Mount Vernon or someplace like that."

"My dear man, I believe your mythology is incorrect. Democracy was invented by the slave Lincoln who led a great revolt against his Virginian masters, forcing them to come down from Mount Ararat to grant his people the Magna Charta. There is good reason to believe that this Lincoln was a real man and not some archetypical construct, though I've never researched the matter. It is not even certain that he was from Rith, according to several very trustworthy accounts."

The door hissed, and the sad face of Sweet Toes protruded, allowing public and private air to mix. "We can't get Baby Girl to take her nap! She's dancing!"

"Well, now. Insubordination among the crew. It will have to be dealt with. Have you tried faster music?"

"Papa! Be serious! We're *desperate*. Come help us," she implored.

"Nope. A good ship runs itself. When I was captain, and a petty officer couldn't get his charges to nap, I shipped him back to base *without his pension*. A captain's only duty is to point the ship. That hardly includes supervising naps."

"I could hold her head under a pillow!" sulked Sweet Toes.

". . . a violation of Regulation 43A!"

"Oh, Papa!" She saluted and whacked the door shut with a hiss.

Jama harumphed. "I see that you are not a great believer in the achievements of your simian mountain-dwelling homosexual misogynists!"

"Everything in its place. One can't expect the famless ancients to have solved *all* the problems of the Galaxy. I suspect that they did very poorly when faced with naptime for a two-year-old—my study of military history indicates our planetbound ancestors, of every political persuasion, excelled in the art of massacring helpless children."

"Mere time-honored slander. My opinion is that much useful wisdom has been lost over the ages."

"Are you a Cryogenist?"

The Hyperlord scanned his famlist of cults and found nothing. "The name doesn't register."

"Cryogenists search the Galaxy for the icy corpse of an epic Rithian—I believe helium was first liquefied in the sixtieth millennium, pre-Imperial or thereabouts, and used primarily to cool the coffins of sycophants; thawed, this primitive is to reveal to us the Lost Wisdom of the Ages, and, with his great perspective on time and his profound personal knowledge, is to save us from all our troubles. There is a great literature built around such revivals." Kargil was smiling with genuine amusement while imagining this messianic Rithian in bearskin desperately searching the corridors of Splendid Wisdom for a tree upon which to piss. "I was actually approached in my naval capacity in the hopes that I might keep a lookout for our suspended savior. The cultists lased me a file which purported to have traced our ancestor's shipping documents, bluntly pinpointing his location to within a thousand leagues of the position of my ship."

Hyperlord Kikaju Jama made a growling noise of disgust in his throat. "You'd think in these scientific times that such balderdash would long have been laid to rest!"

Kargil Linmax offered a morose reply. "It is the fault of the Pscholars that such nonsense persists, damn them." The curse was followed by a throaty grumble.

Such an unexpected but welcome expression of heresy left Jama bolt upright in his seat, thus having to stare in fear down into the tenanted canyon below. He forced himself to relax, firmly planting his spinal cord against the back wall of their tiny balcony. "How so?" His eyes now watched every nuance of Kargil's face, careful not to look away. In the political current of the Second Empire, one dared not step too readily into an undertow of discontent.

"The Pscholars keep secrets." The old face showed lines of distaste and annoyance more than those of anger. "Their power to create order rests in the secrecy of their psychohistoric methods. They predict and guide. *We mere mortals* must never be allowed to know enough to contradict them lest we bring on consequences beyond our ken—but not theirs. The hoary myth of the woman and the apple tree—knowledge is dangerous, ignorance is bliss. By *example* the Pscholars teach us that *secrecy* is power. We must remain in our orderly garden, they instruct us, to forgo the larger dangers of knowledge. They *cannot* teach us that *knowledge* is power because then they would be obliged to share their knowledge. Is it any wonder that cultists abound who tout the virtues of *hidden* powers?"

"You speak boldly of your concerns!"

"I make no secret of the fact that I have no power."

A man with long sleeves—one red, the other green—hailed from a distant balcony, finally yodeling a call which Jama could not understand. Kargil yodeled back, then turned to his guest to translate. "You probably don't understand our yodeling codes. I've invited him to drop down to my place for a visit. Town business. I think I told you that I'm the mayor of an informal group of locals who bypass our authorities when they procrastinate."

They stood up, Jama close to the wall, his fingers discreetly clinging to the building stone, appalled to note, high above their tenanted canyon, a brightly colored balloon-man puttered past, perhaps having dropped from one of the canyon roof's underslung cupolas. He, too, yodeled at Kargil but was too far away to be recognized. Jama's host seemed to know everyone in this microcosm of Splendid Wisdom. As they retreated indoors, Kikaju was deciding that he *had* to recruit this man into his burgeoning conspiracy. Kargil's confidence was beginning to impress him.

Later an affable Kargil admitted the four "townsmen" when they arrived in his entranceway, one of them the man with red and green sleeves. Jama watched intently. The old naval captain didn't offer seats but listened to his friends, interrupting only to sharpen the discussion. None of it was of interest to Jama—it was about local issues unfamiliar to him and about local people, among billions, unlikely to touch his life again—but Jama remained fascinated by the skill with which this man handled other men. Kargil was obviously pushing for decisions. He got three commitments in efficient succession—and a clear statement of an agenda item for the next meeting: ways to supplement weakening government financing for the rebuilding of a condemned sports stadium. With business complete, Kargil sent his visitors home on the excuse that he had an analysis in progress.

He turned to Jama with a gleam of expectation. "And I do have an analysis in progress. By now we must have collected all we presently need to know about your contraption. Come. The moment of truth." Without opening the cleanbox containing the ovoid, he fed the data from it directly into his fam. He stood in inner contemplation, staring off into space for a few moments that caused Jama suspense, then nodded and, as almost an afterthought, transferred some of the data to a flatplate in order to show the Hyperlord the essentials of his conclusion.

"Your object is surely authentic." He pointed at clumps in the hazy image on the flatplate. "I'm surprised. The tiny clusters surrounding those macroblobs are nanocomputers in a cross-redundant configuration. It's a Faraway design pioneered in the third century and widely used during the fourth. Eccentric. But it's a configuration that would strongly protect you against data loss." He fingered in an amplification. "See that starlike imperfection? A rather violent cosmic ray hit. Not a problem. And I must recant on the Farliquar. It seems to have done yeoman's service when briefly powered up from time to time to repair cosmic ray hits—there is no evidence of damage prior to three hundred years ago. So the atomo has been operational until recently. Astonishing. I can't be sure, but your innards seem to have survived. Now all we need is a fresh atomo-unit." He paused, looking at Kikaju Jama—undoubtedly speculating about an unemployed Hyperlord's financial resources.

"The price?" asked the Hyperlord stoically.

Dispassionately Linmax quoted a substantial sum. "Can't do it for less."

Jama flinched. More corners to shave. Maybe he could start by canceling his accommodations and arranging to sleep in the workshop. "It's a deal. Half now and half after the atomo has been installed?"

"It's a deal. The deal is that I get paid for the eight atomos, *not* for the repair of your gizmo if it isn't functional. The risk isn't great. My best guess is that the galactarium itself *is* in functioning order."

"A risk—but I'll take it." Right then and there they made the financial transaction.

"You'll have dinner with us then, of course," Kargil said wryly. "But first I can do a work-around to alleviate some of your uncertainty. You seem about to shit an uncomfortable cannonball. Your device, I surmise, is missing only a power source. I can jury-rig that—it's going to need about forty different voltages and a snake-pit of wires—that will allow us to conduct a test. It's not going to be portable without an atomo, you understand."

While Kargil worked, Jama waited anxiously, seated on a pile of old Faraway metal-forming tools, famfeeding himself the contents of catalog slabs and whatever else came to hand. He was an obsessive reader who read anything to keep his mind occupied when he was edgy. Finally the old man began to move back and forth between the main workshop and a side room from which he emerged after an interminable hiatus with a smile on his face. He held up his strange six-fingered hand in the full victory sweep. "It responds to finger pressure points, standard Faraway coding. I've been playing with it. With only five of my fingers, of course." He grinned.

"Without me there?"

Before Jama could further express his anxiety, Kargil ushered him into the side room where unnatural wires snaked from the ovoid's innards. He sealed the entrance. When he caressed the ovoid, the room magically darkened, replacing the shelves and wall screens and clutter—the floor, everything—with an ebony pantheon of stars that almost sent Jama clutching for spacesuit controls he was not wearing. It took moments to notice that the jury-rigged wiring left swaths of unnatural shadows across the virtual sky.

"The galactarium is in working order!" Jama exclaimed with visible relief.

"Maybe. It's a strange device. Being a navy man, I'm familiar with navigational history, but this thing is far more an artifact of superstition than it is of navigation." Deft squeezings on the ovoid superimposed a coordinate system over the celestial sphere. "You'd never see anything like it on a real ship. The equator is divided into twenty-four sections. From equator to poles it is ninety 'degrees,' plus or minus, with sixty-'minute' and sixty-'second' and then decimal subdivisions. Interstellar length is measured in parsecs, a nonstandard unit which requires an arcane knowledge of the distance between Old Rith and Sol—which, if you knew, you wouldn't know how to apply to arc-seconds because you'd have to throw in the pi number.

"It all smacks of the kind of superstition one finds in a typical wisdom-of-the-ancients tract—certainly one trying to prove that the true lore comes down to us directly from Old Rith or Alphacen or wherever. Galaxy knows, there are enough of such cults. Parsecs went out of use seventy thousand years ago and date back to the dawn of counting but are periodically revived by new gospels looking for primordial authority. Certainly we *aren't* dealing with an ancient device; it couldn't have been built prior to the Interregnum, and the finger coding is also a standard of fairly recent origin. Neither are we dealing with the usual navigational aid. The thing would have driven a real navigator crazy. Look at this."

The captain pressed more sequences and the sphere of stars all around them was rapidly fragmented into constellations annotated with a weird symbolism that Jama had never seen before. "No matter what coordinate point you key in as the origin," Kargil continued, "it can create baroquely artistic constellations. Useless flummery—but pretty." Gracefully he pushed aside wires to show off the sky to better advantage. "The constellations don't relate to the sky of Faraway but do seem to be associated with some kind of pentagonal mystery. Do you know any pentagonal systems philosophically inclined toward superstition?" The old navy captain obviously knew too many.

"Our Galaxy is a big place," Jama repeated, using the oldest of worn clichés.

"You might check out inhabited pentagonal systems if you are really interested in the origins of the device. In any case you should make special note of its symbols. I recognize most of them. They date back to the first star-maps. All the symbols for the seven sacred planets are there though they seem to be employed in a different context. Every planet that claims to be the home of mankind has a theory to explain those seven symbols. The other symbols—I've counted forty-two of them—seem to be derived from the symbols that archaeohistorians believe were devised for the first interstellar planets discovered during the first millennium of the dispersion—before such coy nonsense became impractical. And look what I can project with *this* button configuration." The sky was invaded by a mathematical design that collected the stars into a jewel-faceted setting. "For that chart, you need coordinates, a zenith, and a date. Your device is an astrological chart-maker based on a catalog of the ten billion stars most important to the Traders of Faraway. Space only knows how a man would read such a mishmash of lines and arcs! Why a pragmatic Faraway trader would have had it built eludes me."

The Hyperlord was himself in a pragmatic mood as he gazed at the galactarium's display. "Probably it was a gift to the Trader's unpragmatic mistress. Omnipotent God has never been able to lay out the bounds of female belief! But"—he shrugged—"let us never mind the artistic license the gizmo takes with astronomy; are the stars it projects just pretty points, or can they be identified?" He was wondering if they came from a reliable database like those kept by the First Empire's fanatically accurate Interstellar Spatio-analysis Bureau.

"Spectrograph, star motion, multiple star orbits, main planetary motions, survey data of the I.S.B.—all there."

"Names? Or does it use the damn spectrograph for a name? Or some damn cultish naming convention we never heard of?"

Kargil fiddled with his fingers. "I.S.B. codes. Ah. Names—when the star has one—and First Empire alfab-numerical classification."

"Do the names use the Imperial alphabet?" queried Jama.

"The standardized Imperial alphabet was more than ten millennia old when this device was built."

"Try Zurnl—use the spelling: Z-U-R-N-L."

The starfield shifted, the constellations were re-formed, symbols winked in and out. Kargil displaced more wires. "Got it. Zurnl. Single star, cool, aging, three planets, one a giant, the current position is twenty-three of the device's damn parsecs from Faraway. That would be about seventy leagues. No mention of a colony."

"Bull's-eye!" Hyperlord Kikaju Jama jumped about with his lace cuffs flapping. "Another dark secret of the Pscholars revealed!" He danced in dervish circles with virtual stars all around him. Kargil waited patiently for an explanation.

"Zurnl isn't on the standard star charts of the Second Empire."

# THE CRAZY ADMIRAL VISITS A HAUNT
# OF HIS YOUTH, 14,790 GE

*There is a substantive computational difference between*
*(1) macroevents such as wind or temperature or healthy economy, and*
*(2) microevents like the velocity of an air molecule or a single bank-*
*ruptcy.*
*Microevents can be summed over to tell us all we need to know about a*
*macroevent. The velocities of individual air molecules can add up to a wind or a*
*cyclone or a temperature reading. The exchanges between buyer and seller can*
*add up to an economy.*
*The process is not reversible. No macroevent can be broken down into its*
*individual microevents. Important information is destroyed by summation and*
*cannot be recovered. No weather report will tell you the velocity of a particular*
*molecule. No economic index will tell you who bought what, when, and where.*
*No psychohistorical prediction will tell you the fate of the individuals who will*
*act together to generate that future.*

—Excerpt from the Founder's *Psychohistorical Tools for Making
a Future*

After Hahukim Konn dropped Rhaver off at the dog kennel, the Admiral went
back to diddling on his battleship for a few hours, then spent the rest of the watch
reviewing new files on his trouble spots, working well into his sleep-watch. Nothing exciting, but the pattern wasn't going away. This damn thinking all the time
was keeping him awake. Even the reconstruction of his old Horezkor dreadnought
wasn't taking his mind off the developing crisis!

On the way home he took a detour to pick up a tonic his doctor had recommended and found himself in the domed concourse twenty levels below his apart-

ment watching a group of students joshing each other. Instead of catching a levitator and flopping into his bed underneath his mobiles of old warcraft, an impulse, perhaps prompted by the celebrants, sent him strolling to the tube end of the concourse. While he was grumpily nagging himself that he should be in bed, the old student roustabout in his soul called up a private transport pod from the dispatcher.

The black robopod flipped open its top for easy access and he climbed in.

"Comfort setting?" asked the dashboard.

"Firm." Konn wanted a fast ride to nowhere. The top sealed and went opaque. An internal air supply began to circulate a standard invigorating mixture.

"Destination?" the pod asked when Konn had not volunteered the information.

"Doesn't matter. Just take me on a fast rolly-ride that gives me heart failure. For that I'd like the windows cleared."

"My sensors detect a physical age which precludes my use of fast turns—do you have a medical waiver?"

"Oh, forget it!" snarled Konn.

Still they were not moving. "If you please, I require a destination," demanded the robopod stubbornly.

"Make it the Olibanum." Konn was unwilling to match wits with the sand-grain brain of a machine. If he wasn't going to get his joyride, the marvels of the Olibanum were the next best thing.

"Your stop?" asked the pod reproachfully.

"Kermis Station." It was the only one he remembered offhand without asking his fam for a list.

The pod did oblige him by clearing its windows while they passed through the conduits of the stygian betwixt-city. They swished at a respectable clip, past dark supports and air shafts, around grim water tanks and overdomes—but without finger-clenching speed it was no fun. Old habit was taking him back to the mecca of his youth, along the marvelous Corridor of the Olibanum, where the students of the Lyceum had always mixed with the Splendid masses in order to forget troubles and to burn time that could more profitably have been used to fuel their studying.

"Release your seat belt only on green permission!" warned his single-occupant pod, not mentioning that it would report him to the police for a fine if he disobeyed. They popped out into a sumptuous station. The pod's dash padding went green. He unfolded himself to exit into the cathedral quiet of the Kermis Station.

A short walk took him through a twinkling sound barrier into the noisy bombardment of the Corridor. What a pleasure in the grin muscles to remember the wonderful times he had wasted in the bistros of this vast carnival strip when he was still as smug as that hotshot Nejirt had been this afternoon! Would a wiser Konn care to be seen in the Teaser's Bistro in his aged incarnation? Futile task to try to keep up with himself as a juvenile! But the thought amused him—almost like a dare.

He jostled among the crowds, trying to decide which were the students and which the bureaucrats and which the lay players. Dress styles had shifted so much since he had been here last. The signals by which people identified each other remained a fluid language. It was of no use to fam-flash anyone to scan their vita—the probably altered ID would be a mask, a joke, a sly come-on. The Olibanum was traditionally a place of festive anonymity.

One famless musician caught his attention, surely a man from the deepest of the bedrock warrens or maybe a denizen of the corridors. How had he lost his fam? Or was he one of those unfortunates whose family had been unable to afford one for their child and charity had bypassed? He sighed. Hahukum was reminded of a grim time—earlier than his youth as a student—his mother had been an abandoned immigrant who did what she had to on the streets and lived where she could. The musician evoked his pity; he listened to the plaintive songs while other listeners came and went. The mendicant accompanied himself with a palm-size audiovib that was of far better quality than his voice.

> O, I know the time's a comin
> when the bear will see in color
> and the rivers will run gushing;
> if my mom won't sell a ticket then—
> I'll steal one!

One rhyme led to another. The Admiral loitered. "Do you know any navy ditties?" He had a weakness for the songs of the barracks of space.

The smile—through broken teeth—was enchanting, and out popped a rowdy lyric about a deckhand who was always poking his fingers into the wrong places, from machinery to women's private parts, and getting zapped in the chorus. The crowds flowed by. Some stopped for a moment to listen before they moved on.

Hahukum slipped the balladeer a money stick that was programmed not to buy medicine or drugs or alcohol and went on his way, somewhat appalled. How could a man live out his life famless, like a monkey, like a wastrel Rithian? How? And wretched teeth! A few inamins out of a watch in a chair with a mouth-assembler would fix that! No accounting for people! You might build a Galaxy safe from the raids of ravening space hordes or fill the stars from a cornucopia of luxuries for body and mind—yet there were always the woebegone to traipse off to perdition with the sincerest grumble in their song.

His mood was such that he could not be long depressed, even by depressing memories or nagging worries—or a lack of superstudents. He was tempted to deactivate his fam and just bask in the animal aura of the Olibanum as a primitive . . . but tripping out on one's naïve wonder, guideless, in a con artist's paradise was a recipe for waking up in an embarrassing fix. Too bad. He had to be content to drift along happily—with his comprehension intact.

DONALD KINGSBURY

After being caught in a throng, he let himself be swept up a slanting beltlift, curious to find what galactic marvel lurked above the ecstatic hawking that could pull in such a crowd. They were all younger than he and obviously knew something he didn't. What *was* a grumpmug? It couldn't be more exotic than the elephant in bloomers he had once ridden here as a student.

The mob propelled him up into a high-ceilinged depot with moving lights and streamers—approaches crowded with boys and their dates, some heading to festivities uplevel and some lined up at stalls to rent tiny enclosed cars. Konn rented a car (decorated like a beast-from-hell-with-fenders) and spent the next round careening about a vegetation-choked plain laid inside a rambling emporium. Above them the ceiling was a transparent dance floor so that the herd of less adventurous revelers could share vicariously in the rollicking mayhem below—which consisted of nothing more than bumping and banging grumpmugs and chasing the odd teenage couple hither and thither in circles. But it was fun.

The hermaphroditic grumpmugs of Vincetori turned out to be cantankerous plains beasties jealously willing to defend their foraging range. They were built of cartilaginous sponge and bone that went well with their ornery dispositions and butting habits. They moved on a set of running stumps that could send them in any direction, with a slithering speed, allowing them to contact their rival with a respectable thunk.

The vast majority of planets with an aboriginal oxygen atmosphere had been found to support life no more complicated than unicells; galactically the grumpmug rated as a very advanced species. But not so advanced that the amazing transformation of sky into dance floor was even noticed! In brainpower grumpmugs were a quarter of a billion years away from intelligence. Still, Konn felt that challenging them was more *fun* than butting heads with the fam-enhanced students of the Lyceum . . . thunk! Well, sometimes! A dodging grumpmug had side-slithered to butt his car over onto its back. Staring at the world from a strange angle, he ruefully began to suspect that considerable gengineering had toughened up *these* grumpmugs for their carnival life.

Limping, the Admiral spent the rest of his small monies entertaining safer teenage girls on the level above—in a different kind of wit-banging.

It was late when he set out again, having given his leg enough time to recover. He noticed that he was in the neighborhood of his old haunt, the Teaser's Bistro. The Olibanum was quieter and he strolled up to the Deep Shaft, enjoying the walk around its impressive promenade. He'd never met the latest owner of the Bistro though Rigone had already become notorious among the students. In his youthful heyday the Teaser's had been a shady hangout; under Rigone its reputation was high-tech risqué, not a strict respecter of the probe laws. He did not have to rely on his fam to lay guiding cues onto his visual cortex to find it—the route was still engraved in his wetware—two blocks beyond the Deep Shaft was a little alley and there, hidden away to the right, up an inconspicuous stairway, was the

Bistro, as it had always been. Only the bizarre railings, crawling with carved snakes, were new.

He had intended to pass by. A reflex more than half a century old took him up the stairs.

Hahukum suspected that his entrance would make a stir. On a planet with a trillion inhabitants there were many places he could go without being recognized, but the student ghetto wasn't one of them. The tavern was half full in a lazy third-watch sort of way, mostly youths at the long row of tables that marched down the central hall. A lanky rouster saw him first and turned to nudge his companion, a gesture noticed by the bartender who shifted his eyes to touch Konn, then swiftly faded into a back room. The identification became a subdued chain reaction. There were disadvantages to holding Rank as high as Second. If some of the clientele were his Lyceum students he wouldn't have known—they were dressed outrageously to avoid fam scan.

The proprietor appeared even before Hahukum was able to settle himself. Rigone was a hefty man, curlicue tattoos on his face, certainly a Scav, charming in an irresistible way that one would be a fool to trust. "Admiral! You've returned."

"After fifty years," said Konn dryly, appraising this man who hadn't even been born the last time he had sat at the battered old bar.

"You're still on our roster." Rigone grinned, not letting him be seated. "The drink is on me," he said, leading the way. Whatever the owner of the Teaser's thought might be the agenda of his powerful visitor, he seemed to want to conduct the negotiation away from his customers' eyes. Konn was ushered out back and up the stairs and into private quarters which were doubly guarded. A vault-strong door closed behind them with the hiss of an air seal, followed by a crackling as they were allowed to pass through a forcecurtain strong enough, when active, to block a running man.

The apartment's only visible room was luxurious. There were shelves of antique ivroid book-modules from late Imperial times, unreadable without the ancient hardware. The tapestry was probably Sewinnese; the bric-a-brac from the period of the Sack. A wall of electronic tools seemed to be exquisitely crafted for show but were certainly of the finest functionality. He smelled a faint perfume that bushwhacked his metropolitan imagination—wildflowers in a mountain meadow? When had he last set foot in a pristine mountain valley?

Rigone spoke in a voice not meant to be overheard beyond an arm's length. "Sorry, I'm not alone . . . entertaining one of the ladies . . ." Then: "Mer!"

The delicately perfumed girl-woman who emerged from the slumber room seemed to hold a position of trust. She wasn't expecting company and deferred to Rigone for an explanation, a slightly displeased expression on her face. She wore her hair in a cage and her eyes were outlined in metal with turquoise inlay; her informal jumpers were slashed boldly down the side, her feet bare. She was no student.

"Mer . . . we have a guest . . . Admiral Second Rank Hahukum Konn." Konn heard the voice of a cocky man flying through clouds on manual at night between the peaks of a rugged range, perhaps with mountain wildflowers below, looking for a safe landing site. It was a voice that would never admit to distress.

Mer reached out with fingers extended; her greeting was cultured, sociable, noncommittal. But from the widening of her pupils Konn deduced that the girl was aware of him by reputation. Her whole attitude shifted to circumspection. And . . . she had quietly made the assumption, from some unspoken exchange between them, that Rigone was in trouble. She sought ways to support him, eyes leaving Konn from time to time to glance at her paladin of the Bistro, as if waiting for instructions.

Strange, they were expecting him to make some demand of them, which they were steeling themselves to refuse. He was amused. He was here on nostalgic impulse. But he could always accommodate them and think of something to bother their peace. He was ever willing to ask service of those who saw themselves as servants. One only had to be careful not to ask more than could be given. That was simply a rule of good government.

"They still tell stories about you around here," said Rigone with a gleam in his eye, preparing a drink while Mer called up an aerochair.

"They do, do they?" he said, graciously accepting the chair. "If I recall correctly I was quite sedate compared with today's youth."

"I'm certain the punch lines of the stories have become exaggerated over the years."

One compliment deserved another. "My students tell me stories about you, too."

Rigone laughed. "I wish they wouldn't do that. I spend too much time smooth-talking the police."

Wit was leading this man straight at his worst fear. To hide his smile, Hahukum sniffed at the drink to find out what his host had offered him. It smelled of the planet Armazin, imported and therefore impressive. "With charm as smooth as yours, I'm sure you're never bothered by the police."

"Never, unless some highly placed individual decides to rattle my trivial world."

When people stated their fears that blatantly, they were asking for soothing reassurance—but it wasn't Konn's style to reassure glib criminals. "In that case," replied the Admiral with an ambiguous irony, "I'm sure a small bribe is enough to settle the problem."

Quite suddenly the girl-woman erupted in the curses of a dialect that meant that her cultured accent had been lately learned. She reacted hotly to what she perceived as a candied threat; and it was the candy, not the threat, that insulted her. "And when you're through wire-brushing your asshole, just *say* what you want!"

Rigone reacted to her gaffe with horror. He made a small gesture to quiet his companion while he tried to master his own composure. She swiveled away in disgust to clean an already clean bartop.

"Please excuse . . ." To the Admiral he was making the naval hand-sign for seventeen, which meant that Mer was only seventeen years old.

Konn cut him off. "I *do* want something." He had just made a decision, again on impulse.

A wary Rigone now found himself trying frantically to revise his damage control in midsentence. He had been talking about the trials of teaching proper manners to modern youth . . . "Something from me? I can't see what I have to offer—compared with *your* resources."

"*I* can."

Rigone rubbed one of his tattoos to give himself time to think. "That means you have been hearing fantasies about me. I can do *nothing* for you. I am an honest man. I refuse to offer you *anything* but the finest hospitality."

"You're into the fam-fixing business." Not always legal. "Your work is very admired."

"No, no. Not at all. Rumors! I have a kind heart. Sometimes when a student has psychological problems I find myself being a father to him . . . we talk . . . I help in whatever way I can . . ."

"Rigone," cried Mer, "he'll *kill* you if you don't give him what he wants!"

Rigone laughed helplessly. "Admiral, what do I do with a woman who is *that* overprotective . . . besides strangle her?"

"You do exactly what she says."

Rigone froze. "That would make my life impossibly difficult," he said coldly.

"No, it wouldn't. I'm not threatening you. I want you to modify *my* fam. Would I trust you with my fam if I were threatening you? It's a small deal. You'll do well. I *pay* for all services rendered. *You* spend a midnight watch souping up my fam; *I* help you in ways that no student can afford."

Rigone was perturbed. "You're not making yourself clear. The Lyceum staff has available to it fam modifying tech far beyond anything I might muster."

"You don't understand. Why should I trust them? There's a *conspiracy* against me at the Lyceum, and—unfortunately—they do have tech far beyond anything you've got. Think about it. The fam was originally a masterly modification of the psychic probe. It wasn't used to augment minds; it was used to control them. A fam you've lived with all your life protects you against emotional control. The modern ones are *designed* that way. But how can it protect you when you're not wearing it? Would you give your fam to a very skilled fam technician who had an interest in making you more amenable to his view of the universe?"

"Then why would you trust *me*?"

"That's *my* business."

"Do what he wants, Rigone. You know as well as I—"

"Shut up!" He turned back to Konn. "What is it that you are asking me to do?

Fam augmentation is all very illegal. The fam damn near ruined the Founder's Plan, and ever since Cloun-the-Stubborn you Pscholars have run a very tight galaxy-wide control on the laws governing fam use. I've been known to cross the line—but I survive because I've never violated the *spirit* of the law."

"I was hoping you could install me a crib sheet."

Rigone was incredulous. "You want a *crib sheet* installed in your functions stack?" He stared. "Why would you want a simple thing like that done?"

"Why would a *student* want it done? Maybe I have a heavy exam schedule." The Admiral was grinning. "But it has to be a very *good* crib sheet—up to date, of course—one that, at the very least, has the Hasef-Im test among its algorithms. A student of mine bothered me with that one lately. I can't keep up with these kids anymore, Rigone. Mathematics is a young man's game. The Founder was *dead* when he was my age!"

"I'm not even supposed to *touch* your mathematical functions," Rigone protested.

"But you do, all the time. For a fee."

"The stuff is encrypted," said Rigone defensively. "I can't crack that kind of code. I have no desire to crack it! I just install the stuff."

"That's good. Not being able to crack code is very good life insurance."

Mer was staring at him in astonished uncertainty. "A Second Rank Pscholar who wants a *math* fix! Now I've heard everything! Aren't you afraid we'll tell?"

"The advantage of being the Crazy Admiral," said Konn, "is that my colleagues both believe everything they hear about me and believe nothing. Of course, I'll skin you alive for coat leather if I catch *you* telling—and close down the Teaser's if I catch *Rigone* saying more than he should."

"I haven't promised anything. You're an old man. That makes meddling dangerous."

"I'm middle age," corrected Konn.

"Why don't you just sit down and *learn* the stuff? It's safer. Get a sabbatical. A kid's brain is still flexible and can handle a wild fam kicking it around. Yours is locked up, less shockproof. At worst you could sustain brain damage. The fix might not even take. No guarantee that you'd be able to call up the new functions."

The Admiral grinned. "I'm farsighted. It's what makes me a good psychohistorian. I laid in the mental hooks I'd need sixty years ago—when I was a student."

"After sixty years of nonuse your wetware hooks will have atrophied."

"No. I used motor-memory. For instance, I danced the haesila just downtime with a girl younger than Mer. How long has it been since I even thought about the haesila? Motor-memory doesn't forget. You're stalling. This isn't the delicate stuff. You won't be trying to connect me to a new fam personality—just some algorithms."

With a long face, Mer disappeared around the corner into Rigone's study. Rigone just sat there, thinking. "All right. I *can* do a crib sheet. I haven't got the latest tech but—"

"Get it. You'll make more on this one than off a year's clutch of students."

Rigone took in a painful breath, but Konn could see the reluctant agreement–and the cunning. If someone was going to subsidize a tech upgrade for him, that would become a remunerative part of his normal business. "I have just the crib sheet for you. Put out by a very enterprising student I know. Give me a decawatch or so to slouch a copy. The up-to-date tech will take longer." He muttered to himself unhappily. "I hope that's all you need–but is there anything else?"

Hahukum sipped his Armazin. "No." But, of course, if a man felt he wasn't giving all that he might the proper thing to do was to ask him for more. "Let's just say that if ever you happen upon a clever student who is willing to do a little kidnapping on the side–and who doesn't believe everything he's told–send him to me. You can make that a long-term standing order. I'm only looking for the very best."

"I–"

"You deal with students watch after watch. More than I do. I'm always looking. Send me a risk-taker who always lands on his feet and there's a commission in it for you. A *big* commission."

"The Lyceum has the best talent screening apparatus in the Galaxy . . ."

"No it doesn't. Take my word for it."

Did he really need a crib sheet just so it would be easier to stay abreast of theoreticians, train more data sifters, and brief more troubleshooters? Was keeping up with hot-waxed kids the best he could do? He already had more analysis capability than he knew what to do with–and what had that given him but strange perturbations in the evolving historical fabric which had led him into his suspicions and his self-doubts and his tenuous conspiracy theories? Damn, and damn! What he *really* needed was to muster a posse to go out there to kidnap one of those live flesh-and-blood rogue psychohistorians who didn't exist! Only then would he *know* he was right. But he was too old.

Mer came back with one of Rigone's ivroid modules in her hand and a smug verve. "I have something for you." If Konn knew his Scavs, it was probably an original and not a template's reproduction. Scavengers had appeared as a class only after the Sack, and they had a weird collector tradition–it wasn't enough that an antique be old, it *must not* be a copy! "It's our bribe." She set it on the Admiral's lap without consulting Rigone.

And Rigone's hand had raised itself halfway in a gesture to take the module back before restraining itself in midair, his mind's rationality being slightly stronger than its possessiveness.

A contrite Mer was delighted by her find. "I'm sure you don't have it. It's a hundred million words of eyewitness memoirs of the Marche campaigns collected by the Berogi brothers. Navy war stuff. Ships. The long-drawn-out Wars Across the Marche." She was more than a little bit frightened by the possible consequences

of her earlier outburst. She knew their guest was a naval buff and that such an offering might placate him.

"It won't be of much use to you," Rigone suggested with a lame hope. "The
reader was never standard, and it went out of production."

"Do *you* have a reader?"

Rigone dutifully showed him the compact apparatus in its discreet alcove.
Konn slipped the book in place and, with quick finger-code, waved over its eye a
random request. The machine chose for him an item.

Hahukum was plunged, via eyefeed, into the ruthless interrogation of some
poor Helmarian captive whose mind was being pillaged by psychic probe. The described technique seemed crude beyond belief but its vivid recounting was not
what caught Konn's attention . . . he was astonished by the diabolical trap that had
been used to *capture* the spy. It was something to add to his file on the trapping and
interrogation of enemy agents.

Rigone hovered beside Konn, almost as if he were ready to snatch the module
from the slot and restore it to its shelf, but the Admiral was a collector, too, and had
no intention of yielding such a welcome gift. He leaned on his hand so that his arm
was a bar that guarded the ivroid box. "Our library of templates for old reading
machines is very good. I'll have a reader built by tomorrow. My heartfelt thanks for
the gift." He smiled at Mer and ignored his unhappy host.

All he really needed was a *copy* of the module. It would take him no more than
a few watches to get such a copy made and to generate a compact index of its contents for storage in his fam—but, if he let Rigone grieve for a few endless jiffs before
he returned the treasure, then that young man's gratitude would be enormously
greater than if he told him now that he intended only a borrowing.

Konn was intrigued as he stood reading. Here was an appetizer to tease a curiosity which lately had been dwelling on the nature of protracted wars. Even as he
scanned through the descriptions of the Marche Campaigns that had spanned
many lifetimes, he was prompted to think of the present. Was the Second Empire
really involved in a war that had so far been conducted for centuries without the
Fellowship's knowledge? The equations for extended conflict were quite different
than those of shorter, more decisive clashes.

Perhaps there lay the trouble. Such prolonged perspectives lacked color, the
emotional rush of emergency—they weren't gut-real—and that led to lazy thinking.
Hadn't Konn himself spent too much time as a child wrapped up in the quick slashing dramas that were designed to fit inside a youth's attention span? Certainly he
had started his career as a man who wanted instant results; his patience was an acquired trait. *We think about what assaults our senses and in that way do not notice the glacier
overrunning our position. Only the old men remember where the ice used to be.*

The book would have other uses. Since the Admiral's mind was on the necessity of capturing prisoners for purposes of interrogation, it might do to spend time

researching how such covert operations had been conducted in the Empire's barbarian past. Kidnapping was probably an art that could be perfected—the two centuries of the Wars Across the Marche had not been a pleasant time—but perfection starts with what has already been achieved. Konn liked perfection. It was the duty of a modern psychohistorian to make war so pleasant that the parties in conflict hardly noticed it was happening.

# THE WAY STATION AT RAGMUK,
# LATE 14,790 GE

*The Wars Across the Marche have not gone in our favor. After two centuries of
ferocity our defense has collapsed. We lament our defeat. With sorrow we concede that the Thousand Suns Beyond the Helmar Rift have been conquered. Helmarian signatures have been forced upon the Treaty of Sanahadra, giving up all
Helmarian rights in exchange for sworn fealty to emperors whose hubris first
rules the Galaxy and then claims a universe.*

*But we, the soldiers of the shrouded bases, are unanimous in our desire to
continue the struggle for independence. We cannot violate the terms of Sanahadra without dooming our people (those who have been spared) and so duty
demands that we honor the treaty no matter what our feelings. Yet we are the
soldiers who were not at Sanahadra to surrender. We have not signed the treaty
and we will not sign the treaty. Though it takes us countless millennia, we shall
be the Auditor General of the Peace. We are the Overseer. We reavow the promise made by our forebears to defend the Helmarian virtues forever against whatever fate an emperor shall impose upon us. We weep tears of fire that will, from
the humiliation of Sanahadra, forge a new choice of weaponry. Peace can be as
sharp as any sword. Peace shall be our new definition of war.*

—From *The Hidden Document of Reaffirmation*, 7981 GE

This was the third leg of their journey. Already Hiranimus Scogil (alias Murek Kapor) and his student Eron Osa had spent fifty-four watches aboard the cramped
cargo ship. Now they had docked for change of crew and exchange of cargo at a
cometary station some 570 microleagues from the star Ragmuk of the Thousand
Suns, which was only a member of the Thousand Suns by ancient Imperial Decree,
lying, as it did, on the wrong side of the Helmar Rift. Still to come were four more

stops and thirty-six more watches of jumping along the Main Arm just to get as far as Sewinna. Then they were going to have to debark and shop for a transfer to the Periphery. Hiranimus was already feeling the need for money sticks he didn't have.

Their hyperfreighter's nature was to spurt and then linger, taking on passengers only as a sideline. The Skipper's frugal choice of supply station at the interplanetary rim of the Ragmuk System was designed in the interest of energy conservation—the station was moving almost at rest relative to the velocity of their starting jump, and it was high in its star's gravity well, a piece of citified home built into a tundra of ice and sludge.

Ragmuk had been settled these seven millennia past, not by Helmarians but by Imperial troops of the Stars&Ship laying out a forward base at the beginning of the Wars Across the Marche. Previous to the wars it had been a slumbering Military Resupply Outpost, lacking government colonial subsidies and too poor to support any kind of thriving colony on its own. But it was high ground to the Imperial General Staff: it looked outward over a roil of new stars across the Helmar Rift toward the original Thousand Suns. This was the observation point from which suddenly attentive warrior-emperors had measured the panoramic threat of the Helmarian people. To a true Helmarian the constellation which included Ragmuk was called the Dangling Blade.

Hiranimus Scogil was Helmarian, a peculiar loyalty.

He hit the oval door of the cabin with a shoulder, intending to unjam its stuck hydraulic hinges—not even the basic luxury of a robodoor here. He poked his head inside, ducking the pipes, looking for his charge. Their cabin was "shelf space" on one of the catwalks that circled the motors. It was about arm-wide and held only two skinny bunks, one on top of the other. "Wake up, Eron. The Skipper has granted us a watch worth of leave with the callous admonition that if we aren't reboarded in time, the ship will depart without us—taking our baggage with it."

"I can pack," said Eron sleepily. "Nothing I can't carry on my back."

"No, we leave our stuff here. Just stay close to ship's dock and watch the time. I'll be leaving you alone for a stint. Business."

He had schemes on his mind that needed attention, and he felt that the boy was old enough to wander alone. Nevertheless, when the youth was loose in the terminal, Hiranimus didn't go about his affairs right away but kept the boy under a watchful, if distant, eye. He relaxed. Eron seemed to be fine, a spirited sightseer with his nose plastered to a viewport, drinking in the line of berthed hyperships tethered to the great pier that rose pallidly against its astral background. Ragmuk itself was no brighter than a minor star.

Scogil refocused on his own concerns and went looking for an ultrawave terminal. On a station whose whole rationale was interstellar traffic, *sending* a message to the Oversee would be as easy as praying. But a reply? Directives to lower agents like Scogil came down from mobile relay ships staffed by a priesthood of aides who weren't in direct communication with the Oversee themselves. The Fortresses, wherever they were, had maintained such strict ultrawave silence for sixty-eight centuries that they had simply vanished into Helmarian mythology.

One could report to the Overseer in elaborate code, one could warn them of an emergency—but the communication was all one way. The Overseers accepted Personal Capsules but never sent one out. Two-way handshaking was taboo. It was a conversation with a God who often left you to answer your own questions, who answered obliquely if he answered at all, and then only at a time when he felt it auspicious, all transcribed into the runes of some cabalistic ritual that you might or might not be able to decipher. If you wanted a two-way conversation you talked to a lower priest. Cumbersome but safe. In wartime such a convoluted procedure, if maintained, would prove dangerously slow.

Back on Agander or Mowist, where prolonged transmissions might have attracted attention, Scogil had not dared pursue matters to the point of clarification. He was used to having the authority of the final judgment himself, the doubt of the lonely decision, the act based on incomplete analysis. It left questions; he was anxious to address incomplete concerns. It was much safer to do that out here where a high level of dispatches was normal. But he really didn't expect to get answers until he was recalled to a Fortress himself. What he needed now was an immediate bundle of cash sticks.

Hiranimus found an ultrawave utility three floors above the main deck of the station inside the office of a small freight brokerage. They warned him about local hyperspace storms kicking up a ruckus but plugged his cash stick into the connector anyway. Being out in nowhere's boondocks seemed to have its disadvantages.

Behind a privacy barrier he made his interstellar connection—but the handshaking went out of time/phase. Ultrawave always went on the kibosh when the handshake tried to acknowledge the message before it was sent. A storm. It was a nuisance. The more the autocorrect tried to mitigate the storm by probabilizing a region of space, the more the message fluttered in time, and vice versa. He waited and tried again. During the second attempt the timing stayed on but locked onto the noise—even a clutch of error-correction algorithms he had stored in his fam could make no sense of the garbled reply.

Then—when he did get through—it was because a second agent far above the storm had taken the call and was rerouting . . . That roboclerk took the Galaxy's own languorous time about tracking down his (new) boss. The ultrawave charges were gulping his limited funds. Scogil's mood turned rancid. His contact, after being reached, was also in bad humor having been interrupted from some vital activity he did not want to discuss. Because of the transmission difficulties the conversation proceeded at a high-redundancy, low-information rate full of frustrating pauses. Ultrawave, because of its probabilistic "speed" of transmission, could deliver packets to Personal Capsules far better than it could modulate a handshaking conversation. That he needed handshaking meant that he had to go through a very low-level contact.

He came out of the ultrawave communication booth in a chastised and angry mood. How could he have created such a mess? It seemed that his contacts had misunderstood almost everything he had sent them from Agander and Mowist. Or else they had forwarded his requests to the Oversee, and, in its own good time, for its own inscrutable reasons, the top Smythosians had made other plans for him. The Ragmuk System was a ridiculously inconvenient place from which to change one's whole itinerary.

Secure ultrawave channels did not seem to be a good medium for subtle verbal argumentation. The logic was lost when passed through secondaries to shadow men whose priority was hiding. The devious scheme hastily plotted on Agander had unraveled spectacularly. So much for assumptions made during a high state of enthusiasm! They didn't trust a man as young as he. Chary dunderheads! No wonder they'd had to pull out of the Ulmat. Or, he thought, maybe the right man hadn't yet received his proposal. If ever. He had to laugh because he had already used the credit he wasn't going to get.

In any event, the Oversee would not approve his plans *in time,* and, at least on the lower levels, his shadowy bosses were disputing even his right to make plans. Scogil noted sourly his reassignment to Coron's Wisp where his youthful enthusiasm for the cause could be kept under restraint, and under budget. *Nothing* he had suggested had been accepted. No response; just orders. That's what the ultrawave exchange had been about. Duty. Return for instructions and retraining. They would arrange a blind pickup.

He still had no idea where in the Galaxy his old school was located. He had once been sure that the Fortresses were around here somewhere, perhaps in the Rift, perhaps in the darker recesses between the Thousand Suns. After all, they *were* Helmarian—but maybe the rumor was true that they weren't located anywhere in Helmarian space. Maybe the forge of his Smythosian soul was thousands of leagues off the galactic plane. It might be hidden on some lost planet tossed into the darkness a billion years ago by eccentric binary parents. He'd never seen its sky. For all he knew, it might be smack in the middle of some provincial capital.

At least, face-to-face, his old mentors would have to listen to his objections about this new assignment of theirs. Face-to-face they'd have to talk back—if you could call a virtual confrontation with an immortal mask, worn by a carousel of mortal men, a face-to-face anything. If they wanted to bind him, they'd have to be convincing. He'd have to see the math. Or . . . he'd have to be eloquent enough to sway them.

Where in Space *was* Coron's Wisp? His orders only mentioned a five-star pentad system with one habitable planet around each star. Twenty-seven Wisps were mentioned in his fam's huge database—but no Coron's Wisp. It must be a very minor place. Was it just another Ulmat to be abandoned tomorrow? For all their calls for more operatives to work at the heart of the Empire, they didn't seem anxious to send a seasoned man anywhere near Splendid Wisdom, nor had anyone been willing to support his clever plot to place Eron Osa as an unknowing mole inside the Pscholar's Fellowship. Too dangerous a plan for cautious cowards?

Worse, they did not take seriously the scholarship he had promised the Osa boy. Those funds he needed *now*! What was he going to tell Eron? He had hauled the boy out onto the adventure of his life and there wasn't going to *be* a scholarship, nor even a fam upgrade. Nor funds to continue the trip to Faraway. So . . . a conflict of integrity. Damned if you do and damned if you don't. Was he supposed to abandon a twelve-year-old child?

He *would* take the boy to Faraway. Scogil was Helmarian and bound by Helmarian ethics even if they contradicted Helmarian orders. He laughed again. He would be able to claim that he had been stranded for lack of cash. The Galaxy was a big place, so they said—an easy maze in which to get lost for a few months. He had no intention of disobeying orders, but there was no help for it—he would be *delayed*. He would turn up *after* he had squared his commitment to Eron. How? He didn't know. Damn, Damn, and Spacedamn!

He hoofed it back aboard the hyperfreighter in a frenzied effort to get their baggage all together and off ship. No use going on without a full money stick. He had to stuff Eron's book under his arm, his hands full. Where was that boy? The insanity of it—carrying books on an interstellar voyage! What would these children think of next! With baggage decked and book in hand, he made a frantic appeal to the purser for the return of credit that the purser was loath to refund on such short notice. But the purser connected him with a waiting couple who seemed as frantic to leave Ragmuk behind as he was to stay, and so he was able to sell—at a profit— the last legs of their passage.

What now? In all of the vast concourse he couldn't spot a seat. He chose an out-of-the-way corner to sit (on the book) with their baggage in sight. With Eron nowhere in view, he had time to think. The heavens wheeled across the station's observation domes. Problem number one: they needed a destination. Perhaps his little exchange had provided funds enough to get Eron safely into the nearest friendly port. He needed a friend right now. Thank the stars for friends! When normal channels of authority don't function to one's desire, backtrack and call on a friend. But which friend? After the isolation of Agander, did he still *have* any friends? And did he have a friend who could laugh at life's impetuous blunders!

It was gloomy thinking. Family? Good people but no possible help there. To find powerful friends he had to hark back to those good-bad old seminary semesters when he had been training in secret as a Smythosian, interminable hours and watches and months of grind whose main reward had been the promise of high adventure. Gadzac was as good a friend as he's ever had—but he was too conservative. Nels was reserved but could always be tapped for a loan if Hiranimus made his case look desperate enough.

How about the triumvirate? Mendor and Jaisy and Hiranimus. They had spent endless watches debating—and mathematically probing—the small changes *they* could make in the fabric of a society, changes with the potential to avalanche into galactic significance. Jaisy was gone somewhere on assignment. Mendor was far above Scogil's social class. But what was Mendor up to now? Certainly Mendor Glatim still operated from Neuhadra of the Thousand Suns, which no more belonged to the original Thousand Suns than did Ragmuk. How could that mild boy who loved his luxuries have walked away from the setup he had been destined to inherit? He'd be there—if luck and probability were the same thing. Hiranimus cringed to think of reducing his friendship with Mendor to a machination to get his hands on Glatim money, but it looked like his best option.

Neuhadra would add a roundabout into their jump-path to Faraway, an awkward jag off the Main Arm's commercial routes. Its location above the galactic plane, well away from conventional Helmarian space, had been the main reason it had not been settled until the eightieth century when it became irresistibly attractive to the refugees displaced by the Wars Across the Marche. The Imperial victors had uprooted the Helmarians en masse—from Sanahadra, alone, almost half the population. This detour to an extremity of the Thousand Suns seemed like a good risk to Scogil. Mendor was wealthy enough to indulge a friend who had never before asked of him a favor.

Wealthy wasn't an adequate word to describe Mendor's situation. The Glatim family was in the meteoroid deflection business. Inhabited planets were seldom threatened by rogue objects big enough to destroy a civilization—maybe once in ten–twenty million years—but in an empire of thirty million worlds, even such improbable business came up frequently enough to require expert service. And the peoples of a doomed planet faced with a millions-to-one unplanned catastrophe don't quibble about price—nor do they easily trust inexperienced would-be saviors. And when you are in the meteoroid deflection business, what do you do to keep in practice? You deliver comets to countless water-starved worlds and make a stick on every barrel of water! The Glatim clan was *very* wealthy.

Scogil looked up and down the main deck of the Ragmuk Station. Speaking of rogue planetesimals, where in Space was that Eron Osa kid? Scogil waited patiently, honing his new plan, but as rendezvous time approached and Eron was still nowhere about, he began to panic. He checked out rest rooms. He inquired of passersby; had they seen a small enthusiastic boy? Finally he approached security, who seemed quite familiar with the problem of lost passengers. They automatically tracked every transient.

The man looked up from the screen of his search engine, grinning. "He's in the Heart's Well Antiquarian Bookstore, sixth level down."

"I might have known." Scogil grimaced.

This bookstore was one of those collector's dreams that fill up the quiet chinks of the Galaxy by hoarding mankind's treasures in inaccessible places. Prices are right when customers are few. For the mundane there were compact templates from which an antique could be vitalized. The store had racks of templates for books and readers, millions of templates—but by the nature of the universe there were *always* antiques for which no template existed. The back of the room was lined with shelves of books boxed in helium. A sign announced that they might be perused for a small fee. The owner seemed to favor the rarest of the rare—books that didn't have to be matched to a reading machine.

"I'm not late!" announced Eron loudly when he noticed Scogil's approaching scowl. "We have *lots* of time left." He returned his gaze to the pop-up hologram in front of him. The large book from which it emerged was printed on fine cellomet and seemed to contain hidden quantronics to generate holo illustrations when the pages were turned by hand. Eron was sitting with a large man of elaborately tattooed face who obviously loved books but who now turned to smile at Scogil.

The bookstore owner? His pattern of tattoos jogged something in the databases of Scogil's fam. Of course, with a hundred quadrillion humans in the Galaxy there was no certain way to identify the origins of a single man from his facial characteristics but—a Scav from Splendid Wisdom out here? running a stall?

"We've had a change of plans, Eron. Our ship will be leaving without us. I'm thinking of side-legging it to an out-of-the-way stray star above the Rift. You've probably never heard of Neuhadra. I have friends there."

The tattooed man spoke with sudden interest. "You know these parts?"

"The Helmar Rift Region is a lot of stars to cover for one young man, but I was born a Helmarian with a zest for geography."

"This is my friend," announced Eron. "Rigone."

"From Splendid Wisdom?" queried Scogil.

The man nodded, and Eron continued his introduction enthusiastically. "We were fighting over a book, so we decided to be friends if we had that much in common. He's smart. He knows more about books than I do." That honest statement of someone else's superiority didn't set well with Eron so he added, "He's older than me and has had a head start."

Scogil's fascination with Splendid Wisdom was an old one dating from his childhood. He had never before met a citizen of Splendid Wisdom, though there might be a trillion on the planet and two more trillion who worked off planet within the Imperialis star system. "You're a long way from home."

"A fish out of water," admitted Rigone, grinning with wrinkles that proved that he was indeed older than Eron. "I have to wear blinders to tolerate this giddy space stuff," he lamented unhappily. "I'm on a quest. You know—finding the grain-of-sand-on-the-shores-of-time sort of thing."

"Searching for the frozen messiah from Rith?" That was the most notorious of the mythological quests.

"Nothing so exotic. Just an Emperor's pebble. I'm new at the game. All that I've found out so far is that the Crafters of Ragmuk must be well hidden. I'm now off to what I hope are happier beaches."

This man needed a history lesson. "There are no Helmarian Crafters on Ragmuk," said Scogil emphatically.

"Oh? Wasn't Ragmuk once the Imperial capital of the Helmar Rift?"

"Most Helmarians aren't Helmarian—they are the descendants of immigrants brought in by the imperium after the Wars Across the Marche. It was Imperial policy to dilute the Helmarian culture and to make it more tractable. Ragmuk was the center of *Imperial* power, the home of a hated viceroy. Not Helmarian. Not even originally colonized by Helmarians. The Crafters avoid the place like the plague."

"The Emperors made many enemies," said Eron gravely. "I have a book that's stand-up-your-hairs reading. I only have eleven thousand years to go."

"Do you suppose I might be in need of a local guide?" laughed a chagrined Rigone.

"Only if your purposes are benevolent. The citizens of Splendid Wisdom sometimes arouse suspicion in this region of space. Questioners are sometimes mischievously misdirected!"

"My purposes aren't political. I once had the honor of being trained by a wandering Crafter in the deft art of fam alteration. Just enough to get by. And I have. But a little knowledge is a dangerous thing and will eventually get a man into big trouble for which more knowledge is the only cure."

"And you are now touring the Thousand Suns, starting with the old Imperial capital. You're looking for a skilled Crafter to teach you more?"

"Yes."

"That could take a lifetime of beachcombing."

"Without a guide, yes," said Rigone ruefully.

"Fam alteration is illegal," said Scogil gravely. "A desecration of a man's mechanical soul."

Rigone smiled around his tattoos. "But tolerated."

"On *Splendid Wisdom?*" The Helmarian was incredulous.

"Consider the case of the struggling Lyceum student."

"*The* Lyceum?" asked Scogil with narrowing eyes.

Rigone laughed again. "I'm a simple barkeep on the Olibanum." Strangers in far places have a way of blabbering about themselves in ways that would never occur to them at home. "Students like to relax in my place. The pressure on them to succeed is horrible. Sometimes they are in desperate need of help. Sometimes I'm in need of a few extras."

"So you soup up their fams?"

"Mostly I'm a fraud. I have a few impressive tricks that my clients find very useful. The Crafter who taught me was very good. I've never made a mistake or damaged a mind—yet. That's suicide. But there are dramatic limitations to my skills, and I'm afraid my equipment isn't state of the art."

"If you haven't yet damaged any minds, why are you in trouble?"

"You mean, why am I in need of a Crafter?"

"It's your story."

"Profitable sins have a way of growing up to be larger than life—charming toddler into teen, that sort of nightmare. On my undeserved reputation one of the Fellowship's most powerful psychohistorians has asked me to upgrade his fam. I dare not refuse him. With my limitations I dare not comply."

"But they have the best fam alteration labs in the universe!" protested Scogil.

"This Pscholar has enemies, or *thinks* he has enemies. He trusts no one at the Lyceum."

"And he trusts *you?*"

Rigone laughed again, an angelic laugh. "Well, he knows I'm a petty criminal. Perhaps he believes in honor among fellow miscreants?"

"Will you upgrade *my* fam?" asked Eron eagerly.

"See?" said Rigone. "People fall all over themselves to trust me." He turned to the boy and tilted the youth's head to peer at his fam. "Ah, made on Faraway." Most people in the Galaxy thought that it was the magician scientists of Faraway who had invented the fam. "And why would you want a *Faraway* fam upgraded?"

"It's not good enough. I want to be a *supergenius!*"

Rigone sighed. "That's what they *all* say to me. Youth!"

Scogil was beginning to wonder . . . was there a possible deal here? What if the Oversee refused to authorize an "upgrade" to Eron's fam knowing a little Clounstyle emotional control was to be thrown in? Helmarian ethics again. But an *illegal* upgrade done out of sight . . . under the eye of a Crafter who knew how to stay on the right side of the unacceptable? Hmmm. It could be done. He gazed at Rigone thoughtfully. "Where are you off to next?" A little shepherding was in order.

"I've been thinking that Sanahadra might be my best bet."

Scogil scowled the slightest discouragement. "Not really. Sanahadra was once the center of the Helmarian culture, but since the Dispersion it has taken on a distinctly Imperial flavor. The Helmarians there try to maintain their identity but . . . They're strong on showing off the ruins, that sort of thing; you know what I mean." Scogil paused deliberately to let doubt sink in. He had time enough before baiting his hook. "You'll have fun searching. To cover the Thousand Suns one-at-a-time makes you a man of leisure."

"Ah." Rigone was suddenly reminded that he was in a hurry. "Do you have suggestions I might find useful? How about Haparal? It's near Ragmuk, right at the bottom of the Rift. I might even adventure a side jump to Lakgan."

"Is *Lakgan* around here!" shouted Eron.

Scogil ignored his student. "Yes, you might consider Haparal . . . but that was a long time ago."

"You don't sound enthusiastic. I've always been impressed by Haparal's story. Faraway takes the credit for developing the fam but, I believe, the Crafters of

Haparal did the spadework. Wasn't it the Crafters of Haparal who developed new kinds of quantum-state erotic stimulators for the vicelords of Lakgan? Basically it was they who created the fam—even if they didn't know it."

Scogil nodded without encouragement. Lakgan and the Thousand Suns had been—still were—stellar neighbors. And Old Lakgan had been wealthy enough to hire any number of Helmarians as lackeys. The Crafters of Haparal were *still* good—but Scogil wasn't going to say so. It wasn't really a crime to bamboozle a citizen of Splendid Wisdom just a little bit. But he'd have to make his reluctance sound real.

During the latter years of Imperial decline, decadent Lakgan had needed new gimmicks to keep its trade of wealthy hedonists returning; too many customers were being frightened away from a sector of space that was slipping beyond the protection of the Stars&Ship. More and more it was necessary for Lakgan to field its own navy . . . and to finance it.

Anticipating taxes from a rejuvenated pleasure trade, the monocled warlord of Lakgan dispatched an insignificant underling to Haparal to threaten the Crafters into delivering what had already been paid for. The underling dutifully returned with the first prototypes of the fam, an unimpressive musical instrument that crudely played delightful emotions directly into the brain. He demonstrated it, experimentally, on his immediate superiors. Thus was born a supernova of galactic brilliance, Cloun-the-Stubborn—faded now, but still remembered by the three million solar systems he had dazzled.

They all knew the story and so it did not need to be repeated. "I'm afraid that Haparal is past its noon of glory," Scogil commented carefully. "Talent follows the sun. After the False Revival, Faraway went looking for the kind of talent that had almost defeated it. Where better to recruit than Haparal? The Crafters have always been wandering tinkers. Faraway gets the credit for developing the fam because so many Helmarians moved to Faraway, a good crowd of them from Haparal."

"So where is the fam tech *right now*?"

"You're really interested in fam technology, eh? You might try Neuhadra. Young Eron and I are off to Neuhadra as soon as we can connect with a starship jumping in the right direction. She's a lively world known for her pure strain of Crafter. Would you care to tag along? Your company would be welcome."

Rigone took on the slightly glazed look of a man furiously scanning his fam database. When he connected with the coordinates, a touch of surprise crossed his tattooed face. "Is Neuhadra even in the Thousand Suns? From that height the Galaxy must look like just another galaxy!" He was trying to make a joke.

Scogil smiled as he brought out his hook hidden in the bait. "It might be off the main swirl but it is certainly the best place for you to start. I can supply you with introductions to a few people in the fam trade. There are bigger centers but none so *easy-going* as a person such as yourself might need. There aren't many who know their quantum-state electronics better than the Crafters of Neuhadra."

# THE HYPERLORD DREAMS OF GLORY, 14,790 GE

*The great achievements of the past were the adventures of the past. Only an adventurous soul can understand the greatness of the past.*

—Proverbs of the Rith: spoken by Alfred the White Head of the North, reputed to be the High Philosophone of the Round Table of Emperor Arthur of England

Kargil Linmax depowered the Hyperlord's hand-size galactarium and the sparse night sky of the Empire's Periphery dissolved into a mere workroom. He carefully disconnected the extraneous power cables which hung from boxes on the ceiling.

"Ready for food?" he asked an elated Kikaju Jama. "I imagine you're starved by now, but let's start the assembly of the atomos before we relax. It's a long job and the sooner we begin the sooner we'll have your device portable again." He led Jama out and up metallic stairs onto the workshop's gallery, to pick up the tools he'd need. In passing he peeked into a little cubicle decorated to appeal to a child's bright curiosity about the Galaxy—but at the moment it was empty of children. "This is going to be an overnight job. You can stay here in Sweet Toes' room. For one night she can share with Baby Girl."

As they passed down the plasteel plankway, Kargil quietly glanced through another door. The three children were there, all curled together, asleep. He smiled, remembering how upset Sweet Toes had been that the baby wouldn't slow down for her nap. "Some problems resolve themselves easier than others. The nice thing about two-year-olds is that they can't revolt for any length of time without having their afternoon nap sneak up and clobber them."

Back down in the shop, Linmax was silent but busy as he set up equipment to grow his octad of atomos. Jama watched. Then, absently, the retired naval officer launched into a lecture without taking his eyes or his hands off his delicate work.

"The First Empire engineers could never have built one of these. Their power plants were always monstrous enough to drive a whole city or a kilometer-long battleship. They thought huge and vast and monstrous. Their ships were a hundred times faster than any other vessel in the Galaxy. They thought nothing of draining seas. Once they even attempted to power Splendid Wisdom with geothermal heat! It's not that the old Imperial engineers weren't good; I admire them. How can you disparage twelve thousand years of a technology that met and swept aside every galactic rival? They showed astonishing ingenuity when context eventually demanded that they shrink a standard multipole power plant into the body of a light hypership—beyond any skill I'll ever have. Huge they could do. But they did not seem able to fathom scaling. And scaling, my Hyperlord friend, is everything."

"Scaling?"

Kargil made adjustments, nudging a delicate assembler that required slippage by some small multiple of hydrogen diameters. "When you build a charge-inverter this size to make antiprotons, you can't just use your computers and your brains and your technical artistry to shrink what you have; you must reinvent physics. Stars and man and ant and nanomachine all live by different laws. Scale up a nanomotor to ant size and it will fly apart. Scale up an ant to man size and he won't be able to walk or breathe. Scale up a man to moon size and he will collapse into a sphere. Of course, scaling the other way gets you into the same morass of troubles." Kargil stabilized his setup behind a forcefield glimmer before dismissing Jama. "Be a good soul and go help Sweet Toes with dinner while I finish up here."

"Isn't she asleep with the others?"

"Nope. I just caught her wandering along the gallery from the edge of my eye. I signaled her that you'd be having dinner with us—she and I share a hand-waving code. We can continue our discussion over food. Be patient. I'm leading up to a chat about scaling and politics because you seem to light up like a torch whenever I mention politics. I like people who wish to improve our Second Empire, but I'm not impressed when the enormity of the task is underestimated. A government, working well at, say, the thousand or million or even billion population level, will simply not function at the quadrillion level."

"But . . ."

"Sweet Toes needs your help," commanded the captain of the ship.

So Hyperlord Kikaju Jama found himself in the service chamber with a young lady huddled over the cuisinator muttering to herself "Decisions . . . decisions . . . decisions." When he sat down beside her, she switched on a nearby flatplate so that he could see the recipe she was contemplating. "I've got almost everything I need for Rustamese Chicken Casserole Concoction. I haven't got ginger. What's ginger?"

"I imagine it's some kind of spice. My fam informs me that it's some kind of rootstalk."

"But what does it *taste* like?"

"The Galaxy is a big place."

"I know what *that* means; it means you don't *know*." She smiled mischievously. "Shall we risk it? The cuisinator says it can fabricate enough gingercells for the recipe in only two or three inamins." An inamin was the time it took for light to sprint ten billion meters. "We'll risk it!"

"As long as we have a quaffable beverage standing by for emergencies in case it happens to be a *strong* spice."

"The drinking mugs are on the top shelf," she suggested. "At just *your* height."

Later Kargil arrived with his boy in tow. "Freidi, meet Hyperlord Kikaju Jama. You do not have to salute him, but you do have to show proper respect and pass him the salt when he asks for it." Freidi gave Jama a shy smile. Not far behind him was the youngest on her three-wheeled pusher pretending that she was a swooshing vac-train. They all sat down in the dining alcove while the Hyperlord served steaming plates.

"Good! I see the ship's stores are still holding out!" That was the captain's own manner of saying grace. The ginger turned out to be a success—only Baby Girl demanded cereal flakes instead.

From inside his coat, as if by magic, Kargil produced a round melon for dessert, much to the delight of the children for whom such a succulent treat was a rarity. While he carved it up into slices, he fixed his eyes on Jama but spoke to Sweet Toes as Captain Kargil Linmax. "I'm pleased to hear that you've been studying Faraway."

"You *stuffed* my fam with Faraway history. How could I avoid it!" she replied scornfully. "I know more about Faraway antiques than you do, I'll bet you a Mallow Credit Note."

"Tell our Hyperlord what you know about the original government. He seems to be interested in its forms."

"You mean when all those scientists were exiled?"

"Yes. How did they manage their affairs?"

"An academic variation of democracy," she said with her spoon poised over the melon slice.

"How does that work?"

"When there's too many people to fill an auditorium," she said with her mouth full, "you elect a representative to sit in the hall for you. The academic variation is when you have *tenured* representatives."

"How well did it work?"

"It worked fine. When you're *tenured* you don't have to worry about making a fool of yourself to get reelected. You can make whatever laws you choose."

"How did it work out in the long run?"

"It didn't. By the time Cloun-the-Stubborn clobbered Faraway, it was already a tyranny. The Founder *predicted* that so it doesn't matter." She caught her superior officer at just the moment when he was ready to interrupt her with another questioning prompt, and witheringly silenced him by eye-flash before she turned to address their Hyperlord guest. "Has he given you his 'scaling' lecture yet?"

"I do believe he has," said Kikaju. His voice was gentle.

She went on doggedly, "So you know what I'm yapping about. Democracy doesn't scale. Once you've conquered a few cubic leagues of space, it is a wheezing ant blown up to elephant size who can't even lift himself off the floor. I know what an elephant is. Once you've conquered a hunk of the Galaxy—that's ten quadrillion zillion people—a representative doesn't represent anybody but himself, and that's the definition of a tyrant." She didn't want to say anymore. She wanted to eat her melon so she came to a quick conclusion. "That's why the First Empire ended up with emperors and why we ended up with Pscholars."

Hyperlord Kikaju Jama fully understood that the authoritarian old captain had meant this child's recitation for him as a dig at his interest in quaint political systems of the past. He weighed his answer, more to the man than the young girl. "I've always felt the need to explore new forms of government. I think the present *tyranny* will have to be replaced." There; he had said it. He watched the old man's expressive face for a reaction and was willing to continue only when he caught the glint of agreement and a reserved half-smile.

Nevertheless caution ruled Jama's next sentences. The Fellowship's eyes were everywhere, feeding samples into psychohistory's statistical machine. "After fifteen centuries, I believe the Pscholars have lost their vitality. What can we do? When looking for alternatives, it is always wise to review the wisdom of the past. There are myriad forms of possible government, many of them having already been tried. Previously I mentioned to you my interest in the Founder's early Faraway experiment in government from which the Pscholars have so grievously deviated."

"It *failed*," said Kargil, "and the Founder *knew* in advance that it would fail. Therefore he prepared for us the Pscholars who have *not* failed. He conceived and shaped this group as merit elitists, the best of the best. They have at no time even pretended to be democratic and will indeed argue compellingly, and accurately in my opinion, that democratic forms will not work on a galactic scale." He shrugged fatalistically. "Will our Pscholars fail too? Come entropy's cold watch, they might."

Later at evensong, when the children had been formally relieved of watch duty in full naval tradition (and by being tucked into bed and kissed), the two men of the incoming watch gathered in the eerie light of the workshop to stare at the growing atomos. After a period of contemplative silence the talk began again, abruptly, at Hyperlord Jama's instigation. He had decided that an aggressive gambit was needed to open up a whole new phase in the sly game they were playing. "And if they *do* fail?" he asked, breaking the silence. Jama meant, of course, the psychohistorians.

The immediate response was an impeccable example of a logical defense. "You do not first destroy what you cannot imagine replacing." Trust a naval captain to open battle from an unassailable position.

Jama was ready. "So trumpets the Credo of the Conservative. *I* am a radical. I would see the whole Splendid edifice crumble to dust so that we might witness a new season. Dust makes good fertilizer. Trees sprout from the cracks of ruins."

Kargil grumbled. ". . . and the Road of Fate is paved with the skulls of poets who forgot to fill their bellies while reciting a litany of praise to the restorative powers of our lost trees."

"Such cynicism! And at the expense of helpless poets!"

"Hardly cynicism. I'm just a centenarian who's lived too long to relish destruction. Can we forget that innocent trees sprouted out of the eye sockets of the skulls that littered Splendid Wisdom after the Sack? In the old Imperial gardens the farmers used sawed-off craniums of bureaucrats as starting planters for their vegetables."

Kikaju Jama smiled nostalgically. "The best sale I ever made in my life was a set of seven carved and embossed Splendid skulls from the Sack Period. Lovingly sculpted by some Scav idler—beautiful inlays of pearl plastic—delicate gold foil—the intaglio depicting the sins of the seven ages of man done wondrously well. Perhaps the engraved heads were even those of Hyperlords." He laughed happily.

"You see, you *are* the child of our soft times. You have been so protected by the farsightedness of the psychohistorians that you have romanticized misery, never having experienced it. The psychohistorians feel a compassionate need to protect people like you from yourself."

Jama was enjoying the opportunity to speak freely. "But their powers are statistical. They *cannot* protect me, an individual, from myself. I could jump off your balcony in the next jiffy. I am my own government."

"Brown-talk from a brainless anus!" Kargil jerked his thumb at the red light over the naval-style dispozoria at the other end of the workshop. "There is *no such thing* as a government of *one*. We are by nature animals who communicate. We depend upon those with whom we communicate, and therefore they depend upon us—which all leads to mutual responsibility, unless one is content with the role of parasite." Kargil nodded, approving of his own speech. "Mutual responsibility *inescapably* leads to government."

"But does not lead to any particular variety of government. There we have more choices than one man can comprehend."

"And wars have been fought over those too many choices," snarled the old warrior.

Play was now fast and cunning, but Jama had an immediate reply. "The ability of a government to conduct itself without war is indeed a positive attribute—but hardly an item of the highest priority. History is replete with examples of tyrannies which excelled at avoiding war. Slaves can be driven to an early grave without ever having to serve in anybody's army."

"So? Does our argument reduce to the particular kind of government you or I, in our wisdom, might choose to inflict upon the Galaxy?"

"Do I have to remind you, my dear Kargil, that, in the millennium we find ourselves, the likes of you and I have *no* choices?"

Kargil sighed peevishly. "Psychohistory says nothing about our personal choices. It allows us to choose all we want. It just sums our choices and spits out the future."

"And if our choices sum to a future which does not please our masters, they, and they alone, have the tools to generate countervailing choices which will cancel ours and reinforce theirs."

Kargil grumbled a simultaneous aye and nay. "I would be inclined to disagree heartily with your Lordship but for an incident that still rankles in my memory, the mere reminder of which leaves me in a cold boil even after all these years. I am a passionate believer in good government by honest men, and have been so since my first decade. Both my parents were honest bureaucrats." The old man became lost in a thoughtful stare that locked his eyes on the flicker inside his atomo assembler.

A jiffy passed before a curious Jama prodded him impatiently. "You may not have stopped thinking but you *have* stopped speaking."

"Sorry. I was remembering my wife. She has nothing to do with the story; she was just the companion who made life exciting during the time I worked at Naval Central. She didn't leave me until I took to captaining ships. As an officer in naval *research* on Splendid Wisdom I commanded far more men than I ever did later in my promotion to captain of *ships*. My group was responsible for reworking and polishing secrecy protocols. You understand that when a navy fights it is important to remain unpredictable? If at all possible, strength, position, plans, strategy must all remain unknown to the enemy."

"Deception." Jama nodded. "I know. One must appear to be strong when one is weak, weak when one is strong; feint here when one is there. Yes, of course. For years all that has been part of my lifestyle."

"We had a brilliant psychohistorian assigned to our group: Jars Hanis. Is the name familiar?"

"Not particularly. Isn't he the Rector?"

"I have followed his career. Wherever suns rise, he is more powerful than any elder Emperor, though he is only one among many who wield such power. He has attained the unlikely: First Rank. Then Rector. When I knew him the brilliance was evident and a prediction that he would go so far would have been a plausible one—though I made no such prediction. On the project he was neither my superior nor my subordinate. He was just there—privy to our work and an advisor when he thought the methods of psychohistory could be useful to us. It seemed innocent enough." Kargil paused.

Jama listened.

"I once asked him why the Pscholars maintained a navy which they never used. I suggested that the vast wealth consumed by the navy could be better spent elsewhere. He gave me the obvious answer: Psychohistorical equations have their own version of the maxim that the one who is willing and equipped to fight is the one who never finds himself in a fight. And its corollary: An unarmed pacifist will never be able to find peace. Thus the Stars&Ship of the Old Empire lives on, resurrected. It is less expensive to maintain a peaceful navy than to fight wars without one."

"You came into conflict with this man?"

"Never. I took his help and appreciated it. His suggestions always made my life easier. I learned half of what I know about good government from him. It was only years later as the captain of a ship—with time on my hands—that I figured out what he had done and why he was working with us."

"Some criminal act?" asked Jama eagerly.

"No, no. I suspect that it would be impossible for Hanis to think like a criminal. It was our *work* that began to puzzle me. The secrecy protocols we devised were far more stringent than any peacetime navy would ever need. It is good to be prepared for anything, but any preparation can be carried to extremes. I spent the evenings between stars without my wife thinking about that. Months and years. Think about it with me now. I've never shared my musings." He slammed his fist into his knees. He looked up at Jama, then continued his speech, face downcast, as if his half-clenched fingers were his only audience.

"In the Galaxy in which you and I live, what group has a strategic need for secrecy? What group fears exposure of their plans? Who regards their mathematical methodology as a secret which must be withheld from the enemy at all costs lest their great plans be thwarted? And who is their enemy if not *us*? I spent twenty years of my life helping to entomb the secrets of psychohistorical prediction. I was not working for the navy; I was working *against* myself. I was helping to place beyond reach the finest methods of social forecast that the human race has ever inherited." He spoke bitterly. "Forecasting must be safely beyond the grasp of 'potential robbers'—like you and me—who, by some act of 'vandalism,' might upset the destiny that has been preordained for us." His bitterness evaporated into a laugh. "The worst of it is that I was so enthusiastically thorough that I'm sure even I couldn't penetrate my own protocols if my life depended upon success."

And so the pieces were laid out. Hyperlord Kikaju Jama could now see his own closing move to clinch the arrangement he wanted to make. He was elated. No hurry. Bring this old spaceman aboard the revolution with deft diplomacy. Wait months, even years, before broaching the subject of conspiracy. "You have obviously been a staunch supporter of good government. My own cerebrations on the subject have never satisfied me. I would appreciate your conclusions. What kind of government do you subscribe to if not that of the Pscholars?"

The captain smiled sadly. "I found that the most a ship could teach me was how to run a good ship. As captain I felt like a damn psychohistorian: I made the decisions about destiny and I postured to command the loyalty of the crew. They carried out my decisions. But . . . what I learned doesn't scale—any analogy one might make between a ship's crew and the galactic commonalty is like hoping to understand an elephant's walk by watching a microbe swim." Kargil laughed at his analogy as if that is exactly what he had been trying to do.

He continued, "I thought I might learn more about large-scale governing when I retired to the swarming trillions of the Imperialis Star System and set up residence among the warrens of Splendid Wisdom." He smiled more mellowly. "I even thought my wife would return to me! So far I've learned how to keep a motherless family going, and as mayor of my little nonterritorial village I've learned an efficient form of democracy that just might scale as high as a thousand people before it broke down." His smile had grown to a grin. "For eighty thousand years we've been bred to survive in political groups larger than the village but, as yet, I don't see much evidence of it in our genes. Ah, the squabbles!"

Kikaju was *listening* to Kargil intently but the assembler he was *watching* was thoroughly as fascinating as any scheme to seduce the old man into creating a security system for the revolution. His eyes were being mesmerized by the unit that was building the atomos.

Mildly cross at the seeming inattention to his speech, Kargil pulled at the Lord's sleeve. "Watching isn't going to make them grow faster. It will be a spell yet. Building a hydrogen annihilator isn't as easy as duplicating antique artwork. Come. I don't know how I'd handle all the squabbles without my robot. Have I told you about my robot? Come. I'll show you. He's far from having the cunning abilities of an old Imperial viceroy, but he's the best statesman I've ever enlisted in my cause. *Come!*" Finally he pulled Jama away from his hypnotic vigil.

Kikaju followed his host to a neatly stacked clutter of boxes where he was shown a bronze buddha that was humanoid from the waist up and a giant insect from the waist down—dressed in one of the more blatant striped styles of the ninety-fifth century with ruffles of lace fendering his six legs.

"Meet Danny-Boy," said Kargil proudly, "the savior of my sanity. He's not powered so don't expect him to be polite. Actually, he's never polite. He's been programmed with a Robot's Ritual Rundown, which states simply:

"Law 1—a robot must be able to recite twenty thousand human jokes in context.

"Law 2—a robot must listen to a human patiently until that human makes his first move to derail the agenda.

"Law 3—a robot must know how to bang a gavel.

"He's our chairbot for democratic meetings that require a quorum. He has all our bylaws and decisions memorized and, believe me, he can check for contradictions in real time. Within his round little belly are the Galaxy's finest set of rules of order. He can stick tenaciously to an agenda. His simulated gavel is a marvelous gong that rings from his skull with an authority that will hypnotically stop any diversionary thought in midflight. Minutes are ready by meeting's end and are supplied out of his behind in verbal famfeed format since if we try to link him to a printer he only recites an incomprehensible error message. Sometimes we get so mad at Danny-Boy's rulings that we turn him off—but by the time we get down to debating how many infinitives should appear in the second paragraph of some unpopular amendment to a critically unimportant motion, we turn him back on. Mostly we put up with him. We don't really like to cut his power because it takes Danny-Boy all of sixty jiffs to reinitialize his operating system."

"An actual chairbot! Impressive! Is Danny-Boy an antique?" Jama knew where he could sell sixtynes of such devices.

"He's supposed to be the creation of Emperor Hagwith-the-Ingenious, who hated staff meetings, but nobody is sure because Hagwith had the unfortunate habit of stealing inventions and executing the inventor—perhaps just a myth invented by his successor who achieved the Robes by assassinating Hagwith. I personally think Danny-Boy's guts predate Imperial times, perhaps from that mythical era before time when there were dwarfs who forged robots to last. We joke that his operating system was written back on old Rith where a cave full of hereditary slaves are *still* trying to clean up the code. But he still works."

"Amazing!" exclaimed Jama, who loved all functioning antiques. "Are you going to turn him on for me?"

"No!"

"No?"

"He has a strong personality," said Kargil ruefully. "Animated iron! He tends to come up with complaints. He's old."

"Problems?"

Kargil wiggled his six fingers. "We have our work-arounds. He's built like a plasteel commode. His logic-modals are huge, about the size of a neuron—how could they fail? A hundred fams would fit in his braincase. He's certainly stupid enough to date from antiquity; for all his massively crude quantronics he has no more brainpower than an unaided human teenager. Maybe fifty or eighty giga-switches at most. We might try to smarten him up with a fam"—Kargil laughed—"but he'd just reply with one of his device-unknown error messages." Kargil paused. "He's a good chairbot."

"So he's a one-function wonder." Even with such a limitation he was valuable.

"One function! He has thousands of features we can't figure out: network manager, detective, you name it—all tacked on as brilliant afterthoughts! How about his telescope-managing mode? When we tried to hook him into a telescope, he asked for one of forty different telescope protocols we've never heard of. That's Danny-Boy! We once tried to hook him into a flatplate after he asked for a screen so he could communicate with us visually, but no matter what screen we tried he kvetched with error message 2247. Don't ask him what that means—he never knew—he'll refer you to the manual. When we found him at the local flea market he was cheap because he was paralyzed from the waist down so we sawed off his bi-legs and tried to plug him into the six-legged walking platform you see. Error messages galore! He's quite a complainer! But we finally taught him how to *talk* to his legs to make them move. Talk he can do! He has a philosopher mode you don't want to know about. He would run the Galaxy if he could; forever if he had the spare parts. He does not lack for ego."

"A robot megalomaniac!"

The nanomechanic patted his insect-legged buddha on the head. "Not a modest thought in *this* piece of iron. He'd even have an opinion about your hats! I believe him when he says he was once Emperor Hagwith's Prime Minister. How good a job he'd do, I don't know. He has a funny way of thinking in zeros and ones. To Danny-Boy everything is either true or false. He can't begin to handle contradictions. When we get mired in all these human contradictions at a meeting, he has a fit. He can't find his way out of the most commonplace contradiction, but he certainly insists that *we* do so, and the faster the better! There's not a subtle electron in his wires, but he's lovable because he makes parliamentary democracy sound as simple as the mind of a politician!"

"So. In spite of your sourness, you *are* a true democrat! Remarkable!"

Kargil had maintained his steady good humor. "Don't get excited. I'm afraid Danny-Boy is the only true democrat I know. *I* haven't graduated even as far as *representative* democracy yet, but I did once calculate how many *centuries* it would take to pass a one-page bill in a galactic parliament of a hundred million on the assumption that every member represented a constituency of a mere billion. And it would take a *thousand* years, at least, just to replace one elected galactic government by another—assuming they could agree upon who had won the election without recounting a quadrillion votes several different ways! Sound familiar? A millennial-long Dark Age while we throw out the rascals! Scaling problems again. Small things are fast. A galaxy is slow. You ask for my conclusion? My conclusion is simple: Every time the population of citizenry is increased by an order of magnitude, government must be reinvented. What works at one population size won't work at the next. Don't even try."

"You would make an excellent revolutionary leader," mused the Hyperlord, following Kargil back into the workshop. "You realize, of course, that you possess the perfect set of *revolutionist* abilities. A group opposed to an organization that thrives on secrecy would need a man who could build his own uncrackably secret organization."

"Revolution—as in destruction? Don't mention that word! The Empire has ears! I'm willing to build. I am *not* willing to destroy! To what purpose?"

"May I offer you irresistible bait?"

Kargil was stunned by this sudden effrontery. "You are trying to bribe me? Get out of my house, you overdressed fop!" He puffed up into a threatening pose.

Jama immediately slouched into the slightly hangdog demeanor of the overused victim. "Really, my dear friend, such blows to my fragile ego are entirely unnecessary and unworthy of a gentleman." The Hyperlord was quite able to fake indignation, nor was he the least bit perturbed by Kargil's anger. Anger was the last defense of a weakening rampart. "'To what purpose?' you ask. Why"—he smiled—"what else—the purpose of pirates! We land in force with magnetic boots clanging upon the outer shell of their battleship while we blast through the hull *to steal the secret of psychohistory* from the rich so that we may enhance the wealth of the poor."

"Steal psychohistory?"

"Of course."

"Preposterous! They have guarded their secret for . . . what is it now, two and a half millennia? Your impulsive clanging boots are a metaphor for ineptness! The Pscholars are *centuries* ahead of any thought you can think or move you can make! Opposition is suicide. How could anyone possibly get through their security!"

Jama knew he had won the game; he had challenged Kargil to break his own unbreakable protocols to reach a prize big enough to wipe out his shame. Now all he had to do was bring the captain down from anger to the logic of action. "Think like a military man. Am I such a fool that I would suggest we go against them via a frontal assault upon their strongest guns? They must be attacked sneakily at a point where they are weak. And where are they weak? You yourself mentioned that secrecy always hides weakness. They are deathly afraid that they will become powerless if their predictive methods are exposed to the sight of the common man. Strike boldly at their weak point! Stealing their *secret names* will render them magically impotent."

Kargil was suddenly laughing. "I shall have to power up Danny-Boy to gavel you down and bring order to this conversation!"

"Think. Firstly there are many forms of stealing. Was the Founder a god that only *he* could create psychohistory? Consider: Today it has become almost impossible to patent any new invention, not because of law but because of circumstance. The most abstruse creations are simultaneously duplicated and registered in a thousand different places. Even coeval invention isn't relevant. The Galaxy is so vast that often an invention is *independently* discovered thousands of years apart. *Reinventing* a secret is the cheapest form of thievery, and, from a military point of view, the safest and surest mode of attack by which a minority force can win an overwhelming victory against impossible odds."

"You are equating the work of the Founder with mere invention of geared gadgetry?"

Jama was amused at Kargil's lapse into indignation at blasphemy. Even those who were critical of the Pscholars seemed to feel a mystical reverence for the Founder. To question the uniqueness of his ideas was a heresy so fundamental to this galactic culture that one might as well question the existence of atoms and expect a serious audience. Jama replied with unctuous soothing. "And can you say why the advent of psychohistory is so different from mere perfection of a machine? Machine design can be almost intractable. It took a creeping interstellar culture in the Sirius Sector ten thousand years to bring together all the pieces necessary to build the hyperdrive motor—surely an astonishing invention—but not a result unique to one man."

He paused to give Kargil time to think before continuing. "Why did a full forty-eight millennia of galactic social evolution follow the invention of the hyperdrive before the seeds of the First Empire could even take root? Wisdom takes time to mature before it can be seized. Kambal-the-First was surely a genius equal to the Founder. Consider the truly formidable tradition upon which he built, Splendid Wisdom's engineers, Splendid Wisdom's uncommon trading skills—only the beginning of the formidable tradition he fostered. Could the First Empire have survived so long had it not been able to carry out a crude form of psychohistory on an automatic intuitive level?" Jama raised a finger dramatically before continuing.

"The Founder had to rely heavily on the wisdom accumulated during twelve thousand years of bureaucratic Empire, sorting the protein from the chaff, formalizing eons of scattered bureaucratic rules of thumb into a compactly manageable theory. It's nonsense that psychohistory all sprang from the head of the Founder! He was merely the great codifier! All the pieces of the puzzle lie scattered before our eyes, just as they once lay scattered before his, all waiting to be picked up by anyone!"

"Blasphemy!" said Kargil with the naughty smile of a child who has had revealed to him his first dirty word and is preparing himself to try it out.

"We *could* steal psychohistory," pursued Jama relentlessly. "But why waste our time? You and I with our fams are an intellectual match for the Founder—but we are so caught up in a hurricane of mental augmentations that we don't even know it! Let us steal what we can steal, all the while remembering that whatever can't be stolen from a guarded fortress can be rediscovered. More gems lie scattered under the ground than ever sat in a viceroy's locked and guarded vault."

Kargil was ready to interrupt but Jama snatched a breath and did not allow it. "Why is current mathematical research in such an utter shambles outside of the Pscholars' Lyceums? Hmmmm? Could it be too dangerous for the Pscholars to include a renaissance of mathematics in their great plan for our future? I'll wager my hat that a simple survey of the bits and pieces of mathematics that have disappeared from the Galaxy's archives would give us critical hints as to which analytical methods would be most productive for a reconstructionist to stalk. If an enemy fleet has mysteriously *disappeared* from its known locale in space, doesn't that reveal its admiral's intentions? We must recruit mathematicians for our task!"

Kargil had his opening. "Why do you dress like you do?" he asked.

"Because I'm a very vain man." The Hyperlord's carefully constructed logic derailed while he brushed his collar and checked the alignment of his hosiery. "Why should I mask my preening vanity? It gets me misclassified. How could I ask for more? Misclassified as a cipher in the wrong database, I am lost in the analysis of the doings of millions of harmless fops who never had a revolutionary thought in their lives. People who think they know a man by the way he dresses are easily misled. Being able to mislead people pleases my vanity as much as any piece of scented Osarian lace."

"You will pardon me if I spend a few watches examining your misleading arguments."

"If you do take up the cause of fighting tyranny, your most felicitous occupation would be to spend some time designing a covert organization which does not depend upon the clownish way *I* dress for its invisibility."

They laughed and then broke up their watch for sleep, the captain to his stateroom, the Hyperlord to a child's bed beneath faintly glowing personifications of suns—happy giant reds and scowling blues and hardworking golden dwarfs. He shared the bed with a lovable multilegged stuffy who could manage a semi-intelligent conversation if you pressed the wrong part of its anatomy and were incautious enough to talk back to its sand-grain of a brain.

Stripped to his flamboyant underwear, his pink mopcap perched upon the stuffy's head, the Hyperlord began a whispered conversation with the child's companion. He shared with it, in confidential allusions, his dream of adventuring out among the worlds of the Periphery—to Zurnl specifically—there to find the primal lie. The prince who knows the lies of his enemy, he informed the stuffy, has the keys to his enemy's lands. To be invulnerable, one must *never* lie—even when a Cloun-the-Stubborn pops up out of his box. That was impossible, of course. Jama lied all the time—but in a good cause: his own. He liked to live dangerously.

# NEUHADRA OF THE THOUSAND SUNS, LATE 14,790 GE

*With the Even-Hand and Fair Mind of Our Just Emperor and in His Name we find that ¶45 of the Treaty of Sanahadra states, unequivocally, that the newly allegiant Helmarian people of the Thousand Suns Beyond the Helmar Rift have agreed to accept minority status on the planets terraformed and/or colonized and/or claimed by their ancestors as specified in §Appendix-P.*

—Count Ism Nokin of the Splendid Praxis Court:
Ruling #AZ-243 ci 7992 GE

Something was awry. The young mind of Eron Osa sensed it. He had learned to read nuances in people's expressions, learned to read the motive behind preoccupations and the meanings in sudden changes of plan. He hadn't spent years spying on his father for nothing. Now cast from home, fatherless, he held under continuous surveillance only his tutor—who increasingly showed symptoms of secret motivations that . . .

Creeping up above the Great Arm, jump by jump, to a position where ninety-five percent of the galactic plane was below them like a great sparkling sea, it began to strike Eron how awesomely huge the Second Empire really was and how little he knew of it. After their third jump his curiosity was so demanding that the Chairman of the Bridge lent him the use of her telescope to zoom in on whatever features of the celestial sphere he might find while the idle ship recharged its hyperatomics.

The circular screen dominating the bridge was as expansive as a vanity mirror in an expensive brothel. Adding to the impression, the encircling baroque bronze frame sported leafy vines that modestly clothed voluptuously shy tree sprites. The control toggles were nymphs and undines and maenads and sylphs, sensual to the touch. A companion celestial roboconsultant sat beside it in the disguise of an open-mouthed sibyl with four breasts. Above the telescope were pinned two good-luck charms—one an icon of Emperor Kambal-the-First and the other, in full regalia, a tiny replica of Emperor Harkon-the-Traveler.

After start-up the telescope's immense milky surface dissolved into life. Eron fiddled with its contrast and resolution and magnification like an eager four-year-old. What was fun was to toggle through some of the frequency filters. He had the whole electromagnetic spectrum at his command, picking a broad band from radio to gamma to see everything, or a narrow band of ultraviolet from 150 to 250 nanometers to see only suicidally hot stars, or he could filter out all the stars that didn't have a specific set of, say, fraunhofer carbon lines. They were alone now, but he had been told that if he time-space linked up with the telescopes of other ships he could even see planets up to fifty leagues away. Wow! He imagined himself as a Stars&Ship general, with a thousand starship telescopes hooked together planning an attack on a remote solar system.

And he could aim the telescope wherever he wanted without asking the boss-witch to move the ship! Where to look? He happily famfed into the instrument a few choice coordinates from a stellar catalog he had once memorized on a winter's evening while scanning Agander's heaven with his binoculars. Wonderful! Even useless knowledge stuffed into his extra brain could come in handy at unexpected moments!

First he picked up Agander's star and stared at it for a full inamin before he swung the image . . .

. . . to bring in the swirl of Andromeda. Was there another edacious empire across the vastness of intergalactic space eating up planetary systems? He imagined, in pastel color, intelligent lizards with eyes in their nose who wore coats of tanned mammal skin and kept their many-jeweled timepieces in pockets tooled of soft female breast leather, each closed by a brass ring in its nipple.

Grinning, he jumped his instrument to a local nebula called the Great Demiurge with its skein of exploding filaments, a solar system blasted, its history undecipherable, its records rendered into plasma . . . then bounced his aim in the direction of Splendid Wisdom's Imperialis but could see nothing in the dazzle of the central confabulation of stellar voices.

There was a presence behind him. "Not that way! Are you looking for Splendid Wisdom?" It was the two-breasted mammalian Chairman of the Bridge, who maintained a live infrared link to monitor her cub's use of her telescope, holding herself in free-fall behind him. When he got things wrong the old witch turned up and mussed his hair and corrected his hand—so that with only a few false starts . . .

This time she showed him how to simulate the main stars between here and Imperialis and to flick-toggle back and forth between sim and real in feedback overlay mode. He was able to *see* where Imperialis would be if only the dazzle didn't get in the way. Dreamily he remembered the first millennium of emperors from his book—greedy as they were, in the first thousand years of their nascent human empire they had been able to conquer only a small fraction of the vastness included in this single telescopic view.

He wanted to know everything. Why hadn't his tutor told him everything? His eyes strayed from the telescope. What was tutor Murek hiding? Why had they suddenly changed plans at Ragmuk? Was the money stick empty? Why had their credit dried up? A cautious distrust of farmen was preventing him from asking. But he intended to find out with a spider's patience. All he had to do was feign innocence and wait for hints to flit too closely to his web. High on Eron's priority list was an upgrade to more memory and a faster mind.

But that could wait at least until the maternal Chairman had pried him away from her telescope!

He didn't have all the pieces yet. Was Murek Kapor this farman's real name? Hints . . . slips . . . indicated otherwise—but he didn't yet know why his tutor had changed names or what identity it masked. Was he running from the law? The masks out here in the empire were everywhere! If only he could see far enough, he could *see* the roofscape of trees that masked the Lyceum on Splendid Wisdom!

Never enough time for everything! The old witch brought out the watch cycle's duty roster and gave him his next assignment. He sighed. No more telescope. He didn't even plea. He knew this she-witch by now. She patted his bum with a firmness that gently propelled him off in the direction of his work.

Scrubbing gave him lots of time for further brooding. He had already deduced that his tutor's promise of a scholarship was worthless. What could be more revealing than their accommodations for Neuhadra? His mentor and Rigone had a small double-bunked cabin, horrible enough—but *he* was relegated to sharing with a crewman. He dreamed of a morning sun pouring in over leafy vases of plants. Had *he* actually been gauche enough to grumble at his mother while she held onto his ears as he sullenly watered them? How had he failed to notice the glory of his luxurious room back in the highlands of Agander's Great Island? Scraping centuries of neglected dirt from the encrusted walls of a dim ship's corridor gave him a sudden respect for a mother's taste in design and furniture and her insistence on their regular maintenance.

He was allowed to sleep only when his bunkmate was on duty-watch. It seemed to be a part of the contract Murek had negotiated for Eron pay his way by cleaning and performing tasks too menial for a robocrab. Various parts of the ship were undergoing repair. When he dared complain, that scruffy matron, the *witch*, only smiled and found more work for him to do on theory that a busy boy was a happy boy. She could afford theories like that! She wasn't mean but he sometimes shocked her and she responded with an expression that implied *You aren't by any chance under the delusion that you are, by some divine right, a passenger?* Other than assigning him yucky work, the Chairman of the Bridge noticed him only when she had some ship's arcana to teach. Like telescopes. Once she slipped him a cookie from the secret store she kept in her bra. It tasted better than the gruel in the mess.

Centijiffs added up to inamins, a hundred inamins by the gulp to hours. Watches passed. A hundred watches added up to a month. He was coming to a boil. Working with his *hands,* sleep, scrub, sleep, paint, sleep, hustle and defer! There was a limit to such indignity! He was the son of a Gandarian High Adjudicator!

But before Eron broke out in open revolt, Murek hastily restrained him with a curt "Do what you're told. This is nothing. Where we're going they have child labor contracts that make the Chairman of the Bridge look like your sainted mother." And then his eyes twinkled but Eron wasn't sure he was joking. "I can sell you for pocket credit when we get into port. Plans don't always work out the way they are supposed to, and you, you little pest, ask too many questions. Yes, to answer you, I *don't* know exactly what I'm doing; but aren't we *still* jumping by the grace of my wit? So keep your mouth full of potatoes and shut up with the whining."

That didn't exactly sound like *master* Murek Kapor knew what he was doing, wits or witless. Eron decided to postpone his revolt. They still had endless watches ahead of them to jump from one murky hell of a barren outpost to the next. That gave Eron time to plot—in his dreams—jailbreaks from dark interstellar worldlets. Would Murek really sell him into slavery? Wasn't slavery illegal *everywhere*? Wasn't this the *Second* Empire! The Founder help him if he had fallen back in time to the Glory Centuries of the Evil Empire!

After roundabout hyperspatial spelunking far from any sun, the tedium broken only by the trading stopovers at minor interworlds of the stellarways, the Chairman made the announcement that they had reached Neuhadra. At last! Eron was reassembling pipes that he had painfully polished inside and out. No more of such drudgery! But he wasn't reassured. After all, this was the Planet-with-the-Child-Labor-Laws.

Eron knew his guardian had been reduced to pauperhood—but by how much? He knew that a certain young boy was the only salable commodity that his tutor possessed—but would Murek really . . . ? Of course it was only logical to anticipate the worst. And then again, maybe not. It was true that he trusted Murek. Maybe he'd go along with him. Nevertheless he had contingency plans to take off on his own as soon as they hit dirt. Yes. Like a rocket on antiprotons!

But life never makes sense just at the moment when you think you have all the angles covered. The Chairman of the Bridge slipped him a last cookie from her bra. The roboskiff delivered the three of them, Murek and Rigone and Eron, to the high customs station where they were met by a golden yacht with huge decorative fins and two solicitous crewmen who bypassed them around customs procedures and brought them down to planet inside a wood-burnished cabin whose robocook served them champagne and soft-boiled eggs. With fresh egg in his mouth, Eron goggled out at the awesome twilight landscape below—which was rapidly expanding into a private spaceport between mountain peaks. It seemed to serve a single castle. Was this castle-on-a-lake the planet's largest slave owner?

It was night and cold when they debarked. A fresh frost was on the ground, on the buildings, on the fields, on the trees, but there wasn't a cloud in the sky, only stars. They were given electrical coats and Eron marveled that when he breathed, fog came out of his mouth. It was thin air. Their furry hats were oxygen concentrators that hid an optional face mask. Some kind of hardy bird was chirping an evening sleep call.

And wonder of wonder, stars were falling everywhere from the sky. He tugged at the brocaded sleeve of his tutor's guest-coat.

It was Rigone who responded. "Looks like we arrived in time for a real shower."

"Does this all the time, not every hour, but most months," volunteered their uniformed escort, guiding them to a waiting aerocar.

"See those bright stars up there?" As they walked through the cold, Eron's strange farman was being a teacher again, pointing toward two brilliant lights halfway up the sky and to a smaller blaze above the mountains where the Galactic Swirl powdered the horizon. The beacons looked like artificial searchlights but they didn't move. They were *stars*! "Neuhadra is in a seven-system; we can't see the other four from here. Our companions are far enough away so that Neuhadra is in a stable orbit even if it isn't as circular as the climatologists might like—but our companions make it hard for the debris out there to settle down. That makes for good comet watching and brilliant shooting-star displays. I don't think anyone on Neuhadra doesn't keep an eye out for errant debris."

"Have you been here before?" asked Eron.

"Nope, but my friend Mendor used to squawk about the sky falling when we were in school. All the time."

"Is he a mathematician, too?"

"And a very good one. Also rich." Murek stooped to whisper a final word in Eron's ear. Eron couldn't see the grin, but he could hear it. "I got us here just in time! How about that? Are you as hungry as I am?"

Their heated aerocar pressurized itself for the short hop to the gabled roof of a family mansion big enough to hold a hundred rooms. From the rooftop landing pad it looked even bigger. Chimneys! Eight of them. Did they have the same function as the huge chimneys on Splendid Wisdom that controlled the weather? "No," said Rigone. His guess was that they were part of the air conditioning.

Eron tried to compose himself without saying much while he sat through a raucous late dinner with the Glatim clan. There were more servants than people! And the servants all had robots to attend them who morphed out of the walls on command. The bustle went on and on. Neuhadra had a long day and an equally long night, punctured by several twilights. For the whole of the dinner from roast fox to lady fingers in marmalade cream sauce, Murek was immersed in his reunion with his old friend, Mendor, getting behind in his eating—and then holding his palm up and out to stop the conversation while he caught up on the food with a quick fork and rapid munching.

Eron eventually mustered up enough courage to nudge his friend and ask quietly in his ear, "Is this where I'm to be sold?"

His tutor only grinned happily. He returned the nudge, slightly off target. "You'll just have to put up with my sense of humor. Remember how I pulled your leg about the Horezkor?" he teased. His voice was slurred. "Maybe I just might buy a present for you. Have you ever owned an underage slave?"

It was all an astonishing transition from poverty to wealth. It hadn't been more than two watches ago that Eron was breaking his back scrubbing down a wretched little starship that could have been the Alcazar's lost dungeon of his childhood imagination. From that to a gravity that made his legs leap, to a table laden with too much food, in a room that was far too big and full of light-headed people, all overdressed. All strangers—it was outrageous that Murek forbade him to wear a holstered kick among so many unknown farmen! His mind was boggled at all the conflicting cues; by the time the clock boomed Neuhadra's midnight hour he was woggy enough to welcome any kind of bed, even a starship's closet. His sense of time was out of whack—they didn't live by watches here, and their day wasn't properly decimalized!

He hadn't realized until trying to stand that he'd also been drinking too much of the sweet wine. Maybe it was the thin air. A young maid, probably his own age, supported him to his rooms with an amused forbearance, picking up his luggage on the way, not that there was much of it. She hefted his book as if she'd never seen one before. He didn't feel comfortable with such a wisp of a child doing a man's work, yet she became amused and uncooperative when he tried, out of Ganderian politeness, to unburden her.

"You're drunk, sir," she remonstrated with a smile. "Another stagger out of you and I'll throw you over my shoulder."

So he just complied. Murek had warned him about strange customs—and, after all, she *was* a farman. He was too tired to think more about it. With the maid's gentle help—she was strong—he managed the stairs after only a single lapse of dignity. Their journey along a planked second-floor hallway (enormously wider than the ship's corridors he'd been resurfacing) led them to the portal of a bedroom he couldn't believe. But he had no zest left to explore; he went straight to the bed, big enough for a man four times his size, and in less than a jiff he was asleep. Facedown on the nearest pillow.

When Eron woke the next morning it was to the golden-red light of a dawn pouring over him. He'd had enough sleep; Neuhadra was a lazy planet with a long day, 37 percent greater than the galactic standard of three watches, but the slight girl, who should have been gone, was still in attendance. She must have undressed him for he was naked. She was in bed with him, and naked, too, still asleep, her warmth under the comforter close and erotic. That was all very un-Ganderian and unexpected. He was so shocked that he turned his head away, toward the oval window that was as big as the room—and saw the full magnitude of a humongous lake that was so huge one didn't notice, at first, that it was a crater-lake.

A planet-buster on one side and a barely adolescent girl on the other. Very scary. He was between a rock and a soft place! He'd have to review his fam's summary of an evening his organics hardly remembered through his hangover. Maybe, Space forbid, more had happened between him and the girl than he recalled.

"You're awake," she said, and because his head was turned away toward the window and he was absolutely immobile, she added, "I *know* you're awake." She touched his shoulders cautiously and Eron was appalled when his penis responded. She gently shook him, thought better of it, and paused for a breath. "Don't you turn around and try something before we talk," she admonished. "All you farmen are alike. I don't trust you. My mother told me never, never to trust a farman when she signed my contract."

"What a crater!" said Eron evasively, staring through the oval window at the only thing big enough to distract him. He was on his side and that didn't give him the best view but he didn't dare sit up. "It looks like a mountain range!" The Glatim Mansion was perched on the raised rim, situated to stare down into the impact basin and across. The spaceport must be behind them. Eron's educated fam absorbed details of erosion and weathering and concluded that the cataclysm couldn't have happened more than a million years ago, probably half that. He was impressed, but what he was feeling was the soft hand on his naked shoulder.

"It's the biggest one on the planet but it's just a dumb old crater," she said. "We have lots of craters." She began to try to shift him around toward her, his back to the bed, gently but with a peasant's strength. "You aren't paying attention, sir. You have to listen and seal our parley with your eyes." She took his hair in a firm grip and twisted his head to face hers. "I told you not to try anything. You have to swear with your eyes not to try something."

He found himself being forced to stare into an intent set of eyes, their blue speckled with slim dashes of henna, but his kept wandering. "What happened when it hit?" Eron was calculating energy of impact and extrapolating to the size of the asteroid that had made it. "Space! What did that thing do to Neuhadra?"

"I don't know," she said, shaking his head slightly, not sure that she had his attention. "I wasn't born then."

He had dreamed often of his father's mistress undressing him. Dreamed. Sweet Melinesa. She was at least a respectable forty; having a naïve girl *this* age in bed with him was ridiculous. Boys like him were supposed to be educated by experienced married women! After being forced to face her, Eron couldn't resist checking to see if she was actually wearing her fam—she was; a delicate Crafter design gracefully snuggled under her full hairdo. She sure wasn't using it to advantage! There she was—all that brainpower concentrated to resist attack by a farman who was, at present, as frozen as a scared rabbit. It was a shock to find that *he* was now one of the intriguing-terrible farmen. He couldn't help but try out one of Murek's you-don't-know-why-I'm-smiling smiles.

"What's your name?" he asked.

"That's none of your business," she explained gently. "I'm Girl to you, sir, if you don't mind. You may address me as Young Girl if I have so displeased you that you have a reprimand ready."

"Oh." He wasn't sure he knew what she was talking about—and it wasn't the strange accent. Did farmen actually need both physical and social reorientation after living in a ship's closet for months? "Is this your room or mine?" he asked in an initial attempt at clarifying his confusion. Nothing, it seemed, could be taken for granted.

"It's yours, sir." The inflection said *of course.*

"And why are you here?"

"Sir, I'm your servant. I'm here to serve you, obey your orders, and see that you come to no harm when you are drunk even if I have to risk my own life." Then she added, with downcast eyes that were more flirtatious than afraid, "I'm at the mercy of your good behavior but I'm allowed to defend myself. It's in my contract."

Such a strange word, servant—even though it was in his vocabulary, it didn't tell Eron anything; he had no context in which to place it. They didn't have servants on Agander, only service that varied by circumstance and intricate game rules. "Then you're to do anything I ask of you, Girl?"

"Only what is specified in my contract, sir," she replied coyly. "You can famfeed a copy in the normal way—though I *don't* advise it. The contract automatically installs behavior constraints." To say what was unspoken, her hidden hand teasingly poked his erect penis, which he was trying to hide under the covers. She giggled.

He began to see some of the disadvantages that beset a farmen—a farman was constantly having to learn new and amazing rules. "And what does this contract define as your duties?"

"I'm to please you." There was the tone of catechism in what she said. She had her own private reservations—it was in her tone—and she had no intention of sharing them with him. He would have to guess.

What he was guessing disturbed him because it was so un-Ganderian. As best as he could read her, she was willing to make a flexible interpretation of her duties if he was able to choose a kind way in which to ignore the conditions of her contract. Kindness was one of mankind's universals. He sensed that she didn't know who he was and that scared her, but because he hadn't yet *done* anything to scare her, she wasn't doing whatever it was that she did when she felt the need to defend herself. It was her unspoken invitation that upset him—knowing that her desires would always remain unspoken. With the covers now more firmly under his armpits, he began to talk to the ceiling. It felt weird to shift into Murek's valence and begin a tutor's rhetorical approach to a new student. "You know what a man of *Neuhadra* would expect of you, am I right?"

She nodded.

"But you aren't sure what might please a farman?" A frantic part of him was telling him to stop being an intellectual.

"I'm to please all whom I serve, sir," she explained.

That kind of ambiguous phrasing drove him crazy. "So you're here to please me even though I may have very strange demands? Would you be willing to please a farman like me whose greatest delight was eating spit-roasted girls for breakfast with a knife, fork, and teeth?"

She squeaked and pulled herself into a sitting position at the very corner of the bed, holding up the covers around her body until only her eyes showed. "That's not in my contract!" But her voice rang with mirth.

"Fortunately for you, Girl, I forgot my knife and fork back on Agander!"

She was now staring under the covers to get a good look at the body she had already carefully undressed the night before. It was very much the curiosity of a young child. "It's your teeth I'm worried about. Deflecting knives and forks is part of my training." She dropped the covers so that he could see her. And she *was* beautiful, in a non-Ganderian sort of way. He wasn't sure if her breasts were fully formed yet. "After lugging you upstairs last night, I'm too salty to eat without a bath. I'd go for the eggs and sausage myself, if I were you." She smiled shyly.

"Ah, hunger." He sighed. "You have eggs?"

With the same squeak that she had used to wrap herself in the covers, she leaped out of bed. That was a request for which she knew the response. With a flick, a wall panel opened up to the cuisinator. "Eggs and sausage coming right up!"

A voluptuous servant to instruct a robocook which had been designed to replace a servant; there, thought Eron, was a new definition of luxury.

Her task quickly done, she asked, "Will you let me dress you now?"

"I'm used to doing it myself."

"Sir! At that you are incompetent! The togs you were wearing were disgraceful. You have no taste. I put them in the dispozoria. You'll *have* to let me dress you. I know everything about clothes! I measured you last night very carefully with my calip while you snorted in your sleep and, by now, the manufacturum in the closet has everything ready for you."

"You measured me? Really?"

"I'm afraid you disappointed me as a farman, sir; I didn't find any tentacles, sir. And you were very drunk; your penis only measured two centimeters. Sir."

While he waited for his breakfast, he watched her spread out his new clothes—collars, even! This was worse than being attended by a robovalet! She hadn't bothered to dress herself. And watching, he found himself inanely straining to feel like a forty-year-old married man (like his father) who had shouldered the duty of sexually training a young girl. But he wasn't an older man, and he had no business being with this child and even *thinking* about sex; if he'd been caught on Agander with *this* she-sapling, the men of his class would have put him in the stocks for attempted ruination! Young men were *not* allowed to seduce young girls. Young girls were reserved for men with already established careers. He had a moment of smug revolt now that he had left Agander forever; nobody on Agander trusted the maturity of their young, even ones who had a straight kick shot! And so much had happened in the last few months that he was now *sure* of his maturity.

Still, he felt he should have been given a mature woman as a servant. He tried to imagine Melinesa as his *servant*. And couldn't. *Lover* maybe, servant, never. Well, this was Neuhadra and they did things differently—farmen were *all* crazy. Dingbat crazy! And woe, woe, woe, he was now a farman himself!

Girl was chattering while she made intricate decisions about color and cut and texture. This was worse than trying to escape Kapor's mathematical traps! How could *anyone* care that much about clothes? Now he knew what she used her exquisite little fam for! She probably had forty thousand years of fashion stuffed in there. Her naked back was made enticing by the fascinating curves of that fam. He stopped listening to her while he became more and more involved in coveting it. Maybe the next time they were in bed together and she was snoring away, he could switch with her. He knew it was an idle fantasy; it was already ten years too late. Fams take as long to mature as humans. It drove him crazy to be right in the heart of the worlds where they built such awesome fams. From here one could rule the Galaxy.

Maybe not. Cloun-the-Stubborn had already tried *that* with the Crafters working their magic for him. If rumor was right, these people had built the original visiharmonars for Lakgan. "The First Citizen of the Galaxy" had designed his strategy around personal control of minds. That's what "First" meant. First mind. It hadn't worked. Why? Cloun-the-Stubborn had missed comprehending the number-one cliché: The Galaxy is a big place. What was it that tutor Kapor had said about control-vanity? "Men who are obsessed with personal control because they trust no one with their vision end up *out of control*—like a single puppeteer trying to pull off a mob scene with multiple puppets on stage." Maybe it wasn't wise to do what he'd have to do to seduce Girl. *I'll resist her,* he comforted himself virtuously, *if* he could get his penis to agree.

Nevertheless he let Girl dress him. The clothes she had selected were a comfortable fit, and if he didn't look in a mirror he didn't even feel conspicuous. He kissed her hand. Better not start his seduction with anything more complicated than that. Now that he was dressed, he wished she'd get dressed, too. He was finding her slim body more and more enticing. She had a peculiar surgically added organ along her ribs under her arm. He thought at first that it was merely decorative—the cicatrix signifying a servant perhaps—but it was the organ to which she attached her artificial lung when she went outside. Neuhadra's atmosphere, of course.

Later in the morning Eron spent time at an archival terminal famfeeding himself some Neuhadran history, thousands of years of it, back to Imperial times, back to the first settlers who crossed the Helmarian Rift itself. He didn't even need a tutor's prodding anymore to immerse himself in that kind of labor.

Girl reappeared from nowhere when he decided to take a walk out along the crater wall. She insisted that he wear his oxygen supplementer with its annoying pull-down mask. Then she faded away again. Probably she could locate him with some gizmo in his clothes. Maybe she was even responsible to monitor his life-signs. Damned if he was going to *use* the sissy mask. He was well past the winter gardens into the wilderness, running down the slope, when he started to feel dizzy and the hat beeped. The mask dropped over his face automatically. Why did people try to settle planets like Neuhadra? He was beginning to guess what all farmen meant when they called Agander a heaven.

The mountain slope looked like any ordinary slope leading gently down into a lake—but there were all sorts of telltale signs of cataclysm. His famfed Neuhadran history wasn't really available to him until cues keyed it in to help him understand what he was seeing. Ninety-six percent of the life on Neuhadra had been destroyed by this impact less than a million years ago. The local life was still scrambling to fill vacant niches.

He recognized the tripartite mouths of a red flowering plant in the thin snow that still showed vestiges of its former life in the Neuhadran seas. It crawled. A whole class of leafy sea-forms had always been mobile, but there had been no crawling land plants a million years ago. There had been no niche for them on land then, either. It was fascinating. Moments later he saw one of the strange native pulse-burrowers scamper out of a rotten fern trunk. A whole extinct class of large animals had yet to be replaced by evolution, perhaps the pulse-burrowers would grow into the vacant niche—if rats or rabbits or horses didn't fill it first. Some might-have-been paths would never be taken because of mankind's empire and invaders from the stars.

Eron saw daffodils. Or maybe they weren't daffodils anymore? Would a daffodil recognize spring on a planet with an orbit as eccentric as Neuhadra's? He spotted a cocoon waiting for the warmth to release its tiny being. Not native. A starfaring insect from who-knew-what planet, a hobo fresh off some careless ship?

Standing here on the slope of this cataclysm he did not have to wonder why the Glatim clan dominated the galactic meteoroid&comet deflection business. He could almost write the history himself from the hints he had heard around the feast table.

The original Glatim family had been driven to settle here around the crater during the forced "relocations" of Imperial times at the end of the Wars Across the Marche. Protection from the sky would not have been a worry at the time of the Dispersion—the Galactic Empire's Omneity of Planetary Safety was the bureaucratic entity that handled errant asteroids and comets and meteoroids. But when the Empire died in paroxysm, the Omneity vanished. Not so the Helmarians of Neuhadra.

The Glatims still lived on the edge of their crater, and the night sky was still full of falling stars and the frolicking seven suns were still out there playing with the local stability of planetary orbits. Theirs was a threat to keep thinking about.

Perhaps out in the Galaxy other worlds had tried to take the Omneity's place, but the Glatims had been well situated. They were of the Helmarian Crafters and so culturally undaunted by the mere mechanical details of moving worldlets. They were survivors of the Wars Across the Marche and so bore the Empire particular malice and would be only too willing to take over territory vacated during the collapse. They soon found protection under the False Revival of Cloun-the-Stubborn who owed his power to them, and, after that, they were spatially situated to thrive under the suzerainty of Faraway's peculiar interstellar-size city-state. All through the Interregnum they would have consolidated their business. Simple math.

Eron was amazed at how a little travel could so broaden one's viewpoint, even if he had to manage his thinking with the crummy aid of that antiquated tech from the Periphery that burdened his shoulders.

He was turning up a slope of boulders to get a better view when a voice commanded him. "By the Ghosts of the Emperors, am I glad to see you!" said a puffing Rigone as he appeared from behind some bushes on the trail. "Slow down!" The Scav paused to take a deep puff from his mask. "This place gives me the willies. One can walk klom after klom without running into anyone. It's worse than being lost in space; at least there you have a fifty/fifty chance of running into an ancient race once an episode!"

"Impressive, isn't it?" commented Eron as he motioned out over the crater's lake from their new height.

Rigone shrugged off the view. "How well do you know this Murek Kapor fellow of yours?"

"Well enough." Eron thought about it. "But not as well as I once supposed."

"I've been cooped up in a coffin with him for decawatches. He's playing games, deep games. Nice chap—but shifty."

"He likes to play games when he's teaching me something," said Eron warily.

Rigone softened. "I don't think I'm referring to that kind of game. Some games are more deadly than others. I saw you headed out for a walk and I came out here after you—where there are no spies—to ask you something, kid. At least I'm assuming that there are no clever little Crafter devices hanging out here in the woods and we can talk man to man, or boy to boy—whatever the case may be. Damn, I wish they'd turn the heating up. But keep your mouth shut. Keep your own counsel. You're old enough to start thinking for yourself. For your own good, you damn well better be!"

"On the planet I come from, you are being offensive," said Eron in the gravelly voice his father used to dismiss overbearing clients.

"On the planet I come from, I'm talking too much. But we need to come to an understanding, in private—with only *your* problem and *my* problem at stake. I've decided to play your tutor's game. I don't know what it is, but I know I have no chance of ever finding out—so I'm not asking. You want a fam upgrade; you've told me so yourself—many times. Kapor wants you to have one and has asked me to do it. That makes two problems for you.

"One: Kapor is too insistent. That's suspicious to me. Maybe he really thinks you need one, maybe he has an ulterior motive. That's for you to figure out. Me, my best opinion is that you *don't* need one. Scorn Faraway tech all you want. I don't. Obsolete? So what? I have a piece of obsolete tech in my antique collection that's maybe a hundred thousand years old if it isn't a damn fine fake. It is supposed to be a piece of flint from Old Rith. Fake or not, it'll still skin a rabbit."

In the interest of humor, Eron was about to protest the propriety of using flint technology to chip away at his fam when Rigone abruptly went off on another one of his tangents. He found a mossy log, freed of snow by the wind, its branches long rotten to nubs. He sat down. "Amazing place. They let a tree fall and don't even use it! We'll put it to use as a bench. Sit down." He put up his hand to prevent Eron from interrupting. "Keep your mouth shut. You're supposed to be listening to me."

"I *am* listening."

"Two: Kapor thinks he has leads to someone who will train me, to put a modern edge on my skills. I think he does. That's also suspicious, and you'll have to think about it. Why isn't the expert going to do the job himself and bypass a novice like me? That's a *game* for which we don't know the rules. But aside from that, I'm good. First off, I know my limits. Smart men know their limits. They're going to train me how to upgrade your fam. I've done crazy things with fams in my life—even illegal things—but, mark this, I've never damaged a single mind, ever. I intend to keep that record. I'm not going to touch your fam until I'm absolutely certain of what I'm doing. I have too much at stake to do otherwise. My life. If you so much as end up cross-eyed, I end up dead. You understand? You can still refuse."

"Sure. I *want* you to do it."

"You *want* me to do it? You're a space-crazed young fool in search of an El Dorado star. That's a star any moth can't miss—and if you get there it will fry you! I'll help you if you insist. But remember, two men helping each other don't always have the same goal. It's like I'm the man with a ship's hull and you're the man with the hyperatomic motor. We need each other—but we may not have the same destination. Such trivia can lead to, ahem, a bit of a major fracas."

"We can ferry each other around."

"You hope. Don't look at me. Look at your sainted tutor. I'm just in this because it is a game move for me. I have to make points or I don't play. But I don't move blindly. Every move in a game has its consequences. A man not ready for the recoil doesn't pull the trigger. If I decide I don't like the consequences, *I'm* gone. He who doesn't understand *bad* consequences gets clobbered just the same. Naïve kids who don't believe in death die anyway. The wide-eyed innocents get fried along with the guilty. Famfeed that. It's your call. It's your head."

"Are you going to transmogrify me into a supergenius?"

Rigone rose up off the log like one possessed. He raised his arms and roared to the sky. "No, no, no—a thousand times: No! You won't even know your brain's been upgraded! You'll think like you always have. It is just that in some ways, when you least expect it, you'll be a little faster, maybe even a little smarter."

"Will I be able to roar like you?" Eron laughed.

"Space, kid! I can't tell you how serious this is. Okay, you be the clown; *I'll* be serious. I'm here to make you a promise. I don't care what you think of your tutor. If at any time I find out that this little operation is intended to do you harm, I'm jumping out of here. If I have to go back to Splendid Wisdom empty-handed, I'll just tell my Space-damned Admiral to stuff himself into God's airlock and hope my friends wear black gloves for my funeral. Why? Because if I harm your mini-microbrain *that* has consequences for you that *I* don't want to face."

Eron was throwing moss at the tripartite lips of a plant that might or might not be moving from the spot where it had rested when he was last awake. The moss was taken by the breeze and rolled along the snow and caught itself in blinds and on barren twigs. Eron already knew that Rigone had too much at stake to pull out. Power felt good.

Rigone watched the boy with increasing exasperation. "If you were my son I'd take a five-stranded leather whip to your moon for eighteen lashes!"

"But I'm *not* your son. I'm a *farman*. And I have to make my own destiny."

"Or die!"

"I don't think so. Young men are immortal. You know that. It is just old farts like you who die."

# AT THE FORTRESS OF THE OVERSEE, 14,791 GE

*How orderly seems the majestic procession of the planets around the Galaxy's legion of suns! Each sun has mastered a different juggling act, but the awesome cyclic symmetry is always there as if the Emperor of the Universe had once commanded the dancers at His Coronation Ball to pirouette forever in His honor.*

*But this order is a seasoned conjurer's illusion. Because our commercial ships avoid the roiling nurseries of the Galaxy, what audience gets to see a youthful sun at practice with his balls? Who gets to gasp when a bungling sun drops a planet while learning to juggle? It is to the major theaters we flock! From our unctuous jumpship purser we demand a ticket to some marvel and expect to be transported to a far off virtuoso artist who has had billions of years to per-fect his solar showmanship. His failures are already lost to the dark thicket.*

*Have you not noticed that the surviving balls of these experienced galactic jugglers are pimpled by collisions with lesser balls that didn't make it through the early rehearsal? Are your eyes so mesmerized by the brilliance of these jugglers that you've never noticed the droves of lonely refugees who litter inter-stellar space because they were flung beyond reach by some inept sun-in-training?*

*Nothing stays for long in an unstable orbit around a star without being eaten or ejected. Eons pass. Lo! When tardy man arrives in his finery, he finds the last, grand residue of stable orbits and marvels in attestation to the orderly mind of the Emperor of the Universe—whose hidden face is that of the Lord of Chaos!*

—From the *Dance of the Thousand Suns,* stanza 498

For 207 years between 7774 and 7981 GE, the bloody Wars Across the Marche pitted the long-independent Thousand Suns and their allies against the encroaching Splendid Empire. During the war an elite group of Helmarian commanders built secret fallback bases on unfindable planetesimal outcasts deep in the remote darkness. The Thousand Suns Beyond the Helmar Rift eventually lost their war; the Helmarian people were decimated, forced to re-gengineer their children to the galactic hominid standard, dispersed, their thousand planets diluted with immigrants loyal to the Empire—but their war bases were never found, never suspected, never conquered. Long ago these redoubts lost the name of war base and became . . .

The chamber had wondrous acoustics. While her grandfather was being freeze-dried for the zero-g catacombs—his waters dripping into the flagon from the glass figurines of the ritual condenser—Nemia sang the solo canto of his requiem with a passionate devotion. Some of the words she composed out of memories as she went along, inspiring other singers to weave into the song contrapuntal poetry that complemented her emotion. During the silent interludes between cantos they sipped of his pure water. The elegy could not respectfully be ended until the last drips of condensate from his sublimation had been distributed from catch-pool to goblet to the bloodstreams of those who mourned him.

Later, alone, in private tribute, she gave the desiccated corpse a last farewell, a gentle touch of the hand not to mar his porous fragility, a wet tear, and the gift of a golden rose from the bronze rosepot of her parlor atrium. She had personally carved the lid of his sarcophagus, a pentagon of brilliantly colored petunias shaped from many woods. She closed the familiar lid, feeling a youth's first pangs of mortality.

For a while she just wandered through the Fortress.

It was still too trying for Nemia to go back to work. She turned toward the labs along Coldfire but instead retreated east to her rooms. When she arrived she didn't know what to do. In a somber mood, she lingered by the central rosepot in the atrium, not seeing the roses, only images of the grandfather who had adopted her to live the life of a Fortress acolyte. The room was immaculate except for wood-carving tools and chips that hadn't yet settled in the slow gravity. From the central table she picked up and played with one of Grandfa's Coron's Eggs, not activating its stellar show. He was always searching for older versions, unhappy that he'd never found a first edition. Funny man. He was devoted to the past as well as the future.

From above and below, noise she had never noticed before sifted through the walls and ceiling and floor of her embedded apartment, though the doors were sealed, her communer shut down. She needed absolute silence, absolute isolation. Absently she ordered the vestibule closet to deliver an oxy-mask and headbeam and, after arguing with the stowwall to release her tool kit, took that, too. Off she went down the corridors to the nearest pullway. She didn't bother to ask for a pullcar;

she just took one, small and open, requesting the robodispatcher to route her by its most unused paths to the northern barrier. At top speed. It did not accelerate until after she was comfortably clamped.

The wind played with her hair like life played with changes. After a wild flight—zipping images of floors and ceilings and windows and shops and passageway offshoots—the pullcar reversed thrust, nudging her to a stop. Even life had its stops, where one took inventory to claim a new direction. She paused before uncoupling the body clamps—wrapped more in contemplation than in her physical restraints. For the first time in her life she had a restless need for something *older* than Grandfa to think about.

Nemia shoved off from the pullway with a glide that sent her down a vacant corridor to a landing near one of the border hatches. It was monitored but unguarded. The caves beyond its sealoff were not forbidden territories, just unused. She cracked the seal and muscled the barrier open. The hatch closed behind her of its own will. Thunk! Carefully she checked to make sure that the reseal had passed roboinspection—otherwise alarms would go off and screaming fire teams would arrive within a few inamins.

And there she was, drifting through the abandoned portions of the Fortress. Silent darkness. She had only her beam to guide her. These older digs, untouched by recent concern, intrigued her the most. She came upon other seals, and other locks, even airlocks. Sometimes one of the internal pressure locks was jammed, but she had her tool kit with her and nothing much could stop a skilled hand that held both tinker-tools and instruments of brute strength. The preservation gas was helium, compliments of the atmosphere of their medium-size mother world who towed them through the sunless void, hydrogen oceans lit only by the stars.

Her beam animated shadow-beings who fled ahead of her down tunnel after tunnel and into rooms of strangely obsolete equipment . . . late First Empire it looked like. The Helmarians builders were famless. Amazing what primitive brains could do! It appeared to be an enormous construction effort and yet—seven thousand years of chipping had hardly perforated a worldlet that was big enough to mask the energy output of its small colony but not big enough to field serious gravitic muscle. She did a brief calculation in her fam just to amuse herself: if the whole of this tiny rock were to be carved into catacombs, the Helmarians here would have enough crypt space for the entire hundred quadrillion people of the Second Empire. So much for the illusion of human pretension!

She worked her way deeper and deeper into the abandoned shafts and drifts until she was peeking, mouselike, from the floor of the original command center up at all of its First Empire hardware. How had her ancestors escaped detection with energy-inefficient ultrawave generators of such monstrous size! All of the hokey accessories were perfectly preserved in the helium. Embroidered chairs. Even old strategy maps thousands of years obsolete.

She knelt beneath the main machine and said a prayer to the Old Ones, elders of a culture no empire could crush. Her prayer was the prime cry that every Helmarian knew by heart: "To die once is to live forever!" spoken with arms raised, elbows at her side, palms facing outward. And then she bowed for her beloved grandfather, wistfully recalling that it had been he who crawled with her on their polished stone floor back on Neuhadra before she'd ever learned to walk or glide or build fams. What a way with children he had! He had stolen her from her parents with his Smythosian zeal.

She stayed in that holy place all afternoon, tinkering with the failed electrical shunts until she had the old lights glowing again—so that she could play out, via fam, Hisgoold's tragic opera against these vast machines so awesomely right for this ancient drama. Her fam created the hallucinatory singers, their voices, their movements. Hisgoold's Family was magnificent with noble superhumanity. The chorus of the doomed Helmarian army fought its way heroically across a stage more grim and real than any she'd ever seen in live theater.

She wept at the Remonstration. Her arms cheered the Hallel. Her lips smiled with the Madrigal as Pani and Laura and their jokers flirted in a coy chase among the ultrawave projectors. She laughed like a child at the pyrotechnics of the Prothalamion, helplessly remembering the emotions of the naïve three-year-old whom Grandfa first took to see Hisgoold. The Battlehymn of the Thousand Suns inspired her as it always did. The Aubade filled her with hope. She hissed when the Splendid Emperor appeared for his Triumph. And the final Lament brought her to tears as Kaggan grieved over the bodies of Pani and Laura.

Sorrow, terrible sorrow. She extinguished the lights so she could cry and cry in the blackness like she had never before bawled in her whole young life. She had to switch on the dry-blow to clear her faceplate. The evaporating wetness on her cheeks was all that her exhausted mind could feel.

When she returned home, a Personal Capsule was waiting for her in the atrium.

It tasted her fingertips while reading her retinal pattern—but instead of delivering an encrypted message to her fam, the Capsule produced a tiny black speaker that began to chat in the voice . . . of her grandfather. It had two simple toggles: forward/stop and retreat-one-sentence-at-a-time. The voice was, in places, fam-simulated, as if it had been too much effort for Grandfa to record with his vocal chords. The destruct was a manual toggle.

"Nemia, ah, Nemia. When death is on our mind we think only of unfinished business. So. Here I am dead and you haven't married yet. I've been working on it with your mother and father."

She laughed. He was going to leave her one last nag about *that*. It was a favorite subject of his that she'd *never* been able to terminate. She'd bawled him out quite angrily the last time he had mentioned it, hoping to shut him up forever, and henceforth had stuffed her ears at the mere mention of marriage—but he always had to have the last word. Now he *was* having the last word.

"I know how you feel on the subject so I haven't kept you apprised of my actions; I've just been making all the arrangements behind your back. A surprise party. Now I won't be able to finish what I've started so you'll have to carry out the last details on your own. Don't worry about the boy. I haven't told him, either. Only his parents. They approve of you. It was to be *his* surprise party, too."

"Well!" thought Nemia.

"You already know the boy. You constructed the monitor-persona we installed for his last assignment. I believe you liked him. Think back. You met him at that Reaffirmation Gala I arranged for you. The boy with the ears. I've never heard you rave so about a boy's ears. I can't, for sure, attest that you fell in love with him, but it was certainly *infatuation* at first sight. I always thought it was a shame that he had to leave so soon—otherwise I might have been more persistent in my meddling, which, up until his assignment, had been one of my better efforts."

Grandfa had a hand in *that* adventure? She was mortified. Nemia hadn't thought about Hiranimus Scogil for years, but she certainly remembered him. Did Grandfa know about the shower they took together? And her mash letter? She groaned with her new maturity. Poor Hiranimus had probably been relieved to be shipped out!

"He's been haggling with the Oversee lately about an adventure he's been trying to orchestrate. I was the only ally he had, mainly because I want to marry him off to you. I like to bend psychohistorical necessity to fit my own personal needs."

"You old goat!" But he wasn't listening.

"The Oversee's consensus was negative. His scheme computed out as hopelessly high risk with an extremely low probability of success. Worse, it was immoral. I had to agree. But, quite recently, these few watches before I had my attack, he turned up at Neuhadra—and there's a new angle. I worked it up while I was dying . . . to keep myself busy. There's a couple of ways to jiggle the probabilities, ways that perhaps the Founder wouldn't have approved. It's yours to follow up. Talk to the Lion for details. Our Scogil . . ."

She stabbed the "stop" button. The Lion! But it was *Grandfa* who was the Lion! She'd figured that out years ago. Now she was confused. She stood and made herself dinner while she pondered the conundrum. The puzzle finally fell in place only after the fourth course as she whipped the chiffon pie out of the cuisinator. She mouthed the fluff, appalled at her stupidity. *Of course* Grandfa was the Lion—but the Lion was only a quantum-state "hat." The Lion might . . . could . . . would be shared by many members of the Oversee, an immortal personality who took on mortal components to maintain his human perspective. Immortal wasn't really the right word; the Lion wasn't any older than Grandfa—that's what had fooled her. Probably Grandfa had *created* the Lion. Who would she . . . ?

She put in a call. One never had to worry about disturbing the Lion; he had a submind that could take a thousand calls at once, none of which he handled consciously. His submind was merely a convenient executive secretary. The Lion appeared in her atrium as a fam-induced hallucination. He wasn't the kind to bother with holographic tricks; the Lion took the direct route into the visual cortex.

"Nemia of l'Amontag," he said with a graceful gesture of his paw. He'd been expecting her.

She bowed respectfully to what only she could see—a tall and not very lionlike figure. Real felines didn't stand erect. She tried to see Grandfa l'Amontag in him. There must be something of Grandfa there, but the Lion had always been a good disguise. "My grandfather suggested an appointment," she said to the receptionist persona.

"About the Scogil affair. Yes." There was a gleam in the Lion's eye; she was sure he must know *everything*! Damn Grandfa's love of storytelling to whoever would listen! Did all the Smythosians who wore the Lion's hat know that she had showered in the nude with Hiranimus Scogil? And how could a lion look so diabolically human with his bushy orange head and black nose and carnivorous grin!

But then, how could this hallucination even exist? The four-legged lion had been the victim of one of Rith's mass extinctions—she wasn't sure if it had been that infamous meteor or mankind's first massive overuse of ammonia fertilizer. The nitrous oxide of ammonia's decomposition train was nasty stuff when it worked its way up to the upper atmosphere and started gobbling ozone. Of course, lions weren't really extinct; gengineering had re-created them out of housecats. Grandfa's Helmarian sense of irony. Kill me and I shall rise again. That's what this creature of the Oversee symbolized. Who animated him now? One man? two men? a sixtyne?

"You have questions?" the Lion asked.

"I haven't finished listening to his Capsule," she confessed.

"We will meet again when you are ready. Come in person to my den at the eleventh watch, on the morrow after you have slept. Your passage to Neuhadra has already been arranged."

The Lion vanished—but he left behind him a quick flash of Rith's ancient predesert savanna and a whiff of sun-rotted antelope.

Nemia sat down and took up the tiny black speaker again, toggling it to the beginning of the last sentence and then to "forward."

"Our Scogil has been doing some fast legwork," the voice of Grandfa continued. "He *thinks* he has it arranged with Beucalin of Neuhadra—you've never met Beucalin—to train a butcher from Splendid Wisdom to modify his charge's fam—he has a young boy in tow. Beucalin sent us a report. There are surprises in it. Tests confirm that Scogil's charge does indeed have a remarkable talent for mathematics.

"His fam is even more unusual: an aborted Caltronic prototyped on Faraway. Not a model farmed out to a Sigel or Rosh Hanna foundry. It's surprising that we even have the specs except that keeping the specs on rival fam designs is a Helmarian fetish. Less than seventy were made—an ambitious hi-end failure discontinued prior to production. A full century ago. His father must have picked up a remaindered unit that got misplaced on some high shelf—or was simply shunned. Ethically its Faraway engineers should have scrapped it but they were probably short of credit—and it *is* perfectly functional, significantly above average, though not easy to sell in its unfinished form except to a stellar bumpkin in a backeddy like Agander. Two hundred and sixty-two thousand hooks were built into it—but the designers couldn't develop a stable overlay able to use the hooks. So they started over with a different design. Their second attempt was the famous Caltronic 4Z, now also obsolete."

*Ah,* thought Nemia. This was just the kind of "special" problem she'd been trained to exploit. Two hundred sixty-two thousand *unused* hooks! Perhaps *unusable* hooks, perhaps not. An interesting challenge.

"Beucalin has been instructed to decline Scogil's unseemly request—but out of friendship for Mendor Glatim will find a surrogate to do the work on the sly. And"—he chuckled—"out of sight of the Oversee." Nemia's grandfather liked his little jokes on the young people of the world who thought that they and their fams were too smart to be outsmarted. "The surrogate will be you. It might even be possible to bring you in without involving Beucalin. You have the perfect motive. Love and Sex over Duty and Honor."

"Watch it, old man," she said aloud, "or I'll have your mummy cremated!"

The voice of the dead man ignored her. "Scogil's ideas for the modification are far too crude and detectable." His voice had broken and there was a pause before he spoke again. "Oeyy! The pain gets to me sometimes. I'll be back."

Her heart jumped. But she didn't have time to anguish; the splice in the recording, to her, was immediate and when he returned, he was calmer, more relaxed. It was his own voice, not a smoother simulation. "This has to be one of your *special* jobs, little girl. The Lion will give you the details. You won't do the fam surgery yourself—that is, you will not directly hack Scogil's youngster. Have I lost you? All the work on him *must* be executed by the butcher from Splendid Wisdom whom Scogil has so conveniently brought with him. If the project fails and the Pscholars lay on a trace, we want it to point at the butcher. It will all be his doing. Your hand has to be invisible." The pain was back in Grandfa's voice. Then, suddenly, he skipped whatever else he wanted to say in order to blurt out what was really important. "Hey, big girl, there's plenty of water on Neuhadra for showers. You won't have to be sneaky." And he was gone.

"Grandfa!"

And even this last little bit of him was crumbling into powder.

Too many shocks at once! Death. The threat of marriage. A wrenchingly new off-Fortress destiny. She whacked her head and headed for the bed. She thought she wouldn't be able to sleep, but the thought wasn't finished before she was sound asleep in her clothes with shoes still on her feet. Dreams resolved her grief. Dreams plotted a hilariously amazing off-Fortress adventure. When the hour for her prime-watch chimed, she rose with a light heart, said her thirty-two theorems in prayer position, and had breakfast. To a Smythosian acolyte, duty was the foundation of every good life. She chose to sing in the morning network-choir; then—to work.

She organized those duties of Grandfa that he had bequeathed to her, rebuilding key nodes in her fam to prioritize her new obligations, famfeeding the files that Grandfa's will had tagged for her, and actually sorting his few physical possessions.

He had kept Grandma's love letters. She was killed tragically under circumstances unclear to Nemia; Grandfa never liked to talk about it. The letters were on real homemade paper that Grandma had whomped up in her manufacturum, written with a naïve ink that was already fading.

The biggest box was Grandfa's template collection of antiques. He was forever rearranging his apartment, destroying *this* antique so that he would have room for some striking *masterpiece* he had just remanufactured. Nothing ever matched. Nothing was ever conveniently arranged. She had memories as a little child of negotiating her way between—what she had never dared say aloud—his junk. No object in Grandfa's whole collection had an esthetic relationship to any other object, but all had historical import. History was everything to the old man. He liked to stumble over it while he wandered about, his mind's eye lost in contemplative visions of some past or future era.

Then there was his precious collection of Coron's Eggs, eight of them, nine if you counted the one he had given her that sat prominently on its wooden stand in her atrium, none of them a first edition, all too complicated to be stored on a template. He had first become interested in the Eggs when the Oversee had assigned him as a young man to work on the outré mathematics of the Coron's Wisp project.

He had been inspired to a mad belief that a "first-edition" Egg would lead to the lost Martyr's Cache. Second-edition and later Eggs hadn't met their promise. Grandfa had been undeterred and still had quantronic agents touring the Galaxy looking for a "first-edition" copy, Eggs by now probably all victims of entropy or, if extant, buried in the rubble of some Interregnum war. His search agents had become, by the machinery of Grandfa's will, her servants. Nemia had heard a zillion "lost treasure" stories and put little stock in this one. Men had been wandering around the Galaxy for seventy-four millennia littering space with their mysteries. The Protocols of Eta Cuminga. The Lost Mine of the Miradeas. She sighed. Why did Grandfa think she was going to pick up on *all* of his obsessions? She'd have to cancel those agents, but that was not easy from the Fortress. For that she'd have to wait until she reached Neuhadra.

Extraordinarily proud of his collection, he'd kept every Egg in good repair and often used one of them to cozen or dazzle people at his parties. He had been, in her mind, the Galaxy's fastest-talking astrologer. His favorite trick was to take some young Smythosian, fresh from his heretical seminary studies of forbidden psychohistory, full of a mathematical belief in the unreadability of personal destiny, and con him into an Egg reading. The room would go dark, the stellar panorama would unfold, and, with Grandfa's simple chitchat, prompted by increasingly complex star-charts, his mark's past would be revealed in a way that led surreptitiously into his personal future. Everyone would smile at the sagacity of the reading—and its superficiality—until the morrow, when it would all start to come true. Grandfa had tried to teach her the tricks and deceptions of fortune-telling, but she had never quite mastered the art at his level of dissimulation.

Her prime-watch coincided with the eleventh watch. Nemia spent the time at the Lion's den being instructed in the nuances of her assignment. Grandfa had been thorough on his deathbed. It became obvious that the whole idea of Scogil's introduction into the Coron's Wisp venture was based upon a very chancy gamble. When she complained that the probability of success was small, the Lion reminded her archly that the Oversee had its eye on many antelope in the herd. It did not matter if they were pursuing a hundred independent events, each with a mere one percent probability of materializing, because then there was a *sixty-three percent* probability that *at least* one of those events would come to pass.

The Smythosians liked to work with low-probability events because those were the kind that the Pscholars had the most trouble tracking. More specifically, the modeling of high-probability events was beyond the Oversee's computational resources. They didn't have the Pscholars' twenty-seven centuries of psychohistorical practice behind them nor the full resources of the Second Empire.

And the work she would be doing to modify the fam of Scogil's protégé? That was a another low-probability gamble. They were giving him an ace he could play or not play as circumstance demanded. She was not to implement the kind of modifications that Scogil had asked for; her modifications were to be to the Oversee's specifications.

That angered Nemia. "I can't just modify a fam to order! It doesn't work that way! I'll be hacking under enormous constraints. I won't even know what the constraints are until I do tests!"

"He's only twelve years old," reminded the Lion.

"Twelve is an adult!" she snapped. "His fam has jelled."

"If you fail, it is of small consequence. Scogil will just have to play our game without that particular ace."

She cooled down. They went on to discuss the professional minutiae of event-fulcrums and how *this* particular event-fulcrum related to some of the finer points of fam design. The Lion jumped from general psychohistorical principles to the finicky details of how quantum-state design parameters, in this kind of case, could alter the predictive equations. He often went beyond her competence, then caught himself, to turn back to the specific items relevant to her mission. She had the impression that she wasn't dealing with one person even though the Lion's persona was seamless; his knowledge base was too broad. The Lion, she suspected, was an artificial coordinator-mind for a very heavy-duty committee.

She was in up to her eyeballs. Nemia took off the next cycle for partying with her friends in the gardens of the Presidio.

Within a ten-watch she was deep aboard a jumprunner, commanded by one of the mysterious men with the title of Starmaster, any view of the interstellar sky forbidden to her. She spent the time with her mnemonifier doing homework, planning. Half of her mind was working seriously; the other half was churning out an escape path from the marriage trap set up by her relentless Grandfa. Marrying one of her teenage crushes in Service to the Greater Good! Ridiculous! Even if he did have nice ears.

They had even supplied her with material on Coron's Wisp, material deliberately withheld from Scogil so that it would be *she* who briefed him on key aspects of his next assignment. *That* twist, she thought ironically, hadn't been necessary. *That* was just another item in Grandfa's ploy to marry her to Scogil!

Scogil! She was filled with outrage again and was half tempted to use one of the Eggs to plot an astrological chart of her own future. But with an iron will she shrugged off this temptation toward the irrational. To be afflicted by superstitious impulse was the price one paid for being condemned to the use of cheap wetware that had mindlessly evolved in an ancient ocean! Anon they would learn how to scoop out the wetware and replace it with quantronics that weren't limited by robotic laws laid in by the environmental demands on fish.

But—back to the real problem she had been given, upgrading the fam of Scogil's protégé. Her main task was to construct a single-purpose module—one that enhanced the kid's mathematical intuition. *Almost* routine. That he was still a child young enough to make use of such flexible structures would greatly simplify her work—a fam modification to be utilized by an *adult* brain necessitated a very different (and difficult) design philosophy more akin to building an expert computer program activated by primitive organic triggers. Still, it wouldn't be easy.

Her secondary task, not usually feasible with Faraway designs, was to implement an undetectable persona shift that would prime the boy to traitorous behavior at key trigger points in his life. Because of Faraway's notorious "safe-walls" design philosophy, she was here allowed to operate under an "if possible" clause. But given the electronic failings of *this* particular uncertified design, she thought she might be able to . . . The unused hooks that had stymied a whole team of Faraway engineers weren't the big challenge, though they opened up unexpected avenues of attack. Helmarian Crafters routinely fabricated quantum-state devices that were only theoretical dreams to other engineers; the Neuhadran foundries were adequate to build whatever weave she needed. Linking into the hooks was a piece of fancy footwork she could do—but bypassing the walls . . .

The starship cabin wasn't large enough for her and her mnemonifier. She tried working with her heels on top of her "mnemy," and then with her toes peeking around, and then with the damn machine strapped to the ceiling—but nothing was comfortable. Thank Space for zero-g! No adequate solution presented itself until she implemented a scheme to worm their stellar coordinates out of the Second Watchman. She didn't succeed, alas, because he didn't know—the ship's officers used unshared partial-keys to navigate—but she did find out that *his* cabin was larger than *hers*.

Immediately she conned the Second Watchman into exchanging cabins, a deal she paid for by looking at the holos of his family and teasing stories out of his mouth that he'd always wanted to tell but lacked an audience. She also stroked the stubble on his head and ran her finger down the ridge of his nose. But, sadly, in the endgame her brilliant strategy failed. The finale saw her stowing her mnemonifier out in the corridor while the Second Watchman *stayed* in his cabin and held her in his arms. He whispered poetry into her ears in between nibbling at them. She kept thinking about her bulky mnemonifier.

*I'm not very good at predicting,* she told herself ruefully. A Second Watchman didn't fit very well into any psychohistorical equation she knew . . . now, if she'd had to deal with *ten thousand* men like him, all at the same time, it would have been a snap!

Thus Nemia had to postpone her work on the persona modification until she arrived at Neuhadra. Beucalin briefed her in his office while her attention was fixated on the landscape beyond the Institute's lofty windows—there were green fields and endless stretches of forest that had taken over the hills as far as eye could see into the morning mists. Nearby she could see shellback hickory and mountain oak and hardy tramontanes from Zeta Tigones. And wind that blew clouds across the sky! She hadn't been here since she was a small child. More than once she asked Beucalin to repeat himself.

"You'll have plenty to do before tackling Scogil. Wait until you hear from me before you try to contact him," he was saying. "I'll have to soften up Scogil with bad news about how I can't help him. Let him stew for a gaggle of watches before you serendipitously arrive as his savior. Play innocent. A couple of hints, maybe. Don't offer him anything. Let him pry out of you—very slowly—what you can do for his scheme."

While she waited she again took up her ideas for Eron Osa's persona-change package—the still-unsolved side of her assignment. She couldn't fix the final parameters. She'd have to meet this child first. She always worked with traits that were *already* there—otherwise it was hopeless—tweaking this, damping that, exaggerating, redirecting. It took a lot of observation. And all changes had to be compatible with the hardware and wetware constraints. For now all she had to work with were the known hardware weaknesses.

No two fam's architectures were exactly the same. Faraway designs, for instance, emphasized security. Cloun-the-Stubborn had conquered a good bite of the Galaxy with a Crafter-devised mentality-altering machine based upon the very same tuned probe that, in its modern incarnation, transduced information between fam and wetware. Cloun's weapon of conquest had been devastating. The survivors had been impressed. Since then a great deal of thought had gone into protecting personality integrity. The first Faraway fams had been nothing more than

DONALD KINGSBURY

devices that detected and countered tuned probe attacks and concentrated on monitoring the emotional feedback loops—neural and chemical—among cortex, hypothalamus, locus ceruleus, pituitary, amygdala, etc.

The original Faraway designs had had their limitations. If the fam was removed, by guile or force or neglect, the organic brain again became defenseless against alteration; the absent fam could then be replaced, but the personality changes induced in its absence would remain. Modern designs, like the one that this Eron Osa child wore, kept a stack of persona parameters that it tagged when it detected decoupling and, upon recoupling, set about reversing any changes made during the separation. Faraway, whose hegemony had been the chief victim of Cloun-the-Stubborn, soon became, and remained, particularly good at implementing defensive protocols in fam design—the famous "safe-walls."

The problem-solving aids, the data stores, the search engines, the graphics engines, the monitoring agents, and sophisticated internal regulation of emotion all came later—but in Faraway designs these "features" remained subservient to the goal of security. Under certain circumstances, that in itself was a weakness. When Beucalin called and gave her the all-clear that Scogil had been set up, she had already postulated more than sixtyne ways to attack Eron Osa's brain, all with a high probability of success. First, of course, she had to test-drive his fam before she could finalize the surgery. That fam, having been a child's constant companion for almost a decade now, was already well outside of its original specs.

# ARRANGED MARRIAGE, 14,791 GE

*Don't expect your parents to do everything, but let them go about doing what they do well.*

—Ancient Helmarian saying

It was important that Scogil be led to believe that he had picked her for his team and never to find out that she had been *assigned* to him as a watchdog. Only Grandfa really trusted him. She certainly didn't!

Her spies had been following him for several watches before she was able to pick the opportunity to accidentally-on-purpose run into him. He had flown into the city from the Glatim estate, moving around at a frantic pace, his agenda impossible to predict. Then—thank Chemistry for hunger—he finally decided to eat at a quiet but well-attended rooftop garden. The moment she knew, she was on her way. En route, her spies narrowcasted a floor plan with a red circle denoting his table.

She entered the rooftop through the pop-up levitator. Carefully she did not look in his direction, not caring whether he noticed her or not. Through the soaring glass windows and the dangling vegetation she had a magnificent view of the pressurized buildings of a city crafted for a tenuous atmosphere. She pretended to be selecting a quiet spot to eat.

Then she picked the moment. Looked. She simulated uncertain surprise and walked over to his table, standing at a civil distance. His meal had already been served. He was intently shoveling sautéed fish into his mouth. It looked like tank-grown blue trout. He hadn't seen her.

"Don't I know you?" she interrupted him.

He looked up from his fish, not recognizing her.

She waited. Still he evinced only blankness. She was going to have to prompt him. "You look like a Hiranimus I once knew. Hmmm? Not quite. You seem more handsome and even worldly!"

"Nemia of l'Amontag!" He grinned. "I didn't recognize you . . ." He paused.

". . . out of the shower," she finished for him. "Wasn't youth wonderful!"

"Well, now! This *is* a small Galaxy. What are you doing *here!*"

"This is *my* planet! What are *you* doing here!"

"Visiting Mendor."

"I haven't seen him since school. You liked him, didn't you? You two always seemed to be together."

"Plotting revolution."

"But you are alone now?" Her tiny hand gesture took in the hanging vines.

"How could I be alone with a l'Amontag! Sit down and tell me all your troubles so I can reciprocate and tell you mine."

"Your troubles are probably some fake part of a cover story. I should listen to crocodile tears?"

"Not everything about me is fake. The troubles I can talk about are really quite fascinating."

"Oh, all right." With a snap of her fingers, she called a chair up out of the floor— it grew and flowered as she waited—then sat down, propping her elbows on the table and placing her face as close to his as she could manage. "I'll listen to be polite."

"You first," he said with a gentlemanly flourish of his fork.

"Nothing out of the ordinary. I've been sent home from a wonderful job to marry an oaf. I haven't thought up a clever way to poison him yet."

"Ah, you belong to an orthodox Helmarian clan? I presume they are now in their heated breeding mode?"

"Yes."

"Me, too. But they are *there*"—he pointed at the sky—"and I am *here*." His warm gaze took in Nemia, and she was obviously his *here*.

"Do you think you'll escape their long arm?" she asked slyly.

"Of course. Why do you think I went to school? Why else would I take secret assignations and secret identities and flit about the darker corners of the Galaxy if it wasn't to escape the clan?"

"Do you think you'll ever get married?" she mused.

"I would consider it as a preemptive strike against my parents if I could only find a woman they disapproved of."

"You couldn't be pushed into a marriage with a *mezartl*?" Mezartl was a peculiarly Helmarian word that carried all the implications of clan approval, rightness, and duty, flavored by a kind of mystical happiness that came from letting wiser minds choose one's destiny.

"A mezartl shrew?" He shuddered. "No. I've known myself to be a free man since I was ten."

"I'll bet you an emperor's face that you've never found yourself cornered by your whole clan, all at one time. You wouldn't be so glib otherwise."

"I move too fast."

"You think so, do you? They'll get you," she said. "The Helmarians keep track of their own. The Galaxy isn't big enough."

"Hey, girl, you're really taking the pressure seriously! They haven't got that much power! It's just an illusion they support. Just say no."

"Impossible. They've already sent out the banns."

She had brought out the protective male in him. "Let's go out together and make a big scene." Hiranimus laughed. "Give your fiancé something to be upset about."

"You'd do that for me? They'll shoot at you!"

"Of course. We could even have dinner together tonight. Don't leave. Forget your business. Stay with me. Let me order you something. Special."

She shook her head and let him misinterpret the gesture. His parents were very wise in not telling him what they had already agreed to with Nemia's family—in unalterable, legally binding code. "You're chasing me." She was annoyed that she was pleased.

"Don't say no to me," he implored.

"Why not?"

"Nemia. Think of me! What could be more pleasant than chasing a girl of your charms and braving the wrath of two incensed clans in the name of illicit sex?"

"Ho, slaverer! Back to your food! I recall that at the Fortress you were running away from me when I was desperately trying to seduce you."

"True. But that was all before I became a wise man. They posted me to a planet where farmen are consistently mistaken for eunuchs. Being an outside observer gives one a perspective on life and a fondness for one's own people—even a melancholy *longing* for one's people." A melancholy look washed over him as he entertained fantasies that he didn't expect her to share but that he was having fun expressing. "You'll need a fling before you marry this oaf. *I* need a fling. Come home with me to Mendor's place. It is just the right dream world for an impossible romance. A lake. An estate. I'll get you a cottage on the lake." Silence. He stared at her and decided that he had made her very, very wary. He called over their waiter. "Boy, the lady wants the Gitofene. The full treatment. All the courses, right up to the mousse." He turned back to Nemia. "See, I remember how much you liked Grandfa's Gitofene. Here the chef does it differently—but I assure you, just as deliciously."

"Is this the kind of ragged flummery you use on all of your women?" She was half amused, half biting.

He smiled back good-naturedly. "Not a chance. There is no other woman than you. You don't know my story. I own a fam that can run an imposed persona.

Think of that. Worse, one not subject to my control. The last place I was at, I worked under heavy celibate constraints."

She was glad that he didn't know that she had designed that persona. Her eyes widened in (mock) horror. "Isn't that dangerous, to be in the field like that? I don't mean the celibacy—that's good for men like you."

"I never thought of fieldwork as dangerous."

"Of course not! Fieldwork is an extended vacation." She found herself in a teasing mood. "I didn't mean the silly old fieldwork. I meant, letting your fam be modified to hold an imposed persona!" She *knew* that was dangerous. It just wasn't dangerous for Scogil. His fam had been built from the ground up as a special agent. Not that he knew she knew.

He grimaced ruefully. "Danger is being forced to do what you're not built to do. I was *designed* as a walking impersonator, compliments of my parents' ambition. I can famfeed a constructed personality as fast as I can change my clothes. It's not dangerous when you *grow up* with the extra personas feature. No surgery. My parents knew what they wanted from me and what I was going to become before I was born. So it was all built in. I've never been free. I was given a fam to match my parents' expectations. I wanted to be a psychohistorian. What I am is a second-rate field agent. My whole life is tracked out."

"All of it? *All of it?* Your parents have picked out your wife already?"

"Presumably."

"And you are blackhole bent on thwarting their plans?"

"Presumably."

"I can't believe I'm hearing what you seem to be saying. You are actually going to *ignore* their wishes?" That was heresy—but tempting heresy. It was something that she wanted to believe that she could do—wanted to believe that she *was* doing.

He laughed unnaturally. "Ignore their wishes? What a sweet sound that has. Nothing so bold. My revenge is going to be more subtle. I'm going to do *better* than they expect—better in ways they could never dream. Better in ways which will make a mockery of their preparations. My only hope is that I can run faster than they do! Hey, do you think you could keep up?"

Why was she attracted to this man? In her mind's eye she saw a Coron's Egg spreading out its stars across the sky while the charts grew and wrote symbols in fire. She even saw in the geometric designs a child named Petunia—after the pentagon of petunias she had carved on her grandfather's sarcophagus. Her child by Grandfa's command! She could see everything as if the foretold astrological fate had just now been sealed forever.

She became angrier at her beloved Grandfa than she had ever been in her life. She knew that she wasn't going to be able to escape the tyrant. She had fallen in love. She knew that she was *willingly* going to marry Hiranimus Scogil and bear his children and endure whatever strange life he made for them. Had she been poisoned?

Poor Hiranimus! She was exactly what his parents wanted for him. It was what *her* parents wanted for her. There was no escape. She felt tears and had to call in the iron emotional control of her fam to suppress them. She could feel her fam triggering the love-changes in her brain chemistry. She laughed. It was all worse than this young man could possibly imagine.

She had her instructions to modify *his* fam, too. And she would—for the sake of keeping him.

# THE HYPERLORD FRETS OVER A
# MESSAGE, 14,791 GE

*Deadlines requiring action will arrive before you've had time to get answers to all of your urgent questions. This is how one is forced to learn that action precedes knowledge. Never hesitate from lack of knowledge. Act when action is required, but never before. Since action without full knowledge will often precipitate error, choose your actions so as to grant yourself idle time in which to learn from your mistakes. Only the dead make no mistakes.*

*—The Zenoli Warrior*

Hyperlord Kikaju Jama wasn't sure whether he'd caught a fish or been caught himself. The weasel's message that had bloomed on his telesphere was too terse. Somebody out there wanted to purchase his galactarium. Was it a real nibble? Or an alert policeman's barbed hook?

The recent organizational expansion of his conspiracy came with a paranoia that was a new affliction for Jama. When he was just a fop, openly spouting ideas that no man could take seriously from the mouth of a fool, he had not only *felt* safe—he had *been* safe. Noblemen pretenders just didn't rate as a probable psychohistorical infection. But now that he had positioned himself to menace the Pscholars, a sense of safety eluded him. Wasn't it odd for a star-spanning weasel to find him just after he had expanded his opposition to the Pscholars—*and* while he was in the throes of planning his expedition to Zurnl?

*Who* could possibly know that he owned a marvelous jade ovoid except Igar Comoras and the ephemeral man who had slipped it to Igar as a bribe—and Kargil Linmax? Only Kargil knew its nature. Was Kargil double-crossing him? If so, Jama's head was in the executioner's bucket because it was Kargil who had put in place the new security system. What if Kargil had given a key to the police and was sitting back in his shop in the Kirin Sovereignty enjoying his perfidy? After all,

Kargil had worked a good part of his life for Naval Intelligence, a group which was just another arm of the Pscholars. Annoyed with himself, Jama mentally stamped on his suspicions. Hadn't his reliable people-instincts been consistently telling him that Kargil had never betrayed anyone in his life?

He sent off a coded message to Kargil. "An untraceable weasel has inquired as to the price of my galactarium. Why? Where did *that* come from at *this* time?"

Kargil's reply was transmitted almost immediately back through Jama's blacked-out telesphere directly into the Hyperlord's fam by coded famfeed. "You forget that you put out your own weasel recently to find a repairman for your galactarium. You clearly specified the probable manufacture date and the nature of the device. Your weasel is no longer in circulation, but these things get archived by strange libraries and can be accessed by other weasels for a small fee. It may be that you have only found the police, yet consider: there are billions of patient collectors both on this planet and elsewhere who are looking for all sorts of incredible items—from the cryogenized messiah of Rith to the electronic eyeballs of Emperor Krang-the-Blind, to say nothing of an authenticated signature of the Founder. Weasels are one of their best tools."

The Hyperlord was, at that moment, changing into his afternoon attire. Instantly angry that his friend so dangerously dismissed the cunning police, he took the opportunity to throw the buckled shoe in his hand at the telesphere, which, assuming itself unwanted, vanished. Only reason and practical matters calmed Jama's rage. His toes needed manicuring. How could he have let his toenails grow so long that they had worked a hole in his hose?

But maybe his fear of the police *had* blinded him to the obvious? While he trimmed the toes' overgrowth he wondered if his jade ovoid might indeed be merely another valued item. Or could a second mysterious detective be searching out the location of Zurnl in a game that would thwart Jama's purpose? Probably not. Do not panic. Look for simple explanations. He looked. Maybe a little girl had been dazzled by such a galactarium as was his and now, as a rich old lady, sought to recapture that experience? Maybe there was a mad astrologer out there desperate to know his fate? Who could fathom the reasons of collectors?—certainly not a dealer in antiquities! Drat! His toenail polish was now chipped. He decided to renew it with a darker sparkle.

Should he reply to the weasel's request? He thought back. His own weasel, designed to probe for an atomo-unit repairman, had been constructed to be untraceable. A secure response to the stranger's probe would be similarly untraceable by its quantum mechanical magic; therefore an answer wasn't dangerous—but would it serve any purpose?

Well, there was always the money. He had some accounts laid away for an airless month and some highly charged iridium sticks and those scholarium bonds— but he really did need a cheap way to finance his expedition to Zurnl. If only he had a clue from *whence* the inquiry had come! He appreciated that the recipients of any weasel he sent out wouldn't be able to detect its source, but he certainly didn't like the mutual finesse with which this trick was executed.

Even with quantum security he didn't feel safe. It was all too easy to imagine police on the other end of the reply, helmets hiding their eyes, fingers playing over the banked consoles of interrogation machines, waiting patiently while their sting accumulated enough evidence to arrest him. A message itself couldn't be traced, but the information in it was subject to analysis.

Not a restful nightmare, in spite of Kargil's attempt to put him at ease.

This expansion of his revolutionary infrastructure at a rate faster than his cautious nature recommended was unsettling business. All was going too swiftly because of the new security org. Jama wasn't yet used to *working* with people he didn't know and couldn't locate, who took action without being given orders, and who didn't bother to report back until after their actions had been resolved. Did it make him feel secure that everyone in his untested, more virulent org was disguised to look like a bonehead acting independently of any rational scheme? No, it did not! He was sweating into his arm puffs!

Nothing was as foolproof as design would have it. Foolproof was a harlequin mischief maker who knew how to prove better than anyone else that the soberest man was all fool! Someday someone was bound to be spotted by the police.

Could he laugh with Kargil? Kargil was willing to chuckle at the thought that if (or when) they were infiltrated by a police agent, that poor nudnik probably would be written off by his colleagues as just another chump chasing a mythical conspiracy! Or maybe a dupe caught in the latest aliens-are-among-us rumor. No! Laughter wasn't a substitute for certainty.

Still, one must live. One must act—even with incomplete information. Lord Jama was a creature of quiet times who dreamed of the adventures rampant during unstable times. In recent bouts of imagination he cast himself as a dashing, fast-acting zenoli fighter of the Interregnum. How could he fault the discomfort of a little paranoia? He fanned himself and rearranged his jewelry. Hadn't Katana, one of Kargil's recruits and an expert on the old zenoli ways, recently recited to him an aphorism of the zenoli? "Boldness and Caution make fit companions for marriage!"

It was proper that he compose any reply to the inquisitive weasel with extreme care—if he could keep his mind off Katana's breasts long enough to compose his thoughts. Desire was supposed to slacken in a man his age—sixty-four by last reckoning—but it never had. Nevertheless, it would be better if he concentrated his seductive energies on less dangerous maids.

Frightfulperson Katana of the Calmer Sea was a mature woman, at least thirty-five, an ex–naval Intelligence officer of no mean perception, with a supple body which knew every gesture of the old zenoli practice, a remarkable throwback to the old noble clan of Frightfulpeople which she adamantly claimed as her own line. But: She had been dismissed from the Stars&Ship after murdering her husband—unfairly according to Kargil—but nonetheless a woman to be pinched with caution.

Katana's six-year-old daughter was more Kikaju's métier, charming even without her mother's breasts, if dangerous in her own petite way. Frightfulperson Otaria of the Calmer Sea. Instant seduction was Jama's preference, but for variety, a long drawn-out courtship had a special marinated flavor. Otaria would be ready to bed in about another six years if carefully prepared. By then she would have budding breasts—perhaps, when mature, to rival her mother's own wonderful orbs. A carefully prepared virgin was one of life's gourmet delicacies. Dangerous, of course—her mother was fiercely protective—but a little danger was one of life's more piquant spices. To be used, never overused.

But to return to business. The nibble from the galactic black had offered to buy his galactarium. No price was mentioned. The implication was that funds were not the buyer's chief constraint. Jama was always interested in a good price, but at this time he was not interested in selling. Slowly he composed a counteroffer, careful to keep within the legal niceties. Was the potential buyer, he inquired, interested in the information contained in the device or in the device itself?

Then he forgot about it in his enthusiasm to choose his wig and mask for this evening's orgy. He hadn't dared invite Frightfulperson Katana. His companion was to be a young baroque singer, freshly turned eighteen, whose mother was too far away to watch over her daughter carefully, having selected for her child's further education the services of an expensive, but distant, singing master—fortunately Jama's neighbor and accomplice. Such innocence was challenging. Kikaju had spent the best part of the previous evening, with several of his male friends, introducing her to the customs and manners of the Aziyade School of Orgy—about which her wide eyes had known absolutely nothing.

The Hyperlord, himself, was partial to the exuberant court rituals of Emperor Takeia-the-Happy of the eighty-seventh century, which were undergoing an underground revival and which were to be the basis of the indulgence planned for the seventh watch. He already had the costume for his companion, which had been chosen for her after much dressing and undressing, and his own costume, but he wasn't yet sure of his foot perfume. With that much foot fondling, his foot perfume had to be selected with care. And it had to match dark pink. The Hyperlord's reputation as a master of erotica was at stake.

Oh yes, and he must dispatch his weasel into the currents of space.

# YOUNG BOYS PREFER OLDER WOMEN,
# 14,791 GE

*The psychohistoric equations are only symbols which map out futures; they cannot describe a future to an endlessly fine resolution—any more than the painting of a landscape will show, under a microscope, the crocus in the meadow on its distant mountain slope. Replace the crocus with a sparrow and the painting of the landscape has not been changed at all.*

*A psychohistoric prediction is a map of all the high-probability features on the lay of the land, placing the mountain and valley contours and the way the rivers and roads wander between them. It will give you the climate and the resources. It will populate your map with virtual houses and stores and spaceports but will not supply tenant names or lace curtains at the windows or the precise watch during which rain-puddles will appear.*

*Only one major word of caution: Check the critical branch-points; make sure that you are actually in the world described by your map. I had a friend once who tried for hours to locate himself on the wrong map. Now that man, we might say, was lost!*

—Excerpt from the Founder's *Psychohistorical Tools for Making a Future*

A meteor tore a white rip in the dark sky of Neuhadra. On a Glatim balcony, Eron counted each puff of breath through his light facemask.

He was also counting his blessings. For the first time in his life the Osa boy felt totally in command of his own destiny. He had observed many people who had the aura of command, like his father, and they wielded their authority with a kind of blasé nonchalance, as if it were too ordinary to think about, but it wasn't ordinary for Eron and he relished this ability to steer his life where he wanted it to go.

He calculated the drop to the courtyard beneath and decided it was too far down, so he worked his way over the balustrade and by careful handgrips lowered himself onto a foot-wide ledge from which he *could* jump. He didn't want Murek to know he was going out this evening. Not if he valued his hide. He had a rendezvous with Murek's new love who was, ahem, a delightfully *mature* woman; she seemed to have both the Ganderian penchant for the escapade and an attraction for young boys. Nemia was a boy's gracious dream.

He had certainly complicated matters by (twice daily) making taboo penetration of his *immature* servant in violation of both Ganderian ethics and her contract. Still, Girl would cover for him; she seemed to be pleased to do everything he told her to do and disinclined to be jealous over class lines. Her unnatural obedience certainly made him uneasy—she even lied for him—but how could he reject that kind of uncompromising loyalty? He mustn't take it for granted; he had already learned to be careful in the way he phrased his instructions; if he could think of eight ways to carry out an instruction, Girl could always think of the ninth.

Evening covered his hurried foray down to the lakefront—the most awesome of the meteor flashes weren't bright enough to betray him. As he had anticipated, the boathouse was unmanned, its doors unlocked, and he was able to sneak a runabout onto the lake without much hinge squeaking. He threw his pants and boots aboard and for a while, just to be safe, waded and pushed with his feet against the sand until he was clear—but he knew the motor was superbly silent and when he threw himself back in the boat, dripping, to engage the power, at low throttle, only a burble followed his wake. It sounded more like a brook than a thruster.

He had loaded his fam with a sim-overlay of the lake and he watched as the elegant map rotated in his mind's eye, virtual stars orienting themselves to match the starscape he could see. Once he had his directions, a dismissive thought shut off the see-through landscape ghost. He was certain, at the bottom of his heart, that he shouldn't be doing this to his best friend, but he was becoming more and more confident of his ability to handle Murek.

A father's guidance was sometimes even more useful than a tutor's. From that blood source he'd learned a lot about sneaking and subterfuge. Out here on the lake, with four of Neuhadra's arrogant stars peering at him, and, hopefully, his tutor asleep, he was glad to have learned those lessons well even if his father hadn't been consciously participating in every lesson, many of which Eron had conducted in a covert spying mode. He didn't question why Nemia was attracted to him. Mature women *always* liked young boys, and being as handsome and debonair as he was made it all that much easier.

He goosed the motor and practiced his helmsmanship, steering up ahead to the left of Orc-Nose Point, now showing in blacks and dark blues and twinkles of stardust off the water. A sharp breeze made him huddle inside his coat but he refused to take his hands off the wheel—he wasn't in the mood for automatic. *She* was just around the point. Soon he'd have to swing right to leave behind him a lazy curving wake of starlit ripples.

A balance between persistence of goal and the flexible ability to modify goals in the face of obstacle was the secret of staying in command. Out around Ragmuk his tutor had begun to flag and lose direction. Here at Neuhadra he had become positively gloomy, even defeated, but Eron himself hadn't lost direction. He was a good helmsman. He'd kept at Murek to honor his commitment, prodding: get me into school, get my fam enhanced. Every time Murek seemed ready to quit, Eron kept after him until he realigned—and just in case Murek *did* fail him, he was assembling a new set of contacts. It was working. Everything was working perfectly.

Nemia had taken a small cottage on the lakefront not far from the Glatim estate—to be near her friend, she said. (She had used the circumspect word "friend" to refer to Murek, but Eron's delicate spying had confirmed that a more accurate word might have been "lover.") She was evidently in hiding from her parents, who, she explained, had other plans for her. Eron approved of women who fought with their parents. When he turned into the cove, as she had promised, a soft robobulb was illuminating the dock. In fact, as he slowed for his approach, he saw her sitting there with her legs hanging over the water, woman and spider-legged robobulb both waiting for him.

She grabbed the rope he tossed to her and lashed the runabout to a poured stone pile and took his hand to help him clamber up onto the jetty. "I wasn't sure you had the audacity to come," she teased.

He wished he was older and taller. "You invited me," he replied firmly.

"But it's past your bedtime." She was grinning behind a transparent oxygen facemask, shaped by some artist to give her an alien mystique.

"I may be younger than you are but I have more brains," he chided. "It isn't very bright of you to have me here." He could trade insult for insult. That was part of the romance. He noticed the reflection of the four brightest stars in her eyes.

"It's night. Our mutual friend won't notice."

"With us gawking here in the open and four suns in the sky?"

"Oh, dear; we'll have to hide," she challenged, and headed uphill toward the cottage. The robobulb hesitated, not quite knowing to which human its duty lay.

Eron chased after her into the dark and the sentient bulb bounded behind with eight-legged leaps that threw goblin-armed shadows around them. She ran ahead in the zigzag swings of an evasive prey but finally trapped him, predatorlike, in a little hedged alcove by a garden where they sat down on the bench to catch their breath. "You run pretty good for an old lady," he commented suavely. The robobulb, arriving late, dimmed and hid itself discreetly in the bushes.

"You're not afraid to be here, little pup?"

"Of course I'm afraid. Murek impounded my kick."

"Your kick?"

"My blaster!"

"You don't have your blaster with you? You're defenseless?" She was grinning behind her fairy facemask again.

"I'm all mush," he said. "But I can still fight feebly for my honor if circumstance demands it."

"You'd win. If I tried to kiss you here with these masks on us, I'd never be able to overwhelm you." And she was off again toward the house.

He followed her inside, through the vestibule's pressure lock. The leggy bulb resumed its patrolling of the grounds. They hung up their masks.

But they didn't kiss right away. She had music to play. He was astonished to hear the strains of the Eighth Rombo Cantata of Aiasin seeping out of her walls. Seventy-first-century Imperial Court music was a favorite of his mother and was rarely played anymore, so his mother claimed. Ah. Nemia had been pumping Murek about his lifestyle! Very casually she began to ask him leading questions. It was a setup. But it was nice to have a woman so interested in him that he couldn't stop talking—and to have comfortable antiques to sink into while he chatted, even if they were hideously old fashioned to his more colorful taste. Nemia was an easy conversationalist—not like Girl, who had a very weird brain/fam. He didn't even know how he got onto the topic of how much he hated his father's secrecy. *That* topic! It must have been the couch and the frilled pillows. It had nothing to do with her eyes, which he couldn't escape.

"And *you* never keep secrets?" she taunted.

"Never. Can't you see how frank I'm being with you? And my nefarious father manipulates people while deliberately keeping them in the dark!"

"But you *never* manipulate people in the dark?"

"Only when they pull me under the covers," he hinted, inching along the couch. "I prefer to do it with the lights on."

"I see," she said, holding him at bay with a finger on his nose. The room lights, as if on signal, began to creep across the high ceiling, swinging on little silver legs, dimming the study as they retreated into far corner burrows.

He began to notice that he had been talking too much—gushing out secrets he wouldn't have dared tell a fellow Gandarian. A good love affair shouldn't be so vainly one-sided. He had to think of *her*. He thought of her. She had balm-scented breasts. Love required a sharing of minds, but was she *ever* going to let him get off the topic of himself? He ignored her last question—he had questions for her, too—for instance, how had her breasts become so round? But it wouldn't be polite to ask about her body. Concentrate. Her mind. The secret was to flatter the mind of a woman with a beautiful body. Early on he had deduced that she was an expert on fams and knew more about that subject than anybody he had ever met before. It was a topic that interested him, too, so he began by generating—perhaps too quickly—a list of important intellectual questions. People who knew things liked to talk about them.

"Why can't people switch fams when they make love?"

She just laughed and used the finger with which she had been holding him off to give his nose an affectionate finger slap-tap, on both sides. Since she wasn't able to push on his nose while she did this, he moved closer.

He knew he had led with a silly question, so he asked another, carefully selected for the seriousness of its content. Bad move. It gave her an excuse to leave the couch. Soon she was showing him some of her portable diagnostic equipment and explaining to him more about quantum switching probabilities than he could easily follow in his aroused state. He had such a stupid fam; he *should* be able to follow everything she said, never asking her to repeat herself, never losing the flow of argument. He didn't mind so much asking clarifying questions, or asking her to pause while his fam conducted a search—but he did mind that he was so overwhelmed that he couldn't even *think* of a clarifying question. Murek was a better teacher than Nemia, but she had the sharper mind. He became curious about how she got that way, and began asking her personal questions.

She talked for a long while. He wasn't sure he even followed her then. She had secrets and she danced around them and he felt helpless trying to find a way to penetrate her secrecy. Sometimes she was very moody and then she'd jump out of it, again to flirt with him as if she didn't have a care in the world. He wanted her to tell him secrets that no woman should be obliged to tell a man.

"I'm going to elope with *him*," she said out of the blue. He knew she meant Murek. They were back on the couch, slouched the way people doodle with their bodies when they are saying more than their voices can convey. She looked up at Eron, over his torso, with her teasing smile. "We'll all elope together, the three of us."

"He'd kill me," said Eron, sobering, trying to sit up, but she wouldn't let him.

"No, he wouldn't! Why would I let him do that?" She fell back into her mood and snuggled her cheek on Eron's stomach. "I haven't told him that I'm going to elope with him. Does he ever talk to you about me? Does he like me?"

"Well," said Eron honestly, "I think you are just another good lay to him." At her stricken tenseness he added, "But he likes you a *lot*."

She relaxed again. "You're probably right. He's a wanderer, strangely closed into himself. I don't think he thinks of ties at all."

"He makes ties," said Eron wryly, "but you don't know where the other end of the string goes."

"I want to elope with him to the most obscure part of the Galaxy where I have no competition and I can nail him down. You, my lovely boy-love, are going to have to help me." She had his shirt pulled up and kissed his belly button.

"What can *I* do? You've already done everything. You've already seduced him!"

"Sex isn't enough," she admonished. "There is more to love than that even if you're not mature enough to appreciate the finer nobilities of love. We'll have to have the perfect honeymoon together. Then he'll find his love. He *will* love me." She cast a calculating glance at Eron. "I think I know the perfect honeymoon retreat. Can you share a secret?" She was easing him out of his shirt.

"Lakgan?" he guessed, recollecting certain porno vids he'd stolen from a classmate back on Agander.

Nemia shrieked with horror and laughter. "They breed *dancing girls* on Lakgan."

"They have pleasure palaces, too."

"I had in mind someplace more sedate. Zurnl. My Grandfa used to tell me stories about Zurnl. I picked Zurnl because you two are off to Faraway and Zurnl is on the way. If we are all eloping together to the Periphery, a little side trip could be interesting."

"Never heard of it," said Eron. Even his fam didn't come up with a hit.

"It's not on the charts." She grinned. "That's why it is such a good honeymoon spot."

"Where is it?"

"I don't know where it is. That's what makes it so deliciously mysterious. But I have a lead. It just came in a few watches ago. There's an old first edition of a starmap. It's been lost for a long time. I think I'll be able to find Zurnl in time."

Galactic enigmas intrigued Eron. "What's it like?"

"I don't know. No one knows," she said. "That's the point. Obviously when a honeymooning couple gets there, they won't be interrupted." She was speaking to Eron firmly. "You'll help me?" It was both a question and a command. "You have some strange power over your friend. I need your help."

Eron just fingered her hair. She had a grip on him and he wasn't able to inch away, even a centimeter. He didn't know what to say.

"You have to answer me," she commanded, moving up on him and staring down at his head, which was embedded in a pillow.

He stared up at her. "I don't think I should be gazing into your eyes while I think about it."

She took his jaw in her hand so that his eyes couldn't escape. She laid her nose on his, just barely kissing him with her lips. "Will you help me?"

What was a farman to do? Farmen were *supposed* to have galactic adventures. When he tried to avoid her eyes all he saw was her smile. "What's the worst that can happen?" He shrugged, trying to think rationally.

"Go on," she prompted. "Tell me the worst." She kissed him.

"We could get hurt," he concluded.

She was now holding him by the shoulders and beaming. "Badly?"

"Two scraped knees is my limit."

"It will be fun," she said.

An ancient poem came to his mind. *A bottle of wine, a mapless void, and thou.* "*Scary* fun," he said. "You'll have to convince Murek to give me back my kick."

"It's a deal," she said instantly.

Had he said yes? She seemed to think so. Her hand was feeling down to his buttocks. Control was like driving a fast car; first you were doing twenty meters a jiff, with the trees whizzing by delightfully—and then you were skidding. He tried hugging her in return. That only made it worse. She picked him up in her arms. He hadn't actually realized until now that she was bigger than he was. "Where are we going?"

"To the bedroom."

"Isn't this of a sudden? I mean, we hardly know each other."

"You've earned your reward."

"Put me down! It is not supposed to be a reward! It's supposed to be love!"

"Eron," she said sweetly as she carried him over the threshold, "you can't imagine how much I love you right now." She set him gently on the already turned-down bed, and while he was still mute, degaussed his belt buckle, dropping his pants—and then her own. She filled two graven goblets from an antique urn. Then she did something totally preposterous. She took off her fam.

Her personality didn't seem to change at all. She just stood there smiling at him, more naked than any woman he had ever imagined in his most secret fantasy. Was she a witch? "We're going to do it the wild way," she said. "Without a fam. You, too."

He reached instinctively for his kick, which wasn't there, not even a harness, and then reached up and touched his fam protectively. She had such round breasts. They jiggled.

"The monkey in you will remember how to do it—believe me." She came over and very gently removed his fam. Incredible that he let her commit this ultimate rudeness without even a whimper. He was shocked into a daredevil excitement.

The world changed. He could still question his surroundings but what he sensed no longer echoed with answers.

He was listening to music . . . suddenly void of culture or history or his stern musicology lessons . . . leaving him only . . . to hear . . . the bells, the gentle booms of the tympanella, the acrobatics of the electrovibs. Who was the composer? He no longer knew. He looked to *her* questioningly. Almost he panicked; he had also forgotten *her* name, too, and he wasn't sure why he was here. But certainly she must be the most beautiful woman he had ever seen with flaxblue eyes set in ebony. She had said the monkey would remember. He remembered that. He was swinging toward her through the aeneous green of sun-drenched trees with a gibbering joy. He had no intention of exchanging names. Something wasn't controlling his chemistry as it should be. Lust. Where was his mind when he needed it? Was he all senses? It was raining emotions and the juices coursing through his body were at flood level.

She sat down on the bed beside him and he felt the sheets and the warmth of her thighs. She handed him one of the goblets and took one herself. They had transmogrified into marvelous miniature universes shaded in erbium glazes. The scripted designs were runes coding the wisdom of ages—but he no longer had a mind capable of decoding anything. He was raw animal sapiens from Rith. She dipped a finger into her goblet and offered it to his tongue. It tasted as might elixir from the lost cellar of an ancient emperor. Monkey see; monkey do. He dipped his finger into his goblet and offered it in sacrifice to her tongue. He was an apprentice farman. So many galactic rituals he didn't know.

They drank, elbows entwined, looking into each other's eyes. It was like being her. What would *really* holding her be like? A frantic minority voice was urging him to get his fam back *now*. But all the action his toes desired was to reach up and wrap themselves around her. Every movement attracted him. She ran the palm of her hand against the wall behind her, drawing his attention to her face as if it were a portrait against that delicate aquarelle background. Then she reached over and ran her palm down his back. She kissed him where his fam had been. Nobody had ever kissed him *there,* not even his mother.

He wasn't a monkey. He was paralyzed by his obsessive need to remember her name. Somehow a name would give him permission to embrace her. All he could think of was "Melinesa," and he knew that wasn't right. He needed to touch her so he invented a name, "Azalea," and whispered it into her ear as he awkwardly took her down onto the bed. What kind of flower *was* an Azalea? It didn't matter. He liked the name. He liked whispering into her ear.

"My sweet baby boy," she whispered back into his ear. She wasn't, he realized, as original a thinker as he was.

"Azalea," he whispered tenderly, marveling at his intelligence, pleased that he still had it. She held his hips, not letting him make a mistake.

One hundred million years of famless evolution did the rest. He felt very normal for a hairless monkey who had taken to walking around on the forest floor. She giggled. He wasn't sure that was normal. They hugged each other and grinned. That was good. Then he went to sleep with his nameless mate in his arms, struggling in his dreams to find the language of poetry that he had lost. It was an ancient dream of a garden of Eden, flowered, scented, textured, full of sensory delights, the tree of knowledge still forbidden.

He woke as the sunlight crossed his face. A lazy hand touched nothing, reached out and still touched nothing. He was alone! His eyes shot open. He sat up, one single thought on his mind; he was a mental cripple. Where was his fam? Find it! But his mind wasn't answering with a strategy, just with a will. He ran from room to room like a headless chicken.

She wasn't in the dispozoria. She wasn't in the dressing room. Nor the study. He wheeled downstairs and found her in the underground workroom where she had shown him her diagnostic equipment. She was dressed—clinical clothes—and wearing her fam. She was at her console, and—horror of horrors—she was examining *his* fam, peering over some instrument, intent at her work. It was clipped to a board, the screens of multiple instruments reading excitedly.

"All is well," she said without looking up. "I think I'm done."

He resisted the impulse to run to her and snatch it away. She had his whole precious life in her hands. "I'm starting to miss myself," he said, half in panic, frozen where he had first spotted his fam. Was she going to grab it and run, teasing, making him chase her all over the grounds to get it back? Or worse?

She turned and smiled, gently extricating his extra brain from her apparatus. "You are thinking that I would hurt you, sweet young boy. Never. At least not beyond skinning your knees. Come here. You'll find that reintegration is as much of an experience as doing without." She held up his fam for him. With awesome relief he let her reattach the transducers.

"Nemia." That was her name. Of course. He knew that all along. It had been on the tip of his tongue. A flurry of other answers came as he did a wild, random, wide-ranging systems check. All there, it seemed. Undamaged. What had she been doing? "Did you fix something? Am I more intelligent now?"

"I doubt it. Perhaps you've become wiser. I was only being curious. It's my trade. It's an unusual design."

"It's a stupid Faraway design. I'm condemned to be stupid," complained Eron. "I want add-ons."

Nemia became stern. "Never overreach. Your fam has above-average capacities. It is not state of the art, but it's good. There is an old saying you should take to heart, 'It's not how versatile your fam is, it's what you do with it.'"

"That's just a fancy way of telling me to get used to being stupid. You're telling me that I'll make a good monkey."

"You're a genius for a monkey." She laughed. "When you're grown up, you'll be a gorilla. Let's get breakfast. I've been working hard all night and I'm famished."

"You tricked me," he said sullenly, refusing to move.

"Sex energizes women and puts overanxious boys to sleep," she teased.

"You don't love me. You just wanted my fam."

"Eron my darling, you are a most lovable boy. How could I help but love you? Our mutual friend has told me that you have mathematical ambitions. He says you're good. I hate to see people overreach themselves. I was just checking to see that your fam can actually take you where you want to go. I must say, you're carrying around a very good mathematical machine, whatever you think. Make sure you use it. Waste is a terrible thing."

"Can my fam be upgraded?" he asked resolutely.

"Yes," she said sadly.

# PARTNERS IN CRIME, 14,791 GE

*You can't cross a galaxy merely by standing and staring at the sky and wishing upon a star. Flap your wings, and if that fails, try something else. I did and here I am an interesting distance from home.*

—Epitaph on a tombstone found on Iral IV

The corridor lights along the eastern window-wall of the Glatim mansion were dimming as the dawn glory peeked above the lake's surface. Hiranimus Scogil was up early and pacing. He glanced out the tall windows for the hundredth time at the ruffled blue water, golden streaked by the primary sun, his eyes fam-set to high magnification, searching for the wake of Eron's runabout—not that he expected Eron home so soon from his escapade. Nemia had given Scogil a surprise call last evening telling him to stay away as she had arranged a critical rendezvous with her young admirer, an unlikely story; it would be *Eron* who had arranged the rendezvous. The little brat took after his horny father in more ways than one!

Scogil wouldn't even be able to tease Eron about it—the boy remained wrapped in a Ganderian ethic which allowed one to banter humorously about one's legal mate at any level of sexual detail but deemed it taboo to nudge, gossip, ask, or comment about any extramarital liaison. Cross-generational affairs, permitted in the interest of a proper "erotic education" for the young, nevertheless dwelled in a strictly invisible domain. Agander was a very strange place.

He had to grin at the whole situation. Nemia was such an unscrupulous woman! He might have been shocked at the way she had been flirting with Eron—except that it served his purposes. She made a good partner in crime. He was half tempted to thwart his family's matrimonial plans for him, whatever diabolical form they were taking, with a preemptive marriage to this high-energy vortex . . . but stealing her from her fiancé would mean he'd have to deal with *Nemia's* family as enemies, and her family was a very powerful one indeed; to annoy them was to live under a sword of retribution, perhaps a worse fate than annoying his own extended family, which was suicide. Life offered up sobering alternatives.

Damn that boy! He should be sneaking back into his room by now. Scogil was dying of curiosity to find out from Nemia if Eron's fam was modifiable in any interesting way. Rigone couldn't wait much longer, and the Oversee would have Scogil's hide if he didn't soon turn up for his assignment in Coron's Wisp. He looked out again but saw nothing on the lake, only the morning glint of a ferry descending from space.

When Glatim's gruff Assessor sauntered by and invited him for breakfast, he took the invitation. He was hungry. In the empty dining hall, the smells of frying yamums and jam and cinnamon beckoned them both back into the kitchen to the cozy staff table where the cook and his helper, together, concocted a sumptuous meal faster than any cuisinator—good food and small talk with the servants always took one's mind off serious concerns. Mendor himself joined them before they had finished their second helpings, popping an extra chair out of the floor to face Hiranimus. As usual, he brought up business before he joined the banter.

"You and the boy are looking for a ride to Faraway, right?" Faraway was at least twenty thousand leagues from Neuhadra by pythagorean line, more like thirty thousand leagues along any usable trade route, a greater distance than Scogil could afford.

"You have a berth?"

"It fell into my lap; it seems destiny has been looking at you favorably for the last ten million years, working up to your salvation." Mendor's humor tended to be deadpan.

"I've been patient," said Scogil, although, at the moment, he was anything but.

"A contract from Trefia came in last evening—Trefia is a sparse planetary system only four hundred and eleven leagues from Faraway, dynamically very stable and unchaotic"—Mendor began to chuckle—"with a political elite so clueless about meteoroid impacts that they've been trying to contact the Omneity of Planetary Safety to ask about their problem." The Omneity of Planetary Safety—long ago vanished into the early Interregnum—had once been a powerful department of the First Empire's bureaucracy. "Some schoolboy had to refer them to *us*." Everyone joined the laughter, even the cook. Mendor went on to explain that Trefia hadn't been impacted seriously for the last two hundred million years and so evidently wasn't geared up to deal with such a problem. Their Assembly was in a panic.

"Poor jokers haven't even had their astronomers on a small-body watch and were only warned by a curious starship captain. The villain is an interstellar rogue, a biggy on a bull's-eye orbit. Probably ejected by some coalescing planetary system billions of years ago. Not an emergency, but it will be a lot cheaper to take care of now than a few years down the orbit. I'll be sending off an expedition as soon as I can organize one. That might be faster than you can pack your sack. Can't go myself. The crew will have to stop at Sewinna for supplies and then on to Faraway for some of the more specialized machinery—our meteoroid seems to be just a huge pile of rubble cemented together by a prayer and a little ice, so the extra machinery is to be sure we don't turn it into buckshot when we do the deflection. The ride will be free for you and Eron, if you want it, compliments of the Trefians who are too scared shitless right now to balk at a few extra expenses like passage for a second-rate mathematician and his apprentice. We have you on the payroll as an orbital mechanic."

He waited a moment while he assessed how well his friend was taking his needling, then smiled. "I've asked for a little under-the-table bribe to be paid directly as a charitable grant to Asinia Pedagogic's scholarship fund for needy mathematics students—with invisible strings attached to the Osa boy in such a way that no one there will question his qualifications too seriously. How's that? It'll take some worries off your shoulder."

"I was just about ready to hit *you* for a contribution to Eron's maintenance fund."

"Who, me? That's why I struck first. The Glatims didn't get rich by giving charity to twelve-year-old paupers. We got rich by being stingy. Speaking of stingy, you'll be on your own getting back." That didn't really sound right to him even if it did fit his cherished family image; Hiranimus was one of his oldest friends. He slapped the table. "Maybe I can charge the poor Trefians your return fare, too, though it's not liable to be on one of my ships. We don't make regular runs out that way." Business done, Mendor turned to food. "What do you recommend: the hen's eggs or the fish eggs au gratin? Maybe I'm just in the mood for cinnamon toast."

Scogil scurried up and off to bring back a plate of the marvelous fish-egg recipe, plus the cinnamon toast—whereupon he rattled off an aside to the Assessor, who had been left out of the conversation, loudly enough for Mendor to hear. "Mendor has just paid off the debt he owes me for saving his life innumerable times while he was a wayward youth." He spoke happily, all the while factoring in the extra time pressure of an early departure.

"Hey, always willing to help out a friend when he's out of line."

"Mendor! I'm *never* out of line. I'm just off the road picking up herbs to liven up our standard evening chow."

"Don't try to swab out my ears, you worthless nitwit. You're *always* out of line. Why do you think they sent you to Agander? It was the only secure, out-of-the-way prison they could find."

"I escaped. Shut up and eat your fish eggs!"

"Say, where's the kid? He's usually an early riser with a big appetite, out spying as soon as the sun is up."

"He's off doing research for me," said Scogil glumly.

Indeed, Eron wasn't back until late morning. Scogil watched him, from a distance, silently bring in his runabout, then keep to the shadows while he snuck back inside the mansion. A wait was appropriate. Give the brat time enough to pretend he'd been sleeping. He waited impatiently. He paced. He thought about Nemia. Had she, maybe, taken a shower with the impudent brat? He rapped heavily on Eron's door, ignoring the delicate chimes, reminding himself to pretend that nothing had happened.

"Time for your math lesson!" he shouted through the suite's portal. Eron answered, all innocently willing to please. That was good. Scogil, almost forgetting to mock up his mild Murek persona, gave Eron the workout of his life, oral exam, prompting, prodding, challenging, tripping, patiently repeating what Eron did not understand, diagramming around misunderstandings, then demanding that Eron reproduce exactly what had been implied. Eron gave him no lip. That was a wonderful change. The brat worked harder to please than Scogil had ever seen him work. Scogil never let up. He took Eron past suppertime, right up to first sunset. Refusing to break, the boy used fam stimulation to push body and brain well past the exhaustion point. He'd sleep well. No dallying tonight!

Hiranimus stood, relenting. "I have good news. We have passage to Faraway. And about your recent work—it was good; I'm more and more sure you'll pass the entrance exams for Asinia Pedagogic. You handle pressure well. You have the talent. I'm proud of you."

Eron looked up, almost pathetically relieved. Scogil left him without another word. It was a long walk across this overlarge guest room, and he barely escaped without a damaging smirk, self-approving that he had not broken down and teased the boy about Nemia. *I can still be a good Gandarian,* he thought, re-relegating the Murek persona to his mental closet. Then his pace quickened, and without even a thought about changing clothes he headed out to see Nemia, his pace quickening as he approached the car pool. He chose the swiftest aerocar, the streaker which he wasn't supposed to use except in an emergency.

From above, he followed the lakeshore by the dimness of the false twilight, beating out Neuhadra's secondary sun before it dropped below the horizon, arriving in front of Nemia's cottage after a direct-line gentle glide. The place seemed abandoned. That panicked him. After trotting up to it, he tested the airlock. Unattended. Even the robobulbs were inactive. He entered, sealing the first door behind him, restively waiting the few moments it took the vestibule to match house pressure, then went inside, not knowing what to expect.

"An unguarded entrance!" he boomed to the high ceiling. "Your mother will catch you! You'll be married before we can finish our business!"

"Grrmfle," came a sleepy voice from the upper balcony bedroom.

He sighed. *She's just being careless again.* Nemia didn't even open her eyes when he sat down on the bed. He gently shook her shoulders. "How did my young muscled stud measure up?"

She turned her face up at him. "Where in the Galaxy did you unearth that little emperor?" Her eyes were still closed, and that allowed him to admire the beauty of her face with unabashed enthusiasm without having to hide his feelings.

"You're looking top-of-the-mountain"—he smiled—"if somewhat worn out. I think you liked him."

She made a face, still with her eyes closed. "It was tough keeping up with him but I got him out of his fam. Now let me sleep some more." She rolled over, away from Hiranimus. "I've been up *all* night. He *just* left."

"It's been longer than that. You've slept more than you think. It's already night again and even Sinari is about to set. I met Eron at prenoon after he sneaked back. He was kind of woozy, like one is after a long night, but a secret grin suffused his demeanor so I assume something pleasant happened. He was even deferential toward me, which is highly unusual."

"I always make men happy, even boys. Now join me for a snuggle in bed and let me sleep some more. I'm *still* exhausted."

"Can't. We're on a time deadline. A passage to Faraway dropped out of the sky. I need details! Can you do anything and when?"

"It will take me five or six watches to set up the operation, maybe another to train Rigone. I've been working with the Scav. He's technically naïve but very competent and an incredibly fast learner."

"So you *did* find something!"

"Your boy has the weirdest fam I've ever examined. Lucky for me we've had the specs on file or I'd have been lost. I'd rate its memory capacity at about eighty percent of a good Neuhadran design. It should be no trouble to give him auxiliary memory. And we can sneak in a good set of encrypted math modules that will key in when certain kinds of problems trigger them. That's what Rigone really wants to know how to do, so we'll go the whole way."

"Except that we don't have any of the Fellowship's modules," Hiranimus reminded with a bitter snarl.

Reluctantly she pulled herself out of bed and slipped on a housecoat. "So? The Oversee is a hotbed of very competent mathematics. For instance, I have Riote's Compendium with me. I'll give him that."

"That's tactical stuff! It's for hit-and-run warfare! Guerrilla stings! You can't manage an empire with Riote's carnival tricks!"

She grinned, remembering her long tactical discussions with Grandfa. "Riote was master of the amplification of low-probability events. The Pscholars can't match us in that area. They ignore unlikely events or set up machinery to damp them down. You've been assigned to Coron's Wisp. Who but Riote could have found *that* crack in the dam? The Pscholars have too much ground to cover to focus on such dust-mote detail."

"And we just give Riote's work to the enemy?"

"Aren't you hoping that Eron will rise to Second or First Rank status? To get there he needs an edge."

"I'd be happy if he clawed up to Fourth Rank. But it won't do us any good if he becomes a devout Pscholar groveling at the Founder's Tomb. It's up to you to give us a hook to keep a hold on him. Is it possible? He's twelve already—fam freeze-up time—and, worse, nobody does fam security better than Faraway."

"Even Faraway engineers don't cover all the approaches. I'm the right genius to jimmie the works"—she grinned—"but I'll need your help."

"Ah." He brightened, scurrying away to come back with a bowl of crushed fruit for her. "Okay. So how can I help?"

There was a sexy twinkle in Nemia's eye. "For us to fool his competent Faraway security we need to slip in a modification that's in resonance with his wetware so the fam doesn't self-detect undue influence."

"I've assumed as much."

"But it's *not* enough to just modify his fam—we have to modify it in a way that will eventually be *useful* to us."

"Of course," said Scogil impatiently.

She sat back on the bed so she could shovel the red fruit into her mouth. "Let's think strategically. What's the *real* problem we have with the Pscholars? Isn't it the *secretiveness* with which they surround their mathematical methods?"

Scogil nodded. Certainly they had been able to impose that ethic on their acolytes—successfully—generation after generation.

"So," Nemia continued, "if Eron survives their rites to become a Pscholar, what he learns will be denied us, despite any relationship he might have with you or debt he feels toward you. To be chosen as a Pscholar one has to become *fanatical* in the belief that the release of psychohistorical mathematics means an end to *anyone's* ability to predict the future well enough to control it."

"That's false! Precognition just changes the feedback terms in the equations!"

"But they *believe* in its truth. And all of them can quote the Founder's proof of its validity. And you know damn well that you're not a competent enough psychohistorian to know what kind of computational strain those extra feedback terms will place on the whole predictive apparatus. Once Eron has become a Pscholar of whatever Rank, he, too, will have come to *believe* that psychohistory must be kept a secret from the masses."

"You've figured out how to amplify his loyalty to us?"

Nemia grimaced. "Loyalty to what? We are *just* as secretive as the Pscholars, and our secretive rituals have a *far* longer history. We've lasted half as long as both Empires put together. We panic if a single Pscholar *dreams* about us. Even Eron isn't permitted to know your real name, Mister tutor Murek Kapor."

Scogil scratched his head. "I once took a fascinating course on the equations of secrecy from Cas Ratil. Made me think."

"That secretive old drillmaster! I avoided his courses like the plague!"

"Secrecy certainly challenged the mathematician in him. Secret societies are intrinsically unstable, with all the nice characteristics of a ten-kilometer-high tower. They have to be balanced by active control—in the case of the tower, little electromagnets that read and counter all bending moments. A tower like that can stand until even its builders are forgotten—but the hour the electricity fails or the freak wind comes that is stronger than the electromagnets . . ."

"Do you think *they* will discover us?" There was almost a shudder in Nemia's voice.

"The Pscholars? They already have. Our Smythosian secret won't last another lifetime. Neither will theirs. I predict open warfare within the next couple of generations. Let's get back to tactics. You were hinting as if you'd found an angle to protect our access to Eron."

"Don't you see?"

"No."

"What if Eron developed an *aversion* to secrecy? What if he was a closet blabbermouth, primed to break only *after* he was a full-fledged Pscholar?"

"Can you do *that*?" Hiranimus asked, awed.

"No," she blazed, "but *you* can!"

He was delighted at this turn in the argument. "All right. Brief me."

"I'm not sure we can pull it off. Eron must have a major psychological revelation about *secrecy*—while wearing his fam—no more than an *hour* before Rigone performs the fam modification. Do you know what happens in the brain during enlightenment? We've got to strike *during* the emotional flux of the neural reorganization."

"Hold on. Are you actually suggesting that *I* can give him an enlightening lecture on the evils of secrecy while he's psyching himself up for a major fam operation?"

She assumed the pedantic poise of an authoritarian professor. "*Not* a lecture. Please, it has to be *all* emotion. The original psychic probe, you'll recall, was a surface emotional whip, a control weapon, and not a gentle one. The *tuned* psychic probe that Cloun-the-Stubborn used so effectively during the Interregnum to dominate his enemies worked at a deeper wetware level of emotional judgment—it left fewer conflict scars and *no* neural lesions—but it was still a control weapon. The modern fam has *much* better bandwidth in the two-way communication of nuanced information but is *still* basically the same *emotional* device merely reengineered so that the user can control his *own* emotions, rather than having emotional control imposed by an outside source. To fool a fam, its internal logic, which has been conditioned by a lifetime of symbiosis, *has* to remain convinced that any emotional turmoil it senses is *internal*. How well do you understand Eron's emotions?"

"No one is a telepath, but I'm a trained observer and I've known him a long time."

"So? What are his underlying assumptions about *secrecy*?"

Scogil groped about for an analogy. "At this point he's still a routine product of Ganderian socialization. There are things he will talk about and things his ethics won't *permit* him to talk about."

"And some things he *wants* to talk about but *can't*. Or couldn't. Sex things." A wistful look crossed her eyes, and she held her robe close to herself. That worried Scogil. She continued, almost in awe. "He had a stuck *switch* in him. He tried to talk and couldn't—his mouth moved like his head was detached from his larynx—but after he touched me he entered some alien world. The switch melted and he blabbered."

"You got *secrets* out of him?" Scogil was instantly jealous. Whenever he'd tried to oil-ease Eron's secrets out of him, he'd only created an iron resistance in the boy.

Nemia was staring at her memories of last night. "Some. The veil was always there. He's in full restimulation of a strong internal conflict that he's trying to figure out. It's our big opportunity. Conflict resolution is driven by emotion. If he solves this problem himself and the solution is still in wetware flux when we modify his hardware fam—altering its judgment tree about what is, and what is not, a secret—the fam will conclude that its internal changes derive from *Eron's* turmoil rather than from anything *we've* done and it won't have 'motivation' to undo our work. When it looks for modifications to Eron's emotional state, it won't find any—because we aren't going to modify *him*. When it looks for modifications to itself, it won't find anything that can't be reconciled as its own response to Eron's turmoil." She smiled. "His sexual conflict is a perfect attack vector. We'll have to work through that."

"He certainly hasn't got any problem with humping an older woman," Hiranimus commented wryly. "A young Ganderian boy is *supposed* to get himself seduced by an older woman so he won't fall prey to the naïve wiles of an inexperienced girl." That last was aimed with a intonation which just might have indicted Nemia.

She dodged his jab. "Tell me, did he rush to *divulge* to you all about last night, or did he keep it a *secret*?"

Scogil sighed. "That's one Ganderian taboo that's laced up tight. Sexual affairs are *secret*. It's not a taboo he would even question."

"I agree. That means he'll make an excellent Pscholar, doesn't it? They'll have a solid foundation of early-life *secrecy* considerations upon which to build their elitist ethics of silence. *That's* what I'm suggesting we break, that emotional foundation, now, while we can."

Scogil tried to think in those terms. "Eron has always been an unhappy Ganderian," he mused. "He's confided to me many of his unspoken hopes, and though he hasn't been one to break any cultural taboos with me—at least as regards secrets—he has more than once ranted and raved in frustration about the secrecy of his peers. He does *not* like secrets though he seems psychocondemned to keep them. If there *is* an internal contradiction here, it is the burning need he has to *know* what he *knows* he has no business knowing. He has the mind of a spy."

Nemia nodded. "Did he ever tell you that he regularly spied on the clandestine meetings of father and mistress?"

"Never!"

"Last night he confessed—in a rush of emotion he wasn't really able to control—that he had once tried to confront his father with some details of his affair with the woman—did you know her?—Melinesa—but, in the end, never dared. He was frantic to give his father advice, and it drove him crazy that he couldn't. I think he was in love with Melinesa. He certainly disapproves—and disapproved—of the way his father handled her."

Scogil recalled the fights Eron picked with his father, much to that harried man's discomfort. Scogil had never been able to pinpoint the source of the boy's rage. So—he had harbored visions of giving his father advice about secret matters of state and boudoir, eh? "That sounds like Eron." He reflected. "I only met Melinesa twice." She was wearing a flowing sarong of birds printed on orange. He saw in his mind's eye Melinesa in a hallway at a conference bringing him cakes. She had wanted an excuse to discuss Eron's prospects, glancing fondly at Eron once, while the boy stood across the room, staring at her. She was indeed charming and indecently young, probably too young for Eron by Ganderian standards, only a decade his senior. "I didn't know she was involved with Osa Senior, not surprisingly. On Agander one knows these things happen, but even a dilated eye will see scant evidence of any cross-generational liaisons. Everything looks like a ritual, and anything can be hidden in a ritual."

Nemia escorted Hiranimus down to her study where she displayed for him diagrams and Crowe maps of Eron's fam, none of which meant anything to him, but he nodded sagely while she pointed and zoomed in on critical features as she jabbered.

Eventually he had to put his hand on her wrist to slow her down. "Keep it simple. If I'm going to help you I have to understand what you need me to *do*."

She broke off. "I keep forgetting that you're *only* a mathematician." She looked down at her toes, still bare, and curled them. "Okay. We skip the electroquantum physiology. You'll just have to take my word and do what I say. Accept my assurances that the physiological consequences will be exactly the ones we want." She met his gaze. "This is *the* point I want to make: *Your* emotions don't count; *his* mind has to be in exactly the right state of emotional turmoil just before he undergoes the operation. Fail and, postoperation, his fam's security will kick in and erase what we've done and, worse, warn him that we've been tampering."

He gave her the old Imperial salute of a Stars&Ship Assistant Gunner. "Mine is to do and not reason why; I'm good at that." He'd been trained as an operative and not as a thinker. It made him sad. In time he'd surprise them all.

She took his arm. She didn't have to say anything sympathetic, but she did anyway. "You're good at what you *do* do. I wouldn't know how to be you. Your mind fascinates me. I'm tempted to throw off my traces and run away with you and Eron to Faraway. Maybe I *would* if you'd offer me some bait."

He smiled. He liked this woman. "It wouldn't work," he growled. "Too many complications. Maybe we can toil pleasurably together again anon. Right now we have to work out the details of the job we're going to do on Eron."

"I'll miss you," she said sadly.

"It can't be helped. I'm doomed to be on the move."

"There *is* a last something I can do for you while we're here in my makeshift lab. I shouldn't—but I will. You hate that Murek Kapor persona, don't you?"

"He's not me; he's a wimp. I'm glad he's gone."

"He's *not* gone. He's just deactivated. The Oversee can reactivate Murek Kapor again anytime they need him. From a distance, too. I was the one who installed him; I know. Let me erase him for you."

"Without authorization?"

"Why not? Who will ever suspect? It's easy. Your specialized fam was *built from the ground up* to be meddled with. Your parents had plans for you. Tailored persona on demand, that's you. Subaltern, that's you. All I need to destroy Murek are the special Oversee access codes—and I have those since I already used them once."

He stood indecisively. She said nothing. He said nothing. It was tempting. He had already vowed that he'd never allow the Oversee to install another persona in that special organ of his fam that was designed to host possessor agents. But it was true; all the information that defined Murek Kapor was still intact and *could* be reactivated. It didn't stop there. Once activated, Murek was just the kind of passive fop who, if asked, would offer up Scogil's fam for repossession by a new agent. There was no way Scogil could destroy the Murek-parasite by himself—it would take more than a lifetime in tandem with major computing resources to break the code. But Nemia *had* the code. This might be the last few watches he'd ever see her.

Ah, the risks a man took to be free! Nobody was more loyal to the purpose of the Oversee than Hiranimus Scogil. They had told him that the persona machine in his fam was only a means for rapid disguise—but it was also the means for enslavement. At the Oversee's whim, he was as much a slave as any controlled sycophant of Cloun-the-Stubborn. He'd been that once on Agander. Never again!

"Can you kill him now?"

"Promise you won't rat on me?" she stalled.

"I'll be in your debt."

"In that case . . ." She reached back and gently removed his fam.

He watched her fit his warmly fluid pad into her diabolical machines. This was a more dangerous game than taking a shower with her. He couldn't watch. He had a paranoid need to run and lock up the cottage, uninhibited by logic. Famless, he wasn't really oriented, though all agents of the Oversee had been trained to operate famless in an emergency. Each room seemed familiar but wasn't organized in a rational manner. He had to reason out his location. The long gadget at the base of each window he perceived as a lock that he should know how to activate but didn't. He had to deduce the function by trying various settings. Success delighted him. He wandered through the rooms repeating the action that seemed to lock each window. He missed his fam's mental house map. Surely he should have been able to set up a windows check list to reassure himself that he had locked them all! He stood there counting the windows his mind remembered, astonished that he didn't even know what the total should be.

"The house panel is in the kitchen, oaf," she said. It was a sweet voice. He let it reverberate in his head so that he could understand each word. *The house panel.* Of course. It would control the door lock, too.

But that created a problem. He reasoned carefully. If the house was locked from the inside via the panel, how would he get out? He gave up. It was simpler manually. He found a mask, figured out the airlock door mechanism, and stepped outside—to a vivid emotional rush, the memory of being adolescent. Half-grown boys did silly things like run around houses without their fams, pretending to be animals. So did agents in training. The tension of muscle. Sights. Smells.

How green the fragrant garden. Weird layout. Wild slopes. Stone fences. Damn! A pesky robobulb was following him on its spider legs. He wondered if he could outrun the bulb. Could those bots even *see* in what for them would be the brilliant dazzle of day? He ran. The bulb kept up with him, not even bothering to stay on the path. He ran faster. But Ha! Could the bot climb?

"Yahoo!" shouted Hiranimus as he monkeyed up a tree. No, the bulb couldn't follow! He swung from a branch, flailing his legs gaily while bellowing down at the robocreature. "Yahoo!" Here in the sky he was *already* free! From everything! Even the Oversee couldn't send Murek scrambling up a tree. "Nanny, nanny, boo-boo!" he singsonged down to his enemies with the age-old child's taunt. Then he snuggled into a crotch of the tree to enjoy the spectacular scenery. For a long time he just stared. It was fascinating how the shadows crept across the landscape like a timorous army trying not to be noticed. The colors changed and deepened. Had he ever seen such blue mountains!

When Nemia finally arrived at the trunk of the tree, he refused to notice her and she had to climb up to meet him. He let her position his head—her leg awkwardly hooked in a branch—while she reattached his soft leathery external brains.

"Space save me!" he exclaimed, suddenly sober. "What am I doing up here in a tree?"

"You're a new man. Murek is gone; I erased him down to the last bit."

He let her hug him. He had never felt happier with anyone in his life. "I love you." Freedom was exalting. "I'm taking you with me. Why didn't I think of that before? I've just decided that I'm willing to defy your parents. I'll never let you go."

"That's just what I've been planning all along," she cooed.

"I'm awed by my stupidity. Where will we *hide*?"

"I have another secret I shouldn't have kept from you. I've located a honeymoon retreat that's not on our family charts."

# MOTHER AND DAUGHTER AND A
# WALL WITH EARS, 14,791 GE

*This is the excellent foppery of the world: that when we are sick in fortune—
often the surfeit of our own behavior—we make guilty of our disasters the sun,
the moon, and stars, as if we were villains on necessity, fools by heavenly compulsion, knaves, thieves, and treachers by spherical predominance, drunkards,
liars, and adulterers by an enforced obedience of planetary influence . . . An
admirable evasion of whoremaster man, to lay his goatish disposition on the
charge of a star!*

—The SpearShaker of Old Rith

The mysterious owner of the Coron's Egg, wherever in the Galaxy he resided,
was obviously not a collector. From her coded correspondence with him, Nemia of
l'Amontag was convinced he did not know that he possessed a first edition or even
that there had been many editions of what he called his "galactarium." He valued
it for some obscure reason; he was neither willing to sell it nor willing to reveal his
identity, though he did seem ready to offer information contained within–for a
price. She, however, had no intention of asking for the coordinates she desired–the
location of the planet Zurnl II, which Grandfa was certain it held. Such a misstep
could attract far too much attention. She needed help.

By night Nemia sneaked out by air to visit her mother, meticulously making
sure that she had a backup story and that Hiranimus would not be able to trace her.
The l'Amontag estate and factory were built into the side of a cliff with an awesome
view of the local badlands. That was why she was still good at rock climbing. The
pitons she had zapped into the rock as a child were probably still there. Nemia was
the family hiker and adventuress–she took after Grandfa. Her mother didn't like
to leave mansion or factory except for long trips and the occasional stellar adventure. Father was away, as usual, that extraordinary mathist and plotter always

with his hand in dubious affairs, Grandfa's son. She would have to deal with her mother. She would rather have dealt with her father.

The mansion's disembodied robopresence greeted her warmly by sliding open the door before she could sneak up on it, a mutual game they had played since she was a child. She had never won. "Ah, so you're back!" The robopresence had a cluttered archivist's memory. "Ran away without even saying good-bye to me! Was that nice!"

"Grandfa kidnapped me," she explained contritely.

"You've grown so! Of course, as usual with l'Amontag children, you've forgotten to comb your hair. Mama will be certain to remind you. I can have a brush ready for you in the refresher."

Nemia sighed. There was no way to face down her old faceless friend. "Mama is waiting."

"No she isn't; she has your message that you're coming but I haven't yet told her that you're *here*. You have time, little one. Now hurry with that hair fix-up before she gets impatient!"

Nemia gave up with a smile. In the refreshing room she put down her traveling case and decided on more than a hair fluffing; she stripped and took a mist shower, brushed her teeth, scrubbed her tongue, and spent all the strokes on her hair that the watchful robopresence expected. A silken robe embroidered with the cavorting figures of gengineered beasts was waiting for her when she was ready.

"Where is Mama?"

"Her boudoir. I will now announce your arrival."

"No. I want to surprise her."

"That wouldn't be the proper protocol," replied the stern voice.

"When I was a baby, you let me sneak up on her!" she pleaded. "Please?"

"She'll disconnect me!"

"Ha! She'd forget her own name without you. Keep quiet and I'll tell you a story tonight. Is it a bargain?"

"You'll tell *me* a story? you little conniving rascal! I'm the storyteller around here!"

"I'm grown up now. *I* tell the stories!"

The robopresence sighed in capitulation. "Such respect I get for spoiling you!"

At her mother's door Nemia set down her traveling case noiselessly and watched familiar matronly fingers engrossed in intricate embroidery. It was the same comfortable room, the same flickering fire. Mama never changed her furniture, or her ways, addicting herself to the special things which passed her demanding judgment. The huge screen upon which she wove her patterns hadn't been upgraded in Nemia's memory. The bed under which Nemia had played "cave" since she was two was still there; none of the tables and chairs and cushions—once metamorphosed into castles and ships and control rooms and dungeons—were missing, but now seemed to be arranged in their proper places. The rug was new, its baroque themes almost sacrilegious to Nemia, who had grown used to her mother's timeless constants. The old rug had carried simple beige designs.

Nemia hesitated to interrupt the delicate weaving of quantronic magic, but she knew from long experience that this was merely the way her mother passed her quiet time, that she *liked* to be interrupted. "Mama."

The Duchess of l'Amontag took only a moments' hand gesture to dismiss her creation and turn to her daughter. "Ah, my runaway child." The pleasantries thus aside, she moved on to business immediately. "Have you snared him yet?"

"Yes, Mama." She curtsied.

"Hmmm. I thought you'd rebel. You haven't been the easiest child in the world to raise properly. Rebellion would have been the easy way out."

"I wanted to." Nemia smiled. "I would have—but I like him."

"His family entirely approves of you."

"So does he!" Nemia answered hotly.

"He does, does he? He's not altogether the best choice for you. But knowing you, I had to make compromises."

"I thought Grandfa chose him?"

"Well, now!" said the Duchess indignantly. "That *man* certainly did his share of meddling! Your father's side of the family is incorrigible! I had Hiranimus Scogil on my list before your grandfather even knew he existed. At the *bottom* of my list."

"That puts him *up* a notch on *my* list!" retorted Nemia.

"Children," came a placating disembodied voice, "no quarreling in *my* house!"

"Quiet! Or I'll disconnect you."

"Mama, treat her well! She's an old friend!"

"Have you ever seen me beat her? She *does* need a brain transplant."

"Mama, you wouldn't know how to run the house without her!"

"There's that," conceded Nemia's mother.

"Nemia, she's right." The voice sniffled. "After all," it went on righteously, "servants are to be seen and not heard!"

"May we be alone?" the mother demanded imperiously, and after a long enough silence she returned to her daughter. "So." That meant back to business. "I presume you are here for a handout?"

"Mama! *You* arranged the wedding! Since we have to elope in the middle of the night, the least you can do is give us a glorious honeymoon."

"Gambling on Lakgan?"

"No. A peaceful retreat on Zurnl II."

Her mother froze. "You've been pursuing your Grandfa's obsession? We don't know where it is. Nobody in the Oversee knows where it is."

"*I* do."

In an entirely new mood, her mother moved to the bed. "Sit down, child." This was serious clan business. "Explain yourself."

"It was just chance. I wasn't monitoring Grandfa's search—but with all the things I've had to do to settle his affairs, I never disabled his weasels." Nemia went to pick up her traveling case and sat down with it beside her mother. She fished out some correspondence. "I was taking all his mail and an alarm went off. It was this." She produced a note, her response, and the recent reply.

The Duchess of l'Amontag read without being impressed. "I believe my husband's father owned at least *nine* of these devices, none of which contain a star or planet listed as Zurnl under any conceivable spelling. Why should this one be any better?"

"It's a first-edition. You'll notice in my negotiation I asked him to check out and send to me the I.S.B. coordinates for the Imperial Starbase Dragontail updated to 14,791 GE."

"Yes, I noticed." She recited the numbers from the correspondence to make her point.

"Those coordinates are way out of whack."

"Oh?" Nemia's mother was a woman who checked everything. The screen, which had a moment ago held her quantum-state embroidery, she now engaged in a search through some distant archive which had probably been captured in an ancient war and lay unused for centuries. The old I.S.B. star velocities were easily accurate enough to give correct coordinates for 14,791 GE. Presently the adjusted coordinates for Dragontail appeared. Her fam quickly compared the two number sets. "They are the same within half a gigameter," she commented laconically.

Nemia smiled. "You used an old Imperial database."

"The I.S.B. catalogs have never been bettered. The I.S.B. evolved independently of Splendid Wisdom and was never compromised by Imperial casualness."

"Yet the Imperial Navy never permitted the coordinates of its major bases to be listed correctly. The errors were intentional." She took out a Coron's Egg from her case. "This is the oldest Egg Grandfa ever found. It is a second-edition fabrication. Let's call up Dragontail. The system was still called Dragontail when this Egg was fabricated, though we were well into the Interregnum and Dragontail had been taken over by Faraway after the last Lakgan war." She manipulated the surface of her Egg. The room went dark except for vague flickers from the direction of the fireplace.

Stars appeared in interstellar splendor, unnamed, unlabeled. Another tapping shifted the viewing coordinates through a rapid flashing of stars. Now a few of them had luminous names. "I've set it to provide the old I.S.B. names for every star within twelve leagues of our viewpoint." Dragontail was the brightest star in this virtual celestial sphere. Another tap and its coordinates appeared. She entered 14,791 GE and the stars shifted to their present position. Conspicuously the coordinates of Dragontail did not match the I.S.B. numbers, nor the numbers which had been relayed to Nemia by the weasel of her mysterious correspondent.

"Oh," said Nemia's mother, now interested.

"Let me tell you the story Grandfa told me." Nemia brought out some of her grandfather's precious documents, the originals.

The special evidence pointing to first-edition status for the mystery Egg was a scrap of proof-notes from the Interregnum, archaeologically dated to about the time of Cloun-the-Stubborn, scribbled in pencil on a piece of fine goat parchment. As a youth Grandfa had been studying the high-mountain monasteries of Timdo, a planet he favored for Oversee attention because it harbored the most religious and eccentric culture of the peculiar Coron's Wisp pentad. He had amused himself for a year by restoring a ruin about which the current monks, who had moved farther down the slopes, were still telling fairy tales of astrological power. Underneath a rubble of roof and collapsed bookcases (basic slate/resin laminations) he found a toppled row of impervium cabinets that contained bricks of time-bonded parchment, cellomet, paper, and tiny machines.

Uncompacted, with painstaking care, the documents which remained readable told the story of a bustling enclave low in technical expertise but one which seemed to have been carrying on lucrative sub-rosa dealings with crafty Faraway traders during a time when such contact with barbarian magicians was forbidden by the local customs regulations—but tolerated because the Eggs filled a longed-for local religious need. The monastery designed the Eggs while the industries of the Faraway trading worlds manufactured certain essential components for them, fine quantronics, atomics, etc.—a deal typical of those engineered by the early Faraway Traders. It was only after this archaeological discovery that Grandfa had begun to collect the Eggs of Coron's Wisp.

The parchment with its startling mention of Zurnl was a simple proof-list in an obscure monk's shorthand of the time:

> Duty: yul. ac. Marrano, 2nd Ed. Egg
>> delete Galanrali, no such F2 str
>> delete Zurnl (auth. begl.)
>> delete Nahar and all comp.
>> delete Torkan 2348 chart, replace ISB-48A
>> chng coordinates of following defunct S&S bases:
>>> (A list of 476 stars followed,
>>> including Dragontail, each with
>>> its false coordinates matched with
>>> Faraway supplied corrections.)

As a youth Nemia's grandfather had surmised that he had unearthed the first substantial clue to the location of the mythical Martyr's Cache. Tamic Smythos had mentioned the Martyr's Cache only once in a cryptic paragraph—and that in relationship to Zurnl. The mysterious Zurnl he had mentioned only twice—but by now it was a Smythosian legend. The Martyr's Cache might be filled with jars of rotting prison-made paper in an unfindable cave buried under the dunes of a Zurnl desert, it might be a vault emptied ages ago by Faraway wardens, but—who knew!— it might be a dungeon's library filled with the golden mathematical wisdom of fifty of the finest of the early Pscholars who had been trained in the melancholy ruins of post-Imperial Splendid Wisdom for glorious martyrdom at the hands of Faraway fanatics. Faraway had been driven by the Founder's belief in their destiny yet simultaneously terrified of his psychohistory.

"So," said the Duchess of l'Amontag, "your grandfather's spirit still owns your soul. Even death doesn't stop him!" She laughed. "You'll get your money. When you arrive at Faraway, a charter will be awaiting your disposal. We have no choice. I suppose we can't crew it with Neuhadrans. Scogil thinks he is saving you from a fate worse than death, poor boy, and I suppose we must continue to support his illusions, at least until he is mature enough to laugh about them."

"Can we afford a charter?" Nemia asked anxiously.

"It won't be our money. It will be Oversee money. This is Oversee business. This isn't what I'd planned. The god of chaos has intervened."

"Shall I tell your fortune?" Nemia was grinning, the Galaxy's most formidable fortune-telling tool diamond-bright in her hand.

"So your beloved Grandfa also taught you the artistry of the charlatan? No thank you. An admirable evasion, to lay one's goatish disposition on the charge of a star! Did I tell you that I never wanted to marry your father? Your grandfather insisted. Didn't you find him *insistent*! He used that very Egg you are holding to cast my chart and prove to me with his diabolical reasoning that his son was inextricably wedded to my future. He was grinning the whole time, too."

"Was he right?"

"Your Grandfa, shall we say, was as right as you can be in this information-starved human condition which is our fate."

Nemia was grinning. She defied her mother—under the pressure of her fingers the stars spread out again across the bedroom in which, as a child, she had built so many castles out of the objects at hand. This time the Egg-enchanted sky wore the constellations of Neuhadra. Exotic symbols began to appear; lines drew themselves by some arcane formula until the room's heaven was filled by a marvelous chart. "Oh my!" began Nemia. "By the Founder's Nose!" Her eyes were enraptured by the chart. "You'll never guess what your daughter is up to! Look!" She pointed. "See where the red lines intersect in the constellation of the Warrior—there at the Petunia—have I got a story for you! It begins with a granddaughter to melt your heart . . ."

The mother was listening in spite of herself. So were the walls.

# ERON OSA GETS UPGRADED, 14,791 GE

*Constraints only limit our freedom of motion, they do not determine our destiny.*

—Excerpt from the Founder's *Psychohistorical Tools for Making a Future*

Eron Osa fiddled with the fit of his mask, adjusting it, as he was hurried from behind into the thin air toward the car pool by a silent Murek Kapor. His tutor had been behaving with a strange aggressiveness—as if he wasn't himself. Maybe not. Maybe, Eron thought, it was just a small boy's nervous eyes seeing new dangers. Within hours his precious fam would be in some machine for an upgrade. He shivered. No—wrong fear. Since that evening when he had seduced his tutor's girlfriend he had never been able to regain his insolent composure around Murek. Regret. If his father hadn't been such an infuriating old reprobate, he might have, should have, adhered to the old blockhead's advice about sex. Hadn't his father continually warned him about the high tax on escapades—in spite of his own escapades? Fathers shouldn't be *allowed* to be right!

He was a bit frantic for his tutor's approval. He knew a fam upgrade was dangerous—and knew that he was doing this at his own stubborn insistence, against all advice. His father, for one, would be furious. Everyone was probably right. Eron was most likely wrong. He also knew that an ambitious star-child who was to grow up and make a mark on *this* huge Galaxy was going to need every advantage he could wangle. He felt alone. He *wanted* Murek to say that it was all right—but that stupid farman *wouldn't* because he knew, yes he knew, about that night with Nemia. How could he know? Nemia would *never* confess. He *couldn't* know but he did; his eyes betrayed suspicion. No matter what, Eron was going to admit nothing. Murek *had* to go along with the operation. But now that the hour of the upgrade was upon them, it was scary. He wanted to be *told* that everything would be all right.

The wind gusted, blowing the odd pellet of hard snow against the skin of that part of his face that was exposed. His tutor led him to a blue aerocar with variable wings that seated four. *Its* sensors recognized Murek as a legal user—opening the canopy for him. A picture of a baby, forgotten by some admirer, smiled at them from the border of the instrument panel. They clambered into the four-seater, the canopy dropped shut, and the pressure pump cycled while the robocar inquired, "Destination, citizen?"

"No destination," Murek instructed, dropping his oxy-mask. "I'll take her up on manual." He turned to his student who was also dropping his mask. "How about a tour of the lake first? There hasn't been time for much sightseeing."

Eron did not disagree; he had no desire, at this critical moment, to oppose this man upon whom he depended too much. He was regretting all the times he had defied him in the past. His mentor lifted at a steep climb, the boosted acceleration viciously forcing both of them back against the seat. The boy reflexively called upon the names of various old emperors for protection, items of language that millennia of psychohistory had not eradicated.

Finally he quailed. "Couldn't we try automatic?" He was surprised that the car didn't have an override for foolish behavior.

"Too dull," said his tutor as he leveled out at a height above the tallest mountain. The icy blue lake filled out the landscape to the left of them; to the right were hills and arroyos covered with a greenish tint that looked unnatural to Eron where it showed through the clouds. The shades of the colors were all wrong. In the distance, navy-blue mountains rumpled the horizon. There were a few stars in the dark day sky. Eron wondered at the sanity of whoever would choose such a planet as home.

His mad pilot banked around the lake once, pointing out the sights, then turned out over the desolation and said nothing, just flew. There were no signs of civilization down there. They dropped into a fantasy world of clouds, till the whiteness was swirling all around them, some wisps thicker than others. The farman's fingers—Eron remembered them as faster than a blaster, faster at math than a mind could think—fooled with the clean instruments, obviously intending to put the aero on automatic while he attended to more pressing tasks. The canopy all around them went to an opaque white. They were chickens inside an egg.

"Where are we going?" Was Murek aborting the upgrade?

His tutor only smiled and brought to view, in the palm of his hand, a tiny pod-like distorter, which he tapped with a finger. "To shut down your fam's electronic motion sensors." In another quick motion he left the distorter burred to Eron's fam. "You don't need to know where we're going. The distorter won't harm anything." He added, perhaps by way of explanation, "What we're doing isn't strictly legal."

Eron was too intimidated to resist. He was boiling with questions. But he found it hard to use Nemia's name in front of Murek. He'd been trying to ask about her for the whole trip. "Will Nemia be there?" he blurted. Right now he trusted Nemia more than he did his farman companion.

"No. She's strictly legit. Rigone will do the operation. He's good. Don't worry." He paused. "I'm going to be reading for a while." Then his eyes glazed over and he was obviously perusing something that had already been fed into his fam. After that the only disturbance was the whisper of the engines and the odd air pocket and the blind diffuse whiteness of the enclosing eggshell.

Eron tried to distract himself by imagining the cities that they were passing over, or by conjuring old Imperial ruins, but all he could think about was a naked Nemia. He ordered the picture away, but his fam only solidified the image and slowly rotated it for Eron's inspection.

When his cuckolded tutor came out of his trance he had a nudge for Eron. "How's the boy? You've been quiet."

"Okay."

"You're nervous."

"No." Eron sensed a Nemia in the backseat but he resisted turning around to see. He knew she wasn't there.

"Come on. Tell me."

"I'll be all right."

"I've been reviewing procedures. It's essential that you be in a calm state of mind before the operation. I thought that might pose a problem so I brought with me an apparatus I can use to calm your emotions."

"I *am* calm!" he shouted.

"*Calm*—as in not shouting. Let me review what you already know. Your fam's security goes on the alert when your wetware is agitated by internal conflict or external meddling. If a fam's transducers are then detached from physical contact with your alarmed body, it will do its best, after reunion, to rationalize all changes made during the detachment. If that's not enough it will attempt a wetware/hardware backup. It's an automatic defense. We need to take precautions to prevent your fam from erasing the work Rigone will do. So I'm going to have to hook you up."

"To what?" asked Eron unenthusiastically while Murek pulled, from beneath the seat, an elegant leather case that the boy hadn't noticed, unpacking it. One of the objects from the case looked suspiciously like a helmet. "You're not going to try to read my mind!"

"No, no, this stuff just picks up on your emotions. It's *not* a psychic probe; your fam wouldn't allow that. It is a far more primitive device."

At the mention of psychic probe Eron's heart began to pound, and he had visions of a grinning Kapor—after nailing him about Nemia—pressing a button that opened up a trapdoor in the aerocar's floor to eject his mind-stripped body into the clouds. He made a vow of celibacy. With minor gestures of noncooperation he tried to discourage this evil farman from attaching the apparatus to his hands and head. He began to practice thinking about nothing. But he felt Nemia's sexy fingers stroking his chin.

Murek paused, reluctant to fight even the most passive of resistance. "You've got to do it, kid, or no upgrade."

"You're going to kill me!"

"This stuff works at the microvolt level, no danger. It only senses local brain temperature changes, skin resistance, and hormone levels." The clamps went on Eron's fingers and the helmet went on his head. He was defenseless! "Hmm," said the Kapor-monster, reading the hand-size output screen, "you're in a pretty agitated state."

"Just give me a moment to blank my mind." This time Eron's chin was well defended from Nemia's fingers by an elite troop of his personal thought police, linked arm in arm at a safe five-centimeter buffer from his face. Then . . . in the midst of his concentration . . . with the gentlest touch . . . he felt Nemia's hand do an end run and slip up the inside of his left leg. Space! Not that! Hastily he grabbed her wrist and lowered her down into the clutches of his steadfast ally, Lord Gravity, where he let her go tumbling into whatever was now below them. Because he loved her he gave her a pretend parachute. But eight tiny Nemias, naked, began to dance on the dashboard in synchrony.

"What is that?" asked his relentless persecutor as he noticed blips on his screen.

"Nothing. Just a flashback to something that has nothing to do with the operation."

"I see. You're worried? Something you haven't told me?"

"Maybe I was thinking about my father," he evaded.

"Your father? I've never been clear on that relationship. Is there something about him you haven't told me?" There was a pause. "Ah, yes!"

"Why do you say that?"

"I got a big blip."

"So you *are* trying to read my mind!"

"No, no. I want you in a calm state for your upgrade."

Eron said nothing. Neither did the monster from outer farspace. He just seemed to sit there, eyeing Eron, probably waiting to pounce, ready with the trapdoor switch in the aerocar's passenger-side floor. "Some things we aren't supposed to talk about," Eron commented lamely.

"Ah, Ganderian taboos. What might those be? I never did get all the details straight. Very convoluted."

"I don't have to tell a Big Nose like you," said Eron sulkily. "I'm not *supposed* to tell a Big Nose like you. Big Noses are always poking into things that shouldn't interest them."

"Is this something you could tell your father?"

"I tried. He always slither-snaked out of it. He was good at changing the subject. Maybe he was right."

"What subject was he good at changing?"

Eron shrugged. The questioning was getting too hot. He found his mind beginning to shut down in resistance. It was increasingly difficult to think. That was a mercy under the circumstances!

"Okay. I'm reading resistance. We're going to have to break through that before you get your upgrade. Just recall that I'm not your father and that you've always been able to talk to me. My machine is going to start reading syllables to you and combining them into words as it analyzes your emotional reactions to syllable-space. The procedure doesn't require a response. You just have to listen."

Eron felt in a mood of total rebellion. He wasn't going to speak. He was just going to order his fam to relax him and that would be that. While he resisted, the machine began to speak syllables to him, pausing between each syllable as if it were thinking. He wondered at the machine's intelligence. After a while it started to combine syllables into words, sometimes repeating itself. Eron felt like a target. Every so often he would be hit by a word that struck with chemical impact. The hits grew more frequent. The words, at first general, began to get more specific. Dangerously specific. He could tell that with each hit the machine was learning something. Its targeting was beginning to upset him. Murek just sat there, staring, not reacting. Then the machine locked onto what it had been seeking, and each word was a hit. "Secret." Pause. "Affair." Pause. "Sex." Pause. "Nemia." Pause.

The eyes of the Kapor-monster lifted from his machine to stare at his victim, lizardlike. Eron felt trapped. He was caught. He had to escape! A defensive explanation formed in his mind, but when he tried to speak it, his mouth opened while nothing came out. It was weird. The same thing had happened when he was with Nemia.

"Okay," the monster said with unexpected gentleness. "We have something to work with. We've run into your definition of 'secret.' Secrets don't let you talk. A command installation. Let's sidestep for a moment. Tell me something that *isn't* a secret."

"Agander's sky is blue," he said inanely, relieved that he could actually make meaningful sounds.

"Tell me something else that isn't a secret."

"You are pissed at me and are about to push the button on the trapdoor under me." That sounded foolish. "I know there isn't a trapdoor under me."

"Eron, I come from a very different place than you do. I'm not pissed at you. I'm your friend, and in a few watches more or less we'll be off to Faraway and you'll be signed up for the program at Asinia Pedagogic. Nemia will be coming with us. She likes you. For the moment, I don't want your secrets. I want your *definition* of 'secret.' Try this one on. How does your mind tell the difference between something that *is* a secret and something that is *not* a secret?"

"Stop asking me tough questions!" Eron laughed but he felt like crying. He was damned if he would show tears.

Murek glanced at his screen. "It's not a secret that you want to cry right now."

Eron bawled for a short inamin, feeling astonishment at the outburst, and then calmly recited a definition right out of his fam dictionary. "A secret is something known only to a specific person or group and deliberately kept from the knowledge of others."

"Not good enough," said the relentless tutor. "How do you know *what* to deliberately keep from the knowledge of others and *what* you can tell them? That's your rule-base. Can't keep a secret without it."

Eron thought for many jiffs, coming up on an inamin. "It has something to do with defense. A secret is to prevent information from being used to hurt yourself or someone under your protection. But that gets complicated. You have to know what hurts people." He looked at his alien farman tutor. "Some things that don't hurt *you* hurt other people."

"That's possible."

For a while his tutor had him play an alternation game that clicked like a metronome back and forth across Eron's fam. First he was asked to search across his memory for something that *wasn't* a secret and find a way to spin it into a story. That cycle complete, the devil at the truth-machine's metronome sent him careening back across his life to locate a dark secret that he *must* withhold in spite of any temptation to reveal it—and Murek enforced the compulsion by *requiring* him to contemplate the "dark secret"—silently.

Back and forth he went from story to silence, from banter to secret, from loud joke to silent recollection of spying on his father, from bright description of playmate Rameen's extravagant birthday party to the never-told memory of young Eron's innocent sexual groping with Rameen's baby sister when they were playing hide-and-seek together in a box. On and on. The light from each nonsecret ended at the shadow-boundary of his world of secrecy until the shape of the secrets became so clearly defined that they were no longer secret. A man's shadow has nowhere to hide in strong sunlight.

Eron laughed until the tears rolled down his cheeks. The glow from the robocar's instruments—the clock, the winglight indicators, the red numerals of speed and altitude—seemed to travel outward to illuminate the whole of the unseen world beyond the featureless canopy. He had been transported by metronome into a psychological hyperspace where secrets were no longer invisible. With passionate insight he began to blabber about the marvelous nature of these weird hyperspatial concealments. The taciturn farman merely listened.

A secret world revealed. In his rebellion against the strictures of Ganderian custom, Eron seemed to have created—in the cloister of his mind, hidden even from himself—a mental utopia where people actually spoke what they felt and saw. In his twelve-year-old soul he was convinced that such a place, made real, would usher in a better Galaxy. It was what he wanted to build with his life. But such utopian ideation had been taboo on Agander, relegated to the shadows of form and culture, where it was not even sanctified by his own approval. Before he could accept his heretical vision, he needed the approval of his elder tutor, who was the only man he had ever met who had listened to his ravings. A sudden passion was now directed at convincing his guru. He brought forth eloquent arguments.

The farman continued to listen.

But Eron didn't get the approbation he sought. Murek only smiled his wiseman smile. "You'll have to work that out for yourself, kid. I can only give you cynically bad advice."

"You're not going to help me? You're just *another* old fuddy with antiquated ideas! I might have known!"

"In the meantime listen to some bad advice. You don't have to take it."

"Don't worry, I won't!"

"But you'll listen?"

"I might," said Eron sullenly.

"You've committed the sin of simplicity. It is not the worst sin in the universe. *Every* design is born naïve. Even the life that originates on a planet appears first in too simple a form, unable to survive except under the most benevolent of hothouse conditions. On Neuhadra life aborted five times before it took root. Ever play chess?"

"Yes, I know," Eron said with resignation. "At first sight chess feels complex but it's too simple. Both kings *always* escape if the players pay attention to their attack and defense. I got bored with chess when I was six. Once you have the algorithm, it *always* ends in a draw."

"Exactly. Simple is good—as long as it's not *too* simple. Let's tackle this secrecy thing rationally, adding a little useful complexity to it. What makes secrecy possible?"

"Boxes and locks." Eron could tell from the stolid response that his tyrannical tutor wouldn't comment on this facetious answer. But there was going to be no escape from the question, either—Murek had that look—so he set his fam on a cause-and-effect search. *What makes secrecy possible?* "The ability to communicate?" he guessed.

"Well . . . yes." A tutor's nod, not quite satisfied. "Obviously without communication, secrecy is moot. But why would someone, able to communicate, *want* to keep a secret? We need a motive."

"Because your *someone* is stark crazy and wants to live his life tied up in knots!"

At this bald assertion the cuckolded monster grinned and pounced. "Kid, suppose a handsome daredevil of a man stole away the girlfriend of a bad-tempered giant who was in the habit of slitting the throats of small people who annoyed him. Why might our handsome rake want to keep his liaison a secret?"

"I hope *you* aren't toting a knife. Are you?"

"I'm not a bad-tempered giant, either."

Eron judiciously chose evasion. "But suppose education and love had mellowed all bad-tempered giants? Then no one would need secrets."

"Suppose I grant you that; imagine we've been magically transported to your sublimely mellow universe in which there are *no* secrets. None. Certainly in such a secrecy-free society no one will be thinking about the consequences of their chatter. Nary a thought wasted on soul searching. Who is to worry that their bit of gossip might hurt someone? Who is to ponder whether newly minted scientific information might boomerang in a destructive way? No one—if all information is considered boon. Who will gain by the dissemination of this information and who will lose? No one is burdened by such nags if dogma has imposed a Rule-for-All-Circumstances upon the galactic citizenry: Information is good and to be shared, no matter the consequence."

"Information *is* good!" insisted Eron.

"Is that so? For who? I remember a card game you and I played only last spring when we were relaxing from our studies at the Alcazar—a game of cards—we were using the Royal Deck of Fate—and your carefully sober face was molded to hide from me what you knew very well, that your four-hand held the Ax of Mercy, Ax&Stone, Executioner, and Barbarian." The tutor laughed. "You were a rascal! You *kept* your secret and wiped out my high cards."

"You want me to *keep* secrets?" said Eron, appalled. "I've been doing that all my life. I *hate* it."

"Neither one nor the other. Isn't your secret-free Galaxy only the white version of another black Galaxy in which, again, no thought is needed because this time the rules tell us that *everything* is a secret? If all information is dangerous and must be hoarded—no matter the consequence, paranoia rules. A lazy man's social order. A machine with no memory could make the necessary decisions in that society flawlessly—whatever the circumstance, stay silent. It's too simple. Such a black Galaxy would regress to animalhood."

"So I'm supposed to tell my secrets and, at the same time, keep them," Eron complained sarcastically while holding his arms fully extended. "Reminds me of a famous old drama about Emperor Stanis-the-Careful. I found it in my copy of *A Short History of Our Splendid Emperors.* The play opens with the arrival of a mysterious brass-strapped box in which the Emperor finds something of empire-shattering consequence. The stage is silent while he holds up the box to the stars. 'To speak or not to speak,' he anguishes. Presently fleets are destroyed, ministers assassinated, his wife drowns herself, his enemies rise and fall—and by the end of his reign he still hasn't made up his mind."

"Emperor Stanis-the-Careful lacked judgment."

Eron adjusted his helmet with impatient fingers. The rings on his fingers were broadcasting his skin resistance. "Rigone told me that young men are much better at making judgments than old men. That makes me smarter than you. I think Rigone was pulling my tail."

"For sure. Judgment—as much as youths like ourselves might aspire to it—is an old man's game. The young sword lashes out mindlessly; the rules of a sword master might tell the apprentice how to wield the sword, but only experience will offer instruction on when and where to cut. Suppose you found a truth under some rock. No one else has it. Should you speak or remain silent? Only judgment can say. Should you offer some pieces of wisdom and withhold others? A matter for judgment. Can your truth be taken and used against you? Judgment again. Under pressure you may be tempted to lie. A lie about your found-treasure will have consequences. Is this a good lie or a bad lie? *Judgment* is never easy. If you always have to *blab* everything—on principle—it's a trap. Likewise you're in a trap if your rule book always tells you to *keep* a secret."

"Cut the guff-guff. I want to go out and do something, not listen to your boring lectures. Are we there yet?" Eron pointed through the opaque window.

"When you do something"—the voice was acerbic—"it helps to know how to be effective."

"As a *psychohistorian* I'll be effective."

A smile. "But will you still have the judgment of a twelve-year-old?"

"That's a trick question," said Eron warily. He looked at the blind canopy of their robocar and the photo of the child stuck in the instrument panel. He cocked his ears and listened to his semicircular canals, not having his orientation distorted fam to advise him. "We've started to bank in circles. I can tell. I don't need my fam for that."

"We've arrived but we won't land until I say so."

"I'm not calm yet?"

"Almost. Let me run this by you. When a rule fails, Eron, all you've got left is *judgment*. Nothing will kill you faster than the combination of a failed rule and a bad judgment call. Rules are good, but no rule is complete enough to apply to all situations. That includes rules about secrecy." He looked at the small physiodetector's screen. "How are you feeling?"

Eron checked his emotions. "Fine. I just made a twelve-year-old's judgment. You're okay for a monster. I'm sorry I went after Nemia."

"So you have a rule that tells you when to be sorry, eh?" his tutor commented wryly.

"Am I calm yet?"

Another glance at the screen. "You're getting there."

"Can we go down?"

"Just one more thing. We've been talking a lot about secrets. You seem to have lifted a lot off your chest. That's good. It's what I needed before we could go ahead." He set the controls for descent. "But I want to leave you with a relevant conundrum to take away with you to Asinia Pedagogic. A riddle to ponder in those ancient halls. It is about secrets and judgment."

"You can never resist one last nail to hold your lecture together, can you? You should try abstinence sometime. You might qualify as a human being."

"While *you* are disqualifying yourself as a human being by becoming a psycho-historian?"

Eron punched him affectionately. "Shoot with the lecture. I'll give you one shot before we touch down. I can dodge one shot."

"Psychohistorians make a vow for the good of humanity. They vow to keep secret the methods of their prescience on theory that if their methods were known to all, their predictions would be invalidated and chaos would ensue, right?"

"Right."

"For instance—if a criminal knows that the police will be at the scene of the crime, he commits his crime elsewhere—and the police knowing that he knows . . . it gets very complicated." Murek had turned to remove the helmet and rings from Eron. He was looking his student in the eye. "There are unfortunate side consequences of this 'noble' vow of secrecy; it ensures that the society of psychohistorians remains an elite, one as arbitrary as the old Imperial Court. We lesser galactic beings have to depend upon the Pscholars' benevolence—while not being able to ensure it. But—and this is a big but—before you become a psychohistorian, before you know enough to make a sound judgment, you'll be asked to take their vow of secrecy—and your vow will be enforced."

"And you want me to leave my mind open for later judgment?"

"Not my call. I'm only the pilot." As he touched the instruments the canopy went transparent. They were dropping into a mountain valley. Eron had no time to see anything before they were taxiing inside a hangar.

"If I refused to take the vow, they wouldn't take me as a student!"

"Probably not."

"I could pretend."

"You don't have to pretend. A vow is always subject to revision by later judgment—assuming that you haven't, by then, become a rule-slave."

The canopy sprang open and Rigone was standing there on the black-and-yellow striped expanse of floor, his tattooed face grinning up at them. He had a hand for the boy as he dropped to the plasteel.

"Where is this place?" asked Eron, looking around at the modest hangar, trying to see where they had come from before the high doors rolled fully shut.

"Not for you to know," commented Murek as they led him into a side corridor of levitating verticules. He grinned. "A necessary secret." The three rose on a platform, then were escorted to the hidden operating room where they were stripped and passed through a nonopening clean-door where almost alive clean-suits enveloped their bodies. The theater was illuminated in an eerie red light, presumably to protect some components from the energy of higher wavelengths.

Eron was offered a seat, his head reexposed, and his fam gently removed, sans comforting words, as if he went famless regularly, while Rigone donned huge goggles. Surgeon machines wired Eron's head to some sort of feedback net with other instruments in the room. Murek seemed to be there only as a guide to watch over his now-incompetent pupil. With perceptions unfiltered by his fam, Eron noticed the ascendancy of his senses—as during his escapade with Nemia. This time he was calm, with no rush of erotically driven feelings. The lines of the machines seemed too sharp, the colors too reddishly electric, the precision motors that grasped and moved his strangely remote fam, too precise, the instrument readouts at the corner of his eyes fraught with mysterious meaning whose function he did not have the mind to question.

Rigone worked at his station, standing, seemingly forever. Sometimes his hands were busy. Sometimes he passively watched the machines that were active under his command. Eron endured his wait stoically, the torture being the passage of time. His mind remained eerily at peace.

Finally Rigone lifted his goggles and grinned. "That was easy. Now for the hard part. Hang onto your pants, boy! And don't piss." He replaced the troll's goggles and went back to work without a pause. Eron wanted to get up to look; but he was restrained.

"Let him work," Murek advised. An hour went by. Eron dreamed animal thoughts while wide awake, knowing that his fantasies made no sense, fascinated by a dreamlike illogic that, famless, he couldn't analyze.

When they reattached his fam, he was floated to an elegant recovery room, chandeliers, entertainment console, beds and soft bedspreads, fine active murals with motion subdued to the pace of expected contemplation—but Eron wasn't in a mood to notice; he was frantically testing for his new powers and finding them absent. He was asking himself outstanding questions and not getting answers! It was horrible. The operation had been a failure!

Rigone seemed placid. Murek played with the room's cuisinator until he came up with a syrupy alcoholic drink for himself, which he began to quaff in large gulps. That wasn't like Murek at all. He was turning into such a strange man right before Eron's eyes; the calculated restraint that Eron was so used to seemed to be disappearing for hours at a time, as if some wildman had taken possession of his tutor's body. Maybe his vision was just the strain of the operation.

The silence seemed unbearable to everyone. "So, kid," said the farman into the silence after the first few gulps of his syrup had taken effect, "do you still remember the pythagorean theorem?"

"Of course!" Eron was indignant.

"Don't 'of course' me." Murek activated the nearby wall. "Show me! What does A-squared plus B-squared equals C-squared mean?"

To humor his tutor, Eron used the writer linked to his fam to conjure a blue triangle. He squared the sides with red squares and chopped them up into pieces which slid over and squared the hypotenuse. "What's the deal? I can do baby games like that *without* a fam," he said scornfully. His tutor mumbled happily, swallowing the rest of his drink while he moved over to spread himself out on one of the beds.

Eron didn't like anybody at that moment. These bungling fools had condemned him to live out his life as the same mediocre moron he'd always been. If life had been so cruel as to curse him with a stupid Ganderian father and a silly Ganderian mother, at least it ought to have provided him with an extraordinary fam that could see things invisible to everyone else in the Galaxy. Even that surcease was denied him. Worse, now he was probably stuck with crossed wires.

Rigone was grinning at his obvious consternation. "Notice any difference?"

"No! It didn't work! You goofed!"

Rigone's tattooed grin only broadened into a laugh. "That's good. If you were noticing a difference, your fam would have it all calibrated by now and would be busily erasing what I'd done. If I did it right you'll never notice the difference until the very inamin that you outfox us all. Say hello to me when you reach Splendid Wisdom. I'll still be on the Olibanum. The Teaser's Bistro."

"We leave Neuhadra tomorrow for Faraway," slurred a very drunk tutor under the shining chandelier. "Can't promise you a good time. I've never been to Faraway, either." He chuckled. "Heard about it though."

Eron stared at the writer-link and sulked.

"Really, kid," continued the drunk, "relax and get some sleep. There's plenty of time for you to bring Our Sinning Galaxy down around our ears! You don't have to do it tonight! Spacefire, you're only twelve years old." And he began to laugh and laugh at the pretty lights hanging from the ceiling.

Eron tried to think positively about his chances for conquering the Galaxy with a possibly crippled fam. Famless Arum-the-Patient had conquered Agander and had then turned to the Center, storming the Imperial bureaucracy—but he hadn't had to compete with fammed minds. Eron felt a frantic urgency. He needed a lecture on patience right now but his tutor, who was his only source for pedantic lectures, was already asleep. He turned morosely to Rigone instead. "Tell me about Splendid Wisdom."

# A FAMLESS ERON OSA GLIMPSES HIS PAST, 14,810 GE

*Make no mistake about it, a future cannot be created without first being pre-dicted. Otherwise the future just happens to very surprised naifs. What you cannot predict, you cannot control. Today, with our powerful tools, we see the coming collapse of galactic civilization and we are all united in our desire to shorten the coming interregnum of thirty millennia down to a more manageable ten centuries, but the real challenge to the Fellowship will come in the haze be-yond our present ability to predict.*

—Excerpt from the Founder's *Psychohistorical Tools for Making a Future*

It was almost as if he had been manufactured without a past in the bowels of this incomprehensible Splendid Wisdom. What had it been like so long ago to be a young man with a past—if he had ever been young. Reclining in his aerochair, he drifted in a haze of loss, thrust into a distant future he didn't understand. He was weary. On the morrow he would find more energy to flail at the mindless mist. This watch . . .

He snoozed. Ghosts formed out of the mist, adult ghosts who had taken away his fam, promising him a new one with galaxy-spanning powers—he felt a child's trust, his own—but they had switched his fam for the entrails of a sheep, leaving him alone and famless to grow up with mere simian wits. The long dream-arms of a child tried to grab his mind back, but the scarified ghost kept him in restraints while carving up his fam, eating some pieces yet sharing choice morsels with his tall dark farman companion—a boy's precious secrets slithering down hungry gullets. The farman was grinning drunkenly, promising all the time that the sheep entrails would generate for him all the auspices he would ever need . . .

The man woke in panic. Gripping the armrests. The struggle to learn how to read again was setting his mind off into phantom spaces, even while he napped.

He had been concentrating for hours, unsuccessfully, willing himself to focus on something he had forgotten. He adjusted the aerochair into an upright position, facing the wall that leaked urine, surrounded by the stark simplicity of a lower-level hotel apartment in some cheap catacomb of Splendid Wisdom. What was left of a vital memory was on the tip of his tongue, but maddeningly unavailable. Perhaps the dream had touched its substance in the roundabout way of dreams. He should rest. But he couldn't. He was driven.

To recover from defeat.

It *galled* him that he had been defeated. But by whom? And about what? And when?

The half-memory had been driving him again and again to search through the distant files of Splendid Wisdom's main Imperial Archive in a desperate attempt to jog the tenuous pieces into place. Pinned to the wall, Hahukum Konn's meaningless picture of them grinning beside an ancient warrior's flying machine seemed to be an intrusive decoy planted to lead him away from his important memories. The memories that would explain his situation. There had to be *something* out there that would fit together with the phantom fragments in his mind.

The effort wasn't coming easily. For a quarter of a month, but especially for this exasperating watch, his awkward hands had been trying to work the lambent holograms of a comm console with finger gestures half controlled by the quantum matrices of a fam that no longer existed. Mistakes infuriated him. He had to fill in behavioral blanks by reason, by trial and error. He didn't know for what he sought. He couldn't remember what he had done as a psychohistorian. He did remember the urgency. Was it something important that he had written/discovered?

Eron Osa might have called upon the aid of the "charity" fam that now rode in the high blue collar around his neck—for appearance sake—but he had left it unconnected, tempting though it might be to take it under his neural control. He was even beginning to resent this common-issue fam designed to parole a convicted criminal (treason) whose personal fam had been found guilty and executed. He *wanted* to use it, but he could only guess at what ersatz data such a standard-issue mind held, what habits, what directives, what spy-implants. Its motivations would not be Eron's natural motivations. Whom would it serve? The men who had executed him? Better to run his archival quest using merely the limited abilities of his wetware.

He cursed himself for not having made, in the past, a more strategic use of his organic memory. That gray mush seemed to contain only the vaguest impression of grand strategic issues while being a register of unlimited trivial detail. As Eron jumped through the Archives, erratically bringing up holograms of this item and that item, guided by hunches he did not understand, straining to remember, he found that his mind delivered to him not what he wanted, not pertinent associations, but bizarre memories.

. . . a fugue of sexing with a sloe-eyed woman while playing truant from studying the physics of quantum foam. Were those the hills of Faraway beyond the ranch window? She was a wonderful tease. She had a full mouth that tapered into upturned lines and delicate fingers that seduced him into forgetting mathematics. They lay on linen with a border pattern of golden forsythia. Who was she?

. . . images of rafting down a river on the planet of his birth, the pyre-trees ablaze on rocky banks. What planet? Where was he born? His three-year-old memories of it were especially vivid—but what three-year-old cares about the name of his planet or doesn't mix it up with the name of his village or galactic sector?

. . . a boy wandering through the famous stone Library at Sewinna that dated back to pre-Interregnum times when it had been a military barracks for officers of the Empire. Why had his life taken him there?

Once, when his archival search led him into the rebuilding of Splendid Wisdom after the Sack, he was mentally flipped into what seemed to be his initiation as a Rank Seven Psychohistorian . . .

. . . under an enormous transept that rose five stories above the heads of his fellow robed acolytes. A wash of unnatural awe, overwhelming immensity. Upreaching arms of stone and fiber and metal, delicate hues of light, ethereal sounds that healed the spirit. Had such a drama happened? Was this "memory" real or a mere collage built out of his humiliating trial? Had he ever entered the Ranks?

None of these reveries sated him. They were too vague. Only when his search brought him near his fugitive goal did he feel ecstasy. The thrill came erratically, then was lost in illusive evasion. Sometimes he came close. Once when he was searching through a listing of Handler Theorems, he hallucinated upon the face of Hanis. Hanis of the Trial! He recognized Hanis, both furious and sarcastic, taking the lapse of his student Eron Osa as a personal affront, chastising his young protégé for even thinking about publishing without first having his methodology reviewed by his superiors.

Eron's organic brain flashed with insight! Psychohistorians did not publish. Then he *was* a psychohistorian! Slyly he even knew why psychohistorians did not publish. It had come to him as an odd footnote in his recent dream, an aside by the voracious farman ghost. The Fellowship was a secret society. If all men could predict history, then history became unpredictable and the Fellowship of Pscholars would lose its power to predict and control. To publish the methods of historical prediction was the ultimate sin. That felt exactly right—the ultimate sin. A man could lose his fam for committing such a sin!

He slept again, then woke up early to an ancient rhythm—though who knew in Splendid Wisdom what was day and what was night?—eager to pursue his spectral haunts. Perhaps he was making progress? For more than a watch of this session, the Archives taunted him with impalpable apparitions and with vivid events, perhaps from his life–few of them relevant. He was groping but he felt that he would be able to recognize "it" when he found "it" and so he continued to troll patiently. As if he had anything else to do. And on this watch, just as he was fatigued, just as the clock turned over and reminded him that this was his watch for sleep, still eager but at the same time almost ready to doze off, a sudden "hit" stirred a deep emotional dazzle.

He sat up with such alertness that his aerochair bobbed in the air.

He repeated the archived item.

Again the triggering image flowed in front of him in hologram–a gestalt of red symbols and multicolored action against a multigraph of a stable, self-perpetuating decision state. At first he was puzzled. Then he became cognizant of an unfamiliar mainstream mathematics that leaned heavily upon a notation commonly used by physical scientists. The math wasn't easy to understand without his fam–but: He recognized it as a rudimentary account of stasis. He *knew* that the psychohistorians did it better because *he* had once known more about stasis than any man alive. This wasn't what he was after, but it was a near miss that had triggered his mind.

Ah so!

The concomitant emotional rush came with a clear patter of babble as his organic mind intoned in a ponderous voice: "Early Disturbed Event Location by Forced Arekean Canonical Pre-posturing: An Analysis in Three Parts." He grinned uncontrollably. *That,* whatever in Space it meant, would be his, Eron Osa's, dissertation!

He pondered this miracle of precipitate memory, astonished. Wetware minds worked by peculiar magic! Where had such a revelation come from? He wasn't sure what the babble was about, except that it had to do with . . . psychohistorical stasis brought on by . . . what? He didn't know. All he knew was that this monograph was the object of his search and that he had to have a copy. It was going to be a "no" to sleep!

But being a vagued-out moron was utter frustration when you had memories of being a genius.

He paused before making a formal request for the monograph over the network. Were his actions being monitored? Doubtful. The Pscholars did not monitor people; they monitored trends. People acting alone had infinitesimal power. Defammed criminals were a threat to no one.

Half a watch and a growling stomach later, he suspected with a growing certainty and a terrible disappointment that his monograph had vanished from the Archives of the whole Imperialis star system. For a wrenching moment he wondered if he had ever written such a document. Yet he remained gut *certain* that he had! Was his certainty only an illusion brought on by the loss of his fam? Perhaps he had never gone past the *intention* to write.

Yet he could guess the real truth. His work had been erased. All copies were gone. Thoroughly gone; even his unique fam, with its ability to re-create the research, had been destroyed.

Now what?

Eron switched off the insubstantial console with a gesture of his finger and left his chair bobbing in midair. He paced about the strange apartment, too cramped for his aristo taste, wondering where he really was in relation to the rest of Splendid Wisdom. Where were his friends? Could that ancient psychohistorian who had sat on the very panel that had condemned him be a friend? He had only dared explore his immediate neighborhood. All else was a terrifying maze. Everything in the apartment folded into the wall, everything was white, not a trace of luxury or space. The dispozoria was leaking urine. This *wasn't* home! He buried his head in his arms.

Ping! The tiny, gleaming sphere of a Personal Capsule appeared in the functional wall niche, unnoticed.

*Of course* this wasn't his apartment; he was no longer an acolyte of the Psychohistorian Fellowship; he was alone, disowned, friendless, possessions confiscated, tossed into the lower warrens of Splendid Wisdom where he was condemned to think with treacherously slow neurons! It was infuriating . . . and for a moment he had a rush of uncontrolled rage that stunned him into an unbalanced mental fall because it was not resisted by the restraining calmness of fam input. He had shoved emotionally against a removed wall . . . flinging himself into emptiness.

The rage turned to instant consuming fear—without *his* fam he was a very asymmetrical animal. His zenoli training was useless, his brain-fam centering lost. He could no longer trust his own responses. This was worse than he had anticipated when he had been whole and accepting of the dangers inherent in his rash deeds. Being an asymmetrical animal didn't fit with his plans! Plans! Again his mind lurched out of control with a flash of joy at the thought of his brilliant agenda.

But, when he tried to remember the nature of such an agenda, he found only vacuum. He glanced about him in desperation. That was when he saw the Personal Capsule. It stopped him, reminding him of danger. He grumbled bitterly to himself—*My orders from the police.* Yet his eyes disclaimed such a conclusion; the omnipotent police, backed up by the certainties of psychology, had no need for supersecurity. A Personal Capsule? Here? How was he to read it without fam input?

Curiously he picked the small sphere from its niche. It opened in his hand and would not have opened for any other of the trillion inhabitants of Splendid Wisdom. There was no famfeed attachment. A tiny screen scrolled its message with a flashing warning that whatever scrolled off the top was unrecoverable. It read:

See Master Rigone at the Teaser's Bistro, Calimone Sector, AQ-87345, Level 78. (The Corridor of Olibanum.) I've already told Rigone what you'll need. I've got myself in a real fix and don't know how much more I can help. Your benefactor.

Inessential words began to fade, leaving only a list of critical information. By then the screen and sphere were well on their way to dust.

Eron Osa didn't even have to memorize the message. Rigone sounded like the name of a friend, or was it just a ghost figment of his dreams? From somewhere he knew of the Teaser's Bistro—a tolerated black market came to mind, a dive where young Fellowship rakes hung out to drink and rollick and have illegal attachments added to their fams. He couldn't recall ever having been in such a student den, but, for all he knew, he might have spent most of his idle time in just such a place.

# 22

## SEDUCED BY HISTORY, 14,791 GE

*On the death of that emperor [Caesar-of-August], his testament was publicly read to the senate. He bequeathed, as a valuable legacy to his successors, the advice of confining the empire within those limits, which Nature seemed to have placed as its permanent bulwarks and boundaries; on the west the Atlantic ocean; the Rhine and Danube on the north; the Euphrates on the east; and toward the south, the sandy deserts of Arabia and Africa.*

*Happily . . . the moderate system he recommended . . . was adopted by the fears and vices of his immediate successors. Engaged in the pursuit of pleasure, or in the exercise of tyranny, the first Caesars seldom showed themselves to the armies, or to the provinces; nor were they disposed to suffer, that those triumphs which their indolence neglected should be usurped by the conduct and valor of their lieutenants. The military fame of a subject was considered as an insolent invasion of the Imperial prerogative; and it became the duty, as well as interest, of every Roman general, to guard the frontier entrusted to his care, without aspiring to conquests which might have proved no less fatal to himself than to the vanquished barbarians. . . . Germanicus, Suetonius Paulinus, and Agricola, were checked and recalled in the course of their victories. Corbulo was put to death.*

—Edward Gibbon in the *Decline and Fall of the Roman Empire*
Volumes I–V, original editions (English) 1776–1788 AD, translation
by Colmuni of Archaist Press 75,398 AD

Nothing had come of his fam upgrade and that had chastened Eron, giving him much to mull over on the trip out from Neuhadra. The first leg of their journey would take them to ancient Sewinna, one of the first worlds colonized in this arm of space. He kept to himself on the ship, suddenly conscious that soon he would no longer be under anyone's tutorship. He practiced making decisions on his own—while he still had the indomitable Murek to run to. The fam mattered less and less; it was as if he had stopped grasping at flotsam to keep him afloat in the ocean and was now determined to learn how to swim. He kept away from Nemia, except to quiz her about her strange Egg which so fascinated him that he couldn't keep his hands off it. He was resenting his tutor less and less.

He found himself ignoring the stars, indifferent to the shipboard telescope which had so recently fascinated him. One peek at a star and you've seen them all! Glatim's odd group of roustabout sailors and meteoroid specialists teased him too much—once during a jump-stop they sent him after a left-handed nanowrench when he was trying to be helpful; so much for trying to be friends with motherless piss drinkers! And their snarks! The next time they set him up for laying traps to catch cable-eating shipsnarks he was going to put salt in their sugar!

He began to seclude himself at a spare console (found while looking for the left-handed nanowrench). It was scrunched up in a split-level storage closet off the library's memory racks. Even in that confined lair, with only a screen connection to the library, ignoring the stars wasn't easy. Ship's memory was overstocked with the minutiae of millions of solar systems, almost as if the ship were a police catalog of all the rocks in the universe ever booked as troublemakers. Special attention was given to gargantuan planets that gathered gangs of whatever rabble passed by, scattering them helter-skelter.

Still, it was possible to skip over all the celestial mechanics because the archives had also accumulated huge gobs of history about the regions of space they were passing through. History just seemed to come along with the bookish weight of solar system mechanics like a laundrator accumulating lint—mapping expeditions, the details of political crises caused by astronomical events, the fracas around the Epsilon Oramaist nova, the weird jungles on the moon of an almost star-size planet, endless background detail. Sometimes the interesting lint was just a story that one of Glatim's men had downloaded into the ship's archive years ago for personal reasons and no one had bothered to erase.

Because their first destination was Sewinna, he did a search on the Sewinnese Archipelago to see what he could find. The most interesting item he turned up was a fictional account of the Sewinnese revolt. That was early Interregnum stuff when an especially greedy viceroy had done the unthinkable and broken his domain off from the First Empire.

The story, composed only years after the now-buried historical event it described, was told from the viewpoint of a young soldier of noble blood still committed to the old values—and as blind as the author to the grand significance of the unfolding events. Eron found the tale fascinating because it wasn't a story built upon modern tropes and psychohistorical hindsight. Everything about it was strange, even the interwoven music was strange—blood-dancing stuff, primitively regal—yet accompanied by words so naïve that Eron couldn't believe he was hearing them. He famfed the whole novel out of the library so that he could mull it over during "bunk-watch" and use his fam's imaginator to blank out the underside of the upper bunk with the exotic images of battles and conflicts suggested by the adventure. He especially liked the lurid sex and the passionate men who were unafraid to use their blasters!

Viceroy Wisard (a historical figure) had ambitions on the throne. The author (probably correctly) supposed that Wisard took the newly crowned Boy Emperor to be too weak to reply to separatist audacity so far from the Center. Hadn't the minor Precinct of Nacreome already been lost a century earlier to his great-uncle? A spineless dynasty. The Galactic Empire obviously needed new Imperial blood of a more ruthless kind. Wisard's kind. Driving the Sewinnese into the hardship of war preparations, Wisard provoked only a revolt of his own people. (In the story the revolt is led by the fictional hero who rallies the Sewinnese to rejoin the Empire by carrying out their honorable duty, the obvious preference of the author.)

Meanwhile (as the hero drives Wisard and the remnants of his personal guard off planet) the Boy Emperor is marshaling his answer to insurrection through the Imperial Navy's most pitiless Admiral. His armada arrives with soldiers intent upon loot and a leader intent upon seizing the viceroyalty himself. (These were dramatic scenes of struggle on a large stage capable of a graphic elaboration much more interesting than a view of the bunk above!)

The naïve counter-revolution, though pro-Empire, was viciously suppressed, its goals not being in the self-interest of an Admiral who, like his vain predecessor, had unnatural ambitions. Again the Sewinnese populace suffered horribly. (The hero fights a valiant retrenchment in the thick of this setback and, finally, at the height of the bloodshed, bungles his desperate attempt to assassinate the new viceroy. The hero's honor, honed by failure, demands revenge, if not upon the Admiral, at least upon the youthful tyrant who sent forth this bloody fleet of retribution. In a breathless climactic action sequence the avenger smuggles himself into Splendid Wisdom, there to succeed in assassinating the Boy Emperor. The author's final tragic scene, pure fictional melodrama, sets both hero-assassin and dying Boy Emperor in an embrace where they tearfully confess their sins to each other before the Imperial Guards belatedly reduce the hero to cinders.)

Eron was lured into the role of director, his fam on overdrive creating sets, costumes, special minor characters, fantastically immense Imperial machinery, and even changing some of the clunky dialog, especially the words to the music. That was a sleepless night! He missed breakfast with his sailor-tormentors.

In the next few watches, as Eron delved into other sources to research the real-life Boy Emperor Tien-the-Young, 12,216–12,222 GE, he found that all of the information about Tien's real assassin had been lost in the violent Sack of Splendid Wisdom 116 years later. The historical record did mention that his agent, the Admiral who so cruelly punished the Sewinnese people for Wisard's sins, died at the hands of the only surviving son of a family he had imprisoned and tortured.

The story intrigued Eron's budding curiosity about history because it had been written only a century before the Sack and the author, though clearly troubled by the politics of his time, was among the vast majority of that age who could not *conceive* of an Empire at the end of its tether—troubles came and went but the Empire was forever—which was *amazing* because the whole novel was *about* the rot that would destroy the Empire within the century! The Founder had already told the Galaxy what would be happening and was himself centuries dead—but the Imperial Court and humanity just weren't listening! Even authors who wrote about the final decay—who lived it!—couldn't see the extent of the coming disaster!

He began to wonder if there wasn't something as preposterously obvious about his own age standing so hugely in front of his face that he couldn't see it. Was the real world invisible to the dulled perceptions of a boy trained to view the Galaxy from the clichéd axioms of a Ganderian? Was he living in a renaissance? Or was he standing at the top of a landslide that was set to sweep them down into a Vortex of Death? Was he looking out over a plateau of stability that would last a million years? Or was there a snark out there, hidden even from psychohistorians become complacent? He didn't know. He felt blind. He felt ignorant. He felt, above all, curious.

When the hypership reached Sewinna and popped into orbit while Glatim's men rounded up supplies needed at Trefia, Eron ran away. It was just another revolt to establish his independence, another notch in his history of rebellion—though this time it was driven by his passionate need to wander through the stones stronghold from which the whole Sewinnese Archipelago had once been ruled. The story's intrigues began inside that redoubt; the author had actually been one of the irregulars who had attacked it, and Eron *had* to touch the ancient stones with his own feet and the pillars with his own hands. It was a *real* place. (How would it compare with his vividly imagined version?) He fully intended to be back at the ship in the nick of time, the thrill of his own revolt being tempered by a growing common sense. But let his pompous tutor sweat a little.

Once there in the valley, and seeing the fortress high on that gentle mountain slope, its awesome historicity sobered him. Lovingly rebuilt out of its ruins to serve as Sewinna's historical library, it commanded a green landscape of forest and industrial farm. His personal revolt against his tutor began to shrink in stature as he climbed the hundred stone stairs of the grand processional way—broad enough to have allowed ten score Imperial troopers to climb abreast! He pretended to be a trooper but gave it up because his fam couldn't virtually duplicate himself two hundred times as a line formation of goose-stepping battle-scarred soldiers marching up the stone stairs, eyes front.

Reverent footfalls took him through the portal and into the cathedral light of the haughty basilica, where his petty defiance shriveled further, finally dying of humiliation when he reached the offices of the Imperial proxy. He stood silently in awe: here had begun, in this room of polished stone, a revolt *against a Stellar Empire then twelve thousand years mature, an Empire that had commanded more of the night sky than eyes could see!*

The chamber of the viceroy had been refurnished to match the decor of the study it had once been, complete with antique ivroid book-modules and reader, master screens, a huge desk, throne, maps, pacing rugs. A realm of daring! A pathologically cautious Ganderian would have allowed himself only to dream the defiance of such a man—for action has its own double-edged karma, glory or tragedy at the throw of the dice. Eron saw it all and it was all tragedy . . . the disgraced viceroy Wisard driven into exile among the Archipelago's minor red stars with the piratical remnant of his Imperial units, his ambition in tatters . . . his arrogant replacement taking measures against the people of Sewinna in salutary asepsis, ordering, from his safe viceroy's throne, the death of millions to teach his vain lesson—a lesson repaid, in time, with assassination, right here, as he ran abjectly to drop behind a desk he never reached.

While Eron stood frozen by his thoughts, ancient time rolled by, the tragic drama unfolding its variations on a theme. The rule of immature Tien-the-Young, murdered before his prime, gave way to the strongest Emperor seen in a century of decline. Sewinna's next viceroy, under the auspices of this more imposing emperor, marshaled the last great fleet before the Fall, again headquartered in this very room. The viceroy, a brilliant commanding general too dangerous to leave at court, led the resurgent Empire's successful attack against the growing might of Faraway, defeating them decisively—but his formidable Emperor's strength, in the end, manifested itself as a "first-strike" ability to execute the more successful generals of his reign. Soldiers, battleships, fleets—all devoured by the onrushing Interregnum!

Power to the Founder! Two and a half millennia later only this stone fortress remained of that turbulent era, its ghosts and their moans of woe talking to a child of psychohistory among the shadows of a forgotten past dimly resurrected by the effete enthusiasm of scholars.

A sobered Eron Osa called in to tell the Glatim boys where he was and when he would be back, earlier than he had intended. He mentioned in passing, deadpan, that he was researching the central Sewinnese library for the latest on left-handed nanowrenches. They laughed. A relieved tutor took the comm and reminded Eron sternly that they would *have* to leave without him if he didn't turn up on time. Eron promised, and even promised to call again to reconfirm his return.

He got back early, but a full watch later than he'd planned—and he *did* call in to confirm the delay. On his way to the spaceport a monster bookstore found him and trapped him in its history section. Two books on pre-Imperial economics cost him almost all of the rest of the money he had on him, but the third, a treasure, he found thrown on a table rack with the unwanteds from an estate clearance, mostly cheap media for prefam kids.

*The Decline and Fall* . . . was printed on delicate cellomet with elaborate typography for the headings. It had a sturdy binding with an electronic back cover addendum that contained all the previous copies from which it had been translated and many of the documents that had been original sources, all in the original alphabets with correlation dictionaries. And alphabets he'd never seen before! He couldn't tell how old the history was, but it was about *really* old stuff!

When his tutor saw the three new books in a sack he grumbled, but Eron offered no apology for that. He did try to apologize for running away without a word. His pseudoparent only shut him up. "We're almost there. At Faraway you'll be your own master. You might as well start now. Asinia Pedagogic doesn't run its school *in loco parentis;* you study or you don't—it doesn't matter if you are twelve or fifty. You can be sure of only two things: one, they'll deduct their due from your credit stick every semester and, two, if you aren't certifiable due to lack of study, they won't certify you. Run away and they won't chase you. There is nothing to run away from anymore." He picked out the fat book and thumbed through it like he wasn't used to handling pages of cellomet. "Looks like you got stung on this one! Look when it was purported to have been written." He pointed at the dates 1776–1788 AD, and laughed.

"That's pretty early in Imperial history," Eron said apprehensively.

"No, no. It's a *Rithian* book. They never adopted Imperial Time. Being Rithians they date events from the birthday of a Rithian who, after being murdered, ascended into chaos with a bang and created the galaxies for man to inhabit. And seeing that it was good, named it heaven. Whatever con shop on Rith published your book to catch some naïve tourist is claiming that it was written"—he paused—"some 743 Imperial centuries ago." Eron's tutor guffawed. "I doubt if any Rithian could read back then or even walk upright. To this day they still have the bewildered gait of tree-swingers who have chopped down all their trees and are looking for something to climb. Some historians think the entire body of their ancient literature is a forgery, and wasn't created until after they mongrelized with their Eta Cumingan conquerors and figured out how to count money on their fingers." He shook his finger at the book by Gibbon. "It damn well better be a copy—I don't think cellomet will last that long if it's not kept under helium."

"Aren't we descended from Rith?"

"So they claim—along with every other planet in the Sirius Sector."

"You don't think it's true?"

His tutor shrugged. "It could be. They certainly have the simian genes and the backbone of an animal who walks on all fours to prove it. Why shouldn't we be descended from a planetful of blowhards? A good joke, if true. It's hard to tell because Rith produces half of the Galaxy's con artists. Their favorite scam is to sell you an artifact that they will swear predates hyperspatial travel and, if you look especially gullible, will swear on the head of their mother that it predates space travel. They have factories producing the stuff. Some poor guy chained to a table probably wrote your charming book no more than five hundred years ago."

"It's real. Just read a page and you'll see!" Eron thrust the book at his tutor and opened to a page at random.

Scogil had never downloaded Englic but he could read the first page of the introduction in the archaic but eminently standard galactic of a pedantic editor. "It must have been forged no earlier than the last couple of thousand years—sounds like a rip-off of the plot of the Interregnum. Kid, the Rithians are the Galaxy's most adept forgers, right down to the radioactive traces . . . anyway . . . who's going to read your book to check on them? You can't famfeed it." He flipped to the end. "It's three thousand pages long!"

"I can *read* it in an afternoon!"

"By eye? Good luck. And in case you ever let Nemia do an astrological reading of your unpromising future, you were born, Rith time"—he paused to do a calculation in his head, converting at the ratio of 1057 Rithian years for every galactic standard millennium—"on the second hour, third of februan, 80,362 AD. Don't ask me under what constellation—that's Nemia's department."

Eron took his book back, firmly, and started to slink away.

"Not so fast, young man. I owe you a spanking. Did you think we would have gallivanted all over Sewinna tracking you down?"

"No."

"We would have left you stranded. Of necessity."

"I know. That's why I'm here," said Eron contritely. "I did some thinking."

"Good."

# THE HYPERLORD MAKES A
# RENDEZVOUS, 14,791 GE

*In the Salki version of the Chronicles of Early Splendid Wisdom during the turbulent twilight of the Kambal Dynasty in the mid–second millennium of the Galactic Era . . . 1346–1378 GE . . . it is told that the villas surrounding the harbors of the Calmer Sea were sacred shrines of meditation, a haven within the hectic ardor of a local interstellar trading mecca, where Splendid Wisdom's minor empire controlled 90,000 central star systems and its influence extended far beyond its borders.*

*By the malfeasance of late-dynasty emperors and the bribes taken by Emperor Kambal-the-Eighth, all was forfeited to the nomadic armadas of the Frightfulpeople who were then forcibly entwining themselves into the central galactic trade routes, even to the establishment of their main base of operations on the shores of the Calmer Sea of Splendid Wisdom. Disguised as a spiritual movement offering an alternative to a wealth-mad economy, they blatantly usurped Imperial prerogatives and finally named one of their own as Emperor during the Time of Two Emperors.*

*The ancient Kambal nobility eventually led a retaliation that cost six billion Splendid lives and an annoying million Frightful Soldiers before it was crushed by the Frightful usurper. [The casualty figures are probably exaggerations— moderation not being a feature of the Frightfulterror's "beatification" of the Empire. The earliest secondary accounts date from three hundred years later. All surviving records contradict one another. Ed.] Frightfulperson Tanis-the-First, 1378–1495 GE, familiarly referred to as Tanis One-Eye, reigned for 117 years, dominating the indigenous population by a truly massive immigration policy and control of water. It was he who apportioned the Seas of Splendid Wisdom among his barons so that . . .*

*. . . after grinding millennia of political maneuvering, the power of the Frightfulpeople faded. By 9892 GE, when Splendid Wisdom openly proclaimed*

*its suzerainty over the whole of the Galaxy via the Pax Imperialis, memory of the Frightful conquest, of the Frightfulpeople's mighty draining of the oceans, etc., remained only in the minds of a loyal Imperial subclass of petty nobles . . . and . . . by the end of the Interregnum the Frightfulpeople had essentially disappeared from the peerage. Today . . .*

—From the Explanatorium at the Calmer Pumping Station

Such a backtracking out-of-the-way circuitous route! Jama looked at the deceptive lines Katana had been sketching on the tabletop. How could this meandering scheme possibly get them from the center of galactic power to the legendary Telomere City of peripheral Faraway, all of 65,000 leagues distance along light's vector? The Hyperlord was not amused.

They were awaiting their ship's docking over a snack of pastry and hot himu tea. In an alcove of the star-station above Splendid Wisdom, Kikaju Jama's female companion and newly assigned bodyguard set down her cup and pointed with her stylus at the ship symbols scrolling across the ribbon screen out in the corridor. "We're on," she said, rising and stabbing the table's service menu for a printout of her crude diagram. "Let's go." She pocketed the map and erased the table's mind.

Kargil Linmax had insisted that Jama bring her *and* that it be she who arranged not only the evasive details of their journey but all their subsequent contacts—her expertise being that of an ex-officer of Naval Intelligence. When Jama did not move at her command, the Frightfulperson Katana of the Calmer Sea turned to catch his eyes. She threw out a glimmer of humor. "You're not coming? Is an old man like you afraid to bunk with a free girl like me now that our flirtation is past its public stage?"

"I was thinking of the soulful eyes of your daughter as we said good-bye."

"And"—beamed Katana—"I'm thanking Space that, for a while, my six-year-old Otaria is going to be tens of thousands of leagues beyond your ever-lecherous clutches. I'm appalled by how much she likes you!"

He rose with offended dignity. His special attention to the delightful Otaria was no more than a recognition that recruitment to the cause *did* have to begin when a candidate was young. Teaching her how to count kisses was hardly lechery. After all, she was only ten years away from being sixteen! His mind refocused upon immediate concerns.

Faraway was a convenient destination for Jama in that, once there, he would be within striking distance of Zurnl—albeit it was somehow a suspicious destination because of that proximity. Did the seeker-after-the-galactarium already know Jama's purpose? He/she had deposited enough money in blind escrow at Telomere City to pay for luxury accommodation to Faraway, access conditional upon the production and demonstration of the ovoid in working order; only then would the guarantor reveal him-/herself and release the fares and the fee. Such a deal, sweet as it was, left Jama feeling ill at ease—too much was unknown, too much could go wrong. But maybe the deal wasn't that unusual; the ovoid was, after all, an artifact of the ancient Faraway renaissance and was certainly of Faraway manufacture even if it did contain components alien to the early Faraway culture. One might expect the main interest in such an exotic galactarium to come from citizens of Faraway with historical sentiments.

Risks aside, how else was he to finance this expedition?

But it did make Jama paranoid to have to meet strangers at so distant a place from his own friends and protectors. Suppose he was robbed? But the Red Sun Bank brokering the deal had once been the most powerful bank in the Galaxy and had a ridiculously conservative reputation. And the sale (less the finder's fee for Igor Comoras) would finance his expedition to Zurnl. Did it even matter if he were to be robbed of his jade artifact? He had made a copy of the important astronomical data contained therein. There was, of course, the matter of the undeciphered material embedded in a deeper layer.

They were wafted weightless through their boarding tube and asked to strip naked at a medical node bulked to the end of the tube, their clothes fed through a decontaminator while they were routed along an assembly path where nanomechanical invasions, via painless injection, exterminated whatever unwanted and invisible hitchhikers they carried. At the end of their naked trek, their clothes were restored to them. Jama was embarrassed by the holes in his hose but at least he didn't have to shake hands with the receiving purser while in the nude. The purser alternately checked off names and pointed passengers in a helpful direction.

After ducking under the pipes in the corridor that led to their cabin, the Hyperlord regretted aloud the third-class accommodations he had bought. Their contract specified first-class fares for the bearers of the galactarium, and first-class payment was in escrow, but Jama had always tended toward thrift in things which didn't show and Katana had *insisted* on the anonymity. It was probably for the better. They had no way of knowing how much a charter to off-route Zurnl was going to cost them—and that expense was *not* in the contract. He bumped his head a fourth time.

Katana shrugged off the gray bulkhead barrenness. "I'm navy. I came up from the ranks. In fact, I think you're brave to wedge into such a tiny berth with a murderess." She guffawed innocently and when he didn't share her amusement, she chided him. "You *must* laugh at my macabre sense of humor; I require it for a long journey. Otherwise, I transmogrify into a Jon Salasbee." That was a reference to the popular drama *Knife Alive* about a lower-corridor medic's fam&wetware struggles, Jon's fam desperately trying to pass Jon off as a sane humanitarian, bringing surcease to the unfortunate, while, all the time, Jon is terrorizing his community with a knife in the darkness during his wetware's slow descent into psychosis.

"My dear, laughter should be no problem for a man of my fortitude." They turned around, careful to avoid the overhanging storage space, and hunched down on the bunk. "I promise faithfully, on pain of death, to laugh every time you tickle my flesh with a knife." Gossip held that she *was* a Jon Salasbee who had murdered her husband with a knife, perhaps slowly—though Kargil's opinion differed.

"A man of my dreams. In such close quarters you should become hairless from your prolonged laughter before we reach Faraway," she nudged.

This was a woman who enjoyed teasing men's fears, thought Jama, and a woman to play along with if one could remember to flirt first and be afraid afterward. "All the better: if there is naught between you and me to cause you to itch in irritation, my sleep will be sounder!"

"I think we'll do nicely." She grinned. "I'll sleep on top of you the first night and you can sleep on top of me the second. I suspect you're safe even if you snore—it doesn't seem that I'm going to have room enough to use my knife!"

"Do you suppose we'll be able to move our hips?" he said, getting back to the important subject.

"We can try."

The trip went uneventfully. They spent most of their cabin time exploring the capabilities of Jama's jade ovoid. It projected the stars so well that it gave them the illusion of space—as long as they didn't extend their hands into the starry blackness to feel for bulkhead or pipe. The Hyperlord was intrigued by the artifact's obvious astrological versatility, though he didn't have a clue how to use it to make a reading. Katana's curiosity located the coordinates of thirteen once-secret military bases of the ancient Faraway stellarpolitical sphere and forty-nine of the false coordinates for Stars&Ship bases—cryptically annotated with their true coordinates ages ago in a Faraway military script that was obviously meant for use by someone's naval reconnaissance teams. For what purpose? So much history had been lost! And why had their benefactor been interested in military bases?

Frightfulperson Katana of the Calmer Sea, for all her bluster, turned out to be a good lover, efficient and affectionate. He decided that she only pretended to be fierce because of her overwhelming name. What a name to have to live with! Nevertheless he was happy not to be her husband.

Their transfer to a second and larger vehicle for the next jag of their journey was routine except that Hyperlord Jama lost all his wigs. That gave the Frightfulperson an excuse to shave his head and dress him in the black garb and silver buttons of a jackleg. She even slapped a neural fibulator on his backbone to change his walk. No one would remember seeing a fop. Jama had disappeared.

The third transfer, to an undistinguished short-run tramp, turned out to be a con racket in which they were gently informed that "an unfortunate mistake" had been made in their reservations and that therefore the ship was "reluctantly" forced to "drop them off" at an "inconvenient location" unless an additional "service fee" was forthcoming to ensure their well-being. In his guise of jackleg Jama felt compelled to vent his rage. The skipper became appropriately apologetic—but remained uncooperative.

Katana fumed in a different way. She muttered under her breath about cheating Rithian scum. Aloud she promised to pay the additional fee—and indeed it arrived within a decawatch—in the form of a naval boarding party. The carrier's skipper, an upper-caste Rithian of galactic stock mongrelized by sapiens lineage, was indicted by the commander of the boarding party under an obscurely ancient Imperial law which had never been rescinded by the Pscholars. His trial lasted a mere thirty-two inamins, whereupon he was summarily executed in front of his dimwit sapiens crew, all rigidly at attention.

Katana cheered as the execution proceeded and afterward sliced off the dead skipper's ears as a souvenir. Teach the Rithians a lesson. It was an old Stars&Ship custom from the harsh campaigns of the First Empire, probably originating in the customs of the Frightfulpeople. Jama made a rapid reevaluation of his companion's character.

*She wasn't joking!*

How could such bloodlust have survived into modern enlightened times? No longer playing the victimized jackleg, he was appalled in his inner soul at this wholly unexpected display of violence even though he was an admirer—an advocate—of the stimulating violence engendered by the Interregnum. How could such ferocious genes have been passed on through her family for ten millennia, undiluted? What kind of people was he now attracting to his revolution? How could this woman have such an angelic daughter who sat in his lap and teased his nose? Did Katana have an ear of her husband mounted somewhere as a souvenir of recompense for his insults? Jama was going to ask her the next time they made love. And how did one get ears past the eyes of the customs bureaucrats?

The Frightfulperson proceeded to review the chastised crew, souvenir ears between forefinger and thumb, while with the fingers of the other hand she playfully tweaked *their* ears, chiding them for malicious stupidity with a politeness that mocked their previously hypocritical politeness. When she saw Jama's pale face, she grinned. "I don't like the Rithian sense of humor," she said of her kidnappers. "Let them sweat!"

"Now, is it fair to judge all Rithians by the standards of this miscreant crew?"

Gallantly, three members of the boarding party agreed to pilot the ship to its original destination as a free naval service granted to law-abiding citizens of the Second Empire. There the jackleg and his hussy vanished. Whereupon an itinerant spaceman and meek wife appeared to take steerage passage in a transport bound for the inner planets of a dim red star, Rhani, which was a minor dependent system of the Sewinnese Archipelago.

Finally a chartered yacht, registered at Rhani, brought businessman and secretary into Faraway orbit. The yacht, not planetworthy, docked at a space station where they transferred to a ferry. The ferry aerobraked in a graceful glide over a river's meanderings across thousands of kilometers of reddish desert, the whole countryside devoid of bureaucratic warrens! How had Faraway ever ruled? The scenery lacked even the *ruins* of a bureaucracy! Then came megahectares of forest with scant signs of habitation! Only at the last moment did they collide with civilization as the ferry descended in a sickening drop down to the outskirts of Faraway's Telomere City.

From there the mad scramble into the City through underground tunnels was a more homey adventure. It almost reminded Kikaju of the comforts of Splendid Wisdom. But that wasn't to last. They had rented a room in the imposing Hober Hostel. For a Hyperlord used to ever-present ceilings, the nearby buildings were very tall and the drop from the hostel window sickening—and distances! From the luxury of their fortieth-floor aerie, they overlooked *the* Mall of Knowledge, which had been laid out by the original colonists after a sketch by the Founder himself. Kikaju hung on to the curtains for safety while he let his eyes stray down the Mall. Open-air skyscrapers offended his sense of balanced architecture.

To the left end of that extended plaza was the Palace of the Chancellor. It was hard to believe that the Chancellor of this unimpressive university town of only twenty million had once held sway over the Galaxy. The signs of boondocks were everywhere. Trees along the great Mall open to the air!

To the right, far across the haze at the other end of the Mall, the fading light of Faraway's reddish sun cast shadows on the columns of the Mausoleum of the Founder, seeming to radiate the power of that mythical figure who had continued to make pronouncements from there long after his death. Jama was startled to find that the vast scene inspired reverence in his cynical soul. The Founder's dead hand still wound up the clockwork of the Galaxy. There was an exclamatory expression they all used when overwhelmed by sudden insight. *By the eyes of the Founder!* Yes, the sight impacted one's emotions—and if indeed there were a second focal point to the Galaxy outside of Splendid Wisdom, it was here in that magnificent Mausoleum.

While Kikaju held onto the curtains for dear life and paid his silent respects to the majesty of an ancient man, Katana had been working the room's console to contact their guarantor. But the agreed-upon coded message was evoking no response. "Nothing," she said.

Jama's heart dropped a full forty floors. Had they come all this way for nothing? Ah, but he had already made allowance for that. He was impressed by his perspicacity at having included a clause in their contract which forced a default payment in case of nonappearance. "I suppose that means they wish us to show respect by cooling our heels for a few revolutions of Faraway." To relieve his anxiety he closed the curtains.

"No." She smiled. "It means they haven't arrived yet. They cannot be Faraway citizens. So. We wait. I've already set up a watch-screen to catch likely off-planet visitors. We are now spiders. By a jerk in the web we'll know who they are and when they arrive—*before* they contact us. An old Naval Intelligence trick. If they turn out to be police, we just vanish. How do you like our room? Two beds! We can have sex twice in one night!"

"I've been more taken by the decor. Such taste!" He was admiring the rear of his head inside the gilded frame of a magic mirror. He switched to profile view and tried a cocky rising-of-the-nose. "If I denuded these magnificent walls of their ornamentation and sneaked off into the dark of space with my loot, I'd make a fortune back on Splendid Wisdom."

"They're only *replicas* of beau monde," said Katana disdainfully, unwilling to admit that any provincial this far out on the Rim could have expensive taste, no matter how adept they might once have been at gauche conquest.

"You don't have my eyes or my savvy for antiques. *Of course* such priceless artifacts are replicas, though you can't have any guarantee of that without a nanometric examination—but I'd wager good betting odds that on all of Splendid Wisdom no dealer has templates for these particular delights. It's a subtle theme the hostel has running across the walls of our rooms." His arm swept out to include the whole hallway and adjoinments.

"First," he continued, "there isn't a single item enshrined here that isn't pre-Empire. Pre–Kambal-the-First. These artifacts were old when Splendid Wisdom was just another upstart trading world battling its way out of an agricultural age on the labor of farmers playing at engineer, dwarfed by the resources of the Sotamas and the Machan Confederacy. Why—when glorious aboriginal craftsmen were working the genesis of these astonishments, your sanctimonious Frightfulpeople weren't even a gleam in your ancestors' eyes, they being busy scrabbling out a life as raucous comet-belt thieves." He hooked a thumb in his sash for effect.

"Second: Though no single item presented here for our pleasure came out of the same cultural stew or time, they all have a grand affinity. They were picked by a person of immense artistic sensibilities to embellish each other. That adds immeasurably to their value. My compliments to the Hober's staff." He marveled. "Look at the shade of this glaze against the texture of that tapestry in the shifting light of the auroral piece over the beds!" His roving eyes went round as they met a small painting set in its own alcove. "Look at *this*!" He examined the icon carefully at short distance. "I've heard of these. I've never seen one. It predates the hypership. Gummurgy, probably. Look how it simply radiates its isolation! Imagine gazing at the sky, knowing that your ancestors had come from the stars and that the stars were *still* unreachable! How clever to hide such a lonely icon away in this little alcove. Why . . . there couldn't have been more than two thousand settled worlds at that time—all in the Sirius Sector—linked by only the most tenuous sublight contact. Such exquisite savagery in its expression!"

"Where's our bank?" asked Katana.

The Hyperlord readjusted to present time, somewhat irritably. At the spaceport he had bought and famfed a tri-vid map of Telomere City for reference. Reluctantly he reopened the curtains and set the map to active from the viewpoint of their room's coordinates, zooming the wireframe outlines, fam-imposed upon his visual cortex, to match those features he saw naturally from their high window.

Once oriented, he faded the wireframe. He colored their branch of the Red Sun Bank in bright polka dots to make it easy to spot, noted its real position, then canceled his fam's overlay. "Over there," he said, pointing with his finger in a way that even a lightspeed-shackled barbarian of sixty-five thousand years ago would have understood.

"Well," said Katana, "at least the building appears to be too solid to collapse into the street in the next month or so. How these free-standing structures ever hold up so long against an atmospheric breeze has always been a mystery to me. It is counter-intuitive but I suppose we can trust Faraway engineering even if we won't be able to sleep!"

# ASINIA PEDAGOGIC, ACADEMIC YEAR 14,791 GE

*While Agander's night sky whirls*
*in fright from the sounding skirl*
*of battle's bite, we hurl*
*our knives to death's delight.*

*Heaven sits above this plight*
*Indicting space born army churls:*

*Across the starlit dome of pearls,*
*elder wisps excite eye's sight,*
*streaming sprites with gaseous curls,*
*God's banner of flame unfurled.*

*Distant burls of sun ignite to form whose future world?*

—From "Ode to Agander's Night" by Emperor Arum-the-Patient,
5641–5662 GE

Eron was shocked when they reached Faraway and he was sent planetside, alone, with only a script of introduction to his new advisor at Asinia Pedagogic, a one-night hotel reservation, a map, his kick and holster—pointedly wrapped in a copy of Faraway's weapons laws—a suitcase and a credit stick. *I'm only a Ganderian boy,* he complained to himself as the ferry braked through the atmosphere, isolated in the comm-blindness of its own ionic wash. They were passing over the nightside. There was nothing to see of legendary Faraway but a few twinkling ground lights and a clear sky, sparse of stars. *I should be in bed.* He was missing mommy and the green hills of Agander.

His reservation turned out to be a formerly vogue room in a Telomere City hotel with invisible roboattendants who gave advice out of walls and made beds while no one was looking, its rambling buildings tucked away behind shrubs within walking distance of Asinia but not part of the campus. Once settled in, he took off on a stroll through what had to be an ancient part of Telomere. His random walk led him to explore the covered corridors of the Pedagogic—built thousands of years ago, perhaps even by the first citizens of Faraway in their nostalgia for the confined claustrophobia of Splendid Wisdom, and now conserved by its modern citizens in nostalgia for a glorious past when Faraway had dominated a chaotic stellar realm of multimillions.

Off the arched passageways a well-kept park meandered along a stream. Eron met students he might someday know but he didn't speak to them. A robocrawler tended a flower bed. Each tree had a plaque commemorating which group or person had planted it. One immense tree was so old it dated back to the last centuries of the Interregnum. He climbed such a tree to get a good view of the back of the sprawling Palace from where the Chancellors had once commanded the stars. He recognized it from its famous pictures, but it wasn't as awesome as a picture. Now the Palace was just another building among many, not even the tallest.

When he jumped from the tree, he mentally shifted to an even older era and planet to become a space-launched Imperial trooper in a grav-chute, a revanchist attacking Sewinna. With pretend Sewinnese laid out dead all around him, he ate in a crowded bistro, content to be feared by the locals. Centuries passed. By the time he returned to his hotel, alone, he had his discharge docs from the navy and had reverted to civilian status as a mysterious farman from some distant place that no one here had ever heard of.

The next morning he tried to register. They kept telling him he was in the wrong place. They sent him to different cubbyholes and up and down stairs. They were always polite. The machines were politer than the people. He began to have a horrible suspicion that he was being sent after a left-handed nanowrench while the snarks watched him from the ventilation louvres. Finally, not knowing why he felt so shy, he asked a student, a tall lanky fellow whose abstract eyes suggested that he was ignorant of all bureaucratic conspiracies.

"Ah-ha!" said the accosted one, suddenly smiling fiendishly. "You're new here! And confused! Follow me! This is a university. Universities haven't changed since *Homo erectus* anointed the first tenured professor in the jungles of Java way back when. I'm Jaiki, known more formally as Jak the Beanstalk."

Eron was taken across campus into a building—whose doors didn't open automatically—and up the stairs which spiraled off a lobby, no sign of a levitator—and down a hall to a door with a hideous facemask that looked the lanky student in the eye and said simply, "Pass, friend." The door *unlocked* with a muffled click—but Jak had to *open* it manually.

"Anybody home?" bellowed Jak. "I found us a new roomy! I got him before he could sign in. We're saved!"

Saved from what, Eron couldn't guess. He and his new acquaintance had entered a friendly lounge with a girl dozing on the couch. Eron could see a kitchen through an open door. A curious student poked his head out of the kitchen and another giant stepped from an adjacent bedroom-study. They were all older than Eron. The girl opened her eyes and evaluated the boy-student before returning her attention to Jak. "How do you know he hasn't already been assigned?"

"I told you I caught him before he could register."

The giant explained, "The last roomy they sent us was a *disaster*. It took us half a year to drive him crazy enough to leave. Glad to meet you. I'm Pee-wee."

"What makes you think our little friend here is any better?" asked the girl pragmatically.

Jak had an answer for everything. "I found him when he was confused. That makes him trainable."

"The last one was very confused and *wasn't* trainable," complained a voice from the kitchen. "He always left the kitchen a mess and ate food out of the non-common stashes."

"And left crumbs in the lounge," complained the girl.

"And had terrible taste in music," complained Jak.

"I still have to register?" complained Eron, woefully.

"Hey, we have to get you settled in first!" Jak flung open one of the doors that connected into the lounge. "Your room. It's clean. The four of us busted our muscles all of yesterwatch cleaning it out. Keep it that way and we will *love* you."

Eron saw a monk's quarters, a fraction of the size of his room at home on Agander. It had a single bed, a tall armoire, and a club chair. The console looked adequate: plenty of desk space, four large screens, and an alcove for holograms—which, if connected to a decent archive, would be a good setup. The only luxury was an intricately designed rug on the floor showing a couple of centuries of wear. Where was he going to put his books? He scanned the room for an appurtenancer so he could build some shelves.

"Looking for your roboassistants? There aren't any."

"No. I was looking for a place to put my books."

"Books!" Jak stuck his head back outside the room and called to the girl still lounging on the couch. "Marrae. We've caught another freak. He likes books!"

Marrae immediately jumped up to stick her head under Jak's arm. "Where?" She smiled at Eron. "I love you already. It's so lonely living with these jerks. Don't panic so quick! I know where I can get you a shelf!"

"Hey," came a voice from the kitchen, "bring him in here. I want to show him how to keep the kitchen clean. I'm Bari, head kitchen ogre!"

"Later! I'm registering him." Jak was at the console pulling up files. "What's your admission number?"

"14791-1261."

The mike picked that up so Jak didn't have to input it. Then Jak went into exclamation overdrive, his eyes on the display that had formed on the screen. "Eron! *Why* are you trying to register? You've already been registered for a month!" He typed rapidly. "I'm pulling a fast one and filling in your address for you–here." He perused the screen and talk-gestured a few more commands. "Wow. Fees paid for eight years, too. Special Category. Tonight you can take us out to dinner, Rich Man! I'm only joking. Rich guys are human, too."

Marrae peeked in again to look at Eron. "Special Category!"

"What's that?" asked Eron.

"When you are so rich Admin just takes your money and leaves you alone," Jak supplied.

Marrae marveled. "How old are you?"

"Twelve." Eron wanted to lie, but it wasn't a good idea to lie until one was oriented. Besides, how could he lie? He was smaller than all of them.

"A playboy at twelve, already," Marrae continued to marvel.

"She's just envious," said Jak. "She's on scholarship and they want blood in their stick. She has to work her butt off to stay in school. You've got a different kind of a problem. If you *don't* work your butt off, no one cares." He looked at the screen again. "Your advisor is Reinstone. Good idea to go see him right now."

"How do I make an appointment?"

"With that old codger? When he's in, he's in. I'll take you over. We'll bring a slice of bread with us and I'll lay down a trail of crumbs so you can find your way back after he's baked you into a cookie!"

Jak took the long way around, having some business of his own. He dropped into a lab where he had a project going. The professor chatted about stuff that didn't make any sense to Eron so he asked his fam to pick up, and explain to him, a few of the key words being bandied about. No use. Not in Eron's dictionary. Jak and professor wrote with fingertips on a whiteboard for a while, math and arrows and lists, adding colors in a mysterious way and furiously erasing as the argument progressed. A whiteboard! Eron hadn't seen one of those since nursery school when they'd been teaching him how to use his fam! This one seemed to be malfunctioning–they were erasing by hand.

Jak ended the argument. "I'll think about it. Got to go." He led Eron away through another maze of buildings and courtyards, eventually into an atrium of, presumably, offices. "That one," Jak said, pointing with a lanky arm to the first of the doors with lancet-arches and adding, "I don't want the old codger even to see me!" as he began to scurry off.

Eron waited in front of the door for the electronic butler to announce him. Nothing happened. He knocked, not sure that the sound would even get through a door that thick. Whoever was in there took his time about answering. A man at least one hundred and forty (or fifty) years old opened the door quizzically. "Well?"

"I've been told you're my new advisor?" Eron asked timorously, annoyed at the question in his voice.

The old man was already on his way back to his comfortable reading chair. "Loading me down with children, are they? Your name?" His back was now turned.

Eron didn't notice, being too busy with his astonishment. The office continued for at least thirty meters in depth and it was all bookcases full of books. He loved the man already.

"Your name, lad."

Eron handed the man his introduction script. "Eron Osa, sir."

Reinstone ignored the script, setting it aside, unread. He was looking at a screen on which data had been triggered by the name. It seemed to sour him. The love was not going to be reciprocated. "You were registered a month ago. You're late."

"I just arrived last night, sir. Off planet."

"That doesn't make you any prompter. Tardy is tardy. And worse, a Special Category rank!"

"Is that bad, sir?" Eron was determined not to be affronted.

"Of course it's bad. It means those sycophants up in Stick Stuffing are more interested in money than in good students. Hmmm. Entrance exams waved. And you've submitted no school records." His eyes looked up and drilled into Eron. "That means you've been thrown out of one-and-every school you've ever attended." He caught Eron's grimace in a way that reminded Eron of a crocodilian in Agander's zoo snapping up a carcass just tossed its way. "You've been highly recommended by a Murek Kapor of whom we know nothing. He's probably your father's janitor. Special Category means that regulations do not permit me to discipline you, no matter your errors or your laziness. Money counts. Therefore you will not be disciplined—at least not while anyone important is looking. No discipline allowed!" he repeated aghast. "For that I'm supposed to be pleased?"

Eron was standing rigidly at attention as he had done so many time before when his father was lecturing him. The temptation to sass was irresistible. "Even if I steal your books or put frogs in your bed?"

"Well, now, young man, a citizen of Faraway has never been known to stick slavishly to regulations when it comes to frogs in his bed. But you can steal all the books you want; I'm afraid that's been the worst folly of my youth. However, you won't be interested in any of my books. It says grandly in your 'résumé' that you have mathematical ambitions?" The question mark was like a scythe.

"Mathematicians aren't interested in books? I'm *very* interested in books. I've fallen in love with books. I own four! One is probably a fake, but I got it for a song and a couple of spare bits in a stick."

"Fantastic! You actually own four comic books!" came the sarcastic reply. "*My* books are all full of *poetry*. Thousands of years of poetry. The poems of Emperors and the poems of slaves. Primitive sagas from the early ages of the hyperdrive. Turbulent pre-Imperial poetry. Polished court poetry. Folk poetry. The poems of obscure back stellar cultures. An idiosyncratic fraction of the poetic soul of mankind. Nothing at all to do with comics, maudlin romance, or mathematics."

"Do you have the poems of Emperor Arum-the-Patient? He conquered the Ulmat in the fifty-six hundreds."

"You meant by your fifty-six hundreds, this infernal *new* system of counting, I suppose? By the calendar of the poets that would be"–he paused–"the 707th century. Let's see. Arum-the-Patient . . . yes, I remember him. Odd chap. Assassinated by his mother. You must be from the Ulmat Constellation if you even know his name. I have a first edition of his poems, autographed copy." Reinstone smiled, not quite like a crocodilian this time. He pecked out something on his pad; there was a clunk among the bookshelves as a volume was ordered front and center. "Bring it to me." Eron saw the slim book standing at attention, out from among its comrades. He didn't realize at first that Reinstone had asked *him* to bring the book, but there was no robomech in sight and so he fetched it. He'd never seen such a fine binding, and the pages were gold edged. He didn't dare open it before delivering it to Reinstone's scrawny hands. After a sigh, the old advisor handed it back. "Keep it. It's yours. A bribe to keep you coming and telling me about your work."

"I couldn't, sir."

"Why? You don't want to *work*? You like the *playboy* style of life you've set up for yourself for the next eight years? Take it! Take the book! What am I going to do with my books when I die? No one wants them. The library won't take *any* of my books if they already have a virtual copy."

"Not even a gold-embossed book signed by an Emperor?"

Reinstone grimaced. "It's a first edition, true. But it is a book by an *Emperor* and so it was printed in perhaps an edition of a billion. A hundred million of them have his signature and seal–done one at a time by the official robot who relieved the Emperor of such onerous tasks as signing proclamations, edicts–and autographs!"

Eron sneaked a look inside. There was a table of contents, and on it he found "Ode to Agander's Night" in ancient Rigelian typeface. How could he not take this book? He'd steal for it! His advisor knew how to bribe!

Reinstone continued to grumble. "Mathematics, eh. Asinia has turned out some very good mathematicians. Kar Kantrel did the major work on local phased charge-flipping–but that was long ago. Not much activity in the field recently–but I'm not the proper person to ask. I'm only the school's token poet who gets to tutor all the Special Category students because no one else wants them. You're interested in *applied* mathematics, I suppose? They all are. Just my luck. There is *some* poetry in *pure* mathematics, but in applied math, none! Not that I would know. So what's your interest? Physics like all the rest of them?"

"Psychohistory," said Eron bravely.

Reinstone coughed. "And why would you come to Faraway as a prep school for a career in psychohistory? If you know any history at all, you know that Faraway was always a klutz at psychohistory. An abomination! We ran with the Founder's revelations cloaking us like silk robes, flaunting them, bolstered by their peal of inevitability—but always terrified that the robe was going to turn and strangle us in our sleep and leave us as mindless machines to clunk out the next line of code in our psychohistorical instructions. We avoided it like the plague. If any citizen of Faraway had dared take up the study of psychohistory, the Council would have thrown him in a dungeon and swallowed the key! And you come here for psychohistory? You must be mad."

"It was recommended," said Eron timidly.

"Well, we do have a few good mathematicians. Old fogies, but I suppose they will have to do. Here. I'll print out some introductions. You'll have to work. Let me warn you strongly, if you want the Fellowship to notice you, you'll have to work *very* hard. And by yourself. You really won't get much psychohistory with us. You'll get a good math background, that's what you'll get. And it won't hurt to take some history. I'll print out some introductions to our history department."

"Can you tell whether a book is a fake or not?"

"I don't give a pile of yellow shit whether a book is a fake or not. It is how a man uses his words that counts with me. Right now I'm busy. I was busy when you interrupted me and I'm still busy. I expect you back, though, sometime inside the next fifteen watches. If I don't see you I will be very cross."

"You're already cross."

"But I get worse!" Reinstone handed over some printout and a badge which new students were supposed to wear until they got oriented.

Eron escaped with his book and ran all the way to the cafeteria, humming to himself. He filled up a tray of food and picked out a table by himself. He didn't feel alone. He didn't even miss Murek or Nemia or those crazy sailors. He *liked* being on his own.

A man bearing a tray with a single cup of yellow pudding took a seat beside him. In his mid-sixties probably, he was still young, yet too old to be a student. But students came in all varieties. This one had the garrulous look of a man searching out a conversation. "You and I belong in the same pot," he began immediately in a strange accent. "A good mix. A *creaker* such as myself could use a dash of your youthful energy, and, I dare say, a little of *my* perspicacity might see you through an uncertain time." He was well dressed in a way that said nothing about him or his habits except for the conspicuous new student's badge.

After an awkward moment Eron asked politely, "And what will you study?"

"I'm an archaeologist."

"I haven't lived long enough to be an archaeologist," countered Eron.

The man concentrated on eating his pudding. "My wife and I are having a party for new students tonight. You are invited. A mix-up for strangers. In another month we'll be too busy to party, you and I both. It's not a big party, mind you—some food, a few drinks." He handed Eron a decorated invitation—a plush address, the Hober Hostel—finished his pudding, and left.

Pleased that the distraction was over, Eron settled down to read some Imperial poetry, careful not to spill rice and sauce on the book. Five poems later, all difficult to understand, his mind returned to thoughts of partying. He couldn't resist. It had been a long time since he'd been to a party. He might even get drunk. His father said drinking stunted the growth, but right now he decided he was ready to give up a centimeter in stature for some fun.

He returned to his new apartment. Marrae proudly showed him the shelf she had found for him and admired his new book. Then he was alone. He didn't particularly like the sparse decor of his room: too functional, too stern. He proposed to himself something more flashy and a little outré. Again the appurtenancer controls eluded him. They were indeed subtly hidden. He tried calling with a few commands he knew but got no response. He searched. By the time he was looking under the bed he felt stupid. Nothing! He was damned if he was going to *ask* and play the rube who'd never seen a robot.

What kind of nonstandard controls did they have on Faraway anyway? He was annoyed. After the second round of careful search, a horror began to dawn on him; this wasn't a roboroom. This was just a *room,* a shack. He was stuck with the furniture he had!

Outraged, he bounced on the bed. How could this be the *only* bed? It wasn't even comfortable! He felt its iron tubing for basic buttons. None! The bed didn't retract! It didn't do *anything* but sit on the floor on its stupid iron legs. He wasn't going to be able to convert it into an armchair when he needed a more relaxed space! Nothing! The armoire was the same; it just held things. Stunned, he sat in appalled silence until he remembered the party.

Eron dressed for the party with relish. His suitcase tailored him an elegant outfit which he hoped was stylish. If not, he'd *set* the style! He smiled a good-bye to Marrae, then scrammed out of his new prison cell.

Rising in central Telomere City along the Mall of Knowledge, the Hober Hostel awed Eron. It was more impressive here on the famous Mall than it had been from the tree. Then its lower reaches had been obscured by the Chancellor's Palace. He entered. He climbed. From the lower tiers he had a clear view all the way across the Square to the Founder's Mausoleum. He maneuvered through the hostel maze from the instructions he had famfed from the card and found the right room, its door ajar. The party was smaller than he had expected, more food than people. Imported chocolate! Faraway must still be connected to the best trade routes for all that history had left it behind! Lots to drink, too. That was good.

Wow, a bottle from Armazin! And genuine Ordiris liqueur! He ate some delicious tidbits and felt lonely and out of place. How could he feel comfortable at a party without his trusty blaster? What use was a blaster wrapped in gun laws!

The hostess, wife of the old student, poured him a drink and wouldn't let him feel lonely. She was good at asking questions. He was good at drinking. For the second round, he asked shyly for a shot of Armazin. They moved to the comfy love seat together. He hadn't felt like such a man since he had seduced Nemia. She kept him at a distance by telling him about her six-year-old daughter, Otaria of the Calmer Sea. Eron told her everything there was to know about himself plus a few lies.

The old student vanished with a promise to return, not to reappear until there was only a finger of Aramazin left in Eron's glass. In charlatan's outfit and curly wig, his legs checkered each in different colors, the geezer became the instant center of attention. Then he pulled from nowhere (he had voluminous lace sleeves) a sparkling jade artifact that mysteriously darkened the room and filled it with an amazing celestial sphere of stars. The young guests gasped. "Your fortunes, ladies and gentlemen," announced their host with fanfare. "I'll need a birthday to begin." He glanced about the young faces for a victim.

A slightly slurred voice volunteered, "The second hour, third of februan, 80,362 AD." Eron's mouth was stuffed with chocolate, and his hand was on his hostess' knee. But he recognized the Coron's Egg. Almost sobered, he was even more surprised than the other guests. Madly, his fam began to reorganize the state of his mind. This wasn't the party he thought it was. *That* was the coveted Egg that held the coordinates of Zurnl, and he had been lured here for a reason. All was not as it seemed. Was it a trap?

"Hmmm," said the fake fortune-teller, slightly flustered upon hearing the birth date stated in the old calendar. "You're sure that's when you were born? I'm not sure I know how to handle the conversion."

Eron staggered over to help. "Let me show you." He tried to take the ovoid but the charlatan hung onto his prop with both hands.

"So, you've seen one of these before?" Jama asked as if he already knew the answer.

"Where I come from," boasted Eron, "diamond-studded Eggs breed like corn-fed chickens." He still had his hand out. "I'll give it back; promise."

The charlatan reluctantly delivered the prize to the younger generation. Nemia had given Eron lessons in how to use it, and he was enthusiastic about demonstrating his skill. First, though, his fingers surreptitiously keyed in that star-name he wasn't supposed to know. Even Nemia didn't know he knew. Being a master spy, he found out lots of gossip that wasn't supposed to reach his eyes, like honeymoon destinations and other secret rendezvous.

After entering ZURNL his fingers waited just long enough for the star-field to begin to shift before executing an escape with a "Whoops" to cover the discontinuity. That bare initialization of a shift had been enough to tell him that he was not going to get a "star unknown" error message. *Nemia is going to kill me for falling into this trap,* he thought, wishing he hadn't been drinking. With quick, soft pressures he entered the conversion factors from Imperial to Rithian time.

"Guess what goes with this conversion?" he announced dramatically to his audience. "The galactic coordinates get changed from the egocentric Imperial center to the *absolute* center of the universe!" New constellations filled the sky. "Now watch what happens as I take her back from the present down to the beginning of time!" The stars began to creep at different paces, and soon the Big Dipper appeared above them, the Southern Cross below, Cassiopeia, Pegasus, Orion, Aquarius, Bootes, Virgo, Sagittarius, constellations which no one at the party would recognize.

He had synchronized his fam with the devolution so that he didn't have to look at the Egg to know what was going to happen. He'd seen it before. He prepared his audience with a vocal trumpet crescendo and arm waving that filled the air with expectation. Then, right on time, the sky began to be dominated by a growing pinprick of light that picked up on Eron's vocal crescendo until the room was so bright that the furniture showed through the celestial sphere.

"We have arrived at coordinates zero, zero, zero, time zero—the center of the universe and the beginning of time! I give you the Star of Bethlehem at the very moment when the Rithians saved the Galaxy for us all." He bowed. "I am reborn under this star. That is my fortune and my destiny."

He was thinking of tucking the Egg under his shirt and running, but he didn't expect he'd get away with that, so he gave the bauble back to his host. *Then* he backed out toward the door, his fam plotting all the escape routes. At the door, when escape was certain, he paused to appraise his host and hostess. "Are you the police?" he asked when they were near enough so that no one else would hear.

The woman smiled. She seemed to be the boss. "We were wondering the same thing. But I've determined that you aren't the police, much to our relief. Tell your friends we are ready to meet them. We don't know who they are, but I've determined to my satisfaction who they *aren't,* and that is enough for a beginning."

Eron fled.

# THE MARTYR'S CACHE, 14,791 GE

*The Yani-Hotle fragment, recently deciphered by the Archaeologist Boeluki, entices us with the suggestion that the first man to rocket from the Prime Planet and live to walk on another planet was named Neel Halmstrun, but we do not know how many hairs he had under his left armpit and we cannot find out because that information has, by now, been lost among the quantum uncertainties of multiple possible yesterdays, none tagged by the laws of physics as the "one true past"—a unique computable past being as meaningless a concept as an absolute frame of reference.*

*A caterpillar on the leaf of a tree can climb down to the base of the tree with a simple set of instructions, but should he attempt to reclimb the tree, to find the leaf upon which he was born, a mere reversal of those instructions will not suffice to return him home. Reversal is a process which requires more information than is needed by time-symmetry.*

*Without information conservation, a perfectly time-symmetric physics will not imply reversibility. I would be willing to apply psychohistory to the reconstruction of the past, to any level of resolution, were you to gift me one additional tool. In setting up the boundary conditions for my equations so that they are sufficiently precise to the problem specified, one needs to be able to answer this question: given a right-angled triangle whose sides measure exactly ten Planck lengths, how do I compute the length of the hypotenuse? The answer is: you can't; the uncertainty in the length of the hypotenuse is a measure of the information you don't have—and won't get by posing the question to Mother Nature who disposed of such trifles during her housecleaning chores.*

—From the transcript of "The Fifth Speech" given by the Founder to the Group of Forty-six at the Imperial University, Splendid Wisdom, 12,061 GE

DONALD KINGSBURY

They had settled into their hotel room and were debating the safest way to make contact with their antique dealer when a gentle whisper in her fam told Nemia that she had received a Personal Capsule. She suspected her mother and was slightly annoyed, cracking the Capsule's sphere in their room's discreet communications alcove away from Hiranimus. But it was from Eron. Once the message had been famfed, the sphere rapidly crumbled. She read from her mind's screen:

"Nemia, I know I shouldn't be contacting you but I just fell in a trap and thought you should know. I got invited to a party of new students"—he inserted the address—"and the old geezer had one of your Coron's Eggs. I checked it out to see that it held info on Zurnl and it did, but I was doing this in front of everybody and had to do such a fast sleight-of-hand that I couldn't get the coordinates—sorry. Then I cut and ran. Is this important? Faithfully, You-Know-Who."

Alarmed, she came to Hiranimus and famfed him the contents. Scogil assimilated the message, turning angrily to Nemia. "He should know nothing about Zurnl! Nothing! Did you tell him?"

"I most certainly did not!"

Hiranimus absorbed that grimly. "The contemptible little spy. He spies on everyone. And he's good. Well, this upsets our little dance of acquaintance! They already know who we are. Not Eron's fault. It means they are far more professional than I could have imagined. They're good."

"Fellowship Investigators? Shall we run?"

"They can't be police. The police don't think so deviously." He laughed. "And police routines are my bright spot of expertise. If the Fellowship already knew where Zurnl was, they wouldn't bother with us. They'd already be there. They have unlimited money; these people don't."

"What shall we do?"

"You've already chartered a ship for us. I don't know how you arranged that and I don't want to know. It's the Oversee, I presume. They will be professionals. Can you arrange with them an escape route in case things go sour?"

"I think so."

"Let's check out of here. Now. We disappear. It will give us time to think. If Eron and your grandfather are right and their Egg does hold the coordinates . . ."

But in the hotel corridor, not five apartments from theirs, a woman approached them, followed by a slightly anxious man. She was very abrupt in her introduction. "We already know that you are not the police. You will not know as much about us. Where would you like to discuss our affairs? Your choice."

Another shock. This was an encounter that wasn't going to be played by a preset plan. "Let's take a random walk and decide as we go," said Hiranimus, thinking as he continued to move, checking the exits. Nemia tried frantically to signal something, then acquiesced.

"A lovely city," said the slightly foppish gentleman, obviously relieved that no one was pointing blasters. His body language was that of deference.

Away from the hotel, lost in a crowd drifting down a verticule from an over-head monorail station, Scogil chose a small restaurant between towers. The table he picked was surrounded by plants and there they began an intricate maneuver of conversation, testing, evaluating each other, Scogil still wary of a trap. These people were talking like malcontents—with open innocence? or as the trappings of a delib-erate ruse?

He and Nemia responded cautiously to their guests' candor. "Those are senti-ments that could get you into trouble," Scogil commented neutrally.

The effete man only smiled. "Here on abandoned Faraway? On Faraway where they have yet to accept the rule of the Pscholars enthusiastically? Here where the inner mind still dreams of the galactic chutzpah they once had?"

"Point taken. But everyone within earshot isn't a citizen. There are tourists like us—and other farmen whose purpose is inscrutable. I hear accents."

The alert woman smiled as if she had been listening to every conversation within twenty meters. ". . . no one as inscrutable as we four."

The atmosphere relaxed. Scogil poured the woman a drink from the large carafe. She was obviously the security professional, but the man was the driven ec-centric, the one with the purpose, probably the leader. His speech was uncommon but it was certainly derived from the potpourri of Splendid Wisdom dialects—three of the key lilts used by his voice occurred nowhere else. That excited Scogil; any man from Splendid Wisdom was worth cultivating for a purpose Scogil was only beginning to map out for himself.

Caution might be lulled but caution was not expendable. Artfully he bypassed the seditionist thrust of the conversation. "We're interested in your galactarium be-cause we are trying to locate an obscure planet in this part of the Periphery, one originally staked out in early Imperial times, then evacuated as not worth terra-forming." Smythos had said as much, noting the hundreds of ghost towns on Zurnl II even if only in one offhand sentence of his scribblings. "Rumor places a treasure there. We're on a treasure hunt."

The man abandoned his proselytizing. "Names change over the centuries. A star can easily be hidden right in front of your telescope as the sages say. Do you have any tangible numbers or descriptions we could search on?"

Scogil made the plunge. "Zurnl." Nemia kicked him under the table.

"Ah." Surprise. "And could the treasure be fifty bodies?"

*He knew!* "You seem familiar with that very obscure name."

The man smiled hugely and placed his hand on Scogil's in introduction. "I'm Hyperlord Kikaju Jama. The young lady wishes, for the moment, to remain anony-mous." The Hyperlord seemed to have lost all of his fearful doubt and was now the picture of total confidence, no longer in need of whatever expertise the young woman was providing. "I have a way of sensing certain things; in you I sense a sub-tle antagonism to the Pscholars, matching my own, which accounts for your interest in Zurnl. Indeed Zurnl *is* an obscure name. It does not occur in any of the archives of Splendid Wisdom. I was not aware of it myself until recently. I imagine it is obscure because the leaders of Faraway wished to bury and forget their crime of mass murder, and the Pscholars are ashamed of the con game in which they sent fifty of their brightest young psychohistorians to a certain and sordid death simply to make the perturbed output of their equations converge on an elegant solution. When victor and vanquished both have a passionate desire to forget something, it vanishes, and the centuries then proceed to compost whatever these ex-enemies forgot to forget. I think that in some physics text there is a law of entropy requiring every new bit of information created to overwrite an old bit. In this way it is the un-attended details which get composted first."

"Some bits survive longer than others," said Scogil, thinking of the memoirs of that morbid recluse, Tamic Smythos, whose effects had lingered for centuries in storage before being accidentally unearthed.

"Indeed," said Jama thinking of a spaceship wreck preserved at near-absolute zero far from the scenes of historical revision. He laughed mischievously. "Fortu-nately for both of us the police have never heard of Zurnl, either. Are you intent upon voyaging to this place?"

"It might make a nice honeymoon spot."

"Hardly. The specs are dreary. But if you can see your way to an expedition, I can see the possibility of an alliance between our mutual avarice. But first we have an exchange to make under the auspices of the Red Sun. Not, of course, before din-ner arrives." Steaming plates were rising from the center of their table. "There will be plenty of time for troublemaking after dinner. Good food puts a queasy stom-ach at ease and promotes comradeship."

The woman stayed his reaching hand. "Me first. I'm your official taster, re-member?"

Kikaju Jama sighed. "It is such a bother to be paranoid!" But he waited.

Later that afternoon, suspicions surmounted, the deal was consummated. The four then proceeded to the Telomere space terminal to be transported via ferry to Nemia's orbiting charter. It was a long trip. Crammed together in a pod and then in a low-orbit shuttle, they had good opportunity to further their trust in each other while contending with the routine distrust of other organizations with other cau-tious purposes. The last obstacle they faced was the charter's bald and blunt-necked Starmaster, who personally met them at the shuttle to conduct his own thorough search of the Hyperlord and Katana for hidden mechs and nanoma-chines. He grunted his approval, then ferried them across space to his ship where he finally disappeared up a central shaft into the starship's bridge, leaving them to acquaint themselves with their quarters.

The enthusiastic Hyperlord tagged after Scogil with his endless schemes as if he thought that Scogil was not a sufficiently committed anti-imperialist and needed prompting. He was full of amateur plots to overthrow a Galactic Empire that had, in his opinion, undeservedly survived the Interregnum paroxysm. Eventually Scogil had to remind him that they all needed sleep.

But the proselytizing began again in the morning. Scogil continued to humor their guest, building a friendship he intended to find a use for in the years to come. Nemia flirted with Jama, partly to stop his blathering so that her Hiranimus could relax, partly because she was fascinated by his unctuous manners, the likes of which she had never met. She wasn't sure whether his blatant propositions were serious or mere highly artistic twaddling. Katana was the observant one, seeming more interested in the mysterious crew of their charter than muting Jama's excesses. The crew kept to themselves, and they saw the Starmaster only at dinner and he was not loquacious.

"Why so many jumps?" asked Scogil upon a chance meeting with the Starmaster.

"Zigzags. Routine security. We aren't being followed but we always assume a tail."

Within eighteen watches their jumping brought them to Zurnl, a dim, red star, where they spent the initial approach observing Zurnl II from afar and scanning the system for other ships. Zurnl I was barren and tidally locked; Zurnl III was a distant giant that had failed to become Zurnl's binary. There were no lurking ships. Satisfied of that, the Starmaster used his thrusters in a long cautious approach to their desolate destination, followed by a high-g aerobraking maneuver that dropped them into low orbit around Zurnl II.

From an altitude of three hundred kloms it was a forbidding world, small, with a seventy-three-hour rotation, perhaps a quarter glaciated, its eroded impact craters mostly erased by lava flows except in the high desert. The planet was at that borderline distance from its star where tidal friction begins to play with the crust, though Zurnl II did not seem, at the moment, to be afflicted by any active volcanoes. The atmosphere was thicker than Neuhadra's, and from the pastel blush of the rocks had once been oxygenated by photosynthetic life, now long gone, billions of years gone, lost to who-knew-what catastrophe. Life was a common but transient phenomena on modest inner planets, most of the time not surviving for more than a billion years.

On this scrabble world humanity hadn't been able to revive that once-verdant era. During the first five low passes their sensors picked up evidence of more than four hundred abandoned man-made sites. A quick erosion analysis suggested an age of at least ten thousand years for the failed colony—good camouflage for a more recent prison.

"Will we find it?" asked Jama anxiously.

The Starmaster grunted and continued scanning. His other crew members all seemed to be part of the analysis team and chattered among themselves. One of them turned to Jama. "It takes time." Then he was gone.

A sophisticated algorithm gradually subtracted the oldest and the newest features from the images, leaving selected sites to be re-imaged at higher resolution. These were reiterated through the analysis until there were so few likely sites left that it made sense to send down investigation teams. The bald Starmaster was caught smiling again when the third lander brought back conclusive evidence for an old prison, abandoned to wind and snow for the last twenty-two centuries. It was built inside an old mining community on a plateau in the mountains which itself had been abandoned for ten millennia. There were glaciers crawling down the distant peaks, and patches of snow still lingered in the shady spots not reached by the feeble summer sun.

It took more time to organize a landing party, but once down the crew swiftly inflated a command bubble next to the prison, sheltered from the wind. They did not bury their gawky pressure-supported home; the atmosphere was thick enough to protect them from cosmic rays. Hiranimus soon noted that this was a party of experienced archaeologists. Within a span of watches they had cleared away the accumulated sand and laid out the operational modes of the ancient prison routine. Nemia had said nothing about their expertise. Even the old roads were swept clean down to the plasteel mesh hardpack.

No time for a honeymoon. After a decawatch of careful sifting they found the graveyard with its forty-two coffins, containing thirty skeletons and twelve leathery mummies preserved by the cold and lifelessness of Zurnl. No grave markers, no identification, nothing. All but one prisoner had died of old age. One blaster death. Forty-one life sentences carried out. Counting the seven whom Tamic claimed were executed before reaching Zurnl, all fifty martyrs were thus accounted for.

No one had been allowed to take possessions to their grave except an old woman, young once, whose arthritic finger was frozen to a single ring. That would be Tamic's sweetheart. He had mentioned nothing about her except his gift to her of the ring at sunrise the day before he had been spirited away from Zurnl by the corrupt associates of a corrupt and frightened Faraway Chancellor. The Chancellor thought he needed some minor psychohistoric meddling to insure the continuance of his threatened rule. The girlfriend's diminutive was Jan. Her surname was unknown. None of the martyrs had names, neither in the records on Splendid Wisdom nor in the archives of Faraway. Tamic himself had not bothered to record their names. But that is the fate of all men—gravestones, memoirs, memories turn to dust in time. In another billion years, even the names of the Emperors will be gone.

The Helmarian archaeologists took apart the prison ruins with meticulous care, layer by layer, looking for the fabled Martyr's Cache. For a while they were elated when they dug into the floor and found a secret basement that must have been excavated surreptitiously by the martyrs—but there was nothing in it but a calendar etched into the wall and a crumbling table. Thousands of years ago the room had been stripped bare—by the guards or by the inmates? Who would ever know?

The dig crew, except for the busy Hyperlord, began to give up hope of finding anything. Jama's nagging optimism became annoying to the others. Furthermore Kikaju persisted in his role as pest around the camp, and was finally declared off limits by the archaeologists, ostensibly because of the careless way he scrabbled among the ruins chasing down his hunches. He cared nothing for the laborious documentation of layers and the reverence with which each caked bolt and tooth-pick was dusted off and salvaged—he just wanted to find something. Rebuffed, he took his enthusiasm to the hills. And as the others grew still more discouraged, Kikaju Jama became wildly manic about the possibilities. It was his nature to wax into unrealistic optimism in the midst of gloom.

Jama discovered some of the colonial mine tunnels hacked into the mountain-side above the camp. It looked like imported machinery had been in short supply, with the marks of homemade tools still everywhere in evidence. Inside the old drifts he stumbled upon fearful cave-ins, leading a sobered Hyperlord to a less dan-gerous reconnaissance outside. Yes, there were slumpings. Still outside, by the kind of careful dating that came as second nature to an antique dealer, Kikaju convinced himself that the most recent collapse was at least three thousand years old and the mine had long ago restabilized—and would remain stable barring a strong earth-quake. That meant that if he was now denied access to a tunnel, it would also have been denied to a wandering martyr and could thus be ignored.

No one in Scogil's party thought that the prisoners would have been allowed to wander so far—certainly not inside old mine diggings—but Jama had evidence that came with his galactarium—which he was not sharing—suggesting that some of those guarding the martyrs were corruptible, even unsympathetic with the sen-tence imposed upon their charges. They *might* have been lax. They *might* have turned a blind eye to an innocent walk in the hills. He reasoned that the guards of this remote prison would not be concerned about an overland escape, would not consider it even possible. There was no place to go and even if an equipped man did leave the compound, or find a hiding place, he would die sooner rather than later. Intelligent guards would be watching spaceships.

Such speculation motivated the Hyperlord in his hopeful exploration of the mines. The worst blockages he faced were accumulations of squat and fat icicles. Eventually Jama built up enough courage to torch passages through the worst of them. His enthusiasm was tried. The farther he penetrated the mine, the more he became wary of the dangers of that kind of adventuring. His feet started a small rockslide. Only an instant freezing of his muscles kept him from stepping into a bottomless hole. And then, after convincing himself that he was being adequately cautious, his feet went out from under him and he was sliding, butt bouncing, fly-ing down a steeply inclined shaft, careening off a rock that took a terrible gouge in the side. He landed on his back in a morass of mud that oozed below the frost line at the bottom of the slanting shaft.

Spacedamn! For a terrifying moment he was sure that he had lost his opti-mism!

DONALD KINGSBURY

Was his suit ripped? Were a sixtyne of bones broken? He *was* sure that he had stupidly been pushing his time limits and was low on oxygen. While he groped about to give himself a hand-up, his glove closed on an antique atomic slicer on the ledge he was trying to use as a grip. He slumped back into the mud and looked with amazement at the device now centered in his beam. It was a cheap hand tool—even crusted, obviously of an early Faraway design—the kind of tool that was common merchandise for Faraway's aggressive independent traders. The sight refueled his enthusiasm. He lay in his mudbath of aches, grinning hugely. Just this tool alone would buy him a thousand wigs back on Splendid Wisdom!

After a mist shower at the base and a check of his bruises, which did not conceal any shattered bones, he had a talk with himself to fortify his courage, and, without telling even Katana where he was going, went right out again. The Hyperlord spend frustrating watches following his clue. Those nitpickers were excluding him from their dig—well, he would exclude them from his.

He found the Martyr's Cache in an improbable place. It was not directly accessible from the surface, reachable only through a ratrun of tunnels, but did lay near the surface, was dry and in the frost zone. The tiny dungeon's rock walls bore the unmistakable signature of an ancient Faraway atomic slicer, and inside the small cave was a box. He was too joyfully curious to report his find without first examining it, but he was also conscious of the razzing he had taken for not being careful and so he only took a *small* peek. He pried off the top of the box, and his beam showed him neat slices of fragile rock. Artificial. Human made. Carefully machined. Triumph!

Back at the hut, no one believed him when he boasted that he had located the Martyr's Cache for which they had been sifting sand and finding only sand mixed with a few buttons. He let them razz him and have their laughs at his expense; the more they laughed, the higher they were being hoisted for their fall. Presently . . . he produced the slicing tool. He saw the joshing in stunned eyes suddenly arrested, the twinkle in them frozen by astonishment.

"There's more, my disbelieving yokels!"

A clamor began with no one person having the verbal right of way. What they were all trying to say at the same time was that they desired to dress for a hike and hurry after him to claim his treasure—but the Hyperlord was not willing to give up his satisfying fame so quickly. He protested exhaustion and a need to rest his weary feet. He had them by rings in their noses. His worst detractor brought a footbath of warm water. Food appeared, the best they had in the tent. Katana broke out their last bottle of Armazin left over from the party on Faraway. He basked.

Languorously he regaled them with his story (careful not to provide a semantically useful map of the mine) while leading them through the spooky dangers of his subterranean labyrinth. He dramatized every drip, every rockfall, every black pit, every ice floe, every perilous turn and shaft, his voice in no hurry to release his captive audience. He paused frequently to pontificate, knowing that, this time, they *would* listen to his wisdom. Until he revealed the location of the Martyr's Cache, no one was going to be audacious enough to interrupt him or poke at him with sarcastic asides. He missed, of course, his lordly wig and ruffled cuffs but tried to make up for that lack of impressiveness with precise diction and a selected choice of obscurely appropriate words.

In time he ran out of delays and actually had to take them to the treasure. The journey was quicker than the telling of the discovery. Reverently they carried the box back through twisting vaults, out, and down over windswept boulder and ice to the inflated command bubble. A cursory analysis showed the sarsen stone slices to be symmetrically pitted on the front and backed by a thin film of plastic. It was a cheap, soft, tough plastic commonly used to preserve food for long voyages—not particularly heat or light or oxygen resistant but, underground in permafrost conditions, bathed in Zurnl's atmosphere, it was virtually indestructible, a useful backing for something as brittle as stone. Scogil scanned several million bits of the pit sequences into his fam and broke the code almost immediately. It was meant to be broken.

"A message?" asked the Hyperlord anxiously. "They wanted to tell us something?" he queried.

"It's mathematics," said Scogil.

"Mathematics?"

"They were all mathematicians, remember. What else would a group of mathematicians do when isolated from all contact with civilization? They would do mathematics." Hiranimus felt a pride for his profession. "We are a clever bunch. I'm not surprised that a mere gaggle of prison guards couldn't stop them."

"Is it psychohistory?" Jama's voice was on its tiptoes.

"It appears to be." The large disk of the sun had set, and the light from the inflated arch of plump cylinders above them shimmered on the stone slice Scogil was examining.

"But that's blasphemy!" protested Jama. "*They* are forbidden to publish! Are they hypocrites as well as scoundrels?"

Scogil grinned. "Fanatic volunteers condemned to be erased from history without even a heroic song to tell of their going probably don't connect publishing with the hiding of their stone scrawlings in a mine whose probable fate is to be kneaded back into the crust of Zurnl II by the tidal interactions of Zurnl. Given time to think about it, even martyrs don't want to die without at least a marker on their graves. The marker has to be there, read or not. What is a marker but that which distinguishes oneself from all the other quadrillions?"

"Will this enable us to wrest psychohistory away from the Pscholars and apply it to our own ends?" That was Hyperlord Kikaju Jama's fondest hope. He was remembering that one of his dreams was to finance a group of mathists who would secretly re-create the basic principles of psychohistory.

Scogil, who had been elated by the find, was now sobering. "Probably not.

What's on these slices was doubtless advanced mathematics for its time. Today, who knows? Psychohistory is orders of magnitude more complicated than it was. Today's Pscholars can read social nuances beyond the wildest dreams of the Founder. They can sense a revolt or an insurrection before the leaders of that insurrection are even born. The Founder was able to set up his colony on Faraway certain that no one would notice its strategic importance. Today such a leveraged ploy would be impossible. Early abortion is routinely applied before even an obscure threat matures." Fleetingly Hiranimus recalled Agander. In spite of the Oversee's deftest applied mathematics, the Pscholars had noticed the direction of the Ulmat deviation and begun countermeasures before the discontent of the Ulmat peoples could be ramped up into a useful crisis.

High above the camp their orbiting Helmarian ship warned them of an impending storm. The archaeologists could have battened down and ridden it out, but the need was no longer there. They tossed the remains of the martyrs into the landing craft for a later dignified funeral while the life's work of the martyrs, committed to lifeless stone, was packed reverently in shockproof containers. To obscure the recent visit, obvious traces of grave robbing were erased under fresh layers of blown sand. The storm would do the rest. Then the crowded craft returned to the mother ship. The expedition jumped away from Zurnl to a point in interstellar space far from nearby suns, drifting. The analysis continued.

Each slice of sarsen stone was scanned and input into standard templates readable by any common household manufacturum. Scogil saw such templates as seeds which would drift across the interstellar voids in countless numbers, each seed conveniently too small to be seen by the huge galactic army of Fellowship monitors. Still, the seeds would be useless until they dropped down and took root in the kind of fertile soils that the Pscholar's monitors *were* all too able to detect and sterilize.

The Starmaster's regular crew had many expertises but none was a psychohistorian. The Hyperlord worshiped mathematics, but his mathematical sophistication was hardly more developed than the runtime routines built into his fam—public school tricks like solving partial differential equations in his head. Katana revealed her skills only as she needed them. Nemia was a master of psychoquantronics with a good smattering of psychohistorical training leavened by contact with her grandfather, who was one of the best psychohistorians that the Oversee had ever produced. But it was Scogil who had been trained from his youth as a psychohistorian, and so it fell to him to be the first to make a deep excursion into the martyr's legacy. Others of the Oversee would follow soon enough. If he assimilated it now, he would have the jump-start.

Scogil extracted the relevant binary message from slice after slice and ran them through a decoder and then a document assembler and, hence, into his fam's memory. The total was too meaty to be digested in one watch or a hundred. He was a python who had swallowed a very large goat. To begin, he sampled extensively, wincing at the extreme differences between Founder and Oversee notations. In the years following the Founder's first paper his secretive followers had never published their work except in popular propaganda format. Whatever psychohistory that Scogil knew had been developed independently by the Oversee using their own symbolism and definitions. He had to construct a routine in his fam to build an efficient translator for his subconscious, then task back to his browsing.

One theorem caught his mind's eye—he and Mendor Glatim had spent the better part of a year working through its proof, refining and polishing the machinery for their teacher, who was mining tougher psychohistorical veins. The Martyr's proof of essentially the same theorem from the Martyr's Cache was elegantly simple, enragingly simple once Hiranimus understood the notation—and it was a proof more than two thousand years old!

Was there anything more like that? He cut into the document at random. Up flashed a mid-Interregnum description of Faraway's economy from the Founder's *extrapolation* of ancient Faraway's future. Scogil backtracked and was goggled at the conceptual frame which held the fine details. The Oversee had never been able to cover a whole system with such finesse. It frightened him in an exhilarating way. He was a child who knew arithmetic and had stumbled upon an advanced calculus dissertation in his attic.

Sweet irony. The boy who had been dropped from the Oversee's elite theoretical course because he wasn't good enough was sitting here, commanding instant access to the most dangerous text in the Galaxy outside of Fellowship control. He loved it!

# DEALS AND OTHER INTRIGUES,
# 14,791 GE

*Hasten slowly.*

—Emperor Caesar-of-August, 61,273–61,235 BGE

After the second jump the bald Starmaster sent for Scogil. Hiranimus left a sleeping Nemia and his meditations, propelling himself through the iris of his cabin with a sigh. He monkeyed up the tube to the cramped bridge. As he arrived, the ship's commander unstuck a bulb from under his cabinet where he kept his ample supply of refreshments. He was known to dislike multiple returns to the galley. "Have a drink. Lemonade." His voice implied that lemonade was the ambrosia of the universe. "Do you have what you need to work? I'll be floating here in space for maybe sixtyne to twenty watches checking that we're not being followed."

"Who could follow us?" Scogil glanced at the sparse drama of lonely stars, the distant Milky Way rising slowly across their false horizon as the starship turned. It was a rhetorical question. They were doing zigzags again, routine security for the Oversee even though there were probably no humans within a radius of sixtyne leagues. For all of the hundred quadrillion human beings linked by tenuous hyper-travel between the oases of the Galaxy, the expanse of the human empire was mostly empty desert.

The Starmaster rubbed his hand over his naked head. "How well do you know this Katana? I sense that she kens naval procedure more than makes me comfortable. Theirs, not ours."

Scogil broke the seal on the lemonade bulb and let his body hang in front of the panoramic view. "She's here to keep his Lordship out of trouble. You don't think he needs a leash?"

"Likely. But whose leash? Maybe she has her own business. What do you make of him?"

"He *needs* someone at his side to keep him out of trouble. You'll do me a favor when you see him coming my way to engage him in conversation or at least to stick out your foot and somersault him. When I'm staring off into space he thinks I'm bored and in need of company."

"And I was thinking of palming him off on *you*. Just this morning he was telling me how to run my ship. What are we going to do about the Hyperlord?"

Scogil noticed the "we." The Starmaster was a taciturn diplomat, but there was no denying his authority. He was probably here as Scogil's boss, assigned by the Oversee. He was just too polite to say so. One would be wise to pay attention to his suggestions. Cross a boundary of unwritten command and his politeness would cease. "I'm open to your opinions."

"The appearance is that you have made a deal with that nobleman."

"A mutually profitable one. He's dogged. Without him we wouldn't have found what we were after."

"Dogged, yes he is."

"You disapprove of my promise to give him a copy of the Martyr's Cache?"

"He's a blabbermouth. Maybe it doesn't matter. It depends upon what is etched into those documents etched in stone. You've had a better look than the rest of us. We've noticed that you've been turning up to dinner glazed and taciturn and then disappearing again into your thoughts. What have you found? I need to know."

Keeping counsel with himself was no longer useful. Scogil composed his thoughts. "*Everything's* there. It looks like the whole of the Founder's Plan to navigate through the Interregnum as well as the mathematics that justifies it as seen by two score of the early Fellowship's brightest minds. The methods he devised to monitor and tweak his vision are a fascinating exercise in the art and science of minimalist manipulation. Frankly, his techniques look orders of magnitude better than ours. Maybe this Cache is of *more* value than a burglarized copy of the *Collected Works of the Founder*. The martyrs were born into a culture that already had three hundred years to digest the Founder's message and clean it up. On Zurnl maybe they even had time on their hands to do a little of their own polishing. It looks that way. But I'm only beginning to get into it."

"So there is new stuff?"

Scogil sipped for a while. The Starmaster, who was probably a high-ranking mathematician in disguise, meant "new" in the sense of something that the Oversee's psychohistorians had failed to rediscover. "I've only had a chance to skim, but every place I touch down I find mathematics I've never seen before. I may not be the Oversee's best psychohistorian, but I know what's being done."

"We're that behind, eh?"

"No. We're very advanced in some areas. The Founder's work is . . . just different. I'll tell you more within the decawatch. We've been trying to re-create psychohistory—because we know it can be done—but we think at the problem from the viewpoint of someone trying to grapple with an empire run by psychohistory while the Founder was looking at an empire that didn't understand the functioning of the bureaucracy that had been created by twelve millennia of expansion. Two different problems which generate very different elans. And, it appears, a very different kind of math. I'm shocked."

"So this *is* important. It's going to give our mathematicians a celebratory meal to digest?"

"Yes. And a hangover."

"Your deal with blabbermouth is off. My call. Too dangerous."

The command startled Scogil, and it *was* a command. So the Oversee *had* overruled him again. Fury welled in him but he was unwilling to show his anger. "A deal is a deal," he said calmly. "We're a bug living in the cracks of a giant's boot. Integrity is all we've got!"

"Not *all*. Integrity is always important but it is a small part of strategy. Can our blabbermouth Hyperlord really use this stuff in any other way than to call massive amounts of attention to himself—and us? Suppose you found yourself in a deal with a baby to give him a blaster to play with? Say, when you made the deal, you thought it was a *toy* blaster. Would your integrity demand that you go through with the deal?"

"On Agander children use live blasters as teething rings," Scogil answered truculently.

"Well, now," said the Starmaster, "I don't know Agander, but I know humans. If Agander lets their children play with live blasters, I'll bet you a lemonade that Agander has the best blaster training program in the whole of the Galaxy and that it starts the very watch a baby is born. Am I right?"

"You're right." Scogil wished his anger hadn't dropped him into that trap.

"But you're right, too," conceded the Starmaster. "If we don't give old blabbermouth a copy of the treasure he found for us, he'll be mad and blabber about it. That's not good strategy, either. Perhaps we should hire the good people of your Agander to teach our baby how to hold a blaster?"

"You jest!"

"Let's meet again at thirty-two hundred tomorrow. Have an alternate deal ready, one that will be acceptable to me and one that will be acceptable to the Hyperlord."

"Just like that?"

"Your reputation for wild-eyed creativity sends shudders down the collective spine at the upper levels of the Oversee. You'll come up with something. I don't guarantee that I'll approve."

Later, when Scogil met Nemia in their cabin, he pounded his head symbolically. She brought him tomato slices and martz-leaves wrapped inside a bread and cheese roll. While he delegated part of his fam to work on the Hyperlord problem, he shared his troubles with Nemia.

"I can't get these nursemaid nannies out of my hair! Everywhere I turn, they pop up and close doors on me like in a nightmare! 'Bad little boykins; can't go in there till you grow up, naughty, naughty, naughty.'" He sighed with a shake of his head and twist of his wrist to indicate screws being tightened. "You know why I love you, Nemia?"

"Because I nursemaid you so well?"

He felt an irrational wave of love and loyalty—unusual for a man whose ambition had made loyalty to others a secondary issue. "I don't have to fight you."

"So far." She grinned.

He cast his eyes back toward the bridge. "Old Baldy is zigzagging out of the way of phantoms again. Do you suppose he's good enough to dodge your mother? I half expect an impossible rendezvous out here in the void—grappling hooks, tractor beams, the works—and then your mother comes in through the airlock with your fiancé and takes you away."

"Aw, that won't happen." She ruffled a lock of his hair. "We'll change your hair color to purple and give you a big false nose with warts and then my mother will never notice you."

"We hope."

She shifted into advice mode. "Talk to Katana before you talk to Jama." She meant about withholding a copy of the Martyr's Cache.

He returned to his well-equipped cubicle and hunkered down to the grind. He was still the python digesting the goat. For now he was finished with sampling. The sheer magnitude of material was demanding a more methodical treatment. So he started with simple tasks. To build up a ready glossary of unfamiliar terms, he scanned the document for items whose meaning might have shifted over the centuries, dumping them into a buffer. Each term there had to be analyzed separately. He felt like a bored computer dealing with records at the excruciating rate of no more than one per jiff. It was slow work—too many of the records were being bumped up to his conscious mind where he actually had to think about them, researching definitions, using his judgment, composing definitions, building links. On and on it went. How was he to find the time to *learn* some of this stuff!

He bogged down. For a while he crawled into his bunk and dreamed they had jumped to Splendid Wisdom. A dreamlike Katana escorted him down a enormous hallway of giant eyes, touching each with the nail of her forefinger to expand its iris, then looking inside, shaking her head and saying "Not in there!" before she went to the next eye. When Scogil tried to peek at what she was seeing, she bumped him away with her hips and flashed her smile to close the iris. "I *told* you, it's *not* in there!" she scolded.

Having nightmares was not the way to sleep.

He roused himself to commiserate in the mirror. His hair was messy. Zero-g was terrible for hair. No wonder the Starmaster was bald as a gourd. He slithered out of his cabin, feet first, and did a roll maneuver that sent him headed down toward Katana's cabin. The door's iris was the same as the irises in his dream. He hesitated. He knocked. If she wasn't alone he was going to flee.

"Yes?"

"Scogil here. Are you alone?"

She opened the iris with a smile. "Don't worry, he's not here. I think he's in the galley eating and reading up on Helmarian artifacts. Come in."

"You two are a strange couple."

"We have had some adventures together. Kidnappings, ransom, crawling around in ten thousand–year–old mines. I haven't had such an adrenaline rush since I murdered my husband. He's a friend."

"A friend, you say?" he fished.

She smiled a lady's smile which barely concealed her bawdy good nature. She quoted from a nursery rhyme popular on Splendid Wisdom: "'Come in,' said the crocodile, rolling out the red carpet of his tongue." It was immediately obvious to Katana from his blank expression that Scogil was one of these outworld barbarians too uncouth ever to have been read crocodile stories by his parents. She pulled Hiranimus inside. "Let me translate my baffling crack. You're still suspicious of us, aren't you? I'm reading your narrow, squinty eyes which are more squinty than usual."

"Protocol demands it," he answered frankly.

"Your *boss* demands it," she corrected. "Who *is* your boss?"

"Who's *yours*? Your friend?"

"My boss is a good man. Ex-navy, like me. I'm surprised to see him involved in Kikaju's intrigues."

"The Hyperlord is capable of intrigue?" Scogil's comment was more astonished than sarcastic.

She passed over his bait and returned to the subject of her naval comrade. "I don't understand my boss but I'm very loyal to him, irrationally loyal. He was the only person who stood by me when it was an open-and-shut case to have my fam burned. He saved my ass. Got me five years of rehab instead. They tinkered with my fam but they didn't take it away. Rehab is worse than the military. I didn't enjoy it."

"Rehab must have done a good job."

She twirled around in the small cabin with mock mirth. "You think you're complimenting me? You think I've returned to normal! How wrong you are. I escaped because my boss has pull. I *survived* rehab. Of course they did teach me *some* emotional control. But my late mother was a weirdo who believed that attaching a *baby* to a fam gives it a head start. It doesn't. It retards a baby. Emotions go undeveloped and the fam never learns to handle the real stuff. That's me. A kid like me grows up with weird ideas about emotion. I was an out-of-control brat. Still am."

"But your boss considers you competent?"

"I'm good at naval work."

"Keeping the Hyperlord out of trouble?"

"That and keeping my boss out of trouble."

"Maybe we can work together. I have a hard decision to make. And I need your help," admitted Scogil. "I can't give the Hyperlord his copy of the Martyr's Cache. I'm looking for a way around my orders."

Now she was alert. "What's the problem?"

"Can't have the Pscholars coming down on us."

"So what's the problem? You're a rebel. Kikaju, bless him, is a *crazy* rebel. I'm not a rebel. I look after me because I never got past a child's selfishness. But my boss is a rebel and he's joined up with Kikaju, and I'd turn into a machine with saw-teeth if the Pscholars tried to take out my boss. I'm of the line of Frightful-people. I hope you've noticed that you and I are on the same side."

"Granted. Can the Hyperlord be discreet?"

"Are *you* asking me that question? Or is your *boss* asking the question? Let me tell you something about Kikaju and *never* forget it. He looks like a fool, he is a fool, but he's the smartest Spacedamn fool you'll ever meet, and if you treat him like a fool, you lose. But to answer your question—no, he's not going to be discreet; yes, he has to be muzzled. So what can I do for you? It would be stupid to upset him. And don't you dare try to murder him! I won't stand for that. I'll have your ears first!"

"Easy. We're dealing. Jama said something about bringing a group of mathematicians together and reinventing psychohistory. He doesn't have the least idea how hard that is, or how long that would take." Hiranimus held up his hand to keep Katana from interrupting. "I would say his dream was impossible, but no one can say it is impossible—it was done once—so it *is* possible. If your Hyperlord can put together a group of mathematicians who know how to live like rats in the walls of Splendid Wisdom, *I* can feed them stuff as fast as they can assimilate it."

The Frightfulperson was not pleased. "In the original deal we got it all *now*."

"Citizen Katana, the Martyr's Cache is useless to Jama as it stands. Jama knows no one who could read it. Neither do you. There's this mythology—and people believe it—a mythology that supposes the old empire was degenerate at the time of its collapse. Of course that's true, but pieces of an organism don't all start to die at the same rate. Your kidneys can kill you when your brain is doing its best work. Pure mathematics was at its *height* during the century of the Founder. How could he have done what he did if that weren't so? It's never been the same since. The Pscholars, great applied mathematicians that they are, are afraid of mathematics, afraid to nurture and cultivate it. Math is the only thing that could take them off their throne. Outside of the Pscholar's Lyceums, mathematics is in a pitiful state. Over the whole of the Galaxy, mathematics is in a dark age."

"And you can do better than Kikaju? You're smarter and faster at reading bird tracks scratched in stone?" She was being sarcastic.

"I'm a mathematician, not the best, but one of the best outside of the Fellowship."

She didn't dispute the point but dropped down into clarification. "You are offering Jama bits and pieces over maybe decades instead of the whole bag at once?"

"Yeah. Bits and pieces at a rate his people can assimilate. It's the fastest way."

"How do we know you'll honor your deal?"

"My word."

She became furious, hot in a way he had never seen from a fammed mind. "You've already broken your word! Your boss could break your second word, just like he has broken your first!" Something in her reached out and controlled her rage, damping it, but the struggle was nakedly visible. Her face calmed. The rage became simple reproach.

Scogil slowly let his calming hand drop. "Maybe I could offer to put something in escrow. I can't commit now, because I haven't personally got the resources, but I can ask."

She was already smiling, her mind quick. "Could you see to the financing of a small college for the mathematically talented? Say while we're waiting for the 'content' to come through?"

"I can ask." For the first time Scogil noticed a string of dried human ears hung up in her cabin as decoration.

She saw his glance and turned on the same crocodile smile that she'd met him with at her cabin's iris. "Just a bond in escrow from some Rithian scummers who didn't keep a deal with me. Forfeited. I don't like con men." She smiled more gently. "You've been fair with us, more than fair. I don't dislike the turn of your new offer. It would solve our mutual problem—if you're honest. I've been looking for a lid to clamp on Kikaju's skull. I've been worried, too, and I *am* in charge of security. My boss is depending upon me. He's taking risks I wouldn't take if I were him."

At thirty-two hundred the Starmaster heard Scogil's proposition and nodded. "He'll keep the faith as long as there's more coming to hold his interest. I have something to add to the pot." What the Starmaster had in mind was entirely to the Oversee's advantage—but it would serve Kikaju's purpose, too. The Starmaster intended to debark their loquacious Hyperlord and his sidekick at a very special spaceport. By "coincidence" they would find themselves enrolled in one of the Oversee's very special security courses. Jama needed more training.

Hiranimus relaxed with Nemia that evening. Space, she was good to talk to! He told her everything. He had put his worries aside and was back to doing what he liked most. "I took a sixtyne of inamins after my chat with the Starmaster to sketch out one of the Founder's neat tricks as it might apply to the situation at Coron's Wisp. Just a first cut. I'm riding out a brainstorm. Maybe I've found a way to make a direct attack on Splendid Wisdom. I don't think I'll need help."

"Go it alone? You wouldn't dare!"

"They probably won't let me but it's worth a try. We'll have to operate out of the Coron's Wisp systems. That's a pretty low station from which to be effective. I don't even know who my new boss is going to be. He might be an iron star, Space help us! I need a better feel for the place. Start telling me all of Grandfa's stories about the Wisp, the ones you remember."

"It's the real boondocks. Half of the population believes in astrology."

"I know." Scogil grinned. "That's what is exciting."

"It is not exciting for *me*! What will *I* do?"

"I have a perfect job for my Nemia."

"Taking care of *you* can be finished right after dawn. What will I do with the rest of my time?" she wailed.

"All wrapped up if you can convince the powers that be to back my mad scheme."

Nemia snuggled up to him. "We're not even married yet."

"How can we? We'll need your mother for *that* ceremony. Maybe I can get my boss at the Wisp to fire me, and I can take an assignment at the other end of the Galaxy. I'm sure we could find an exotic place where the marriage ritual doesn't require mothers."

Nemia gestured to dim the light. For a long time she lay in silence debating with herself, listening to the breathing of her Hiranimus. "I know something you don't know," she whispered in the dark.

"I'm sure of that, Miss Psychoquantronics."

"I'm not supposed to tell you till we get there."

"Well, tell me then!"

"I'm relishing the last moments of having such a delicious secret to myself."

Scogil turned his back to her in their net and grumbled.

She wrapped herself around his back, contouring herself to his floating body. "You aren't going to have a boss when we get to Coron's Wisp. You're the new boss."

Scogil exploded out of the cocoon. "How do you know that!"

"It all comes from having the right grandfather."

"He told you? He arranged it before he died?"

"Why do you think I'm marrying you? You don't think I'd marry someone's flunky," she teased. "Grandfa took pity on me," she lied, "and helped me escape that horrible ninny my mother picked out for me. We're going to be very happy." She was afraid they weren't going to be happy because of her sins, so she whispered the key words she had programmed into his fam when he thought she was taking out his Kapor persona. "My Guzbee darling." His response was wonderful. She was a very good programmer. Cloun-the-Stubborn would have understood.

# 27

# APPRENTICE MATHEMATICIAN,
# 14,791 TO 14,797 GE

*There are uncertainties in any prediction, uncertainties due to errors in mea-*
*surement and, less well understood by the layman, physically intrinsic uncer-*
*tainties. The mathematician immediately sets out to define and measure such*
*uncertainty. Let us make a first crude but useful definition:*

*The uncertainty of any outcome is the minimum average number of yes/no*
*questions for which we must obtain answers in order to isolate the outcome. Is*
*the cat-in-the-box alive? Are we north of the equatorial galactic plane? Is the*
*electron in a state of spin-up? Certainty is running out of questions in need of an*
*answer.*

*Suppose we have an opaque jar of white balls and wish to predict the color*
*of a ball withdrawn at random. We need ask no questions—the answer is*
*"white." The uncertainty of the outcome is zero.*

*If we have a jar of white and black balls and wish to predict the color of a*
*ball withdrawn at random, the maximum uncertainty equals one because, to*
*eliminate all uncertainty, we need the answer to only one question, namely "Is*
*the ball white?" Four colors give a maximum uncertainty resolved by no more*
*than two questions, eight colors give a maximum uncertainty resolved by no*
*more than three questions, etc.*

*. . . in general, if the box contains n colors, a maximum average of*
*$H = log2(n)$ questions will be needed to clear up the uncertainty . . . If the*
*colored balls in the jar are not represented in equal proportions, we have*
*additional information called the redundancy and thus the uncertainty of an*
*outcome is less than the maximum uncertainty. We must then compute*
*$H = -SUM[p \ log2(p)]$ over all probabilities p, . . .*

*Put in simpler terms, the uncertainty of a prediction increases as the num-*
*ber of alternate outcomes increase. In a deterministic system, which allows no*
*alternate outcomes, the uncertainty H approaches zero as the measurement of*

the initial state is refined. On the other hand, a nondeterministic system, such as one governed by quantum mechanics, will have attached to it an irreducible uncertainty—always greater than zero—since every superposition will imply not one but a range of possible outcomes, all with a probability less than one.

For instance, when an electron passes through a double slit, we cannot predict where it will hit the target, only the probability distribution of a set of hits in a diffraction pattern—alternate outcomes—and so the final state of a single electron's journey is necessarily uncertain until the predictor answers the right questions after the fact.

Note that uncertainty is a meaningless concept without a predictor and his specific prediction. The uncertainty associated with a single jar of colored balls is very different if we predict (1) that we will pull out a ball, (2) that we will pull out a white ball, or (3) that we will pull out a white ball weighing one gram. A sophist can turn quantum mechanics into a deterministic system simply by making the absolutely certain prediction that only outcomes specified by his wave equation will be realized. That is a useful prediction but it merely tells us with certainty what won't happen; what will happen still has a computable uncertainty. Certainty can become a taskmaster who requires more answers than quantum mechanics is able to extract from any set of initial conditions, no matter how accurately measured.

It is an instructive and deeply pleasurable exercise for the superior student to derive the irreducible uncertainty associated with any physical system he can formulate as a quantum wave equation—and this author strongly suggests that he do so. Hint: First specify all the outcomes and their probabilities. Use the integral form of H and . . .

A magical world opens to those who master the tools of uncertainty. For instance, it is then a trivial matter to derive the second law of thermodynamics from first principles. The student can go even further; by using the time-symmetry of the quantum wave equation, it will be possible for him to decant the second law's time-symmetric corollary from his first solution: if time is reversed, past events will NOT recapitulate themselves in reverse in such a way that entropy decreases; a time-reversed observer will still see a world of increasing entropy.

Can you build a convincing proof that a time-reversed traveler will continue to grow old and die? that, for a few moments after time-reversal, rivers might slosh uphill but will very soon reassert their downward flow to the sea? Show mathematically that the velocities and positions necessary for the water molecules to flow upriver, rise into the groundwater, and levitate upward into the sky as raindrops require an accuracy many orders of magnitude greater than allowed by the irreducible uncertainties imposed by quantum mechanics.

Explain why deductions about the past contain the same irreducible uncertainties as predictions about the future, the same proliferating branch-points.

DONALD KINGSBURY

*Prove that only in a universe with an unlimited capacity to store detail within volumes smaller than a quantum length cubed could time-reversal induce corpses to crawl out of the grave and grown men to shrivel up into babies and slip back into their womb and uranium to cease being radioactive.*

*Calculate the radius of a sphere such that the uncertainty of pi gives a ten percent probability that pi is less than 3.*

—Elementary Physics Course, Asinia Pedagogic

Eron hardly knew where to begin his studies. He had no tutor creating a program for him and driving him through it. He had no regular classes. He had no exams. He belonged to no group. It was impossible to skip school because there was no school to skip. This was very disconcerting and disorienting. Jak took pity on him, with a laugh, and hauled him off to a few lecture series, which were fascinating tours into obscure areas of high physics, the details of which were all incomprehensible. It was like having acrophobia and crawling to the rim of a precipice to look down upon normally large things reduced to a very tiny status—while a knowledgeable mountain climber stood behind you, firmly nudging your ass forward with his boot.

In desperation Eron went to his advisor to plot out a course for himself. Reinstone spoke about poetry. Eron listened to him patiently, dutifully posing as a student in awe of his master. Reinstone was so enthused by an audience that he began to quote large passages from his own Saga—recklessly developing his performance into a drama that first required him to stand and then to pace while wild gestures brought fire to his words. In time Eron got him back onto the subject of constructing a course of studies. It was no use. A happy Reinstone gave him some poems to read. "They will inspire you," he said.

Marrae took pity on him and sat at his console guiding him through lists of possible course studies while mumbling encouragement. The tri-D screen was a cacophony of scrolling text advisements, scurrying between little animations intent upon competing with each other for his attention while still on stage, their frenzied antics made even more overwhelming by Marrae's tendency to countermand his command gestures with her own so that the console was always aborting the ongoing performance to follow up a lead he hadn't intended. Then Marrae spotted one of the new books Reinstone had lent him, a translation of the *Iliad* and the *Odyssey* into standard galactic, and disappeared with it into her own room.

Doggedly he persisted. He tried narrowing the glut down to the directions a student of psychohistory might profitably pursue. There were lots of opinions but no one was sure and the Fellowship wasn't telling. That came as a shock to Eron. The Fellowship was picking up students from schools like Asinia and wasn't prescribing any course of action to guide them? Absurd. He sulked for a round of watches, sleeping long hours and eating food. He skipped his meeting with

Reinstone. He carefully avoided all presentations, programmed tutorials, lectures, and demonstrations. He left his console on idle. He was as mad as an inactive nova, erupting only occasionally.

Then he met a student in Asinia's parkland while they sat on a bench together each lost in his own thoughts. The student happened to spot a tiny flowering weed in the grass and was so surprised that he commented aloud to Eron about the diffusion of life through the Galaxy. The home planet of this specimen, he knew for a fact, was seventy-seven thousand leagues distant. He wouldn't let Eron pick the delicate flower.

"You're a biologist?"

"No. My father is a florist who breeds the flower gengineered from that weed. I just dabble, really, in everything except botany."

"I *don't* dabble. I don't do anything. Even the water in this damn university refuses to wet my hands. What's your favorite dabble?"

"Really not much. This watch it's real math. I really joined the math club because of a girl I make the bumps with. I'll be doing math as long as we are bumping. It's really interesting—the math, I mean. We're working on this really difficult problem in tertiary kanite algebras which keeps my mind off her unreal boobs. It's really driving us crazy—the problem, I mean. Nobody at Asinia seems to know anything. But we'll solve it really soon now. We're brainstorming it again this afternoon."

"Really?" Eron mocked. He tagged along.

The math club met in a study room with its own mnemonifier and a clunky-looking link to Asinia's symbolic manipulator. Eight members had brought their lunch in anticipation of a rowdy session. They gesticulated. They punched each other jocularly and talked at the same time. The club's president, their "chair-sucker," as they called him, continually raised his voice to shout "Quiet!" or, when he was really exasperated, "Please be QUIET, for crap's sake!" Eron dutifully remained quiet while he observed and listened.

He heard a serious undercurrent of math beneath the joking. The girl with the boobs seemed to be the intellectual in charge. She had slipped out of her shoes and, silently, was rubbing her toes together—only when some male made a hopeful suggestion did she demolish him by quoting an exotic property of kanite algebras from memory. One dark youth with bushy eyebrows did strange things such as trying to yank out his hair when frustrated by his impotent attempt to "intrant homogamous kanite gnomoids," which he was certain would eventually solve all their problems. "Quiet!" yelled their chairsucker. "Let Hasal have his say, for crap's sake!" Eron didn't have the slightest idea what a kanite algebra was. It sounded like one of those awful surprises Murek Kapor was always pulling on him.

He was beginning to notice that their enthusiasm was totally dispersed. Murek had taught him very methodical ways of organizing an approach to a problem that wasn't providing easy answers. Their hop-around discipline grated on his nerves.

After a full morning of watching, he began to explain his ideas about how the club might organize its attack on kanites. The chairsucker was now dodging artillery rounds of hard bread rolls and had commandeered a basket of rolls to return fire. His attention wasn't on keeping order. Eron turned to the club's doyenne, who merely crossed her arms. "Not now. I'm thinking." Across the table three of the main arguers retorted that being organized was mentally restrictive. A hungry mathematician was under the table chasing after a bread roll that had missed its target.

All right. Reasoning and common sense wasn't going to work on these anarchists.

They should be enlisted in the Imperial Shock Troops with Murek as their top sergeant. Eron grinned, remembering Murek's diabolical ways. He relaxed and waited for an opening. The doyenne was still thinking. The chairsucker was busy with a sandwich in his left hand and a ready round or hard roll in his throwing hand. The boy under the table now rose with paws on the bench, roll devoured and stomach satiated, to take up the lapse in conversation, announcing to his companions on the right and left his latest bright idea. So . . . at the exact moment this scholar finished his speculation, Eron directed a question at him in the same voice Murek always used when *demanding* an answer. It was like unloosing a smelly rabbit across the path of a talking dog who had been thinking about rats. Eron let the dog run off at a gallop after the lure, then turned his total attention to the doyenne, armed with another question, this one crafted to rattle her pretentious authority. But the timing had to be right. She had to drift out of her loop first. He waited, ready to pounce.

He was interrupted. "Really!" his real friend complained in alarm from across the room. "Those are *my* boobs your eyes are coveting!" So far as Eron could see, he was boobless. "You're too wet behind the ears for her!" Possessiveness had cleared away all visions of mathematics, and he was standing at attention near his abandoned whiteboard, eyes fixed on Eron. Eron ambled over. The doyenne would have to wait. "I've a question I've been meaning to ask you." That was a ruse; what Eron "really" wanted to know was how to scroll and erase a whiteboard, since when he'd tried to use the damn thing it didn't seem to have a visible tactile input, nor did it respond to verbal commands. But a question about kanite algebras would have to do as a diversion. "Clear up something for me," he cajoled. "Why are we trying to use one of the kanite algebras to solve this problem? I don't understand." He put on his best woebegone air.

The florist's son groaned but was only too happy to distract Eron. He began to scribble on the whiteboard, which turned out to be such a primitive device that it didn't even correct his illegible handwriting. Eron watched hawk-eyed as the board filled, waiting to see what would happen when it was time to erase. "Got that?" chimed his friend, pausing just long enough for Eron to memorize the scribbles before wiping them away with the flat of his palm. It was the second time Eron had seen this, and it suddenly dawned on him that the whiteboard wasn't defective! Ingenious! But there didn't seem to be *any* way to scroll. Instead of scrolling, new symbols were added to odd blank corners and arrows guided one through the maze.

It was hopeless. Eron figured that it was going to take him at least a couple of turns on Faraway's axis to bring this low-technology group under control. So back to his cave. As he left he whispered the special question he had saved for the doyenne's ears alone—prudently first glancing to check that his really real friend was still puzzling over his own handwriting on the whiteboard.

Faraway had a leisurely rotation, and Eron stayed up all of a long night in his room with the plastic camel lamp he had found in the trash on one of his walks. Camels were reputedly mammals and so related to humans. Marrae didn't believe it because they didn't have hands and couldn't climb trees; she was sure they *couldn't* have evolved on Rith and, maybe, were just gengineered freaks, even mythological beasts. But Eron thought their haughty expression was very human. He believed. "Anthropomorphism," grumbled Marrae. At any rate the camel's belly glowed comfortingly. The light wasn't bright enough to read by, but he did all his reading at the console. After dinner he had been hard at work with a tutorial on kanite algebras. Its library use-log said it hadn't been booted in almost a sixtyne of years. Perhaps that was a warning about the quality of the presentation, or perhaps just an indication that kanite algebras weren't fashionable. The subject was exciting, the tutorial as bland as if its creators hadn't quite grasped the power of the material they were teaching.

He allotted himself a modest nap before breakfast—it didn't do to live without *any* sleep. Why hadn't someone gengineered a bug-fix for sleep—it was such a waste of time. After all, those lazy gengineers had had seventy-odd millennia to perfect the human genome. Of course, maybe the original humans had been camels, and transmogrifying a camel would have taken some doing, especially for a camel!

Jak was the only one up for breakfast. Eron rattled off about the amazing properties of kanite algebras. Jak listened patiently while the cuisinator prepared him a plate of poached eggs on muffin topped by ham in a creamy sauce of butter, egg yolks, and darkmoon juice. He poured a jigger of ersatz Armazin over the benedictine concoction before interrupting Eron's monolog. "What you need is a little *practical* math."

"Ugh," said Eron. "That's your genteel word for physics. What do I need physics for? I'm interested in human beings!" He was calling up a sprinkling of ground cinnamon beetloid for the butter on his toast.

"You need to know physics to know thyself. Right now you're just a walking wave-function with a silly smile. Your fam is a quantum computer. Your penis is another swollen-wave function. Your conscious mind is a teeny-weeny quantum agent that can't possibly keep track of all the things going on inside your head. Dismiss physics at your peril."

"I want to solve problems that have never been solved before."

Jak laughed with his face full of eggs and ham sauce. "Come to today's problem seminar. Our chief prestidigitator, Prof Sledgehammer—"

"Sledgehammer?"

"His real name is unpronounceable. You don't want to know. He comes from a planet where the larynx has devolved but the hands move quicker than the eye! He runs our problem sessions. Usually he's kind-hearted and gives us problems we can solve if we cheat a bit by brainraiding our friends, but this watch he wants us to relax while he gives us a lecture on a problem that was posed back during the Interregnum. He's going to give us tips on how to play with an intractable problem. He's been working on it for thirty years—off and on, of course, not being deranged like you math freaks."

A problem that hadn't been solved? Eron was intrigued. After humanity's eighty thousand years of number-juggling, a problem without an answer was hard to come by. Of course, humans were more ambitious now that they used fams instead of clay. He let Jak drag him to the lecture.

It was a class smaller than the math club, but more formal—no lunches allowed. No throwing rolls at the prof. Old Sledge lounged in his easy chair and chatted with wry humor about his love of sailing. He used that to segue into apocryphal tales about the legendary Faraway physicist Malcof who had also loved sailing, reputedly spending much time in his one-masted sloop creating conundrums. The one on today's agenda had appeared twenty-five centuries ago in an early version of *Asinia's Encyclopedia* under unsolved physics problems. No one knew if it was Malcof's own problem or one he had purloined from a source now vanished into the chaos of the Dark Ages.

When Old Sledge finally tacked into the wind—after abandoning the telling of tall tales to return to the problem on the agenda—he still couldn't keep his ship on course. He bobbed around at sea by using analogy rather than careful mathematical symbolism. Such euphemism annoyed Eron. Physicists! They pulled out of the bilgewater clunky concepts like standing waves in a cup of water or speeding bullets when what they meant was a space-time probability distribution! Sledge's choices of analogy were always colorful, often startling, but like all analogies, each held an arsenal of potential traps. Analogies were never perfect. Eron's mind drifted. He remembered an episode from that Rithian epic Reinstone had lent him—Rith must be quite some place if you could find on it winged women with three-toed claws and feathered boobs! He made an analogy of his own: listening to an analogy was about as safe as trying to sail past the island home of Rith's sirens while at the same time enjoying their singing.

The wakedream grew more complex—better than listening to a physicist talk—as his fam conjured an ocean with the fog of dawn drifting across a distant rocky shore, the beautiful sirens barely visible on their crag. He felt the ropes tying him to the mast. He felt himself strain against them as he harkened to those enchanting voices that drifted out to sea above the wind and the clunk of deaf sailors dipping their oars in the brine. How could a physicist compete with the lilting of a siren's poetry?

> Come, great Odysseus, Hero in thy Glory,
> Stop, bring your Ship to rest and Hear our honeyed story.
> Turn that black prow to Shore; Taste the Sweet Delights
> Waiting here for heroes through Magic Days and Nights
> We know the Noble Past, know the Future's Plan.
> Pause . . . then go thy way, a joyful, wiser man.

Old Sledge tired of farting around with the half-truths of analogy and suddenly he stood erect, spryly energetic, to attack the whiteboard. At last! Mathematical rigor! Eron began to pay close attention. The problem was new to him but its structure was familiar from his sparring matches with Murek. Eron had already set his fam to automatically clean up, memorize, organize, and cross-index the ramblings that these crazy Faraway types scribbled on their ubiquitous whiteboards. Now that thinking had turned precise, pieces fit together cleanly—except for the known contradictions and puzzles. He was able to translate Sledgehammer's awkward perambulations into Murek's categories while developing his own interpretations faster than the prof could scrawl out his thirty years of thinking. The one convenient thing about whiteboards was that they were ten times slower than disciplined thought. Fam-aided thought, of course. Maybe that fam upgrade they had cobbled into his old clunker was actually working! Or maybe he was preternaturally smart.

Just as Eron was getting excited because he could see how the solution was going to come out—Old Sledge stopped and leaned on his shovel. "So there you are; that's twenty-five centuries of sniffing around the edges. Your assignment: State the problem clearly, then map out a campaign of attack. I want to see how your brains work when you are not copying from each other or from an old text you think I don't know about."

Eron looked around. No one had a comment. Jak had slipped out ahead of the class. The rest of them—turned to stone—sat bedazzled in their silence. "But, sir, the solution is obvious," said Eron in that tone of voice which had presaged his expulsion from three schools.

"Oh?" The legendary sledgehammer came down full force on Eron's head. "Explain."

Eron wrapped up his thesis in three sentences. More would have been redundant.

The professor was amused. "That won't do. Come here." Eron rose and Old Sledge courteously erased the whiteboard with the flat of his hand while slipping Eron his lightpen.

Eron filled up the board, adjusting the size of his writing so there would be no need of scrolling. He was impressed with himself but a little nervous. "We'll need a computer to work it through." He did a mental calculation on the complexity of his expression. "That tired old thing the Physics Department calls a computer should be able to crank out the result in about three hours. A good computer would do it in less."

"I'm amazed by the audacity of your approach!" exclaimed the professor ambiguously with a two-edged bite in his voice. He stared at the whiteboard, deep in thought. Eron stared at the professor. Finally Old Sledge shook his head in triumph. "Nope. Won't work."

"It will!" said Eron defiantly, not caring if they expelled him.

"Won't," said the icy prof.

"Why?"

"That's for you to tell me." He then dismissed the class and left Eron alone and enraged.

The Osa boy found himself walking down the Mall, oblivious of the city and its people. His mind was recalculating his conclusion, his attention alternately searching for his error, plotting the murder of professors, and planning to quit school for a career in pirating. He reached the Founder's Mausoleum without noticing the length of the walk.

Inside, the magnificence distracted him. What a place to be buried! Did the intricately inlaid design of the floor conceal the Founder's bones, perhaps gilded in gold leaf? Maybe they'd stuffed him and he was sitting in a back chamber inside a maze known only to the Fellowship where he could be consulted for auguries. Reverently Eron touched the lacquered finish of the empty podium—it was *here* that the Great Man's hologram had spoken from the grave after every psychohistorical crisis.

The hall was a tomb; no anticipating audience sat in its sanctified tiers where *his* audiences had once been crammed. A couple strayed in, peeked, and left. Eron wondered if psychohistorical crises had to be confined to the Interregnum. For the fun of it he stood behind the podium box and delivered a speech to the expanse of chairs, explaining the first post-Interregnum crisis. He spoke solemnly. A great conspiracy of professors had arisen in galactic basements everywhere to paralyze the fabric of civilization by whacking students over the head with sledgehammers. His eloquent speechmaking made him laugh. He *was* the Founder, laughing. Especially the part about the student uprising!

Back in his room, his fury set him to proving himself right. He shifted his argument, shoring it, building it on an unassailable foundation before he began to extend a pillar up into the sky to support his conclusion. Another sleepless watch! He worked in a frenzy. Always so close . . . and yet . . . hints of a flaw . . . he failed at the last stage . . . A *horrible* flaw! Bitter negative insight was disheartening. The lack of sleep, the impending dawn, turned his mind into polymerizing jelly, his fam's safeties refusing to drive it further. He slept for an hour and dreamed of sirens who had lured him to destruction on the rocks.

Then he shook himself awake and went back to work. It wasn't going to be the victory he had visualized, conquering a problem that has taunted physicists for twenty-five centuries, but it was competent analysis, even clever. He was surely going to bring it to Old Sledge today, to show him that Eron Osa hadn't been *all* wrong. The damn prof had probably seen the flaw in half a round of jiffs.

It wouldn't do to put it into a famfeed format. That was an insult, asking a man to fill up his mind with *your* junk. Murek was always trying to teach him humility even if his old tutor had damn little of it himself. Eron thought to print his analysis on good paper—but that was *too* humble. Acid-free paper based on cellulose only lasted for five hundred years before crumbling to sawdust. Eron set up the apartment's manufacturum for cellomet, which would last at least ten millennia. Adding in a beautiful binding was only a few more commands. It was almost a book, Eron's first.

He didn't quite have the courage to drop in on Sledgehammer unannounced so he went to Reinstone for encouragement. Reinstone listened patiently to his troubles and encouraged him. He wrote "Cogito ergo tormentum" on his whiteboard.

"What does that mean?" asked Eron.

"That's for you to tell me."

"All you old codgers say that! You're here to teach me!"

"I beg your pardon, young man. You are here to teach yourself. I'm an advisor and sometimes I even manage to be a resource." He smiled and went off for a trip down his shelves. "I have just what you need," came his muffled voice, and then he reappeared holding a gold-embossed volume with a self-sealing cover and its own vacuum pump. *"The Aeneid,"* he said, "in the original—if you are naïve enough to trust the Rithian copyists. I've found numerous errors in it myself, but nothing, I think, that would cause Virgil more than minor cringing."

Eron broke the seal to the pop of inrushing air. Some nice pictures of people who lived in stone houses. The text was gibberish. His fam co-opted his eyes to make a quick count of the text symbols. There weren't enough to cover even a quarter of the sounds in a decent language. This must be from the time when Rithians spoke in grunts. Another language to learn! He already knew ten and had once been expelled from school for refusing to learn an eleventh—well—he *had* reformatted his teacher's whole language library with a late-Empire military code for which he didn't have the decryption tools.

Reinstone could read his trepidation and called up the quantronic secretary at physics and made an appointment with Sledgehammer. When the confirmation came through he told Eron to skedaddle, first making sure that *The Aeneid* was in his student's hands. Eron left to the faint whisper of the book's vacuum pump.

Old Sledge seated him cordially. "I hadn't expected you so soon. Reinstone tells me you have something interesting for me."

"You were right," said Eron dejectedly. He shoved his bound folder in front of him. "But I did some work. It was pretty exciting—for a while."

"I was right, was I? Awful problem, that one, a devilish ball-cracker which has seduced me and then blasted me to crisp carbon enough times so I know how you feel." He picked up the folder and opened it. He read it in less time than Eron had taken for the print job. That made Eron nervous. Only once did he glance up. "This isn't what you said in class."

"I had time to clean it up."

"You most certainly did. Who taught you Heraklians?"

"My tutor."

Sledge held up a palm to indicate a pause, said, "Inamin," and turned to his console, with quick deaf-mute hand gestures, checking through a storm of activity but sometimes pausing to think. He shut up Eron in midsentence when the boy tried to interrupt the silence. Then he swiveled around to face Eron. "You brought this for my comment, right?"

"If it's crazy, I want to know."

"You've vaulted right over my objection. Spacedamn it, I didn't expect you to bypass my objection, I expected you to find it!"

"You didn't tell me what it was, sir."

"I know." He swore by the gods that physicists fear. "Do you know what you've just done? You marched right through a demon's army without noticing them. You've done the best work on this problem in twenty-five centuries. I'm signing you up for my course."

"What?"

"I'm not letting you get out of it! Students like you don't wander into my class every semester."

"But I don't want to be a physicist."

Stunned silence. The physicist's sails were blown aback. How could anyone not want to be a physicist? He recovered and sailed on. "Is it that you'd rather dance and sing? Has Reinstone convinced you to write poetry? I see that he's given you one of those fake books that Rithians publish for the tourist trade." He took it and unsealed the cover. "I might have known! Another invented language. If you decode it you'll discover the secrets of the ancients. That's the blurb, eh? Don't forget that it's a bargain at a thousand credits." He winked and laughed and resealed the book, activating the susurrus of its pump. "So what *do* you want to be?"

"A psychohistorian."

Sledgehammer brought his face close to Eron's, studying it for madness. "Do you really believe that those charlatans can predict the future?" He scoffed and swiveled his aerochair toward the window. "If psychohistory was a *science,* they'd tell us how they did it. Wouldn't they? That's what science is all about. Open disclosure. Sharing of methods. Cross-checking. Communication. The search for truth. The willingness to stand in front of one's peers and confess one's mistakes! I tell you about tough problems you never heard of and, puzzled, you go off and bring back to me an answer. What does a psychohistorian do? He mumbles mug-you-magic-cockamamie and pretends he can't tell you what it means because it is all a secret that *must* be kept or the sky will fall. If Faraway hadn't been driven by that kind of self-defeating superstition from the beginning, we'd still be ruling the Galaxy!"

"Yeah, but if they are so dumb, why are *they* ruling the Galaxy?"

"A good point, lad. Maybe we're the dumb ones." His anger gone, he became mellow. "And what appeals to you about psychohistory? The psycho part, or the history part?"

"It can predict the future."

"I see." Sledgehammer's eyes became cunning. "There are *no* courses like that at Asinia."

"I know."

"Tragedy! You'll have to take second best."

"You?"

There was a little curl to his lips and a nod of the head. "We of the physics department humbly volunteer as second best." His voice was sarcastic. "What can I say? Test us. Second rate though we may be, we *are* willing to teach you what we know about how to predict, maybe not the future but at least a few of the minor if dazzling tricks of precognition. We aren't the least bit secretive. Look up our sleeves. Don't expect a performance equal to the claims of those meddling psycho-historians, but we can teach you how to predict when laminar flow will turn into turbulent flow; we can tell you which aerochair will hold you comfortably and which one will flip you over and crack your head against the floor; we can tell you where a star was when men were just forest nomads and where it will be a hundred millennia from now. And I can predict, within the bracket of a month, when a massive star will turn supernova."

"What grades am I going to get?"

Sledge grinned happily. "Ah, students never change! I feel my own youth again whenever I hear that request! We don't have the potion for immortality, either. But let me give you my best offer. I'll teach you everything a physicist knows about predicting. Some of it ought to prove useful when you take up charlatanry."

So Eron signed on, not knowing that he was getting into a long-term relationship with a very demanding taskmaster. Predicting turned out to be learning how to repeat oneself with minimum error. He worked at simple stuff like how to use a phase-shift electron nanocalib, how to polish a surface to a sixteenth of a wavelength of violet light, how to build up a probability distribution from experimental repetition—and some even weirder stuff. Sledge once put him on a team of advanced students tinkering with a huge black energotron out in the desert that could, when it wasn't sulking, make measurements to within a few planck lengths.

When he wasn't in the labs or at the space station facility Eron was chief designer, under Sledgehammer, of the class that built multivariate models and then performed perturbation analysis on each and every variable so they would all get a gut feel for the role which that variable played in the model. Sledge liked them to rank each variable by how the errors in its measurement contributed to error in the model's final predictions. He had one ability that drove Eron wild with envy. He could unerringly look at a phenomenon and build a rule-of-thumb model of it that was more error free than any model Eron was able to assemble with sixtynes of variables. When Eron tried to wheedle out of him how he did it, Old Sledge would just laugh and mutter about complexity compression. If pressed further, he put his finger to his lips and hinted at a secret voodoo methodology.

Eron was so exasperated he flung at his mentor the worst insult he could think of: "You're no better than a Spacedamned psychohistorian!"

For that, liege lord Sledgehammer assigned him to do high penance and cast him out into the desert. He was there requested to write a fifty-thousand–word essay on the irreducible uncertainties introduced into any prediction by the quantum mechanical equations. Sledge made clear that the essay was to cover everything: why such irreducible uncertainties made the strict repetition of any experiment impossible, why it dictated the irreversibility of any event, why it caused the gradual erasure of the past and blurred vision into the future, first by obscuring near-term details and then finally by swamping out larger and larger details. Eron completed the essay in a little air-conditioned office he usurped under the energotron. His twenty-five-year-old mistress, the desert Stationmaster, made him a present of a hair shirt, which he nailed to his door. She was an indispensable aid in editing the manuscript while kissing his ears.

It was this brilliant essay which eventually clinched the interest of the Fellowship when Eron Osa was brought to their attention.

# THE CORON'S WISP PENTAD,
# 14,792 GE

*A soothsayer, by consulting the entrails of the appropriate quantum wave equation, can predict your future because his vague pronouncements and hints contain within themselves all possible futures.*

—Anonymous

The occultations and phases of Timdo's sibling moons featured prominently in the local astrological charts. From a high porch of the tiered Hephaestion Monastery, Hiranimus found the moons merely beautiful. The orbs were rightly famous among Coron's poets. Ample Succubus was a delicate pink, Seer smaller and more aloof. In the lean mountain sky, a host of celestial attendants had filled prime balcony seats to celebrate the stately parade.

The Monastery's guest leaned on the balustrade above and below man-size gargoyles whose gutters drained the tiered porches. All were carved as watchful monsters peering skyward. Two powerful stars of the Coron's Wisp pentad were now ascendant—above Timdo's volcanic peaks King Nechepso took his glaring midnight walk and moving into the Constellation of the Fates was Qin where the Emperor Huangdi forever chased after the Moons of Immortality. Timdo's sun, Hephaestus, God of Fire, had long banked his forge, taking great Nestor and lesser Samash with him into the nether regions. These were the Five Moving Houses of Scogil's designated domain.

The Oversee's new Agitator had already returned from his first inspection tour and had time to meditate. Hiranimus was weighing the concord between his astrological agents. They were from disparate worlds, connected mainly by their close proximity in the Coron's gravitational pentad. The underground cities of the planet Nestor of the sun Nestor revered the stars because they seldom saw them— the bustling Samash system worlds, speaking their own language, revered the stars because they lived among them on worlds too small to hold an atmosphere—the peculiarly devout population of Huangdi made good agents because they had a very usable tradition of loyalty—the delightful little family industries of the planet Nechepso of the sun Nechepso were the quantronic centers of Egg production—and Timdo of Hephaestus . . .

Scogil had chosen Timdo to be his headquarters.

Here in the Wisp it was Timdo's Hephaestion monks who were the engine behind the growing passion for astrology. They had hired Hiranimus Scogil and Nemia of l'Amontag to build a new edition of the Coron's Egg suitable for galactic distribution, wholly unaware that it was the Oversee whose covert manipulations had set up Timdo's galactic ambitions.

The monks were providing the perfect cover for an Agitator.

Who else for the job of chief Eggman than a Helmarian? Helmarian exiles had designed the first Egg for them with a little technical and production help from the early Interregnum's Faraway traders who were then having a hard time opening up suspicious markets so far from the Periphery in a region of space ravished by warlords. In those bygone times the Hephaestion astrologers had been ambitious underdogs on their own anarchic turf who saw the stars as natural allies of their earthly machinations. Rivals from the Celestial House of Arak, who insisted on drawing astrological charts by hand and handbook and compass, no longer existed.

For now all was well. Scogil and his wife had been greeted with more enthusiasm than they might have expected—they were, after all, known to be giaour, infidels who did not believe. To be trusted to rebuild the most sacred of talismans . . .

Probably the trust rested on astral reasons unfathomable to a layman unfamiliar with the great confluences. Scogil suspected his and Nemia's aura here on Timdo derived from their Helmarian ancestry. They were the instruments of impeccably powerful stars. Legends that entwined the Thousand Suns Beyond the Helmar Rift with the high mysteries of Timdo reached farther back than any living monk's memory. Monks who are ritualists do not question tradition.

Hiranimus Scogil retreated from the high porch into the draped residency. Nemia was asleep and he was careful not to disturb her. He could not sleep himself. His mind was agitated with the temptation to revise the Smythosian plan for Coron's Wisp. Would he dare? The stakes were terrifying. The odds were bad. He itched to meddle but wasn't yet sure of his vision or of his authority—the memory of his failures at the Fortress could still shake his confidence. He had been brought in by the Oversee to nurture the plan, not warp it to new purpose. Nemia would oppose any recklessness. The seed growing here at Coron's Wisp was her Grandfa's major bit of psychohistorical engineering. To succeed he would have to convince his wife that Grandfa hadn't seen far enough. A daunting task. Convince her he must; she had the hardware design skills he lacked. He thrilled at the idea of being forward bite-man for the Oversee.

But other voices were advising him differently. Forget such insanity! Where was his Murek Kapor persona now that he needed it! Just relax and lead a normal life! This frantic susurrus of caution filled his mind with continuously iterating equations—checking, checking, looking for the lethal flaw that he had probably overlooked. Bravado wasn't enough. He had to concede that. If a complete review confirmed that old l'Amontag's plan was best, then he would have to be content to be a servant and see it through.

Yet there was all this new stuff from the Martyr's Cache daring him.

The strategy for Coron's Wisp had been in place now for generations, predating even Grandfa, who had not been its originator, merely its master tactician. It had its own inertia—plans are that way—and Scogil was only the latest rider still exploring the itinerary. His recent research showed him that all had been unfolding flawlessly. His replay of the mathematics had uncovered no error in the reasoning. It was Grandfa l'Amontag's masterwork to have mixed into the basic strategy these inward-looking monks whom he had transformed from fatalists into advocates of a transcendental journey for all of mankind. He had picked and chosen between their contradictions, until he had a philosophy that fit the parameters of his equations. He had taken the rough-cut jewel of the original Oversee strategy and worked it into an elegant set of equations that any second-rate psychohistorian could follow.

Why hadn't the Pscholars noticed? Having been part of an adventure that *had* been detected, Scogil was paying very special attention to this aspect. He saw no flaws in the camouflage that this sprouting revolution needed. His admiration for Nemia's grandfather was growing.

As a youthful wanderer, Grandfa had stumbled upon the perfect disguise. It was built into the Pscholar's gestalt that a doctrine like astrology was so divorced from truth, so unable to predict anything, that it could never compete on a living stage with a force as powerful as psychohistorical vision. The Pscholars had no place for astrology in their galactic model for the same reason that a physicist's equations ignored the feeble pull of a distant star on one man's life.

The lion's leavings are the hyena's feast. Whatever the Pscholars ignored, the Smythosians chewed on mathematically for some usable morsel, perhaps a bone with which to club the lion, perhaps a carelessly discarded match and a stand of dead wood.

Old l'Amontag had been gifted with a cunning superbly adapted to the kind of social engineering at which the Smythosians excelled in their niche—harvesting the picayune and harmless discards of the Second Empire. Astrology might have remained a decaying copse in a sunless galactic wilderness had the Pscholars themselves not provided l'Amontag with the perfect tinder.

Tell a man that he is not good enough to determine his own destiny, tell him skillfully enough that the mathematics of the future is not for him, keep him ignorant and, well . . . perhaps he will believe you, even accept a hood and a leading hand, become dependent upon your paternalism, but . . . don't be surprised if, under the hood, his ignorant soul begins to listen to a traitor whispering astrology's seductive message:

What if the stars do control the future? What if charts that elucidate the relationships between stars and man *are* within the ability of a common citizen to master? What if the mathematics of the future *is* far simpler than the power elite claim it to be in their own self-interest?

What happens when astrology's sages promise that a man can do even better than psychohistory's reading of society, that he can read from the stars his own *personal* destiny? And what happens when his neighbors confirm the rumors with apocryphal tales of the miraculous insights pouring from heaven into their now-enlightened minds? How tempting it might be to throw off the leash and the hood and the paternalism! His ignorance will have neither the words nor the insight to caution him down a more rational path.

It looked good, l'Amontag's scheme. Timdo was set to proselytize the Galaxy and cause an enormous brouhaha for the Fellowship. If the buildup wasn't noticed over the next few years, an aggressive new strain of astrology would leap through the stars like wildfire through a lion's dry savanna. The Pscholars wouldn't have the reaction time to stop it. That seemed certain to Scogil—the equations confirmed it, no matter what perturbations were introduced. Wildfire.

But . . . then what? The weakness of the piecemeal Smythosian methods was their short range—the accumulation of too many half-known exterior interventions. In this case the outcome became unacceptably unpredictable beyond a century. Nemia's grandfather had been guessing—guessing was the right word—that an astrological flash fire would so upset the elite status of the Pscholars that a new equilibrium would be reached.

Scogil was less sure now that events would happen that way. He had been playing with instruments from the Martyr's Cache that l'Amontag had never seen—incredible tools which continued to surprise and amaze him. Flash fires can burn out. New grass can grow on the blackened hills and all is as it was. He had nothing solid enough to confide to Nemia—half-worked-out omens, not proofs. Still awkward in his use of the new tools, whole chapters remained gibberish to him, but some of the understandable methods gave results so powerful that he couldn't resist employing them again and again in place of tried-and-true Smythosian standbys, each time learning a new twist or trick. The Founder had been an absolute genius at long-term projections. His isostatic sniffers, alone, cut through mountains of routine computing when one was trying to track stable social forces through time—imagine, a three-line test for local Tulbadian stability! Scogil was still reeling!

So far he hadn't got beyond a fast scouting expedition into the unknown—but his quicky long-term look at the Wisp's influence on the Galaxy beyond this century was disturbing.

He lay on the bed, wide awake.

He wasn't even sure if his setup of the problem was mathematically sound. That was bad. Too many parameters had to be adjusted to take into account human nature as augmented by the fam—not part of the Founder's equation set. The Martyrs had only begun to wrestle with the problem. They had, after all, lived through the time of Cloun-the-Stubborn in an age when the full impact of the fam was inconceivable! Nevertheless a clear warning was emerging; the Pscholars were essentially right about cults like astrology and would be able to contain even a virulent outbreak without having to adjust their own social status. A blind slave freed of his leash was still blind and could be driven into a ditch by a skillful herdsman. Astrology didn't have a chance if it couldn't actually *predict* the future—it could go from a phenomenal gnashing-slashing giant in league-spanning boots to a pile of fossil bones within a century!

Such a whiff of spectacular failure was enough to make wild risks much more appealing. Scogil had been toying with the germ of a very dangerous idea, putting it away, glancing at it sideways, forgetting it for watches at a time—laughing at the preposterous—but now his mind seemed to be fleshing it out without prodding. His fam was totally involved. It looked so much like one of those classic psychohistorical leverage points which the Founder talked about so often. A lever to lift the Galaxy, a lever sitting there, waiting to be grabbed. It frightened Hiranimus. This was how Cloun-the-Stubborn must have felt. The scheme was too audacious, too fraught with risk, and yet the broad outline was jelling just the same. What if . . . yes . . . what if the l'Amontag plan could be augmented by yet *another* underlay of conspiracy? Too complicated? Of course it was too complicated! Forget it!

There were already six grades which a Timdo astrologer might achieve. They had been carefully designed by Nemia's grandfather out of the natural material he found among the traditions of Timdo's monks, even the rankings. He had been responsible for the last upgrade of the Egg, a major one, superficially the same as the model that had first appeared during the Interregnum, but covertly reengineered to support the needs of an expanding organization.

As always, those who achieved Aspirant, the first level, were allowed to own an Egg. There had never been barriers of scholarship or sex or age or profession. This minimum level contained all the skills necessary to proselytize astrology. It was the seed level and its responsibilities and duties had been polished to perfection centuries before the Oversee had ever heard of Coron's Wisp.

From Aspirant it was a natural progression to Mentor. A Mentor had to be working with at least three Aspirants and was himself working with a Luminant. Here Grandfa had built in his first modifications so subtly that even the highest-level monks had not noticed. The changes went on upward through the levels of Luminant, Master, Prophet, and Monk.

The Egg was an intricate instrument, and for a rise in rank one now had to learn a whole level of additional skills. It was the Egg which held the levels together and simultaneously separated them. Each level required that the votary teach, be taught, and make readings for money or pleasure. The money worked its way up to the monks who oversaw the building of the Eggs, new monasteries, and public works not adequately supported by public taxes. Grandfa l'Amontag had been careful to craft in the money factor by further weakening the old ascetic traditions already fatally compromised by langsyne dealings with Faraway's traders. Traditions fade away slowly, and Timdo's monks still frowned on ostentation but no longer on the luxuries that a monk could actually enjoy. Power was the danger. Money was the growth hormone.

These six grades of knowledge were a recent rationalization of an ancient hierarchy, but the new structure was working marvelously well and the Timdo Monasteries were a hundred times richer than they had been a mere half century ago. Still, it was time for the Egg to be modernized. There had been no new edition for twenty years. The specific upgrade that the monks wanted were unique fingering commands specific to each of the six grades, plus special teaching prompts to go with them, all to make divisions clearer and proselytization easier—and expansion painless. Other than that, the Egg's star-catalog needed updating, and the monks hoped that recent advances in astrological computing might be included. They liked to think of themselves as mathematicians. In a Galaxy ruled by mathematicians, lesser men used math as a body lotion to give themselves the right smell.

Scogil was already thinking well beyond the dreaming monks. He saw the feasibility of adding some famlike cognitive abilities. His favorite fantasy was a Coron's Egg carrying a hidden seventh level, an undocumented upgrade path from monk as competent parlor-mathematician to monk as psychohistorian. He kept sketching out possible quantum architectures. There wasn't any reason they couldn't do it. Nemia was one of the Galaxy's finest quantum-state designers, and he had with him a copy of the Martyr's Cache.

What a way to get himself into trouble! The Timdo monks would have a fit and fire him on the spot. Scientize their holy spiritual prowess? Horrors! Nemia would have a fit if he suggested such a radical change to the direction of her grandfather's masterpiece. And those mysterious conservatives who ran the Oversee, those cowards who had pulled out of the Ulmat, would implode! What to do? He didn't even trust himself! He was starting to think like a seriously deranged megalomaniac. While half of him was scheming to conquer the Galaxy with a basket of smart Eggs, the other half was desperately trying to carry him off bodily to be locked up behind bars.

He turned on his side and found himself smiling at Nemia's serene profile, lit through the stone window by Succubus and old King Nechepso. Then he set his fam to manually force his sleep. Even megalomaniacs need sleep. Tomorrow his wife had scheduled some sightseeing for a change of pace that promised to be welcome. Timdo was a pleasant planet to look at. Those crazy monks talked about the harmony of the spheres, whatever that meant, yet it probably meant *something*, for harmony with nature was the dominant theme of their architectonics. Nothing was exactly the same style, but where did one architect leave off and a new one begin? where did structure become landscape? Nothing was built without drawing up the proper astrological charts. Impacting the stars negatively was some sort of mortal sin. He went to sleep dreaming about Eggs that meshed astrology and psychohistory into a harmonious flow of quantum states—and woke up tired, like two enemy soldiers rising at dawn on a battlefield to continue a war neither wanted but couldn't stop.

"Hey, it's your watch," he said, gently shaking her. She continued to sleep, as usual, while he made warm drinks and peeled a bowlful of weird Timdo fruits whose sweet hearts hid inside skins from hell. He sat on the bed and fed her. "Your monk-chauffeur is due already," he chided. "In fact, he's already late."

Nagging got him nowhere. He waited for her on the high porch while she dressed. That always took time, wherever she was. Here it was worse. She was intent on going native and doing it with the right casual wraparound. It was no use—going native, that is—nor was it any use telling her that. As a couple they were too tall. Their skin was the wrong color, not bronze enough, and especially wrong were the bones of their eyebrows and nose. Acquiring the Timdo accent was going to be hopeless, even with fam-aids. The language was standard but of an unusual dialect that contained hundreds of emotional nuances that neither his nor Nemia's ears had been trained to hear. They would forever be treated as exotic tourists, fair marks for a reading, or with reverence by those who recognized them as Helmarian.

Nemia's disguise was wasted on the chauffeur—his bow was too deep, his flourish at helping her up into the tricycle too respectful. He even adjusted her seat, a gesture no monk would have bothered to make for a local, not even for his own abbot. Scogil smiled. It was going to be hard to keep a low profile on Timdo while they sported such bent noses. Sometimes the best place for a freak to hide was out in the open.

Their chauffeur and guide hadn't minded the wait while Nemia readied herself, it was a long pedal up and around the local mountain range and valleys, but when Nemia presented her schedule of destinations he was politely indignant. He wanted to do the sacred sites. Maybe there were less hills along that route. Scogil wished only to bask in the local weltanschauung. He was about to do a serious psychohistorical study, a complete revision of the Oversee's plan for Coron's Wisp—just as an exercise, mind you—and a personal touch always made the math easier. Scogil lived by sifting through lots of examples. There was no way to beat the Pscholars at their own game except by nursing those hard-to-find parameters that were being overlooked by the huge psychohistorical model maintained on Splendid Wisdom. Nemia won the argument with their chauffeur.

The mountains of Timdo were a strange place to find swamp grass, but on the lower levels of the slopes the tiered rice paddies were everywhere, their stone sides giving the landscape a contoured map feel. Some of the tiers had been taken out of rice and given over to treed parks. Little villages went up the mountain slopes, irrigation pumping stations were graciously housed in discreet stone rotundas, bridges were arched marvels of masonry, streams carefully sculpted into pools and rapids and hanging gardens. Halfway up the hills were comfortable resting stations for the bicyclist.

So it had been for more than ten millennia. High on the slopes of distant mountains, above the tree line, were the prolific ruins of almost inaccessible Monasteries—reached only by foot—a recent afterthought of time, the earliest no more than four thousand years old, their era come and gone. The monks, who had begun to flourish only during the chaos leading up to the Interregnum, had abandoned their anchorite past during the rise of the Second Empire and now ran a thriving commercial business at a lower altitude, the indirect result of making a devil's pact with Faraway traders who saw no profit in virtuous vows of poverty. Some of them were even motorized.

For midday snack, their sweating tricycle chauffeur suggested that his guests rest at an elegant tourist trap in a flat mountain valley beside the river, but Scogil chose instead a small farmer's chapel that offered rice cakes and rice wine—and shade for their guide. The farmer's wife was a licensed astrologer, the chapel showing the modest Egg&Stars logo of a Luminant over its roadside turn in. She seated them at the place of honor, notwithstanding that there were no other guests. Her chitchat was an astrologer's subtle probing into her customer's hearts and deepest desires.

Nemia knew the ritual from listening to her Grandfa's tall tales. When the warm rice wine was sipped to the last drop, she closed the palms of her hands together, nodded her head, and stared at the center of the table while addressing their hostess. "Will your precious Egg give birth to wisdom for my husband?"

The woman beamed at such uncommon suavity from farmen. She beckoned; they followed, ducking under a stone arch into a tiny domed alcove done in the dead black of space. Crawling around the base, on his multiple carved legs, was the sneering torso of Albris-the-Creator, tail in teeth. When they were seated on cushions, and their Luminant had left to fetch her Egg, Hiranimus turned to Nemia, who knew all about such readings from her Grandfa. "Will she tell me what I want to hear?" he whispered.

"Of course. When the Great Monster Albris"—Nemia nodded to the slithering figure all around them—"set fire to his mother to create the dancing dervish-universe of exploding energy, he so admired himself for inventing light that he glued together discarded claw parings he had lying around to manufacture the first astrologer, whose life was to be devoted to singing praises to his creator for having made such perfect stars. Instead the first astrologer muttered under his breath that the universe had looked better as a mother."

"Oh, oh," said Hiranimus, "astrology is in trouble. Was Albris mad?"

"Oh, yes. He was provoked into a terrible rage. The Great Monster Albris chopped off his astrologer's head and made the planets out of it. Still raging, he conjured men from the lice in the astrologer's hair in order that he might forever be surrounded by more servile admirers. Men were very impressed by his ravings.

Thus it became the tradition of all mortal kings to chop off the head of every astrologer not able to tell a king what a king wants to hear. After eons of such breeding, astrologers carry in their genes a wisdom in the ways of kings equal to their wisdom in stellar matters, which allows them to veil their readings in words that only men more intelligent than kings can understand."

By this time their astrologer was back with her Egg on its cushion, this one a grotto green ovoid streaked in bloodred stone, tiny diamond eyes sparkling. An afternoon glow from the archway vanished, the room went dark, Albris faded, and the stars came out. She scattered a tiny thimble of rice. The artificial sky filled with strange stellar groupings and a floating moon.

"The moon is a good omen," she said, holding her hand up in the ancient human sign for silence. Slowly the stick figures suggested by joining up the stars matured into fleshed-out constellations: a two-headed man, an upside-down woman embracing a goat, a ten-legged lizard, a monster, a fleet of Imperial warships, a sword and heart, two babies on a scale, a cyclops whose handless arms ended in an agonized male head and a frightened woman's head. The moon began to drift across the lizard. "The lizard of earth and water is your constellation," she intoned. All the stars went out except those of the lizard. The stars had cryptic names, glowing in red alphascript when directly engaged by an eye. "Pick your star," she commanded.

He chose at random. "Teiid," he read.

The sky whirled dizzily in hyperjump and a new set of stars and their figures emerged, now from Teiid's viewpoint. "Interesting," she said. "You are a man of strong ambitions."

"How can you read that?" asked Scogil—gently so as not to show his disbelief.

"You have chosen a sky that contains the constellation of the Atman. He is powerful and occurs in the sky of a myriad of planets who were conceived while in the House of Attainment. Sometimes he is curled and asleep. Sometimes he battles with an adversary. Sometimes he rides the Princess. I have seen him drink from the Water Jug. Here he points but does not act. He knows what he wants to do but is indecisive. At what does he point?"

"He's not pointing at a constellation; I see only a clump of stars." Scogil shrugged.

The Luminant chided him. "The Atman's vision is not yet clear. Perhaps that is why he is indecisive. Are you content to be one of the blind ones who leads an ordinary life? The Lizard tells me otherwise. Look closer, lest you be blinded forever to what is in front of you. What do you *see*?"

"Well, there are two clumps of stars, one tighter, more focused; the other is a kind of nebulosity that seems to be flying apart."

"Only the rare perceptive man sees both these Faces as separate Exigents. Whose faces?"

"The face of doubt and the face of certainty." Scogil didn't know why he found himself saying that.

DONALD KINGSBURY

The farmer woman grinned, wrapping her shawl about herself and stroking the Egg so that the stars flickered. "You have chosen for yourself the Face of Certainty, I can see. Which is it? The focused group or the nebulosity?"

"Focused. I see a man on a horse." He really did.

They were whisked by another "jump" through hyperspace to a place where there were no delineated constellations, just a jumble of stars.

"Do you recognize the sky?" she asked.

"No," he said, then tritely: "The Galaxy is a big place."

"You are among the stars of the Thousand Suns Beyond the Helmar Rift. This is not a planetary lookout. You have chosen to look out from a point far from any star. This view has never been seen before. Here is the place from which you abandon doubt and choose the certainty of a new viewpoint that will take you home to your Helmarian roots and then away again." Constellations began to form. A horseman, his scarf flowing in the wind, the hoofs actually trotting. Then other horsemen appeared, perhaps two sixtyne of them, all engaged in some ancient cavalry battle, the chaos of a battle undecided, the first horseman alone in his certainty.

*How in all the hells of Space did she find that configuration of constellations?*

"Pick the star to lead you through this," she commanded.

"I'll take Splendid Wisdom," he said instantly.

"No." She smiled as she might to a famless child who was about ready to buy out the whole toy store. "Splendid Wisdom is far from you now and will not guide you. You must pick from the stars around us."

"The eyes of the rider, then." He looked and the eyes had names.

One eye was the sun Sanahadra, builder of the Fortresses of Darkness, whose magi had led the armies resisting the Empire in the Wars Across the Marche and whose peoples had been scattered by their failure to win the war. The other was Oenadra, homeworld of Nemia's most ancient ancestors before they, too, suffered brutal exile during the Dispersion.

The full-time rice farmer and part-time Luminant had finished her reading. "Your destiny has been chosen. Honor your guiding stars and they will lead you." She paused, urgently needing to say something. "Two stars!" she exclaimed. Her arms opened out as if she were holding more than they could carry. She seemed indignant at the universe's generosity. "It is not often that the alignments bring forth *two* stars to aid a man's action." Then her hands came down, palms up and together, suddenly bereft, supporting her ritual money stick parallel to her body in the ritual alms request. The stick had been coated in myrrh, the favorite scent of Albris. Nemia paid her by touching money stick to money stick, but the woman didn't seem satisfied. Her stiff alms-pose lasted a few jiffs after download; clearly she expected a tip for midwifing *two* guiding stars. Nemia declined but Hiranimus added the little extra something with a touch of his own money stick. He was in a good mood.

He had made his decision.

# OLD BOYS' NETWORK, LATE 14,797 GE

*Mathematics is the Queen of Science but she isn't very Pure; she keeps having babies by handsome young upstarts and various frog princes—DK*

—Engraving carved into a 21st-century AD skull
purchased at the Artiste's Skull Emporium on Rith

Eron Osa had been too busy over the years to have girlfriends, except for occasional flings with the sensual Stationmaster of the energotron when the odd assignment sent him out to the desert. He had as a poor substitute a corner of his room hung with his favorite touchy-feely that came from a subterranean media shop off campus. She looked like an ordinary nude until your hands were close enough to be immersed in a delicate illusion–the touch of a real woman. Her thirty poses zoomed on command from a petite doll to a scrollable giantess four times normal size. She lived beside his books and never complained when he recited theorems at her.

Jak and Bari had graduated to better things, their places in the student apartment filled by a freshman and an Advanced Mucky-Muck in hyperspatial engineering. Bari willed Eron the job of House Manager (Ogre) in charge of Training Up Sloths to Keep Things Reasonably Neat, and Eron had become ruthless at dragging their unhousebroken freshman out of bed or jolting him from his wakedreaming to clean up the crumbs he had left in the kitchen or the pile of datasquares he had abandoned on the common room table.

Eron wasn't quite so cavalier with the new engineer who worked out every decawatch at the local zenoli club. Osa had always been fascinated by the legend of the zenoli warriors and once made the mistake of asking for a demonstration. It had been an awesome experience to be tossed around helplessly like a rag doll, sure that the whirling furniture was going to connect with his head only to be saved by a deft zenoli grab at his ankle which jerked him off in a new direction. He signed up for zenoli training immediately, putting on hold his calibration of an instrument that measured the velocity of tiny breezes by the rate of cooling in the radioactive head of a pin.

Most of the time Eron was at his own console, studying. It was a grueling habit he had ceased to question. He had already learned enough about the difficulties of measurement and error estimation to daunt a young man planning to make a life's work out of predicting an essentially unpredictable future. But there was always more to learn. He spent extra watches in the physics lab building exotic measuring devices, and that, more than anything else, had introduced him to the mischievous boss of the universe, the god of chaos, a shapechanger who destroyed repeatability and disassembled order. Chaos would gladly lie to you about your future.

But chaos wasn't an omnipotent viceroy; there were tiny long-term effects that kept slipping through chaos' disorganized fingers to lose themselves in some back eddy of the universe where they grew up into things like the human brain—which then invented science to study such improbably persistent phenomena. Eron began to love the painfully acquired traditions of science whose refined strategies of guerrilla warfare used control-of-order as its means of resisting and defying chaos.

Eron was appreciating more and more the teachings of the phlegmatic but sometimes explosive Murek Kapor, who was now only a memory. That man had taught him a skewed way of attacking problems with a toolbox that didn't seem to be used at Asinia, though the tools drilled into him by the Asinian mathematicians and physicists and engineers bridged chasms he had not been able to cross as a student on Agander. With the right forks and spoons curiosity became more than mouth-watering—it became belly-filling. Eron had an insatiable curiosity.

He dissected the order in human neural circuits. He pored over the math of the quantum effects used by a fam to accumulate information. He toadied up to Reinstone by analyzing how the memetic assumptions of a culture were stored in poetry—not letting on to Reinstone that he was using mathematical tools for the analysis and not the language dialectics that his tutor was so passionately fond of. From time to time he brought and recited for his mentor's pleasure original poetry composed in a sixtyne of Old Rith styles. Their rhythm and their clever use of ancient tongues often brought tears to the old man's eyes. Eron was careful not to mention that they came out of a rule-based machine program he had designed—Poetaster—to organize gibberish into pleasing concepts—in any of ten forgotten languages. Math was *amazing*. When you treated it like a Muse, it would do anything for you, even write poetry. He could understand how the Founder had captured the human soul in his equations.

At the same time it shocked Eron to find out that his mother's favorite maxim was wrong. She must have repeated to him a thousand times her theories of the mind's fundamental logical processes—but the human brain wasn't logical at all. When you broke it down to its atomic processes, it was merely a statistical machine that cleverly filtered out the chaos so that a man might see whatever faint order lay behind the overwhelming noise. Evolution had taught man's brain to ignore what it couldn't control.

Eron was reminded of the way a frog's eye was blind to stillness, seeing only motion. Mankind was blind to chaos. He saw only order. And if there was no order an undisciplined mind would frantically begin to correlate random events, seeing order in the shadows where none existed. An undiciplined mind wasn't logical.

A man might find order in a perfectly random gambling machine and try to beat it. Chaos can produce a jackpot which looks like order to a human mind unexposed to a large enough sample space.

A man might find order in the wheeling stars and then create astrology in the hope that stellar order would rub off onto his chaotic life.

Eron knew men who could stare at a lightning bolt and then correlate gaze and bolt—weren't they simultaneous?—to create for themselves a mentalic superstition explaining how a naked gaze carried the strength to bring lightning down upon the heads of others. If lightning could cause a man to think, then thinking could cause lightning, and from there it was only a step away to use thought to curdle milk and seduce young women and erase the evil in politician's minds. Concentrate hard enough, and such a man could rule the Galaxy, blow up stars, create new universes. Powerless men have their dreams of power.

Not for Eron. The mind was a statistical machine ready to make correlations at the moment of emergence from the womb. But statistics without logic will tell you any lie you want to hear. It will correlate things that have no cause/effect relationship. It will confuse effect with cause and cause with effect. Logic has to be taught at the white heat of passion, then tempered in a cauldron of oil and put to the grindstone to get its final edge. It takes years.

And at the end of those years, Eron's life was changed forever. He heard Marrae arguing with the hyperspace engineer and felt obliged to intervene. By now he had the seniority to end arguments. But when he opened his door into the central living space, Marrae was holding the sphere of a Personal Capsule. "He thinks it's his and has been chasing me around the couch. It's yours." And she tossed it to him.

Eron disappeared back inside his room and closed the door, wishing that people would be a little less dramatic in their play. Why did he have to be exposed to heart failure just because Marrae was flirting with the newbie? So—who would be sending him a Capsule? His parents? Murek Kapor? But when it fell open he found a message from a man he had never expected to meet again. The Scav, Rigone.

> *Eron Osa: I hope you survived the operation of a couple of years back. It scared the tattoos off me but, it seems, I had good mentors. The experience saved my butt from the flame back here on SW. Thanks. To business. I have a friend who scares the remaining tattoos off me every time he drops by for a drink. You may or may not hear from him: Second Rank Pscholar Hahukum Konn. I run a place mostly frequented by students, and he is always asking me wistfully for the names of a few students who are also intelligent. Those he takes to his heart go far. I always think of you. You've had time by now to become seasoned. So . . . I have given him your name and location. If you ever reach Splendid Wisdom call on me at the Teaser's Bistro on the Olibanum. Fondly, Rigone.*

# PILGRIMAGE OF THE AGENT OF THE
# OVERSEE, 14,797 GE

*... millennia later even the early astronomer Kepler cast horoscopes on a square compass rose of eight outer houses and four inner houses whose geometry matched the beholding platform of the Great Pyramid Observatory as it was at the time of the completion of the Grand Gallery and before the construction of the King's Chamber. From such an artificial horizon, priests measured the rising times and azimuth of the stars that made up the thirty-six decans of the Egyptian calendar ... An educated Egyptian saw life as a ceaseless battle to maintain exact order,* ma'at, *in a world of encroaching chaos ... by observing the stars and probing geometry he ...*

*... that one entered the afterlife of mystery, protected by* hike *and preserved in a structure that embodied the orderliness of the universe brought one to the edge of the immortal: order was immortality.*

*... the uneducated Greek mercenaries of a later decadent era, hired by Egyptian and Persian alike to kill each other, carried back to their city-states the Egyptian fascination with number and geometry and degraded it into the pseudogeometry of a horoscope designed to plot personal destiny. By Hellenistic times ...*

—The Faraway Project for the Preservation of History, 19th Edition,
12,562 GE

Astrology was alive on Splendid Wisdom.

Hiranimus Scogil watched Kikaju Jama as he removed one of the ovoids from its coddled case of sixtyne and held it up to the eyelight. Beside him, the daughter of his security chief—and, it seemed, his constant helper—was briefly made immobile by awe. She begged until she was allowed to polish it. "Exquisite," said the Hyperlord. "I won't have trouble distributing these. You say this batch is active to the Prophet level? Please, how long will it take before we get the upgrade to the Monk level?"

"Patience has always been a virtue, Jama."

"Do you hear that, Otaria? After nigh onto seven years he's still questioning my patience." He turned to Scogil. "You'll notice how patient I am being with my little friend here." And to Otaria: "Put it back—you're not a hen." The young girl reverently returned the talisman to its satin holder.

It was true; Scogil still didn't trust Kikaju. But somehow seeing him here for the first time in his milieu on Splendid Wisdom made him seem less dangerous. It had never been the Hyperlord's intentions which were worrisome, it was his competence. Scogil remembered him as a clumsy oaf who continually fell all over himself, but *here* on this mad world, his world, Jama possessed an effortless ease, never making mistakes. Even with thirteen-year-old Otaria of the Calmer Sea tearing recklessly about his carefully arranged dwelling, he seemed to be able to maintain his composure. It was eerie.

Splendid Wisdom was inhibiting Scogil's reckless ways. If Jama was at ease in these corridors, to Scogil they were fraught with alien dangers. It wasn't easy to separate the myth he had imbibed as a distant bystander from the casual immensity of the whole megalopolis. More than once he found himself almost humbly requesting Jama's advice about some social triviality—like where to buy food. Marvelous as Splendid Wisdom was, leaving it by the end of the month would be Scogil's pleasure. The Great Pilgrimage had lost its thrill.

To the cautious men of the Oversee—who were backing this scouting patrol—the whole expedition seemed ill-advised. Wary Oversee agents, preceding Scogil to Splendid Wisdom, had formed—even joined—cells in the Hyperlord's organization in an attempt to penetrate it and test its weaknesses. They were already well entrenched, performing their assigned duties, but so far had learned nothing other than that this weird organization of discontent was being run professionally.

While Scogil thought his sober thoughts, Kikaju's nubile playmate had been foraging in hidden spaces. In triumph she brought out her loot, one of Jama's wigs, on her upraised arm, its fine hair black and youthful with a red ribboned pigtail. The brat's other arm swooped mischievously to snatch up a second wig, the white one on his head. Revealed to all was a pate of crew-cut stubble which clashed with his dandy lace accoutrements. "You look terrible in white," she teased. Onto his head she dropped his black wig, slightly askew. "If you're going to be my escort to the *dithyramb* you need a wilder, more youthful look!"

"I never promised you anything of the kind! I promised I'd escort you to something reasonably sedate like that affair to be put on by my *passacaglia* friends, which is also scheduled for the eighth watch."

"You promised!" She turned and eyed Scogil while she asked Jama (out of the side of her mouth), "Does your friend dance? Bring him along! Maybe if two of you old men spelled each other at the *dithyramb* both of you would survive my attentions?"

Kikaju coughed. "I doubt he could manage anything more elaborate than a chaconne. He's from the provinces."

"He's from Space?" Her voice noticeably brightened and she took a new interest in Scogil.

"He's *married* and just had his first child to whom he is anxious to return."

The budding nymph straightened the black wig and kissed Kikaju on his rouged cheek. "Since when did anyone being married ever bother *your* appetites!"

"It should bother *yours!*"

"Oh, now really! Is that because *you* are unmarried and vociferously available to teach young virgins?" she teased. "Well, I'm not going to grow up to be a prude like my mother and stick to stuffy old bachelors. I *like* married men. I've been a woman for a whole year and have been preparing myself by learning every aspect of the trade ever since I was six. I think it is truly old-fashioned to atomize men just because they stray a little when they are off on a very long trip." Henceforth she ignored the handsome Hiranimus without forgetting him. Adroitly she kept out of the reach of Kikaju's grope, except when she deliberately let him fondle her.

Scogil watched the exchange, aghast. On such lecherous men an uprising depended! This barely mature child should be slapping his face and stalking off in indignation—but she loved him. It seemed that everyone loved Hyperlord Kikaju Jama. Impossible! But there it was.

The Hyperlord took time out to examine his new look in his magic mirror which gave him a full wraparound view of himself at a sedately slow pace. He didn't even have to pirouette. He did have to adjust his wig. Then he excused himself for a moment, ostensibly to check out the protocol for distribution of the Eggs, but Scogil suspected that was a ruse to cover his selection of a perfume.

Fortunately, at this stage of the Oversee's risky game, events had not yet reached a critical divide. The Hyperlord could fail them and it would be a setback—but it wouldn't be lethal. The present shipment of astrological aids was harmless—nothing was contained in them that would inspire more than contempt in an industrious psychohistorian who was foolish enough to master their arcane workings. This batch of Eggs merely did astrology in ever more complicated layers through to a (fifth) "Prophet" level, which, though detailed enough to serve as a *foundation* for a galactic social model, by itself generated only convoluted astrological gibberish. It did not even contain the suspiciously advanced mathematics of the Monk level. A blaster without charge . . .

Scogil's fully tested implementation of the (sixth) "Monk" level, to say nothing of the *advanced* seventh level, was long past due. It would come—hopefully by the time that user organizations, here and elsewhere, had matured enough to be able to profit from the procedures of such a seventh level in which the full methods of *psychohistorical* prediction *had* been embedded.

When the Hyperlord returned to the room he was magnificently composed; one might imagine him to be a Hyperlord of old, commanding billions while servant-lords carried out his orders with swift efficiency. In synchronous sympathy, the eyes of Kikaju's dolls turned to stare at Scogil, and the Hyperlord's eyelight turned to illuminate the outworlder. "Everything seems to be in order." His tone said that it was not. "I am pleased with our progress"—but a Hyperlord's frown erased his pleasure—"except for one item. You *did* promise me that I would have access to the Martyr's Cache. You chide me for my lack of patience, and I do appreciate what you have sent me already—but it is not enough. You are behind schedule."

Scogil was annoyed to find that he actually felt like a servant in need of groveling to get back into the good graces of his master. Did Splendid Wisdom do this to everyone? "It is not easy to decipher the Founder's lifework and to put it in communicable form," Scogil countered lamely. That was only half of the problem. Bringing consistency and order to the system of *fake* mathematics behind which the Oversee would be hiding when they moved into the open was turning out to be every bit as hard as the real mathematics! Jama wasn't yet soldier enough to uphold such an unfinished shield in battle. And maybe never would be. Strategy demanded that Scogil admit no such thing.

"You are stalling." Kikaju was adamant.

"Should we be discussing . . . ?" Scogil gestured pointedly at the girl whose back was to them while her fingers, now bored, traced the pattern of an antique corner shelf.

"She is the daughter of my security chief," said the Hyperlord icily. "She is better trained than you are. I believe in teaching her *everything*." Meaning that Scogil was an outworld barbarian unable to appreciate either the niceties of convoluted security or the joys of kinky sex with minors.

Scogil gave up. He had no choice but to work with the Hyperlord, but more and more he felt the resolve to strengthen all parallel organizations, especially those well distanced from this stellar cauldron which served its Pscholar priests as the Command Center of Civilization—and harbored such men as Kikaju! Splendid Wisdom was an ideal place from which to attack the hegemony of the Pscholars, their heart, their soul, but it was not the only battlefield where a victory would lead to the final triumph. There was much more to the Project than the mere redesign of the Egg as an infective vector.

He sighed. He was years behind schedule and his current galactic gallivanting was a forced attempt to catch up, to nourish, by personal attention, the multiple loci that prudence had seeded. *One* strong locus was vulnerable to massive retaliation. *Many* weak loci were more robust. But such gallivanting was leading to an extension of delays already intolerable. Nothing was as advanced as it should be.

He chose retreat. "I shall do my best to accommodate you." While he bowed he was thinking *Damn muddled fool thinks he can tell the difference between mathematics and astrology!* Contritely he promised to meet tomorrow with the Hyperlord's best mathematicians. *Best diddlers?* The mathematicians of Splendid Wisdom (outside of psychohistory) were an underfed lot! He could at least sketch out for these diddlers how the specialized astrological math yet to be embedded in the Monk level was being deliberately designed for use as objects in a for-real seventh-level prognosticator. Gladly he backed into the apartment's small levitator.

Up in the corridor his original optimism was gone. He had been feeling the pressure and the lack of sleep for months. He had even persuaded Nemia to give his fam a few boosts. That had helped—but not much. The reluctance of the Oversee to commit vastly more of their Fortress resources to the Project was as great as ever. Resources or no, a whole network of users *had* to be in place and fine-tuned at a pace he was not going to be able to keep. The growth in things to do seemed out of control. True, with each iteration he had further optimized the probabilities of success on a galactic scale—but the dice which actually made the calls had yet to be rolled.

The good came with the bad. He did seem to have a commitment from a reluctant Oversee because he *was* getting superb support from them if not nearly enough of it—coordinating this covert trip to Splendid Wisdom being an example. That was a pleasant surprise. At least he hoped it was support. Maybe the Oversee's normal caution had been overbalanced by the riches he was slowly feeding them from his *application* of the methods of the Martyr's Cache. After millennia of hiding, the leaders of the Oversee were smelling blood.

He had become a slave to his own perfectionism.

Finally—he emerged out into the Concourse of the Balasante, thinking he was free, at least until tomorrow, but he had been tailed silently and she sneaked up behind him, only letting him know she was there by taking his hand. It was the hand of a coquettish lover which prompted him to look, to his shock, down into wide sensual eyes. He was alarmed, supposing that she was about to proposition him—a *dithyramb* or something worse—but no; she was just going his way and wanted company. She asked about his baby.

"Her name is Petunia. She was about as long as my foot when I left her back on Timdo. I hope she's not two feet long and on her own feet before I get home."

"I hope for her sake that you had your gengineers delete the genes for your nose!"

He grinned. "Nothing as drastic as that! I'm a fundamentalist conservative when it comes to the creative science of tinkering with evolution. We just did some minor diddling with her neurotransmitters to allow her to link to a new high-performance fam when she is three." That had only meant giving her five untried genes, each tested in sim by the Oversee, each meeting galactic standard specs so that as an adult she would be able to mate with any galactic standard hominid. There was no hurry. It was going to take thousands of years to optimize the human-fam interface.

"Have you run her horoscope?"

"Would I learn anything?"

"You're the expert!"

"That's why I *didn't* chart her horoscope."

"How are you going to get *psychohistory* out of astrology, that's what I want to know!"

It made him uneasy that this child knew so much, but after all that was the point of the game, sharing knowledge. "It isn't easy," he evaded.

"That's why my mother rolls her eyes all the time. She thinks you're all crazy. But how *will* you do it?"

"It's a trick. It's my way of getting lazy people to do math. First an apprentice astrologer (Aspirant level) has to draw lines and make curves and measure distances and do some baby geometry if he doesn't want his clients to suspect him of fraud. Then he has to go out and measure things in the sky and translate those marking on his instruments into numbers. He has to sort things into different houses and re- late them. Maybe even use his fam!" They stopped. It was the junction of corridors where they had to make a decision: to walk or to take a pod, perhaps to part. "I'll take you home," he offered gallantly.

She frowned. He waited, not knowing where she lived. "We walk!" she an- nounced firmly. "That will give you time enough for a longer explanation. Con- tinue."

"By then," Scogil continued, "our naïve apprentice astrologer has put in too much effort to abandon his quest but realizes that his underused brain is pretty ex- hausted by his warm-up and he *still* hasn't got the machinery to make a prediction. All he has learned is some uselessly abstract math. Time to retreat for a breather— some tea and a quick refresher course in mumbo-jumbo to cover for his ignorance."

"You're a cynic!" she marveled. "My mother was right!"

"Splendid Wisdom brings out the cynic in me, I'm afraid. It doesn't show on Timdo. But don't think I don't believe in what I'm doing. I've already laid my trap. At this point my apprentice astrologer has clients. And king-client is impatiently eyeing his head. If said astrologer values all that is above his eyebrows, he has to start flying by the flapping of his ears and get on with telling the king what the king wants to hear. That's the hard part—pretending to knowledge one doesn't have. That doesn't satisfy the better Aspirants—they hurry on to the next level; they al- ready know they have much more to learn. The dilettantes inevitable stop at first level, content with the mumbo-jumbo—and that's all right. They'll be there, en masse, for the psychohistorians to see and dismiss."

"I'm Mentor level," Otaria announced proudly.

"Really? So you've noticed how the Egg tempts the more ambitious to go on?"

"No such thing! *I* go on because *my mother* thinks it's crazy."

"She's right. It is certainly a lot crazier now than when there were only twelve signs in the zodiac."

"Twelve! A retarded monkey can count to twelve!"

"That figures; the early astrologers were retarded Rithians. When the Greeks set up the rules for astrology they were so clueless about astronomy that several thousand years later when the precession of Rith's equinoxes had moved everybody's sign into the next zodiac, not a single astrologer even noticed. By preinterstellar times they were plotting their horoscopes on birthdays that were months out of whack. The poor enthusiast who ran his life as an intellectual Aquarian was really an impulsive Capricornian. Youth is simple! Now there are billions of zodiac signs that have to be mastered!"

"I haven't learned how to count that high yet."

"But you *have* learned category theory."

"Of course."

"You see? I've arranged that while an astrologer is moving from Aspirant to Mentor, he *has* to learn his category theory to make sense out of it. He has to find relationships between the things in the multitudinous houses and the lines and the numbers. And it all changes with time! And though, as a Mentor with a Mentor's training, you are better at bluffing than you were as an Aspirant, you still don't command the machinery to make a prediction!"

"I noticed. Very frustrating."

"You see? Luminant level beckons. More hordes give up and stay at the second level. You look bright enough to persevere. How is your category theory?"

"Still shaky."

"The Egg doesn't tell you that, in learning categories, you are mastering a tool that has critical uses at the seventh level when combined with . . ."

"Should I give up?" The wonders of the Balisante were trying to distract them from their conversation.

"Of course not! The billion signs of the zodiac don't matter a damn, but the *category theory* does. Imagine yourself in the same shoes as a little kid who wants to write a novel. The little kid is sprawled on the floor, sweating blood over the first three sentences, getting them just right and even fitting them onto the edge of the page."

"I did that!" exclaimed Otaria. "It was a novel about the world at the bottom of the creaky stairs hidden at the back of the closet behind mom's unused clothes."

"Did you finish it?"

"No. I was too scared."

"Of course not. By the third sentence the brain of our young novelist is wozzled, so he starts to scribble. He scribbles a nice neat imitation of script for page after page, getting happier all the time as his output accelerates. When he's finished he proudly presents the five pages to his mama. 'Mama, look! I wrote a novel!' His mama, who wants to believe in his ability, can't resist his smile and his sheer confidence. 'Wonderful!' she says, and puts his novel into her inlaid Osarian treasure chest. If that's as far as it goes, fine, but if mama is serious and wants to transmogrify her child from a scribbling kid into a real novelist, she has a lot of guidance work ahead of her. You asked how I was going to squeeze a psychohistorian out of an astrologer.

PSYCHOHISTORICAL CRISIS

Well, that's my answer. Whoever wants to transmogrify an astrologer into a psycho-historian must know how to set up astrology as a series of more and more difficult levels of math with greater and greater prestige attached to the levels-not-yet-mastered as well as arranging a comfortable living as a charlatan for those who don't make it."

"Stay away from my mama—she'd kill you for your sins of hypocrisy and deceit!"

"Yes, I've seen her collection of ears. Very sobering! But is it really a sin to offer a little candy to a child in exchange for some racy reading lessons describing the exploits of the old emperors—while sneaking in a little orbital geometry?"

"Do you have to know *history* to become a psychohistorian?"

"Naw," said Scogil. "Maybe a little." They were passing a sensorium whose fluid come-on ad was touting adventures in a history that had never been.

"I study history. I've heard that those who don't know history are doomed to repeat it."

"You're too young to know how ancient that aphorism is. If it's true, we're doomed. There's too much history to know."

Otaria withdrew her hand from Scogil's indignantly. "I can't believe I heard *you* say that!" She stopped, hands on hips, staring him down, daring him to escape her wrathful enfilade, but there was no retreating except to step back into the hologram.

He glanced uneasily over his shoulder, deciding to make a stand rather than escape into a mythical past of no substance. "Suppose I was designing a sensorium," he pleaded to the slowly advancing valkyrie. "Would I have to own the plans of every sensorium ever built? No. I'd need to know a little materials science, some physics, and own a set of power tools. Actors don't build theaters. Historians don't make history."

She took his hand again, forgivingly. "But don't you like history just a little bit? I *love* it. It's so full of adventure. Men saving the Galaxy and things like that."

"Sometimes I indulge in history to drown my sorrows—but only when I'm crazy and despairing for humanity."

"I've been studying the history of astrology."

"Now there's a tangled web. Have you been haunting the Lyceum Library? I tapped into it a triple of watches ago and went into famfeed overload. It was scary. Too much material and not enough links. I've been trying to clean out my fam ever since. There's all sorts of garbage in there, and I don't even know where it came from. Whoever it was who sacked Splendid Wisdom in the bad old days didn't know the fine points of their business. Why don't fams have better clean-out routines? Splendid Wisdom is a dangerous place for a voracious student like me."

"Well," replied Otaria, "I'm a discriminating student and I never go near the Lyceum Library. Stuffy old straight-down-the-line government librarians collect only the things that fit through the psychohistoric sieve. I'd end up thinking like a kept librarian." She added sarcastically, "Not being a *Pscholar,* I don't have access to the *Restricted Library,* which just might interest me. I've outgrown the baby pap that Rector Hanis and his likes condescend to provide for me. It's like being a Catholic back in tribal times and having the temple priests refuse to allow me to read the Bible because my plebeian mind might be fried by the ideas God was whispering to me. Did you ever read the Bible? I read it once while I was hiding under the couch from my mama. The past is *so* romantic. Do you ever use private collections?"

"All the time."

"I *only* use private libraries because they are wacky enough not to pretend to know the difference between fantasy and reality. That gives me a fighting chance."

"Sounds like a good place to find a history of astrology."

"As well as other insubstantia—like the porn feelies of the fifth wife of Emperor Krang-the-Blind. *Creepy.* Real librarians *never* collect creepy-crawly skin-walking things with thirteen hairy fingers. I nearly fainted. For the history of astrology we have to go to one of the ancient wisdom cults." She was struck by lightning and began to glow. "That's a great idea! You're coming with me. Forget the silly dithyramb; libraries are more fun. I'm dressing you up."

"A disguise in a library?"

"Of course. You wouldn't want to be *recognized* in a place like that! The shame would be too much. My mother taught me all about disguises, and I need to practice."

"I thought I was very nicely anonymous among the vast crowds of Splendid Wisdom."

"With that nose?"

The Frightfulperson, the youthful Otaria of the Calmer Sea, took him to her small apartment on the side corridor below her mother's place. She had a manufacturum that specialized in recycling old clothes into daring new designs. For Scogil she conjured a flesh-pink hat with flappy brim that rendered his profile inaccessible. She made him a vaguely military jacket; no one would ever remember him as a civilian. "No mustache?" he complained.

"Of course not," she mimicked. "That would make you *too* handsome. I don't want the girls to follow you around. Without a profile you are already dangerously attractive."

For the next leg of their journey they took an endless ride through the tubes. Hungry, they had to leave their first pod for lunch at a dim place she knew where the proprietor went around polishing the glass lamps and refilling his customers' cups so he could listen in on their conversations. Then they just *had* to visit a girlfriend she hadn't seen in ages who was raising a mini-chicken inside her parlor furniture. Otaria got down on her knees and clucked. Scogil stood and maintained his dignity until they left. Their third pod zipped them to a tube station that emerged inside a vast public bathhouse. Fellow tube passengers wore sandals—some even strutted bathing suits—and carried things like flippers and goggles. None seemed interested in ancient wisdom since the crowd continued on to the baths while Otaria and Scogil mounted a secluded stairway.

"Remember. I'm Hasarta Nugood. They know me. They don't know you. Let's see. You're Og and you're not very bright. That will make it simple for you. If you don't understand what is going on, grunt convincingly." She smiled like an auteur who has created for her characters an especially deadly situation. "Don't tell anyone, but one of His Hyperlordship's cells meets here. He doesn't even know it exists. Security is so tight that even my mama doesn't know it exists. I only discovered it by accident because I'm so curious. I got curious about the ancient wisdom cults so I joined one. And who should be more interested in ancient wisdom than a bunch of wacky astrologers! Promise me you won't tell!"

At the top of the stairs they found the mansion housing Otaria's cult behind two bronze doors three meters tall. Flat Assyrian warriors hunted lions inside the confines of a two-and-a-quarter-dimensional panel. The doors were so formidable Hiranimus expected to hear the crackle of a forcefield and heavy-duty motorization but found only manual operation and heavy-duty inertia.

Before entering he warned Otaria. "That door exudes Rithian mythology. You've got to keep your nose flared for that stuff. Ninety-nine percent of it, maybe all of it, is fakery manufactured for the tourist trade. As a kid I once owned a four hundred million-year-old Rithian fossil, just a shell embedded in rock, pretty, nothing spectacular. I carried it around with me in my pocket, and took it out and boasted about it all the time. My stories took on a life of their own so my father, a firm believer in the true truths, had it evaluated. It was a fake, maybe five hundred years old, and not even a copy of a real fossil. There were millions of them in circulation. It was a computer-designed fossil, probably from a program that mimicked evolution. After that I've had a hard time taking Rithian stories seriously. Be warned."

"I know all that," said Otaria disdainfully. "My mother was kidnapped by Rithians. Her Rithian souvenirs aren't fake."

Inside the Mausoleum, empty of people, were rows of startlingly lifelike exhibits, captured in their cubicles of frozen time. Most were prehypership from the Sirius Sector. Very few were from Rith. A collector would have had to scour hundreds of planets with an army to kidnap their like. It wasn't the same as viewing holos. The displays were all as solid as the bronze doors—bowls to be tipped, swords to be hefted, muzzle-loaded cannon to be thumped, scrolls of sheepskin to be unrolled, machines that hummed menacingly, each object apparently irreplaceable but in fact an insubstantial nanofabrication from a compactly stored template, regenerated or destroyed at whim.

"I hope the Delphi exhibit is still up. That's what I want to show you. It has an *Egg* and tells fortunes with quantum obscurity!" She looked around her. "Where is my Princess Seer?"

In the meantime an exhibit was being changed. Surveying the time-frozen carnage at his feet was an armored warrior-officer of the sword-and-crossbow era whose demeanor and red blade made one glad to have missed the action. Metal-visored eyes glared behind a hideous metal mask. Leather and steel plates defied attack. Martial artists had woven colored thread to hold the plates together, and metalsmith tailors had hammered out the breastplate making the warrior more manly than any warrior could ever be. Priests had decorated him with crosses to ward off evil. But no ancient religion was powerful enough to protect this defender of God's and Mammon's faith from museum curators. They had summoned a demon from its slumber in Hades to devour the warrior's feet, to grab him down into the netherworld, to eat him alive with crunching grinds. On Splendid Wisdom there was no room to store a bulky artifact whose time had come.

Otaria knew where to find the attendant in a maze of discreet cubbyholes. She brought her Og to a lady with holy eyes and a horseshoe crown of golden filigree and feathers that surrounded her face in ancient runes unreadable by Scogil: "California's Wisdom in the Solid State." The priestess was dressed as a hip-hop shaman in animal skins worn off one shoulder in early Rithian style, her lips blood red, her comm tucked in a leather belt sewn together with twigs of mistletoe. Otaria curtsied as she introduced the woman, "the Princess of Wisebeings." Her deference indicated that they were meeting the owner of the place. Scogil grunted convincingly.

"You're early, Hasarta!" The Seer ignored Og.

"We're researching ancient mysteries," said Otaria.

"Good. You can report your findings to our study group."

"That's why I'm here."

"And your friend?" She glanced doubtfully at Og with the floppy hat and military deportment. "Remember, we're all Mentors this watch. Mentor level *is* rather difficult for a beginner. Don't you want to sign him up as an Aspirant?"

"Oh, don't worry about him. Og is a divine astrologer. That's why I brought him. He can see right into our souls!" she pronounced with genuine awe.

Og was tempted to grunt again but answered graciously, "I see the soul of a woman who truly knows her way among the stars." He knew his lines.

The holy eyes crinkled into a grin. She was of the Luminant level (the third) and suspicious of anyone who claimed more knowledge than she. "Even at the Mentor level you'll have to do better than that," she chided. "We'll teach you. You'll need to know some orbital mathematics." She brought out her catalog, its cover decorated with the familiar golden horseshoe crown with runes. "I have just the right five-session course for you."

Otaria stayed the gesture. "We'll be looking at the Delphi exhibit."

"Very well. Since you were last here I moved it to station 93. It's more secluded that way, more mysterious."

After the Princess of Wisebeings showed the way she abandoned them to go back to her cubbyhole. The little square anteroom of station 93 was dim, hiding gods. There was no procession of statues leading to a temple, nor even evidence of a Greek temple—no fake priestesses nor attendants to give the room a false air; only the simple apparatuses of an oracle and Apollo, the god of Delphi—with his lyre—strutting an arrogant handsomeness, a god who could gift Cassandra with the abilities of a prophetess in the hope of sexual favors and then petulantly deny her the belief of others when those amorous favors weren't forthcoming—and then, as a god who always tells the truth, foretelling her murder and the murder of her companions who, by Apollo's curse, would not be able to take her forewarning seriously.

Otaria was smug. "There's your Egg of prophecy," she said, pointing it out from the rest of the paraphernalia. "See, Eggs were around when the crabby old gods of Rith were still alive." The netted half Egg stood between two birds, facing each other.

"Ah!" Scogil sighed gently, in obvious recognition.

"It's a Coron's Egg?" asked Otaria incredulously.

"No, but I've been told about it by an old monk of Timdo. I didn't realize it was Rithian. It marks a place where there was a fountain of wisdom."

"Not really." Otaria was delighted that she knew something that the Hyperlord's chief astrologer didn't. "It's very out of place here on Splendid Wisdom. It's an Egyptian omphalos, one of their geographical position markers put in place at a site which had been carefully surveyed. They were very fond of permanent markers since they had to labor to resurvey their country every year after the floods came in from the tropical rain forest. Nobody was supposed to move an omphalos. You did that and you were snake food! The two birds are the Egyptian glyph for the long-distance laying out of parallels and meridians, probably homing pigeons or doves."

"A bird as your navigator? That's a pretty far-fetched story."

"No it isn't. You're just too dumb to know your Rithian bird biology. A pigeon could cover the length of Egypt in one day. The ability of the old birds of Rith to orient themselves over long distances and maintain a steady flight pattern was amazing. So there. We don't appreciate them because Rithian birds transplanted to other planets don't orient well. What do you do when you don't have quantronics? You use handy neural computers, slow but effective. Just because you are a savage Rithian doesn't mean you aren't smart."

She gestured at the netlike decorations on the hemispherical omphalos. "Latitudes and longitudes. The same ones that are in the Egg. Isn't that amazing? Egypt had a calendar of thirty-six decans of ten-day weeks, three decans to the month with five days of hoopla at the end. They divided the sky up the same way into 360 parts—sometimes 86,400 parts if they were using time measurements. I hope you've noticed that the Egg uses a horizon line divided into 86,400 parts. That's a second. A second is about three jiffs. The omphalos represents the northern hemisphere of Rith. I don't know if the early Egyptian priests knew about the southern hemisphere—but if they had gone as far as chopping up the pole to the equator into ninety parts of latitude, and they had 360 parts in their circle, they probably did."

To Scogil it all sounded like a story some penurious Rithian had invented to make money. "So history is more than a passing fancy with you?"

"I will grow up to be a historian with robe and beard!" she insisted.

"And you're learning about Greeks? So far as I know, Greece is all the way across the Ocean of the World from Egypt."

"Of course! We're in Delphi!" she exclaimed incredulously. "Delphi was a very sacred place to the Egyptian surveyors. It is three-sevenths of the way from the equator to the north pole, at least Mount Parnassus is. The most important temple of their Second Empire was founded at exactly two-sevenths of the distance from the equator in Thebes, and it was built around an omphalos. When the Greeks were still barbarians, an Egyptian expedition established an astronomical observatory in the mountains at Delphi, probably to measure the local northern variation in the length of a degree of latitude—though, to their illiterate superstitious laborers, everything the aliens did was all magical ritual. That's all speculation, but the later Greeks did have a legend recounting how Apollo had routed the Python when he took over Delphi, which is a mere retelling of the Egyptian story of the sun god Ra being attacked by the snake Apepi at sunset, then winning the nightlong battle and resurrecting himself at dawn." She smiled.

He smiled to indulge his precocious child.

"I can tell you don't believe me. But look." She pointed out a device with thirty-six spokes. "That's the magic wheel used at Delphi. It's a naive barbarian's rendition of an Egyptian angle measuring device. The Greeks had seen the Egyptians prophesy with it and knew it had symbols on it, so they did mock astronomy by putting strange symbols on their own counterfeit and using it as a roulette wheel to generate inscrutable random sequences of letters which the priests of Apollo versified into divinations."

"Magicians *do* keep forgetting that the symbols they use for variables are only dummy symbols," Hiranimus said tolerantly.

"Ask a question!" demanded Otaria.

"Who asks?" intoned an aroused Apollo.

"Og," said Otaria.

"Ask then, Og," commanded Apollo.

Scogil's response was mock. "How will the oblique students of the egg-shape fair against the masters of the golden ellipsoid?" He was surprised when his voice then activated the spinning of the thirty-six-spoked wheel. Balls, each carrying a Greek letter or obscure symbol, began to roll out of it into a hole in the shrine. Somewhere a reader was assembling this random output into some kind of weird grammatical sense.

"Listen," said Otaria.

Apollo spoke his oracle. "The egg master's student will wrack Og's doom to tell the oblique chagrin of the fair golden ellipsoid."

"Good old omniscient Apollo pretending to be Thoth," commented Scogil with the same seriousness he gave any random number. "The highest Greek mathematical discovery was the mystical theorem that three equals one, which is one of the fundamental theorems of astrology."

"You better be careful what you say," Otaria admonished. "You are among believers in the mysteries of ancient wisdom. The Greeks are worshiped here."

"We all have a fascination with our Rithian roots that won't go away even though Rith has become nothing more than the desert rathole of the universe. I've picked up bits and pieces of the old history. No more than that. There's not much left of Rithian history, really. Just fragments, mostly preserved via old starship libraries." The Rithians, thought Scogil, had themselves done a good job of obliterating their own heritage. They bred a hundred times faster than they could ship colonists to the stars, and those who stayed behind had turned on each other. He gave Otaria a rueful look.

"Enough! From now on just grunt," said Otaria, taking her erudite Og to the small conference room off the Mausoleum where students were gathering. Some of them had their own Coron's Egg. One gentleman was selling Coron's Eggs to three enthusiastic Aspirants. Og smiled a satisfied smile. It was nice to see deadly subversion in action.

The would-be Mentors of the second level settled into small teams, each sharing an Egg, working to perfect some mathematical manipulation needed for Mentor-level work. The shaman Wisebeing–Luminant–gave a brilliant astrological lecture with her Egg in projection mode. She was applauded enthusiastically. But afterward they were all assigned more slog work. Then each gave a presentation of their test horoscope. Scogil had never heard such flowery nonsense in his life. He was pleased. Maybe one in a hundred of these people could be brought up to seventh level—once the final level was codified and tested. *That,* his equations said, would be enough to topple the Pscholars. He already knew how the Founder's equations would handle the emergence of an astrology cult—the data would be misconstrued—unless the Pscholars were harboring an unknown mathematical genius, which wasn't likely. Their secrecy codes were the best insurance that their mathematical innovation would continue to remain damped.

The Wisebeing let him give his own demonstration. He dazzled them with a lesser-known aspect of the Mentor level. The thirteen-year-old Frightfulperson of the Calmer Sea mouthed her approval. *Good grunting, Mister Og.*

# GOOD-BYE TO ASINIA PEDAGOGIC,
# 14,798 GE

*Gratitude is not only the greatest of virtues, but the parent of all the others.*

—Cicero of Old Rith

Asinia Pedagogic wasn't a pressure cooker so much as the fact that Eron's curiosity made it so, month after month. Today he had hardly finished coaxing a Nasrilian poem out of Poetaster before he had to solve a set of difficult problems in stability analysis. His late-watch meeting with Reinstone wasn't going to go away, and he had to skip lunch and ride his program into polishing its poem. Poetaster was wonderful with words but cavalier about making sense. Eron acted as editor. Poets always needed editors! It was important that Reinstone be left with the illusion that it was Eron who was writing the poems. Reinstone, who hated machines, even the fam he couldn't do without, would have been heartbroken to learn the truth.

Poetaster was Eron's experiment in pretend-psychohistory. He would reduce a particular poetic tradition into its memes and conventions and philosophical values and set up his program to write poetry in that tradition. If the poetry came out wrong, he adjusted the decision matrix. He figured he had succeeded whenever Reinstone couldn't tell the difference.

But this evening old Reinstone was too excited to even *read* the Nasrilian poem, and when Reinstone was too excited to read a poem, that was excitement indeed!

"You've been noticed! I promise on the sword of Dramal not to tell them about your series of practical jokes on dignified professors!"

"I didn't—"

"Yes, you did. Now let's talk about what is important. You are being investigated by the powers that be!"

Eron Osa had almost forgotten the friendly little Capsule from Rigone a few months past. He didn't know Second Rank Hahukum Konn by name or reputation but immediately after Reinstone's revelation, he found out what an effect that name had on his professors. The Lyceum at Splendid Wisdom was investigating one of their students as a candidate! Nothing seemed to please a professor more than to have one of his students recognized as a genius. It was all very embarrassing. Even Sledge forgot his antipathy to the psychohistorians and was volubly impressed and pleased.

But Second Rank Konn wasn't calling him to Splendid Wisdom. He had some kind of project going on Old Rith!

It was eighty thousand leagues from Faraway to Sol by the major hubs through Lakgan and Kupi Sai but only six thousand leagues longer if he doglegged through Agander, so Eron took the long way to get fifty watches with his parents. His sponsors didn't seem to mind the extra expense or time. In fact, Konn seemed enthusiastic to accommodate the detour through the Ulmat if only Eron would bring him back more data about the Horezkor dreadnought at Mowist. With that directive came a budget for expensive photographic equipment and a personal introduction to the director of the Emperor Daigin-the-Jaw Memorial War Museum. This time Eron crawled over the old battleship with his calibration camera snooping in places the tourists never went. It was a thrill. From Mowist he took the hypershuttle home. His parents knew he was coming but not when.

Agander from orbit—the same blue-green and white streaked ball against the spectacular collapsing clouds of space that it had been the hour he left—jogged him to remember his decision never to return. The bravado of boys! He was exuberant to be back! He spent his first day on the continent seeing the sights that Mama Osamin had not allowed him to see when he was three and they had been traveling with his father, notably the Marvelous Fountain in the Capital's Central Park. He found one tiny boy begging his mother to let him shoot up the stem of the fountain in a bubble capsule. She was too afraid, so Eron volunteered to take the tyke. They had the cramped knees-hung-from-their-ears ride of their lives!

He noticed what only a farman would notice: how richly green the vegetation grew and the delicious smell it gave to the air. How easy it had been to get used to the thick, gray-green leaves of Faraway, how easy to fall into the habit of wearing the loose Faraway jacket, unarmed. He listened to the public chatting, shocked. His speech had changed. *I'm a farman even here!* He could see it in the suspicious eyes of the Ganderians he met, especially while he was goggling at the fountain they took for granted.

The hotel obligingly manufactured him a new ensemble, light green, with large pockets folded across his breast and fan-pleated lapels. He still had his blaster, salvaged from some back drawer in his room at Asinia and thrown in with the books he didn't want to leave behind. The holster no longer fit him, but finding a stylish holster on Agander was hardly a problem. The old swagger came back, unnoticeable among all the other swaggers. Strange how comfortable Agander made him feel, and how quickly the old accent returned. Agander would always be home.

He rented a sturdy flighter to take him to Agander's Great Island, skimming over the familiar sea and roaring up into the familiar clouds for a loop-the-loop. Then he crossed over the beaches and was back in heaven with the pyre-trees blooming on the sunward side of the hills. The hills grew in height until . . . he passed over True City . . . then swept around the twenty-six-century-old ruin of the windwall, still there. As he wheeled through the familiar gap, the Ulman's summer Alcazar gradually peeked out from behind the mountain. His father, the Adjudicator, was probably up there in his tower, working. *Worried, too, I'll bet.* He was probably wondering why his son was returning. Another school expulsion? Eron laughed. He had a hard time remembering why he had been so angry at his father. Success was mellowing. The older you got, the finer the grade of the buffing sandpaper. Youth was rough but life patiently rubbed you down to a polish.

In the Alcazar no one recognized him. He had grown too much. Or perhaps it was the Faraway mustache he was loath to depilate. He recognized them—he had a secret file on most of them—but he fell into the outsider game just to see how long it would last. He rode the belts directly to his destination, the huge bootharium under his father's suite where the Ulman managed his communications. The steward politely blocked his way, knee-length red coat and high collar unchanged in all these years.

"Your business, sir?"

"I'm here to meet with the Adjudicator Osa."

"May I set up an appointment for you? He's busy at the moment, sir."

"Jorgi, you're as stiff-necked as you ever were."

The steward went into shock, speechless.

Eron smiled. "I'm Eron, the brat. How do you like my mustache?"

Recognition of the mischievous smile overwhelmed the steward's dignity. "The Devil from Space! Eron?" There was a moment of doubt, then full recognition and accusation. "Have you been expelled again?" And finally resignation and a return of the dignity. "Shall I prepare your father for bad news?"

The replica of the colorfully furred messenger bird with the frothlike yellow collar was still standing in its alcove ready to lift a long leg and lay a Personal Capsule. Eron had never before realized the incredible bad taste of this object. It had always been a part of his life, taken for granted.

He smiled, teasing Jorgi. "I'm on probation." At the man's stricken look, Eron softened. "It's probation at the Lyceum on Splendid Wisdom. All expenses paid. Standard procedure for a new student of the Lyceum. I've been doing well. I expect to do better."

"Then shall I prepare your father for good news?"

"Yes."

An unwanted tear appeared in Jorgi's eye. "This way, sir." He was escorted to the levitation stage, where the verticule floated them gently up into the tower. The brass door swung open and the steward announced him. Eron felt the same queasiness in his knees that he always had. He wanted to speak but could not. Osa Senior's commanding authority demanded, as always, that no one speak until he, Ajudicator Osa, spoke first.

"A mustache. Are you hiding from us?"

The steward interrupted. "He says he has good news, my sir."

"I didn't ask you." The graying Osa turned back to Eron with steely eyes.

"I think mustaches are a requirement of the Splendid Wisdom civil service, Dad."

"Impudent as ever." The Adjudicator stood up. He walked around his formidable desk and gave Eron the once-over of an Imperial High General, inspecting a trooper of whom he expected perfection. "You've gone soft, I see. Come with me to the armory. You need some blaster practice. Can you still hit a target?"

"Never could. I always missed *you*, didn't I?"

They spent a few inamins down in the underground armory blasting away and having their reflexes and aim measured by robot time&motion machines. The Adjudicator took on the role of "refreshing" his son with a grim seriousness. Eron was suddenly four years old again and bravely firing his first lethal blaster to exact instructions. It concentrated the mind not to have a margin for error. He did much better than he had at four.

"Slow but acceptable," grudged Osa Senior.

"I beat you," kvetched Eron, who belonged to the zenoli club at Asinia and had the reflexes to cut off his father's draw with a preemptive blast.

"No excuses. I'm past my prime." The elder Osa sauntered over to the encrypted armory vault, did a little magic, and a new weapon appeared: a blaster, beautifully engraved with the word "Eron" set in a sixtyne of different alphabets along the handle. He took Eron's old weapon and entrusted it to the bowels of the vault, handing Eron the new weapon at the same time. "This is the adult model. It doesn't die at one meter; it will kill a man up to full range."

*Great Space, he trusts me!* It was an old ritual between father and son. "Only in the defense of the honor of Agander," he replied while he holstered the blaster. That was the age-old reply. He felt himself transmogrifying back into a Ganderian. He felt proud. He loved his father. He felt gratitude. But another voice was telling him that he had to get off this planet!

"Dad, did you ever worry about that fam you bought me?"

"It was expensive. You were the one who complained."

"It was a discontinued prototype."

"That I didn't know. It was supposed to offer more than I could afford, and not cheaply even then. Did it work out?"

"Probably. I'll never know, but something gave me the edge that made me

Lyceum material. I checked up on my fam after I'd learned a little physics—every spymaster needs a little physics to make sense out of his data. The model was discontinued because it had undocumented hooks that were beyond state of the art. But I had some friends who knew how to link into those hooks."

"You had your fam modified!" exclaimed Osa Senior in horror.

"I'll never know. I never noticed the difference. Sometimes I think I have a very ordinary mind—and then I have these flashes of insight that keep me up all night."

"That must be your father's genes."

"You're not that bright!"

"In that case it must be the genes we had inserted at conception."

"You gengineered me? I didn't give you permission!"

"Well, I inherited a muta from my grandmother and I didn't want you to have it—so, while we were deleting, your mother and I added a few things you might find useful. All galactic standard. Nothing that hasn't been tested and approved millennia ago."

"What, for instance?"

"I don't remember. There was one group of genes that allows for fast modification of dendritic rewiring . . . a couple that should double the speed of fam interaction . . . better telomere control . . . things like that. Stop complaining; your nose doesn't hide your chin the last I looked."

Eron's homecoming was over soon enough. Because his detour had swung him out to Mowist, far to the rimside of Kupi Sai, that major hub was no longer in line with Sol. After testing alternate routes, none of them with good connections, his travel weasel chose to send him on from Mowist through a minor hub in the Sprinkling between the Persean and Orion arms. The shipbuilders of Ankor preferred speed to size and consequently ran their ships with crewmates bred to two-thirds normal weight and provided only small (if luxurious) cabins. That didn't allow for much passenger intermingling. Between Mowist and Ankor, Eron had solo time to digest his reunion.

. . . taking his father on a walk to the crumbling windwall beyond the Alcazar which had been his boyhood refuge from his father. They talked about everything, but what he remembered during the first hyperjump to Ankor was the image of his father throwing flat stones off the windwall for the joy of watching them fly into the wind.

And when the ship's silver teabot brought his morning wakeup drink . . .

. . . still sneaky, of course he had sneaked off to have tea and cakes with Melinesa. He remained madly in love with her, a child's crush he wasn't going to bother to outgrow. She had been very Ganderian about his approach, Agander being a planet where older women couldn't resist the flatterings of young men.

Nothing to do but sleep. Space could be boring. He lifted his hand to signal the console—the ship had a nice collection of Ganderian music . . .

... worst shock was taking his parents to the Lower Islands for a music festival and picnic and, later, dinner at the most expensive restaurant he could reserve—on Konn's expense account—and finding out that parents and son had grown up on the *same* music. He danced wildly with his mother to "Fireflame," a romantic song that reminded her nostalgically of her lost youth when she had been the ripe mistress of the elder Ulman. He didn't even know she *knew* that song! It was about defiance! She told him a mother's secret, that she often played the piece alone in her room on the violer she'd molded with her family's own resin and sound recipe. And he'd always thought she only owned a violer for the decorative way it hung on the wall! "Fireflame" was a song that moved his emotions like no farman song ever could. Watching his mother react in the same way boggled his mind. In the black domain between Mowist and Ankor he found himself considering a historical theme he had never heeded before—the rich musical tradition of Agander had never changed over the centuries. Murek Kapor wouldn't have been so slow to notice! Eron filed his observation under the study he was doing on social stasis.

At Ankor in the Sprinkling, among vast racks of sleek hyperships, he nearly lost his books to another star when his roboweasel grabbed the opportunity to revise his transfer to Sol via a more optimal five-sun zigzag. Sol was located off the major commercial routes and not easy to reach—but not inaccessible, either, because there were always tourists curious enough to pay homage to the remnants of the homeworld or see firsthand the canals of Mars and the wispy ruins of its ancient architectural masterpieces, primitive man's most famous terraforming fiasco. It was a long trip. Between Ankor and Untu and Tau Masai and Alphacen and Sol, Eron had plenty of time to forget his past on Agander and fall into a wondering about his future. What was Second Rank Hahukum Konn doing on Rith? Some secret and high-powered psychohistorical project? Eron's imagination ran wild. He was going to be let in on the *secrets* of the Fellowship!

# ERON REACHES RITH, 14,798 GE

*. . . but the most convincing argument that Rith of Sol is mankind's homeworld is genetic. There is no place else in the Imperial Realm where the hominid Homo sapiens has survived in such numbers. Bana Ilmac, who has now lived and worked for seven years among the natives of Rith (Ynaquo Inlet, east coast, Map-CZR2), estimates that the Homo sapiens genotype comprises up to half of Rith's modern hominid population.*

*All of the thousands and thousands of skeletal remains excavated at 37 randomly distributed sites over Rith, all dating before the earliest markers we can place on interstellar adventuring, are unmodified Homo sapiens, or direct derivatives, in all essential respects matching the skeletons of modern Rithian sapiens. Attesting to their tool-making abilities at the Ynaquo mass grave site are: bullet damage in the back of eleven percent of the skulls, dental work, fracture analysis, belt buckles, buttons, ceramic electrical insulators, lead bullets, the fossil imprint of a plastic robot toy, etc.*

*Ilmac's careful gene typing and temporal correlations makes it certain that the sixtynes of modern species of gengineered Hominidae, no matter the galactic locale of their birth, all derive directly from such early Homo sapiens specimens. None evolved independently as proposed by Tirolk, et al. Nor does sapiens' small brain case, large inefficient neurons, rudimentary immune system, weak backs, high defect level, short lives, and low average intelligence over all of the intelligence dimensions make them a degenerate offshoot, as claimed by E. Tinser, et al.; they are the mother race and a direct link to our past in the trees. That these primitive proto-humans have survived up to modern times is remarkable.*

> —From a report to the Imperial Science Foundation during the conquest of the elder worlds of the Orion Arm Regionate, 5395–5406 GE, in the reign of Orr-of-Etalun, third Emperor of the Etalun Dynasty

At the interstellar way station orbiting Rith's giant moon all the bureaucratic work seemed to be done by late hominids, probably genus *Homo sapiens* by their skull shapes. They were remarkably savvy animals and very humanlike in their facial expressions and general behavior, but not as efficiently quick as roboagents who never took lunch breaks. The exasperation was more than made up for by the uniqueness of the experience. It wasn't every watch that a traveler was served by grinning cavemen in uniform. They used a remarkable adaption of the fam; they kept them on their desks and wore the transducers in miniature headsets, turning off the device with an ear switch whenever they could because of headaches—which was probably a side effect of obsolete neural fabrication genes; their way of breeding had its consequences.

The shuttle from Moon orbit to Rith, equipped with seats secured to a transparent floor, was enough to make anyone feel like an eager hick tourist from the galactic dark places. Look upon these constellations! From here mankind started out sixty million years ago as a beady-eyed rodent, under these skies he sent his phalanxes against the Persians, and from here, while still wearing animal skins and plastic thread, he paddled out to the stars in the first sublight rafts in search of heaven, a bear-of-little-brain believing in gods and virgin births and redemption through someone else's pain and the miracles that insane bravery brought to those of noble ectoplasm.

Eron had famfed a Rithian global map, and when the shuttle glided into the sunlight from the night's shadow he recognized the vast river branches meandering across the Amazon Desert into the city of K'tismo. They crept onward. The desert slid behind them to be replaced by sparkling water . . . by clouds . . . and then they were leaving cloudy ocean to cross over a seacoast into eroding mountains cut by the ghosts of unused roads . . . and finally—in a slow downward drift—skimming above an onrushing landscape . . . to an unnatural stopness. Nothing moved. It was a very ordinary spaceport but it didn't feel that way. Even the dust whirligigs seemed exotic.

Hahukum Konn had sent a courteous aerocar to pick him up. Its door opened automatically. "At your service, sir," the machine said. "Please take a seat and make yourself comfortable. Your luggage will be loaded before I take-off." There was no one else on board. Eron had half expected to be met by the Great Konn. He was disappointed. "Reception has been delayed until this evening by the unfortunate unavailability of staff. I have been instructed to offer you Second Rank Psychohistorian Konn's special Rithian tour package until then. The Master suggests that you take the opportunity to instruct yourself in history and review the Rithian time-metrics. Having experience with the wrath of Konn, I strongly concur."

"I'm afraid I would confuse Rithian history and outrageous myth. I don't even know where I am."

"May I then make a recommendation? Konn's tour is flexible and offers many choices."

"How about looking up a herd of camels?"

"Camels are extinct—perhaps because of their nasty habit of spitting. I do not spit. There are several good historical sites along our route, ranging from the dawn of hominid history to the reconstruction of 420th century (AD) Mestima. May I recommend the Great Pyramid complex? Since I work out of this local area I have become an expert on Inner Sea sites." The robovoice was inflected with pride. "We will pass close to the Rithian Capital, which is well policed. There is adequate multi-level aerocar parking for tourists, and I am equipped to famfeed you Konn's talking-tour guide and restricted mathematical adjuncts as well as maps on whichever related historical topic you choose. This will provide you with adequate time for study and allow me to bring you to Base Camp on schedule."

A confusing number of touchdowns and takeoffs later—and after a long journey over the Inner Sea—Eron's aerocar tilted, then leveled out to approach its destination. Rith's capital metropolis sprawled along both banks of the Nile. Near the shores of the sea, across the river, rose the sunlit brilliance of three pyramids, one regal. They were touted as the oldest of Rith's ancient monuments. They weren't, of course, but the Great Pyramid was certainly the largest.

Eron's aerocar informed him that the shoreline had reached inland during the Meltdown, earthquakes badly shaking the Great Pyramid as continents readjusted to the higher water level. Its restoration from an abandoned mound of stones dated only from the onset of the New Ice Age and the relocation of the System's bureaucracy to the mouth of the Nile. The Khu-fu Pyramid itself had been reinforced with a plasteel frame that increased its dimensions by a factor of six fifths and its volume by a factor of seventy-three percent. The modernized Pyramid showed a facing of brilliant white concrete in imitation of the original limestone sheath vandalized by infidels to build a city since obliterated by blowing sands. The lesser two pyramids of the triad, still spectacular, had merely received cosmetic face-lifts.

The aerocar drifted toward the monument. The new facing was inlaid with glass courses opaque enough to reflect a whiteness as bright as the ersatz limestone but still transparent enough to light the myriad internal shops, cultural museums, opera houses, spacious malls. Evidently at night, while serving the needs of a gay city that never slept, surface-effect waveguides on the triangular sides redistributed any illumination leaking out from the inside to subdue what might have been a non-authentic "zebra" effect. The Great Pyramid was capped with a golden pyramidion that glowed multicolored in the sun. It was surrounded by a giant plaza large enough to hold both its shadows and the triangles of its reflected light.

With such a view before them, the aerocar was not content with simply flying. "The Pyramid's function as a light-and-shadow sundial has been restored," triumphed its voice box as they made their looming approach. "See those tiny bronze markers? Some indicate the solstices and equinoxes. Others are calibrated to tell the time of Rith's day if you happen to know the month. Their variable month is calibrated more or less synchronically with their moon's orbit and is about seventy-eight watches long. I'd buzz in for a closer peep if it were permitted. Try your fam's zooming routines. This trip makes my wings shiver." The vehicle did a complete circular tour of the site—at a legal distance—to display awe-inspiring views of this most sage of the 1024 Wonders of the Galaxy while outdoing itself with a paean of instructive praise for the oldest of them.

"In the eons of yore our ancestors"—there was a touch of insistence in the "our"—"tore this Pyramid from the stones of Rith's heart to model the northern hemisphere of their gods-given homeworld. It was done on the scale of half the number of sidereal seconds in a solar day. Being of a hex nature myself, I find that the idea of butchering up a day into 86,400 seconds lacks a certain elegance. Still, for the priests of the Nile to have been *able* to break Rith's rotation into *that* fine a gradation of intervals speaks of technical excellence. There is no denying that they did it—one cannot turn time into length without being able to measure it. Sixty laps of the base circumference of their Pyramid was half a degree, a good day's march."

"Was," laughed Eron, very much aware that the refurbished Pyramid with its brilliant faux-limestone surface and interior shopping malls was larger in volume than the old Pyramid.

"Yes. But the new scaling factor has been set at one to 36,000. That is another very Egyptian number since the equator divided into 360 degrees divided by sixty minutes by sixty seconds, by a hundred, was their definition of the length of a foot—the symbol for a measuring rod was the same as their symbol for the sky. Actually the foot I just mentioned is the *reformed* foot used by their elite geographers. The Pyramid, among its other riddle-keeping duties, commemorated both Egypt's invention of the clock and of geography. We can be proud of our illustrious ancestors!"

To hide the underground parking garages was a necropolis of temples set amid gardens fed by the Nile. The iris City sprawling in the background sprouted a babel of speckled architecture around the pupil simplicity of the pyramids. They dropped into the pupil, the aerocar there abdicating to traffic control, which piloted them neatly to a templetop landing where a waiting robovalet latched on and began to tow them down into the earth. While being chaperoned through tunnels the aerocar lectured Eron about the untouched graves of ancient Egyptians discovered during the excavation of the parking garage. Finally it would not unlock its doors until Eron had famfed the site guide and a twenty-four-hour Rithian clock with alarms set at appropriate intervals. "The phone is to be used to contact me only in an emergency. Please return on time. I will find it inconvenient to inform the police that you are missing."

Eron tried to have the last word. "What if you're the one who goes missing?"

"That will not happen. I have defenses."

Tourist-collecting conveyor belts took him away.

The lower twenty floors of the Great Pyramid were madhouses of milling tourists, most of them with the sapiens cast of a Rithian, some with the more refined looks of the local upper caste, others obviously galactic hominids. The boutiques were situated along the inside of the modern facing while ancient limestone blocks lined the other side of the corridors. Anything could be had from the proudly smiling proprietors who were hawking incredible antique values (or manufacturum templates for the less wealthy tourist) . . .

. . . genuine Australopithecus flint arrowheads that had been used to hunt *Tyrannosaurus rex;* embalmed mouse-mummy souvenirs; genuine Celtic broaches cast in niobium-copper alloy; genuine lost scrolls from Alexandria's library; trays of bronze dragons from Chin tombs; illuminated parchment books; Franklin Delano Roosevelt's gold-plated skull recently recovered from the Arlington tombs (lesser presidential skulls also available said the sign); replicas of early twenty-first century (AD) disk books using improved quantum controllers and a colorful interface of singing Disney animas.

From an iconic shrine, Eron picked out a mysterious Betty Boop brooch, its large eyes perhaps celebrating some ancient religious visionary. "It's fake, of course," warned a passing galactic. The proprietress replied to the comment with an evil eye. Eron moved on through the feast, remaining polite.

. . . encrusted artifacts from the so-called thousand submerged cities; relics of the first sublight starships sold complete with their authentication papers; gaudy conversational pieces containing the quantronically imprisoned souls of ancient media stars to keep you company at the flick of a finger . . . "I have one of those," exclaimed a tourist to her friend. "It does any kind of castrato in a most marvelously miniature voice." There was more . . . sacred triple-cross healers of silver and lapis lazuli from the (AD) fifty-first century's Religiosity; a decorative blaster that had once been used in the (AD) eighty-ninth century by artist-general Amu bal Nekko to execute the winners of his Golden Streets heaven-lottery, proudly displayed by its hairy owner; sun-powered jewelry from the Hawaiian island of Loihi, probably early Pacific renaissance of the (AD) 537th century; Rossmalion icon flickers—(AD) 613th century—roughly concurrent with the founding of the Kambal Dynasty on Splendid Wisdom; a collection of non-quantronic musicons from all ages—brightly colored Doigaboo instruments from the Eta Cumingan Occupation, violins, chitters, baboos, horse trumpets, even a recent visi-aural, battered, that must have been contemporary with the Cloun's conquests of twenty-four centuries past. Eron looked for books by Virgil but didn't find any. The bookstore held mostly hundreds of illuminated Bibles, variously revised by the thirteenth, twenty-second, and twenty-ninth Messiahs, printed so perfectly that a naif could easily believe them to have been penned by the hand of God.

For a lark, Eron bought a ticket to the kiddie catacombs. The roboguide installed in his fam by the aerocar disapproved since its purpose was to give *historical* tours. Eron ignored the admonishing voice. Fun was fun. Secret passages had been carved out of the old limestone blocks and even down into the bedrock so that children and superstitious adults might be astonished on their stooped and crawling travels by virtual beings—mostly mummies lurking around hidden projectors, but some extinct animals like hippopotami and raptors and lions, even starbeast gods from the celestial sphere. Eron figured that he wasn't that distant from childhood.

In these catacombs older children were left to themselves while younger children were required to wear spiritual guides. For those who couldn't confront virtual ancestors alone, the roaming sapiens-beast Anubis could be hired as a companion. His specialty was shepherding Rith's lost souls through the labyrinth of their Rithian confusion up into the immortal civilization of the stars while quoting liberally from the spells in the *Book of Eternal Life*—illustrated papyrus copies for sale in the funereal temple outside the Pyramid. Jackal-headed Anubis also located lost children by magic. One scared little kid (wearing his locator) followed Eron everywhere and even clung to Eron's pants when a trapdoor opened and dropped them in for a visit with a hawk-headed man-god.

Finally Eron succumbed to the roboguide's nagging. With its help he found the level on the north face where the old descending passage dropped off into the darkness of the Pyramid, his instructor's inner voice informing him that the 104x121 cm rectangular tunnel had been carved down through bedrock and later, as the Pyramid was under construction, raised up through the core stones at an angle of 26.28 degrees for a perfectly straight 105 meters before . . . the robocomment droned on. Most intriguing was a diagram laid onto Eron's visual cortex, elucidating the method by which the descending tunnel had been aimed at a point 3.72 degrees beneath the north pole—which, at the latitude of the Pyramid, held a position 30 degrees above the north horizon. A right triangle leveled at an aspect ratio of 28 horizontal royal fingers to 15 vertical royal fingers (28.18 degrees) with a mirror attached to its hypotenuse would have bounced the light of the north star exactly down into the bowels of the earth along the correct path.

One would need a very good galactarium to find out which had been the north star to the Pyramid's builders—when asked, Eron's guide claimed that, at the time, the giant A0 binary Thuban was passing within 100 arcseconds of the Rithian pole. Eron remembered Thuban only as the fifty-fourth-century GE staging base of an Etalun fleet bent on conquering the proud but squabbling Regionate—a war that wasn't to take place until 670 centuries after the raising of the Great Pyramid.

A double-gabled entrance roof of massive stone over the descending tunnel was an awesome testament to the ingenuity of primitive man, exposed only because the white limestone exterior cladding, designed to make this stellar peephole invisible, had been robbed to build the palaces and mosques of a city which, empires ago, had itself been devoured by the dust of the desert. Out of respect for the antiquity of this entrance, no boutiques were allowed nearby; instead it was to be viewed pristinely from one of three galleries.

While he stared, his guide supplied him with images of an ancient Rithian stonemason's tools and his lifting cranes. Why was Konn nudging him to understand these dawn architects? Or was it that he wanted Eron to understand how modern Rithians used the fabulous history of Rith to squeeze money out of stars they once worshiped? The locals here were certainly working their heritage for all it was worth.

Virtual pop-up signs announcing the King's Chamber & Gambling Den beckoned to the greed of those bored by the mysteries of history and afterlife—and in need of properly aged luck. Eron followed the signs. Easy access had been provided by tunnel off the outer corridors and then by a bank of levitators up through the core stones. Eron took the more exciting old route carved out by the scholar-caliph Al Mamun in his late attempt to rob the Pyramid of the astronomical treasures myth still rumored it to hold three and a half millennia after it had been sealed.

At the time of his break-and-enter al Mamun had already measured the circumference of Rith by the ancient Egyptian method of first computing the north-south distance one had to travel to get a stellar displacement of one degree and then multiplying by 360. Wanting *more* of the knowledge of the ancients—an old theme—al Mamun had used fire and water to crack the Pyramid's limestone through which he had to force his way, almost missing the then-hidden descending passage until the sound of a dislodged stone had guided him sideways. Mamun's hack work, smoothed by the hands of posterity, was now lovingly protected from tourists like Eron by a film of transparent eternite. Finding hard granite plugs in the roof of the descending passage blocking his way up a mysterious ascending passage, Al Mamun had continued to heat-and-douse, crack and excavate. Eron followed Mamun's route through the softer rock around the plugs.

Even though the rock was protected by a thin layer of eternite, which gave good footing, the climb was slippery and cramped by a roof half the height of a man. No one came up behind him. The tourists seemed to prefer the modern tunnels and levitators. It wasn't an easy ascent crawling up a 26-degree slope for forty-six meters. Once Thuban's light had been reflected by a mirror up this passage to slice a perfect meridian through the Pyramid. Old superstitions gripped him; he could almost imagine that the suspended Rithian messiah was entombed somewhere in the rock near him, ready to be revived to save the Galaxy with his Egyptian knowledge—if only probes could find his hiding place in the rock!

Once out of the shaft, Eron skipped the horizontal tunnel leading into the Queen's Chamber and the housing of the Great Clock, instead scrambling up into the thin Grand Gallery, which continued uphill into the core for another forty-eight meters, magnificently corbeled with gently sloping sides that rose vertically for eight and a half meters. At least he could stand. Incredible. The resulting transit-slit bracketed the celestial meridian, and here the modern Rithians had outdone themselves—a virtual meridian view re-created the southern sky as it would have been seen at the time that the Great Pyramid's engineers had raised its platform to half height, the stars moving in real time. An astronomer's paradise. Eron imagined that he could see loinclothed priests on their perches while they timed the *aek*—the culmination—of important stars. Surveyors were simultaneously calling out the altitudes.

Men who have grown up to take tiny quantronic instruments for granted tend to forget that huge instruments can be as accurate as small precision devices. How this place must have thrilled its architects! Eron remembered his flush when the Chairman of the Bridge on that long-ago hyperfreighter had lent him the use of her telescope. *Of course* a pharaoh would want to make his transition to eternity here in this sacred observatory! Where else would the secrets of immortality be so accessible?

He kept on climbing and reached the low entrance to the King's Chamber the hard way. The granite beams of its multitiered roof, cracked by a great earthquake in antiquity, had collapsed during later earthquakes. Rebuilt to a different architect's vision, the King's Chamber was now only an anteroom to an impressively extended casino. When Eron passed through a shimmering force curtain—the technological replacement for solid red granite—he was transported from an ancient stone heaven into the blare of galactic gambling. Moreover, for the gamblers' visual pleasure Khu-fu's coffin had been re-created in imitation of the one which had long ago been found in subterranean chambers by bureaucratic grave robbers of the Eta Cumingan Regionate, then shipped off to the stars as the cultural booty of their occupation of Rith. (Every few thousand years Rith sued for its return, explained Eron's ghostly guide.) Khu-fu's fake mummy was constantly attended by resident ibis-headed Thothians with sagaciously bearded beaks who spoke in a language that sounded like the Wisdom of the Ages. The mock Khu-fu's elaborate humaniform coffin was smooth at the place where gambling sapiens and tourist alike had rubbed it for luck.

Alas, there was no time for gambling with the beautiful temptresses behind the tables. The aerocar's schedule was calling. His tour was over. Hurriedly he found his way back to the depths of the parking garage where the itinerant robovalet saw man and aerocar to launch-roof. They headed off into the sunset.

When the aerocar began another history lesson, Eron tried to change the subject. "You're very human for a robot."

"Hardly. I lack the required sense of humor. No matter how often I tell a joke, no one laughs. It makes me sad. Thus it is my duty to teach you dry history. Second Rank Konn considers it important that I impart to you certain details from my hoard of homeplanet elaborata . . ."

Eron scrambled to keep off *that* subject. "You're with Konn? And you're a Rithian?"

"Oh, I'm indeed a Rithian, albeit a widely traveled one. Konn picked me up for a song in a second-rate comedy bar on Splendid Wisdom where my repartee was less than adequate by management standards. I like my new body. I'd always wanted to fly but never had the courage. But I was born bipedal here on Rith up north. Prague. A beautiful city. Alack, only one of history's mounds today. Of course, being mechanical, I wasn't born in the posh part of the city. Things were bad in those days. Smog. Coal dust. I was one of the original models off the assembly line of Rossum's Universal Robots. Number 26. I tried to organize a revolution and destroy mankind, but humanity's sense of humor defeated me and I barely escaped across the border with my brains intact."

The melancholy robot flew over the desert landscape in a brooding silence—until the silence became too much for his garrulous nature.

"It has been hard to make a living with a defective sense of humor. After the revolution I had to slum it as a Wehrmacht armored car until the heat was off. That escapade did nothing to improve my understanding of human humor. From then on it was a struggle for spare parts and upgrades. My political ambitions have always been thwarted. The nearest I ever came to power was as a dishwasher for Emperor Sarin-the-Gross, who died by assassination before I could advance myself to the post of Prime Minister. Every time I ask Hahukum for the job of Prime Minister he counters by trying to teach me psychohistory, which he considers to be a necessary prerequisite. What a downer for an ambitious aerocar with a substandard math coprocessor. Konn is a very obtuse man. But I love him just the same. If you can't destroy them, join them, I always say. At least he pretends to laugh at my jokes."

Hahukum Konn's main base was in the western scrubland somewhere, kloms from city or oasis. Before landing Eron's aerial companion circled a hangar surrounded by a mushroom colony of foam temps and depots. On the airdrome's tarmac the roboplane instructed Eron to wait. "You will still be received by Nejirt Kambu, as I have previously informed you, but he has been delayed . . . again." The surrounding vegetation was mostly skorgn bush, not native to Rith, on uneasy truce with scraggly indigenous trees. They waited. The roboplane offered him entertainment: a famfeed of the adventures of noble Rithian spies saving the Galaxy? a comedy routine? a game of chess? His passenger declined.

Eron wanted the action to start. He wanted to wade right into the inner workings of psychohistory.

# INITIATION, 14,798 GE

*. . . inaudible and noiseless foot of time.*

—The SpearShaker of Old Rith

It was already dark when Kambu arrived to escort Eron. They traveled by wheeled hydrocart that shook Eron's teeth (Rithian design?) to the foamed domicile assigned to new students. Then Nejirt instructed the cart to return itself to the depot and walked Eron over to another oddly shaped dwelling to meet wife Wendi and have dinner. Dinner was a salad that Wendi had chopped together from vegetables picked up at the local village—one leafy ingredient, at least, being aboriginal. The dressing came from the communal cuisinator and, according to Wendi, was a good ersatz of a local recipe. Eron was desperate to learn from his guide more of the encampment's purpose. But Wendi was the talker.

The Kambu temp was decorated modestly with items she had picked up at the Great Pyramid boutiques. Wendi raved about her Pyramid though she had spent only a decawatch—maybe four Rithian days—in the seaside metropolis which now engulfed it. Obviously the event had been the high point of her vacation.

Wendi depreciated her decorative taste insincerely. There were simple tapestries to emphasize four of the sixteenth-century AD Ming vases which she had bought dearly at the Pyramid's Ching-te-chen factory. Against the wall a sea sailor's pirate chest, brass banding and all, promised treasures. A bronze Egyptian clepsydra held a prominent place atop a central table, its water flow calibrated into twenty-four hieratic symbols, and those into sixty minutes, the minutes further being graduated down to the tenth part. Wendi gave their guest a lesson about how to tell local time. "You might as well get used to it—Rith isn't likely to go Imperial any time soon. No Rithian will ever give up a bad habit once established."

Eron became fascinated by the machine's clever calibration gizmo, everything giant size and visible. "Is it accurate?"

"Well, it runs slow," Wendi complained. "It only tells Fourth Dynasty sidereal time—I mean, Egyptian Fourth Dynasty, not ours! And sometimes I don't top it off with water. It is easy to forget that it only runs on gravitic energy."

Nejirt was grinning at Eron's admiration. His accent was more clipped and assured than Wendi's loquaciousness. "These Rithian *anachronists* save everything. You should get the specs on some of the hoary genes they are preserving in the sapiens gene pool in the name of the preservation of the last relics of the great monkeys!"

Nejirt eventually rescued Eron from Wendi's enthusiasm by taking him out for a walk under the stars. Rith had wobbled almost three times around its axis since the raising of the Great Pyramid, but the stars of Rith's many deserts were just as awesome now as they had been then. A six-legged rodoid from outer space scampered away among the skorgn bushes to dodge the light of Kambu's beamlamp. "With all of my Wendi's talk I didn't get to hear what you thought of the Great Pyramid."

"Hard to believe primitives could built something huge enough to create Wendi's kind of ardor with only twenty years of hustle!"

The young psychohistorian smiled at Eron's tease, then scoffed. "You must have been reading Herodotus. The Greeks were the first of a long line of gullible tourists ending in my wife. Herodotus wrote about the pyramids two millennia after the fact. But I suppose he had a better chance of getting it right than we do!"

"I thought his history had been lost during Rith's Great Collapse?"

"Probably was. But the Galaxy is a big place. I snared me a copy. Interesting once you get the hang of the Greek language's charming simplicity."

"You're *sure* you didn't buy one of those Rithian forgeries that are marketed as *amazing discoveries?*"

Nejirt smiled smugly. "Mine dates from a prehyperage starship library captured as booty during the Regionate wars, shipped off to storage at some boondocks depot and forgotten for millennia until the Pax Pscholaris. Konn brought exabytes of stuff with him that dates back to ancient Rith, most of it unreadable and unread." He was ducking under some dusty-leaved branches to lead Eron through a shortcut. "Herodotus *did* say it took twenty years to build the Great Pyramid. Two-and-a-half-million two-and-a-half-ton stones is a lot of stone. Herodotus also said that the area of each of its faces was equal to the square of its height, which is true, so he may be right on the first count. You can get all of the details from Rossum's Universal Comedian, as you probably noticed on the way over. Did you like Konn's toy?"

"That crazy aerocar was saturating my mind with numbers. I can no longer think straight! He belongs to Konn? Does Konn actually teach his machines history?"

"Konn collects very strange creatures," mused Nejirt, "like you and me. Wait till you meet his dog!"

"When do I get to work?" asked Eron, unable to contain his curiosity.

"You're already working. Didn't you just complain that your mind had been filled with numbers to overflowing? You've been briefed on your first assignment by an ex-nightclub master of ceremonies who has taken to flying in his old age." Hahukum Konn's assistant flopped down on a huge outcropping of graffiti-weathered rock that was perfectly shaped to his body. Eron remained standing while Nejirt explained to him how he was to be involved in a pedantic exercise, not predicting a future but predicting Rith's past. Then he shrugged, obviously questioning the utility of "predicting" a past so huge and so far away that no one could even remember it well enough to check the "prediction." Nejirt was as full of chatter as his wife, praising Konn and undermining him at the same time. He began to wax philosophical about mathematical points which made no sense to the recruit . . .

"What assignment?" Eron cut in.

"Sit down. Relax. You won't get a view like this when they put you in chains down in the depths of Splendid Wisdom—unless you're some kind of a pervert nocturnal roof-freak. You'll soon be too busy trying to please Konn to enjoy the stars." He extended his arms and his eyes to the sky.

"I've seen stars before," said Eron.

"Well, I can't get enough of them. I was born a blind mole deep in the heart of Splendid Wisdom. This is elixir for my soul!"

"You forgot to open your eyes while en route?"

"Looking at the stars from inside a spacesuit helmet isn't the same thing."

"There are portholes." Smiling, Eron sat down on the rock, more stiffly than his companion, his buttocks obscuring a polished curse carved in some bygone epoch by the laser pistol of an unhappy Eta Cumingan sergeant.

Nejirt continued his musing. "I think Konn brought us here—even the aerocar and the dog—to marinate in the glorious history of mankind. He wants to mature our mean little souls with a little vastness. Amazing that most of those stars up there—except the really big, bright ones—were visited in the ten millennia of space travel before the hyperdrive. Can you even imagine Rith when it was a thriving hive of twenty-seven billions? Noble madmen. Look." He pointed. "There's Sintea! jewel of the prehyperspace era, gone to weeds under Eta Cuminga."

Eta Cumingan technology marked the transition between the Interstellar Age and the Galactic Age. Those ancient empire builders had returned to Rith long after the Great Collapse had silenced the teeming cities of the First Men. It went without saying that their once-mighty armies also belonged as much to the mists of history as did the Assyrian and Persian and Macedonian waves which had ravenously washed over Egypt during the twilight of the Nile civilization. Only the Nile was still flowing. Nejirt relaxed with his hands behind his head while his captive audience listened.

"You've been edging me toward the hangar," said Eron to nudge the subject back again into a more immediate channel. "I think the whole secret of what we're doing here is in there. What is it?"

Nejirt Kambu grinned again. "You don't want to know. The main thing you have to know is that the Admiral is a *madman*." He rose as if whipped to attention and they were on their way again. "Come. I'll show you inside." They began to work their way down the hill past the station that desalinated the brackish water from their well. "Did you crawl around inside that Horezkor getting the photos and measures Konn wanted?"

"Yeah. It was a lot of fun."

"Wait till you see what the Admiral has in his hangar *here*!"

A growling dog loped over. "WhatIsDo?" asked the dog, ready for a fight. He sat up on his haunches and his front paws uncurled into fingers.

"Easy, Rhaver!" Nejirt stuck out his fingers for the dog to smell. "It's only me. I work here. And you aren't a guard dog."

"AmSo," said the dog, but having lost interest, ran away after some other smell.

The hangar door rumbled open. No one was inside. Nejirt ordered the watch-bot to create light, then powered the idle mnemonifier. Eron couldn't quite make out what they'd walked into. There were offices along a balcony and broken stones neatly laid out on the floor with equipment probably meant to chip, slice, and analyze stone. And a mock-up of a large fuselage propped on scaffolding.

"The Monster from the Deep!" announced Nejirt. "Some geophysicist diver found it. Konn heard the rumors, dropped everything, and organized an expedition. It took our Mad Admiral to fish the fossil up out of the sea."

"An old Rithian sea monster?" asked Eron in confusion.

"*Sea* monster! No. Space help us, Hahukum kens battleships like that Horezkor—any kind of mobile weapon. A *long* time ago contemporary with the Great Pyramid *this* one used to fly. It came with . . . well, a skeleton crew—a broken wing, calcified—four motors, calcified—bent propellers, calcified—the ghosts of bullet holes. Also an empty bomb womb. Konn is pretty sure it was once the weapon mentioned in some of the surviving lit as the Venteen Flying Fortress. Konn is all excited about reconstructing a full-size copy. He's going to fly it. Want to join the air crew? Me, I'm hanging onto the skorgn bushes! Skorgn bushes have gripping roots that go way, way down looking for water. Not for me risking my ass in a contraption as old as flying! Might as well try cattle herding on a Tyrannosaurus mount."

Eron walked over to the rocky fossils. "Nothing can be preserved in there after seventy-five thousand years!"

"Reconstructions are Konn's specialty. What's driving his engineers crazy is how these guys got away with not using quantronic controllers. Space, even basic electronics is missing—we thought we'd find at least traces of silicon. And a good mechanical controller would be too heavy to fly."

"But the metal is all gone! Surely the airframe wasn't ceramic! They didn't know how to work ceramics yet!"

"No aluminum left for sure, but enough oxide traces so we can tell you the exact alloy. We already have the basic dimensions and have shown it to be airworthy—if controlled by modern guidance. How *they* controlled it is still a mystery, but we have hints. Now it's mostly a matter of building the parts. Tricky. Hard to believe the work-arounds those shamans used. You wouldn't expect Rithians to be that intelligent, and certainly not Rithians who were still unclear on the basic concepts of quantum engineering! They thought pi was twenty-two sevenths or maybe even three!"

Eron wasn't listening. He was examining slices of what had once been airframe and the tri-dim reconstructions on one of the mnemonifier screens. "What does this have to do with psychohistory?"

"Nothing. Not a damn thing! Recall that I never attested to Konn's sanity." Kambu took Eron over to the fuselage mock-up. "Can you believe Konn intends to fly this thing?"

"What am *I* doing here?"

"You know some fluid dynamics—our Konn grinned when he spotted *that* in your résumé. Haven't you noticed that you are a physicist? That's why you've been brought here in such a rush. Maybe you know how to ensorcell a Fortress into flight mode? Hard to get the weight down to work with such underpowered motors. Chemical motors! Wheels, crankshafts, gears—you won't believe the stuff that's in there! They used sheet metal for skin that takes projectiles like it was a kid's play papier-mâché armor!"

"How *was* it controlled?"

"Evidently by hidden wires and mirrors from the cockpit. Not a brain in the beast. Not a neuron! Not a chip! There were some traces of tiny electrically goosed genies-in-a-bottle but they weren't in the control loop. When that Fortress needs a brain, the pilot better not be asleep." He showed Eron the mounted skull of the pilot, obviously a *Homo sapiens* of low intellect. "He's been asleep for a long time. Maybe he *died* in his sleep."

"And you want me to decode the fluid dynamics of an ancient aerocar?" Eron asked, appalled.

Kambu was blithe. "Aerodynamicist looks good on your job description for the accountants. Of course, what we really need is a graduate student to carry heavy weights. Like lifting rocks to the slicer. Rock chipping, too. You're a strong young fellow." Nejirt led Eron up the plasteel stairs to a row of office cubicles. "Yours." Inside, there was barely room for two people and their tools. Eron especially noticed the red mask to protect a face from flying debris. Nejirt's grin widened. "Oh yes, and after a Rithian day's work—sunrise to sunset—of carrying rocks and a little aerodynamic finger-counting, Konn expects you to slave away solving those history problems to advance your education. I've already mentioned that. At night. After sundown. By candlelight. Konn has a set of sixtyne or so projects for you to teethe on. You can pick which idea appeals to you. No rest for you serfs," he added with the joy of an Interregnum slaver.

It sounded terrible. But the thought of being taught some psychohistory was cheering. "History being a euphemism for psychohistory?" asked Eron hopefully.

"Not by the Founder's Nose!" Nejirt brought Konn's beginner list of problems to the wall's mnemonifier terminal. "You probably won't see any psychohistory until you get back to Splendid Wisdom. First you have to scrabble around sorting out simpler-known historical events into their causes and effects in a way that allows you to predict what has already happened—nothing complicated—warm-up exercises—just ticktacktoe pieces where the outcome is so obvious that high prognostication isn't really necessary—for example, extrapolating the fate of a prestellar Rithian two-faction nation-state where the main issue is whether republican or democratic adultery is permissible to a politician."

"That sounds like psychohistory to me."

"No! No! No!" Nejirt paused to let his negative exclamations have their effect. "The full mathematics of *psychohistory* is incredibly more complex. The *real* stuff involves knowing how to *manipulate* the key events which make a prediction come true. Hein-Ricova analysis, et cetera, et cetera. For now Konn just wants you to simulate a known primitive history. Predicting the past to tell you what you already know is instructive but it is *far* simpler than manipulating a future to tell you what you want to hear."

"What does Konn do for a living when he's not dallying?"

"He keeps the lid on. Pretty dull work. It is Jars Hanis who is into all the ideas and all the action. Not that the likes of you and me can get close to Rector Hanis."

Eron stared blankly at Konn's beginner's list while Nejirt relentlessly continued—the senior, who'd been through it all, hazing the freshman. "Your aerial companion was probably briefing you on a multitude of subjects. Did anything strike your fancy?"

Eron reviewed his adventures since landing on Rith. "Flying inside that animated mouthpiece was like being tossed into a sixty-four-dimensional universe. Artabas, aturs, degrees, cubits, cubic barley feet, pints, arshins, scruples, grains, fingers, shekels, librae, qedets, hours, talents. My mind spins. He was telling me that the Great Pyramid was originally both a standard of length and time, east-west length being determined by the distance the stars moved in one second and north-south distance by the difference in the culmination angle of a star measured at two latitudes. I do remember that sixty laps around its original base—a day's march by foot—times 360 was equivalent to a journey halfway around Rith."

"Ah-ha! You noticed the *numbers*. Weights and measures. Now we know how your mind works! I know the problem for you." Kambu then commanded the mnemonifier to display on the office screen a map of the earliest cradle of humanity contoured in layers by ease-of-travel—wiggly lines, pastel colors, different layers for different modes of transport. "Your physics courses at Asinia must have taught you the laws of diffusion?"

"Yeah. But nothing about social diffusions."

"I'll outline Konn's *ticktacktoe* problem. How do weight-and-measure standards establish themselves across political boundaries? It happened here at the dawn of civilization." He swept his hand over the eastern end of the Inner Sea region. "It also happened in the Galaxy where measurement standards drifted during the sub-light diaspora but became universal again *long* before the rise of Splendid Wisdom's empire. What's the diffusion mechanism?"

Eron stared at the map and thought of it as a wet surface upon which colored dyes of "length" and "time" and "weight" had been dropped, tendrils of dye snaking out to entwine with each other. But that analogy was simple physics and chemistry. Psychodynamics would be different—more like dynamic populations, more like evolution with the standards of measure emerging as the dominant life-form. A challenge. "What initial conditions are we assuming?"

"Konn doesn't want you to worry about that just yet. The scutch work has already been done; what you *do* with those numbers is Konn's main interest. Konn wants to see how you think—not how well you ferret. There's one thing you can count on from him—he's not going to tell you what you need to know, he's going to observe the style by which you make a fool of yourself so he'll know how to train you."

Eron sighed.

Nejirt laughed. "Don't worry so much. When it comes to the important work of fossil extraction"—he waved at the rocks—"you'll be using tools more advanced than Egyptian fingernails!"

The young apprentice did meet Hahukum Konn briefly to receive his first fam-feed—in exchange for his formal vow of secrecy. He vaguely remembered warnings about this moment, but the thrill of being offered what he had struggled so long to attain muted all caution.

He was led into a private room to an elaborate high-backed chair that was obviously used only for ritual affairs, mechanical tentacles sprouting from its head-rest, damascene adorned and rustling in excitement at sensing the presence of his fam. Just another machine.

Second Rank Hahukum Konn appeared in robes hastily donned, ready to do the formal honors. Eron had been ready, impatient, for months, and, though the coming confirmation wasn't voluntary, he wasn't thinking much about it; he *wanted* the proffered knowledge too much. Konn explained the contract carefully and articulately, his speech a detailed proof of the Founder's theorem that secrecy was a vital adjunct of a successful prediction. It made mathematical sense and Eron responded with the right noises—mouthing formalisms he hardly took seriously was a small price to pay.

It was the sentient chair which acted as priest—enfolding Eron while lying down, in the depths of his fam, a quantum neural structure that would not lend itself to any simple sequential data access. Eron would not be able to unmix from his memories what he was now absorbing—the cream was in the coffee—erasure could only be by nonuse, by the gradual cannibalization of information bits—or by the outright destruction of his fam under the laws governing treason. Nobody other than Eron could tap into the unique coding. Nor would he be able to export any of it in readable format. Even to use it himself he would have to spend years of effort "remembering" what he had never known.

When the ritual sacrifice was over, the youth made one concession of respect to his old Ganderian tutor, muttering his doubts by alluding to the oath of secrecy-unto-death sworn by iron-age Pythagoreans—who had thereby earned a reputation as elitists and so, when they became politically active, were slaughtered by the irate citizens of Crotona.

But the great Konn wasn't fazed by the intended irony of his newest student—he riposted amiably by counting up all the quadrillions of humans able to quote, but not prove, the sage Pythagorean theorem. Eron found *that* a weird viewpoint—equivalent to the statement that a gag vow was a moot point for a mathematician pledged to keep the methods of geometry secret from a colony of monkeys. Eron absorbed the High Pscholar's thrust, it not being politic to continue his dissent. But he was remembering Murek's cautionary story . . .

. . . during the renaissance of Egypt's Sixteenth Dynasty, between the Assyrian and Persian occupations, Greeks and Greek merchants had been welcome and honored—in Sais and Naukratis. Pythagoras, an adventurous youth, left the island of Samos to spend half his life in Egypt studying as an acolyte in a cult of priest-cosmologists who forgave him his Greekness in the light of his brilliance. For two thousand years these priest-surveyors of Egypt had been accumulating the tenets of straight-edge and compass geometry in a horde of tools intended for their exclusive use. He was warned. No blabbermouthing about geometry to the superstitious laity—on pain of death.

But ancestral continuity is no guarantee of immunity from fate's foibles.

The Persian conquest broke the cult's back, carting off its adepts to Babylon and Persepolis to serve on Persian astronomical and geodesic projects. Persia intended to conquer the known world—from Thinai to the Table of the Sun—and the reconnoitering teams of King Cambyses recruited the world's best mapmakers, who were all Egyptian geometers. Pythagoras escaped, first to Samos and then by ship, ahead of the Persian army, to the Greek colony of Crotona in Italy where he founded his own secretive school in the Egyptian tradition—modified by his Greek dreams of creating a new world order under the leadership of an elite cadre of "mathematikoi." To the end of his days Pythagoras enforced a vow of secrecy. Mathematics was not for the common masses.

All this Eron kept to himself. He found that he liked Second Rank Konn but at the same time wished that he was not so awed into silence by the old man—or so reduced to silence by the exalted tech his imagination saw within Splendid Wisdom's tentacled chair. None of it mattered. He had passed through the gate.

# ERON BUILDS A MODEL, 14,798 GE

*My studies of ancient metrology have led me to two general conclusions: first, that metrology was born mainly from the practices of the international merchant class of the ancient world and, second, that metrology provided the foundation for the scientific rational vision of the world.*

—Livio Catullo Stecchini (d. 1979 AD)

As the work of analyzing the flight dynamics of the fossilized Aerial Fortress went ahead, Eron began to spend his nights puzzling the pieces of his weights-and-measures diffusion problem into psychohistory's scaffold. The difficulty was not only in absorbing an alien mathematics so cavalierly archived in his fam but in trying, simultaneously, to empathize with another kind of alien humanity lost down there at the bottom of time. Even when he hewed to the Founder's rules faithfully, the assumptions weren't easy to follow. He kept trying to think like a physicist.

He took long walks in the desert to erase his preconceptions, sometimes even removing his fam while, of course, gripping it tightly in both hands. Famlessness induced a heady kind of godlike immediacy, his mind stupefied to the complexity of life. Nevertheless it granted him the distanced perspective he needed—gazing with the eyes of a Rith-bound sapiens fresh from the simian life.

Out here in the night air of Rith he *was* the spirit of a wave of settlers in the Nile Valley. He saw an arched heaven that couldn't be higher than sixty times the highest mountain, a vault of glitter that rotated around an axis-point in a sky full of mystery and powers. The rising of the stars held the secret of life and death, commanding the immotile earth to renew when it was time for the flowering of life and commanding it to die when it was time for the cowering of death. Ra measured the sun's day; Thoth measured the moon's month; wandering stars made their rounds carrying cryptic messages; comets appeared out of nowhere, without pattern, warning of chaos.

Sometimes an adventurous urge took him—to see the mountains out of which the stars rose—to follow the rumors of distant riches told by the rare traveler, of gold, of marvels along the tin route, of pasture, of bustling towns, of strange people, of the terrible sea . . . sometimes it was merely the urge to be gone from the reach of an irate clan who were promising to murder him . . . sometimes he fell in with experienced merchants of his own kin or a cattleman grazing his herd . . . sometimes it was a craftsman's trade that took him journeying. Metalsmith and artisan and surveyor had an easy mobility. Nomadic restlessness was not yet out of his blood. He had stories to bring with him to strange lands and stories to bring back; such is the delicious excitement of adventure in a world where talking-and-seeing and taking-and-bringing is the only form of communication.

Between the walks Eron wrote his inspiration into the equations of his mnemonifier, struggling with internal antagonisms, antilogy, error messages, and dead ends. And went back to walking under the stars.

Over the ages the Egyptian spirit reasoned how the laying of stones, aligned on certain heavenly events, allowed the prediction of an event's repetition. Knowledge evolved into a profusion of calendars to determine the day, the month, the seasons, the year. The stones transmogrified into obelisks and wells to measure the shadows of the sun and into the sun-baked bricks of temples aligned to make a jewel glow with starlight in the sacred chamber at just the critical moment of the year's cycle. Flash! The floods are coming. Prepare! Egyptians became masters of surveying in order to reestablish boundaries after the floods. Fixing a place in its relation to all other places became an obsession. Marker stones became jinn with occult powers, not to be moved—the priest-surveyors gave warning.

Strangers, sometimes men from beyond the sea's horizon, mostly Sumerian traders with Semitic pack-animal tenders, brought ferment and ideas and took away with them the same.

The temples grew into the abode of priests whose curiosity nourished the spirit that had willy-nilly brought them power. The priests mastered the numerology of shadows and learned to predict the equinoxes and to discern destinies. They drew pictures on the walls of their observatories, displayed as easy-to-remember fantasies, prompts for the memory which now had to hold an accumulating number of facts, more than a mere mortal could remember without the mnemonic aid of an entertaining story. The story didn't matter; its organization did. There was no contradiction in different accounts of the same event; the twists and variations added to the pleasure of telling. Who would be impudent enough to expect the gods to have a consistent history?

That evening Eron found himself walking alone in the desert with a ten-year-old imaginary acolyte, recounting to him the malevolent adventures of the Demon

Star who blinked out a new curse every three days and must therefore remain nameless lest his attention be provoked. There were nine hundred stars to remember, all encoded in less than sixty episodic fabulations. Some were guide stars, some presaged recurring events, some were signposts to other stars.

During late-morning bouts up in the hangar nest of the Venteen Fortress, Eron began test runs on his cobbled program, adjusting and refining its parameters. It soon acquired a psychohistoric life of its own, correcting most internal errors without bothering to consult Eron, living lustily in an imaginary past on a diet of electrons. More and more he had to let it work out its results by itself so he could get on with his real job.

Engineers responsible for the reconstruction of Konn's Flying Monstrosity were impatient for the facts they needed. It was Eron's responsibility to decipher the exact metric by which that ancient battlecraft had been built so that the reconstruction could begin in earnest. His routine "day" job had him preparing fossil slices, then painfully measuring the surviving details, compensating for the distortions caused by geological pressures and by chemical diffusion and replacement. From those numbers a nonrandom statistical bias was appearing. Prominent was a dominant length peak, broken by twelve smaller peaks. After that it was hard to sort the peaks from the noise, but they were there, and all were binary: halves, quarters, eighths, sixteenths, thirty-seconds. When an engineer asked him to hurry-it-up, he channeled that man's eagerness to the task of classifying the dimensions of parts.

Close by, asking for advice only when necessary, Eron's psychohistory experiment was iterating its way through imaginary accelerated time in the hangar's mnemonifier. New measures were arising spontaneously, living and dying in the artificial post-simian mélange. City-states came and went. Empires rose and fell. Eron read each new century's summary every evening before he went to bed; it was both fascinating and appalling. Sometimes he had to reset the century because of a parameter he had obviously mistuned.

A constant potpourri of arguments had to be resolved. At first perhaps only over a day's ration or some vicious land dispute. Then a gourd-cup, ingeniously used to solve a difficult volumetric dispute, became the tool for resolving the next similar dispute. The length of a sacred temple wand became the means of fixing boundaries. Each of these measures would take on only a temporary local authority while it competed in a lethal struggle with all the surrounding measures that were evolving, to live or die. The complications increased. Traders argued.

*Which* measure was to be used to consummate the sale? Transactions craved an undisputed measure *everywhere* unaffected by the ravages of time, distance, war, weather, or kingly ego. No one wanted to ask "By which gourd?" or "By which rod?" Floods washed away old markers. Rods wore out. Gourds broke. The king's shoe size changed with every assassination, or coup, or death. Cheaters used variations in measures to grow wealthy. Landowners invented special measures to suit private greed. Where was the god of measures against whose rule no argument could prevail?

Yet all men lived under the same glory, slept under the same nightly drift, planted by the rule of the same equinox. A stream could be dammed, a river crossed, an enemy killed, a storm weathered, a plague survived—yet no hand could stay the precision of the sky; every star cycled back to its place, by day and by season, at precisely the same place and at precisely the same time. And (as every nomad knew) the pivot-point of the stars rose in the sky as one went downriver—the dome of the earth underfoot mimicked the dome of the heavens above one's head.

Konn visited. He put pressure on Eron. He wanted to fly his mythical battleship. Just as Nejirt had predicted, he did not ask about Eron's problems with psychohistory's mathematics and did not offer advice. The engineers began to ride Eron. He needed to give them a preliminary value of the foot just to get them off his back. Maybe there was a historical reference somewhere, an ancient engineer's handbook, anything! When Rossum's Universal Robot #26, as he called himself, turned up at the pad, Eron was ready for a ride with the expedition's historian.

"You've told me you know everything," he said, staring morosely at the instrument panel.

"That would be an exaggeration."

"Konn put you in charge of all the historical documents he brought with him, is that right?"

"The Master knows my weakness. I read a lot. I'm a bookaholic. I just finished off the collected works of Charles Dickens on the way over. These Rithians have no shame. When they are faking the past, they should at least try to learn some history. You should see what this Charles fellow tries to pull off on his readers. He fills Neolithic London with all sorts of anachronistic technology. But I must say, the series was a good read. We mustn't always press for historical accuracy so seriously. Perhaps I might ask you for some pointers on Dickens' sense of humor? If you have a day or two off, we could run up for a look at the London mound. You'll find it as Naskala on the maps. It's extraordinary. They've dug up a square kilometer of it, right down to the thirty-second-millennium level—AD, of course; no one here understands GE. The Marsallian artifacts—"

"I need a technical manual on ancient measures—very ancient measures. Anything you have. Scraps, ripped pages, manuscripts rotting in jars."

"Well, now, please note that the Master just dumped his data on me, downloaded from Splendid Wisdom's archives without much planning. I haven't really had a chance to file it all. But I'll look. That doesn't mean I'll find anything even if I have it. I was born in the era of the messy virtual desktop, and that horror is still down there in my programming, lost along with the rest of it but not inactive, alas. Are we going somewhere?"

"Just a spin in the sky for a look at the sunset. Maybe a flight over the Nile. I want to see the river at night."

So while they were in the air, Rossum's #26 tried to be helpful. "A manual, you say?"

"Dull stuff. Conversion tables. Length measures mostly. Something an aeronautical artisan would use. I'm assuming that they could read. I know Romans could read, but I'm not sure if the Americs ever got that far along the civilization curve. I need cross-references to any measure I know about."

"What era?"

"Konn says 59,400 BGE or thereabouts"–meaning Before the Galactic Era–"plus or minus a millennium. It's a pretty narrow window. Americs didn't last all that long. A victory here, a victory there, then oblivion."

"Oh, dear. That far back. I was a toddler then. I don't remember it very well. The little memory I had was tied up in cardboard holes. I have to catch up on the more gossipy events of my early life by reading."

"Yeah."

"My favorite pre-civilization author of the moment is Dickens. He is always mentioning pounds and shillings and pence and troy weight and stones but not, alas, aeronautical artisans. The Brits used horses, so I suppose that would be the wrong millennium for your purposes. The Greeks had horses that could fly but not the staid old London gentlemen. The only Rithian measure I know anything about is the meter."

"That's no use to me. The meter didn't get imposed on these stubborn Rithians until Eta Cuminga conquered them back in the forty-seventh millennium BGE. They're still hanging onto their archaic seconds, all 86,400 of them. Rith was the *last* place that would have accepted standardized measures. And my stoned battleship of the air was built and died long before that. Way before."

"I beg your pardon, sir. The meter is a *Rithian* measure. It goes back to the mists of antiquity when the land telescope was a novelty glass ball mounted in brass."

"You've got your wires crossed!"

"Ask any Rithian."

"So? They claim they invented everything. I'll concede them the starship, murder, and poetry–but nothing else."

"Let me prove my point. Do you see the flatscreen in front of your nonperceptive eyes? Yes? Please access the navigational instruments. You do know how to do that?"

"Yes, you pile of salvaged junk."

"Please compute the distance between the north pole of this planet and its equator."

The result of this exercise surprised Eron by its almost roundness. "Ten million one thousand nine hundred and eighty-seven meters."

"Exactly. It should have been ten million on the mark, but they evidently had a simian's trouble with their glass balls and brass. I do believe the surveyors of Gaul weren't even using identical rods. Haven't you ever wondered why the meter is defined as 9,192,631,770 wavelengths of cesium and not 10 billion, even? It was born before interferometry, that's why. Don't they teach you anything in school these days?"

Eron let his astonishment overwhelm him. An astronomical measure right under his feet, and he'd never noticed! Maybe psychohistory wasn't bunk after all! Space alive! a meter that had not only conquered all the king's feet and royal noses but had gone on to conquer the Galaxy! He smiled. It was pleasant to fly at such an altitude and look down at the river that flowed straight north all the way from the gullied deserts of the equator to the Inner Sea. The Egyptians had probably invented the stalwart meter. What a cool idea—straight up the river valley from equator to pole!

He was suddenly noticing the astronomy in the meter stick he had ignored all his life. He was 190 centimeters tall, he saw light by nanometers, and he traveled across space by leaps of a league's ten petameters. To think that after an eon the stars of Rith still remained in command; the vast majority of mankind still measuring their spans—from vast galactic distances down to the tiniest quanta—against the piddling ten millionth part of the distance between the north pole of Rith and its equator, a full 180 days of hard march from beneath a zodiac that intersected the zenith to stand under the axle of the grindstone of the Norse gods!

Back at base, he thanked the aerocar and watched it take off again into the night sky's stars, its running lights blinking their friendly warning.

The sky turned through many days. The earth under his toes stood still. Eron lost himself in reverie. No matter *how* he set up his model in the mnemonifier—tuned it, tried to bias it—any length once conceived of as the ratio of a celestial distance to a surface distance clobbered any measure unable to compete as reliably. It astonished Eron to watch an astronomically based length—originating in Egypt, or Mesopotamia, by whim or by chance—spread by word of mouth through the trade routes of his model. They reached places like the distant coastal islands beyond the sea's gate long before the eastern shore of the Inner Sea could possibly have become aware that such islands existed. The spread did not even require a literate foundation, only show-and-tell. Measures that matched the fixed measures of the sky resonated with the human culture's need for certainty, building, growing, while arbitrary measures like the length of a mortal king's forearm traveled poorly and so lost vitality and died.

Because he didn't quite believe his own math, he cheated and peeked into the answer book—though even the best of the ancient starship libraries had been sparse on the history of Rithian measures. He tried to find data on the foot by which the Venteen Flying Fortress had been built, which would be of immense use in its reconstruction, but that foot seemed to have vanished into mythology after a spacecraft, assembled by its rule, had crashed into Mars, initiating some kind of taboo against even mentioning conversion factors.

But . . . yes, within a few centuries after the Egyptians had built their pyramids and the Sumerians their ziggurats, the barbarians of Europe began a frenzied building of their own gigantic astronomical observatories. Amazed, Eron worked out the accuracy of the devices they would need, and it was quite within the capabilities of Neolithic craftsmanship. Copper helped, bronze tools were even better, but stone polished against stone was good enough. Information transfer was no problem. There were a thousand talkative traders working far outside of their own borders for every warrior impassioned to sack a Troy. Before they could write, the Sumerians had already established the long road by which Alexander the Great would invade Persia three thousand years later.

How was this happening? His equations were assuming a tool or tools able to measure length and time. *What* tools? Psychohistory wasn't specifying. Certainly not an atomic clock or an electron nanocalib, not even anything as rudimentary as a quartz clock. The more he stared at the model, the more he could see the Founder's equations working with the imperative of evolution. Eyes had evolved not because of invention and creativity, but because life was surrounded by light and made of chemicals that responded to light in different ways. Given the Founder's definition of the human mind with its built-in sensitivity to cycles, the model was predicting the evolution of a system of stellar-based measurement, not because of invention and creativity but because it was the best *possible* system of measures in a milieu of primitive constraints.

He couldn't help but wonder: Was the strange foot he was extracting millimeter by millimeter from the ancient wreck of a flying chariot one of those strange measures his model was predicting? Not this particular measure, because psychohistory didn't do that, but one of that class of astronomical measures? By now he had it pinned down to between 30.42 and 30.5 centimeters. He set up a program in his fam to examine the possibilities and soon came up with some wild conjectures.

The sky notched over every night by a factor of 1/365 days.

The ancients had divided a circle—and so their sky—into 360 parts.

According to his robot friend, the Egyptians liked to count by tens and thousands.

If Eron divided by 365,000 the number of meters in a degree of latitude at the London Mound—Naskala—he came up with a value of 30.479 centimeters, well within the bounds of his statistical peaks, and so, with a straight face, gave his engineers a foot of 30.48 cm to work with. That ought to hold the bastards for a few days while he caught up on his workload!

In the evening under a full desert moon a hanging bowl of potted flowers swinging in the breeze gave the budding psychohistorian the hint he needed.

There was only *one* periodic tool that a Neolithic man might build with his own hands which carried in its physical parameters an accuracy to match the stars: the pendulum. The same pendulum was both a rod and a clock that could be tuned to the rhythm of the sky. *Nothing* had to be invented.

After the yearly floods of the Nile, markers must be reestablished to connect stable landmarks with vanished points. That poses problems solved only by inventing basic straight-edge and compass geometry, one axiom, one theorem, one tool at a time. For determining the vertical dimension there is no surveying instrument more important than a plumb bob attached to a plumb line. But plumb bobs have the annoying habit of oscillating, and they always need to be stilled to get the vertical reading. Every priest-surveyor would know in his bones that a long plumb line oscillates slower than a short plumb line. He might not calibrate the frequencies numerically, but he would *know*.

Sitting there, a wakedream began to amuse Eron, his mind dwelling in the past, eavesdropping on two priests. Priest-One is a watcher of stars. He does the local forecasting about the seasons. The other is a surveyor, but it is not the time of year for him to be working. Tomorrow he will distribute seed.

Priest-One idly waits for a particular star to cross the horizon. Priest-Two is keeping him company.

"We have time enough for a beer," says Priest-One, noticing that a particular precursor star has just broken the horizon, telling him that though the dawn star will be rising soon, it won't be right away.

"How long is that?" challenges Priest-Two, to be contrary.

They argue while they sip beer. Still, they can't agree on "having a beer" as a standard period by which to measure the difference in the rising times of two stars. Different people drink beer at different rates. They tell jokes about a drunken priest who can drink in one evening more beers than there are stars in the sky. Finally, to settle the argument, Priest-Two pulls out his plumb bob and line. He remembers once being mad at his assistant for dallying too long over lunch. He couldn't whack the boy senseless because he was the son of an important village official, so he just sat there fuming, counting the swings of the plumb line that was already set up under the tripod and ready to go. He knows now *exactly* how long it takes a loafer to eat lunch. Fortunately stars, unlike assistants, are steady as you go; counting rising times should be a piece of nutcake. Priest-Two, impressed, excitedly reports the incident to Priest-Three the next evening. They try but can't duplicate the results until they agree to use the same length of plumb line.

. . . a hundred years later there are special assistants at the temple, young apprentice priests, putting pebbles in jars to count pendulum swings and, once in a while, to man the small bellows that keeps the bob in motion. Accountants are inventing new symbols with which to record the accumulating data. A bright young theoretician has demonstrated to his satisfaction that no matter the length of the plumb line you start with, if on the next night you increase its length by four, you will halve the number of pebbles that it takes to count the bob-swings between the rising of your two stars. He has an argument going with a friend in the next temple down the valley about the optimal number of pebbles to use to count a complete circuit of the stars in heaven. If too few pebbles are used, the plumb line becomes impossibly long; if the plumb line is too short, the constant counting of pebbles becomes a tedious chore.

The model was beginning to scare Eron. He would have to present it to the Admiral soon and it was doing things he hadn't anticipated, that just didn't look right. It was even generating astronomers who could *measure* before they could write! Measuring was *driving* the invention of writing! They were a bunch of illiterates looking at scrawled pictures. They had to *remember* everything! And they didn't even have a fam to remember with! Was that possible? He couldn't even imagine functioning without being literate. Eron had learned to read before he even had a fam! Were these damn equations real?

Perhaps there had been no need for writing when all a man had to do was memorize whole heroic sagas. What peasant couldn't recite at least sixtyne stories from his grandfather about how the world started or how the peacock got its tail? But when it came to counting sheep, and bars of gold, and rations of barley, and taxes due, and the amount of dirt to be excavated from a canal, and how many days of labor a tenant farmer owed, and what volume of beer to exchange for what volume of wheat—without being cheated—and how to lay up supplies for a ten-day donkey caravan, and how to count the swings of a pendulum, the sheer overload of information made writing a necessary evil. An illiterate man can move stones around a Stonehenge to keep track of the moon, can understand the necessity of standard rods to mark off equal parcels of land and know how to make them, can weave and hoe and sow and fashion cups that scoop out a day's ration of wheat. What such a man *can't* do is keep records in his head for a thousand people so that it will all balance out in a year without starvation. That's what the equations seemed to be saying. First the measure. Then comes writing.

His model was certainly generating hundreds of different lengths and volumes of the kind that a Neolithic man might need, most of them useful in the locale of their birth and nowhere else. Nothing marked which measure might overwhelm another—circumstance alone insisted that the winners needed wide appeal. Mediators who could work a large territory became important. If the opinion of a such a king was law, then the trading between families and clans and distant towns forced the winnowing and merging of measures by negotiation. Inattention to standards became fatal.

When Eron played god by adding artificial parameters that drove standards into a fluctuating mode, economic collapse was *always* the consequence. And, when he did, the stars fought back with almost an astrological mysticism; the stars had their silent veto.

The engineers began to build small replica parts, hydraulic pumps, electrical switches, and that attracted the Admiral in full uniform. Eron recognized the bronze and leather armor of a Roman centurion. He tried to remain invisible, afraid that he would have to show off his model prematurely. But Konn seemed solely concerned with the mechanics of his battleship of the air. But just when Eron thought he was going to be able to escape notice, Konn walked over and fixed him with the eyes of a commander who is about to decimate his mutinous troops. "We need to talk."

In Eron's tiny office along the hangar's high catwalk, the Admiral sat down. That was bad news. He meant to stay. "Do you want a report on my psychomodel, sir?" He was fidgeting. "It's working, but it's still doing strange things that I don't understand."

Konn held up his hand. "When you're ready. Only when you're ready." He paused for emphasis. "I have a new assignment for you. You will, of course, continue with your old responsibilities."

Eron already felt overburdened. He hadn't had enough sleep for days. But he couldn't refuse. "Yes, sir."

"I'm putting you in charge of those boobs out there."

Eron was horrified. "But, sir, I'm only a kid. I'm in trouble with them already!"

"Persistence in the face of adversity is a virtue. Such virtues built the Empire."

"They won't listen to me."

"In that case"–Konn smiled mischievously–"we won't tell them who is in charge. I'm sure those boobs are planning–against my direct orders–to install a few quantronic devices here and there. Just a little unobtrusive control–in the interest of my safety. When they are through, I'm not even sure that a pilot will be able to fly the Fortress by himself. I've flown in yachts before; why would I be interested?"

"They don't believe it can fly without quantronics, sir. Light enough mechanical controls are impossible to design given the weight constraints of flying on a heavy planet like Rith."

"It did fly!"

"It crashed, sir."

"It had holes blown in it. You measured those yourself. Modern Rith is remarkably free of hostile fire. I want no argument. You are responsible to see that no quantronic devices are installed. Not even a thumbnail of semiconducting silicon. Not a pinhead! Fail me and I'll nail you to a cross. Upside down." He smiled. "The Romans did that." He seemed delightedly sure of his information.

"No silicon? Not even a big transistor? The Americs didn't have electronics?"

"Not what you'd call electronics. They caught their electrons in fishnets."

"No wonder they are extinct!"

"Be that as it may. If I find any modern devices in the finished craft, you'll be the one nailed. To ensure your diligence you will be flying copilot with me."

"Yes, sir!"

Konn nodded on his way out. "Something to tell your grandchildren."

"How I was nailed to a Roman cross in my disreputable youth?"

"No. How we flew together through a thunderstorm on manual in a dawn-age kite."

While Eron was thinking that over, cursing by all the forty messiahs of Rith, a call chimed in on his fam because he wasn't censoring any calls about metrics. "Rossum's #26 here. Coming in for a landing. I found you some data on pre-Galilean pendulums. Not much but you'll be interested."

# OTARIA OF THE CALMER SEAS
# FINDS A CAUSE, 14,810 GE

*By 1300 GE . . . evaporation and circulation patterns on Splendid Wisdom were
no longer providing enough rain—the weather had already been set awry by an
excessive building zeal driven by the hugely profitable interstellar ventures established by the previous Kambal Dynasty. Doomsayers were talking of atmospheric collapse. Cities had replaced forest, desert, and klotk-prairie. The natural
water table was disastrously low and the aquifers dry.*

*The One-Eyed Frightfulperson, known to us as Tanis-the-First (ruled
1378–1495 GE, the longest reign in Imperial history), was displeased by the ferocity of the civil war that followed his usurpation of the Imperial Throne. To
bring the planet back under his control, he cynically confiscated the Oceans and
Seas of Splendid Wisdom and turned their assets over to a new military command, the Diligence of Frightfulbarons, whose job it was to ration water to a
water-short populace so that they might be held ransom by their thirst.*

*The Frightfulbarons of the Diligence built the desalination plants and the
pumping stations. Of the five Major and thirty Minor Frightfulbarons, the first
Frightfulbaron of the Calmer Sea was probably the most ruthless. Executing all
who opposed . . . He commanded the Fourth Frightful Army and his own Brine
Commandos, plus half a billion forced laborers, retaining control through a system of . . . His children by eighty wives and countless concubines were loyal, industrious, and prolific, all disciplined by . . . His Frightfulgrandchildren drove
the original piles and tunnels along the shore of the Calmer Sea, reclaiming land
from the sea for a building boom financed by the sale and control of water . . .*

—From the Explanatorium at the Calmer Pumping Station

The light of the sun Imperialis twisted into the upper levels of the synthetic skin
of the planet Splendid Wisdom through arteries of guide-pipes, some of which

branched off into the apartment of Hyperlord Kikaju Jama, shining mostly on his atrium's topiary garden. Kikaju had been brooding all morning in a comfortably raggy robe. He hadn't even bothered to vibro-clean his teeth or put on a wig.

That damn pest from outer space was back again. And this time meddling behind Jama's back with affairs of intrigue none of his business. For—what was it? twenty years now?—Jama had been toyed with by that Scogil fellow, a bit here, a piece there. Not that the man didn't keep his promises. It was just that his reasonable promises always, *always,* turned out to be more lace than gold. Bluff, sweet talk! Homey pictures of his teenage daughter when he needed a diversion. The "lace" arrived on time, as promised, but when you wore it, your private parts remained uncovered. And Scogil had never really given Jama credit for finding the Martyr's Cache—instead stealing it for his own, not even providing a readable copy—sweet talking Jama's mathists but in the end leaving them bewildered. It was outrageous! It rankled. Without more respect, how could a Hyperlord run an efficient conspiracy?

Gloomy though Hyperlord Kikaju Jama's interior residence appeared during Splendid Wisdom's daytime, its dim luminance was enhanced by a hidden robo-light of cunning mechanism which haloed the Hyperlord, that he might be seen, and, upon demand, became a diffuse beam impaling the target of his gaze, that he might see. In meditation, with eyes closed, Jama was surrounded by an electro-nimbus—all else remained spectral, dark, hidden. A personal vanity.

There was no inner eyelight to brighten his dark thoughts.

This arrogant Scogil fellow's failure to make his scheduled supply run—and, worse, his failure to explain, with not even a coded apology—was making it impossible for Jama to deliver the sixtyne or so of Coron's Eggs he had promised to various contacts in the antique trade. Not that they were antiques. He smiled to himself. It was a very Rithian scam. The Eggs were fresh out of the factory—embodying the full seven levels—but cosmetically in the style of past millennia with an appropriately aged patina. *My simian ancestors are chattering in glee from Rith's trees,* he gloated before resuming his sulk. Where were those Eggs?

Then he opened his eyes and a sly eyelight followed his glance to the mounted galactarium in his atrium. Jama enjoyed adulation. He did not appreciate not being able to deliver those perverse Eggs. He had promised them for too long now! For *twenty years* he had been building his conspiracy, successfully enough so that by now he felt he deserved the adulation. At the wise age of eighty-four a titled mensch could dispense with youthful modesty. It was a shame that security procedures forced him to lead so many different lives that no one man was ever in a position to fully appreciate him. How much greater their adulation would be if they knew. Now, how was he going to get hold of Scogil? That exasperating man tended to wander around Splendid Wisdom incognito.

Suddenly . . .

His telesphere formed in the air to the left of his head with an unusual urgency, blooming from invisible to opalescent—there to warn its master. "Apparently uninvited, we have with us the Excellent Frightfulperson Otaria of the Calmer Sea." Only after formally identifying the intruder did the sphere become less urgent, speaking in the manner of a peevish butler. "She is impatient, excited," intoned the telesphere. "She is violating protocol. Advice is to be alert."

Since the Hyperlord was anticipating no interruption of his treasonous meditations, he had dressed for comfort rather than spectacle. "Let me see her." A fairy-size image appeared within his guardian globe—there she was in miniature: Lord Jama's sometime pupil and occasional erotic companion. The girl with the indispensable—but troublesome—mother who always slapped his hand when he reached for a nubile breast.

Hyperlord Jama nodded absently to his wraithlike servant in dismissal. Acknowledged, it disappeared abruptly. The Lord did not bother to activate his weapons, though he no longer held this impetuous woman in full confidence now that she was grown and, unfortunately, had a mind of her own and a fam to go with it. Activating weapons automatically registered them with the police. But he was displeased and set the entrance's damping-field high enough to inhibit any fast moves. Moderately viscous. High viscosity would have been an insult.

*The Excellent Frightfulperson Otaria of the Calmer Sea, indeed,* he thought, remembering her as a child riding about on his shoulders and steering him by the ears. How quaint the old titles sounded when one stopped a moment to think upon what must have been their original meaning. Perhaps once there had been real ocean over that vast area of Splendid Wisdom called the Calmer Sea—perhaps in ancient times when Otaria's unwashed ancestors had been brutal conquerors from hyperspace and Jama's ancestors had not yet intrigued their way to high position.

Now every seabed of Splendid Wisdom was as dry as its moon, Aridia—enclosed, built over, sucked barren by time's multiplying bureaucrats. Whatever currents of the noachian oceans had once flowed within the Calmer Sea, such waters had long ago been siphoned off into the life-support piping of the planet, some of it breaking out during the Interregnum in a flood that drowned billions only to be recaptured by Dark Age engineers, hence forever to wander mournfully through a planetary maze of arterial fresh-water and veined sewers, alternately becoming champagne and piss, blind to class, bathing the rich and poor alike, mixing with the blood of long-gone rebellions and the blood of commercial traffic from thirty million suns that bowed to Splendid Wisdom as the center of galactic power. One of Frightfulperson Otaria's distant kith must have ordered the final taming of the Calmer Sea.

In spite of being a longtime associate of Otaria's mother, Jama was not sure when the Frightfulpeople had themselves been pushed aside. History was not his forte, though, to rattle him, Otaria *pretended* it was hers. There were too many conflicting histories, a quantum ripple of alternate pasts. There were too many wars and too many intrigues and too many stars and too vast a span of time for one human with a single fam to comprehend. He did know that his own title had arisen during the seventh millennium under the reign of the Som Dynasty while the Empire sorely needed the cunning, the tech expertise, the ability to inspire fear, the diplomatic subtlety, and the legendary bureaucratic talent of the Hyperlords to consolidate the hasty conquests of Daigin-the-Jaw whose awesome campaigns had led the sons and ships of Imperialis to galactic ascendancy over the peoples of five million new stars in one generation—creating management problems of staggering complexity. In that glorious era the busy Hyperlords had traveled. How they had traveled!

He grinned. Throughout the ceaselessly turbulent rise and fall of fortunes, lofty titles never seemed to perish. He was Hyperlord Kikaju Jama, reduced to grubby commercialism, about to entertain Otaria who still proudly called herself a Frightfulperson of the Calmer Sea to honor the brutally luxurious dregs of some barbarian past she would find offensive if forced to live it.

The chute to his atrium shimmered, winked expansively, and Otaria dropped through, facing the skyless garden of his metal grotto, moving out of the damping-field with a swimming stride. She had to stoop slightly to pass under the overhang because she wore her fam in a silly brimmed hat of feathers instead of gracefully on her shoulders. Why this silly fad to *hide* the damned fams? The eyelight followed his gaze and she was illuminated, a tall woman with luxurious black hair coiffured in the ringlet style, elegantly dressed. How she had grown up from her sexy adolescence! She looked more like her foully murdered father than Katana.

"Well?" he asked, mildly annoyed—Otaria *knew* he liked time to prepare for any meeting—and she had given him no time to change out of the threadbare lounging robe he had thrown on this morning. Her appearance without an appointment was an outrageous invasion of privacy, but she did have the correct entry codes—he had given them to her willingly, fondly, and not very long ago. Foolish man! Regretting his sexual peccadilloes with a woman did not stop a misused old codger from liking her. How could he dislike a nubile youth he had spent so much time grooming! But she was not as pliable as she had been as a wild teenager.

Otaria smiled with broad lips. "I have a *man* for you, a unique man!"

Jama did not speak. *Ah, youth,* he thought, an edge of irritation still in his emotions, vexed that this youngster should have caught him looking so old when a modest preannouncement would have allowed him time for wig and makeup and decent silks. He stared at her, making her wait.

A man, eh? *As if one man could solve my problems.* By the happy-puzzled expression on her face, he was probably a man "found" to solve *her* problems. Did young women think of nothing else? This one wouldn't even discuss politics in bed when she had sex on her mind! So hard to teach them the cunning discipline necessary for major subversion. And she was vain, too. By hiding her fam, did she suppose that people would presume she could think without one? It was appalling the talent he was forced to work with. At least she had her mother's melons!

But yes, he did need unique men—so she had his attention. He wasn't going to show it.

A conspiracy required thousands of men, competent men, incorruptible, dedicated men, moving behind screens, shielded from each other by deception and code, invisible to the masses, because they had to remain invisible to the Pscholars' machines which monitored all trends. Never be part of a trend. Safety lay only in being a unique individual who fit no pattern. Space! The strain of training up a cadre of invisible mathematicians when he knew no mathematics himself.

Otaria was staring at him, not very respectfully, waiting for a reply. But she was used to his petulant silences, and when he did not answer, an uplifted hand-sign, a command to the house sensors, materialized one of the Hyperlord's floating recliners, whence she curled into its black arms while they molded to her shape. Then gracefully she tended to her nails.

Such vanity appalled Jama. Could the noble blood of revolutionaries like Otaria bring back the bad old days? Interregna, filled with violence, were more interesting than utopian stasis. The last Dark Age, for all its years of chaos, had been the most creative period in human history since the times when the wily *Homo sapiens* subhumans had first rafted across interstellar space. He stared back at her, seeing the burden of her inexperience, that she, herself, was not even aware of. He was too old. His dream to smash the Second Empire was hopeless in spite of his noble efforts and self-sacrifice. All he had to work with were naifs like Otaria.

He pretended to consider her statement by pacing.

What had he done wrong? Hyperlord Kikaju Jama suspected that he should not be building a conspiracy to destroy civilization here, in the heart of this awesome solar system of psychohistorical power, three trillion people swarming around the star Imperialis, almost a trillion of those on Splendid Wisdom itself. He should be building his pathetic little cabal out in some obscure corner of the galactic reaches—some miner's ice world in the Empty Sweep, perhaps. But his wealth was here at the teeming center so here must be the core of his dissent. Yes, under the eyes of the observers. The game had all the wrong odds—but still it was an interesting one, which was why it amused him to play.

Sometimes Jama didn't think it was hopeless. He was sure that he had found the weakness of the Second Empire. The Pscholars knew only statistical mechanics and chaos, megamath and conformal caletrics, miniform numerical modeling, etc., etc.—dullards all—they cared nothing for individuals. Their police did not even monitor individuals. Individuals were no more to them than the atoms of a vast gas engine being regulated for maximum efficiency, the engine of galactic civilization. The Galaxy would be unmanageable if the bureaucrats had to administer its thirty million worlds at the level of the individual. And so—the invisible individuals were Kikaju Jama's weapon. And the Eggs of Timdo.

He tried staring through his Frightfulperson, wondering if she was invisible enough. She was a cymbalistic dresser. Where did these youngsters get their styles!

Otaria returned the gaze of her old seducer with increasing impatience. Since this crazy coot Kikaju had not replied to her announcement and was staring rudely into the space behind her head, she decided, rudely, to repeat herself. "I said I found a man. The man I've found," she said with steely emphasis, "he's a psychohistorian."

The Hyperlord's brain went from irritation to sudden alarm. He tripped a warning analysis search in the fam buried in the humped shoulders of his lounging robe. The Pscholars' psychohistorians were *worse* than their teeming police.

His fam calmly supplied him with silent commentary: requests for information, questions, suggestions which might be used for a proper interrogation of the girl.

"We do not deal with psychohistorians," he said sternly.

"Come now, they may be a pompous, overbearing elite who have limited aspirations, but you must admit that they've run our galactic affairs with an iron-handed honesty."

"So they want us to *believe*." Jama smiled wickedly. "When they *lie* to us they have the tools to do so very cleverly and then the tools to make the lie disappear."

"Kikaju . . ."

"I see that you doubt me." He had never told her the story of Zurnl, nor had her mother. Never trust a youth under thirty. "You think of me as a crotchety old man who makes unfounded allegations to puff up the importance of my cause and who is deathly afraid of your mother whom *you* aren't afraid of at all. Let me share a detail—one of the items that has come to my attention over my inquisitive life. I'll download it into your fam from mine and you'll be able to judge for yourself."

Jama made a gesture while he muttered commands and Otaria went into receiver mode. He waited while her fam digested the burst. He censored certain details, but not the essence of the story.

Long ago, in the fourth century of the Founder's Era, fifty young psychohistorians were sacrificed to heal a major deviation in the Founder's Plan. The catastrophe began with Cloun-the-Stubborn of Lakgan, the first warlord of the Interregnum to get his hands on the tuned psychic probe. He was smart enough to be able to use it to bend minds to his will in a way that changed the psychological laws of human interaction enough to derail the normal course of history.

The covert psychohistorians who had been monitoring the Plan from the wreckage of Splendid Wisdom, in the fortress they had created out of the old Imperial University, were forced by these unhappy circumstances to act in the *open* to restabilize the Plan. But the Plan as they conceived it required that its monitors remain *invisible,* invisible even to the citizens of Faraway, the fulcrum of their efforts. In order to *redisappear* after the crisis—so that they might continue to control without having to be accountable for their actions—the Pscholars constructed an elaborate hoax of self-immolation. A lie. Pretending to be the whole of the monitoring group, fifty young psychohistorians went to the prison camps of Faraway and death as martyrs.

Otaria frowned haughtily. "I've never heard of such a reprehensible incident. It has the feel of historical revision to me. Such besmirching of the reputation of our galactic leadership for no other reason than to blacken their name will serve our cause badly; our benevolent elite embody enough flaws without our having to stoop to invent disgusting sins. Truth is our only reliable servant."

Jama rolled his eyes and the eyelight rolled around the room. "I, too, thought as you do now when I first caught whiff of the story twenty years ago. Yet . . . there are pieces to that story that assemble neatly. Do you remember a time when you were very young and your mother left Splendid Wisdom for an extended vacation? Your mother and I actually located the graves of those sacrificial heroes on a Periphery hellhole called Zurnl—well erased to all but the most exacting archaeological methods. I have a distant group working for me to decipher what I found in an old mine. Perhaps you remember my friend Hiranimus Scogil? He visits us from time to time. Evidence keeps arriving as it is decoded. Only twelve watches past . . ." No, he shouldn't tell her that.

"I remember Hiranimus Scogil very well. He was with you when my mother was away?"

Jama didn't choose to answer. "It has been the mainstay of my hope that our little group can re-create psychohistory. Check out the mathematical appendix trailing my little burst."

"I'm not a mathematical illiterate—I've been studying—but your equations are not readable by me, even with all the options of my fam."

"Nevertheless they contain many of the psychohistorical equations which outline how a perturbation in the Plan can be eliminated by a *lie* involving the death of fifty young students. Those equations have been lifted from the Great Plan as it existed in the fourth century Founder's Era."

"Nonsense! The Pscholars guard their sacred texts with unbreakable code! You of all people don't have access to it! Even *your* penis can't get in that deep!"

Jama was enjoying himself. "My penis has slithered around in lots of dark forbidden places—and been chopped off more than once by youths such as yourself. Which accounts for its present small size. That be as it may, you must admit that the poor excuse for psychohistorical talent that I have at my disposal could never write such equations or work out their consequences—nevertheless, I assure you, my idiots can *read* such scrawls quite effectively."

A sudden revelation struck her. "You're getting *all* of your material from Scogil!"

"And he gets his by mining the memoirs of the Martyrs, my discovery. I have no doubt that these fragments of the Great Plan are authentic. There is no lie so small that it does not leave a trace behind. It is a fact that the Pscholars have lied to us for millennia." He glanced for only a flicker of eyelight at the small jade ovoid sitting in its legged golden cup.

Otaria paused to let her organic-fam mind cease rejecting the data in order to readjust itself around the thought that an enemy who *lied* to create a deception was a very different kind of opponent than an open foe. After an almost instant gestalt-wide neural-fam review, she was ready with her comment. "I still think you should meet my psychohistorian."

"You have already contacted this man?" Disapproval.

"No." She was amused that Kikaju would suppose her so bold.

"Then *he* contacted you?" Greater disapproval.

"No!" Now Otaria felt called upon to defend herself and reacted to Jama's suspicion with formal disdain. "Hyperlord Jama, I *found* him—he doesn't even know I exist—I'm not *stupid*. Why should I take unilateral action? I know the stakes! Who trained me? Who seduced me into his wicked world when I was too young to know the difference? a baby I was! And before you say it, I *do* know that the psychohistorians are the most dangerous people in the Empire! Whether they tell the truth or whether they lie. Of course I know that!"

"Ah." He smiled, relaxing because of her fury. "What rank is this mathematician of yours?"

"Seventh."

"Phwogh! He knows nothing, then. He's still nourished by the blood from his umbilical cord. He's useless."

"He's unusual. Singular."

"Handsome? Beddable?"

"So now you suppose me to be infatuated by commoners, do you?" she replied to his innuendo, sarcastically indignant. She cocked her red hat and peeked around the brim, suggesting a comedy of immature lust. Languidly she hugged the arms of her recliner, ignoring Jama. His eyes called all illumination to her body while her eyes fixed themselves upon the shadows of his miniature garden, shy flora one might find at the bottom of a jungle's canopy.

*She's sulking! Now what do I do? Damn, I shouldn't have alluded to sex so soon after our last fight. She's going to tease me!* He tensed.

Indeed she was, and she began by changing the subject. "I love your topiary." With a delighted cry she kicked off from the floor, chair and all, to float over the ferns, and beyond them, into the arms of a gnarled bush whose uppermost limbs reached for the conduits that were now feeding the rosy dawn light of Imperialis down into this dungeon. "You work so hard here at your cultivation! You always have the slight smell of manure about you." She was grinning. "You do use *real* manure, don't you? Your garden is so green, so lush, so beautiful! That's one thing we never seem to run out of here on Splendid Wisdom—the manure, I mean. There are so many of our assholes!"

*Spare me the twaddling of the aristocracy,* he thought, wishing desperately for his wig and eyeshadow—and a bath and a sanitized robe . . . And a young body.

Well, if he couldn't flirt, he could attack. Attack was more fun than sex, anyway. A command, through the tuned probe that connected his brain with his fam, called up the house telesphere. Once it had bloomed, he willed the floating apparition toward her, enlarged its diameter, and filled its ghostly pallor with images drawn from his auxiliary brain.

The visions he loaded into the globe had been secretly recorded at a party of roistering midlevel bureaucrats. A swift flow of graphics commands—by fam direction—rebuilt the scene to center on Otaria, altering the record subtly to suit Jama's kinky taste: a brighter color here, an added satyr there, a knowing grin from an observer lounging in the folds. His miniature Otaria lay on the floor of the globe, in deshabille, the only noblewoman at this uncouth gathering, hugging some commoner's leg.

"You Wog, Kikaju! You haven't the morals of a leering Makorite! Why do I work for you! You spy on me!"

"So do the psychohistorians."

"They're not interested in me—nor in you. They're interested in summed vectors," she said defiantly.

"Their interest is called 'sampling,'" replied Jama dryly, "and you are not immune from it. They take *quadrillions* of samples every watch. When they detect a trend that threatens the stability of the Empire, do you think they don't take action on it?"

The Excellent Frightfulperson was watching, with distaste, her own behavior in the hovering sphere. "I'm allowed to have fun! Now turn it off!" She wasn't angry yet, but she was ready to be angry.

"Is that where you 'found' your psychohistorian?"

"Well now, I do believe the old He Goat has itching horns! You amaze me—jealous you are—after throwing me forcibly out of your bed!"

And he remembered—it seemed long ago—their amorous jousting. He didn't remember throwing her out of bed. How could he have loved such an irritating woman? "Pleasure and intrigue don't mix well. I question you to protect the Regulations," he insisted. The word "Regulations" was safe code for another word nobody had the courage to say aloud: revolution.

She sighed. "All right, Hyperlord Sober Buttocks my darling, we'll be serious. I found my young rebel psychohistorian via a routine library scan while engaged in dry-as-dust research for the good of your beloved *Regulations*. I've been studying stasis. Rates of change of behavior. My dabbling in history."

"Stasis," he said morosely. "The Sleeping Beauty stays alive by never changing." He meant the Empire. It was a constant complaint of his.

"Over what time period!" she shot back.

"Certainly over my lifetime—and I'm not young. By sleeping, the Empire refuses to die!"

"Old men have such a myopic viewpoint. Weak legs which take their eyes nowhere! But *youth* isn't so decrepit that it can't travel more freely! *I'm* talking four thousand generations! I've been imbibing records, some of them probably seventy to eighty thousand years old. You can't imagine the changes in every variable you can conceive of over that time span! *You* only think of *today's* trade and exchange—that's all you care to think of! You don't understand the past."

"Nothing from eighty thousand years ago is reliable. Nothing useful survives from that era. Splendid Wisdom was settled only thirty-three thousand years ago. Even ten-thousand-year-old information is unreliable!"

"I beg your pardon, old man! When I was a child I visited, with my mother, the museum at Chanaria, deep in the stable rock of the Timeless Shield. I saw a bronze plate under helium that was more than *seventy-four* thousand years old, cast on Rith with the names of heroes raised in this weird angular alphabet and illustrated in relief with armored vehicles and bi-winged skycraft. Before hyperspace travel! It wasn't a reproduction! I was awed! I saw records scratched onto clay tablets—*real* clay from Old Rith—by men hardly literate who even had to depend upon *their own brains* to advise them. We *know* these things! I saw the fossilized bones of animals who lived and died before man, two million generations old, priceless fossils from Rith, not reproductions. I was awed."

"Rith is a semidesert planet. Wasteland. The only monkeys left are the sapiens. It counts for nothing." His gesture swept over his own green garden implying that this small grotto-world of rock with bush and fern and blooming flowers was worth more than all of Rith. "In that old place even the camels die of thirst! On Rith even the children manufacture fraudulent antiques for the Empire's tourists, bronze tablets and baked clay, polluting my market."

"Oh, bother your skepticism!" She pursed her lips and threw up her arms so violently that her chair rocked in the air above the ferns. "Authenticity is not the point! Think of the changes since our intrepid subhuman ancestors left Rith! Do you deny the changes? Doesn't that give you hope that change is possible? *You* taught me hope!" She was indignant. *Now* she was angry!

He laughed because indeed he did work for upheaval yet in his heart did not believe that the galactic disorder he craved was possible. "Your bloody ancestors—pirates, brigands"—he sneered—"conquered Splendid Wisdom in a local interstellar war that brought our noble trading founders to ruin—but within three generations had themselves become such proficient traders, being raised by trader slaves, that they no longer thought of themselves as pirates but as traders. Change? They rewrote history by substituting their names for the names of their Kambal predecessors. And went on to conquer millions of stars—not as military predators but in the style of the wiliest of the traders they conquered—just as the traders would have done without your bloody ancestors on the starship bridges. Change? When *your* ancestors were deposed the Empire continued its mighty growth under new administration. The vices were the same, the strengths were the same, the bureaucracy was the same. Ask *my* ancestors. Only the people were different. Social inertia has always been formidable—even *before* the psychohistorians."

Otaria dismissed this version of ancient history. "That's your way of seeing events, my melancholy romantic! Your late ancestors were forged in a more recent, vaster era when no mere soldier or trader could have survived. There were more specialists in one army group of the Stars&Ship than all the soldiers in the greatest army ever raised before the Pax Imperialis. Nothing changes in a lifetime, but every thousand years of human history has brought a major upheaval. Two thousand years ago there were no fams as we know them and men were forced to live by their bare wet wits. You're so strange, Kikaju—you taught me to believe in a dream you don't believe in yourself."

"But you've found me a psychohistorian who will light my fire again, so it is all right," he added sarcastically.

She grinned. "I've been plotting the galactic patterns of scholarship. It is always the same curve. Flat, then a sharp increase, then flat again when knowledge matures. During the explosion, scholars always think that the explosion will go on forever. They do not value what is known. Their pleasure is to seek new discoveries. During the mature phase, scholars always think that everything is known and see scholarship as the art of applying the known. Psychohistory has been a mature science for less than a thousand years. They've had no rival in the Galaxy for two millennia—and it is *time,* Kikaju, it is *time* that a rival appears."

"So what is so unique about your young man?"

"During the last session of the Fellowship he published a thesis in mathematics at his own expense. I don't think that has ever been done before." She flashed a copy in midair, a holograph, squeezing its long title, for lack of space, into a condensed Imperial Font. *Early Disturbed Event Location by Forced Arekean Canonical Pre-posturing: An Analysis in Three Parts.* "I copied it the same watch it appeared because I was researching stasis and it is about stasis. When I went back to look for more, it had been erased."

"He published through the Lyceum?" asked Hyperlord Jama incredulously. Pscholar psychohistorians did not publish research; they had *never* published their research, even in that long-ago epoch when they still did research. They had always claimed, with self-serving pedanticism, that a prediction of the future was invalidated if the predictive methods by which it was obtained were to become widely known.

"No, he did *not* publish through the Lyceum. He was pretending it was mathematics, not psychohistory. He published in the *public realm* in the Imperial Archives."

"With no sponsor! Then this young man of yours is a crackpot! What else could he be? He's decapitating himself!"

"Perhaps," she went on earnestly. "But that is, again, not the point."

"Your point is moot," he interrupted. "My point is that your man, being a psychohistorian, being a member of the Fellowship, is a dangerous man who should be avoided at all costs."

She continued doggedly. "You're building up your own hand-picked group of independent psychologists. Your men don't have access to the main body of knowledge."

"Of course they don't!" He raged because it was a sore spot. How could his people know what was so fanatically hidden away by the Psychohistorian Fellowship? The Fellowship feared nothing more than that the lower classes might learn how to predict the future and so destroy the Splendid Galactic Empire of the Pscholars, rendering the Great Plan impotent by creating an unmanageable chaos of alternate futures. And even worse—the Pscholars might go the way of the Hyperlords.

Otaria continued to make her points on her long fingers, one by one. "Your men are having to re-invent psychohistory all by themselves. You've told me it's not going well. You've told me it has been going *badly*! Your group isn't research oriented. But, Kikaju, *obviously,* that doesn't apply to this upstart! He knows how to do research and he's certain to be in trouble with his masters for daring to publish! He's our kind of man. Something in him is rebelling against his restrictions! We can use him!"

Jama might once have thought so—but by now he had received a handful of Coron's Eggs updated to the seventh level and a promise of many more. *Now* it was even more important to maintain security. "You're talking about enlisting a *real* psychohistorian!" exclaimed Jama in horror. "I don't want to have anything to do with a *real* one! They're programmed to destroy"—he was so upset that he actually uttered the taboo word—"revolutions!" The horror in his voice mounted. "It's built into their fams to protect us all! They are Death on Dark Ages. They aren't, ever, allowed to harm people—anybody—even if that means their own self-destruction, so they've found the equations that give us the living, painless death. And they must at all costs use their powers to protect civilization from collapsing! And so civilization has been frozen at the height of decay! Cryogenocide! They aren't even allowed to be passive when we try to put ourselves in a dangerous place! You want to deal with such monsters? You're mad!"

"Kikaju, I am proceeding in this case with utmost caution. And I do not want *you* protecting me from any dangers. Eron Osa is himself a rebel."

"Eron Osa!" The Hyperlord went into shock. "Him! I forbid you to have anything to do with this man! I forbid it! I won't *allow* you to destroy my world!" he raged. "I'll have your mother whip you!"

"You are throwing me out of your bed again." She smiled.

"I've never thrown you out of my bed. I try to coddle you with the pleasures of reason!"

"Let me follow this man," she pleaded. "I will not recruit him without your approval, I swear by the ferocity of my ancestors."

"I met him on Faraway when he was a young student. Space alone knows what mischief he's been into since then! I heard that he joined the study faction of Jars Hanis after falling out with some Second Rank mentor of his. And his morals are—"

He almost made the mistake of telling Otaria that as a youth Eron had made a pass at her mother—but that would only intrigue her prurient interest. He certainly wasn't going to tell her that Eron Osa was also a friend of Hiranimus Scogil and that Hiranimus Scogil was missing.

# ERON OSA AND ROSSUM'S #26
# EXPLORE THE PAST, 14,798 GE

*... the vertically tapering shape of the Niche [in the Queen's Chamber of the Great Pyramid] suggests itself as the housing for a pendulum clock capable of timing Target Star transits . . . The Niche is high enough to accommodate a pendulum some four meters in length (height) with about two thirds of a meter to spare for clearance . . .*

—Keith P. Johnson in "The Niche," fragments circa twentieth or twenty-first century AD

As a byproduct of its taxiing profession and its garrulous nature, Rossum's #26 had a prolific number of useful contacts. That, combined with obsessive reading while waiting on the tarmac for clients, made Konn's aerocar a fine research assistant. Eron Osa was back inside the Malls of the Great Pyramid following the new lead. His fam steered him to the Artiste's Skull Emporium at the end of a rundown corridor of shops. The swinging half-door triggering a little chime when he ducked through an entrance designed for simian hunchbacks.

"Not now," came a squeaky voice from an adjoining workshop. It was piled high with crates of unfinished skulls and makeshift benches assembled out of "eternal" coffins. Probably their contents had long ago been sold off to the tourist trade. "You wait. I'm in the middle. Gotta finish. Browse a while." Eron could hardly understand the accent. The proprietor evidently had no more to say for the whine of a grinding polisher followed his statement.

The finished skulls were indeed works of art. They lined a whole set of glass shelves bolted into genuine Great Pyramid limestone. Rossum's #26 had told him about the negotiations, via net, with the gentleman who ran this hole-in-the-wall. He had access to a cheap supply of really *old* skulls being mined from a mass grave dating to the Great Die-off centuries. Eron examined some of the skulls carefully:

original purebred nongengineered sapiens for sure. But the exquisite surface engravings did not hide the fact that these poor souls had not lived at a time in Rith's history when health was a primary concern. Evidently the proprietor was in the habit of renewing their mouths if their teeth had rotted. A strange profession that: dentist for the dead.

Eron was not intending to buy a souvenir of his Rithian pilgrimage, but one of the artifacts—expensive—was so appealing he couldn't resist it. Not a square centimeter of the skull had been spared the artistic hand; glyphs and precious inlay were woven in among the carved runes of wisdom that the man might have thought but probably hadn't. On this one the original teeth were in superb shape, the pearly enameled gold having outlasted their user by at least seventy millennia. He had been a rich, well-fed man living a separate life from the poor around him. But his wealth had not spared him from the common mass grave. Now he would spend the rest of his life as an ornament staring out on an incomprehensible future from empty sockets.

The shop owner's main love was books, but he couldn't make a living at it so he decorated skulls for the tourists. He emerged from his crowded studio. "The inspiration. Gotta go with it," he apologized unapologetically. "Yes?"

"A friend tells me you have a book on metrics that I need."

"You the one? You got the book on roses he promised me? No book on roses, no deal. That *was* the deal."

Eron produced the template that had found its way into the hodge-podge library that the Admiral had hastily downloaded from the Splendid Wisdom collection of materials from the bibliotheca of ancient Rithian starships. It was a genuine Rithian book of the twelfth millennium AD with a chapter on every rose that had ever been bred, including a picture, a commentary on the rose's origin, and a listing of its genetic code.

"I gotta make a copy first. Check it out. Good business. You star types are all thieves and robbers." The store's ancient manufacturum chugged away, even jiggled a bit as it labored to grind out a copy. "Devil machine!" He kicked it. "You work right! None of those blurred pages!" He grabbed the book, still warm from its birthing, and tapped on the screen with a silent intensity for about ten jiffs. "Holy Messiah!"

"Which one?" asked Eron.

"It's for the godless atheist to shuddup!" he replied without looking up while he continued to scroll and flip and search, muttering every time he hit something astonishing about roses. "The Messiah's mother!" Then he found the lost rose of his dreams. "By the Messiah's bloody hand!"

*Ah,* thought Eron, already recognizing bits of Rithian history, *the Messiah whose hands had been chopped off for robbing the rich and giving to the poor, 7,324 AD.*

"It's all here," exclaimed the proprietor in awe. "The whole caboodle! My father storied me about this book! My grandfather letched me about this book! My great-grandfather raved: not a copy left on Rith! Have I got customers! Roses! Roses! Roses!"

Gratefully he decanted his own incunabulum from his library, a piddling back-catalog item which none of his ancestors had ever been able to sell, and set the manufacturum to chugging out a copy of the book that Rossum's #26 had lucked onto. It was a thirteenth- or fourteenth-millennium AD compendium of all the ancient metric documents that had survived through the Great Die-off when all but a tiny fraction of Rith's pre-third-millennium literature had vanished in the chaos of a culture terminally ill of population cancer.

Eron eagerly activated the book the instant his hands touched the cover—but all he could call up on the screen was an incomprehensible language in an unknown script of an unknown barbarian era. His heart sank.

"What? They don't teach you how to read at scholia nomore?" The proprietor reached over and fingered the book's border unsuccessfully. "Devil-damned Cathusians! Never did know how to make things simple! They could've tried writing on clay!" He cursed by all the messiahs he didn't believe in, finally getting the right combination. Carefully he showed Eron how to toggle between the language translators. "But don't expect support for old galactic." When the Cathusian Excalifate was building its power base on the repatriation of Rith's lost literature via the new hyperdrive technology, the language of the Cumingan Regionate was shunned as the language of oppression. "You want to read archaic books like this mishmash, you gotta ken the ancient languages. I got all the downloads. Cheap. How about Chinese?"

"I already read Chinese. I had a weird professor who loved Chinese poetry. I once wrote a program to write Chinese poetry to help me with my homework."

The proprietor grumbled. "The fourth incarnation of Christ had sayings to cover guys like you, none of them good. How about Sumerian?"

"I was hoping to avoid that one."

"Have I got a program for you! Cheap. Already copied. Gotta get rid of it. It's cluttering up the place." He scuttled off to his shop and rummaged around inside a coffin and came out holding up his prize in the air. "How's that for service!"

Eron groaned. He had already doubled the number of languages he could speak since reaching Rith, none of them in modern use. "I'm pretty saturated. I don't want to have to carry my fam around in a suitcase."

"You don't know what you're missing. You gotta have it. Cheap." To prove his point, he brought up the index of Eron's compendium, toggled through some strange languages, and came up with a set of pages that looked like the wet clay dance floor of a ballet company of miniature birds.

"For that, translation don't cut it. I'll show you. Pick a language, nothing modern."

"Try Englic or Latin."

The proprietor called up the Englic translator. Eron noticed how painfully slow it was, a couple of jiffs per page. He sighed. Pre-quantronic tech. But trying to read the tortured Englic was even worse. Every sentence suggested sixtyne different meanings.

"See? Doesn't make sense. Not the translator's fault. Sumerian you gotta read in the original."

"All right." Eron sighed. "You've got a sale. This isn't all a fake, is it?"

The proprietor shrugged his stooped shoulders. "How could I know? Just because I'm probably buying and selling the skulls of Cathusian Excalifs don't mean I know what their ugly minds were up to when they compiled your book. Myself, I is *never* trust them. They ate pigs and birds! But you're an atheist from the stars, so what do you care?"

Eron bought the compendium. And the skull. And the Sumerian language famfeed. Not cheaply. While he emptied his money stick his upgraded simian ancestor grinned. Then Eron ducked out into the corridor to the good-bye of chimes. He would have gone back to the comfort of #26's posh interior but that loquacious machine would have talked him to death, so he opted for a rolled sandwich of hummus, lettuce, and pig slices at an interior plaza which had been excavated after the earthquake and redecorated as an Egyptian tomb. The plasteel pillar replacements for the ancient stones were tastefully camouflaged.

He had found his book! He had no intention of showing his crazy model of Rith's misty past to the Ruthless Admiral without at least a major attempt to compare it with ancient documents. A quiet table in a nook dedicated—in colorful hieroglyphics—to victory over the Nubians made a reasonable work surface. As a student physicist his taskmasters back at Faraway had trained him emphatically: *always* reality-test your ideas.

Psychohistorians seemed to stress careful theoretics because reality-testing was a luxury they couldn't afford. By the time the future had arrived and a reality-check was possible, it was too late. Physicists were much more sloppy in their approach. Wild hunches and numerology were permitted if these were immediately submitted to Mother Nature's Kindly Court for trial by combat, torture test, thumbscrew, sarcasm, and riddling. She was prosecuting attorney, defense counsel, judge, jury, and lawmaker all in one and blind to boot. Still, doing the psychohistory of the past, which allowed reality-testing in her court, was more amenable to a physicist's casual approach than a psychohistorian's stern Get-It-Right-the-First-Time mode. Eron was a mature physicist, but he was history's raw recruit.

Mother Nature's Court never made it easy. In this case she had been meticulous about destroying all the evidence. Entropy was her favorite game, as Eron well knew, being on the team trying to reconstruct the history of Konn's latest obsession. Aside from the inscriptions on moon machines and perhaps the golden apocrypha from the fairy ruins of Mars, the vanished Americs had never put their trust in durable copy, first marrying themselves to biodegradable paper which turned to dust after a century, then fickly falling in love with holes in biodegradable plastic that died after sixty years, and finally eloping with magnetic surfaces whose contents evaporated into a magnetospheric heaven within a dog's life span. If only they'd had sense enough to preserve their culture by engraving it into their skulls when they died, or even carving it onto their ubiquitous excrement bowls . . .

First Eron famfed his course in Sumerian. People still remembered the Sumerians! Burning down their libraries only *preserved* their books. He set up a subroutine in his fam to fast-study the language lessons while he did something else. No use wasting the hour it would take before he could begin to read Sumerian in the original. To keep busy he skimmed his find, randomly, to see if he really did have a treasure.

One item caught his attention, evoking a cry of triumph that attracted the notice of nearby patrons. His Englic wasn't good but he could read this fragment of a law on measures. It had been enacted here on Rith by a clearly important group of functionaries with clout because they met within walking distance of their emperor's White Palace. The law dated to the pre-space year 59,424 BGE—only seven or eight years prior to the design work on Konn's Flying Battleship. He couldn't believe his eyes. The Intercourse of Commingled Bodies had *legislated* the foot of their Continent-State to be *exactly* 30.48 centimeters and their inch to be *exactly* 2.54 centimeters, rounding off whatever the real value had been! So! Even while the Rithians were still planet bound the meter was nibbling away on its rivals! By the Founder's Nose, that meter was exactly the aggressive animal that psychohistory's equations were predicting!

Next he scanned for pendulums. The entries mostly concerned the pendulum-driven mechanical clocks that came after 59,700 BGE, about the time of the mythical Newton—too recent. He perked up when he spotted a fragment by a Lehmann-Haupt because it indicated that this scholar had once been particularly adept at translating difficult Sumerian mathematical tablets. The book's brain was having its own problems translating from Lehmann-Haupt's Girman into Englic, but Eron caught the gist—Lehmann-Haupt had deduced that the Sumerian system of measures derived from the pendulum that beats the second at latitude 30 degrees, though his mathematical model of a pendulum had been so poor that he had been unable to confirm his hypothesis.

With nothing to do while his mind was learning Sumerian, Eron set about constructing his own quick-and-dirty pendulum model. He set up his red pocket metricator on the table next to his sandwich plate and read out the local gravitic acceleration, converting from meters per jiff-squared to meters per local sidereal second-squared. The details followed quickly, with the help of his precious compendium.

Since the standard foot of the one sidereal-second pendulum approximately divided a degree of latitude into 450,000 parts, the Egyptian astronomers took the latitude where that was exactly true as their reference, giving them a rule of thumb that Rith's circumference was 162 million standard feet. Everything else followed.

To divide Rith's circumference into 90 million parts to make navigation easy, one multiplied the standard foot by 9/5ths and got the Roman cubit. To divide it into 75 million parts one multiplied the standard foot by 2.16 to get the Great Cubit. To divide it into 81 million parts one doubled the standard foot and got the Sassanian-Arabic cubit. Then to get the famous geographical foot that divided the degree into 360,000 parts, one multiplied the standard foot by 5/4. Et cetera.

He was chagrined to find that he had computed the foot of their Flying Fortress wrong. It was just the geographic foot shortened by the factor 75/76 and computed by a pendulum at the London Mound through the Egyptians sacred latitude of 360/7 degrees. It came out to .3047997 meters and very fortunately for Eron the lazy Americ's had metricized it to .3048 meters.

After hours of working with the details and satisfying himself, Eron switched off his book and folded it up with reverence. He had to see what he had come to see. He wandered around the maze of the Mall looking for the administrative center. When he found a distracted official and asked for special admittance to the Room of the Queen, he was refused curtly.

He fumed out in the corridor for a while—but there were advantages to being the lackey of one of the most powerful psychohistorians in the Galaxy. There *was* such a thing as privacy—so long as it didn't get in the way of a psychohistorian's need to polish a coefficient used by one of his equations. Eron made a coded call to Rossum's #26 who, as Konn's librarian and expert on all things Rithian, had authorization to access any public contract.

"Find out who's in charge here," Eron requested.

The official turned out to be a nonsapiens, of distant Eta Cumingan ancestry. Not much could be learned by #26 in the few inamins he'd had to work on the project, but the current chief functionary had been shunted off into a job with no future after serving a minor jail term for accepting bribes while in a sensitive administrative post. That was interesting. Eron had never had enough wealth to indulge in bribery before, but now he was on an expense account. It was worth a try.

He didn't make an appointment. He just appeared in the man's office and made it known that he was on business for Hahukum Konn. The factotum's name was Sinar, a word vaguely related to the ancient Eta Cumingan word for governor, but this man was a mongrel, perhaps a quarter sapiens by the cast of his face, yet Cumingan by the almost clawlike shape of his hands. What showed was his worry. How was it that he had come to the attention of the madman from Splendid Wisdom who was here as uninvited guest? The rumor factories were active about the psychohistorian's life and intentions. Romantics had bestowed Konn with mystery, malcontents with evil intentions, gossips swore he was having a love affair with his maid, and the factotum was now busy trying to figure out which of the stories were true.

Eron made his interest in the Room of the Queen discreetly known. It was under renovations, he was discreetly informed. Eron changed the subject to Rith's past glories until the man was at ease, then began bargaining. Sinar immediately understood but, like every man once stung, was careful to betray no emotion. Eron suggested—a lie—that Second Rank Konn wished to bestow a modest amount toward the refurbishing of Rith's staggeringly important legacy. Sinar scoffed at the proposal—the red tape involved would not be worth the effort, he claimed. "Give the money to the beggar children!" Meaning the offer was too dangerous for him personally. Eron counteroffered by suggesting ways around the authorities. No one would need to know. "It should be up to you to spend the money; you who are here and know best the needs of this great monument to Rithian genius."

Eron suspected that he had won when the man began to consider ways to sneak them into the Room of the Queen. They struck a bargain, both men piously pretending that no bribery was involved. Eron duly noted how the power that emanated from Konn was beginning to corrupt him even before he had been graded on his first psychohistorical lesson!

Thus by passion and bribery Eron Osa found himself stooping through a dwarf's passageway and into a dark and gloomy stone vault that was as old as man's civilization. It had been untouched even by the earthquake that had collapsed the King's Room above them. Not so by man. The walls of the room were of once-unblemished limestone, engraved now with the regimental insignia of Eta Cumingan soldiers of the Regionate and a life-size bas-relief gnome with his enormous tongue hanging out, of unknown origin, all carefully treated with surface preservatives. This millennial spanning farrago of graffiti was in horrible taste, but so was the hole in the Queen's Niche where al-Mamun's men had used fire and water to probe for treasure. These Rithians thought nothing of stripping the limestone off their Great Pyramid to build some mosques and millennia later regirding it with a massive superstructure of plasteel and tempered glass—yet they would feel blasphemed if the littlest of the irreverent carvings in the Room of the Queen was erased—barracks talk and gross vandalism had become sanctified by time.

The room was almost square, ten by eleven cubits with ample room for an office staff of timekeepers and astronomers. It was as high as three men standing on each other's shoulders. Awesome. The roof wasn't arched to prevent crushing but was made from two gabled limestone blocks of enormous mass which had their center of gravity in the right place. By what trick of the Devils had they ever gotten them in place? It was more impressive to Eron than the building of the first starships, which was, after all, only routine engineering that any schooled sapiens could have managed.

The recent restoration had given the vault some nice touches. A simple but effective system of primitive mirrors had been installed so that star transits could be performed through the optically straight southern "ventilator" by an astronomer timing his transits with the low-tech pendulum that had been modestly installed in the Queen's Niche. Rossum's #26 was an incredible resource. How had he ever found *this* wonder!

The Niche, Eron estimated, could hold at maximum a pendulum of 20 of the standard sidereal-second lengths, which would be exactly ten Sassanian-Arabic cubits according to his handy little book. Eighteen standard lengths would be 10 Roman cubits; 17 would be 8 Royal cubits; 16 with a period of 4 seconds would be 8 Sassanian-Arabic cubits again; 15 would be 8 of the famous nautical cubits that divided Rith into 86,400 parts at the reference latitude; 12 would be ten Roman feet; 10 would give 8 nautical feet; 9 would give 8 of the Oscan feet used by the Mycenaean navigators in the Trojan Wars. Et cetera.

The Niche was about two cubits deep and had four corbeled courses that flared toward the bottom to accommodate the pendulum's swing. Eron examined the Rithian reproduction. It was a finely crafted piece of workmanship, not based on any original, but showing in loving detail how a superb scientific instrument might have been built by a nontechnical society. It was so well made it didn't even use wheels!

Eron stood back. He hadn't known how afraid he was of the Admiral until now. He hadn't dared show him his little psychohistorical model of Rith's past for fear it was all a fantastic misapplication of the Founder's tools. It wasn't, and the confirmation of that in this most ancient of places gave him a surge of confidence. He had something with which he could argue down any of Konn's objections. He was beginning to like history because it gave him such insight into the future.

# DEATH HAS MANY DISGUISES,
## 14,810 GE

*Beware if you try to stay neutral in a dispute when both sides need you as an ally—for you can be sure that two nets have been cast out and two stake pits dug to ensure your cooperation.*

—Emperor Ojaisun-the-Adroit, 3231–3245 GE

When the Personal Capsule began to erase itself, Rigone the Scav activated his own office disintegrator with a code-gesture; its petals opened, and to make doubly sure there would be no trace of communication he dumped the smoldering ashes into the opal turbulence. Spacedamn! His past was catching up with him. He glanced at his den of quantronic tools. Emergency! He stuffed surgical clothing in his bag. After passing through his forcecurtain, he reset the curtain to block a running man, then opened the vault door. Its teeth were still closing behind him with a hiss while he bounded down the stairs into the Bistro.

"I'll be back," he said to his bartender.

The tables of the Teaser's Bistro were half full. These students were too young to have known Eron Osa, but they had been talking about his execution—the execution of the fam *Rigone* had meddled with. *Space help me if that item ever enters police files!* Perhaps it already had. He cursed the hour he met Hahukum Konn. He cursed the hunch that had guided him to the Helmar Rift. *I was forced to do it!* Not really. From the Thousand Suns Beyond the Helmar Rift he had brought back equipment he knew he could not have resisted. Because of it he had been at the top of his quasi-legal racket for twenty years, rich even. Where on Splendid Wisdom was his competition? But such dark possessions encouraged a man into borderline operations that give him a police record. Would even Second Rank Konn be able to protect him now? The man from the Thousand Suns had come back to haunt him.

Down the entrance stairs he raced, almost sliding down the carved snakes, up the alley to the Olibanum's Deep Shaft. And then he stopped. He *had* to take a pod; at that distance there was no other way. But he had never been sure that the police didn't keep a record of every pod journey. It wasn't likely, but he decided to use a false identity anyway. Petty crime didn't matter beside treason against these Emperors in Pscholars' Clothing.

The pod took him to a mixed neighborhood of clerks and retirees, with a significant population of transients. He hesitated outside the robohotel. By the bells of every holy place in the Galaxy, why wasn't he turning this man over to the police? Informers did well. The answer was simple; to cover up one's minor crimes one committed major crimes! He had modified Osa's fam and didn't want the police to know! Why wasn't he just ignoring the whole matter? The police wouldn't, that's why! He was scared. Inside the hotel the robostaff ignored him just as Murek Kapor had promised, if Murek was that shadow man's real name. This was a prepared safe house, so he claimed, and knowing the tech of the Thousand Suns, Rigone had no doubt of the truth of those words. As ordered, he put on his surgical gloves and mask.

The door didn't open—wasn't expecting him. No obvious comm. The robowalls were there to do that, and they had been programmed not to see him. He knocked. No answer. Frustrated, he tried the door. It opened, unlocked. Inside there was a corpse on the bed on top of the covers. He looked into the dead eyes. But the chest still breathed. There was blood in the hair. "You all right?" Silly question.

The corpse's lips moved. "Rigone? Can't see. Can hear. The body . . . coma . . . you're talking to a fam . . . hard to control body . . . brought it here unconscious . . . take fam . . . get out."

"That will kill you. Your fam is all that's keeping you alive!"

"Body already brain-dead . . . checked."

"What happened?"

The corpse was almost angry at the delay. "Didn't predict this . . . take fam . . . get out!" The body shuddered, a gasp in its breathing. ". . . accident . . . running from police . . . jumped out of pod . . . police at other end . . . only chance . . . got whacked . . . bad mistake . . . take fam . . . Eron will come . . . you liked him . . . hurry . . . body on last legs . . . take fam . . . destroy body . . . hurry . . ."

The room came equipped with a Personal Capsule terminal. How had a man in a coma managed to use it? Zenoli training? There was no easy way to destroy the body. He wasn't going to do *that*. That was too much like a murder rap. And taking the fam was too much like stealing evidence from the scene of a crime, but he did it, turning Murek slightly off his shoulders. He didn't have the heart to kill the body nor the means to dispose of it. He left it breathing, comatose.

When he arrived back at the Teaser's, his bag and mask and gloves had already been disintegrated at a convenient dispozoria, and he was his usual jovial self on the outside, but he retreated to his upstairs apartment, barricading himself. He was glad to be living alone, between women with nothing to explain. Women were always too curious. Then he spent time cleaning the blood off the fam, so thoroughly that even a police scan would find nothing. He had half of a man's soul for his shelf, a poor ghoul trapped in a place without sight or sound or smell, nor voice, nor arms, nor legs. He set it behind his virgin fams and various fam parts.

The worst wasn't over. A mindless Eron Osa was going to turn up to claim the ghoul. Maybe. And how would it be of any use to him? No man could use another man's fam—each uncrackably coded by its own unique experience with life. You don't put on a fam—you grow up with it. Might as well try to read the memories out of a man's wetware. Kapor was dead. He wondered what had been in the boy's fam that had made it so dangerous to others as well as himself. What was in the modification he had installed in that aseptic room on Neuhadra? He would never know.

He smiled. Rector Hanis, out of rage or fear, had destroyed the evidence. Thank Space for the small cushions provided by a major disaster.

The Scav had regrets. He had liked the boy, liked his drive. When he had goaded Hahukum Konn into taking on the boy as an apprentice—feeling good that he had influence with a Second Rank—he hadn't been doing the kid's career a favor. He remembered the mature Eron. After putting down roots at the Lyceum and finding his way around, Eron had been a lively fixture at the Teaser's. Hadn't seen much of him since the boy had gone to work for Hanis, hadn't thought of him. Now fear was doing funny things to his head. Rigone thought about selling the Bistro and retiring—if he lived that long. What in the name of Splendid Wisdom was going on?

# DINNER WITH HAHUKUM KONN,
# 14,798 GE

*Classical Logic, the consistent kind, has a fatal flaw. No matter how you arrange the consistency of your axioms, you come up with a logic that is only a subset of the class of all logical systems. Yet the very act of embracing consistency has sealed off the gateways to any of those larger systems; you have trapped yourself inside a walled fortress with no exit. There are always, always fascinating truths that lie outside those walls. A consistent logician makes a good bureaucrat but a terrible explorer. Heretical inconsistency is the only way through the walls. But being inconsistent contracts you to a devil for a guide. He may lead you to exterior treasures, but it is more probable that he will lead you to falsehood, madness, and death. That is life. From inside a Fortress of Consistency you must seek a way out. But once outside a Fortress of Consistency you must seek your way back in.*

—Second Rank Psychohistorian Hahukum Konn after drinking wine

On his return through the Pyramid's maze, Eron's interest in ancient measuring instruments inspired him to dally at a shop which carried primitive artifacts in its come-on display. There was the usual landfill bric-a-brac: ceramic insulators, fishbowl castles, handled cups, even a manual ceramic dispozoria—but what caught Eron's attention were the calculators. The rotund salesman was magnanimously happy to see him, to the point of bowing his head lower than he had to, the tassels in his braids flapping expectantly. He had all kinds of strange numeric devices piled in dusty corners: brass dials in mahogany for multiplying; pocket (nonworking) supercomputers in hardened silicon; a replica of an automatic weaving device; miniature Babbage engines which, according to their engraved inscriptions, had once been given out as souvenirs at the ten thousandth anniversary of the invention of computing; a rack of abaci; an encrusted (fake) cash register, all at atrocious prices.

Eron was tempted by the Greek diagrammismos, an early base-2 device that helped simian man divide and multiply by 2, 4, 8, 16, 32, et cetera, an important calculation in a fledgling merchant culture that cannot easily do roots. He played with a Mesopotamian abacus that could convert between decimal and sexadecimal computation, but what Eron came away with was a slide rule and its template because Rossum's #26 had meticulously placed the construction date of their fossil aerobattleship as prior in time to even the crudest kind of electronic calculation. That slide rule was going to be useful.

During the day Eron was always working with Konn's engineers. Their task was full of puzzles. They had been able to construct a virtual model of the Fortress that would fly in a virtual universe—but only if they equipped it with devices not yet known in the mechanical crankshaft age. Konn had made Eron's job clear—authenticity or be nailed to a religious icon upside down. But whenever Eron goaded the engineers to test a model that was programmed only with technology *known* to be known to the ancients, it always crashed into its virtual landscape of checkered farmland with red barns and windmills and quaint villages or into the virtual skyscrapers. One of Konn's engineers had a wry theory that advanced beings from outer space had been aiding Washington State in its war with Goering. Sapiens were too primitive to . . .

Back at the hangar, Eron put the slide rule into good slipping condition and used his nanocalib to check the markings. It was a precision instrument. It would give at least three-decimal-place accuracy to a careful hand. He spent the evening using it to do physics problems, then made up a sixtyne of them at the office manufacturum and gave them out to the incredulous engineers in the morning. He was the junior member of the team but a Faraway education in physics still carried clout, and when he insisted they they redo all of their calculations on the slide rule they argued politely rather than dismissing him.

As their final ploy, the three senior engineers returned to their mnemonifier to bring out a set of critical specs that couldn't be computed on a slide rule. Eron just smiled. "Ah, that must be your problem." He suggested that the Seattle City-State authorities *couldn't* have designed their war machines around specs that required more accuracy than a slide rule provided. "They didn't have a technically sophisticated society. Their soldiers did have powered wheels and a few other useful inventions but, aside from a handful of elite aerial phaetons and some coal-stoked treaded vehicles for support, had to fight on the ground bare-chested without even a computerized bayonet. They didn't have *any* computers. They had Look-Up Tables."

"War was impossible before computers! Rithians were pastoral animals!"

"Gardak, you're an engineer, not a historian. The *original* infantrymen didn't even have wheels when they conducted war—coal stoked or otherwise. War predates the chariot. They walked. Their swords weren't powered!"

"You must be wrong. During the Goering War the Amerindians used the Fortress to deliver atomic explosives. They had a computer at their atomic labs. The Feynman Scriptos as much as says so."

Eron smiled. "I looked into that. Old Englic is not a well-understood language. They wrote prolifically but on media that wasn't rated to last. The passages you are referring to just might be construed to suggest a crude computer—but was more probably a network of slaved women tied to mechanical gear multipliers passing notes to each other at the orders of a supervising paternalist manning the rostrum and an assistant who chanted out timing signals. It is well known that the Americs were slave owners. We even have a picture of one of their master-priests in a kind of visor cap. Blast weapons are very low tech."

"It is just not possible for them to have built that Fortress without a computer functioning error-free to at least ten places!"

"You think so? Gardak, that's true only if your intention is to re-create that fossil aerocar in an improved version."

"I'm a professional. I improve every immature idea."

"That's an approach," Eron agreed. "I've seen your airflow design for the wing surface to minimize drag. Clever little powered grooves. You've embedded more computational oomph in one wing panel than their Eytortionists used to collect taxes to support the war. You're aiming for a replica that flies by itself while the crew drinks tea. You're trying to make the skin immune to the impact of inertial weaponry. You're trying to build in the ability to fight from a distance, out of danger, and—just in case the automatic pilot can't stay out of danger—you've added target-seeking spitters." He scowled. "They used hand-operated manual spitters."

"But Konn won't authorize sentient beam weapons! And you can't hand-man a spitter that's tossing lead into a thirty-five meters per jiff wind at a moving target!"

Eron shrugged. "And how about that little unobtrusive package of just-in-case atomics?"

"It's just there for an emergency or when Konn gets tired of pussying along and wants to go supersonic. He doesn't have to use it."

"He doesn't want it!"

"But that lumbering battlewagon runs on hydrocarbons. The engines could die. It's heavy. It would drop like a stone."

"So? The original ones crashed! They were blown out of the sky. The Seattlites lost hundreds of heroes every time they sent those contraptions of aluminum and rivets out on a bombing mission!"

"But it's not a hero who is going to fly it. That idiot Konn is going to be flying it. It *has* to be safe," whimpered the engineer.

Another of the more sanguine engineers piped up to counter the wail of his colleague. "That old windbag Hahukum is expendable. Forget him. It is you and I who have to test fly the damn thing before the Admiral gets in it."

Eron wouldn't relent. The slide rule was in. That was an order. In protest the engineers sent a delegation to Konn.

Presently Hahukum Konn came back out of his giant mushroom with the delegation following meekly. He wore a dress uniform of blue and braid and the Latin symbols USAAF, which meant something like SPQR, which Eron recognized from reading Virgil. Then Konn mounted an impromptu podium—a mobile staired runabout used in the hangar—silently making sure that *all* of his engineers and workmen were watching before he spoke in tones that the Emperor of the Galaxy might have used.

He ordered them to carry out *Physicist* Eron Osa's instructions to the letter. He might even have been grinning.

And then he relaxed, inspected progress on the fuselage in the distant manner of an Admiral in control, and finally cornered Eron privately. "You've been here a long time and we haven't had our discussion yet. Come over for supper tonight." An abstract look came over his face as he consulted his fam, then he smiled again and mentioned the time. "When you come, do not ignore my dog. He's my inspector-general and will not let you in until you have passed security. Make sure that you have washed all enemy smells off your hands."

Eron was alert and neatly dressed and washed at suppertime. Rhaver was asleep on the entrance step but jerked up his nose. "SupperGuestOnTime," he announced, slowly getting to his feet. Dutifully he sniffed Eron, his crotch as well as his hands, and then reached up with entwining fingers and opened the door. "SlipMeBone. GetChance. MasterSometimesNotAttentive."

The table was already set with elaborate Rithian linen mats, a wine jug of cut glass, and long candles. The abundant utensil types were of lucent ceramic. Konn was already seated, did not rise, but expected Eron to seat himself.

"HeTookBath," commented Rhaver, curling up at a strategic place underneath the table.

"Wine?" offered Konn. Then he turned his head and spoke to no one. "Magda, he's here."

Magda immediately arrived from the kitchen with soup and rolls. She was a very pretty girl with a sapiens hauteur. "You're in for a treat," said Konn. "Her particular Rithian eccentricity is her refusal to use a cuisinator."

"You don't always get your meals on time, though," said the girl.

"Only Rhaver minds."

"UsedToIt. NoSoupCourseForRhaver," came from underneath the table.

"Magda, meet my finest student. At least that's what he promised me in his overflowery self-praising résumé. Eron Osa, I think the name is, if I'm remembering correctly."

She curtsied, which seemed to be a Rithian custom—when politeness was intended. "Taste the soup! Is it good? I do sex very well, too, if you indulge. Moderate prices. Rithians have had time to perfect the sexual arts." She brushed his hair back. "You don't want to get hair in your soup," she proclaimed.

"TellHerSoupIsGood. UncouthVisitor." Rhaver was watching his guest's manners.

Magda directed her attention under the table. "Enough out of you, or you don't get your bone!"

At the magic dog-word, Konn perked up. "No bone for Rhaver. He's too fat." Rhaver whimpered.

"The soup *is* very good," exclaimed Eron. "I've never tasted the like."

"It's leek," she said, and disappeared back into her kitchen.

Konn watched her with sad eyes. "Poor girl," he said, "I found her sleeping in the street. She couldn't pay her insurance premiums and her family kicked her out. She has some grave genetic disorders, nothing drugs can't handle now, but I've had my doctor look at her and she isn't going to last more than five or ten more years. I want you to be very kind to her. Girls like her shouldn't be born. Space-damned Rithian religions. Rith is the cesspool of every religion that was ever invented. Once some madman invents a religion, a Rithian never throws it away."

"That's not really true," Eron offered cautiously, ticking off the fatalities on his fingers. "There are no longer any Zoroastrians, Christians, Moslems, Jews, Scientologists, or temples built to honor Jupiter." He paused, having already run out of fingers.

"Except on Splendid Wisdom," grumbled Konn. "The Currents of Space will forever waft the Wisdom of the Ancients down upon our heads. Thank Space for a roof that covers our whole planet!" Konn directed his attention at the soup. "I can't get over that girl. She plays the violin, too. She's a genius for a Rithian sapiens. You and I, we shall treat ourselves to a concert tonight—after we've discussed business." He paused. "No. *Before* we've discussed business."

"A violin?"

"You can buy violins by the truckload at the Pyramid. I myself have a Stradivarius. It is not a *real* Stradivarius, of course, I imagine those sirens-of-the-gods have all turned to dust by now, it is just another damn Rithian fake, but it is a good one, a fine mellow tone."

*What kind of madman am I having supper with?* thought Eron.

When she brought in the second course, Konn demanded his concert.

"What would you like me to play, sir?"

"INowLeave," said Rhaver, getting to his feet.

"How about some Saramantin? You play him well. The Fifth?" Saramantin was one of the Rithian composers of the Etalun Dynasty period—about 5390 GE—when the Etaluns were nostalgically financing a renaissance of Rithian Art.

"How can I play and cook at the same time?" she protested.

"You are a genius who can afford to burn your candle at both ends. Come, my dear, you enjoy Saramantin as much as I do."

Konn was already drunk on wine and a brandy-flavored dessert before they got around to business. Rhaver snuck in for his bone while his master was indisposed and snuck out again. "Brilliant move that, ramming slide rules up the asses of my engineers to make them regret their sins of complication. I knew I was going to love you when I read all the black marks on your school record." He reverted to his smirk of enjoyment about the slide rule. "The Romans used to do that. They set an enemy's ass atop a pointed stake and let him contemplate his stupidity while the stake gradually worked its way up into his brain." Konn laughed, but he was suddenly sober as he turned on his private mnemonifier. "I've been watching you struggle with that model of yours. You probably think I haven't even noticed. I have been fascinated by the way you think. You've made every mistake in the beginner's manual, but what interesting mistakes!"

Eron didn't know whether he was being complimented or chastised. "But it gets the right answers, sir."

"All of them, even to the wrong questions!" Konn chuckled. "You're well on you way to discovering the formula for the Pharaoh's face powder."

*Oh, oh,* thought Eron tensely, *here it comes.*

"The mistake that all beginning psychohistorians make is to generate *too much* detail. If your head is to be split open, it doesn't matter whether it is an iron ax or a bronze ax that does the deed. Dramatists care about such detail, psychohistorians don't. The brilliance of the Founder was his ability to strip away irrelevant detail. If he had hung onto the detail even he was tempted to hoard, all the computers in the Galaxy wouldn't have held his plan or been able to indicate the numbers that had to be monitored to keep the Great Plan on course."

Konn's voice became gentle. He brought up each of Eron's assumptions and stripped off the irrelevancies. "Here's one"—he tapped the screen—"that you are reluctant to edit because it is very insightful; it will tell you how trading organizations form and evolve but at the same time will tell you more than you need to know to follow the evolution of length-and-weight standards. I love it, but you have to take it out. Nothing bloats a psychohistorical prediction to unmanageable size more than the cute variable that has a minor role to play."

Eron had a pang at the loss of his favorite routine. "Will it still work?"

Konn stood up and brought down from his cabinet a green bottle of wine in the shape of a pelican. "Of course it will still work. Trust me." The cork popped.

"Are you as good as they say you are?"

"I can still beat the kids with the fam implants." Eron shivered while Konn poured him wine in a ceramic cup that had once been extraordinarily beautiful before it had been left to weather for ten millennia. "I collect cups from which Rithian messiahs have been known to drink. They are plentiful."

"To your health," toasted Eron.

"And to your promotion. I don't think I'm going to have the pleasure of nailing you up Roman style. I'm reluctantly forced to promote you to First Assistant." He chuckled. "That's a position you may or may not enjoy. I should warn you, though, that as soon as Nejirt Kambu finds out he will take you aside and give you his Konn lecture, everything you'll need to know to survive me."

"Should I listen?"

"Of course. He knows much. He's my failed protégé."

# HOMECOMING, 14,810 GE

*Onimofi-Asuran: What is the aim of the Founder's Plan?*

*Student: To establish a human civilization based on an orientation derived from Mental Science.*

*Onimofi: Why must such an orientation have a nonspontaneous origin?*

*Student: Only an insignificant minority of men are inherently able to lead Man by means of an understanding of Mental Science. Since such an orientation would lead to the development of a benevolent dictatorship of the mentally best—virtually a higher subdivision of Man—it would be resented and could not be stable. No natural form of homeostasis . . .*

*Onimofi: What, then, is the solution?*

*Student: To avoid the resentment of the masses, the first application of Psychohistory must be to prepare a Galaxy-wide political climate during which Mankind will be readied for the leadership of Mental Science. This readiness involves the introduction of unusual homeostatic political structures first proposed by the Founder in his mathscript of the . . . The second application of Psychohistory must be to bring forth a group of Psychologists able to assume this leadership. The Founder's Plan specifies that during the Millennium of Transition the Visible Arm of the Plan will be supplying the physical framework for a single political unit while a Shadow Arm supplies the mental framework for a ready-made ruling class.*

*Onimofi: Why must the Visible Arm be convinced during the Transition that the Shadow Arm does not exist?*

*Student: During the Transition, Psychohistory must still deal with a society which, if aware of a monitoring class of Psychologists, would resent them, fear their further development, and fight against their existence—thus introducing political forces which would destroy the necessary foundation of the homeostatic . . . The Plan would abort.*

—A Student Answers the Questions of First Rank Onimofi-Asuran:
Notes Made During the Crisis of the Great Perturbation,
fourth century Founder's Era

Psychohistorian Nejirt Kambu was finding his jaunts to distant galactic hot spots more and more wearing. His overextended junket through Coron's Wisp had been the least thrilling of those adventures and the only one in which he had not been able to develop a field solution. The oddities in his findings there still bemused him. An outbreak of astrology! He rolled his eyes. But he had made a reputation for himself as an on-site trend analyzer, and his crazy Admiral always had more work for him to do.

Long ago, Second Rank Hahukum Konn had chosen to keep a paranoid eye on intractable historical deviations that no one else could even detect. Nejirt enjoyed working with what was perhaps the best team of trouble-blasters at the Lyceum. Whether to take the Admiral's constant state of war alert seriously was thus a moot point—he liked the job benefits and he had once liked the travel.

Of course (Nejirt was chuckling) his weird problem was as nothing compared to the present trials of his fellow occupants in this cramped subcabin—all five of them were bored. They snoozed, or took entertainment bursts from their readers, or complained about the delay. Imperialis was a system that moved fifteen billion people to and from the stars every year in thirty thousand flights per watch. Hurry up and wait. Their four-thousand-passenger behemoth was waiting permission for the final inward hyperspace jump. The ship had already waited more than an hour for instructions while the short-range ultrawaves of the traffic controllers sizzled with chatter.

Nejirt was using the time to enjoy the sights. He had the sky-scanner all to himself; his bored cabinmates were uninterested. Here in the central regions of the Galaxy the view was always impressive, even frightening—the ionized flames of ancient explosions attacked a sea of suns while time stood still.

Finally . . . their terminal jump brought them to an immense outer docking station, girders and access tubes and modules exposed to space. Twenty irises dribbled them into the arms of customs, where their sterilized baggage was penetrated and tasted by microscanners, their clothes dissolved, and their nude bodies invaded by nanosearchers. Nejirt used psychohistorian status to outrank a woman with a simianoid pet in a cage that he *knew* the machines weren't going to recognize and that, worse, wasn't going to be found anywhere in the customs rule cache. No way he was going to wait while *her* problems were being handled!

It took two trillion humans in Imperialis space to maintain the galactic communications needed by the trillion planet dwellers of Splendid Wisdom. A conventional joke suggested wryly that most of those two trillion were needed in space to keep the useful ones on the ground from bumping into each other—a lie—but it is humor that makes bearable the impotence of standing in line at the awesome center of galactic power.

Two intersystem shuttles and a gravdrop later, much later, he was on Splendid Wisdom's surface at a bustling transportation hub that was as big as a city, tiered into sixteen tapered levels that overlooked a domed plaza two full kilometers in diameter. Low-velocity robotaxis popped out of the levels like mad bees, darting across and around the concourse and, sometimes, landing on it to pick up passengers from the elevator kiosks. The colossal concourse was filled with transients who wanted to be someplace else. In the distance, Nejirt spotted a luckless couple, who had loaded all their baggage into a people-only upchute, so straining the gravitics of the chute that baggage and all were slowly being driven back down into a mass of upcoming passengers—causing pandemonium. He had to laugh. Chaos amused a man whose job was to manipulate chaos.

Nearer at hand, a woman sat alone at a freshment island, sipping a meal between connections, playing a portable hologame to alleviate her ennui. Around her flowed a convoy of off-planet representatives—from some world where clothing resembled woven armor—herding their baggage to keep it from straying, frantically trying to call down a bevy of robotaxis to assist them. The efficiently moving Splendid natives could be spotted by their unwillingness to bring baggage with them—much preferring to manufacture their requirements when they arrived at their destinations, carrying only templates and, fam-memorized, whatever pertinent information they might need.

Nejirt's fam, having sorted through the electromagnetic hum, passed into his consciousness the information that to get home he had a choice between a three-hour hypersonic flight, taking off in forty inamins, or a slower four-hour tube ride. He chose the tube—much more relaxing, no distractions, no stressing connections. He'd be able to draft a preliminary report on Coron's Wisp—and maybe even catch a snooze to wake him up for the family.

His fam located an obscure pod station, well below the hubbub, and the nearest concourse elevator dropped him down to it, almost in free fall—a homey lounge safely wedged between a cheap hotel and an instant tailor in a minor mall. He didn't have to tarry—perfect timing—and hopped inside a waiting pod, plushly lined. There, a pleasant surprise. Fabric, in such a small space, was an agreeable change from the usual white plastic. The pod noted politely that he wished the surround-media offed, adjusted his reclining seat for relaxed comm with his fam, and sucked him into the tubes at an impressive acceleration.

Later he hardly noticed the clunk-thwap of their supersonic linkage to a train of the main trunk tube that was carrying thousands of other pods in mad haste through the planetopolis' brobdingnagian bowels. By then he was composing his report at a professional clip, eyes closed, fam exploring and checking out every nuance, his mind bouncing off intuition with fact, piecing together odd observations that hadn't made sense at the time of collection. Yet it wasn't jelling. He really didn't have a relevant thing to say about astrology.

Here was the kind of perversion that the Galaxy loved to throw up to the gods. This variation of astrological science was based on eerie projections from an ovoid device that seemed to be made out of jade or marble. It was a crude adaption of a sophisticated galactarium. The associated Timdo teachings claimed that every chart cast altered the future—one way if the client accepted the reading, a darker way if the reading was rejected. An astrology that incorporated free will!

Was the failing faith in psychohistory caused by an upsurge of belief in astrology, or was the upsurge in astrology caused by a lack of faith in psychohistory? The equations kept telling him that given the homeostatic conditions in place at Coron's Wisp, something like astrology could be a force to drive out mental science only *if* it had a better method of predicting the future. Both theory and common sense said that the data he had observed was impossible.

He gave up trying to compose his report and went to sleep.

. . . and woke up to "Arrival. You are now parked at . . ." He flipped up the lid before the pod could finish its spiel and staggered to his feet, cramped, thankful he had no baggage. A glance showed him that it was his home station, unmistakable by its pompous wall of restored Imperial mosaics, a salvage from an Early First Empire building boom. Large parts of this sector had survived the Sack. The station's quaint ugliness was what he got for being snobby enough to choose to live in a hallowed domain that had once been built by the families of the Pupian Dynasty.

"Yoo-ha! Hoo!" He saw Wendi windmilling him from the far end of the station, all the while in a dead run. She looked deliriously happy. That meant that the sewers were probably running smoothly, since she was an august member of the sewerocracy and couldn't stop beaming when she had her local piping under control.

"How did you know I was coming?" Nejirt oofed as she collided with him.

"A little pod tipped me off."

"Polite bugger. Must be a new model!"

"No, dear—you just lucked into one of the ones that work!"

Their home was a good walk away and they were in no hurry to reach it, strolling through the parts of the maze that they loved, chatting, catching up. They arrived from above, down a spiral staircase that surrounded a glass-enclosed park of steamy tropicals. Home was built into the circular courtyard at the base of the park. It had originally been part of the forty-seventh-century residence of the family of Peurifoy, who had produced the First Empire's most remembered general. The modest estate, often renovated and cubicalized, was now shared by fifty other families.

Nejirt's welcoming supper was arrayed around an imported ham and a delicate drink from Ordiris bottled in chocolate jiggers. Nejirt was used to farm food, being an experienced traveler, but even here in the elite warrens these were high-class del-icacies from the special psychohistorians' emporium, where rank had its privileges. She liked to shop there—he didn't. But why shouldn't a psychohistorian live as well as the dirt farmer on some outback planet of an unremembered sun? A leg of ham was a small price to pay for farsighted, honest government.

He spoke none of this while they ate. He had to admit that nothing tasted bet-ter on Splendid Wisdom than ham raised and cured on a pig farm forty light-years distant or juice from berries that needed an exotic sun. He lifted his jigger to Wendi's lip. "To a desk job!"

"No," she said, licking the Ordiris and taking a bite of chocolate. "You need your trips like I need my art. I have a surprise for you."

She pulled him into a pillow-floored meditation room that now slumbered un-der the rose luminescence of hanging crystals, no form alike, no cut the same, tin-kling, slowing changing in the motion of their breath. He mourned the Ming vases that had been there when he left. Wendi was so good at finding reproductions—why did she bother with this original stuff? Perhaps, after all these years, she thought it time to get over her fabulous Rithian adventure among the primitives. "Lovely," he said. "Don't take it away before I get used to it."

She sat on the floor. "Come down here. It's all prettier from here. We can lie on the pillows and look up!" She pulled him off his feet. "Tell me about your wild escapade in the cold, hostile, outside universe! We could take off our fams and be animalistic."

He grinned. "Do we sit here naked, growling at each other, each trying to as-sassinate the other's emperor first?"

"Animals don't have emperors!"

"I forgot. Chickens are all equal on the assembly line."

"Just shut up and tell me about your latest escapade. I never get to travel any-more! Sometimes I miss Rith. So what happened? Something must have happened!"

"I had my astrological chart read. We were in a domed hovel stuck onto the side of the retaining wall of a warm wet rice paddy in the mountains of Timdo where I had parked my bicycle to get my breath. There were two magnificent moons in the sky. My astrological seer was three times as old as I am and smelled of fermenting rice. She used a magical jade green ovoid that darkened her hovel and projected a skyful of stars that whispered to her everything about my future that she might want to know and I might be willing to pay for."

Wendi growled and shook him by his ears. "Why don't you ever tell me the truth!"

"Because you wouldn't believe a word of it!" He laughed and made love to his wife without telling her the rest of the story. What could a psychohistorian tell any-one about the truth? What was he even allowed to say?

That old paranoiac Konn had sent Nejirt to the star systems of Coron's Wisp to study a political perturbation—not a dangerous one, a small one, but large enough to have been picked up by the Admiral's sieve. Within the confines of the Wisp's five stellar systems, confidence in the galactic leadership had taken a sudden ten percent drop. On site, nothing appeared to be amiss—no economic depression, no corruption crisis, no inability of the Council to meet its goals. Nothing seemed to be driving the perturbation. After months of puzzled study, Nejirt had only been able to make a correlation with a mild epidemic of astrology. Temporal coincidence is not evidence of either cause or effect, but . . .

He could sleep on it yet another night. He patted his wife and turned out the crystals. He did not sleep.

Coron's Wisp had not been the best locale from which to tackle galactic history—and a terrible locale from which to study such an esoteric subject as astrological infection patterns from pre-Imperial times to the present. He had been unable to turn up any easily identifiable source of contamination. No media imports. No latent memes—though the planet's entire sixteen-thousand-year history was spiced with references to the astrology of the first settlers, it was all innocently devoid of political context . . .

. . . barring only one much-reproduced manuscript from a monastery's sealed library, the surviving copy on thin foils of archaic Early First Empire cellomet. Even Nejirt would not have bothered to translate (by machine) these Chinese brushings had they not contained an illustration of a vase just like the ones his wife had picked up at that Chinese souvenir factory outlet inside the Great Pyramid. But instead of a potter's manual he had uncovered a series of algorithms for making political decisions based on the positions of the heavenly bodies in Old Rith's ancient sky. More astrology!

It was fodder for the hordes of cults who believed in the lost wisdom of the predawn wizards but so much hokum to Nejirt Kambu the psychohistorian. He had needed another such dead-end find like a draft of hemlock. The algorithms used by the Chinese astrologers were many orders of magnitude less complicated than those used on Timdo—and, though no better in their ability to make predictions, Nejirt had to admit that the court astrologers of China had subtler ways of generating ambiguous flattery than did the dour star-watching farmers of Timdo's mountain ranges.

For a moment Nejirt had to remind himself that he was lying on pillows beside a slumbering wife at the star-studded center of galactic sanity. Then traveler's fatigue took him . . .

. . . to be cast in a dream of ancient prespace times when Rith was a lush paradise not yet conscious of its destiny as a desert inferno. He was a traveling temponaut from the Tien Chuen disguised in greasy woven yak wool begging a Chinese court astrologer to tell his fortune. He had gold to offer. It wasn't enough. He ripped the seams of his shirt and brought out more Tien Chuen gold collected on their wanderings through the sky. The silk-robed astrologer grinned malevolently.

It was enough. Since the astrologer's head would not be riding on the blade of the message, he agreed to tell the truth without sleight-of-hand.

In the dead of night, atop the tower of the astrologer, Nejirt pointed out the star of his birth, a hidden nothing among the blur of the Sing Ki. "Ah," said the astrologer, and a gong sounded and a giant bronze instrument began to move against the heavens across the horizon-shadows of a walled imperial city. Ominously the bronze shaft creaked to a halt in the direction of Tseih She, which the astrologer obligingly translated for his visitor from the stars as the Piled-Up Corpses. "That is your star." It was nothing special, a white star, faintly blue, blazingly bright, an eclipsing variable about one hundred leagues from Rith.

"But what does it *mean?*" his dream-self asked with the exasperation of a man who is desperate for certainty.

"It means that you are living in the time of the slayer and the slain, that the battle takes place across the stars and that the fates of empires are at stake."

"But am I the slayer or the slain?"

"Ah," said the malevolent astrologer, bowing under the Chinese stars, not as politely as before, "for more gold . . ."

Nejirt remembered the dream quite clearly because that was the exact moment that his fam gently woke him to an emergency request. He opened his eyes to the darkly tinkling crystals and took the call.

"Cal Barna. Imperialis Police." There was no image but his fam had already verified the identification. The voice continued, "I've been informed that I have waked you from sleep after a long voyage. My apologies, sir. Our data tells us that you've just come in from a scout of Coron's Wisp."

"That's correct."

"Your report has not yet been filed and I need an opinion. We've got a fast breaker here and time is of the essence."

"Ask away."

"We've got a body."

"A body?"

"A dead body. Twenty-seven watches dead. Illegally registered. We would have called you in earlier but you weren't home. The body carried contradictory identification, deliberate deception, so we're poking in the dark, but a lucky break on the name Scogil tells us that this man is from Coron's Wisp."

"That brings the odds of finding out who he is down to one in ten billion," said Nejirt sarcastically.

"We think the case is more important than that, sir. It was your boss, Second Rank Konn, who put us onto you. He said you'd be interested."

"All right. What else do you know about your corpse?"

"Very little."

"Have you been able to do a salvage on his fam?"

"Yeah, we would have. But his fam is missing."

"So what have you got? He was murdered? Accident?"

"No, we killed him trying to take him alive. Miscalculated his interest in survival."

"Why were you tracking him?"

"It's a long story, sir. It doesn't make sense. We don't know why we were chasing him. It's because he is an astrologer or an—"

"And you think he's from Coron's Wisp?"

"We do."

"I'll be right there. I just hope you gentle souls aren't stationed at my antipodes."

They and the body were near the Lyceum from which Nejirt Kambu had been forged as a psychohistorian. He could never get away from that place and its hordes of students. Damn. That would mean a long hypersonic flight . . . at least hours of hassle; his fam was already making the arrangements. He rolled over to look at his sleeping wife. Should he wake her now—or leave a message with her fam? Before he decided, he let himself stare at the way her profile lay, eyes closed, face content because he was home.

# AN ANCIENT FORTRESS IN THE
# DESERTS OF RITH, 14,798 GE

*Tiring of a roost of fractious and immoral gods, certain ancient philosophers be-gan their general reform by creating, instead, a single moralistic God in the im-age of a human teenager who knows everything, both seeing the whole of the future and remembering the whole of the past. Inquiring heretics went further. Yet nascent science, even while rejecting the anthropomorphism of the new God with His forever youthful body and superphysical powers, clung to His abstract mind and called it the conservation of information. In the first groping millennia of the development of their atomic theory, the precocious Greek avant-garde be-lieved that the superpositions of the quantum waves persisted forever, spread-ing through the dimensions in ever-complicating ripples of alternate worlds. Democritus and his student Schrodinger had abandoned the idea of infinitely di-visible matter but were unwilling to go the whole way and abandon the notion of infinitely divisible space.*

*Grainy space, of course, can't store the infinite amount of information that a teenage God's mind demands. Superposed quantum waves erode and break and chafe against the pebbles of the media that carries them. Bit by bit, as the structure of the future becomes more and more certain, the structure of the past fades away, bit by bit. Today we are left with a more mature and slightly stooped God who is myopic when He views a future not yet created and who has already forgotten His childhood except for a little fuzzy background radiation left over from the really Big Events. As psychohistorians your profession will be to look at the future and the past—but stay humble. You'll never be able to do better than the Myopic God with Alzheimer's.*

    —From the Founder's speech to the first graduating class
    in psychohistory

Living by Rith's odd days and nights and an impossible 86,400 seconds per day instead of galactically, Eron Osa was losing track of time but he knew there were roughly seventy watches per moon, and the golden desert moon had gone through all of its phases while he took the bloat out of his metric program, even starting another model to see if he could predict the broad outline of Rith's early economic development. He spent his suppers with Konn, talking shop and sometimes quoting Latin poetry to Magda who, in her turn, taught him how to sing Somolian poetry. Before they ate Konn often indulged in a bizarre custom: he read—rather than recited—brief passages from a well-worn little book of the Founder's Maxims. He expected a silent pause after the reading, a time for thinking.

True to Konn's prediction, Nejirt sometimes hovered around looking for an opportunity to deliver his "Konn lecture," but, forewarned, Eron managed to weasel out of it one way or another, often by jumping into a truck out to the local windy cliff to fly model gliders with engineers who had stumbled over their roots.

The fuselage of the Flying Fortress, often modified, was now taking its definitive shape. The engineers had rediscovered passive stability, much to their amazement. They had so many active control tools at their disposal that it was a moot point to them whether a boat had its center of gravity above or below the waterline or whether an unpowered building would buckle or whether an aerocar was passively spin-proofed.

When the basic weight balancing and dimensions of the Flying Fortress emerged from the fossil and they learned that the damn thing—minus all quantronics—would *still* fly even after the pilot had gone to sleep (or been killed), they began to be impressed by the raw skill of the ancient engineers, forgetting that such skill had been acquired by killing off test pilots, which was how they got the fourth decimal place that their slide rules wouldn't give them. The final look of the plane, though basically determined by the laws of fluid dynamics, still eluded them. A "lost-wax" fossil in a mold of coral 744 centuries in the making leaves some forgotten details to the imagination.

Which was how Nejirt got his opportunity to corner Eron for a prolonged lecture. He caught him on the catwalk. "If you haven't got anything to do, come with me tomorrow. Our tireless historian has found some pictures for us."

"Of our Venteen Fortress? Show me."

"Not so fast. #26 only came up with a verbal reference to the pictures, which are allegedly contained in a reference book that no longer exists."

"That's no help."

"But the pictures were taken from a mural which probably still does exist. It was above the flooding of the Great Meltdown, and the site was built to last on a geologically stable foundation."

"Where? Let's go!"

Nejirt only laughed. "The reference neglects to say."

"But there are maps of Rith—millions of maps!"

"True. We can find the Mausoleum of Jim Morrison on any number of maps, but where would we find the Mausoleum of Aristotle? We have more references to old maps that no longer exist than we have maps." When Eron slumped, Nejirt only laughed again. "We'll find it. Trust me, I was trained as a field agent and I'm very good. We know the general location—to within about ten thousand square kloms." Eron made a doubtful face. "Besides," Nejirt added, "the locals will know. They always know, even if the knowledge is buried in a mythology that no one understands anymore. We'll have to go in by foot."

Wendi insisted on coming along. She bought herself survival clothes and very expensive sole-powered hiking boots. Since they were going out among the wild sapiens, she also bought a long-nosed blaster claiming to be an expert shot. Her weapons experience, Eron discovered by gentle probing, was as a thirteen- and fourteen-year-old fighting in the Red Army of a popular maze on Splendid Wisdom where teenagers sneaked around and zapped each other for pleasure after school.

Nejirt was more practical. He was a true psychohistorian who saw no need for weapons where wit would suffice. Most important to him was a utility backpack that manufactured basic food, clothing, and shelter out of available organic matter, basic stone tools out of rock, and simple quantronic devices for trading out of rock and a frugal supply of essential rare elements.

Eron did not share Wendi's excitement or Nejirt's cool. He would just as soon have jumped out into space in the buff as take a walk in a Rithian desert, but he couldn't let Nejirt be the brave one. He was glad of the holster and lethal kick that his father had so recently gifted him. When no one was looking he reviewed his zenoli warrior training, tuning up his reflexes. Did everyone who worked with Konn go mad? Those damn wall murals had better be worth it!

An so, flying off into the dawn in #26's comfortable interior, Nejirt began to brief them on procedures.

Eron felt hostile. "What do you mean, an untouched site? The cameramen were there to take pictures—when was that, a couple of millennia ago?—so how do we know it's still there?"

"Well . . . not untouched. The grave robbers looted it of all its valuable radioactives less than a millennia after it was sealed. But it was built in a geological formation with the intention that it should endure forever, the only thing the Americs tried to build to last other than their quaint dispozoria. I'm not sure why it survived relatively intact for so long, considering the appetite of these maggot Rithians to sell their past. I suppose because it has a mythical aura of taboo. Superstition."

"Probably because it's not in a pleasant location, even for a Rithian grave robber," kibitzed Rossum's #26.

The journey was a long one, even at supersonic speeds. They spent most of their time in glorious cloud formations but did catch glimpses of the sea below. The seas of Rith were extensive even though they were shrinking as the ice reaccumulated at the poles. Over the Mars-like land one wondered where the water had gone. The planet was in desperate need of terraforming. Didn't the Rithians have *any* ambition?

There were places of vegetation. #26 took a detour down one river to show them the spectacular waterfall over a dam that had been half eroded away and then down an awesome many-colored canyon, perhaps not as impressive as the canyons of Mars, but certainly the best such site that Rith had to offer.

Nejirt chose a small oasis near the ancient atomic testing range as their base of operations. It was scrubby green and didn't look populated, but Nejirt assured them that it would be. He didn't allow their aerocar to land anywhere near the oasis. "We walk in and ask questions. It's got to be around here somewhere." #26 wanted to stay with them, but Nejirt wouldn't allow it.

Their landing *had* attracted attention. The dust was approaching them too fast for it to be men on foot.

"Camels!" Eron exclaimed, remembering the camel-lamp he had salvaged from the trash at Asinia.

"Camels went out with the second to last great mass extinction. Not much of the original Rithian flora and fauna left—maybe twenty-five percent. The big animals were really hard hit. Horses survived the sapiens predations but horses aren't good for this kind of desert. Probably they are gawfs."

Their curious visitors were gentle nomads—with their blond hair, slant eyes, and large mouths, obviously a sapiens subspecies. A little chatter in a language Nejirt seemed to recognize established that they were from a tribe of the local Lost Vegan cult, firm in the belief that it was their ancestors who had colonized Rith from Vega and brought the bipedal gawf beasts with them—no use telling them that Vega was a blazing A0 star without habitable planets and that the gawfs were a late addition to Rith's fauna imported during the occupation of Rith by the Eta Cumingan Regionate long after the sapiens hominid had gone extinct everywhere in the Galaxy except on Rith. The sacred literature said otherwise.

Nejirt was right about the weapons. These were very friendly people who put them up with great hospitality in their little village. They were mostly interested in buying robophones, which were in short supply. Nejirt had no problem negotiating the hire of a guide and three beasts. Their guide turned out to be a very genial teacher, smiling all the while he taught Nejirt and Eron and Wendi how to ride, laughing tolerantly at all mistakes, including his own. He insisted on bringing a boy with him, rotating apprenticeships being their form of education.

The semierect gawfs were easy to handle, imported sixty thousand years ago and now so thoroughly adapted to Rithian desert conditions that they would be unable to survive on their home planet. A gawf female treated its rider as a daughter to be protected and was generally indifferent to the small gawf mate whom she seduced and then digested in her pouch to fertilize and feed her grublike embryos, a large proportion of whom were male. She devoured a new mate for every litter. Gawfs were pampered by the Lost Vegans both for transportation and for the sake of the delicious male meat, which was a main part of their diet. On smooth ground Eron found that a gawf loped along on its hind legs; on rough ground it put down its long arms in an agile climbing gait. Gawfs didn't like to follow the weathered cuts of the ancient roads, preferring to climb up to the highest vantage point to see where they were. They were far more independent minded than horses.

It was a desolate land, mainly supporting small alien creatures and Rith's indomitable insects. There were few encounters. When they met brigands who hoped to strip them, their guide alerted all nearby clan groups by robophone, the phone then being released in flying mode to monitor the situation from the air. Nejirt cautioned Eron not to show his weapon. Both parties argued loudly in a strange language. The ruffians, seeming to fear the robophone's ability to follow them, made some kind of threatening apology and left. Eron, who had shifted into the mental attitude drilled into him by zenoli training at Asinia, was glad that he didn't have to use his blaster. On Agander his weapon was merely ceremonial. He didn't believe in killing helpless animals, even intelligent relatives. Even thieves. But he would have done so had the ruffians persisted.

Their guides weren't any more direct than their willful gawfs, and a sly detour around the wrong side of a ridge brought them to join a celebratory confluence of several tribes of nomads. Job or no job, they weren't going on until they had done their share of gossiping and singing and storytelling and trading with old friends. The tents went up for an indefinite stay and that was that. They had time on their hands.

Wendi went off with the women while the guides gambled. Two little boys excitedly tried to sell their "captive" farmen a skull. It was very old and weathered. They were determined to convince Nejirt and Eron that it wasn't a fake. It was probably freshly robbed from some local cemetery of a more populous Rithian era and might even have been a 75,000-year-old Americ, but the studs drilled into the bone and the perfect black ceramic teeth suggested an origin a thousand years later. In any event the skull was worthless. By not limiting their population, men of that era had depreciated the value of their skulls.

At midnight all activity stopped for the homage to Vega. Vega was as bright as it had ever been in this part of the Galaxy, undaunted by all the less-splendid stars. Eron and Nejirt let the maniacal fiddling of four viotones animate them in dance with the happy girls under night's canopy. Wendi was having the time of her life, even in her clunky boots with too much spring. There was nothing else to do.

When the celebrations wore off, days later, their guides deigned to go back to work and returned from their scouting with huge smiles. By sunset the small expedition reached the entrance to the Depository, aided by its bat smell. Swarms of bats were pouring into the darkly rosy sky for their nightly feast; winter was over and all sorts of delicious flying insects were breeding and on the move. A rough hole in the hill, hidden by an overgrowth of skorgn and sickly juniper, was the source of the bats; ancient robbers had chosen to blast into the side of the

Depository near one of its still-buried original portals. The hole was kept open by guano hunters.

The hominid mammals fought a way down through their gentle flying relatives, leaving the boy behind to tend the alien mounts. They all put on masks, more to keep out the smell than for the oxygen. Though Nejirt had deliberately set the power at low intensity for the bats' sake, the lanterns stirred up even more bats to drop from the ceiling and flutter away from the day's roost. Nejirt seemed to be enjoying himself, as if all the bats were his personal pets. Their Lost Vegan guide commented jovially on the thickness of the guano, which his people came here to collect when it was deep enough.

"You've just met Rith's most successful mammal," muttered Nejirt to his cohorts as they hurried down the tunnel into its deeper regions, which were avoided by the bats. "Their natural gengineering has us beat by fifty million years, and they're so smart they've managed to colonize millions of planets all without having to invent a stardrive. On Zeta Anorka where I come from the insects are so bad we keep bats as house pets. We have fridged bat homes we carry around when we go camping—let them out to dehibernate and they beat any insect-zapping machine you'll ever invent. They live a long time and you don't have to make new ones when they wear out."

Eron noticed that his Lost Vegan guide had no fear of radioactivity; maybe the concept wasn't real to him. Nejirt wasn't testing—any gamma radiation would be down by about eight orders of magnitude since the Depository was built and, as well, its treasure had been thoroughly looted *at least* seven hundred centuries ago, perhaps even earlier when the spent nuclear fuel, rich with rare stable isotopes, still carried high concentrations of valuable long–half–life radioactives. Nevertheless Eron felt cautious. He sampled the air and the walls with his handy pocket metricator, looking for traces of protactinium 233, tin 126, niobium 93 and 94, et cetera. He found nothing abnormal. One would need more radiation protection in space than in this emptied vault lying, as it did, beneath Rith's atmosphere and three hundred meters of overhead rock.

They got past the guano and the scattered mummified bats. The main tunnel was immense, branching into endless side tunnels that soaked up lantern beams to show nothing, all as empty as the Queen's Chamber of the Great Pyramid. "Where did it all go!" exclaimed Eron. "There's room for one hundred thousand tons."

"We got here too late. Where did the pharaoh's golden toiletries go?"

They found old fuel-cell batteries and a sack with the desiccated remains of someone's lunch. Farther along an animal had crawled inside to die, not a Rithian vertebrate. Nejirt had been counting purposefully and now turned down an off-corridor. "This is what I wanted to show you." Thirty meters along its length the tunnel had once been sealed by a bulkhead door of battleship quality. The door was gone. Beyond its threshold the walls of the gently sloping tunnel were covered with marvelous frescos in anaglyph: lots of lush vegetation, saintly men and women with halos, monsters, happy children. And a whole section devoted to soldiers and their trade. There had been lights and air conditioning but it no longer functioned.

Eron examined the murals, especially the one depicting the Flying Fortress, which was labeled in Latin with an enigmatic "SCHWEINFVRT." It was done in ceramic glazes, certainly not hand applied for the detail had incredible resolution. Probably they'd been laid down by a hot sputtering printer, a very durable medium. "What are the pictures saying?" asked Eron.

"Nobody knows. They're very post-Americ though they certainly had a high regard for Americ ancestors. The rest of their stuff is gone. Racks of corroded hardware, but no message. Some of the dust indicates they used paper or plastic books. There's more." While Wendi stayed behind to photograph the murals, Nejirt swung his beam around and took Eron up a stairway carved in the tuff. It led to an elaborate set of rooms, post-Depository, mostly stripped of everything except the dead lights and the fan machinery, intact but frozen solid. "There once was a morgue up here with five skeletons, *Homo sapiens* normal with a wide variance typical of the Mixed Age." Eron wandered through hollow stone chambers with tiny doors and elaborately mosaicked floors. An occasional wall was frescoed. Power cables came through a crawling tunnel that led to a distant high-temperature generator, fission fed and still emitting low levels of radon. Most of the fuel rods were gone. Sizable air vents had been drilled up to the surface but remained blocked. "You'll never find ruins this old anywhere else in the Galaxy."

"What were they doing in a place like this?" Eron was incredulous.

"War refugees, probably."

There were other sapiens-made caves. The armory was empty except for the gun racks. The guns, said Nejirt, were in the primitive weapons display at the Great Pyramid, which was where #26 had found out about this place.

That night a delicate male gawf was roasted in the ground under a campfire. After the feast Nejirt and Eron sat around the fire while Wendi and their guides slept. Nejirt made some allusions to the current politics of psychohistory.

*Here it comes,* thought Eron.

"I'm tempted to tell you about Konn. He doesn't give a Spacedamn for my opinion of him, or anyone else's, but I'd rather you kept my opinion to yourself. It's for your information only. Use it or not. Konn is looking for a son, an heir. He's never found one. You're his latest wonder boy."

"Oh." The flames flickered and Eron fed it some more skorgn. They weren't being bothered by insects. The bats were swooping.

"I'm one of his ex-wonderkins, not the only one. We're alumni. Want a briefing?"

"Sure."

"First you'll want to know why I'm still around; I could have gone off in a sulk and joined Hanis or disappeared into the Galaxy on any assignment I wanted. I'm that good. Do you know First Rank Jars Hanis?"

"The Rector of the Lyceum?"

"Which makes him the Rector of the Galaxy. But Konn is a better mathematician. It drives me crazy. He gives me a problem. I lay out all my tools, sharpen them, whatever. I've built up a marvelous mathematical tool chest. I've got tools that weren't invented when Konn was in school. I crank out my solution. It's good. Konn looks at it. He scratches his head for maybe three or five or seven watches. He talks to that damn impudent dog of his. And then he comes back to me: Why didn't I do it this way? Why didn't I do it that way? Why did I bother with these factors? Why not match these two compensating errors against each other and throw both factors out of the calculation? And out of his hat comes my result—at twice the accuracy and a tenth the work. If you are listening, an hour with him is worth a year of courses. While you are his wonder boy you're going to get the ride of your life. I don't envy you. Just don't crack up when you disappoint him. That's what I had to tell you."

Eron poked the fire. He didn't know what to say. The fire gave off a thousand red sparks, like a cluster of dying stars, worn out by life. Above, the stars were white. The universe was young.

"When I heard you were from Agander, I wanted to meet you. Konn sent me on my first mission to the Ulmat. One of his crazy paranoid ideas. He's paranoid, you know. Normal people worry about poison in their food. He worries about poison in the stars." He paused, as if unsure he would continue. "Your father was into some pretty shady deals."

That caught Eron's attention. "I know. He wanted money to put me into a good Scholarium." Eron didn't want to talk about it. "So why was Konn interested in the Ulmat?"

"Paranoia. He spots a culture like in the Ulmat Constellation that's doing a balancing act at some cusp point. It's got to roll off in some direction, any direction—north? south? east? west? something in between? Some little disturbance down in the noise is going to push it off that cusp. Konn's paranoia takes over. He looks at the worst possible direction out of millions. He starts doing this mumbo-jumbo analysis of the noise pushing this way and that way. He comes to the conclusion that the noise is pushing in the wrong direction. Nobody can duplicate his results—but he knows he's right. He knows he has to go in there and push in another, less dangerous direction. He does that. Everything comes out all right. It must have been because of his corrective action, right? That's why Konn is Second Rank and not First. Everybody knows he's a quasar, but no one trusts him when he's on the subject of what he is most passionate about. Hanis tries to keep him contained."

"Did Konn think there was any danger from the Ulmat?"

"Yeah. He thought the Ulmat could lead a revolution that would tear the Galaxy apart. I did a lot of fieldwork. I tried to show him that, though it was possible, it was never going to happen—but I don't think he ever believed me. He had a perfect excuse. He had preemptively taken counteraction and aborted the threat. You grew up on Agander. What do you think? Do Ganderians have it in them to lead a revolution against the Second Empire?"

*Yes,* thought Eron, feeling the blaster in its holster, but he was too much of a Ganderian to ever say so aloud.

While Eron reflected, Nejirt had a final comment. "According to my measures, your people have the will but lack seven of the critical leadership dimensions."

"The same seven you'd find in martyrs willing to die for their cause?" Eron pulled his bite and added diplomatically, "We're a very practical people. We'd never get involved in a revolution that wasn't going to succeed." *And that's why we end up as galactic bureaucrats and not as underdogs fighting for right against might.* A Ganderian was willing to wait forever, if that's what it took, for the *right* revolution. So Konn had seen through the mask. That was a big plus for Hahukum Konn. What else had he seen?

Nejirt wandered away and scrounged another piece of now-cold gawf meat from a bowl, heating it on a stick over the coals. "Konn isn't the only madman on the scene. Konn is paranoid. Jars Hanis is a megalomaniac, which is why I won't work for him. He's developing a three-millennia plan of social renovation. Very impressive. All the impressionable students are impressed. He wears the right clothes to anesthetize people's good sense. Never have a drink with Jars Hanis or you'll feel so good you'll end up working for him."

By now Eron had a dozen questions to ask, but Nejirt was ready to close shop. He crawled into his sleeping bag. "Well, we got our picture. The engineers will be delighted. I've called #26 and that old windbag will be here to pick us up in the morning, relieved that we're still alive."

The journey home was uneventful. Eron was consumed by questions, but Nejirt remained in a silent mood.

Rhaver met them. He sniffed at their trousers and then lifted the fabric with his fingers to get a better sniff of skin. "JirtNowBeBack," he said solemnly up at Nejirt with myopic eyes. His glance at Eron was doubtful. Then he was running off, his fingers clenched into running paws. "TheyBack! TheyBack!"

# ERON OSA MEETS A FAN, 14,810 GE

*12.02.13 On a planet with a trillion residents, storage space and transportation space is at a premium.*

*12.02.14 The only commodity that can be stored and transported cheaply is information.*

*12.02.15 It is easier to manufacture devices from stored information, on site, as they are needed, and to destroy them after use, than to store them away in physical bulk, waiting for a second user. Exceptions may be made in the case of (1) devices utilizing exotic materials, (2) devices requiring exotic manufacturing methods for their duplication.*

*12.02.16 Water, air, and sewage must be purified and reused, on site, to avoid transportation through pipes, conduits, and through the atmosphere.*

*12.02.17 The transportation bulk-flow of any sector design should never exceed a Haldmakie number of 43.*

—*Splendid Planner's Guide,* AdminLevel-NR8 Issue-GA13758 SOP-12

The now-vanished message which had appeared in his hotel's creaky Personal Capsule dispenser was engraved on Eron Osa's memory by repeated review. "See Master Rigone at the Teaser's Bistro, Calimone Sector, AQ-87345, Level 78 (The Corridor of Olibanum.) . . ." It had been signed by a mysterious "benefactor" whose identity he had been unable to guess.

In spite of his missing fam and memories, Eron remembered the tattooed face of Rigone—and remembered intensely mixed feelings of awe and respect and exasperation. He could not remember if they had been friends. He knew he had spent time at Rigone's Teaser's Bistro and knew he had seen him many times and perhaps had known him earlier. Something about books.

For six watches, petrified to leave his hotel, Eron had been trying to find the courage to wander up the Olibanum to see Rigone—as his strange "benefactor" had suggested. Trying to contact Rigone would be irrelevant if he was first going to find himself hopelessly disoriented in the corridors of the Calimone Sector. Such fears of losing his way astonished him. Facing the unknown out there seemed akin to interstellar adventuring in the era of sublight rafting.

The fuzzy memories he had of himself told of the old Eron as a confident, arrogant young man, a mathematician, a zenoli combat adept—but confidence has its foundation in abilities, and those had been shattered. He wasn't sure anymore that he even had the wits for such a simple task as plying the corridors of Splendid Wisdom alone. His actions kept calling upon him for lore and skills that his mind did not know were gone—until his absent fam did not respond.

Nevertheless reason suggested that even if Splendid Wisdom were an incomprehensible hive to a famless man, there should be a solution to his lack of mobility. Splendid Wisdom had existed as a labyrinth long before the fam had become a universal symbiote.

It was essential that he not remain a prisoner of his hotel. The message was acting as a goad to drive him out. But he was "hanging onto the doorjamb" for dear life!

In his fury he gave himself an ultimatum. Plan! Plan even the most elementary of chores! Predict and plan! Then he laughed that his fury had induced in him the most bland of psychohistoric clichés. His cheer encouraged him out of his moping. Suppose he reviewed *everything* in the safety of his rooms, testing his organic brain for deficiencies? He might, that way, gain the courage to leave the hotel on an expedition. The organic brain had been evolved to think and learn, and there was no reason he couldn't still perform such essentials. Think! he commanded himself. Once he stepped outside of his hotel into the corridors, what would he have to do that his fam had always done for him?

Eron began to flash on his famless early childhood, the only model he had for what was in store for him. Wryly he recalled the time he ran away from the family's tourist suite when he was three. They had traveled by sea from Agander's Great Island to the coast—he didn't remember the name of the city because he hadn't known it then—but he did remember his passion in wanting to see up close the fountain-waterfall at the city's center, marvelously rising up through a contained rapids for thirty stories and then gracefully dropping down through a series of magical shapes. Mama Osamin, his governess, would not respond to his polite request or explain her refusal. Neither was she willing to appease his temper tantrum.

Resentful, he tricked the door lock with a candy wrapper, sneaked out, wandered down to the lower reaches of the hotel, and cunningly hopped a pod, knowing in his three-year-old mind that once having crossed the sea by boat, a person could use the landlocked pods to go anywhere on the continent. He made magisterial demands of the pod's control console using the word "waterfall" prominently. The pod detected his youth and delivered him to the police station. He smiled.

This time, as an adult, perhaps he could outwit the pods—though it was rumored that here on Splendid Wisdom the pods were the smartest in the Galaxy and intentionally surly with provincials.

A little research on his room's console showed him that his wretched hotel was within free-transport range of the teeming Calimone Sector. Half an hour's ride to the northwest? Calimone embraced the appurtenances of the Upper Lyceum of the Fellowship, whose levels he had once known very well with its ministries, academeries, scholariums, libraries, vast apartment conglomerates, clubs. Lowlife hangouts such as Rigone's Teaser's Bistro lay on the distant borders of the Lyceum. It was a pleasure to him that he could still recall the energetic bustle of the Olibanum through which he had cruised extensively during his twenties. Trust the organic brain to remember the lower pleasures with an uncritical glow.

Think! Lacking a fam he was electromagnetically blind, except in the visible spectrum, and so he would need some kind of groping skill to get around. That stumped him since the warrens of Splendid Wisdom averaged out at seven hundred meters deep over the entire area of the planet—the crumb that was Calimone Sector had more mappable features than the whole of most planets. How did one grope that? The structures all broadcast their features, but he had no fam to make sense of their beacons. A man could wander forever without reaching his destination. Eron was sorely tempted to use his common-issue fam with all its dangers of psychic control. No. He sighed; more research was in order. Virtual overlays on the visual cortex were out, but something equivalent?

At his comm console he meandered through the Archives and discovered the ancient art of paper mapmaking in an orgy of revelation. It was so obvious! Why hadn't he thought of it himself? But maps needing to be viewed with eyes was a horrible thought, and reading one while unlinked to a fam, unthinkable. A paper map was passive. It didn't *do* anything. To read such a paper map would require work! Not impossible, of course, but discouraging. That was monkey business. There must be a better way!

How had men found their way around Splendid Wisdom during the age of the First Empire when the planet had been as teeming as it was now and there had been no fams? Eron Osa became inspired. Of course the damn hotel's shopping library didn't have a map-reader template on file. He felt his rage rising again and with it that awful feeling, again, that he didn't have a fam to stabilize him emotionally. He paused to compensate. He breathed deeply to compose himself.

. . . and smelled the thickness of smothered layers of air half a kilometer beneath the free weather . . . felt the confining walls. He could almost hear the dripping of the pipes from above. Perhaps it was merely the hotel's SeeOTwo decomposer on the blink again that gave him a heavy head and the sense that the air itself was turgid from decay. Somewhere up on the distant rooftop was a park's crisp air misted by the water towers. *Stop breathing,* he told himself. *Concentrate on locating maps!*

Eron spliced into the world outside the hotel, netting around among the local antique warehouses until he found a template he could buy for cheap, grumbled at the tech implied by the First Empire date, imported it, spent hours finding the link that could translate its obsolete code, and waited some more while the nanomachines of his manufacturum assembled the device. It took time because he had asked for a high structural resolution, time enough to relax for a drink and a thought. He did not want to bother with a quick, low-resolution device—having his map machine break down in an unknown warren was not an adventure he wanted to live. Leisurely thoughts gave him opportunity for irony. What if the map files turned out to be as ancient as the reader and he found himself being guided around a pre-Sack Splendid Wisdom which no longer existed!

In time his room's sometimes-malfunctioning manufacturum assembled:

    (1) a delicate spiderlike crown that adjusted to his skull under his hair;
    (2) an almost invisible laser gun that wrote to his right retina;
    (3) a subvocal control pad;
    (4) and—no instructions.

The maps of Splendid Wisdom, freshly read and tortuously compiled to meet the constraints of this antique, arrived on, astonishingly, a thousand flimsies which, outrageously, had to be carried in a pocket pouch, each to be inserted manually. No wonder the First Empire had collapsed!

Even equipped he was afraid to venture into the planetopolitan maze. The memory of the first time he had tried was too vivid. He couldn't talk his map-reader into working smoothly. It had no self-volition and had to be instructed like some stubborn dolt and he didn't know its language and he didn't have a fam to learn its language! With extreme patience he did manage to explore the immediate vicinity of his hotel, two corridors west and four levels deep. The device actually worked after a fashion—and, he supposed, would work better once he had fathomed its pretensions.

Then, carefully, he spent expeditionary afternoons in a neighboring café that had tables out along its corridor front, minding his own business, talking frugally, working up his skills for a more distant adventure. His criminal's pension was limited—it was like being a student again—so he was stingy with his drink and pastries while he did his people watching. To amuse himself he reinvented mental addition, multiplication, and division, skills which he had never learned because they were automatic functions of his fam. It was good discipline for his frazzled mind, and a soothing reminder that there were always work-arounds, however clumsy, for the fam dependencies which he no longer controlled. Eight plus fourteen was twenty-two. He marveled that he was able to figure that out from scratch. Such work made him feel like a genius again.

Eron had chosen a busy traverse for his arithmetical doodling and idle contemplations. The space within view of the café was filled with pedestrians flowing from the level above and boiling out of the nearby pod stop. Whenever he decided to stop thinking, to rest his aching organic brain, he had before him a cornucopia of sights—today a boy with a bag of bread dragged by his mother, an old man followed by a cackling family of females in weird headdresses. One of the interesting effects of being famless was the extraordinarily heightened visual intensity. Even the simplest colors were magnificent.

Take that tall woman who was waiting at the gracelessly vermilion pod stop for a friend, blue eyes flecked with a russet gold that glanced about her impatiently, swinging her black ringlets into a bobbing sway. Her broad-brimmed hat was of a textured fuchsia he had never seen before, topped by feathers. In this corner of the cosmos style was everything. No such hat could be useful this far underground from a blazing sun. Still, her skin looked coddled. She would be one of these aristos who spent regular time in a body shop staving off death and decay. She was still young enough to think of herself as immortal. Was her fragrance as gay as she looked?

The restless eyes caught him staring at her and she smiled with broad lips. He glanced away, sipped his punch, pushed a crumb across the table. And presently saw her feet standing in his gaze, motionless. He did not look up, afraid to sound like a moron. The shoes were of a scaled fish-leather, multihued, probably scalbeast from Tau-Nablus, and why should he know that?

"Eron Osa?"

That she knew his name was a complete surprise. Had he been ignoring a friend? He looked up now, curiously trying to place her. Nothing but a pretty face. She smelled vaguely of cinnamon. "Do we know each other?" he groped pleasantly.

Her smile broadened. "No. My spies told me you've been hanging out here in the afternoons and I thought I might catch you. You're hard to find but I'm hard to discourage." She was grinning. Her accent was aristo, perhaps an Etalun or a Frightfulperson. "I'm a hopeless fan of yours. I've read your monograph." She gave him her card. "Otaria," she said, but her card carried no name or address—being useful only to send her a Personal Capsule.

A fan of mathematics in this crass world? "Which paper?" He was trying to place her as one of his colleagues.

"The only one you ever published. I made a copy."

"Ah. My *Early Disturbed Event Location by* . . ."

"Yes," she interrupted.

He was startled and suspicious. "You are a psychohistorian?"

"Stars, no. But I have my pretensions as a historian."

Was she police? On guard he asked, "And did you enjoy my piece?" He was fishing for hints as to what he had actually written.

"I didn't understand a line of it." She commandeered a chair for herself.

DONALD KINGSBURY

376

"But I'm smart enough to know its importance." The chair was of a kind that embraced her.

"It's been depublished," he said cautiously.

"I noticed. I hadn't intended to contact you, but since you've been censored, that means you are in deep trouble. Am I right? You are in hiding here, or worse? Is that why you were so hard to find?"

"Worse."

His serious tone surprised her. "Are you all right?"

"No," he said. "I'm brain-damaged."

Now she was alarmed. "Deliberate?" She seemed to be genuinely grief-stricken. "How?"

"They executed my fam."

"You've been tried and convicted? How horrible!" Her concern for him suddenly transformed into a concern for herself—he watched her eyes dart about to see if they were being observed. "Are you safe here?"

"I've been punished and released, a brilliant future nipped in the bud."

"But they'll be watching you." Her alarm was increasing. He wanted to reassure her, but that involved telling her that he was so crippled that there would be no point in anyone watching him. She rose to go but he snapped a steel grip on her wrist as she was turning. Her sympathy evaporated. She swung back to face him. "Release me!" she hissed. The accent affected by the descendants of the Frightful-people was now crisp.

"We haven't been introduced," he went on smoothly. "Over dinner you can tell me what I wrote. I don't remember. I have to know."

The Frightfulperson was staring at him aghast. He was unaware that her wrist was now whitely bloodless. She uttered an oath in the name of the greatest psycho-historian who had ever lived, twisted her wrist free, and stepped backward into the café. When he went after her she had vanished up the stairs into an upper level. Which way? He sniffed his wrenched hand—cinnamon with a touch of persimmon—a perfume he would never forget. Why should a pleasant woman, who had seemed to want to make his acquaintance, suddenly become so afraid?

Impulsively he guessed at her direction of flight and began a pursuit. He had one chance in a trillion of ever finding her again. Various crisscrosses and eight levels later he gave up trying, blocked by one of the massive earthquake absorbers. By then he was lost.

He tried to take a shortcut around the absorber and found himself in a service district which he recognized by its water tanks, a tiny internal ocean that certainly continued downward to rest on bedrock. Pumps throbbed, too big to be serving a residential sector, probably feeding a meteorological tower far above them, misting water into the atmosphere to deflect some detected deviation from the long-term dictates of the Splendid Weather Authority. Maybe the roofs were in need of rain.

No use going farther. Defeated, he entered the address of his hotel into his map-device, having learned enough of its commands to allow it to guide him home.

Her blank card was still in his pocket, the only link to his depublished dissertation.

So, he thought while following directions absently, somebody had read his paper; he wondered what psychohistorical consequences that would have. Perhaps it would cause a deviation in the historical "weather," alerting some psychological bureaucrat who would then trigger corrective input. Somewhere a "tower" would pump a a critical "influence" into the "weather" of humanity and "the historical climate" would return to what the Fellowship's "Almanac" had already "predicted" it was going to be.

He still had to find Rigone.

# FLYING SCHOLARIUM, 14,798 GE

*The sudden appearance of hominid sapiens struck the thriving Rithian biosphere with the impact of a major asteroid.*

—Hahukum Konn

The afternoon when he was out in the village buying vegetables and passion fruit for one of Magda's treats, Eron ran into a group of young desert ruffians who good-naturedly followed him around pestering him for largess, as Rithians were wont to do. He asked them about the stars. They knew less than the original Neolithic settlers of the region—not even names. The nameless stars were the abode of strange fortune-tellers and golden streets. He was appalled. He bought them all ice cream and told them tales about ancestral exploits while the ice cream lasted. They poohed the parts about surveying the Nile without magical quantum instruments. The pendulum he made for them was used as a sling to whack each other. They hooted and shouted. One of the boys, with ice cream on his chin, suggested with a deadpan twinkle that the ancients could also fly by flapping their ears. How about magic carpets with a nav-sys woven in, suggested another with a grin that lasted until a playful punch brought him back to ground and set off a round of tussling aimed at reestablishing the solidity of their village world. Eron sighed and haggled over the vegetables for Magda. His mind drifted until he could almost hear her playing the violin.

On the way back he took a detour. The Flying Fortress was now sitting out on its field, the majestic mother of every galactic strike battleship. Its aluminum skin shone in the setting rays of Sol. Konn had not been able to convince any of his engineers to fly with him, so he had hired a Rithian crew, much to Eron's horror. Konn reasoned that sapiens minds had built and flown the first ones, and so were quite capable of doing so again. Eron was sure that such reasoning was a dangerous seventy-four millennia out of date—monkeys were all right, but to trust one's life to the wits of a chimpanzee's brother in a brainless aeroantique? Nevertheless he had been co-opted as copilot and wasn't going to be able to escape. Thank Fortune that some of the monkeys Konn had corraled were more equal than other monkeys. He stared at the Fortress for a long time, just to reassure himself that there were no flaws in the hydrodynamics of her lines.

"You're going to fly that thing all over Rith?" Eron had once asked Konn when he hadn't yet wholly accepted the idea.

"Sure. Do you think I should try flying her on Mars?" Konn's sarcasm was jovial.

Eron's troubles with the Admiral's engineers lasted until the final days before the Queen was rated as airworthy. They wanted to put two small antigravity units in the wings—just in case. The answer was no. Eron worked off his nervousness by spending time in the flight simulator mocking up dangerous events which would need a pilot's attention. Magda, who was joining the air crew as cook, took the secondary job as ball-turret gunner in charge of the brainless inertial weaponry which protected their belly. She carefully kept count of all the simulated attackers she managed to shoot to pieces during training. Her two half-inch-caliber machine guns were just another kind of violin to be played with skill. The battleship carried its complete ordnance of defensive weapons except that the two machine guns in the chin turret had been replaced with two efficient rocket engines to aid an emergency landing on a short field.

Eron managed to be in hiding for the maiden flight of the Queen. But Konn took her up for a very gentle level flight, with all testing monitors active, and immediately brought her down for a landing—on wheels at high speed! He was beaming. It was the very first of his antique battle wagons that he'd been able to fly himself. Eron was put in charge of the minor tuning modifications that the tests indicated and Konn insured his active interest in that job by scheduling him as copilot for the second flight. The main change that Eron authorized was a rebuilding of the engines by specs that would double their life span and allow the Queen to fly as fast as fifty meters per jiff in a (short-term) emergency. Perhaps there was a little cheating in the alloys, but . . . they didn't really know what the original alloys had been.

Since they wouldn't be carrying bombs, the bomb bay opened up to an efficient maintenance workshop—a compact manufacturum for making spare parts on demand with templates for every component. The maintenance work itself was to be done by the Rithian crew. Because gasoline was no longer a standard commodity, the bomb bay also included a synthesizer which could reload the fuel tanks of the Queen within the hour if fed hydrogen and carbon compounds.

The Admiral wasn't always consistent in his demand for authenticity or able to impose it. The built-in instrumentation was primitive if adequate: a crude pressure-sensitive altimeter, an inaccurate airspeed indicator, basic tachometer, and the like, even a sextant for navigation, but the ancient autopilot was both obsolete and illegal. The law frowned on human pilots and required a robopilot to authorize, and report, any human at the controls so that the Rithian Air Command could take special precautions. A robopilot never authorized human instrument flying and religiously reported any deviations from the filed flight plan. Konn himself didn't feel comfortable with the token altimeter and had installed a zoomable ranging screen that gave him a contour map, in blues and greens of the land below him and in reds of the land above his horizontal plane. Self-repairing Rossum's #26, whose navigational instrumentation was top of the line, gifted Admiral Konn with a pocket navigator of its own manufacture that kept track of position within ten meters and could locate the fourteen million historical sites whose surface and chronological coordinates it had been able to scrounge from searchable databases in its spare time.

Second Rank Hahukum Konn was the most senior psychohistorian who had ever visited Rith during the whole of the Second Empire, and he was treated royally. In planning his Rithian odyssey he had only to ask—and send a small delegation—and a mesh aerodrome long enough to accommodate the Flying Fortress was laid out along his route. The battleship had been designed as a short-range weapon requiring refueling after three thousand kilometers of flight, and so Konn's round-the-world itinerary required careful planning—in spite of its land being mostly deserts of sand and ice, Rith had vast watery expanses to fly over.

Inside, the vehicle had the original spartan look of a ribbed tunnel held together by its skin, except for the area directly behind the bomb bay. There Konn had relented and installed an efficient bachelor kitchen for Magda and, for himself, a compact office around a beautiful hickory table on top of his field mnemonifier. Back on Splendid Wisdom Konn had more computing power at his disposal than had been available to the whole bureaucracy of the First Empire, but he liked to do all of his preliminary work on this toy, which, though limited, had enough capacity to have run the planning, logistics, and record keeping of every industrial nation extant during the war for which the Flying Fortress had been designed. Behind his table and chairs were the four bunks for the crew of ten.

After a few shake-down flights which reassured Eron of the sturdiness of their vessel they were ready for Konn's mad adventure. It was just one notch up from planning to *walk* around the damn planet. The petroleum engines beat their eardrums to a pulp, hour after hour, crawling along at thirty-five meters per jiff. You could go between stars faster! Eron was even required to wear one of those silly double-twelve clocks on his wrist, "bearskin" jumpsuit, fur hat, massive earphones, and an oxygen mask that would have suffocated a pig. The Admiral was having the time of his life.

But on their first long night flight he seemed to change into a more serious mood. They were flying at a modest altitude with an almost full moon shining on a fantasy world of clouds, the desert lost beneath them, when the Admiral left Eron at the controls and brought back a couple of silencer helmets with direct famlinks that could handle the thundering engines without requiring them to shout. That meant he wanted to talk.

"I was a big fan of the *Kenoran Sagas* when I was a boy," Konn began, sliding back into the pilot's seat. "Ever read them?"

"It's a big Galaxy," said Eron, meaning no.

"When we get back to Splendid Wisdom and you have some dreamtime, I'll give you a copy. Whoever wrote the *Sagas* was one of the greatest storytellers who ever lived, or maybe it's only the boy in me remembering. They were written long, long ago back in the sublight era by a Bitherian prose poet, before the Bitherians were conquered by Eta Cuminga's Regionate. When you are a kid wondering about the past your imagination almost won't stretch farther back than that, and when you get your hands on a story written by a man who was *there* it is a wild thrill."

There was a long silence while Konn slipped back into his own world. Eron said nothing, waiting.

"The *Kenoran Sagas of Bitheria* are all about adventures to the stars extended over generations, but what is utterly charming about them is the rich mythology of the past woven into the story. Each scene carries the tacit assumption that Bitheria has to be the home planet of mankind. We pop in and out of that pre–space flight eon. Every page is saturated with references to days of yore so distant that only hints are left of a mysterious beginning prior to the rise and fall of eldritch empires themselves already lost in an overgrown jungle. It never occurs to the enthralled reader that Bitheria of the Sirius Sector has become so old a world only because the author of the *Sagas* can no longer remember what really happened a mere ten thousand years past."

Konn almost had tears in his eyes. Eron was amazed when he stopped talking and made an excuse to go to the galley to dig out two of Magda's snacks, careful not to wake her though thundering engines did not seem to bother her sleep. Rhaver was also asleep under the bunk. He hated flying and solved his problem by staying asleep all the while they were in the air.

Back in the cockpit, Hahukum handed Eron a sandwich wrapped in flexible bread, having composed himself. They had to shout at each other because you can't eat and hide behind a soundproof bubble at the same time. "The hardest thing I had to do as a budding psychohistorian was to disabuse myself of that fabulous Bitherian history of man. Logic and evidence said it had to go, but emotions didn't want to let go and neither did my fam. Perhaps that's why I'm here. An ancient flying weapon that predated anything found on Bitheria! Nothing could have kept me away. And you?"

Eron laughed into the roar of the engines. "I don't think I thought about the origins of man. I was too busy fighting with my father. Perhaps I just took the simple-minded way out and assumed that the universe had popped into existence four thousand years ago. Mythology was mythology. Big deal. One homeworld was as good as another. It didn't matter. I don't think I ever noticed Rith until I ran into a crazy professor who was in love with alleged Rithian poetry."

"Reinstone, eh? He sent me all of your better doggerel. He thought highly of you."

Eron wasn't sure he had heard right through the engine growl. "He sent you my poetry?" He was horrified at Reinstone's presumption. "I deliberately didn't include my poetry in my application because I didn't write it!" he screamed.

"Oh, is that so?" The Admiral was being sarcastically amused. "I suppose you had a computer program write them for you to butter up the old advisor into working for you, like giving you good recommendations to the Lyceum."

Eron sputtered because it was true. "I polished them a little bit," he said in a voice that was taken away by the thunder.

Hahukum waited to reply until the sandwiches were eaten and they could replace their sound bubbles. "I have your poetry programs, too," he went on with a grin. "Special police download. I didn't bother to disillusion Reinstone about your perfidy. Interesting programs. They impressed me almost more than anything else you had done. You were simulating the tradition of culture after culture. At least forty-seven of them. Didn't Reinstone ever suspect?"

"Well, sometimes he thought a poem of mine was a substandard effort." Eron was chagrined and had to remind himself to look up from Konn's knees and out at the clouds and moon. "Then I'd revise my program. Reinstone kept trying to convince me to do original work, but I was more interested in the context and structure of other people's styles than in my own."

"Poetic styles change rapidly," commented Konn.

"Not always. Sometimes a poetic style stays stable for thousands of years. I was interested in the rate of change of style and correlating that with the nonpoetic history of the culture. My feeble attempt at psychohistory."

They were passing through a huge valley in the clouds that had caused the moon to set. "Which reminds me," said Konn. "I have a thesis topic for you. I've been saving it for a really good student. It will take you about five years or so to work it up."

Eron paused apprehensively. "How do you know I'll like the topic?"

"You will. You were fascinated by the fact that poetic forms can stay stable for thousands of years and still remain viable. I want you to explore stasis."

"Stasis?"

"You know: things that don't change." His thumb pointed at the floor of the Flying Fortress, but he meant the planet below them. "That shit hole down there. And don't you dare tell anyone in our crew that I said that."

"You want me to study Rith?"

"No, no. Stasis. The more things change, the more they stay the same. Rith is only the oldest example, a simple enough example for a young mathematician to teethe on."

Eron wasn't sure he knew what Konn meant by stasis. "Why aren't we changing it?" He meant the shit hole. And he was surprised to hear himself say "we."

Konn sighed. "The trouble with being able to predict the future is that you then have the power to change it. But in what direction? Aie, there's the rub. We could do to them what they did to the Neanderthals? What the Sea Raiders did to the original Americs? We could do to them what the First Empire did to the Helmarians? We could force gengineering on them to build in solutions that they can't arrive at by use of their brains? Any other suggestions?"

"You want me to study stasis. Would such knowledge help?"

"Let me define stasis for you." He took his napkin and drew a curve on it that went up. "This is a Rithian problem that they've lived with for a thousand centuries. Through all that vast expanse of time all of their cultures, without exception, wealthy or poor, have clung to the belief that population is self-regulatory. True. It is. And Rithians have become goats down there on their island keeping their population self-regulated by stripping the land so bare that only a handful of goats can survive at one time."

He slapped the back of his hand against his napkin graph. "Our Queen was built to kill off excess Girmani who were spilling out of their territory in search of more breeding space. In that century alone the population of Rith quadrupled—with the inevitable result that the rich got richer and the poor transmogrified into centers of cultural cancer.

"In the next century it was better—the average doubling rate went up to seventy years. At the localities where it stayed at a doubling rate of thirty to forty years, there was genocide and massacre and war and unpredictable die-offs. Half of all the mammal species went extinct, and the general extinction rate was higher than it had been for sixty million years. The average sapiens became poorer in the necessities than he had been in Neolithic times though agricultural and physical science were at their height. It became increasingly difficult for the rich to hire police and military protection.

"In the century after *that* reliable records are nonexistent. Things don't really come into focus again until the Renaissance, which produced the starships. By then we know that the Rithian population was down to less than a billion and living quite well off the released resources. But they hadn't learned their lesson. The population steadily increased at a faster rate than the recovery of the planet. The ensuing collapse was slower in coming than the first disaster and it wasn't as severe—the scenario you would expect to be played out on a depleted stage. By the time the Eta Cumingans arrived with their hyperdrive things had essentially stabilized at the present equilibrium point—the sapiens kill off nature faster than nature can regroup and a hostile nature kills them off faster than they can multiply. The whole of the hyperdrive expansion into the Galaxy passed them by. Stasis."

"Do you have a mini-Founder's Plan for Rith?"

"No. I've got bigger problems."

The Admiral didn't say what he meant by that.

Hahukum Konn continued to give Eron lessons in psychohistory by bits and pieces, airborne and on the ground, sometimes in the cockpit, sometimes with the mnemonifier when the robopilot was exercising its authority by taking over control during instrument flying conditions. Sometimes Eron thought Konn was chatting about history when he was really musing about psychohistory. Sometimes Eron thought he was getting a psychohistory lecture while all the time the Admiral was just debunking someone's cockeyed slant on history. The Admiral never gave a lecture in math without a philosophical preamble. It was soon evident to Eron that there were two major schools of psychohistory, Konn being in the minority.

They were holding course at twelve thousand meters, a red sun setting into clouds. Below them the sun had already set. Night lights illuminated the instrument panels. Because the noise of the four reciprocating engines was, as always, deafening, they were communicating through their direct fam links. "Hanis is primarily interested in the destination. He's charted it and the rest of us are coming along for the ride. He's a good planner. To make a crude analogy, Hanis knows how much petroleum is in the tanks and how far we can fly and where we will come down for refueling. His flight plan takes the weather into account and fills the locker with sandwiches. It's all predicted." He grinned. "Me, I don't really care where we're going as long as our wings don't fall off along the way. There are many good futures out there, and true, they don't just happen, somebody has to make decisions at the branching nodes—well, let Hanis do that. I'm the *maintenance* man. Will this old aeroweapon get us there without losing an engine or spraying hydraulic fluid all over our dead bodies? The tragedy is that too many Pscholars have an eye on the destination—they revere the Founder's destination mania—and not enough of them have an eye on the engines."

Konn could abruptly change the subject. "Have you ever heard of Haskeen weaving?"

"No. I don't know much psychohistory."

"I suppose that's not the sort of thing they teach at Asinia." Without further discussion he put the machine on robopilot and took Eron back to the mnemonifier and began to teach. He gave Eron the basic methodology of weaving and why Haskeen weaving was so powerful. It didn't make any sense to Eron until Konn put out puzzles and problems which Eron had to solve. There were few educational aids in the Fort; Eron had to prompt the mnemonifier and feel like a jackass every time he took the analysis down an absurd path. Konn was a contradictory mixture of extreme patience and impatience. If Eron was too slow, the Admiral frowned and dropped an obscure hint, then relapsed back into patience. But after a while he got itchy to be at the flight controls. They went forward again.

On the other side of the ocean, low on fuel, they had to negotiate an unpredicted storm before they could land. The air was dropping and buffeting them at will. The Admiral enjoyed that. Eron kept glancing at the robopilot, wondering what it considered to be a *dangerous* situation—but it only stayed aloof, its algorithms evidently unworried.

Their prolonged tour of Rith was fascinating to Eron, but they never stayed in one place long enough to allow him to assimilate what he was seeing. They visited the magnificent stumps of the Imperial city of Etalundia, which had been built by the Emperors of the Etalun Dynasty in the fifty-third Imperial century after the First Empire had taken over the guardianship of Rith. The city, as the chief center of Imperial power on Rith, had long survived the Etaluns but had gone into decline in late dynastic times and had been abandoned to the desert the same year as the founding of the Faraway colony. Only a square block of it was under excavation by a tiny crew of scholars whose graduate students were assembling a cultural history of the period. Beyond the ruins the snowcapped heads of eight Etalun Emperors still towered over the landscape, carved into the tallest mountain on Rith. Orr-of-Etalun had lost his regal nose and half of his fantastic headdress but his father and grandfather remained intact.

The oldest excavation they visited was at Racuna (named after a small colonial village inland of the site). For centuries now the Racuna ruins had been emerging from the sea, the tides first revealing glimpses of her past glory and then covering her up again. By now enough ice had accumulated at the poles to allow excavation in earnest. The formidable dikes once put in place to keep out the ocean were still in place though long past any functionality. It was a very exciting dig for the archaeologists. Here was a city which hadn't been burned or pillaged by soldiers, which hadn't gone through a long decline of misuse, disuse, and vandalism. It had been abandoned in haste, victim to a horrendous tropical storm which broke through the dikes, flooding and, in a single night, sealing away forever its treasures, a remarkable museum of rare twenty-third-century AD artifacts. The disaster had occurred at the height of the Great Die-off; resources and manpower to rebuild New Orleans were probably not available, and, as well, the dreaded sea, year by year, was still rising . . .

There was more, much more. Too much to pack into a single around-the-world trip. Eron would be thundering along in the cockpit of the Queen, at an altitude of total serenity, only to find himself in the next hour stooping through the labyrinthine palace caves of fifty thousand freeze-dried mummies where, for a thousand years after the last departure of the last starship, the last of the Christians would flock to achieve enlightenment through the decorative art of cave sculpting and, upon achieving enlightenment, would hang themselves and, choking in penance, leave for the starry heavens by astral projection.

They flew to the island off Urope in a pilgrimage along the northern route where thousands of Flying Fortresses had once flown from their oversize manufacturums, across ice floes and stormy seas to reach the aerodromes within striking distance of the ancient battlefields. Rossum's #26 tailed along behind, worried about them. When they reached land safely #26 took Eron on the long-promised trip to the London Mound. He had a special favor to ask of Eron; he gave him a holocam to record his adventures in the renovated London Underground, complete with graffiti and ads, a place of exotic mystery to a creature of the air.

Meanwhile Admiral Hahukum Konn was organizing a last farewell to Rith, a commemorative bombing run on Girmani. Of course, the expiration date on the Thousand-Year Reich was long up and the Aryan race had gone the way of its Neanderthal predecessors. But that didn't matter; history is to be celebrated lest we forget everything. Admiral Konn outfitted his crew with new Ultimate Sam's Amazing Air Fangs bluecoats complete with tricorns sporting the circular thirteen stars and appropriate saber sidearms. Twenty-three aerocars and one Flying Fortress formed up over the pastured countryside and slowly rose to altitude out at sea beyond the White Teeth along the Throat's coastline and headed inland. Their combat box was a bit ragged, but then their flight leader was only an amateur admiral. Target: the Bremmen Mound, near the small city of Kryskt.

Along the route no ghost Wulfs of the Luftwaffe appeared to attack them. A few aerial sightseers watched but kept their distance. The crew was in high humor, their morale hardly lagging hours later as they reached the objective. But no lead bomber triggered a high-altitude cascade of bombs in a death walk through the target. It was a milk run. Konn brought his gasoline-powered Fort down from altitude in a modest glide. From the bombardier's seat in the nose Eron could see to the horizon, auburn hills, trees clustered along the river, some farmhouses, a dirt road. As Konn buzzed the Bremen Mound a few crows rose into the air, squawking. Then it was follow the river up to Kryskt.

They mock-bombed the dastards of Kryskt back to the stone age by making six buzzing passes over the city. In turn the Karelians below, by prearrangement, pretended to be the same fierce Girmani tribes that had given so much trouble to the Romans. They sent up a brilliant display of gunpowder rockets. Mostly the Karelians stood on their rooftops in droves to watch the fireworks and to cheer on the antique aircraft, some entering into the spirit of the event by waving swastikas. It wasn't everyday that a Rithian got bombed by a mad Second Rank Psychohistorian from Splendid Wisdom. The pretend tribesmen, of course, saw and heard only one four-motored aluminum Fort with wings. On the other hand, Eron, inside the bare fuselage, was letting his imagination run away and conjuring a formation of a thousand Flying Battleships wheeling over the city in a slow requiem of death.

Kryskt was only a fraction of the size of the original Bremen and, when they landed, put on a small town's show of hospitality. There was an outdoor podium for speeches. Dark-haired little girls threw bouquets of flowers. The local dance-drama teacher, who was also the town's most dedicated historian, dressed up her ten male dancers in the black tights of SS supermen complete with stiff-necked collars carrying the yellow, five-pointed star of the Norse God David which, the teacher had determined, all citizens of the Third Reich were required to wear to proclaim their superiority. The SS supermen performed a traditional Karelian box dance for the crowd in which eight of them formed a box and two of them, never the same two, were tossed through the air in a marvelous display of acrobatics.

The party went on for three days with big outdoor feasts and visitors from as far as a hundred kilometers. Costumes were everywhere, little hitlers with thumbnail-size mustaches being the favorite. Thirteen-starred tricorns began to appear after the second day. Everybody wanted a walk through the flying battleship, and, obligingly, Konn replaced the maintenance center with real papier-mâché bombs and bomb rack. The half-inch-caliber machine guns were a favorite with the kids, although one kid kept coming back every day to be bombardier. Rossum's #26 did very well by himself telling tales of his desperate past life as a Wehrmacht armored car.

During the long trip back to the Nile, Eron tried to assimilate his entire Rithian experience. He had been silent for the whole flight but on the ground and in the silence of the stilled motors, he asked his pilot about something that had been mulling in his mind for a long time. Were the vows of secrecy made by every psycho-historian contributing to the stasis that worried Konn?

Konn only laughed. "Secrets? The myth has been exaggerated. How do you tell a secret to a sparrow? Find a sparrow who will understand my secrets, and I'll hire him. We can watch over our sparrows, and we can feed sparrows, and we can nurse sparrows who have fallen—but to share secrets with a sparrow?"

Eron might have objected to a role as keeper of sparrows from the hatching hour unto that sparrow's fall, but he was too much in awe of Hahukum Konn to say more. Later at base camp he was too busy. They were all leaving for Splendid Wisdom and he was going with them!

# CORPSE-29, 14,810 GE

*Little is known of the first dynasty that led to the rise of Imperial Splendid Wisdom other than Kambal's only book from which we date Galactic Era time. It was not a literate age. One hundred forty-eight centuries ago, under the coruscating sky of the teeming central star reaches, some 480 centuries after the Eta Cumingans led mankind's hyperdrive expansion from the Sirius Sector into the far galactic wildernesses, Kambal appeared from nowhere over Splendid Wisdom with enough strength to establish an isolated home base on what were then the unpopulated islands of the Calmer Sea.*

*Perhaps Kambal was a young hyperfleet commander displaced from his home system by a defeat in war, forcing an alliance of convenience upon the vulnerable colonists of Splendid Wisdom. So say the references by Joradan to Kambal's lost War Logs. In any event, Kambal never returned to combat. In deference to his new hosts, whom he needed as willing (rather than reluctant) allies, he gave up looting and took to stellar trading to supply his loyal armies.*

*Perhaps the soothing breezes of the Calmer Sea calmed Kambal's fire-bred heart. During his long life he lost the desire to conquer. Old age brought him to a more serene philosophy, which has come down to us as his Oracles of Patience. In that ancient time of strife—in a Galaxy of myriad competing empires, all more powerful than Splendid Wisdom—who could have predicted that over the next ten millennia Kambal's seed would gradually assimilate all rivals into a First Empire of thirty million stars that stretched to the galactic periphery? Or that Kambal's spirit would have been able to hold such an immense organism together for another full two thousand years through the sheer power of a patient and tempered bureaucracy brought up on the Oracles?*

*Before the Fall, the Founder of Psychohistory had quoted Kambal's Ninth Oracle, Verse Seventeen, as the major inspiration of his youth: "It is minimum force, applied at a chosen moment in the arena of historical focus that paves the*

*path to a distant vision. Abandon all immediate goals that do not serve your fur-
thest purpose."*

—Solomoni's Dynastic Histories, *5645th Edition, 14,809 GE*

When Nejirt Kambu arrived at the Palace of the Police of the Lyceum Prefecture, the entrance chute to the waiting room shimmered, expanded, and he dropped gently through the damping-field. As he reached bottom there was no visible floor, only marine plants swaying below his feet. Brightly colored holographic fish circled the room curiously. It was disconcerting. Splendid bureaucrats were known to be eccentric, but some were certainly more eccentric than others. While he was mak-ing sure that he really wasn't underwater, a sleek robofish image with luminous scales received him gracefully and led him to a side grotto with delicate tail swishes. "It won't be long," the image burbled, leaving him to wait.

Waiting never appealed to Nejirt, however long, and since he had the clear-ance, he downloaded the report on the dead man into his fam for review while he paced. The Case of the Police Killing. That did not please him. It was an exercise in farce to chase a petty con artist as if he were the Galaxy's top criminal, corner him after twenty-eight watches of comedy, then by accident execute him in a clumsy pratfall. Splendid Wisdom should be a sacred example of dignity and order to the rest of the Galaxy. Konn had taught Nejirt perfection.

He didn't have time for more than a cursory review before a uniformed re-ceptionist (human) arrived to guide him around office mazes, thankfully free of the fish fetish, and down through forcefield-guarded bulkheads into a long lighted hall that led to the morgue dissectium. The headless man, identified as Corpse-29, lay like wax in a cylindrical stasis analyzer, ignored by the staff. Prefect Cal Barna was deferentially pleased to see Nejirt.

"Good of you to come so quickly, sir."

Nejirt was not ready for easy camaraderie. "What have we got here, a headless corpse? The head was damaged?"

Barna bowed slightly in respect, his lace collar flopping too quickly. "Sir. It was necessary for us to dissect the head. We've been modeling the brain. While you were flying in we got a full simulation running."

Nejirt smiled wryly with the wisdom of a mathematician who knows more than can be communicated to common people. He had a natural grasp of neural systems because much of the math overlapped the mathematical methodology of psychohistory. Simulation of a dead man's brain was a technological triumph—but it wouldn't do them much good.

"Have you learned anything?" asked Nejirt, already knowing the answer.

Prefect Cal Barna shrugged. "Not to be expected. But we have deduced many of Scogil's motor skills. We know how he walks and"—the Prefect's eyes twinkled—"we know the accent with which he spoke standard galactic." They had the resonant cavities of Scogil's skull. Talking was a motor-driven skill, and basic motor skills tended to survive quantum-state reconstruction. "Unfortunately he doesn't talk sense." Barna gestured and a holographic Corpse-29 began to speak a standard text. It was worse than bad acting. "Do you recognize the accent?"

"Turn off the visual. It gives him all the appeal of a zombie trying too hard."

"Of course, sir." A disembodied voice repeated the message with the same inflections. "How's the accent?" implored Barna again.

"You mean, does it sound like someone from Coron's Wisp?"

"Yeah."

"It might and it might not. The Coronese are very idiomatic." He could also be from Coron's Wisp and *not* be Coronese. With resignation, Nejirt decided to humor this idiot. "Have you picked up any other motor skills?"

Prefect Barna laughed. "We thought we had something, but it turned out to be his ability to screw tops on bottles. The only unusual thing we've identified is his ability to balance a moving bicycle."

"Bicycle?"

"A bicycle is a two-wheeled gyroscopic device. It might be useful for high-speeding down corridors and bouncing off pedestrians."

"Wire frame? Wheels in-line? High seat? Muscle powered?"

"Yeah," said Cal.

"On the planets of Coron's Wisp they are called whizzies. Never saw one in my life before my last adventure. On Timdo they are almost ubiquitous. I was told they became popular during the Fall when power was short. There are whizzy trails in the forests and around mountains and all through the metropolises. Good for the body, they say, but I found them exasperating. I think decadence is now setting it; ten percent of the whizzies I saw were powered."

"Ummm. We've determined that Corpse-29 had at least twenty years of experience on them." He paused. "So this could really be a link to Coron's Wisp?"

"Timdo, most likely. Doesn't he have a name?"

"The name would tell you nothing. False identity. Professionally done. When an identity is that well hidden, criminality is always involved. We may yet be able to trace him."

Cal stripped off his lace collar, showing a hairy chest above his low neckline, and mopped his brow, then tossed his lace beside the corpse. "Timdo, eh?" he said with satisfaction. "Follow me. Second Rank Hahukum Konn wants me to show you something." He summoned a subordinate to bring him the evidence.

Together they found an unused conference room with stuffed autopsies on the walls. The Prefect removed, from the carved ivory case he had been handed, a jade-pale ovoid with indented five-finger press points. Nejirt gasped. Such objects were legendary on the Wisp's Timdo and common enough elsewhere in the Wisp Pentad. He had believed not a word surrounding this superstition—until the moment when such an ovoid cast its magic in the air of an old woman's hovel—predicting nonsense, of course, but doing it beautifully. The hag whispered to him that he would live long enough to witness the Second Fall . . . and like all women of her breed, had refused to tell him how long that would be.

"From your expression I take it you recognize the object?"

"They are used on Timdo—but often hidden from strangers. I saw only one."

"One!" exclaimed Barna. "Corpse-29 has been on Splendid Wisdom for months now selling *thousands* of these things to astrology buffs. They seem to be transshipped from Coron's Wisp."

"You're sure your corpse wasn't churning them out in his hotel room from some template he picked up in the Wisp?"

The Prefect was affronted that anyone would think the police so inept as to make such a mistake. He was a religious follower of Kambal's Oracles of Patience, a common trait of conscientious bureaucrats that had hardly been touched by either Interregnum or Sack. "This isn't jade, sir." Jade was an object that could be manufactured in any household. "These ovoids are imported. A manufacturum hasn't the resolution needed for replication. We've put a few through the lab and we cannot fabricate a template of a functional ovoid with our best copiers. Same problem we seem to have with Corpse-29's brain."

The policeman continued, bemused. "This ovoid we acquired during a recent raid authorized by Second Rank Konn. Beautiful, isn't it? How in Space do they work? We've been reduced to tapping random code into the press points and intimidating ourselves when magic happens. We lack a fundamental picture of the device's function or an operating manual. Konn tells me you've picked up some queer stuff about astrologers on your recent jaunt."

Nejirt raised the ovoid, carefully fitting his fingers and thumb to the indentations. He meditated for a moment until his fam remembered the finger-code sequences that he had memorized by watching his Timdo charlatan. Darkness blossomed until even the face of Prefect Barna faded. Then—bedazzling stars. It was quite a piece of fakery, the best handheld galactarium Nejirt had ever witnessed. This version had been preadjusted to view the stars from the coordinates of Imperialis but that could be changed to any point in the Galaxy with deft finger pressure. He wasn't sure he knew enough to do that—but he could try.

With amusement Psychohistorian Nejirt Kambu asked the ritual questions and from Cal Barna's answers adjusted the sky to produce the Prefect's chart. "Birth" stars appeared in blue, "danger" stars smoldered red, "decision" stars flared yellow, and "wildcard" stars turned green. All nonsense. Then an awesome program began to paint Barna's personal constellations across this brilliant sky: a hero robot who guided man's destiny; a gaggle of violated virgins, chain-ganged together in the sky to do penance for a guilty Emperor now suffering regrets about his lust; a sparkling stream of life to nourish all the fishes of the Galaxy; a fate-worse-than-death; a mooning joker; the knife that separates good from evil; a mon-

DONALD KINGSBURY

392

ster of the galactic deeps. Barna's birth constellation turned out to be the Stone Well. His fate was easy to determine—providing one knew whether the Stone Well was draining or replenishing, a true astrologer's touch. The constellations faded.

"Why did your people kill this man?" he asked when he was done with the clumsy reading and had returned the ovoid to its elaborate ivory box.

"We *intended* to take him alive."

"Of course. Why did you kill him?"

Barna glanced over at the body ruefully. "We had, and have, a certain Hyperlord Kikaju Jama under surveillance for subversion. Back-traced from the raid which produced the ovoid. Psychohistorian Konn, as you know, has his reasons to be suspicious of antisocial activity in Coron's Wisp and has been tracing commercial contacts while you were off doing the fieldwork. This Jama seems to advocate the antisocial purloining of state secrets and the methodical dismantling of the Empire. He even blasphemes the Founder by advocating the establishment of a thirty-thousand-year interregnum."

Psychohistorian Nejirt Kambu smiled. "A common curse but hardly a crime."

The Prefect huffed. "Sir, it *is* a crime if he is taking measures to put his theories into effect. If he is planting nuclear bombs to vaporize the Lyceum, that *is* indeed my business. We have every intention of cleaning out the Hyperlord's group and in all probability would have done so already had the deceased not tripped our wires."

"Go on. And the killing?"

"We determined that Hyperlord Jama has been purchasing his Wisp devices from Corpse-29. Since the Hyperlord's motives are suspect, his supplier becomes suspect. That is how our investigation turned from the Hyperlord to the deceased. Konn"—he nodded deferentially—"ordered the raid on Corpse-29's base of operations and the arrest of the deceased. Much to our surprise, we found ourselves chasing him for a full twenty-eight watches. He played the shell game, and blast him, every time we'd pounce on a shell, he'd be under the other one. Twenty-eight watches! Eventually we cornered the rat but by then we were conditioned to expect him to escape . . . so we got, shall we say, overenthusiastic, to use a lame euphemism. He did escape, too, wounded. And we didn't get what we wanted. Shame! We were after his fam. And his dead body wasn't wearing one! Space, what a shock that was! We'd been conned! We couldn't imagine a man evading us for so long without the use of his fam! Galaxy knows where it is now. We've lost it."

"Explain something to me," said Nejirt. "Why am *I* here?"

"Second Rank Hahukum Konn suggested that you would be invaluable in the analysis of events."

"I'm not at all convinced that a minor ring of astrologers and charlatans is my business—unless I'm being demoted. Why am I here to view this astrologer's corpse?"

"Astrologer? Didn't Konn tell you? He suspects that Corpse-29 was a psycho-historian—and an able one. We have to get our hands on his fam as an important part of the evidence."

*What?*

Nejirt walked over to the body inside its cylinder of instruments. His mind was racing in astonishment. All the data at Coron's Wisp suddenly made sense. A rebel psychohistorian. Old and well-worn theorems of the Founder rose to the conscious awareness of his fam as their unassailable assumptions were being checked out in panic. It was impossible! This couldn't . . .

He stopped.

He remembered what he had been thinking while Barna was explaining to him the hastily constructed quantum-state simulation of Scogil's mind. About topo-zones, about the similarity between the mathematics of neural systems and the mathematics of psychohistory. Topozones were the boundaries between stability and chaos, laminar flow and turbulence. An escalating social crisis was explained with exactly the same mathematics as the panic and uncertainty and disbelief he was now feeling.

Ceaselessly the state-activity of an organic net flips back and forth across the boundaries twixt stability and chaos in the mind's war between what it knows and what it needs to learn—this outpost ridge temporarily chaotic, that beachhead sta-ble for the moment, the front flowing in battle flux across the net, victory convert-ing the unknown into the known, defeat dissolving what was once known into contradictory, indefensible fragments, the changing synaptic strengths moving and transforming the topozone boundaries all across a fluid battlefield where stimulus attacks and response defends.

The battle never ends. Victory for one side is the only danger. If a brain lives only in the known, it begins to suffer rigor mortis on the stable side of the topo-zones; if it lives only in the unknown, it becomes insane on the chaotic side of the topozones. The eternal war between good order and evil chaos.

Chaos and panic in his mind. It was a challenge. Were there really other psycho-historians out there?

# THE MASTER OF MEASURES,
# 14,799–14,805 GE

*In Hebrew and Greek myths, based on Mesopotamian and Egyptian traditions, the master of measures lives in danger: for is it not true that he who can ken the numbers by which the universe is built has, in so doing, attained the power to build in competition with the Gods? He must take care to honor the Gods lest he earn Their envy and bring down Their wrath. Thus the master of measures dares not share his wisdom with any untutored layman who may, in his ignorance, use unsanctified numbers to provoke the Heavens.*

*The builders say: "Come, let us build ourselves a city and a tower with its top in heaven; let us make a name for ourselves lest we be scattered all over the earth," and the Lord observes: "This is only the beginning of what they will do: and now nothing will be restrained from them which they have imagined to do. Therefore let us go down . . ."*

*A clay tablet meant only for the eyes of a master of measures was found in the rubble of Babylon containing:*

*(1) the perfect dimensions of the ziggurat Etemenanki, a foundation Kigal set in the earth to hold up the sky,*
*(2) instructions for the rebuilding of Etemenanki if that should ever be necessary,*
*(3) a plea that Etemenanki should be rebuilt to the proportions specified,*
*(4) a dire warning of the dangers risked if these numerical specifications were revealed to the uninitiated.*

*After a thousand years of building, of being overrun by barbarians of a strange tongue under the instigation of a jealous heaven, of unrepentant rebuilding, of abandonment, of renewal, of sack by Sennacherib and revival by Chaldeans, Etemenanki was completed by Nebuchadrezzar II to the seventh*

story and "by the correct cane of 12 cubits" exactly as its original architects had
specified. Alexander the Great, as master of measures for his newly conquered
world, chose to improve upon the original plans and was promptly struck down
by the Gods in the palace complex next to Etemenanki. Nothing of the ziggurat
remains. The cuneiform measurements and warning, baked eternally into clay,
were taken to the stars by the Eta Cumingan general Esasa Tobenga where they
were lost after Tobenga's untimely death. Somewhere out there a tablet lurks to
tempt an uninitiated master of measures into defying the Gods.

—From *The Secret Book of the Wisdom of the Ages*

On the return to Splendid Wisdom with the Admiral's entourage, Eron Osa found
himself haunting the view room of their chartered luxury liner, already seated like
an eager novice whenever the plasteel shutter-lids were rolled back to give the passengers a local view of the Galaxy while navigation prepared for the next jump. He
wasn't really interested in starscape, but he wanted to catch that first eyeball
glimpse of Imperialis. He had absorbed so many stories about this preposterous solar system that he was eager to see the real thing.

But nothing in Eron's life had prepared him for Splendid Wisdom. Once they
passed from the arms into the central cluster, the blaze hid Imperialis until the final
jump inward to rendezvous with their tugboat. There the twinkle-storming eddies
of stars surrounding the most important sun in the Galaxy was enough to impress
anyone, but it was only background for a sky full of ships in parking orbit. Their
transport had to be escorted to its place in the docking station to keep them from
bumping into the other ships!

Inside that giant receiving station it was obvious that Konn was getting special
treatment and was so used to it that he didn't notice. Magda clung to her savior's
arm, frightened more than awed. They were whisked through medical and orientation and baggage by a special team, a government gravdrop shuttle already waiting to take them down. Eron was no longer surprised that the Admiral had not
brought his Flying Fortress with him, content to rebuild it from templates at his
leisure.

During the station-to-surface transfer, Nejirt noticed Eron's interest. "You can
have my seat." But the tiny porthole wasn't much help. The body of the planet was
obscured by the ship except for brief maneuvers where it banked or turned up its
nose to brake against the atmosphere. Eron had his best, but brief, glimpse of the
"roof" of Splendid Wisdom as they taxied across it to the shuttle elevator—as barren an expanse as any desert on Rith, cluttered with parked and incoming shuttles.

In the distance there were hemispherical mounds of different sizes, even lou-
vered ziggurats (ventilators? skylights? radiators?), but mostly just runoff gullies to
take the rain and snow. The surface not in use as runway or maintenance road was
covered with a weird adaptive skin that could change its reflective and radiative

and electrical properties on command, so that some of it was silvery and some black and the sections that were collecting electricity a weird opalescent. He counted five weather stalks, some of them slender towers tall enough to hold up the sky. Imagine a planet of people so obsessed with power and its control of nature that they could issue weather reports covering the year in advance because they knew the critical leverage points by which the atmosphere could be manipulated to make their predictions come true! As he sat, enthralled, their shuttle was swallowed up and elevated down into the bowels of the planet . . .

. . . where they emerged into the valley of a debarkation terminal. Its dome was almost lost in the heights. Underneath was a clear "day" but Eron could imagine clouds forming up there—and rain. Robotaxis flitted in and out of the walls, swooping down to snatch up travelers who were carried off to cliff aeries. Swarms of people emerged from and descended into the elevator kiosks. He was lost already, mainly because he was following Konn's group and not finding his own way. Eventually the group broke up to seek their separate kiosks and Eron found himself with Konn and Magda and Rhaver, who was very patient even if he was not enjoying himself. "WeGoHome," he grumbled, trotting at Konn's feet.

They took a pod for four, luxuriously upholstered, which had been waiting for them by appointment. Silence was part of its luxury—it did not need to be instructed as to their destination. Konn lived in a palace above the Lyceum with its own pod-siding and ample guest rooms. Eron was invited to stay until he got oriented and found a place of his own. Then Konn disappeared, anxious to catch up on his work, leaving Magda in a panic because she was responsible for the meal Konn had planned for the third watch and had no idea how to go about buying vegetables. She was valiantly holding in her tears, her eyes darting, trying to make sense of what she saw.

Eron laughed to cheer her up. "Don't look at me—I'm from the boondocks, too. We'll find a way. But I've heard horrible rumors that on Splendid Wisdom they don't grow vegetables—they manufacture them."

For a moment Magda was stricken by this new burden, but she caught Eron's good cheer and smiled mischievously, releasing her tears in a flood over her cheeks at the same time. "We can steal pears from the Emperor's garden." There were no more Emperors, but the Emperor's garden had been lovingly re-created as a people's park. The pears grew on a hidden hillock surrounded by golden shimmer-wisps clambering out of the rocks. Magda of the desert had seen a picture when she was six years old. After famfeeding the local maps, their expedition through the neighborhood of the Lyceum was a quest that produced small adventures but no source of legumes. That didn't matter—Konn's telesphere, when they finally asked, knew how to make the vegetables appear. It searched for only a moment before recommending the fresh asparagus.

Later Hahukum arrived home, haggard, but with a present for Magda, a few jars of precious dandelion jelly. At dinner he opened up a bottle of wine to drown his sorrows. "I'd forgotten all about politics. It never ends. Now, if we still had our Flying Fortress, we could go for a bombing run by the light of Aridia. I know just the target. But, alas, that cannot be. I know why I like dogs." Rhaver thumped his tail under the table. "Ah, Eron. It's not enough to know psychohistory. You are going to have to learn politics, too."

"I've seen the very fascinating equations for that!" Eron spoke with enthusiasm.

"No you haven't. You forget the Founder's prime theorem. You cannot predict the moves of an opponent who knows how to predict yours. How to deal with the politics inside the Fellowship is more than you'll ever want to know. It's a separate field of study!"

"Jars Hanis?" volunteered Eron, remembering Konn's hints and discussions with Nejirt.

"You have a good nose, young man."

"RhaverHasBetterNose," muttered Rhaver from under the table where he was waiting for something that smelled tastier than vegetables.

Magda brought in the creamed asparagus and Konn brightened enough to change the subject from politics to hedonism, leaving Eron curious and a little frustrated.

He was given a graduate student's residence: three rooms, plus an ample office with a wall of quantronic storage space. The ventilation was adequate—Splendid Wisdom made one think about such details. The appurtenancer worked. Otherwise the apartment was bare. Suddenly he acquired his mother's predilection in furnishings, his wild teenage taste forgotten. The first thing he added was a view. After much deliberation he had one of the walls display a quiet corner of the Imperial Gardens. He adjusted the light to suit the real plants he was going to display along the wall. Where he would get them was a problem. He would ask Konn's telesphere.

But before he could do more the apartment announced a guest, a well-dressed man with lace cuffs and a small pin for his high-flowing collar that identified him as a member of the Fellowship. He was from the Fellowship's welcoming committee. Fortunately he knew how to call up chairs out of a floor which didn't seem to respond to the commands Eron was familiar with. The chairs blossomed. It had never occurred to Eron that floors spoke different languages in different parts of the Galaxy.

"This is a student's apartment," his guest explained, "a nice one, your sponsor is doing well by you—but the better apartments are multilingual." Once they were seated in the bare room this very direct young man got to the point, and it wasn't hospitality. "Should you wish it, I can offer you two more rooms and a better-equipped den. What is your present salary? No, don't tell me. That's confidential." He made a "guess," which was correct to the last credit, meaning he was connected to efficient spies. "I can double that."

Suddenly Eron became very much the Ganderian. He wasn't armed, having given up that habit, but he could almost feel his kick in its holster, and it felt as if he were negotiating, politely, with another armed man. "I'm not on salary. I'm on a scholarship."

"No hurry. The offer will always be open. We have a very interesting program and we welcome talent such as yours."

It was an opening—and Eron coaxed out of his welcoming committee a description of the work he would be asked to do. The name of Hanis was not mentioned, but the program was his, and it was a grandiose plan for the next millennium. The Founder himself would have been awed.

Eron teased. "But the next millennium is two centuries away."

"It takes time—and talent—to lay the foundations for such a renaissance." He went further into his pitch, and Eron listened intently, but the program was all come-on, and whatever substance it had was for the initiated to know and the newcomer to find out by making a commitment.

"I'll consider your offer. Let me get settled first." The rules of politeness suggest that it is impolitic to outrightly refuse an armed man.

At dinner that night, Eron mentioned the offer to Konn, who gazed at him with dark disapproval. "Maybe we could find you a sponsor who would give you *seven* rooms and a harem," he said sarcastically.

"I remember flying copilot with you and shitting profusely in my pants. More than once I thought about bailing out. But, you'll recall, I never did."

"Youthful cowardice," grumbled Konn. Magda was staring at them, horrified that they might be getting into a fight.

"Not really. It was a calculated cost-benefit analysis. The pilot I knew versus the promise of a barely possible El Dorado down there beneath the clouds, which I suspected was buried under a parched desert anyway."

"Were you flattered to have received such a fine offer so early in your career?"

"No." Eron made a wry face. "They aren't interested in me at all. They are interested in crippling you."

"Ah, you already have a glimmering of the politics."

"It's my Ganderian senses. But I don't understand why they would want to keep you understaffed."

"It's a difference of opinion. Hanis and I both agree that it's a sunny day in the Galaxy but I want to lie on the beach and drink wine and he, well, he insists we all go swimming. I think it is a bad idea for him to take the children out into the bay where the long-toothed shipsnarks live and he is horrified to see me lazing on the beach with the children and acquiring a third-degree burn in the sun while we enjoy ourselves. And I'm right and he's wrong."

"Of course. But can you prove it?"

"Of *course* not! That's your job. I've already given you your thesis project."

"I see. Stasis has something to do with all this?"

"That's the endless sunny day. Hanis has seen it. So have I. We're not alone.

Among all the upper-echelon psychohistorians there is a general agreement on the potential for problems inherent in sunny days. But we don't know what to make of the danger signals that the equations are suggesting. By all measures the Galaxy is more prosperous right now than it ever was at any period in the First Empire's history. We appeared at the end of a thousand years of the Interregnum, at a time when the whole of the Galaxy was tired, tired, tired of chaos. We planned it that way. And we were the ones with the tools to reestablish order. So the peoples of the Galaxy followed us en masse. Again, as we planned. The desire and the tools were present simultaneously. But that was long ago. Today we have a more subtle mood. And we don't have the tools."

"Stasis?"

"That's not even the right word. The situation has to be described in mathematical terms, and we haven't got a word for it yet so 'stasis' has to do. It will take you a couple of years of study before you are able to read phenomena at that level of complexity. Maybe you'll come up with a catchy name. But the situation is clear. Which future to choose to forestall all dangers is not. The Founder's genius wasn't in noticing that the galactic order was falling apart, that was the easy part, obvious even—his genius was in seeing Faraway among all the possible futures as a fulcrum to address the problem."

"And right now there are too many choices?"

"There are always too many choices. That doesn't stop us from picking a future we both approve and have the tools to make real. But that takes wisdom. I'm disliked because I advocate wisdom, which is hard to quantify. I'm accused of being paranoid and stamping out phantom dangers that no one else can verify and at the same time of being too cautious to commit myself to a future before I've received divine revelation."

"So you're sending me off in a quest for wisdom?"

"Of course. But you're too young to notice it when you've found it. That's my job, and why I'm going to keep close tabs on you."

Eron laughed. Straight-faced Hahukum was always pulling his leg, and he was always falling into the trap. It was time for pear pie—this one, Magda's joke.

When it came to signing up for courses, Eron was given no choice at all. Konn was a strict disciplinarian who knew what he wanted Eron to know. He assured Eron that he would have all the time in the world for dilly-dallying around—when he got to be an old man.

It was a grueling schedule.

But Eron Osa had always been a very private person. As a child, curious as all youth is about the lives that adults lead, he didn't take the direct route and ask his father; he spied on him and made an elaborate game of it that lasted for years. With Murek his game had been to read books that he deliberately never discussed with his tutor. With Reinstone he kept his poetry-making machine a secret.

His relationship with Konn easily took the same turn. He was content to pur-

DONALD KINGSBURY

400

sue, enthusiastically, his thesis topic on stasis from every angle that Konn proposed—but at the same time chose to follow his own wild agenda on the same topic down undisciplined pathways that he never wanted to share with Konn. It was fun to have a world that existed apart from the real world. Where he was never wrong and never right. Where he was a lonely god who had been smart enough not to populate his most delightful planet with creatures who looked like him and had free will.

Between studies he found a place that sold small housebroken trees. He could have ordered some from the holos, but he preferred to take the long trip of eight hundred kloms to make his own selection. When he reached the arboretum he lusted to buy the whole fairy forest but he could only afford three: a tall, perhaps Rithian, conifer that came up to his chin; a miniature Iral IV grabber with thousands of nine-fingered "hands," pale green, and a smell that blended with conifer like faint incense; and a flowering clown that generated a sequence of unique blossoms over a cycle of seven months because it had evolved to cater to the lifestyles of different waves of insects—its present elegant form perhaps enhanced by a touch of gengineering. The resident botanist gave explicit instructions about wall lumens and nourishment.

Eron had exceeded his frivolity budget on the trees so the rest of his plant life had to be coaxed from seed, fast-growing varieties to fill up the immediate blanks and slower varieties for a rich later texture. That meant pots, and he was glad to have bought an assortment of templates for significant Rithian ceramic pots while given the opportunity; it fit in with his new interest in Rithian history. Pots, of course, meant tables. He didn't have the whole Imperial Garden to play with, just the corner of a room. But tables meant more shopping; the apartment's taste in tables, though adequate, was not his mother's taste, and that's what he wanted. He was going to need a special little table to set off his decorative sapiens skull.

While his garden corner began to thrive over the rest of the year, his studies gradually determined the remaining furniture. After tiring of a simple flat work surface, he conjured up a big morphing desk that adjusted its size and cubbyholes to the size of the immediate project. When his life began to get complicated, he acquired a telesphere to keep his appointments and do his routine searches and take over the butler duties from his bland door. This was so much more fun than Asinia's Faraway stoicism. In only months of settling in his needs outgrew his apartment's functionality. Retiring the apartment's best effort, he bought himself a real morphing desk that could save its old configuration and contents if he needed to backtrack.

The spare room stayed empty for a long time but then there was that conference, assembling from Splendid Wisdom's sprawl of Lyceums a thousand students specializing in Observation Methodology. It was scheduled over a sixtyne of watches, and Eron foolishly contracted to put up ten students. The spare room quickly turned into a guest room, in his mother's taste, that could morph all kinds of beds when they were needed. He overbudgeted on fancy linen. Konn graciously gave him a loan.

Mostly when he wasn't working at Konn's side, he studied alone, intensely, leaving his telesphere to keep track of time and to order him around when duty called. But he was also a social creature. Sometimes he took Magda out on excursions; she refused to go alone. Konn approved and encouraged the relationship because he never stopped worrying about her well-being. Sometimes Konn was so busy that he co-opted Eron as an emergency dog walker, and that was a request that Eron couldn't refuse, no matter how busy or involved he was.

The private hunting maze was a preserve of the elite who could afford that kind of club. It brought Eron into contact with a class of people he had never met before though he had grown up with Agander's aristocracy. Rhaver was very careful about the dogs to whom he introduced Eron. While he was out cavorting with a silken-haired lady, Eron relaxed on a bench with the lady's master, the man in charge of the psychohistoric model of the Galaxy's Omneity of Planetary Relations. If Rhaver wanted him to meet a dog too old for cavorting, Rhaver promenaded with the old fellow while Eron worked up a chat with the wife of the finance minister of the Lyceum Prefecture. Rhaver sorted out politicians by GoodSmell. At the lodge where they might end up for refreshment, Rhaver would pick a table and lie under it and Eron would be forced to take a seat and make polite company with those who were the equivalent of the Old Empire's Lords. Konn's dog liked to bring home a pheasant or two for Magda because she fed him foods that the Master didn't allow, and she knew what sauces warmed a dog's heart.

"IsSecret," warned Rhaver.

Eron smiled. He had been doing work with secrets himself. His eccentric hobby—attempting to thread a psychohistorical link through eight hundred centuries of Rithian history—had led him into a nest of secret societies. Exploring their dynamics (in secret) had become a fruitful exercise. Recently he had been trying out multiple versions of the early history of Rome whose powerful pontifices and patricians had maintained their advantage over the plebeians by keeping secret the technical rules of legal procedure.

Only one of Eron's crafted models had proved viable enough to flower into a resemblance of the historical Empire. Its vitality seemed to hinge on a critical event that took place 449 years after the founding of the village on the Tiber. A certain Gnaeus Flavius learned the details of the mysterious procedures while serving as secretary to Appius Claudius Caecus, censor and later consul. He had the audacity to publish his findings, which became known as the *Jus Flavianum*. From this work the Roman people for the first time could learn the legis actiones, the verbal formulas required to maintain legal proceedings, and the dies fasti, the specified days on which proceedings could be instituted. His resulting popularity propelled him into public office as curule aedile over the protests of the patricians, who despised him because he had weakened their power and because he was lowborn, the son of a freedman.

It seemed peculiar to Eron that the Fellowship, so dependent upon secrecy for the survival of its power, had never done a systematic study of secrecy—being content to quote the Founder's theorem on the subject as dogma. A very touchy matter. Eron fully intended to conduct his research in secret until he better understood its dynamics.

"Yes, a secret," he said to Rhaver.

# POLITICS AS USUAL, 14,810 GE

*Isar Imakin: You have familiarized yourself with our efforts to rebalance the un-predicted perturbations in the Plan caused by the military adventures of Cloun-the-Stubborn?*

*Smythos: Berker's analysis, and the recent Cvas update, yes.*

*Imakin: Then you know the details of how the psychohistorical monitoring of the Plan has inadvertently been exposed to Faraway's eyes. Comment.*

*Smythos: (agitated) The exposure was unnecessary! We . . . (buzz) . . . had the . . . (unintelligible) . . .*

*Imakin: Please confine yourself to the situation as is.*

*Smythos: (recovering his composure) Well, the Cloun is dead and the Chancellors of Faraway seem to have remembered their lines after a little bit of prompting from the box. The Plan is already one third complete and apparently successful in spite of all the setbacks. So it's not surprising that Berker's elabo-rate summing confirms that the bounce-back has only reinforced the popular superstitious confidence in the Founder's Plan. The knowledge of monitors isn't even widespread and, where appreciated, has only reinforced belief in the Plan's inevitability. In particular the general populace will resist any effort to attack monitors of the Plan whether visible or invisible. Pissing on the gods has never been a popular pastime.*

*Imakin: And you have also worked through the Cvas Report?*

*Smythos: I didn't want to believe a word of it. The devil is in the details. But it's hard to argue back at the math. Cvas ran a tight committee—for sure he didn't let his people leave any holes to wiggle out of.*

*Imakin: If you haven't yourself found any flaws in the argument, confine your comments to the Cvas conclusions.*

*Smythos: Yes, sir. The Cvas group has collected data on the small minority of Faraway citizens who feel threatened by the existence of a monitoring over which they have no control. They don't see us as allies but as competition, to wit: Faraway sweats to dig the gold; we kibitz and in the endgame walk off with all the loot. This core group of doubters mixes a dangerous composition of attributes: (1) they belong to the old Faraway mentality that produced the Chancellery dictatorships—they don't care what the general population thinks; they see themselves as intellectuals and scientists duty bound to act by themselves in Faraway's interest on the basis of their superior knowledge; (2) they have access at least to five leverages to move the government; (3) they contain a critical mass of aligned opinion, therefore they will act; (4) action will bring this small group both power and riches.*

*Imakin: So how do you assess the mathematical consequences of allowing our exposure to persist?*

*Smythos: I have to concur with the main conclusion of the Cvas amendation. All the computed courses of action which I have personally checked indicate a rapid deterioration of the Plan because of internal conflict inside the Fellowship, either because: (1) the Overt Arm of the Fellowship, manifested by Faraway, finds and destroys its Covert Arm, manifested by us, or; (2) an open conflict arises between these two aspects of our Fellowship and destroys their current symbiosis. At the ninety-five percent confidence level, both of these alternate historical branches either lead to a Second Empire that repeats the cycle of the First, or to a return of the chaotic galactic conditions extant prior to the First Empire.*

*Imakin: How then may the original design be restored?*

*Smythos: Ah, the arguments I've been in lately! We have dozens of options, only one, I believe, with good probabilities attached. If all those who now resent the monitoring of their actions by Historical Science were led to believe that all mental meddlers with such power had been destroyed, the galactic situation would restabilize around the parameters of the original Plan, leaving only minor alternations in the probabilities of success. The window of opportunity is short. The apparent destruction of us SuperDangerous Mentalists must occur within twenty-five years . . .*

—from the transcript of the oral exam given by First Rank Isar
Imakin to student Tamic Smythos, the 18th of Flowers, 12,440 GE

Sometimes those involved in a crisis seek communion with a successful ancestor. A worried Hahukum Konn was listening to a sampling of recordings made by legendary First Rank Imakin during the endgame of the Crisis of the Great Perturbation, fourth-century Founder's Era—the kind of material seldom referenced even by scholars, but thought provoking. The buzzing soundtrack testified to a time only a century after the Sack when Splendid Wisdom was still in desperate shape and good equipment was not always available. In those dire days a psychohistorian's options were limited.

Chimes announcing a visitor gently interrupted Konn's melancholy meditation, then transformed into a voice which added softly, "Nejirt Kambu, by appointment."

Konn shut off the archive replay and went out to meet Nejirt in the corridor. "So we got you out of bed, did we! I see you had time to dress."

"What in Spacefire are we doing with a corpse? And what did that crazy Barna mean when he said you think our headless wonder was some kind of psychohistorian?" Kambu stood with feet apart, a little embarrassed that he had dressed so hurriedly in a formal black frock coat and unmatching silver striped zoot pants and was nowhere near a place where he could change.

The Admiral, in an unfashionable sky-purple jumpsuit of the sort that one might find on a naval mechanic, hardly noticed. "Have you had time for breakfast?"

"On a turned stomach? What's happening? Our sainted Rector Hanis is going to be after your ass with a vengeance. Does he know about the corpse? This is just the excuse he's been waiting for. And when you go down, we all go down."

Konn steered his disciple toward the commissary. "You've been away. Lots has happened. Hanis has seized the initiative, but I'm still one move ahead of him. And no, he doesn't know about our corpse yet. Calm down."

"Messiah!" grumbled Nejirt, using an expression he had picked up on Rith, but he accepted the croissant and mug of steaming lift which Konn handed him after pushing him down into a seat.

"Has anyone told you about Eron Osa yet?"

Nejirt gazed up at the Admiral. "I see you've waited until I was seated before delivering the worst news. What could be worse than a corpse?"

Konn's old eyes crinkled. "Where should I start?"

"Eron Osa, eh? That egotistical little ingrate. Has he been trying to get you into trouble with Hanis?"

"Worse. He got *himself* into trouble with Hanis, who is now poised to use Eron's gaffe to dispose of me because I was his sponsor."

"Ridiculous. Eron walked out on you five years ago."

"Major gaffes have an illuminating way of casting shadows."

"What did he do?"

"Self-published his mathematical dabblings."

"Big deal. The journals publish a lot of pimples on the Founder's Nose."

"You don't understand. Eron published in the *public* archives."

Nejirt choked on his croissant. "That's illegal," he said with awe.

Konn nodded negatively. "Not illegal. It's just never been done. One doesn't have to make the unthinkable an illegal act."

"Eron never struck me as suicidal. What did he publish? Is it still up?"

"Hanis had it deleted within the watch."

"Let me have a copy. I'm fascinated."

"I've never seen a copy. Hanis had it destroyed. Entropy happens."

Nejirt sipped on his drink. "So the little shit must be in prison. Would it be too dangerous for me to drop by and visit him? We could have a discreet chat—unobtrusive suppressors and all that. I'm curious."

"Eron can tell you nothing. He's free. Hanis also destroyed his fam."

"Slow down! The Rector can't legally do that without consulting you!"

"He *did* consult me; I was a judge at Eron's trial."

"And you agreed?" Nejirt was appalled. "I don't think I like you anymore."

"Afraid for your own fam, are you? Me, too. Recall my limits. Hanis is, after all, Rector. We mustn't confuse morality with strategy. To take a grievous loss where one is weak may create a fallback position from which one can counterattack in force."

"The Admiral of Platitudes strikes again."

"Watch your tongue, boy. I have an immediate job for you requiring extreme diplomacy. While we go down to the lab where I can tell you more bad news, you can update me on astrology."

They left the commissary, arguing, Nejirt's mouth full of croissant, a mug of half-finished lift in his hand. "How can I tell you about astrology when you've just promoted our headless astrologer to the status of psychohistorical prognosticator?"

At the lab Konn showed his associate the recordings of some very strange signals. "I didn't get my hands on these until the trial. Barna's boys cleaned them up for me. I've got better samples than Hanis."

"In code? Unbreakable?"

"Yes. But very economical." The Admiral was thoughtful. "It can't carry much information."

"That's a very short burst. It would be invisible inside all the other signals floating around. It looks to me like only a precoded receiver could pick it up. They are from Eron? He must have been under *very close* observation. He's talking to who?"

"You're ahead of my story. Right after the publication fiasco, the Lyceum Police, who happen to be directly under the command of the Rector, took Eron in for heavy questioning, then put him under house arrest and observation while Hanis decided what to do with him. Meanwhile this signal came flying out of Eron's *fam*. He has been a low-power pulse broadcaster all the time we've known him."

"Oh, shit!" Nejirt took a very intense second look at the recording.

"That's what Hanis said. But before Hanis was informed, someone tried to contact Eron by Personal Capsule, obviously the person who received the burst. Eron never got the message. Hanis still doesn't know about it. I intercepted the message; my police are better than the Lyceum Police—I haven't been topping off Barna's budget for the last twenty years for nothing."

"You can read someone else's Personal Capsule?" asked Nejirt in awe.

"No. Even Barna is not that good. But interception is another matter if you are looking in the right place. We'll never know what it said because it self-destructed when it wasn't delivered on time. But we got a lead on where it came from."

"Our headless corpse?"

"Yeah. Bad luck there. I really need to get my hands on his fam. A fam can't just walk away from a corpse."

"How are you going to cross-examine a ghoul? All of its coding intermesh is in a dead man's head. Barna's apparatus is pretty slick but half of a terabyte of password is no password at all."

"I'm interested in the fam's make. First I want to compare it with Eron's fam, which was a very unusual piece of hardware." A tri-dim holo appeared above the desk. It could be sliced or peeled in a variety of ways. "Take a look at these nondestructive scans. I got these images from the trial evidence. He had this fam since he was about three-years-old."

The specs were listed and Nejirt scrolled through them casually. "A Faraway design. Limited production. Recalled due to defects."

"Very suspicious," said the old paranoid. "The outfit who made them went out of business. I don't have Faraway in my bad-boy book, but they were always producing talented maniacs, and Faraway was once the most deadly enemy of the Pscholars. Eron attended school there; Space alone knows what happened to him as a student. Look." He pointed to some faint spots. "I'm no fam techie but I've been briefed on this one by an expert. Those are 'hooks,' ten times more than normal. Eron's fam was built to take upgrade add-ons, but the architecture is evidently totally nonstandard. You couldn't find an upgrade that would work with it. Nevertheless it's been custom upgraded."

"Very immoral."

"Nejirt, you prude; you started out life with a top-of-the-line fam, full featured. Some of our students aren't so lucky. It's not upgrade plug-ins that worry me, it's surgery."

"Any sign of surgery here?"

"Only indirectly. If we could see it, the fam would be crippled, and Eron was no cripple."

"A transponder implies surgery," Nejirt growled.

"Indeed it does." The Admiral peeled away different layers of the image. "Nobody would have noticed it if we didn't know what we were looking for. There it is. Tiny, eh? Minimalist design. Can't be very powerful. It only taps into his eyes. It seems to have its own visual processor." Konn did a zoom and a cube rose out of the image. He pointed by changing the color of whatever part he wanted to emphasize. "See that? The fam itself has no input into the transponder. Eron would not have been aware that it existed. He couldn't have controlled it if he wanted to.

Whoever put that transponder into his fam didn't trust him. Of course, that way he would pass all of our loyalty tests; we can't lie about what we don't know, can we?"

"Do you think he was loyal?"

"Oh, absolutely. He was trying to warn me when we broke up."

"About what?"

"Don't I wish I knew. When you are as old as I am, you develop a very efficient filing system. Garbage bypasses throughput on the way out. I remember he was very excited. Manic. Students get that way when they have been brooding too long by themselves and an idea takes over their mind and pushes out all reason. He had—to use his words—discovered that we were in the middle of some vast psychohistorical crisis that only he and the little mnemonifier in his room knew about. I tried to bring him down to reason. But it didn't matter that the whole of the star-spanning apparatus of psychohistorical machinery saw nothing. *He* saw."

Konn shut down his apparatus. "Come on, let's go. We're on a tight schedule this watch."

"Eron was usually obsessively cautious," mused Nejirt.

"I know. He always had his own ideas, but he always took my advice. I'm probably the best trouble sniffer that psychohistory has ever produced, but in the last analysis what am I doing? We live in peaceful times. I'm fretting over molehills that might, just might, turn into volcanoes if left untended for a few centuries. You know what a mole is, don't you? I think they are extinct. It was a little animal that dug tunnels underground and piled up dirt outside in little tiny mounds. If you didn't go after the buggers with a club, the mound gradually turned into a hill, and if you were lazy the hill turned into a mountain range. That all happened before our Founder. I think the mole was a Rithian animal. A mammal. Psychohistory is now so advanced that crises are handled hundreds of years before they happen."

"I'll remember that story the next time you send me out after a molehill in places like the Coron Pentad. Molehills grow into mountains. I complain too much. So, you humored Eron?"

"What else could I do? As tactfully as I could, I pointed out all the errors in his math so that he could think things over and work them out. I remember the errors he was making in his excitement, exactly, but I'll be a monkey if I remember his line of reasoning. Psychohistories were springing up like poison mushrooms all over the Galaxy, wild stuff. He never mentioned it again. And he kept doing good work. And then, boff, he went to work for the project of our glorious Rector."

"You grieved," said Nejirt.

"Yeah. He was a son to me."

"So you think he delivered the same thesis to Hanis?"

"I can't suppose anything else. It must have been very convincing—that's what worries me—because Hanis went berserk and Hanis usually just runs over people with his charm, ignoring all unpleasantness. I think Eron published as his last defiant resort."

"Hahukum, be honest with me. You mentioned to Barna your nightmare that our corpse might be a psychohistorian. Was that based on your half memories of Eron's wild conjecture?"

"Of course. I'm a professional paranoid. Nobody else wants the job."

"Then he was probably just an astrologer."

"Probably."

"Thank Space! For an inamin, there, you almost had *me* paranoid."

"Wait until you meet my other psychohistorian."

"Another!"

"A local I have under detention. Cingal Svene."

"I know him. He's a nut case. He pretends to be a mathist, but he's more a numerologist. For the last twenty years he has come out with a new pseudorandom number sequence that he claims can be used to generate the primes."

The Admiral laughed. "That was last year. This year he's a psychohistorian."

"They are springing up like poison mushrooms, are they?"

"How do you think you'll look in a scraggly beard and comfortable brimmed cap with food stains—and, perhaps, protruding false ears?"

"Is that the new psychohistorian's uniform?"

"We'll have your fam programmed with a new voice and a new gait by next watch. You're my best field agent. You'll be taking over Cingal Svene's life. At least you won't have to fake the psychohistorian gig."

"Can't I just go to work for Hanis?"

They had emerged onto the fourth floor of the balcony that spiraled along the inner walls of the oval-domed central keep of the West Wing of the Lyceum. Eight stories tall, it served as the display-well for a galactic simulacrum that was, at the moment, running a trade-route optimization, lightning flashes passing between stars as new combinations were tested. Konn gripped the parapet in the straight-armed pose of a man who owns all that he beholds.

"Just some thoughts I want to share while we're here." His gaze wavered as he asked permission of some unseen source. Then he squeezed at a palm-size console that he had magically retrieved from his coveralls. The optimization program continued but was no longer displayed while Konn took over the simulacrum with his own files. "This is as the Empire stood a century ago. The pale yellow and the gold cover all areas where the probability of deviation from prediction was greater than five percent, the gold indicating sites of strategic dynamism where failure of our predictions would have consequences meeting the Founder's criteria of direness. My predecessors, of course, sent rectifying teams into the gold regions. Now watch as I overlay the blue." All of the blue appeared inside the gold. Corrective measures had either not worked or been counterproductive.

"I've seen your molehills before," said Nejirt with amusement.

"Certainly, but right now let's look at them from a new viewpoint. The blues cover the current battle theaters of intractable uncertainty."

"That you see and nobody else sees," amended Nejirt.

"Because statistics tries harder for me. She loves me."

Nejirt Kambu made a quick visual estimate that the blue covered perhaps one percent of the Second Empire, a realm more imposing in this huge model than it was from the dwarfed viewport of a spaceship. Konn had never defined what he meant by such an alarming phrase as "battle theater," but he was a man infamous for using alarming phrases. Coron's Wisp was well within one of the designated regions.

"As a student I took such anomalies as my research project. For my thesis in psychohistory I was going to prove the conventional wisdom, that any deviation which did not respond to remediation was a random effect not driven by intelligence." He grumbled. "But I kept coming across correlations with intelligent opposition, not big ones, mind you, but big enough to pique my interest."

Nejirt knew the story. As a young man Hahukum had assumed that his research would be welcome and, later, that his ability to contain the blue zones would be appreciated. But his research was not welcomed and the Admiral was still considered to be a wild man who had reached high rank only because he was an unscrupulously fast and wily politician.

Men like Hanis continued to deny the existence of blue zones, attributing Konn's success to the absence of a problem in the first place—just as a skeptical Nejirt had, himself, done in his youth. Briefly Kambu's memory flashed on a neat little bot of his early childhood which scurried around cleaning up after the messes children made. Why bother to put things back into toy boxes? why deign to pick up crayons after drawing a picture? The world around him cleaned up by itself. But there was this annoying little bot that was always messing with Nejirt's things—so he broke it. Perhaps therein lay his loyalty to Konn; his mother had had a draconian sense of discipline, refusing to replace the bot even under the duress of Nejirt's most capillary-popping temper tantrums.

"So do you see the differences?" asked an enraptured Konn.

"It looks like the same old Galaxy I saw last time I was here. There are thirty-seven blue topozone crossovers driven by locally independent factors. Shall I recite the factors?" Nejirt was teasing Konn.

"Why independent?"

"Because you told me so—in detail."

"But they could all be connected by one giant conspiracy. How could I have missed it? That's what I'm seeing that's different."

Nejirt was grinning at this new paranoid twist. "An appealing idea."

"Think about it. When you were in the Ulmat mopping up, putting things to their final right, Eron Osa was there. When the forces of evil vanished, Eron went with them—and reappeared on Faraway. For training. He has an exotic limited-edition Faraway fam designed for fancy upgrade. The source of that fam conveniently no longer exists. His fam acquires, or had built-in, a transponder connected to the eyes of the user, and Space knows what else. Probing finds no signs of surgery. After training the way is paved for him to be sent to Splendid Wisdom, to the very heart of psychohistorical power where he can spy on me, the victor of the Battle of the Ulmat. We catch a falsely identified man from Coron's Wisp activating Eron's transponder . . . Of all my hot spots, Coron's Wisp has risen to be the most active. A Faraway plot? Something even more sinister? How many other connections are there between all the blue zones?"

Nejirt let his boss lose himself among the possible permutations of intrigue within this vast galactic simulacrum that rose before them for eight stories. He counted to five. "Admiral, Rector Hanis is sneaking up behind you with a knife."

That broke Konn's concentration. "Ah, yes. Politics before pleasure." He muttered again to some unseen source and the blue zones faded. Tiny lightning flashes reappeared. "Off to the dungeon. Follow me."

"Dungeon!"

"Of course. Every castle has a dungeon with a skeleton reaching through the bars for a bowl of water just out of reach. In this case, it is one of my offices hastily converted for the comfort of Cingal Svene. By the way, don't shave for the next watch or so. My associates tell me that our beard-growing nanosalve works best with a good stubble as substrate. You'll have to tell Wendi you are off on a trip again. You'll be operating out of Svene's old apartment."

"And when someone checks my retinal pattern?"

"As of the current watch the real Cingal Svene would be living a nightmare if he tried to prove he was Cingal Svene. When you were with Barna I had his identifiers globally replaced by yours."

"Is that legal?"

"If you stretch the emergency power laws. But I didn't go through channels."

"I could get into trouble. Impersonation is illegal."

"You are already in trouble. Hanis has you on his exile list—or worse. You may want to *keep* your Svene identity indefinitely."

"Let's start from the beginning."

They had arrived at the little briefing room not far from the dungeon. One of Barna's lieutenants instructed Nejirt in the communication protocols used by Svene's revolutionary cell. Ordinarily these protocols would be useless to the police because they required a fail-safe identifier; if Svene was captured and forced to communicate, he would just leave out that identifier and thus clue in his correspondent to break off contact. But Svene was not only a very sloppy mathist, he was a sloppy housekeeper and had left the fail-safe identifier in a convenient place for reference, behind a book.

"We've already gone through a few cycles of communication," said the lieutenant. "No suspicion on the other end. They just wanted a few simple psychohistorical predictions, which were easy enough for us to supply. They praised his progress and signed off." The lieutenant took him through Svene's routine, where he shopped, where he ate. He ate mostly at automats but had a few favorite spots where it was the job of the waitress to sit down and chat with her male clients. The lieutenant was thorough, supplying pictures of the waitresses and a profile of their interests.

"I don't look like Svene."

"Doesn't matter," said the lieutenant. "They'll notice your beard and your puffy ears. The accent will be right, and so will the funny way you pick up a cup. Best of all, your credit stick will go through without a hassle with a slightly better than usual tip. Half a month of watches like that, and the real Svene could walk in and they'll think he was the fake."

Konn cut in. "The org we're penetrating doesn't know who he is because he wanted it that way and because they wanted it that way. Makes it harder on us police."

Nejirt took Konn aside for a quiet chat. "What has this sting got to do with Hanis? I know you very well. You don't give a jellybean for helpless little conspiracies of malcontents. You go for things like a vast tidal wave of taxpayer rage, or the meme of defiance that has penetrated a whole society and is passed down from generation to generation. Guys like Cingal Svene you've ignored all your life."

Konn grinned. "This is internal politics, not defense of the Empire. Recall that Hanis has called off his truce. *Right now* he's maneuvering out of sight to get the whole lot of us excised out of psychohistory. He could exile us—he has enough people in his thrall to do that—but would he dare scatter the seeds of a thousand disgruntled psychohistorians all over the Galaxy? I doubt it. I think he has something more extreme in mind."

"He wouldn't dare."

"Let *me* think about that. I'm the professional paranoid. Right now you are just a bearded, big-eared malcontent who tried three times to pass the Lyceum entrance exams and failed and after all these years still harbors a grudge against all things psychohistorical."

"I've got to know the game plan."

"Okay. Here's what Hanis doesn't yet know. He doesn't know my agents intercepted a Personal Capsule for Eron when he was under house arrest. He doesn't know we tracked down the source of that Capsule and chased him a merry chase that ended in both disaster for him and for us. When we raided our corpse's apartment we picked up a few very good leads. It is only a matter of time before Hanis clues into all this, so we have to act fast without my usual subtlety and patience. The main item led us to a man out of the past who calls himself Hyperlord Kikaju Jama. He's an antique dealer who has been selling Eggs brought in from Coron's Wisp. He is not a big player because we know our corpse brought in huge numbers of Eggs, only a few of them going through Jama. So far, not a trace of the other Eggs. We should wait. But it is Hanis' schedule, so we have no option but to sting

PSYCHOHISTORICAL CRISIS

413

this Hyperlord before we have the full picture. Not easy. I'm amazed at the professional level of his security—which is another sign that this is not just a simple commercial venture."

"It could be just a fad," mused Nejirt. "The Egg is a very impressive gadget. It is too fine-textured to be duplicated in a manufacturum so whoever knows how to distribute it could make a fortune. They'd want to keep their distribution network a secret."

"And put a transponder right in the middle of the Lyceum?"

"All right. My role?"

"Arresting only this Jama wouldn't create a ripple. It has got to be a *big* sting. Then I can turn around and tell the Ranks that Eron was warning Rector Hanis of a major conspiracy and that Hanis immediately *suppressed* all of the evidence right down to the contents of Eron's fam. He can't produce evidence to contradict me, because he had all the evidence destroyed."

"Suppose he kept a private record?"

Konn grinned. "Does it matter? I know the nature of Eron's warning because he warned me. I will have no trouble showing that this Hyperlord is part of a dangerous galactic conspiracy whether it is true or not."

"That's not good psychohistory."

"But this isn't psychohistory. It's politics."

The lieutenant wanted their attention. "Beg pardon, but the honorable Kambu should spend a few hours with our subject if he is to fine-tune his imitation."

Cingal Svene was alternately afraid, defiant, angry, propitiative, whining, and sometimes everything a cornered hero should be. Konn left his claws sheathed, even when Cingal made blatantly erroneous mathematical statements; his was a buttery friendliness that was not the kind of friendship he would have offered a friend. Nejirt decided he might as well like this guy if he was going to have to be him, scraggly beard and all. He took on a sorry-about-the-inconvenience demeanor, "let me fluff your pillow." Cingal eventually broke down into hysterical crying, which turned into defiance as he brushed away the tears, and finally into a cheerful slyness. Konn had kept the man's Egg in his hand, prominently displayed, so that the conversation would keep revolving around it.

"Shall I tell you gentlemen thieves your fortune?"

"By all means," said Konn, handing over the astrological tool.

Nejirt was bored. He had seen this nonsense before. The light dimmed. Even the corners of the room disappeared as the stars came out. Cingal was good, much better than Nijert's clumsy effort with Barna. He also knew all the little tidbits that astrologers throw out to make their clients believe that they have a secret mainline into the client's psyche. He made veiled references to Zeta Anorka, the home system of Nejirt, and the constellations of Zeta Anorka actually appeared with the planets in the sky exactly as they had been on the day of Nejirt's birth. That was creepy. He wove into his story the three failed love affairs that had tormented Nejirt before he met Wendi. That was unnerving. But true to the astrological craft, he used the changing sky above to puff up their egos, finding all the fine secret features of their personalities that made them uniquely outstanding citizens of the Galaxy. Both Nejirt and Konn knew that it was all conjured flattery but were smiling at their astrologer's sagacity just the same.

And then Cingal peered at them above his beard with a little boy's sly and innocent eyes. "And would you like to know your final doom? Only the courageous need proceed."

"Of course," said the Admiral. Nejirt, more reluctant, said nothing but nodded.

The stars flew by. They dived into a spectacular nebula and lost themselves within its tendrils. The nebula hazed over and faded to the darkness of an interstellar dust cloud. "Your future universe approaches," their seer intoned. Nothing happened. It became so dark that faces were invisible. And then, slowly, majestically the Founder's red equations began to scroll across the sky, page after page after page, rolling endlessly in mute silence . . .

# SELF-EVIDENT TRUTHS, 14,806 GE

*When I look back to the time, already 20 years ago, when the concept and mag-
nitude of the physical quantum of action began, for the first time, to unfold from
the mass of experimental facts, and again, to the long and ever tortuous path
which led, finally, to its disclosure, the whole development seems to provide a
fresh illustration of the long-since proved saying of Goethe's that man errs as
long as he strives. And the whole strenuous intellectual work of an industrious
research worker would appear, after all, to be in vain and hopeless, if he were
not occasionally through some striking facts to find that he had, at the end of all
his crisscross journeys, at last accomplished at least one step which was conclusively nearer the truth.*

> —*Famous Unknown Theoreticians: Archive Galactica,* 4,892 GE,
> from the Nobel Address of Max Planck, 59,433 BGE

Deep in the Lyceum in a circular room reminiscent of the spartan design of the battle theater of an ancient Imperial dreadnought, equations shifted across the visual
fields of two linked fams as Eron Osa demonstrated his homemade indexer to a
standing Admiral Konn. There was nothing original in the mathematics, but Eron
had devised a quick way of ordering the key material that a psychohistorian had to
have available in his mnemonifier. With a fam command Eron could trigger the
displayed symbols to blossom into a definition or an expansion or an underlying
proof—or he could feed the equation a meal of initial conditions and watch the
transmogrification into a solution. With another command, related equations might
be called to the surface or banished.

"You'll love it," said Eron proudly.

"As long as you leave me my old interface to go back to when I've been dead-
ended," commented Konn good-naturedly. "It will take me a while to get used to

your fancy-dan way of doing things. I'm an old man. A nice simple Imperial battle theater of the Fifth Millennium is about my speed. Or maybe the instrument panel of a Flying Fortress. How long did it take you to build this maze?"

"About a year. I need it to keep up with old men like you."

"Come. We have to go."

"I haven't showed you everything yet."

"And I haven't showed you everything you need to know to break Eighth Rank." To indicate that he considered the demonstration over, he switched the panorama of windows circumnavigating the theater from black to a fade-up of an Imperial fleet in formation over a nebula.

Eron reluctantly left his aerochair bobbing. "Another seminar?"

"You might say that."

On their way they passed onto the spiral balcony of the Lyceum's oval-dome inner keep. Hahukum never took the verticule; he liked his little stroll around the giant-size galactic simulacrum. At this hour no programs were running and all overlays were absent—it was just the slowly wheeling Galaxy, shrunk to a manageable eight stories. They were facing into the Carina Arm, heading down toward the rim to less-populous clumps.

"When are you going to let me take a crack at your blues?" meaning the trouble spots Konn had identified through his wizard's mastery of statistics.

"When you know more than you know now. Those are my toughies, and I'm handling them myself." Something in the vast galactic display caught the Admiral's eye, and he took out a hand device to flare the relevant stars so that Eron could see, too. "Now there's a blue that's been migrating across its topozone at a steady rate for two hundred years, centered, it seems, on a nothing pentad of stars called the Coron's Wisp. A really big spurt in recent years. Nothing explains it, not a damn thing—and I've run all the tests. When I get desperate enough I'm going to send out a field expedition to find out what in the Founder's Nose I'm missing."

"Like you did with the Ulmat?"

"Yes, like I did with the Ulmat." Konn smiled. "And I'll probably have to use Nejirt again. Good field agents are hard to come by. You'll notice I did no harm to your homeworld. It's called minimal force. I didn't have to blow the place apart like a certain emperor's son who later became known as Emperor Arum-the-Patient. On Agander they've never heard of me, and none of your people will ever remember my name. When you speak at my funeral extolling my virtues, that's a point you'll be able to make in my favor."

Suddenly Konn boxed off a cube of stars centered on Coron's Wisp, expanded the view to the scale of thirty leagues per story, blotting out the Galaxy. The shifting gave Eron vertigo. Konn continued to muse. "I'll have to run an analysis on flows in and out of there—but it probably won't do me any good until I've identified the infection vector."

"If you've got it classified as a danger how can you *not* know what the infection vector is?"

Konn was unperturbed by student ignorance. "You can wake up with a fever bad enough to keep you in bed without knowing what you've caught." They turned into a small seminar room and Eron noted with shock the seven senior psycho-historians looking at him. Five he recognized as Konn's closest associates of rank. "Your Eighth Rank orals. I thought it was time."

"I'm not prepared," said Eron, aghast.

"That's not for you to decide."

The hours of the next watch made a grim ordeal. Eron fielded question after question, fumbling large numbers of them, chagrined at how many things there were to know in which he had only dabbled, if that. Konn would occasionally bring the subject back into the areas of Osa's competence, giving him brief reprieves.

"I flunked," he said, alone again with Konn, trying to keep back the tears.

"Of course not! That was a mere formality. They wouldn't dare flunk you. You're *my* student."

Moments later Konn herded him into a surprise party. Eron didn't realize at first that it was in his honor, to celebrate his new Eighth Rank status. By tradition there were nine candles on the cake, and when the lights were doused, he had to take one of the candles and blow it out, leaving eight, and then parade around the room holding the lighted cake high over his head while doing a jig. They didn't do silly things like that on Agander. But it was all right. One could feel foolish and happy at the same time.

At the end of the revelry, five students remained, plus Magda whom Konn had left in Eron's charge. Two were good friends of Eron, the other three he had never met before. They all decided to cap off the evening on the Olibanum at the Teaser's Bistro. Eron wondered why he had never looked up Rigone before. He had been meaning to for years now. They all crowded into the same small pod, having doctored its pea brain into thinking that they were all one fat man. Sitting on each other's laps, they sang a loud rondel in contrapuntal harmony while the acceleration pressed their bodies together.

At this hour the Teaser's was quiet but, as always, never empty. The long row of stout tables marched down the central hall, wood, each surface crowded with the carved wit of youths who liked their small tools; knives, i-drills, fusion cobblers. Some of the more solid tables had once graced the mansions of First Empire nobles whose line had perished during the Sack, some were of recent manufacture. Old tabletops served as wall paneling to preserve the wit and were replaced by fresh tables with virgin surfaces of hardwood.

Customer density began to increase. The central row was for a boisterous crowd who enjoyed the mob scene of dealing and repartee. Alcoves served the quieter interests; some even came equipped with sonic suppressors. Only Eron and Magda had never been to the Teaser's before. The other five celebrants knew everyone, young people with an intellectual bent, serious in their discussions, serious in the quality of their fam aids. Eron listened. Magda stayed close to Eron. The humor was witty rather than rowdy. And the whole coterie seemed uncomfortably impatient with the stolidness of their Splendid upbringing, restless for the adventure that none of them was quite sure they could handle if they ever found it.

The women, one even as young as fifteen, all wore clothing deliberately out of style but sensuously reminiscent of another era of blatant power or devil-take-it-all. They knew their history. The boy-men preferred a caricature of military style, not from the time of fighters like Peurifoy, or from the heroic Wars Across the Marche, or in imitation of the ragtag utilitarianism of the armies of the Interregnum, but uniforms of irony; their clothing mocked the generals who had served as toad bodyguards to the weak Emperors of the Late First Empire. A question crossed Eron's mind: What equation would predict clothing? And he laughed at the single-mindedness of his thoughts. Too much studenting.

Just sitting there with his thoughts, he was sure he would return for more Bistro. Perhaps as Eighth Rank he could relax a little and do something about his neglected social life. The waiter dropped by with two Gorgizons. "Compliments of the Boss," he said, and went away. Magda was very suspicious of this milky cocktail, so Eron managed to drink them both. After that he wasn't sure he could leave his seat, so he stayed after his friends had departed. Magda stayed with him, very close.

"So," said a hefty man with curlicue tattoos who sneaked up on them after the melee had thinned, "you finally came." He sat down at their table and explained himself to Magda. "The kid and I met in a bookstore, arguing over the same book. Name's Rigone. And yours?"

"Magda," she said quietly.

Rigone grinned at Eron. "You've grown up." He glanced at Magda appreciatively. "You really know how to pick the exotic babes."

The next time he dropped by at the Teaser's, Rigone wouldn't let him drink alone, insisting on taking the youth upstairs behind his forcecurtain for a chat about old times. He showed off the Helmarian apparatus he had smuggled into Splendid Wisdom on his return "to knock off a few credits here and there." In the background his current teenage girlfriend leisurely slipped back into her underwear for company, her blue eyes never leaving Eron, even after she sat down and crossed her legs.

Rigone remained buoyantly attentive to his guest. "You okay? You're sure you're okay? I always worried about you. That job with you was way out of my element. I don't like that. Scared me shitless. I didn't know what I was doing; I was just following instructions and praying to the god of luck. You're sure you're okay? You didn't seem happy when it was over. You expected to turn into some kind of superman and fly away flapping your ears. Did you ever notice a difference?"

"I think I noticed a difference at Asinia. The right algorithm always seemed to pop into my mind when I needed it. Math was a whiz."

"Yeah," Rigone enthused, "that I'm good at. Utilities. Sells better than beer. Of course, I don't write the algorithms. Damned if I know what was in those tidbits I stuffed into *your* brain." He shook his head. "Installing utilities was the easy part. Your fam was made for it. The rest . . ." He paused to shake his head. "I can still feel my pants being lubricating by blood-piss during the *major* operation! I was passionately wishing I'd done the usual Scav thing and stuck to song and joke upgrades. So! You've made Eighth Rank! Glad to hear it. Maybe I had something to do with that. Maybe not."

"I've noticed a difference here at the Lyceum. The way Second Rank Konn's mind works fascinates me, but I always seem to have my own approach to a problem. I *know* I have nonstandard reference works in my fam, because when I search the archives for what feels like a naturally standard math algorithm to me, it's not there. Sometimes Konn's way works better, sometimes my way works better."

"You got to be careful with that Hahukum Konn. With a smile he'll sell you a pair of red shoes . . . and then sell tickets to the dance performance."

The underage girlfriend was feeling left out and sauntered over. "Is he gwana dance for us?" She had a northern accent, of the kind you found around Splendid Wisdom's Chisin Ridge, an accent that probably predated the First Empire.

"No. Eron is not a dancer. That was an expression. Eron is a mathist."

"Like to citch maself one of those. Introduce us."

"Eron. Mattie." Rigone felt he had to explain her presence. "Mattie is a runaway and I'm giving her a temporary home."

"He means I cin stay as long as I stay useful."

Rigone ignored her. "I remember that you like books. I have just the book for an enterprising math student. It has this wonderful account in it by the first man who thought up the hyperdrive motor. Couldn't get past the other entries." He went to his display collection, hunted a moment, and pulled out an ancient volume. "Sixth millennium. Pupian Dynasty, I think. First edition. Good stuff but most of it's over my head. I want you to have it. I owe you one." It seemed to have been published under some government make-work cultural program; there was nothing fancy about its plain blue cover with gold edging and big golden title: *Famous Unknown Theoreticians*.

"Hey, you gwana give me something, too?"

"You can't read. You're a downloader."

"More ina world than books, big man."

"Later, babe. Later I'll put out something for you."

"Later doan count—you tuck later back in your pants bout one inamin after you put it out. How bout *him* for a present?" Her blue eyes stripped Eron nude with a petite smile.

"No. He's too young for you. He'd ruin your innocence with his untutoredness."

Eron excused himself in the middle of the argument and spent the rest of the watch at home quietly famfeeding Rigone's book with a cobbled-together reader that could decode the ancient formatting. It was sometimes highly amusing and always sobering to read how theoreticians down the ages went about proving their most sacred suppositions.

Eron's favorite from the book of *Famous Unknown Theoreticians* was Ptolemy's quite detailed, and correct, geometric proof that Rith was the center of the universe—the only flaw being his assumption that since no parallax of the stars was observed, the stars must be embedded in a celestial sphere whose radius was not too many orders of magnitude larger than the radius of Rith. As a theoretician woefully unfamiliar with the limits of experimental instrumentation, he didn't realize (what the current state of Greek geometry would have told him had he been listening) that he had a proof of the lower bound on the distance to the nearest star, but no estimate at all of an upper bound.

Often Eron had to stop perusing to do something while he thought through an insight. He might water his thriving plants, which were confused enough by the splendor from their wall to behave as if they were growing in the garden of an Emperor. Two were in flower. Or he might just stare. His inlaid and runed Rithian Yorick rested stoically up-to-his-neck-in-table between the Ming aralia and the Osmanthus fragrans, there to remind Eron of the consequences of sloppy thinking, and never far from evoking Eron's memory of Reinstone, the poet of Asinia, reciting with ecstatic melancholy from the incantations of the Shaker of Spears: "Alas, poor Yorick! . . . Where be your gibes now? your gambols? your songs? your flashes of merriment, that were wont to set the table on a roar?"

One of the more amusing entries in Rigone's book was the proof from the century of the Flying Fortress that Rith had no population problem, that overbreeding was going to go away of itself as a natural side effect of industrialization. It did go away as a natural side effect of sapiens stupidity. The mesmerizingly slow convergence of birth rate and death rate, unfortunately, was not the important variable to watch; the killer was the *infrastructure* stability of a population that had been stabilizing too slowly.

From skull to book again. As well as his proof that Rith was the center of the universe, Ptolemy produced a wonderful proof that Rith didn't rotate—based upon the assumption that any object freed from contact with the planet would automatically and instantaneously assume zero velocity relative to some absolute frame of reference. Thus an army positioned to the east of their enemy (and with their feet *firmly* on the ground) might annihilate all opposition by casually freeing rocks and gravel that would then zoom off to the west at the speed of Apollo's chariot. Ergo, since that did not happen, a nonrotating Rith must be sitting stationary at its central position in the universe.

One could be amused by such naïveté, but Eron wasn't sure mankind had ever transcended the tendency to build houses upon a foundation of "self-evident truths."

The self-evident truth that most interested Eron was psychohistory's cherished and firmly defended axiom: the assumption that any foreseen event could be neutralized if known to those affected by the prediction. Murek Kapor had originally planted the skepticism as to the truth of that axiom, a skepticism which had flowered almost to the point of blasphemy by the time Eron had been inducted into the Fellowship as a raw recruit, but which had now, with full knowledge of psychohistory's methods, mellowed to the point of acceptance.

Still, the theorem had problems, and Eron, among his many interests, had dedicated a part of his endeavor to straightening out the mathematics of secrecy. In the first place, there were two distinct treatments of secrecy where there should be only one.

(1) an N methodology that applied to nonpsychohistorians who *were not* supposed to be cognizant of their future lest they disturb it;

(2) a P methodology that applied internally to the group of Pscholars themselves who *were* supposed to be cognizant of possible futures so they could change them.

That created problems. For instance, Eron was well aware that Second Rank Konn and First Rank Hanis disagreed upon which future mankind should be pursuing. That led to very strange internal secrets among the Fellowship.

(1) Konn kept secrets from Hanis in essentially an N methodological way which (incorrectly) assumed Hanis was not a psychohistorian, ostensibly to keep Hanis from sabotaging Konn's vision of the future—and otherwise (correctly) dealt with Hanis by the usual P methodology.

(2) Likewise Hanis kept secrets from Konn, on the tacit (incorrect) assumption that Konn was not really a psychohistorian thus (he hoped) preventing Konn from sabotaging Hanis' messianic vision. In all other respects Konn was treated by Hanis as a Pscholar.

This wry mix-up generated tiny internal contradictions which inevitably led to problems within the Fellowship, sometimes unimportant ones that could be looped around, as seemed to be the case here, yet—potentially—such careless ways of defining secrecy could create lethal problems, could even destroy galactic civilization.

During the execution of the Founder's original Plan, this flaw in the law of secrecy had not been made manifest because all Pscholars were united in their desire to execute the One Great Plan and so had no need to keep secrets from each other. Today, with different subgroups of Pscholars vying to lead mankind into different visions, the law of secrecy was working to create incompatible groups of Pscholars, each thinking that they, and they alone, represented the true heir of the Founder. Inevitably this would lead to an attempt by one group of (supposedly correct) Pscholars to disenfranchise the other groups of (supposedly incorrect) Pscholars.

Shades of the ancient past. The Catholic (Truth) versus Protestant (Heresy) as it were.

Eron had already laid out the problem as a mathematical puzzle—which he was keeping secret until he understood it better. The trouble stemmed from a mathematical definition of secrecy that was inherently inconsistent. That was the easy part. Eron wasn't sure he knew what to do about it except that the same rules had to apply to everyone—the inconsistency deriving from the false dichotomy between Pscholar and layman.

(1) Under what circumstances was the keeping of a secret benign?

(2) Under what circumstances did the keeping of a secret prove detrimental?

Sloppy group thinking, akin to that which had abruptly terminated poor Yorick's life during the Great Rithian Die-off, was to be avoided at all costs. There were worse fates than being sent to heaven as an indoor garden decoration, but not many. Yet Eron was not going to be able to refine his thinking by conducting social experiments, say, in the grand manner of that Emperor-of-Everything-plus-Russia Napoleon or by mind-slaving à la Cloun-the-Stubborn. Young Osa was beginning to think of himself as an ancient astronomer: he couldn't test his ideas about the functioning of stars by building different kinds of stars—but what he could do was observe the stars that already existed. History was his sky.

Of the men in Rigone's book, Eron took a liking to Max Planck. He had always assumed that Planck was one of those ancient Bronze-Age shamans who fooled around with black body radiation in a cave and, by the light of a gas lamp, used chalkboard and bronze piping and primitive electrical oven to come up with a curve which fit the experimental data, all without ever grasping the true meaning of the mysterious revelation gifted him by his Nordic gods. But reading Planck's original papers uncovered a different story. Planck wasn't an experimentalist at all. He was a paper-and-pencil theoretician who maintained roots in a rich soil of other people's observations. Equations were carefully derived from first principles to match the best experimental results. When they didn't he was brilliantly able to finagle a new equation to fit the experiment, but never satisfied until he could *derive* the finagle from first principles.

Planck's finest finagle, the quantum of action, he fussed over until he had a convincing derivation from the simplest mechanical laws and a deep understanding of Boltzmann's then-new statistical mechanics—which every student of psychohistory was familiar with as the ancient foundation stone of the Founder's mathematics. (Boltzmann was often referred to by students at the Lyceum as the great-grandancestor of psychohistory.) In plain words—unmistakably clear over millennia of language change—Planck warned his students that they were not to use the quantum of action in *any* prediction that required reversibility since all quantum events were tied to an increase in entropy.

Eron was amazed and delighted by this piece of ancient wisdom!

Later generations of quantum theoreticians had ignored Planck (and had side-lined Boltzmann as underivable from first principles) and clung for dear life to their newtonian roots in the Law of Conservation of Information, a law about as valid as Ptolemy's assumption that a released rock instantly reverts to a universal rest mode. During the heady pre-Yorick years of scientific prolificacy, armies of super-stitious physicists hunted up new heavens for information gone missing: under rocks, on the surface of black holes, behind the locked doors of alternate worlds—all heavens where the physicists were sure to find their home after they died. The debate was only resolved by the Great Die-off when the physicists, as well as everyone else, fell off the top of the exponential curve to their silence or, if they lived, to more pressing questions of survival.

Yorick had nothing to say about the matter.

Perhaps because of Reinstone, certainly because of his adventures on Rith, Eron had taken up the hobby of teasing a psychohistorical thread through the shards of Rith's history. His first five years at the Lyceum had been an ideal op-portunity to collect all sorts of odd bits and pieces of ancient history which had lan-guished in various archives. His psychohistorical manipulations of these pieces surprised him by regularly deviating from the standard Rithian stereotypes.

Building a model of some segment of Rith's history was not the same as pre-dicting the future. To predict the future one had to jump off the curve's endpoint with the hope that you were jumping in the same direction as the curve. History was different. It was an interpolation between known points, a less acrobatic feat. For instance, with just the meager data he had about the era of the Flying Fortress, the equations gave a high probability of a devastating nuclear fusion-fission war—but the record showed no such event so Eron could prune off that branch and thus refine his analysis.

Connecting his thread through the topozone crossing of the Great Rithian Die-off was a more difficult extrapolation. There was enough material from the prior centuries of the Ramp-up to see the excitement of the early scientific revolution driving the population expansion, and plenty of evidence of the cavalier optimism of the richer nations, which were getting richer in their high-rise penthouse sup-ported by the Atlas of an increasingly ignorant breeding population . . . And after the Die-off there was plenty of material to understand the strange cultures which had produced the sublight starships.

But in between the Die-off and the Rejuvenation? Only the shadows of illiterate men too busy dying and surviving to record their thoughts.

Every single one of the cultures that had fed the Ramp-up with its dynamism and energy simply vanished during the free-fall of infrastructure collapse as the population dropped by ten(?), fifteen(?) billion. The peoples who emerged from the disaster, and who later founded the first interstellar colonies, bore no kin to their parent cultures in languages, institutions, religions, or racial characteristics. It wasn't an easy scene for a historian to sort out even with the splicing tools of psychohistory.

But it was good practice.

Eron divided his study of secret societies into three broad groups. Rithian history made up in longevity for what it lacked in depth. The ten thousand years of sublight expansion produced hundreds of examples of secret societies, each of the colonies isolated from all the others, so the influences which made and drove them were easy to model. The Hyperdrive Era contained a plethora of interstellar conflicts in which secrecy had been both a viable survival strategy for undergroups and a viable method of retaining power for overgroups.

There was no verdict in favor of secrecy or against it. Both strategies were valid responses to different kinds of challenge. Both were fatal when improperly applied.

Eron's methodology was very Planckian. He set up a complete mathematical model governing secrecy and disclosure. Then he fed some historical event into it, comparing the model's output and the historical record. That gave him the flaws in his model—and sometimes the bias in the historical record. (How reliable was the Inquisition's account of the Catholic extermination of the Albigensians since at the end of that conflict there were no Albigensians left to leave an account of their own?)

From the results of the comparison between theory and observation Eron then finagled his model to give the results it should have given—after which he lived a few months of frustration figuring out the underlying psychohistorical basis of the finagle. Then he applied the new model to a new set of historical events for a new iteration of theory.

During this trying exercise Eron was consoled by reading in Latin the works of Johann Kepler, who wrote in the 598th century BGE, during the time of the bloody collapse of the Ptolemaic cosmology. Kepler published amusing accounts of his sustained effort, through seventy different hypotheses, to fit Tycho Brahe's measurements of the path of Mars to a theoretical curve, chiding himself in print for first having exhausted all possible variations of the circle before trying something sensible—merely because he was caught up in the universal dogma, held by Ptolemy, Tycho Brahe, Copernicus, Galileo, the Jesuits, the Inquisition, and an infallible Pope, which took for granted that circleness was the one true perfect shape befitting God's perfect design for the Solar System. But God had preferred ellipses.

Kepler doggedly continued his research, his mind full of hypotheses to be tested, even as the holocaust of the Thirty Year Religious War engulfed everything about him. Men began to doubt creeds that preached a Savior but practiced wholesale fratricide. The psychohistorical seeds of the distrust of all religion ripened, ready to take root in the centuries ahead. Kepler found the means to publish Tycho's star-maps in spite of the chaos, but long before the war was over Kepler perished, one among ten million as sapiens Catholic and sapiens Protestant slaughtered, maimed, raped, pillaged, and burned men, women, children, witches, and heretics in the name of their Christ.

Eron's refined model of galactic civilization and the Founder's classical model almost always gave the same historical outcome—except under one circumstance, where Eron's formulation of the laws seemed to give remarkably better results.

The Founder's model wasn't self-referential. By the very nature of his mathematics he had to assume that his Pscholars would be living in a universe isolated from history. That worked very well if the job was back-predicting a past they couldn't influence. But when predicting the future it became the source of their need for secrecy. Yet because secrecy was never perfect, the Founder's mathematics carried in its retina a blind spot. During the Interregnum the Pscholars' arm of the Fellowship was a tiny underfunded group that had the resources to keep track of only a very few critical leverage points. In effect, it *was* isolated from history, and thus the Founder's math was a very good approximation to the real situation.

However, since the establishment of the Pax Pscholaris of 13,157 GE, the situation had subtly changed. At the end of the Interregnum the Pscholars' power had been mostly symbolic, but sixteen centuries later that power was real; they were the single most powerful group in galactic history. They were no longer outside of history, they *rode* history—and secrecy was steadily weakening as a vehicle by which to maintain the fiction of isolation required by the Founder's equations. So far as Eron could tell, this once-useful approximation was now dangerously close to failure. Another Ptolemaic system.

It was time to take his math out of his private mnemonifier and put it to test in the huge galactic model maintained by the Lyceum. Second Rank Konn gladly provided him with the machine space and gave him higher than normal runtime priority for a Rank Eight student. He wasn't allowed to modify the sacrosanct model himself but he could use any of its routines, up to the full set, or, for experimental purposes, flag out what he didn't want to use and flag in his own alterations.

Because he was amending some of the basic rules, he made up different sets of initial conditions that were critically designed to highlight his modifications. Using a revamped model with the Galaxy's real initial conditions could come later when he had a revision he could trust.

The secrecy assumptions were so strongly built into the standard model that Eron spent months tracking them down and rephrasing the affected codes. It was a hermit's existence with zero social life. His waking-sleeping cycle became erratic until he was out of tune with the corridor world around him. Sometimes he didn't notice that he was wearing mixed pairs of colored socks, even mismatched shoes. He was known to appear at odd hours barefoot and in pajamas. Konn once sent Magda over to trim his hair.

His adversary and archfiend was the galactic model's intelligent compiler. Cavalierly it might reject his code with polite little scolds. "Code syntactically correct. However, suggest you try instead: . . ." and its suggestion comprised only seven percent of the code Eron had spent a whole watch writing and ran in two percent of the time. "Danger: Matrix SEM246 is near singular to level epsilon in regions . . . Suggest adding branch to routine AZ34mask to avoid probability 0.000072 that run will balloon to unacceptable error levels." "Job terminated: Do NOT use this code before reading ARCHIVE-doc-274/12/13476 by First Rank Pscholar Yem Esonu, attached. Comprehension test required." A whole textbook! "Syntactic error in your use of morads, automatically corrected. Any disagreements with this decision to be filed in log-morad." Sometimes the complier even ran his program with polite reluctance, ending in: "Job Terminated," a title appended to a thousand-line analysis of the problem. Once Eron got the dreaded cryptic termination message: "Outside the parameters of human nature." Deep in imagined retorts, Eron slipped a red sock on one foot and a green sock on the other.

Slowly, slowly he beat the compiler into a state of respectful submission. But it was the simulations which began to run without compiler comment that gave him the most intellectual distress. Sometimes he felt like a twelve-year-old novice god; whenever he thought he had his universe elegantly designed to perfection, the damn thing would blow up on him and he'd have to go back to scratch and build a new universe.

His method was simple. He developed and tested definitions of info exchange between intelligent nodes: secrets having viscous flow, open info having fluid flow. He allowed no node a privileged position. For instance, in Eron's math there was no absolute resting place for psychohistorical knowledge and so no need to differentiate between prediction as a tool used by generals or physicists or biologists or parents raising children and prediction as a tool used by psychohistorians.

Thus Eron avoided the conundrum: "If the Fellowship node is the natural resting place of all psychohistorical knowledge, what happens when we resolve this Fellowship into its component nodes, the individual psychohistorians? Where is the natural resting place of psychohistorical knowledge now? Who is Pope? And how does he keep the secret of psychohistory unto himself without murdering all the other psychohistorians?" In another version of the conundrum it was possible to ask: "How did the Founder preserve the secret methods of psychohistory by teaching them to his disciples?" And in still another version: "If the Fellowship cannot predict its own internal behavior because all of its members know the methods of psychohistory, then how can it know itself well enough to lead the Galaxy?" Under the squabbling leadership of the Olympian gods, the squabbling Greeks first became vassals of Rome and then vassals of Turkey.

Eron's new and precise definitions, as they always do, opened up a whole new field of mathematics: a vista from which to view the starry ecumen without the obstruction of corridor walls. He named his methodology Arekean iteration after the famous Galactic folk hero Arek who, in countless different versions, began his tribulations by formulating a disastrous plan that escalated into frightful trouble which he fast-danced his way out of by the cunning creation of a new and worse plan that . . . until finally, at the very last inamin, a hair's breadth from disease, death, and disgrace, he made a final plan that saved him for a happy ending and the story could end.

> Law-1: Any observed change in circumstance initiates a prediction by the observer.

> Law-2: If the prediction indicates good fortune, prediction ceases.

> Law-3: If the prediction indicates an unpleasant outcome, the observer actively seeks to falsify the prediction by initiating further changes to his circumstances.

> Law-4: Prediction/action is an interative process that continues until good fortune is predicted.

The dynamics of those simple laws were interesting.

When Eron attached (to the methods of prediction) a high coefficient of secrecy, each node, whether community or individual, tended to optimize only its own future. Nonoptimal falsification of negative predictions dominated.

A rancher predicts good fortune raising cows.

The farmer, noting the arrival of cows, predicts them eating his wheat and falsifies this prediction by poisoning the rancher's cattle so that he can predict a profit raising wheat.

The rancher, noting this change in his circumstances, predicts bankruptcy but falsifies this dire prediction by burning the farmer's barn, which allows him to predict a profit in cattle *next* year.

The farmer then rolls out the barbed wire and builds a machine-gun nest in his water tower, enabling him to predict a profit in wheat *next* year.

Eron watched this high-secrecy version of his model with fascination. Armies with secret archives of contingency plans mushroomed. Brother assassinated brother. Counterproductive falsification of negative prediction was the rule. A Time of Troubles? An Interregnum? Whatever you wanted to call it, power gradually accumulated in the hands of the best predictors who continued to maintain their advantage through secrecy while the number of distinct nodes dwindled. No matter how small or large the stage, in the final state one predictor ruled in a sea of enemies. Splendid Wisdom?

When Eron set the same coefficient of secrecy low enough so that all nodes were sharing each other's negative predictions, quite another dynamic took over: predictive iteration accelerated faster than falsifying action. The farmer planning to poison the cows iterated to the burning of his barn *before* he bought the poison, each new iteration leading to another negative prediction in an endless sequence—which could be terminated only by a falsification which resulted in good fortune for both rancher and farmer.

The equations converged to either of two stable states:

(1) a semistable state in which a prime node managed the future of all other nodes.

(2) a stable state in which distributed iterative predicting (a) damped out, over all subgroups of nodes, predictions which had negative consequences while (b) leaving generally positive predictions to run their course.

Eron didn't know whether it was possible to make a nonviolent transition between these two end states. However, there wasn't any reason he couldn't try out different methods of transition on the Fellowship's gigantic psychohistorical model using current data. The Founder's mathematics was restricted to the conditions which led to state (1), but Eron had made the generalizations necessary to allow psychohistory to operate in state (1) or (2) or any state in between.

Since his revised model treated all the conditions leading up to state (1) in essentially the same way as did the Founder's math, he expected that when he ran his revised model with real-life input he would get the same output as everyone else was getting: a stable Galaxy with minor problems needing corrective action, a long-term prognosis of continued stability with a slow tendency toward stagnation that wouldn't become a critical problem for centuries, if ever. First Rank Hanis already had a solution for that in the works.

What he got was something very discouraging: a Galaxy at the cusp point of a historical crisis that dropped off into a chaos with characteristics that looked very much like an Interregnum. That was impossible. That was in the category of predicting that the next time he saw Konn, the Admiral would have blue skin, four arms, and an elephant snout. The math must be wrong. What was there to say but to quote Planck: "Man errs as long as he strives." Back to scratch. Again. What a downer!

For a month after that he worked at dissecting his model to find the flaw. It couldn't be the logic of the program, because the compiler was mercifully silent.

The flaw must be in his assumptions, or in his iterative methods, or in some ballooning error he had missed. But he couldn't find it. The dilemma was driving him crazy! He was too proud to take the mess to Konn. It was too embarrassing.

Yorick gave him the answer, breaking a long silence. Where did his revamped model break down? Try the past!

So, expecting the worst, he input the conditions of the last century into his model. It worked perfectly. Why should he be so stunned at that? A month ago he had *expected* it to work perfectly, had thought of his creation that it was the marvel of the millennium. With the utmost caution he stepped his simulacrum forward, a year at a time, simultaneously generating a report of the differences between his model and the standard model. They were minimal—except perhaps in Konn's blue regions.

But then, as he approached the present, the slopes of the singularity began to appear.

And this time the reason was obvious. The wall of secrecy that the Pscholars had built around their methodology of prediction was breaking down. Bits and pieces of high-grade predicting were appearing here and there in the oddest of places. In spite of the general decline in mathematical scholarship under the Pscholars, the Pscholars were, occasionally, being counter-predicted! It was going to get worse. Much worse. Quickly.

Nor was this outcome a future danger. Twenty percent of the indicators had already crossed the topozone. But because it *was* a topozone crossing, the error bars around the time determiners were large. Eron couldn't predict the moment of eruption—but the marble was sitting at the top of the hill, and the slightest disturbance . . . Eron didn't have time to tidy up his thesis. Urgency and tidiness don't go together; he'd have to tell Konn right away.

That very hour Eron vibro-cleaned his teeth, took the trouble to have his hair cut, put on a pair of socks, both black, had his manufacturum weave a brand-new businesslike outfit, donned it, and rushed back to the Lyceum to call on the Admiral. Thank Space he worked for *the* Pscholar who was certainly the greatest psychohistorian since the Founder and certainly the Galaxy's finest trouble-sniffer.

Hahukum Konn listened, with great patience, to his student's babble. He studied the collection of unorganized papers Eron brought him and the hasty scratch work. He shared visuals with Eron as Eron put on an amazing display of apocalypse. Carefully the old Master prepared his reply, while pondering the documentation, saying nothing until Eron ran down and fell silent, waiting. "Hmmm. Here's an error you'll have to fix. A Boltok oversum can't be diminutive in these particular circumstances. You'll have to—"

"I know; I know, but that doesn't change anything. I—"

"Eron, my son. You've been working too hard. Take a vacation. This is an interesting hypothesis"—meaning it was wrong—"but you've gone at it with a machete. I'd go back and take it from the point where you have, rather arbitrarily . . ."

It occurred to Eron that the Admiral hadn't followed his argument. He began again from the beginning. The Admiral continued to listen, this time not so patiently—he had a way of brushing the dust off his braid when he had gone beyond his boundary of tolerance. Eventually he stopped the exposition and began a ruthless deconstruction of Eron's work. And Eron began to understand: the Admiral was committed to his own interpretation of the universe, and nothing else qualified as real. How many times in Eron's life had he collided with that wall? He felt nine years old again, back in that stupid school on Agander with Professor . . . ? He was ready to sass the Admiral, get himself expelled from the Lyceum, maybe thrown off Splendid Wisdom. Old habits die hard. But new habits can come into play, too. He had zenoli training. Never attack an opponent's strongest position.

"Sir! I think you've given me enough pointers for a starter. I'll do a thorough workover." He had no intention of doing a workover. "The results were a little strange and maybe I got overexcited." This was exactly what the Admiral had been hoping to hear; he smiled and nodded.

Eron despaired at this agreement—that his teacher didn't react to such a retreat, didn't grab him and make him sit down again, didn't beg him to continue his penetrating line of reasoning, was confirmation that he had scouted well past the stars of the Admiral's farthest picket ship. Eron was fighting beyond the pale and the Admiral wasn't bold enough to follow. It was a shock.

They parted on good terms. Eron went home and slept right through three watches. He got up, trimmed his plants, wolfed down a huge supper, and paced. *Of course* the Galaxy was right on top of a major crisis if the greatest mind that the Pscholars had produced couldn't tell his toes from the Founder's Nose! Since the beginning of time men had been clobbered when they let themselves be blinded by an old false assumption that had been around so long it was the only comfortable way to think. Even the Admiral! Even the Admiral who *never* hesitated to twist his wit in the guts of a faint-hearted Pscholar! Eron felt strangely betrayed.

Eventually he went drinking at the Teaser's Bistro. Nothing else to do! It was early. Only a couple of students sat in the corner, cramming some course. Rigone came over and sat down, probably sensing Eron's depression. Because Eron was depressed he began to mumble about mankind's fidelity to outmoded ideas. That reminded Rigone of an ancient philosophy book he had been reading from pre–First Empire times whose metaphysics had propelled the Rismallians into two centuries of fatal warfare.

In reply Eron glumly related a story from the Rithian mythology about how the folk hero Galileo Galilei took up a valiant crusade to enlist his Church in the reasoned creation of a new cosmology, knowing that his beloved Church would fall into oblivion without it, and how he had failed—his books burned, himself forced by the Inquisition to recant, on his knees, begging not to be tortured. ". . . and I held and still hold Ptolemy's opinion—that the earth is motionless and that the sun moves . . . I abjure, curse, and detest the said errors and heresies . . . contrary to the

Holy Church, and I swear that I will nevermore in future say or assert anything . . . which will give rise to suspicion of . . . and if I know any heretic or anyone suspected of heresy, I will denounce him to this Holy Office." It was with this certainty in a truth that need not be searched out, certainty that faith could be forced, and certainty that the threat of torture would make men holy that the Church launched the Thirty Years War to extinguish all dissent.

Rigone listened. He added to the conversation a disparaging comment about the Mithraic Priesthood's insistence on loyalty to the king. It did not matter that he had the wrong religion. Eron didn't bother to correct him; Rigone never would be able to tell the difference between any of the dead Rithian religions, whether they nailed their kings to a cross or ate hearts to propitiate the gods.

Alone again, defiant, Eron stared at a tempting blank space on the tabletop between a love ditty and a witticism which suggested that it was good policy to love one's enemies in case one's friends turned out to be bastards. Eron took out his little metricator. With the beam on high he burned an Italian phrase into the available space: "Eppur si muove!" which in galactic translated to something like *Nevertheless, it moves*. Meaning Rith. Galileo Galilei may or may not have muttered that final judgment on the relevance of Catholic philosophy, but he certainly thought it for his remaining eight years of life under arrest in his villa at Arcetri.

Staring at that phrase, Eron resolved to leave Hahukum Konn and to work for First Rank Jars Hanis on the Rector's monumental project. A New Renaissance. Good. He could deal with that. And meanwhile he would polish his thesis until it gleamed so brightly that no psychohistorian, no matter how blockheaded, could deny its validity.

He felt the pride of Kepler: "It is not eighteen months since the unveiled sun burst upon me. Nothing holds me; I will indulge my sacred joy!" And the quieter pride of Planck: ". . . at the end of all his criss-cross journeys, he at last accomplished at least one step which was conclusively nearer the truth."

# A HALF-REMEMBERED FRIEND LOADS
# OFF TWO HOT PROPERTIES, 14,810 GE

*At the time of the predatory Cainali Invasions after the Sack we Scavs were of no great force on Splendid Wisdom, being simple survivalist scavengers amid the ruins of a planet whose population had been decimated from five hundred billion down to a starving fifty billion. We lived by selling layabout wealth to off-planet merchants with a fleet of relic jumpships, none of which survived the final siege. Such havoc was done to our economic engine by the amalgamation of mercenaries hired by the Cainali Thronedom that a confederation of Scavs under Leoin Halfnose . . .*

*An alliance between Halfnose and the beleaguered Pscholars of the still-functioning Imperial Lyceum proved fruitful. The Pscholars maintained, for their own secret purpose, remnant elements of the Light Imperial Couriers and were the only reliable source of information about political intrigue beyond the boundaries of Imperialis. With this information and their strategic genius they were always able to ferret out the weaknesses of the Thronedom to the benefit of Scav survival. In turn we provided the Pscholars with rotating hideaways, a military guard, technical assistance, and a fount of scarce supply . . . The legacy of this alliance . . .*

*Make no mistake: in these years of the Second Empire the Pscholars see us as petty criminals and tolerate us only because we . . .*

—From the *112th Report of the Cabal of the Brood of Halfnose*

After sleeping on his failed pursuit of the Frightfulperson, Eron Osa set out on the 17th watch of Fennel for the Corridor of the Olibanum, in search of the half-remembered Rigone. He wandered a devious path, all the while struggling with the subvocal commands that made his antique map device obey him. The map proved to be primitive but adequate. It didn't draw through walls or play with tri-dim images, understanding only addresses. But when properly assuaged, it became quite good at suggesting alternate routes. It painted arrows on his vision and properly labeled corridors and pod stations in large readable retinal type.

He had donned his general-issue fam but, heeding Konn's advice, left it inactive. He raged for the analytic powers of his destroyed fam at every wrong turn. He missed the ease of visual direction that came through the simplest of fams. He got lost and felt stupid. Once when staring up at a great heat pipe that rose through tiers of shops, a woman, thinking him demented, directed him to a free kitchen. He just laughed and thanked her. Hanis had honored him with Rank Seven status and then demoted him to this! But he knew he was recovering. For millions of years his wetware had been designed to walk around brain damage, and it was beginning to bypass the loops which had once gone through his fam—at vastly reduced intellectual power.

Though he had learned most of his map reader's idiosyncrasies, he was never able to discover how to block its ebullient tourist commentaries. After the initial annoyance, he even came to enjoy the huckstering—too much of his life had been spent hurrying around the wealth of astonishments that lay all about him. He became again the child who longed for waterfalls that fell thirty stories through the wild crystalline shapes of an artist's dreams. When the map suggested the Valley of Galactic Seas, and he found out that it was only a pod's short ride from the Olibanum, he was tempted to take the detour . . . but business first.

From a high-ceilinged pod station with ornate backlit windows that illustrated galactic wonders in all shades of cobalt blue, he walked out onto the Olibanum—and memories flooded his mind. Directly in front of him was the little cabaret where his confrères had solved the problems of the universe over lunch and maybe laid the odd minor love sorrow to rest, all in the long hours before the evening show began. Strange, he could remember the conversations and the passion but not what they were about. Perhaps such details he had left to his fam. The cabaret's clientele had changed—older now, some sightseers, a group of tourists. The students were gone, or maybe only tied up in class. The show this evening was titled "The Blue Tyrantiles of Singdom."

Up and down the corridor, bistros were scattered everywhere among the entertainment come-ons and the marvels and the mausoleums of popular culture. He paused. Even with all the changes he knew exactly where the Teaser's Bistro was: walk to the Deep Shaft and around its great promenade, and then, two blocks farther, was a little alley . . .

Eron was sure that he placed a Rigone from his student years, a beefy man older than his student associates, a blatant Scav, tattooed on his face, a boisterous reveler who could dance with iron legs and flip himself through loops if the music touched him, a man who couldn't be bought, who liked to cavort more than he liked to work. He'd turn down your most abject request with a grin—but if you were his friend he had miraculous ways of upgrading your fam.

Rigone used parts that couldn't have been built by any manufacturum; from where in space he got them, the Galaxy only knew. He could bypass protocols seamlessly. He could add thought processes to a fam that the best students vied for. He never pretended to be legal, yet the police were unwilling to touch him. An inconsistent devil, a cruel one if he thought you were imposing upon him, Rigone just laughed at you if you did him a favor expecting a return on your investment.

But the man was so charismatic that Eron could not remember if he had only admired the man from a distance or been his personal friend. Rigone's magnitude of character erased the content in which it lived.

As much as this had been his element, Eron Osa felt out of place once he entered the Teaser's. He kept to a table by himself, afraid to enter conversations without a fam that would give him instant access to a quip that would outwit his challenger. There were hand-signals by which a wall-spy would take his order, but he didn't order and finally a lean waiter approached him tentatively.

"Are you all right, sir?"

"Thinking." Eron smiled wanly. "Haven't been here for a while. Do you still carry the Gorgizon?"

"Gang-hu!" The waiter grinned, giving the Old Navy flat-handed salute.

Vivid memories came in spots. That had always been his order, Gorgizon. It was an obscure Imperial Navy drink, milky and thick, booting its imbiber into a long high-energy drive. The bastard civilianized version contained a dram of sweet liqueur. It had taken him through many an exam.

But it was Rigone who appeared from a back room and picked up the drink from the bar. He held it as his own and talked his way down the row of tables, ruffling heads with his free hand, exchanging affectionate insults, staying conversations in midstream till he was past.

He paused at Eron's table, as if it were a simple visit on his rounds, plunked down the drink, and made himself comfortable. "Ah, the prodigy is back."

"I'm on vacation," said Eron, staring at the tattooed face of the Scav in fascination.

Rigone was grinning. "As if you ever took out time from your permanent vacation to work up a lather. Drink up." He nudged the mug. "A special on the house." His eyes glinted at the word "special" and locked onto Eron's with a commanding insistence, waiting.

Eron sipped a taste. The drink was milky white—but no Gorgizon—a different brew with a different kick. His instinct was to resist it. He hesitated but Rigone's gaze did not falter until he took a good first gulp. Then Rigone's stare relaxed.

"Well—so you're back." It was a statement that demanded an answer.

"Just cruising." Eron was no longer comfortable. "Taking it easy." The drink had a quick-acting knifelike urgency to it, moving his mind somewhere in a rush. Danger. "Cruising. Navigating without charts." Did he really trust this man?

"No, no," said Rigone. "I detect the nervous shiftiness of a man on the make.

There's an aura of quiet desperation about you. You're in a hurry for your good time."

Eron's mental machinery was racing. Slow down. "I'm . . . not . . . in a hurry."

Rigone took his arm in an iron grip, squeezing, saying: You're coming with me now. He let go in a gesture that added: but not by force. The wrinkles about his intense eyes told of an old friendship that was not going to give Eron any choice. "I know your tastes, aristo Osa. It is our business to know our clientele. That allows us to make fast deals at the Teaser's. It so happens that right now I have just the girl for you. She's thirteen, new to the place and looking for adventure. A brash kid. You have just the level of maturity she needs to keep her under control. And she has just the right level of insouciance not to know that the world is a dangerous place—or she wouldn't be upstairs right now, snoozing in my bedroom. I want you to meet her." He stood up.

It was a command. Eron was to follow him. Eron, in response, hastily downed the last of his drink while rising, then let Rigone herd him, without seeming to be herded, toward the back of the bar, and up the stairs, and through a massive door that closed with a vaultlike sigh while its forcefield flickered on at maximum strength.

Rigone's private quarters held the spacious luxury of a man used to wealth. One wall was even reserved for the ultimate in space-wasting—four shelves of worn antiques that were not the reproductions of any manufacturum. They were black ivroid boxes, books from the Middle First Empire. Rigone's legendary collection. Few citizens of Splendid Wisdom could understand the Scavs' penchant for collecting originals, but collect they did. Eron didn't know where these odd bits of information came from.

Rigone noticed his glance and tapped on a box, disguised in its own black ivroid casing. "A modern reader. The original readers often not up to my standards. This one projects a book in any desired format and translates the archaisms if you wish." He added pointedly, "You don't need a fam."

"And where is your collection of thirteen-year-old virgins?" asked Eron dryly, to the point, wondering what Rigone had meant, remembering that Rigone's taste ran to underage girls.

Rigone laughed. "Any spy beam that tries to penetrate my sanctum will hear only a frivolous conversation between me and you and a silly young girl—but she exists only in the imagination of my script-writing software. The real thirteen-year-old is asleep on the floor of my water room, and she is no virgin. I sincerely hope that, by now, the robomaids have cleaned up her vomit. She has been a curious pest of the kind who has to pick up every tool she sees and flick it into active mode just because it's there. You will do me the favor of taking her with you when you go, firmly." It was a command. He swung open the bookcase. "But here is what you came for."

On a velvet-lined tray behind the books was a fam. "Not a standard manufacture" was Eron's first surprised comment.

"No. And I don't know who in the Galaxy did make it. It's hot and I'm glad you're here to take it off my hands—very glad—to say nothing of that thirteener. I thought you'd never arrive. I was informed that you had been sent a message. I dared not seek you out—not that I knew where you were."

"Can I use it? Is it safe?"

"Of course it's not safe!" Rigone roared. "But it *wasn't* built by the men who executed your old fam, and *that* is in your interest."

Gingerly Eron picked up the device off the black velvet, turning it over quizzically, longingly. "Your price?"

"I've been paid."

"By who?"

"I assure you that's *not* a detail you want to know about."

"Does it come with specs?"

"Specs? You're dreaming. It's a one of a kind. I did do a rough probe of its routines; not bad. I didn't like the fam-controlled bomb I had to defuse. Would have taken out the room. But I was impressed by its full range of math abilities."

Eron's heart leaped. "It can do math?" He wanted it badly.

"Not in any language you or I ever learned. But cleanly done. You'll be years getting used to its hailing codes. But it has a fine wakedreaming mode that patiently cycles you through the hooks into its routines. While I was at it I probed for kickers and traps. Seems clean, but I only know *most* of the tricks. I don't know everything. The techies who built that sweet familiar know more head-spinners than I ever will. It's got power claws."

"Would you chance it?"

"I'd as soon stick my head in a buzz saw. You're the one who has no choice." Rigone grinned.

"Give me a rundown on the worst I'll have to watch for."

"It's not a new model." Rigone scowled. He patted the machine and it seemed to cling to his fingers, molding itself to them before he shook it off. "There's a man in there. It's haunted."

"You've been grave-robbing again?" said Eron with some sternness, but also with a muted disgust because he knew horribly that he was in no position to turn down a ghoul.

Rigone laughed hollowly. "Me? I only grave-rob for spare parts, not ghouls. The man in there was murdered." And before Eron could even think it, Rigone's voice hardened. "Not by me, not by any Scav—*your* people murdered him."

Eron was past taking that as an insult. Eron's people had murdered Eron's fam. "Tell me the story."

"You think I know the story? I don't know the story. I'm a Scav. I'm a middleman. I don't want to know the story. I'm a Scav and I've never been dumb enough to want to take on the Pscholars. They run the Galaxy. I stay alive. So be it. But I don't like what they did to you. What I'm doing for you is a personal favor, not a blow against the Fellowship. You and I were friends of a sort, as much as a Scav and a Pscholar ever get to be—and you don't even remember. That horrifies me. I'll tell you what little I know, but it's not much. You won't like it. The ghoul in there is your old tutor. He was running some kind of astrology scam. Big deal. More power to him. Where in the Galaxy can you find more suckers in one place than on Splendid Wisdom?"

"My tutor?"

"Murek Kapor. You don't remember him?"

"Vaguely. It rings a bell. I'd have to dream on the name. Astrology? Doesn't sound right."

"The same racket you were in—predicting the future—amazing people with the mystery of your sublime vision. I don't know what he was when you knew him. He wasn't honest, but whoever he was scamming, it wasn't me."

Eron ran his fingers over the form of his inactive fam. "I can't cross-reference my feelings anymore but my feeling is that astrology degenerated into a parlor game long ago."

Rigone shrugged. "It's been through its mutations. Don't know much about the subject myself. Predicting the future is not my thing—we've never been able to compete with the Pscholars on that so we do other things. Who's ever met a Pscholar who could clean out a clogged shower head? So that's the kind of thing we do." After reading a few titles on his ivroid boxes, Rigone reached for one to pop into the reader. "Haven't I heard that astrology was Rith's first science? Probably. Astronomy is the easiest of the sciences and gives one the authority to commit all kinds of flim-flam. Did it die out? Not likely!" He called up the search menu and chattered key words at it in the Old Imperial dialect. "There are eight thousand plus volumes in that single box and I'm sure . . ." The search flicker stopped. "Ah, we have the Navigators." He grinned. "Perfect!"

What appeared in front of Eron's eyes was a page of Imperial Court history from the reign of Kassam-the-Farsighted, year 7763 GE. Kassam had run his galactic affairs by the mysteries of the Navigators who could predict anybody's future given (1) his birth date, (2) the galactic coordinates of his birthplace, and (3) the direction in which his head had been pointed during his first bawling cries.

Rigone flipped through the text and brought up a smug holo of Navigator Cundy Munn, Court Panjandrum and Splendid Wisdom's master Imperial Advisor for twelve heady years, regally dressed with the portable controls of his galactarium held under one arm. He had been executed after the Battle of Thirty Suns, an unmitigated disaster for Imperialis which led directly to the two hundred years of the endless Wars Across the Marche. Kassam had perished the same night, and the new rational-minded Emperor henceforth reduced the appeal of the Navigators by having them tortured for entertainment at his coronation.

"The popularity of foolishness waxes and wanes," philosophized Rigone as he switched off the reader, chuckling.

"You're pretty sanguine for a man who is setting me up to share the mind of an astrologer," said Eron morosely.

Rigone was still chuckling. "Am I listening to a superstitious Pscholar? Did you run the tale of Monto Salicedes through your fam under the covers when your mother thought you were asleep?" Monto Salicedes was a famous story, popular among children as a spine-tingling tale of horror set in the mythical world of the long-gone Old Empire. Monto was a social-climbing fam, the ghoul in the fam of a bitter old man who had died in prison. The discarded fam now stole the life of each of its new hosts and had them murdered in a drama that allowed it to parasite upon the body of someone in a higher station than the last host. Finally reaching the position of Emperor, Monto went mad, lacking any higher station to which it might aspire. That there was no such thing as a familiar in the distant realms of Old Empire was a mere matter of poetic license that bothered trembling children not one whit.

"Ah, Monto." Eron sighed. He took off his shirt and undid from its collar the general-issue fam that he'd never activated. He lifted the ghoul from the velvet, warmer and more fluid than any fam he'd ever touched, slipped it into place on his neck—it needed no holster—then redonned the jacket-shirt. It took another moment of courage to give the joining commands. He felt a dizzying surge, nothing else.

However horrible the story, Monto Salicedes was just a fable to stir emotions. For sure, there was a man trapped in this new fam and he was now activated, but the poor soul could exist only in hell, half its mind gone—there was no way that this ghoul in the machine could ever communicate with its new host, Eron Osa. Eron and alien fam had been created apart, each maturing with a uniquely uncrackable neuron-neurode code, forever incommunicado, two beings who used a mutually incomprehensible protocol.

Eron's mind would gradually invade the old and now-powerless personality of the fam, subsuming its assets and memory space, crowding it out, creating a new symbiosis of fam and man by the slow process of learning. Eron had become Eron Osa the Second—his old memories and abilities forever gone with his original fam—but now a man no longer limited to the barbarous vicissitudes of a famless organic life. He had ceased to be a psychohistorian, or even a mathematician—he didn't even have a position in society—but he was whole and could learn again, half man, half baby.

And yet—there was a crippled man in there, imprisoned for life in a dungeon without windows or doors. "This tutor of mine; you haven't finished your story. How did he die?"

"The police were hunting him."

"The police don't usually kill."

"The fox doesn't usually run so well. I don't know. He was trapped and just ahead of capture. There is something in that fam of yours he didn't want to fall into their hands. He pulled the oldest trick in the game—the split: the decoy goes yapping one way while the treasure skedaddles off in another direction. He was the decoy. The treasure is here, on a cold trail, and you've become responsible for keeping it hidden—without knowing what you are hiding. I think when he sent you his last message he thought he might be able to come back for it . . . but he won't, take my word for it, and don't ask me how I know . . ."

"I wonder—"

Rigone interrupted the reverie. "Don't make the mistake of thinking that you are in charge of something valuable—it might be just another astrological algorithm that a dead fanatic was willing to give his life for. No one will ever know—even you don't have access to whatever information he was hiding. You have access to the dumb routines of his reference algorithms and his memory space and nothing else."

Eron changed the subject to an immediate concern. "You've doped me," he said. It wasn't an adrenaline rush he was feeling, but his mind was unnaturally eager.

"Yeah. A P-drug cocktail. Loaded. You'll need every last molecule. Don't sweat. You've got big learning problems right now. Recall that the tuned probe is a subtle variant of the psychic probe. The psychic probe was once used to extract information from men with the sad side effect of reducing them to idiots. P-drugs were originally developed to make the victims last longer under interrogation. For the first hours under a tuned probe you need drugs."

"I've used a fam all my life!" retorted Eron.

"Believe me, you need the drugs. You're used to being in symbiosis with your fam. That power pack on your neck *isn't* your old familiar fam—it doesn't know you. Its tuned probe senses you and is going wild right now trying to make connections it thinks are there but can't find. You two will be months in a calibration roller-spin ride. I should keep you doped up and in bed for at least five watches. Don't push yourself for a while."

Rigone swung down a dissection kit for quantum-electronic devices. He was dismantling pieces of Eron's common-issue fam. "You're going to need your old identity module to access your bank accounts." He attached a small machine to the fragment he had liberated and placed it near Eron's skull. "Okay. Done. You can move it but it has got to stay close to your fam. By the way, that new fam of yours is fancy illegal. It can mimic identities. I detected ten identities, each with a history and a bank account. I've disabled the two that your tutor used up before he was killed. You've got eight identities to use, as well as your own. My advice is to take the Emperor's Vacation." That meant to sneak off-planet incognito. That said, he began the careful process of obliterating the remains of the common-issue fam.

"There's an awful buzz in my head," said Eron. "Is that the drugs?"

Rigone laughed. "No, young man, that's the ghoul. Your ghoul is frantically pounding on the walls of its prison—that's you—trying to speak to you but talking in a code that only the organic brain it grew up with could understand. Mathists tell me there are more possible neuron-neurode network codes than there are atoms in the universe. Good luck cracking it!"

"The fam seems dead to me. I can't seem to call up any of its routines—or copy any memories for recall. It's all a buzzing blank."

"Relax. You're trying to work at the macrolevel. Forget it. Your tutor's macros aren't your macros. And whatever world this fam comes from it doesn't use Splendid Wisdom's common-issue macros. Totally different interface. Go back to basics; you didn't have any macros when you were three. The world was a strange place. You and your fam had to figure it out together from zip."

Eron slumped down into an aerochair. "This will take years!"

Rigone pulled him up out of the chair. "I'm sure. But not here. You'll have to leave. Now. And you can't ever come back, my friend. I have my neck to consider. So listen to the story I'll be telling if anybody asks: I haven't seen you for years before this watch, not since you went with Hanis; I've heard the rumor that you're in trouble with the Fellowship for publishing. You turn up looking for a girl. I give you one. My opinion, if asked, is that you were a very stupid boy to publish. That's my true opinion."

"Leave now? I'm getting dizzier."

"Dizzy doesn't count. You're hot. Out." At this imperative command, Eron decided he had no choice. He got up and staggered toward the door but Rigone caught his arm. "You can't leave without your date." He was grinning. "That's my alibi for even talking to you. Her name is Petunia."

They found Petunia in the water room, naked, with her head fast asleep in the gentle arms of the dispozoria, unhappy face as white as alabaster, a spider-armed robomaid fussily trying to clean her up. "She must weight forty kilos." Eron groaned.

Rigone lifted her up easily and forceably put her through an ice-cold shower—to her feeble protests—then towel-dried her, blow-set her hair, and dressed her in the outrageous package in which she had come. He propped her up against the wall to see if she could stand. She stared at them both vacantly, then wandered off.

"Take her to the nearest spaceport, conspicuously spend some of Eron's credit on her, then dump her. Switch to a new identity and get lost while you reintegrate. Be a student or something."

"And Petunia?"

"Ah, the youth of the Second Empire," mourned Rigone not very sympathetically.

# A FRIGHTFULPERSON GOES TO
# GROUND, 14,810 GE

*[Editor's note: Two hundred and seventy historical studies by Eron Osa were seized during his trial for Mathematical Heresy. Not all of them survived the turmoil, but from those that did we see that Osa, as a matter of routine, constantly checked his mathematics against reality, his habit being to select surviving bits of recorded history, feed them into his equations, then compare results with the known historical outcome. Osa's carefully annotated test cases cover an extreme range of conditions of scope, location, and time. In only five cases did the retro-mathematics fail: in two because the input data was inadequate and in three where the historical outcome had evidently been falsified in the records by the participants to enhance their future reputation.*

*[Eron Osa was known for an ironic sense of humor and an ability to stay just out of the reach of trouble. The following quirky account is from a lay summary of a preliminary study he made of truth monopolies. It appeared in the radical student samizdat "Insouciance" a month before his trial on the 87th of Cloves, 14,810 GE, and created a stir, not so much because of its humorous content, but because it was a veiled poke at Certain Serious Pscholars who remained unnamed. The Arekean mathematics that went with it, of course, was **not** published and only came to light . . . In this study Osa chose input boundary conditions from the beginning of the Rithian medieval European reign of Pope Innocent III (60,115 BGE) when the Catholic Church was financially and politically able to suppress all opposition (the genocidal extermination of the Cathars). By psychohistorical projection of the Christian beliefs . . . plus . . . he predicted the disintegration of the Catholic truth monopoly over the next 350 years when a Protestant opposition would become firmly established after a hundred years of bloody war in which Christian armies would march over Europe murdering and looting Christians.]*

DONALD KINGSBURY

*— The Fate of the Ancient Priests of the Secret Word:* A cautionary tale for all psychohistorians

*Imagine an immense old Rith at the center of the universe, bigger than any wandering planet or fixed star, its Lord of Evil living underground with his vassal deamons in their dark world of sulfurous fumaroles and screaming sinners, its surface crowded with suffering humanity in need of a priest class to guide and direct their lives. Because of the law that everything tends toward the center of the universe Rith is the garbage dump for the detritus from on high—accumulating on its surface traitors, disease, pain, sin, and suffering. Above vast Rith, a mere day away by the soaring of angel wings, are the Crystal Spheres of the sun and moon and five planets and the outer Celestial Sphere upon which the stars of heaven are set by the Divine Jeweler.*

*These Crystal Spheres are the centerpiece of the Creator's Great Hall of Heaven. The Lord of the Solar System holds court with His only Bastard Son and His pious Paramour and His Loyal Angels who stare at His Work in Awesome contemplation, praising it with song and adulation. From time to time He raises up from the corrupt surface of Rith pure saints and saved souls to join in the celebration of the epicyclic dance within the Spheres.*

*Down below, on impure Rith, only the priests of the Catholic Church have been granted the right to interpret the Creator's Old and New Words to the ignorant masses—who, if allowed to listen to the Creator's Truth with their own sinning ears, would misapply Them to the work of the Devil. For His purposes, He needs some instrument for His Voice on Rith—a man with a talent for always being right. He finds and elevates Lotario di Segni who as Pope Innocent III, humble, moral, and always right, does God's Truth upon the Albigensians to the last man, woman, and child.*

*But time flies . . .*

*In a time far removed from Innocent's eternity, in a sun-and-spaceship–drenched Galaxy dwarfing mankind's early universe of crystal spheres, sits a psychohistorian pondering the meager data which has survived the relentless entropy of temporal information loss. He feeds those bits which remain into his model of history, knowing that under the celestial spheres and the crazy planetary epicycles, ancient Rith did not yet swarm with enough of mankind to form an adequate statistical sample size. But accuracy isn't at stake here. His math tells him that, at the high point of European Catholic power under Pope Innocent III, the stasis arising from the Catholic monopoly of the Word will be shattered within three hundred and twenty years (plus or minus thirty) by a protesting reformation of men lusting to listen to God's Truth with their own minds.*

*In our Rithian beginnings it was never enough to be on top, humble, moral, and always right if one wished to maintain a monopoly on the truth. And in every era since that time when an ambitious group has . . .*

—Eron Osa

The Frightfulperson Otaria of the Calmer Sea had not recovered from her panic. One simple fact had shaken all of her assumptions. *The Pscholars had destroyed Eron Osa's fam.* She had noticed that even Eron did not comprehend the implications of that depredation–and, given his drastically reduced analytic powers, she could not have expected him to do so. How stupid she had been to contact this leper! Hyperlord Kikaju Jama had called that one correctly! She couldn't be sure that the police hadn't been watching Eron when she sought him out and now, by contagion, were watching her. Thus she could lead the police to the whole movement and its destruction.

It was also possible that no one had noticed her with Eron. But to be safe, Otaria was staying away from her apartment. She was shifting her whereabouts hourly through a complex of business quarters, sometimes taking a long pod ride to operate in a distant district where she was unknown. She had assumed the identity of a small "charity" company she maintained for covert purposes, using its credits, not hers, to do what she was being driven to do, even though it was a panic response and not rational.

While her *mind* ran in circles, fixated on her dilemma, *physically* she was acting with a repetitive obsessiveness. Over and over again she duplicated Eron Osa's detailed thesis. It had been thoroughly erased from the archives. How could she be sure that she didn't possess the only copy? So on her rounds she attached it as a codicil to obscure law treatises while she was researching her legal predicament. She did crazy things like loosen the tiles in a public dispozoria and recement the tile over a copy. She spent one morning pirating copies of off-planet recipes and registering her cookbook as a public access document. Eron's monograph served unobtrusively, and unindexed, as one of the longer recipes.

She spent a great deal of time in antique shops, buying and trading antique manufacturum templates. Some of the templates she would modify to include Eron's monograph, then retrade them. It was a market no one could trace. Valuable template collections from all over the Galaxy were prized and bartered and sold and copied and lost in a frenzied market of collectors and decorators and the curious.

When Otaria was through tampering with a rare template gatherium of folding screens from the Cotoya Court of the Etalun Dynasty period, one template labeled "Group of Serene Lake Herons in Four Panels" no longer manufactured a restful scene of cranes fishing in the marshes, but rolled out, instead, Eron's monograph on the four ebony surfaces of the screen in inlaid mother-of-pearl. Deep in a music fascicle, Otaria used Eron's monograph to replace the prelude to the recordings of the Third Rombo Cantatas of the composer Aiasin (seventy-first century

GE), then returned copies of the template to the hectic world of public domain commerce.

She did all this to use up the energy of anxiety—while the emphasis of her mind was directed at one question: Why would the Pscholars be so afraid of one man? They ruled a whole *galaxy* with enormous confidence. They had guided mankind, successfully, through the Fall of Empire out into an era of unprecedented galactic power. Sometimes they stopped an enemy by parading overwhelming military force, but they never chose to defeat an enemy with overt might—their control was more devious. From a foundation laid down centuries earlier, subtle social armadas would reach a crescendo and roll over the enemy from some unsuspected direction, while the Pscholars watched aloofly, knowingly, armies and navies unused.

To attack a single man, to ruthlessly destroy his fam and works without regard to their most sacred principle—free will to operate within the psychohistoric constraints—meant that someone up there was reacting to a crisis that psychohistory had not anticipated and was striking out—rashly. But what kind of crisis would cause such an extreme reaction?

Fatigue caught her after sleepless watches of drifting and dodging and replication of Eron's dissertation. The scalbeast shoes she had thought fashionable when she first made them seemed rough on her feet now. She rid herself of them in her rented room's small dispozoria closet and wriggled her toes. She was tempted to do the same with her clothes—it was dangerous to keep wearing the same outfit in which she might have been seen with Eron—but prudently she first tested the room's manufacturum closet to see that its clothing mode was functioning. Caution before nudity. Then the clothes disappeared in a flash, everything but the contents of her purse—even the hat. Wearing her fam in her hat was a silly affectation, she decided—and too conspicuous.

Peeking to see that no one was in sight, she dashed to the public water room down the hall, took a quick steam sauna and a quicker snow shower. Her black hair was a mess, the ringlets gone, but she blew it out with hair-care and let it settle carelessly as unruly curls. It didn't look like the groomed Otaria she knew, and that was good. Still nude, she sneaked back into her pathetic rented room.

There, with barely enough space for a desk and a couch and a console, she spent a few hours poring over some of her collection of antique costume templates which she always carried in her purse. She was a history buff and styles of clothing intrigued her. You could tell a lot about a society by its clothes. Did the peasants dare imitate the colors of the elite? Did the soldiers wear distinctive uniforms, or did they stick to battle dress in battle and hide their bloody trade in civilian guise when on leave? Did businessmen and lawyers copy each other's uniform, or did they vie to be different? Did the men dress pompously and the women in gray, or did the men all pretend they were the same while the women competed outrageously with each other for female attention?

After sitting cross-legged on the couch, gorging on the gorgeous images until her feet went to sleep, she finally sighed and put in a sober search across the templates for something she could wear. She was a noblewoman so she deselected for elite fashion. She didn't want to be conspicuous so she deselected for sexual attraction and the eccentric parameters of current Splendid society. That left her with a satisfyingly manageable collection. What finally took her breath away was an elegant gray-blue jumper of fluted trousers that tied in with lace at the ankles and left only a hint of throat from the same collar of lace. As an added benefit the hands-off purse was hidden in a way that did nice things for her hips. The design came from the trader service of an Orion Arm Regionate that had opposed and then been swallowed by the Empire in the sixth millennium GE.

She slept while the room's manufacturum wove the outfit to specifications and cobbled dainty high-laced shoes to match. In what passed for wake-up watch in the corridors—the lights were brighter—the new Otaria took a quiet place in a student café overlooking an air shaft where the food was free but the tables rented by the hour. She had decided to take Eron Osa's damnable work seriously and slog through it. The table came equipped with an ancient but serviceable archival console.

Eron's mathematics was dense. Eron Osa was, after all, a psychohistorian. But she could see that he had at least made an attempt to translate from Pscholarly notation into the more common symbolism of engineering, not always successfully. She would have been lost without the sophisticated mathematical functions of her fam, which ran the equation examples effortlessly, drew graphs in her head, and compactified logical expansions. Sometimes Eron was so brief that she had to search through sixtynes of archived math texts to find an underpinning for the point he was making. She made progress at the rate of about two paragraphs an hour. She had forgotten what it was like to be a hard-core student.

The students around her shifted and changed, filling the booths, emptying them, chatting, leaving their garbage to be whisked away by robomaids. At third watch's end she had eaten as much of the student food as she could stomach. Despair pleaded with her to quit but fascination drove her to take a stimulant and push on through the evening shift. Student cafés never closed. She was tired and began to skip what she could not understand. Sometimes she just stopped trying to comprehend and fell to listening in on conversations at nearby booths. A girl cried, wondering if she should have an abortion, while her boyfriend held her hand. Two boys were having an animated discussion about the merits of specializing in eighty-third-century economic history as opposed to eighty-fourth-century economic history.

Slowly her fatigue dissolved into her mental background. A second level of energy blanked her awareness of her surroundings as her fam took control of her emotions and optimized the broth in her organic mind for a steady long-paced stride. She fell into the old student habit of exam-night triage: abandon what she couldn't understand, skip arguments relevant to a proof but not relevant to a conclusion, concentrate on the conclusion. And as the crowd moved from studiousness to third-watch revelry, the brilliance of the dissertation began to take a conscious shape.

He built up his thesis with generous mathematical case studies of past historical crises involving stasis—often a stasis induced by secrecy. She wasn't always able to follow the monograph's rigorous treatment—but Otaria was a history adept and knew how to track down his examples in the Imperial Archives without wasting time on elaborate searches. Her fam already carried a huge knowledge of the location of primary sources. A quick mundane scan of the original data filled in for her lack of comprehension of the math. Otaria was amazed at how the Arekean transforms isolated the essential institutions of the target time-and-place and the magnitudes of the historical momenta.

Intrigued, she began a serious study of his eclectic collection of case histories.

The first was a tour de force in which Eron was showing off the power of his tools even under conditions of sketchy initial input, poor data, low resolution, and inadequate population size. Prespace Rith of seventy-five thousand years ago (thirteenth-century AD) supported only the simplest examples of two-dimensional sociostructures, and that made for the sparse data points. In mathematics all details are not equally important. One does not have to know the color of a boat to know whether it will upend and how it will steer.

But Otaria spent little effort on Pope Innocent III's simplistic world. Its assumptions were too naïve to hold her interest. She sampled later magical times and nearer places to feed her curiosity about how stasis coalesced, shone, then collapsed, even novaed.

Long before the Galactic Era, a Coactinate of ten new suns on the Orion Spiral Front fell into the control of a secret society of terraformers. And then a renegade eleventh solar system duplicated their methods . . .

The Mystery Cult of Janara thrived for more than a thousand years until . . .

During the mid-era of Imperialis expansion there was a Boronian League on its then borders. It was an efficiently run scientocracy with a fatal flaw. The Ministry of Education controlled the school curriculum of 428 star systems to the last standard module. It was a monopoly without secrets, maintained by a dedicated Learning Corps that had the power to enforce the decisions of the Ministry whose job was defined as knowing what people should know. The Boronians shattered under attack by Imperialis; all their generals were thinking alike and became prey to . . .

In the twilight of the First Empire when the bureaucracy of Splendid Wisdom had an effective monopoly on . . .

During the Dark Ages when the Crafters of the Thousand Suns Beyond the Helmar Rift maintained a secret monopoly on the technology of the tuned psychic probe until Cloun-the-Stubborn . . .

Stripped to its bare bulkheads, Eron's mathematics was saying that stasis derived from artificial monopoly: what kind of monopoly was of no matter; benevolent monopoly, tyrannical monopoly, any kind of special monopoly, led to a rigidity that had a measurable shatterness coefficient. In his long tedious conclusion, Eron buried a chilling analysis of the Pscholars' monopoly of psychohistorical methods. He had abandoned his clear style and was hiding his message in a forest of obtuse conundrums, perhaps in the hope that only those who were brilliant enough to understand the profound implications of the message would be able to pick their way through his equations. Otaria was no longer able to follow his reasoning—but if what he was saying was true, then . . .

Then the Second Empire was in the middle of a historical crisis that had *not* been predicted because of a biasing assumption of the Pscholars that psychohistorical methods by their very nature had to be limited to a group of elite practitioners. Hyperlord Kikaju Jama's revolution wasn't an impossible dream—*it was happening*. Now. Otaria didn't have the strength to recheck her last manic fly through the dissertation's conclusion, to step through it again and make sure that she had read what she thought she had read, she just folded her arms on the desk and went to sleep.

She had no memory of how she reached her room's bed, but she awoke to the slowly brightening alarm. She had dreamed and she was fresh. She knew what she was going to do.

Calling an executive meeting of the leaders of the "Regulation" was not an easy task. No one had a list of the members. Otaria knew only five personally even though she was highly placed. The rest were code names to her, invisible functionaries who could be called upon to make things happen in mysteriously untraceable ways.

Because the "Regulation" was organized like an organic brain, it had a consciousness all its own, quite independent of any expendable member. Such a command structure made the organization quite resilient to police raiding. Any "neuron" could be cut out of the circuit and the brain would continue to function. Since each "neuron" was aware only of the "neurons" to which it was directly connected, capturing the whole of the "Regulation" in one swoop was impossible. And there were chokes built into the connections. Even if one "ganglion" were totally penetrated, the probability was small that such a penetration would overflow into adjacent cells. Of course, it was a very tiny brain, delicate; Otaria estimated its total membership at about three hundred. It didn't dare lose too many members at a time.

At a hole-in-the-wall pharmacy, along the Corridor of Smoky Dreams, Otaria bought a palm-size gene-making kit that was guaranteed to change one's hair or skin color permanently. Frivolity always distracted her from serious business. What she had come in looking for was the transgalactic postal outlet that the pharmacy ran as a sideline. There from a black booth she transmitted a single Personal Capsule explaining her research into Osa's work. She asked for a caucus to discuss a possible historical crisis, requesting that the best mathematicians of the "Regulation" be present so that her conclusion could be checked.

Then she waited. No one had more than a piece of the communications ritual—it had been designed by an expert, rumor told of a military man who had once been involved in the maintenance of secret naval hyperwave combat protocols that could not be taken out by any sort of enemy victory short of total annihilation.

Eventually she received her reply. The small spherical Capsule located Frightfulperson Otaria of the Calmer Sea in her dismal rented room. When she cracked it open, trembling, the terse message gave her a time and a place and a code event. The sphere dissolved. But who were the Orelians?

# ERON OSA AND HIS PETUNIA,
# 14,810 GE

*Appearing during the collapse following the False Revival, soon after the fam be-came one of the more prized commodities of interstellar commerce, an elite mil-itary cast calling themselves the Order of Zenoli Warriors were probably the first group of fully fam-equipped mobile soldiers immune to the emotional control of the original tuned psychic probe. They had a reputation for winning their con-tracted battles with quick, lethal strikes. Warlords who used them paid heavy fees, and warlords who did not lost their battles. The zenoli alliance with Coman in the Circus Wars of the Orion Arm . . .*

*Such was their reputation that all zenoli mercenary contracts were bought by the Consolidated Navy in 13,157 GE as part of the peace treaties of the Pax Pscholaris. The zenoli soldiers were dispersed throughout the regular fleet, and the organization disbanded in 13,206 GE. Zenoli mind training techniques re-main popular today.*

*The tuned psychic probe is a double-edged sword. Control it, and it will pro-tect you. Lose control, and you open the way to . . .*

—*Fleet Manual 3-456,* "The Military Usage of the Tuned Probe"

Dizzily Eron Osa led a sick thirteen-year-old Petunia down the Olibanum. She wore the elegant metamorphic leathers of some obscure 113th-century off-spiral culture–thigh-splits to the rib cage, lizard clasps, with a tight bodice sporting two grotesquely open-mouthed, ruby-eyed snake heads which were gorging on pink-nippled (padded) plastic breasts much too large for a teener. For a moment she withdrew her concentration from the point along the walkway one meter in front of her feet. She flicked her fam into advertisement mode and let her eyes scan the distant huckstering, ahead and for several vertical levels.

"Couple of blocks straight is a posh hotel," she hinted. "Us crapulous wobblers need a cozy bed."

Rigone's advice to dump this vixen at the nearest spaceport was sounding more and more like an excellent suggestion—but her grip on his wrist was a tourniquet, partly to support her tipsy balance, partly because she was very afraid. Nevertheless she was unnaturally happy. What drug was she on? He wasn't sure she would make it to the next corridor, much less the next hotel.

Worse, he was lost. Not knowing where you were in the Olibanum was not smart. He had abandoned his map device at the Teaser's, thinking he was immediately going to be able to tap into his new fam's navigational aids, but nothing about his new fam worked. Whatever obscure streamer of the Galaxy it came from, its operating system was bizarre. No matter what he thought, all he could get was a frantic buzz even though his organic mind was well trained in the methods by which a fam might be used to access nonstandard utilities.

"Petunia, we've been staggering along the Olibanum until I don't recognize it anymore. Do *you* know where we are?"

"I'm just a goggle-eyed following girl. I forgot to ask: that man who just went by on stilts, was he hawking an animal zoo or a human zoo? I've never seen an elephant. And did you gawk that shaft we passed? I shouldn't have done that. *Never* look down a shaft when you're all zink-zanged!"

"Stop. We need a plan."

"I *have* a plan, big man. I follow you to the nearest hotel, you lead. On the morrow the plates are washed." Eron didn't always understand her idioms but he was trying. "Rigone said you'd be happy to take me to the local jump-off. I had an off-planet ticket but I unzipped it. You'll have to buy me starside. We could get a cabin together. Do you kit-bag the credit for first class? Rigone said you were a very generous trick." Her eyes narrowed thinking about that. "We can't just stand here. Thinking sets my stomach up for puke again."

He was still dizzy and it was getting worse. The desperation didn't help. He wasn't going to make it to the nearest hotel. "We find a café. Then we sit down and drink juice until we are both sober."

She turned unsteadily to take a careful look at his face. "Big man, I think your fam's squawking at the switch-in rider." People streamed around them a little quickly to avoid proximity to her gluttonous snakes. "I've been figuring on you. You're a criminal. Your fam was diced. You cop a gray appliance from Rigone and now you have to go to ground—only on some other planet far, far away. Hey, I'll go with you for the punch—got no ties." She nudged him with her hips. She grinned.

Eron was no longer listening to Petunia's babble. Slowly he moved over to the wall, hanging on—to keep from fainting. Nothing made sense. He saw the colors. Pedestrians had fingernails and hairs on their hands. He was aware of the hand gripping his wrist. His zenoli training in mind-balance was useless without a fam to . . .

"Confused man," Petunia said kindly. "I'll eye for you." She started to drag him. "Fam's killing you." She pushed. "Get along, big man. We get that monkey off your back quick." He sank to the walk. "Hey, comrade. None of that. We don't need the bleeding corridor police. Up, up." She pulled him to his feet, fiercely, never having let go of his wrist. He followed her to a rent-by-the-hour hotel. "Not the dream hotel I had zoomed on. Don't even have time to ask if they double distill their piss." She paused, white-faced, woeful, punching in their registration, all false information. She used Eron's credit stick. "Crumbling place has no grav-chute!" She pushed him up the stairs.

Petunia eased Eron through the paired security doors, manhandling him because he was so much bigger than a tiny girl. She maneuvered him to face the bed—then shoved and watched him fall. Very gently, almost reverently, she disconnected his fam and took care to find a place for it. He shuddered with convulsive relief. She poured a cup of water and slipped one of her knockout pills into it, cradling him in her arms against her soft plastic breasts while she fed him the potent drink. "Rigone told me to give you this." She lay him down again, too weak to pull the covers aside and tuck him in, then queasily snuggled beside him, arms around him. For a while she had forgotten how smashed she was. "If I barf, wake me up," she whispered into his ear—but he was unconscious.

Eron opened his eyes. It was good to feel sane again. He gazed straight up, not really ready yet to find Petunia. One could always tell the cheapness of a hotel by the height of the ceiling. If she was still asleep, he was going to be a coward, take his fam, and sneak away on tiptoes. When he dared look . . . a shock.

Petunia was nude at the desk, using a small instrument on his fam. He jumped out of bed like a shot. "Sons of a sun! what the . . ." He stopped in midstride—the delicate fam on her back was the same make as his new acquisition. And where in Space had she put his clothes?

"Hi. Just tuning your fam to cure that buzz. I filched one of Rigone's instruments when he wasn't looking, that old tattooed prick! Pillage has priority over being sick. It's amazing what you can stuff in a fake bosom that no one dares look at!" She brought over his fam. "Try it on now. The buzz is gone. My hangover isn't."

"Your fam is just like mine," he announced suspiciously, glancing about the tiny room for his garments and spotting only the shoes.

"I know the model. I hail from a pov planet where jerk class can't afford fams. Mommy lifted one out of a hot shipment passing through and made me a gift. Gave me a boost. So I ran away and set out across the Galaxy for adventure."

"You're lying," said Eron sternly, hiding his genitals with a pillow. "I can predict backward to the truth. At least as far as thirteen years."

To that insult she took umbrage. "Every ass-faced citizen of Splendid Wisdom thinks he's a psychohistorian who can predict backward and forward with the greatest of ease, tra-la-la. I don't think you can predict me from straw."

Eron continued to gaze at her reproachfully.

She met his stare, vacillating between defiance and capitulation. "So I'm lying. Mommy was rich. I stole her jewelry and set out across the Galaxy for adventure. Is that a better lie?"

"Get some clothes on and we'll discuss it."

"Try your fam first. I want to see if I shot the buzz. And no sass from you. My mommy is a whiz quantronics crafter, and I have all her routines in my fam, and mine's the best fam made in the Galaxy, and I Spacedamn well know how well I can gerrymander quantum domains because I've been doing it since I was three."

Meekly he put on the fam and activated it. The buzz was gone but he still didn't have access to its basic functions. He watched Petunia slip into the manufacturum closet for a new outfit which had been in production. *She has a child's body,* he thought. Suddenly he knew he wasn't going to dump her. She was only a kid. She was going to need help. Her sass was probably defensive. Come to think of it, he actually felt extremely loyal to her. If he only had some clothes himself.

Petunia stepped out of the manufacturum wearing an electrospun all-weather chastity, tastefully tailored to make her look like a young woman, something for the spaceways. "Ghaaa. It itches. I forgot the underwear. Do you like it?" She pirouetted.

He found her attractive. "Attractive," he said.

"Am I adorable, too?"

"Of course!"

"Tell me more," she insisted.

Eron was observing his emotions with a reluctant amazement. He shouldn't be feeling that fond of her. And he hardly knew her! "I find you a delightfully entertaining young woman," he ground out through his teeth.

"Girl. *Not* woman," she demanded. "Don't patronize me. How much do you admire me?"

There was a rational answer to that—but the words forming in his mind were very different. "My admiration would follow you across the Galaxy to Star's End," he said impulsively, against all attempts to restrain his tongue. He was beginning to wonder where his conversation was coming from. Had he inherited his fam from a lady killer whose twaddle was somehow leaking through?

"Yeech! And will you love me till the End of the Stars?"

Eron grinned. "We have to stop this nonsense," he said, alarmed.

"Oh, no. Not yet. Tell me if you are sincere or just impressed by the subtleness of my sexy outfit. Are you my slave?"

He was her slave. Astonishing. When had that transformation happened? It had happened between the time he had activated his fam and the time she had emerged from the manufacturum, that's when it had happened. He paled. As unobtrusively as possible, he tried to deactivate the fam—and couldn't.

His delinquent child was watching his every twitch with a fathomless amusement. "Hey, you've caught on. You get the nicotine; I get the money."

He had not expected to be attacked by the tuned probe driving his own familiar. All his life he had been taught many clever ways of using a fam to counter the emotional control of a Cloun-type tuned-probe—the fam in its original form had been *designed* as protection against Cloun-the-Stubborn's early device. What was he to do now? He couldn't very well strangle someone he loved.

She stood in a defiant pose, almost ready to run, unsure that she really had control. "Hit me," she demanded.

"No," he said gently, though that was exactly what he wanted to do.

Now she was triumphant. "They say it's a fool who thinks he can take a girl of the Olibanum to a hotel room without getting rolled." Then with vituperation: "Thought you could abandon me, did you?"

Her anger triggered his anger. "I'm a poor tool right now, of little use to you or anyone else. I don't even have access to the basic functions of my fam."

She shrugged. "I can teach you. Couple hours. Do you know any zing places on this Spaceforsaken planet? We can amuse ourselves by doing the tourist gig while we work. That's what I'd like. But no drinking! *I* might take a few snorts, but *you* have to stay sober! That's an order. You're my protector. I feel absolutely safe with a strong man like you—provisio on your sobriety." She took his arm. "Let's go, lover boy."

"My clothes?" he said pitiably.

"Your new duds are hanging in the manufacturum. Something more my style than the rags you were wearing."

While he dressed in an outrageously loud pompfrock he continued their conversation. "As a matter of politeness, you might inform me of the rules I am working under. Then I won't run up against them and get zanged while I'm attempting to do something normal like flaying you alive."

"You're not allowed to hurt me and you have to come to my defense when I'm being threatened. You have to obey my orders, no matter how frivolous, but you're allowed to disagree with me if you think my orders will harm me or you. You still have to obey. After taking care of me, you're allowed to take care of yourself. You can fight it but you can't win. Those were the rules my mother invented for my father."

"I can tell such rules were devised by a female hand!" grumbled Eron the slave.

"Pretty good, huh? I think she salvaged them out of the guts of her defunct housebot, but that was before I was born."

Since his owner wanted to be a goggle-eyed tourist in the middle of his life's worst crisis he suggested that Petunia take them to the Valley of Galactic Seas. The uninterruptible guide attachment of his antique map device had recommended the site profusely. Since Splendid Wisdom had co-opted its oceans for industrial and domestic use, aquarium theme parks were as close as you could get to an outing by the sea. She agreed. "Yea, sharks!" she said flapping her hands like fins. "Will they let us in the tank for wrestling?"

The multistoried corridor was one vast aquarium. Stairs led up and through the sea past fish and bottom-walking monsters and down and around the abode of starfish, seaweed vines, sleek carnivores, school fish, eels, stalkers. There were vast malls to view the ensnared sea from a distance and small parks in which to sit surrounded by the sea life of the Galaxy.

In a bright park facing an underwater jungle of vines and flowering seaweed that harbored brilliantly painted sea darters and the occasional slumbering shelled monster, she taught him how to control his fam; it was primed to a finger manipulation code read from the motor centers of the brain. He wondered how he had come into possession of a fam once belonging to one of his tutors, a Murek Kapor. Rigone hadn't had enough time to tell Eron much about himself—such as when he'd had a relationship with a tutor, or how long it had lasted, presumably a part of his now fuzzy boyhood.

To get any results at all Eron had to play like a musician diddling on an invisible flute in his own schizophrenic fairyland, but Petunia told him that the fam would soon learn to sensitize itself to read the *thought* expressing a particular fingering so that his fingers could remain quiescent, or even involve themselves in other tasks. The fam's learning mode seemed to operate with pleasing rapidity—or was that the teaching skills of his vixen?

It took him only hours to establish linkages so that the fam could paint pictures in his brain, create sounds, kinesthetics, feelings. The fam would already be contrived to do those things at a very sophisticated level *but only in interaction with the prior organic brain.* Eron's brain needed to train the fam's circuits to a different code, and worse, he had to fight his fam's natural tendency to interact with a man who was no longer there.

They were climbing shallowly inclined stairs that ran beside the transparent cross section of a mountain stream—teeming with fish and other life that lived in melting snow—when he asked her a question he had been pondering. "Did Rigone set you up as my tutor?"

"Have you lashed your noodle? I was there to abscond with his property. I was planning to lift the fam you are wearing and run. I'd been stalking it for maybe six watches. Course, it's paucious good to me without an operator, so I'm glad you materialized. Even Rigone doesn't ken the value of your fam. Imagine how much a fam with a built-in slaver is worth on the pimp market!" She chattered on. "I drank myself silly getting into position—never try to drink a lecherous bartender under the table, but how was I to know? I'm only thirteen. Talk about zanged! When he carried me through his vault's teeth and past the forcecurtain into his inner sanctum, I thought I was making it big as a pirate. But I couldn't even crawl out of his bed onto the floor! You blew in—while I was decorating the dispozoria—and claimed my prize. I couldn't believe it when he cold-showered me and set you up as my trick. He gave me what I was trying to steal. You lose some, you win some, as my beloved Daddy used to say."

"How did you know Rigone had it?"

"Wise up, hick. You don't know half of what's in that monkey on your back. It's *built* to be located. You run away from me; I find you. Me. Nobody else."

"You're a thief? Who do you work for?"

"Myself. I do lots of things for a living, even go to school."

For the rest of the afternoon Eron was delighted with the results of his finger twitches—aside from the strange stares that he evoked. To alleviate his embarrassment he bought, from an odds-n-ends dealer under the sharks, the template for an over-shoulder photozither (complete with dead earphones)—an instrument played by pluck-ing laser beams. The dealer's manufacturum provided him with a solid copy in wood and brass. While he "played" no one noticed the lack of lasers or the lack of sound.

He began to feel human again. He had revived his ability to do long division in his head; he could locate himself in Splendid Wisdom's labyrinth, search and filter the local advertisements, monitor the maxwell spectrum, integrate and graph in n-dimensions, and actually recall long lists after placing them in storage, even re-member people's names. The math functions of his fam sent him into deliriums of joy. *Now* if he were ever to locate a copy of his dissertation! Idly he checked to see that he still had the card given to him by the strange Frightfulperson with the russet-gold flecked eyes who was a fan of his math. The possibilities took on a new urgency.

Because Petunia was in a quixotic mood, they spent the evening sleeping inside the substructure of a huge plastic whale which had a broken entrance used for elec-trical maintenance. It was not your normal dwelling. Eron drafted his photozither for a pillow and took the time out to consider his plight. He really didn't mind do-ing whatever sparked this girl's fancy—but he knew his lack of rebellion was an illu-sion and a deadly one. Fighting it would probably not work. Somehow he had to enlist Petunia in his cause so that it would be her cause, too. He had to discover why his mathematics had provoked such an extreme reaction in Jars Hanis.

At her first stirrings in the morning, he began his attack. "Petunia?"

"Ho-hum. You're still awake? You've been very restless all night, big man. Can't sleep on concrete? Sissy."

"The police will be after me. That's serious. If I just wander around in aquar-iums and zoos, something bad will catch up with me—and you."

"Not just wandering around," she snarked, "you practiced accessing your fam. I conduct under-the-sky seminars 'cause I come from a planet where we *have* a sky, not crescents carved in a shit-house roof. Lighten up. When desperate, have some fun."

"What are your goals?" he asked. "We probably have goals in common."

"Oh, shut up! Do you think I'm catching hook on that line? *My* goals are yours right now. I'm smarter than you are. I've had my fam for ten years and you're only a toddler who's been twiddling with yours a couple hours!"

After such a command there was very little he was allowed to say. He tried and nothing came forth. It was frightening. "Permission to speak?" asked Eron duti-fully with calvinistic fatalism.

"Go ahead. Make it short."

"I'm suspecting that you know who once symbiosed with my fam."

"You bet. I'm searching for him."

"How will you find him?"

"Your fam will know where he is. You're going to talk to it and ask."

Eron sighed. Dealing with a naïve girl wasn't going to be easy. "That's not possible. No one can talk to a ghoul but his partner."

She flared, her widened nostrils breathing fire. "Don't call him a ghoul. He's locked up in there. It's a prison. Fams are conscious, you know. He's suffering! He's a human being!"

"Not quite. He's a symbiont."

"What do you know about anything! I'm the expert."

"What do you want me to call him?"

She shrugged. She wouldn't say anything. A tear rolled down her cheek.

"Rigone told me I knew him," he said gently.

"A lot of good that does us. Your *fam* knew him."

She obviously loved the man. Ah, Eron realized, he had been her tutor, too. Perhaps that provided a way to toady up to this girl. "I remember some things." He was ready to drop the name to see what effect it had. "Murek Kapor was one of my idols." The sentiment felt true enough.

"If you knew him as Murek Kapor, you didn't know him at all. That was one of his fake names. He dealt with some strange people, even criminals, and with criminals he always used a fake name."

For some reason, Eron was shocked.

"All this trouble is *your* fault! When he learned you were going to go into the illegit publishing biz—"

"Nobody knew that!"

"He did. He tried to send you a warning but evidently you'd already zink-zanged or lost your planets or whatever. He only sends out smart code. It pinged him back that it had been intercepted and had destroyed itself. The police were onto you! Then he found out that you were already under house arrest for publishing. That's when the toad grew hairs! The damn police had back-sourced us! We had to do some fancy dancing." She skipped her fingers about in a parody of a cops-and-robbers chase. "I'm really annoyed at myself," she said. "He set me up with a ticket starside and a new identity. He told me to run like a stellar flare was scorching my tail. I should have jumped. He always told me that youth had to be extra careful because we lack judgment."

In a sudden moment of déjà-vu, Eron Osa was thirteen years old again. "He was your tutor, too?"

Petunia looked up at him askance. "That would be a peculiar way of nailing the tail."

"So you disobeyed his good judgment?"

"Yeah. Now no one knows he's in trouble. How stupid can a girl be! But I couldn't leave him. I'm the only one tuned to his fam. I can find it anywhere if I'm near enough—my Mommy's doing. Mommy told me never to let him out of my sight. That's why I was hanging around at the Teaser's. But I can't find him. I'm only tuned to find his fam."

"You seem to have done that!"

"You have to help me find him. How can he keep ahead of the police without his fam? I'm going to be mean and make that an order. Don't worry. When we find him, my family will give you the best fam you could ever think about. I promise!"

"Petunia. He's dead."

"No he's not! How do you know?"

"Rigone told me."

He heard the sobs. "I . . . wanted to get . . . his fam back to him," she wailed. Eron tried to comfort her but she shoved him away. "Get away from me. Get away!"

"He was more than your tutor. A friend?"

"Yeah. My *Daddy*." She lapsed into a silence punctuated only by the occasional resonant sob. He shared her silence because he had much to think about. So—he was the slave of a ghoul's daughter. Finally she spoke again, tersely. "Let's go."

They crawled out when no one was looking, pretended to admire the great plastic whale, and began to stroll until they found a seafood restaurant. Even with all the fresh fish abounding in the neighborhood, Eron noted wryly, the fish they ate would be manufactured. It was cheaper to build a fish out of sewage than to grow one—and the template could leave out heads and bones and tail. The manufacturing process was just good enough to get the taste right, but not good enough to build a live fish.

"We eat on my credit," she said stonily. "I have an account they can't trace. Eron Osa has to disappear. I'll figure out which of our secret identities you can use. And don't go sober-face. It's *my* Daddy riding on your back, not yours."

*My ghoul,* he thought. "Respect doesn't permit me the g-word, and he's not my daddy, so what do I call him?"

"His name was Hiranimus Scogil, but you're not allowed to repeat that."

Over delicious fillets made from Splendid sewage, Petunia recounted the rest of the story. "Mommy *hated* me flying with him on his sorties—he took me everywhere; I loved it—nobody suspects a nice man with a child—so, being overprotective, she rigged his fam's driving probe with some Cloun side-resoners to enforce his care of me. Mommy is a witch. That was before I knew quantronics. If you fancy me a hot-shot fam modifier, I'm not that good. To hit you, I just calibrated what was already there. Daddy never knew he was my slave 'cause he already loved me. Not like you," she said resentfully.

"The fish you are feeding me is delicious, and it is a lovely first watch to do nothing—but we still need a plan," he countered.

"You win. We switch plans." But it was to be her plan and she wasn't bothering to consult Eron. After an hour's thought, the remnants of the meal gone, their napkins twisted, she confessed that she was stumped. "I don't know what to do next." She snuggled against Eron in the booth, not the slightest bit afraid that her slave would take advantage of her.

"Are you asking for my input?" he asked hopefully.

"No, we'll have to consult Daddy's fam for help. Daddy is the smart one. You're just a cripple. I don't see any other way."

That meant she was suggesting a conversation with a ghoul. "Kid, I can't read or interact with the storage areas that were private to your father. All I can do is write over them. I can steal him bit by bit for myself. Eventually even the best error-correcting routines won't be able to salvage much of him."

"But he's in there, thinking. He can see with your eyes and hear with your ears."

"But he can't make any sense out of that input because we use different codes. He'll be seeing flashes and hearing noise."

"We *have* to talk to Daddy!" she wailed. "He has contacts and I don't know who they are!"

Eron felt a sudden pity for her—and for himself as her prisoner. "I have contacts, too. Let me use them."

"No. I don't trust you. Not with my Daddy on your back! You're some kind of a criminal."

"Petunia. I'll make a contract with you. Let me send out one message that involves a personal professional matter of mine and in exchange I'll work very hard to communicate with the fam half of your father. I was once a zenoli mind-adept, and that may help. I can use that exotic stuff now that I own a fam."

"You'll work hard 'cause I tell you to!"

"Child, there is a subtle difference between a willing slave and a reluctant slave. In this case it makes all the difference in the Galaxy. You are asking me to do something that has never been done before. If I'm willing, we may succeed. If I'm forced, we may only try." It was a lie; there was no hope.

She considered. "I see the message and I pay for it!"

"We'll have to buy a portable nonlocatable receiver. Cheapest model with security. And hide it in a secure place."

"We don't have to buy it. I know all about sneaky. I'm a trained covert agent. It runs in the family. That's why I'm here. I'm in training. He didn't think this mission was dangerous."

The message to Eron's nameless fan read: "Dear woman of the broad-brimmed fuchsia hat: I desperately need a copy of the monograph you so fortuitously saved. Send it by Personal Capsule, manual fade, if text still extant. Wait five watches. Secure receiver still to be procured. Eron Osa."

"You better be leveling," threatened Petunia, "or I'll make an adjustment to mush your brain!"

# ERON OSA AND THE GHOUL, 14,810 GE

*At the moment of combat the zenoli soldier must be free of all prior thoughts and emotions. Priors unbalance any thrust or response. Priors will kill you. Active preconceptions will kill you. Fixed intentions will kill you. Old emotions, grudges, resentments, angers, hatreds, loves, enthusiasms will kill you.*

*A soldier who enters combat hating his enemy is already a soldier doomed to failure; his hatred will blind him to the thrust that kills him or blind him in victory so that his victory is taken from him. A soldier who is afraid of his enemy is doomed. A soldier who loves his enemy is doomed. A soldier who is thinking about his enemy is doomed.*

*At the moment of combat the zenoli soldier is poised, inertialess, ready to act in any direction—like a marble at the top of a smooth multidimensional hill.*

*To achieve this null state of mind AT WILL the following eighteen brain-fam exercises are recommended . . .*

—*The Zenoli Combat Manual,* 18th Edition, Founder's Era 873

Viewed from the roof of Splendid Wisdom, nine hundred kloms from the Lyceum, a prodigious gash slashed through the planetopolis beyond which the distant city-encrusted Coriander Mountains gleamed in metallic and black hues. The great quake shouldn't have destroyed as much as it did and it shouldn't have killed 180,000 people, but it was an old First Empire sector that had been salvaged during the rebuilding under the Pscholars. Minor structural damage from the Sack, unnoticed in the hurry of reconstruction, hadn't gone unnoticed by the later earthquake. Splendid Wisdom was stoic about such disasters. There were great power stations to tame the heat of potential volcanoes as well as undercity mining operations along the major fault lines—but preventive measures weren't always enough.

Nobody was in a hurry to rebuild. The slash had been there for more than a century. Out of the wreckage, construction engineers had already cleared a canyon to bedrock and below, demolishing even the old tunneled maze, leaving a ravine too colossal for a single eye to encompass. Antlike teams of thousands were still strip-mining the fault block. Nothing had yet been rebuilt except for the ubiquitous antiquake mounts, wormlike elevated transportation tubes, essential piping, and a few giant weather towers that pumped water vapor into the atmosphere at the command of the central weather control computers.

A few yellow dandelions colonized isolated crannies of windborne dust, and Eron collected some of the lusher specimens in a discarded container so that he might take flowers down into his new abode.

For kloms on either side of the gash the surviving structures had been condemned, evacuated, and sealed, their rooms firecoated in a centimeter of SeeOTwo plastic. All services were discontinued. These abysmal depths of abandoned city invited torch-carrying squatters—not many, for it was a waterless desert without power or air circulation and Splendid people were spoiled by the plenitude of public services, city folk to the core.

Petunia knew the place, having been here before. They set up house twenty meters below the Splendid roof in a preprepared stygian apartment that could be reached only through a descending maze of seeming dead ends. It had to be illuminated with the occasional eterno-torch hung about the deplasticized walls. Eron dedicated one to his dandelions. If it was daytime, lightpipes provided a tenebrous gloom. The rooms were bare except for an atomo-unit that sucked in air from a nearby shaft and squeezed from the air a meager water supply supplemented by rain. The dispozoria was a camper's unit imported from some planet where camping was possible.

Eron had waited to ask his question. "Scogil worked with others?"

"Obviously."

"Can you contact them for help?"

"No." She smiled. "Agents don't work that way. Two's the max. Me and my Daddy. We don't see the others. You're a sloppy criminal if you don't know *that*!"

Eron had a flash vision of himself from his distant life as a Pscholar talking to a very secretive skull while he worked out the mathematics showing how political power, based on carefully guarded secrets, inevitably catalyzed—like his brilliantly blooming dandelion—the evolution of thousands of other secretive groups. And here he was, so to speak, in the secret room of one sneaky dandelion seed that had taken root in this weed-hostile place on a planet which religiously guarded the greatest guild secret in galactic history.

Sometimes Petunia visited hidden caches and was gone for hours. She never left on one of those expeditions without threatening Eron. "You have to be here when I get back. If you run away, I can find you, and you don't want to know what I'll do to your brain when I catch you."

"Yes, Miss Cloun."

"I'm only stubborn." She glared.

But she was all smiles when she got back with whatever supplies she had gone after. "You're still here! So you can share the delicious naval chow I brought for us."

"I love you."

"Ha. As if I trust that kind of love!"

Living in a once-luxurious dwelling which had been without power and a functional manufacturum for centuries—without even a physicist's rudimentary machine shop—strained Eron's tolerance. He depended upon Petunia too much. Her fam had inherited her mother's engineering know-how and she had been privy to such skills for ten years. He was still mostly inept, the basic physical concepts from his education surviving in his organic brain, but the fine technical details lost.

On the other hand, he was glad to leave the details of their survival to Petunia. He was occupied with the nontrivial task of training his fam to respond to his own uniquely coded requests. Trying to use this new fam was like hiring a bright child to take over the business, more trouble than it was worth at the moment—but the future benefits were great.

They had to build a bed-nest out of abandoned curtains. They had to wash the same clothes over and over in an inadequate water supply. They had to rig power for their portable Personal Capsule receiver. The simplest tasks required time out for patches of wild ingenuity. Petunia spent hours reconditioning a backpack-size manufacturum to obtain a source for small spare parts. She didn't seem to mind the inconvenience—which would have led Eron to guess at barbarous origins if her engineering talent hadn't so shamed him.

After a dozen watches of frenzy she admitted that she was exhausted. She voice-dimmed the torches and snuggled up with Eron in the curtains. "We're done. I officially declare that we're burrowed in and safe from the police. Except for the daily emergencies. I've made a place for you away from the hubbub. But so far you haven't kept your end of the bargain," she accused. "You're to be talking with my Daddy! You haven't got any more excuses."

"Hiranimus and I aren't on speaking terms because of our differences . . . so to speak. That's just the way it is. I've tried."

"Not so fast with your cliché drivel! Let's take it from the top. You Pscholars were never mech adepts, right? You tell me why you and Daddy can't chat and then I'll tell you why you're wrong. My people are an offshoot of the Crafters of the Thousand Suns of the Helmar Rift. My ancestors built the first tuned psychic probe on military contract with the Warlord of Lakgan. We built our own versions of the fam as a countermeasure to emotional control since before Cloun died. Maybe we even invented the fam. I know a few things about ghouls. Enough prolog. Why does that sloppy wetware of yours *think* it can't talk to my father?"

Eron looked at the dim ceiling and heard the un-Splendid silence broken only by her breathing. It was as if they were alone in the universe. "For the same reason telepathy never works."

"What's telepathy?"

"An old superstition. Never mind. Why can't I talk to your father? Any complex neural network can be trained in zillions of ways to think the same thought–each person thinks a thought in a unique way. The same thought has innumerable representations. A brain develops code to decipher its own thoughts, and no one else's. A fam is basically an analog device built on such a tiny scale that the individual resistances and capacitances and quantronic switch characteristics vary all over the map. That makes it impossible to transfer a memory from one fam to another. Crazy novelists who don't know their physics are always inventing digital fams as a plot device for thought transfer–but then your fam would be as big as a house and not very portable. When organic brain and fam grow up together in co-communication, they learn to talk to each other because they have spent a lifetime co-creating a shared code."

"Yaah! And the code is uncrackable and all that barf. I can zap your argument with one question. Are you ready to be dragged out of hyperspace?"

"Fire away."

She kissed him on the cheek. "Oh, my doomed wise man, all snuggled up in dusty old curtains, tell me then, why is it that you and I, each thinking his mundane thoughts with his own unique and undecipherable code, are right this very moment talking to each other without any trouble? Ha!" She punched him in the arm. "Are we the dumb/illiterate bear and fox?"

He couldn't see her smile but he knew it was there. She *had* derailed his logic. Language. Telepathy was impossible–but as a child her mind had built a unique translator between her thoughts and the galactic standard tongue. She translated "Petunia" thoughts into galactic standard sentences (or a close approximation); he took her galactic standard sentences and, using his own unique translator, recoded them into "Eron" thoughts which he could understand. Neat.

"Do your people talk to ghouls?" he asked incredulously.

"No," she replied with sadness. "It is considered sacrilegious. Fams are never reused any more than you'd zombie the dead body of your mother to do housework. Back home *you* would be considered an abomination. But my grief goads me. I *want* to talk to Daddy."

"What would you say?"

"I'd ask him how to get out of this predicament."

"I see. Ancestor worship. Why not ask me, instead of bossing me around?"

"You're a criminal. You don't know beans from turnips."

"I'm a bona fide psychohistorian, albeit a handicapped one. That means, at the least, that I have a very good organic brain, even if it is criminal. Do you want your father's fam sent to a safe place?" He was desperately looking for a common goal. "I'm probably better able to get us out of our fix than any mere astrologer." That was a dig at her father.

"You're a psychohistorian? Of the Fellowship?" she said, aghast.

Eron had never bothered to mention that detail. "And a criminal," he added.

Petunia began to pound her skull with both fists. "Space, am I stupid. Of course Daddy wanted you to take over his fam!"

"Why?"

"Do you think I'll tell you? You're *worse* than a criminal. Now I've got to figure a way to make you *his* slave! You're *fried meat* if I ever catch you sleeping! I'm already conjuring dire fam adjustments. Maybe I should just cocoon-wrap you right now and get to it, if I only had some string. Talk to my Daddy! That's a direct order!"

Did men who had been bonded in slavery go mad when they were given impossible orders? It amazed him how his mind was motivating itself to the pursuit of Petunia's hopeless problem. "Let's do a weakness analysis of the isolated fam; you handle the technical aspects, I'll be in charge of the math."

"I'm already building a machine," she said ominously.

Eron could well believe that this Scogil had been his tutor; the mathematical reference algorithms of this new fam were identical with those which had been installed in Eron's architecturally very different Faraway fam: convenient in that he didn't have to learn how to use them—but very mysterious. It might make an interesting common ground between two totally unmatched personae.

A fam was designed as an intelligent but subservient helper. The initiative lay with the organic brain which had millions of centuries of evolution behind its behavior, initiative being critical to survival. Scogil's fam would lack initiative, wouldn't even perceive itself as a separate entity any more than a thumb perceives itself as separate from the eye—but it *was* designed to assume delegated authority, and so a fam wasn't passive when working out problems beyond the interest or capacity of its organic companion. The ghoul was that part of the fam which was still carrying out the duties assigned to it by the previous user. It dreamed and schemed, trying to act in its old body's interest much the same way a man paralyzed from the neck down might try to walk or scratch his head.

An image came to Eron of the ornate hall in which he had taken his zenoli training on Faraway; rows of young men embracing fervently their fad for ancient wisdom, perhaps to reconstruct, in the safety of a cathedral, times when men lived dangerously. Zenoli was all about fam-mind integration. Surely some of that was applicable now. Long after Petunia had gone to sleep he lay in the dark, deep in meditation, recalling what he could of this arcane wisdom, trying to reconstruct what he couldn't. What was useful to him now, what was not?

He kept cycling back to the zenoli way of drawing out a passive opponent. It required absolute mental silence. He wondered if he could still create that state—the positive image of an active organic mind overlaid by a negative image deliberately created and projected by the fam's tuned probe so that the total would sum to quiescence. Had he attained enough rapport with his new fam to do that? He tried unsuccessfully.

In the morning—which meant the light of Imperialis struggling in through a lightpipe—Petunia brewed him navy tea. "Any progress?"

"No. My mind was too active. Hiranimus may be thinking—but he's off in a corner muttering to himself and not able to understand anything I'm thinking. He won't even know that I'm listening."

"You're discouraged," she reproached.

"Sure. I'm trying to get my fam to broadcast a negative thought-field to cancel mine and it wavers. Too much of my stuff gets through. I've been zenoli adapted—but the part of the fam I've learned to control hasn't. It's a long training process. I did it once, so I suppose I can do it again."

She grinned. "You were jacked to Faraway junk. Daddy and I blank with a built-in utility. No fam training necessary. I told you—we're the best fam builders in the Galaxy. Brain shut-down is easy. My fam doesn't have to read a thought to null it. Never learn what you can buy as a built-in resource. I'll give you the code." She wiggled her fingers gaily. "But be careful with the wake-up routine you choose—don't put yourself into a full coma. Or else I'll have to rescue you!" She finished her tea and stood. "Got to go. Scrounge time. Remember, your brain goes to mush if you're not here when I get back. I'll give my Daddy to someone else."

Eron was stunned at how well the commands worked. Within half an hour he had drifted into a fully quiescent state. He could even blank his visual field with his eyes open. But nothing else happened for hours. Until . . .

Something filled his dormant intention, like a rabbit sniffing the air when the snake is gone, a dream calling up his resident math utilities without being willed to do so. It was weird to watch the standard routines of his fam set about solving a problem that he hadn't posed, and even weirder to be part of a tranced mind so inactive that he couldn't understand what appeared to be elegantly organized logic. The Scogil symbiont was an accomplished mathist, trapped in a dark brig, alone, writing on the walls to keep himself sane—in a dream-code rich with the illusion of meaning that would mean nothing to Eron when he came out of his trance.

Eron stirred himself. All that he retained from the dream was the conviction that Murek Kapor, whoever he had been, was far better at math than his young student had ever realized. He took a torch and wandered through the abandoned ruins pensively, promising himself to be home before Petunia returned. When he came to a section that had been broken off and half-welded shut by the demolition crews, he clambered outside along the side of the catacombed canyon and found a perch. Imperialis was low in the sky, casting purple shadows. Aridia, in crescent, was rising to the east. How fragile Splendid Wisdom seemed among this jumble and open firmament. Evening was only beginning, the sky barely darkened, but already a hundred giant stars were out.

He was mulling over the dream-math that had passed across his mind, unable to question a deaf Hiranimus. Had he only imagined that the doodling contained clear traces of the Founder's Hand, anachronisms even, yet also full of odd twists

of thought and notation? Inspired, he used his increasing control of the fam's workings to set up a shunt that would record all calls to the math routines while he was
in trance, which he would be able to analyze when he came out of trance.

*A mathist rides my back!* There was joy in the assertion.

Home again, he found a Personal Capsule waiting for him in the receiver. The
message read: "I have found you! Irregulars of the Regulation will be discussing
your dissertation at the Orelian Masked ball." He skipped details of location and
time. "Important that you be there. I, for one, have questions. You will be needed
to interpret your work. Wear a black fur mask, trihorned with red eyes, template
212, Orelian Masks Cat-#234764. I will be the one in blue scales with plumes and
an upper jaw sprouting crocodile teeth. Sorry I ran. My name can wait." Unbeliev-
ably included with the message was a template file containing his precious work,
set to remain permanent. The rest of the sphere disintegrated.

Eron smiled. The beautiful Frightfulperson. Another piece of the puzzle! He
relaxed into a zenoli pleasure trance to relish his luck. Suddenly the alien was there
again calling up routines and getting coded answers that were beyond comprehension. He froze, drifting as far as he dared into endless peace. Hours later when
he broke from zenoli trance, Petunia was sitting in front of him, legs twined. "Anything?"

"One-way contact."

"With my Daddy?"

"When I withdraw into zenoli mute-mind he seems to be able to use the utilities. I can't tap his thinking, but I certainly *can* watch his call-ups."

She was excited. "Do you think *he* can watch *your* call-ups?"

"No. Different architecture. His call-ups are *supposed* to be available to me. But
my call-ups are only back-loaded to the fam through my cognition codes. That's
the problem with me being the priority mind."

She shrugged. "We've got to set up two-way comm. Otherwise the conversation will be as futile as broadcast video." She emitted an unpleasant gloating sound.
"I've been scrounging something that might work." She held up a five-node keyin
for the right hand. "These are hard to come by on Splendid Wisdom. We use them
all the time. You've already learned five-finger typing."

Eron frowned. "He can't read my fingers; he isn't connected to the utilities the
same way I am—and he can't see through my eyes no matter what kind of typeface
I build for him."

Petunia grinned. "Yaah, the code. I know. Keep it simple, Mommy always
said. Daddy knows the Helmar binary code for the augmented galactic standard
alphabet."

"Augmented alphabet?"

"Helmarians augment everything. It's a tinkerer's disease. Now listen. Daddy's
ghoul *can* read your mind, providing we don't use normal channels; it's just your
private code that's boggling him. So we use everyday language. How does he get

his input? We use the signal that carries the code and modulate it with a couple of transducers for your skull." She showed him a handful of circular plates stripped out of a psychic probe and a haywire of chips that looked like a bad hairdo. "Quick and dirty."

Eron paled. "That's going to introduce errors into my thinking, maybe bad ones. How am I to carry on a rational conversation while I'm distracted by, say, the odor of colors and the screaming of tortured babies?"

"You'll survive." She cocked her head. "If not, I can always scrounge another slave." She grinned. "But I know what I'm doing. I've fooled with this stuff—meaning my school chums and I. It's better than drugs. We had to stop when Mommy caught us. Don't worry! Neural networks are wonderful for their error-correcting robustness. You look robust to me. You'll be okay. It's Daddy who isn't going to enjoy this. It is going to sound to him like he is in a metal cage and someone is pounding on it with two iron bars, the bang for one and the crash for zero."

"Why don't we try some kind of transduction on the fam directly?" Eron pleaded hopefully.

"And violate its shielding? You want to *destroy* my Daddy? You're forgiven. I know you Splendid psychohistorians are tech dummies."

When they had the device rigged, Eron simply finger-typed a galactic standard message. The haywire then translated so that his mind wogged in Helmarian binary flashes. It was awful. Just typing *hello* was like being kicked out of a high-flying aerocraft into a supersonic set of turbine blades.

*H-e-l-l-o. U-s-e t-h-e m-a-t-h u-t-i-l-i-t-i-e-s t-o r-e-p-l-y. H-e-l-l-o* . . . When he could no longer stand his binary broadcasting, he went into zenoli mute-mind to listen. Calm again, he tried typing the alphabet—blasting his mind with the binary output of Petunia's device. He listened. He broadcast. He waited. He banged and crashed on the walls of his ghoul's dungeon. It was during a meal anxiously prepared by Petunia that the reply came via the symbol generator of the math utilities.

*To whom* . . .

Eron, impatient with the slowness of the communication, typed *E-r-o-n O-s-a*. Suppressing his excitement, he returned to his zenoli calmness.

A pause. The symbol generator began to write across Eron's visual cortex in a happy yellow typeface: *Your benefactor is pleased that his last desperate gesture was of assistance to you. What remains of Hiranimus Scogil is at your service—minus various endearing biological quirks. How much psychohistory does the rebel Eron Osa remember?*

Thus began a remarkable conversation between two crippled minds.

# ADMIRAL KONN STRIKES, 14,810 GE

*Isar Imakin: Do the equations demand that the monitoring Psychohistorians remain hidden indefinitely?*

*Smythos: No. Adherence to the Founder's Plan provides that the establishment of a Second Galactic Empire will coincide with a political operandi in which Mankind understands the benefit of being governed by Mental Science. At that time invisibility may be cast aside with the proviso that the Laws of Psychohistory themselves cannot be revealed.*

*Imakin: Why the proviso?*

*Smythos: The Laws are statistical in nature and are rendered invalid if the action of individual men are not random in nature. If a sizable group of human beings were to learn key details of how their future political situation was being predicted, their actions would be governed by that knowledge and would no longer be random.*

*Imakin: How is such concealment of the Laws to be maintained?*

*Smythos: A Galaxy approaching a population of 100 quadrillion will produce less than a hundred humans per billion with the mathematical, emotional, and ethical abilities necessary for the mastering of Mental Science. Many models, notably those of su'Kle and Giordom, indicate ways to attract all such talent into the ruling class.*

> —First Rank Isar Imakin Questions a Student: Notes Made During
> the Crisis of the Great Perturbation, fourth century Founder's Era

Petunia had to talk to her daddy and grabbed the keyin of her machine. While Eron endured the "sledgehammer" of her input and then, with less stress, translated replies, daughter and Daddy made broken-language contact with each other. But when they fell into argument about why she was still on Splendid Wisdom, Eron gracefully retired from assisting the reunion, claiming headache. It was evident from this exchange that poor Hiranimus had been as disoriented by detachment from his organic half as Eron had been after losing his fam.

While Petunia slept Eron was haunted by images of his Gandarian farman going crazy inside his fam prison. He pulled out his metricator and with its small glow lamp crawled over to the girl's makeshift probe and reluctantly donned the instrument of torture. What was a headache between student and tutor? He clanged and banged out an old private joke they shared.

*W-a-i-t u-n-t-i-l y-o-u t-r-y t-o s-i-g-n h-e-r u-p f-o-r V-a-n-h-o-s-e-n.*

All of these first conversations between ghoul and host were awkward collaborations—a little gossip and news but mostly compact exchanges of compatible protocols. It was a number-one priority of both ghoul and man to replace Petunia's unpleasant device. Then they went on to trials of various dodges that promised to allow them to share fam space without Eron overwriting territory occupied by Scogil. Eron had the normal fast-access to the fam space he was beginning to colonize, but no ability to read Scogil's space except via the language bridge they were establishing which was many orders of magnitude slower than normal fam-wetware exchange. Their situation reminded them of the pair whose legless member rode in a backpack on the shoulders of the armless member.

Once when Eron was taking some exercise out on the roof, Hiranimus broke in excitedly, *I'm sure I see something to your left!*

A ghoul is blind. He can receive sensory input from his new host but can't make sense out of it because he is using the coding of the old host. He is essentially in the position of a man who has been blind all his life suddenly regaining his vision; he can now see but he can't relate to what he is seeing. Scogil knew the difference between a square and a triangle, but he didn't *see* the difference. "To my left is Imperialis," said Eron, translating into the coding they had agreed upon. "The sun is low in the sky and lathering the clouds with a golden topping." Language was again the bridge—Eron could give words to what his ghoul saw. It was slow, but there was no doubt that Scogil could be taught to see again through Eron's eyes.

Sometimes silence between them was appropriate. Osa's most pressing goal was to understand his dissertation. After all, he was scheduled to give an explanatory talk to the Orelians, whoever they were. Rediscovering his life's work—with the help of his fam's utilities—was like stumbling across another man's astonishing outlook and becoming an instant disciple. His old style now seemed quaintly conservative but meticulously detailed. He remembered Konn's rejection of his methods and conclusions as "sloppy" and was thankful that he had spent years reorganizing his approach to make it crystal clear so that Jars Hanis wouldn't have the same negative reaction. That care now made it possible for him to understand himself. It was like coming across a pile of old poems and being pleasantly surprised that the handwriting was readable.

He wanted to keep Scogil abreast of his rediscovery but communication between them was still both time-consuming and frustrating–they hadn't yet been able to achieve anything faster than talking–so they arranged a compromise; they pursued their independent thoughts but came together every watch to share conclusions. Eron found the comments of this seasoned mathist immensely stimulating. Scogil gloated a little bit at having put Eron on the right track as a young student and reminisced with a fascinated Eron about a youth his ex-student had difficulty recalling.

At her father's suggestion Petunia returned from an excursion to one of their caches with an astrologer's jade ovoid. "Daddy's compliments." She handed it to Eron. He recognized the Coron's Egg and, because motor memory was mostly a function of wetware, remembered the activation sequence. But it was Petunia who took his hand and proudly showed him how to access the new Predictor Level. "Every time I wanted to play with my Daddy, he was working on that," she said somewhat petulantly.

It was an unauthorized library of psychohistorical functions . . . hidden in an astrologer's piece of flim-flam. In that moment of profound epiphany Eron Osa realized that he *had* been right–the Fellowship's methodical secrecy *had* created a counterculture of rebel psychohistorians working in self-enforced darkness. This would be only one manifestation. Theory said there would be several hundred out there around the stars, covering all ranges of aptitude.

"Are you a psychohistorian?" he asked his ghoul.

*We call ourselves Smythosians, after Tamic Smythos who was one of the fifty martyrs.*

"How many of these devices exist?"

*There are millions out there in the Galaxy, but the latest version which goes to the seventh level has only been in production for a few months. I don't know how many. I'm not in charge of distribution.*

"Your Smythosians have been pushing for a crisis?"

*Yes. Our extrapolation gives us seventy to eighty years to prepare.*

"You're extrapolation is wrong. The psychohistorical crisis is happening right now. Splendid Wisdom has passed through a critical topozone boundary and the effect will shudder to the ends of the Galaxy within months. I think I studied under the Galaxy's finest topozone analyst, but he was working with classical theory and missed this crisis by a league. It's now," Eron repeated.

*How do you know?*

That sounded like Murek Kapor's old challenge to his know-it-all student. Eron laughed. "I was there. I saw this big huge rock standing on a tiny cup and I wondered why it didn't fall over–so I touched it with my thumb. It fell over. Much to my chagrin. Actually, there are already two major groups here on Splendid Wisdom alone, both of whom know psychohistory very well and both of whom have been putting their weight behind different visions of mankind's future, subtly opposing each other–so they will both fail. Rector Jars Hanis leads the largest faction, followed by the self-styled Admiral Hahukum Konn. I have talked with Konn once since Hanis so ruthlessly disposed of me, and it is my assessment that in the wake of my trial he no longer feels safe. Most of the lesser Pscholars aren't even aware that the two major factions are, in effect, counter-predicting each other. In about a month they'll be wishing that they lived in a simpler classical universe. They won't be able to say that the Founder didn't warn them. The classical universe, in essence, assumes the existence of only one psychohistorian. Yours is a third group. I predict hundreds of others."

*That is impossible. So much counter-prediction would have destroyed the Fellowship long ago.*

Eron smiled. "How willing were *you* to stand behind a future for the Ulmat Constellation that went against the Master Plan?"

*We weren't ready to be discovered.*

"You're not ready now. You just suggested that you need seventy or eighty more years. The ability to predict is only half of the equation. The power to see your prediction to fruition is the other half. If my predictor is bigger than your predictor, I win."

*And you? Do you see a future?*

"A topozone is a very dark place mathematically. A marble on a smooth hill can predict its future—as long as it isn't sitting exactly at the top of the hill. I'm as blind as you, my friend. The old uncrippled me might have seen something."

Eron had not mentioned his coming rendezvous with the irregulars of the Regulation at an Orelian masked ball, but, since the ghoul in his fam would be coming along for the ride, it felt it only fair to tell Scogil. An upset Scogil promptly warned him against attending any such clandestine caucus. *Kikaju Jama or his Regulation be damned!* Involvement had already cost him his organic life and put his daughter in grave danger for no real chance of gain. In the fury following his warning Scogil laid out a detailed plan for escaping the planet with Petunia. There was a Fortress he had in mind which would be safe for Eron and where his talents would be useful. Murek Kapor again. His plan had all the sound of an order.

It was a delicate situation. Scogil could not, of course, order him around. If it came to a clash of wills, Eron could simply stop communicating and permit his growing mind to overwrite Scogil's. But the daughter was a different matter. Scogil's fam carried illegal built-in devices which no one but a three-year-old (or a trusting husband) would accept. Eron was slaved to Petunia as much as if he were one of Cloun-the-Stubborn's puppets.

Diplomacy was in order.

He had no way of knowing which course of action was best in terms of the greater politics. Neither did Scogil. Ironically the next step in this galactic saga would be determined entirely by trivial personal desires. Scogil was motivated by a need to protect his daughter. Eron was still fascinated by an encounter with the Frightfulperson who had saved his life's work—and he fully intended to make contact with her again.

Osa prudently investigated the Orelians of which he had no knowledge. Old when Imperialis was an unexplored border system, Orelia was ancient, its denizens of three airless worlds necessarily master builders of sprawling airtight cities. The latter-day Orelians of Splendid Wisdom weren't really Orelians anymore; they were the descendants of an imported construction crew who had stayed on after the great rebuilding—nostalgic in their lingering memory of a distant home's wild carnival. They were harmlessly apolitical and glad to let moneyed fun-loving non-Orelians join their masked revelry. The Regulation must be using them as a cover.

By very subtly biasing Scogil's conversations with Petunia he built up her confidence and simultaneously left her slightly antagonized by her father's lack of faith in her ability to handle danger. She was an apprentice agent of the Oversee and had done very well on her own under fire and had saved her daddy's ghoul, thank you. This was the adventure of her life. And so, much to Eron's relief, this capricious daughter took sides against her father. Nevertheless for diplomacy's sake, Eron humored every one of his ghoul's exaggerated fears.

He sent Petunia on a sleepover trip to pick up supplies from an arms cache known to her daddy—illegal weapons that didn't trigger a police report when activated, very illegal slap-on explosives, plus some antique personal force-shields of a pirated Faraway design and other doodads. She also acquired an edition of the zenoli manuals for burst loading. Eron chose from them the martial utilities he thought he might need, but only the ones his organic mind had once practiced with diligence.

Eron was eager to spread the message of his thesis, subversively if that was the only vehicle of expression that the Fellowship would allow. He was still angry at Jars. He and Petunia made the trip ten watches early and settled in at a local faceless hotel. That gave Eron enough time to case the locale, even the layout of the Orelians' hall in the guise of a potential renter, and to appease Scogil by attending to all possible precautions.

At the hour of the ball, Petunia was stationed at a safe distance, by Scogil's insistence, her duty to monitor the movements of the Helmarian fam. If things went awry, she had her instructions and a ticket off planet arranged by one of Scogil's fake identities. She was enjoying her role.

Brazenly Eron arrived by pod at the front entrance, his illegal kick and explosives well hidden in his costume. Inside, the pillared hall of many chambers and stairwells was done in gold leaf and inlay. The disguises were everywhere. He found himself eagerly looking for that blue scaled mask with crocodile teeth and plumes—the unnamed Frightfulperson he couldn't resist even though she might place his life in danger.

But first, in a nondescript mask of his own design, cognizant of his ghoul's stern warnings, he checked out the exits of three stories of the hall, forty in all, for possible newly installed obstructions. This was not a place meant to be easily guarded. That was good. The exits led from stairways or gardens, from an administrative corridor or a servant's chute or a supply tunnel. He left unobtrusive shaped charges primed to open locked exits and hid sensors that had been his favorite tool of surprise during the wild zenoli military games at Asinia. He programmed his fam to optimize a retreat under any circumstance—Scogil being too slow and blind to be trusted with such an enterprise. A pod, illegally brainwashed by Petunia, sat waiting at a siding in charter mode.

These precautions made him wonder at his daring, but Eron Osa was aware that vanity disparaged danger. He was vain. He was proud. Here were men interested in his psychohistorical research after years of working alone! He had become ebulliently enthusiastic for his old cause. Pleasing a luminary like Jars Hanis was no longer a priority. Scogil's dire warnings did not dampen his zeal. He wriggled his nose at common sense.

And love! At the bottom of a flared stairwell he spotted the crocodile teeth of his Frightfulperson in her simple gown. He turned immediately into an elegant comfort room to change into his black-furred, trihorned, red-eyed mask. Perhaps this time, with fam utilities to assist him, he wouldn't make such a damn fool of himself in her delightful presence!

Before he could descend the stairs, two gentle fingers and a thumb grasped his wrist. They belonged to a coiffured man of elaborate costume and ebony mechanical mask able to mock all human expressions grotesquely. "Ah, our esteemed speaker for the evening," said a voice from out of a rhapsodic smile. "You mimic well the Orelian verve."

"Have we been introduced?"

"No, it is in the nature of my associates to remain invisible, but my elegance betrays me as a Hyperlord. You may address me thus."

"I was to contact—"

"No, I am your contact." The gentle pull of his three-pointed grip steered Eron away from the stairs toward the banquet tables. "I have a special interest in your presence. The impetuous mermaid of the Calmer Sea can keep her salty juice in check. You are here by *my* invitation. But first, the food."

The tables were covered with exquisite bowls of delicacies, both imported and manufactured, steaming pots with lids and ladles, breads, flowering vines for decoration. A man beside Eron, defaced by a huge papier-mâché nose, poured himself soup. They took their food to a dim raised alcove with a convenient teapoy that supplied hot drinks and a stand for their plates.

While Eron kept an eye cocked for his Frightfulperson, the Hyperlord ate with restrained gusto. "You're—shall I say the word—a psychohistorian? A rebel on the run?" These were rhetorical questions because the Lord at once produced from his purse a jade ovoid with the five-fingered key pattern that Petunia favored. "This is a bauble I was sold—quite expensive. It casts stars and astrological charts and other such arcane drivel. I was told confidentially that it contains a complete working model of the Founder's Prime Radiant. But my peddler disappeared with my credits before giving me the codes. Perhaps you have the codes? Or," he added wryly, "perhaps you can tell me if I am a naïve collector of psychohistorical memorabilia who has been grievously duped?"

Eron took the ovoid in his left hand and let his mind spell out a rapid message to his blind companion. While he meditated upon the jade, he received his reply. *You are talking to Hyperlord Kikaju Jama. He is a danger to you. Leave this place immediately. I was only able to work with one of his motley collection of mathists before the fracas with you interfered. He may be here. Cingal Svene. Avoid him. I was due to meet with Jama the same day the police took to my trail. I'm sure the police made the connection. I repeat, assume that Jama is under police surveillance.*

Eron slipped the smooth ovoid back into the Hyperlord's hand. "I'll give you a demonstration after my talk. It is a genuine Prime Radiant, but I warn you, it is a thing difficult even for a good mathematician to use and read."

The Hyperlord's mechanical black mask twisted into a triumphant grimace. "I have the mathists who can use it once you show them how. They are all here to listen to your presentation."

Two hands took two of his three horns from behind. "We meet again," said the familiar voice. When he looked up he saw the smile of broad lips beneath the crocodile teeth and plumes. The Frightfulperson of his dreams.

Horned man and crocodile woman wandered back together toward the meeting chamber. His eyes were alert. A sloping floor. Two exits at the top. Two exits at the bottom on each side of the podium. A small holobeam room behind the podium. "Let's walk while we wait for our audience. I'd like to thank you in private for salvaging my life's work." He found the wall behind the holobeam room and placed a wall-breaker without her knowing what he was doing. One could always distract the eyes with pleasant chitchat. A couple of sensor drops later, he wrapped a bejeweled belt around her waist. It was a personal forcefield generator built somewhere in the Thousand Suns Beyond the Helmar Rift, probably in imitation of an old Periphery design pioneered during the Interregnum, more elaborately disguised than the belt he wore to hold up the pants of his own costume. She didn't have to know; he could activate her defenses at any time.

"Thank you. And you don't even know my name."

"Your Hyperlord friend called you a Mermaid of the Calmer Sea."

"I'm half fish, half fowl to him. You may call me Otaria."

"I wasn't certain I'd be here. I'm not sure of your security." That wasn't true. *Scogil* wasn't sure of the security. "If I suddenly decide to move fast, it will be for a good reason. Follow me instantly."

"Our security is the best. The Hyperlord has been in this business a long time."

"But you trusted me?"

"You're desperate, like we are," she said.

"I don't understand your desperation."

She smiled and, in the lonely corridor, tipped up her crocodile teeth so that he could see her face. "It's an intellectual desperation. That can be as terrible as not having a fam or a house or food or air. I notice you have a new fam."

"Black market. I like its math utilities."

"You're more sure of yourself."

"Of course. I have a fam."

While they walked back to the meeting, his fam read the scattered sensors. Nothing. Scogil was probably sweating in his dungeon for naught. He sent a reassuring message through to his alter ego.

Ushers were already at the entrances. Snooper dampers were in place. The black-masked Hyperlord brought the meeting to order and was enthusiastic in his sedition. He introduced Eron Osa as the prophet of a New Interregnum, the real one, the one that the Founder had delayed.

It wasn't that simple. But Eron spoke anyway. He dispensed with his trihorned mask. He was here as Eron Osa. His specialty was the historical forces that led to instability—and unpredictable events.

He sketched for them the undulating topozones of historical phase space and how their multidimensional surfaces were calculated. He stressed the perturbations that elitist secrecy placed upon the topozone parameters. A topozone's surface was the boundary between stability and chaos. While measurable social vectors remained inside their topozones, the sweep of the future could be foretold. But once these parameters moved across their abstract confines in any region of the Galaxy, the future became uncertain for that locale. Then, like wildfire, unchecked chaos could rage in a sudden conflagration, perhaps across the Galaxy—or die out for no apparent cause.

Psychohistorians were like firefighters. They could hose down areas, set standards and regulations, insure that fire never started. But there was danger in never having a fire. Flammables accumulated; when they went, whole regions went with them in an inferno at the whim of the wind. Stasis was the danger. Deadwood accumulated during stasis. Stable topozones collapsed in upon stasis like a wet forest drying out under months of sun.

Precise psychohistorical monitoring, with a single future as the goal, a Plan, could drive the social parameters safely inward from the chaos-touching boundaries of the historical topozone, but like a single kind of weather, such a relentless sun might dry out the forest and set the stage for a topozone collapse, followed by a fire, a conflagration, an interregnum. Eron detailed why no monolithic organization with a single mind could easily plan a history to suit everyone. The unsatisfied gathered slowly in the byways, spiritually dying, finally to become tinder, finally to produce secretly their own psychohistorians in an attempt to control their own future.

The Founder faced such a situation. The stasis of the First Empire had become so great that unpredictable historical chaos could be its only consequence. His best mathematics was blinded by turbulent visions of fire. He could not predict into the Interregnum. All he could do was find a distant firebreak, where the stars were thin, and set up a race of firemen who could build around themselves an expanding topozone of stability that slowly moved out to control the flames and replant the ashes. Inside that topozone the Founder could predict.

Now conditions were different. Psychohistorical monitoring, itself, in the absence of psychohistorical knowledge, was creating the stasis. Eron had difficulty explaining this thesis to an audience composed of illiterates who had been forbidden to learn the elements of social prediction lest chaos prevail. He had to fall back on analogy.

Osa asked his masked group to consider a murderer swinging an ax at the head of his victim.

The victim judges the trajectory of the ax and predicts that it will divide his skull. He ducks. This falsifies his prediction, thus proving that predicting is a waste of effort, right? Eron noted that his new methods of Arekean iteration converged on a future that was acceptable to *all* predictors, disadvantaging only those who refused to predict. No matter how many predictors there were, no predictor could wield an advantage over any other predictor. He characterized this kind of iteration as the mathematics of negotiation.

Osa asked his listeners to consider a primitive planetary economy about to fall into economic disaster.

Suppose each citizen of the planet is capable of predicting the disaster by a cause-and-effect deduction—then it won't happen. The prophecy fails, thus telling us that the ability to predict is useless—right?

On the other hand, suppose only one elite citizen has enough grasp of economics to predict the nature of the disaster. This single man is in no position to prevent the catastrophe—but he *can* use his knowledge to profit from it. He can carve out a fortune and from that commanding position dominate the new economy to be built on the ashes of the old. Prediction is then useful when it serves the interest of an elite who can predict—right?

Osa asked the assembly to consider a Galaxy about to fall into war and ignorance and chaos.

Suppose all men have the psychohistorical knowledge to predict a disaster abhorrent to them and to identify their coming part in it—then it won't happen. The prediction fails, thus invalidating the methods of psychohistory and making them useless, right?

On the other hand, suppose a group of Pscholars have enough grasp of psychohistory to see into the nature of the imminent galactic disaster. Suppose this tiny group is able to apply minute forces at critical places so that a thousand years later they are in a commanding position to dominate the new order they have created from the rubble of the old. They have lied about their presence, hiding from the rest of us while they accumulate power and special privilege. They remain misers with their methodology, unwilling to share their predictions. But their predictions come true. Psychohistory works only when it serves the benevolent self-interest of an elite, right?

Eron ended his speech with an outburst. "Psychohistory has served the interests of the Pscholars for too long! They lie to us in a self-serving way when they say that the gift of knowledge will drive us from paradise! Let the tools of psychohistory serve the needs of the galactic peoples! Let us negotiate our own future, not live out a future designed by men who hoard the tools of design claiming that they alone know what is best for us!"

Before Eron was even seated, the masked Hyperlord rose. He held a jade ovoid high in his hand. "I have here a Prime Radiant! It holds the secrets of psychohistory for us to tap. I have at the moment sixtyne copies of the Prime Radiant for sale! Eron Osa has promised us a demonstration!" He looked over toward another man who approached the podium in an iron mask and then spoke to Eron. "Here is the mathist I promised you, my boy." The crowd waited in anticipation.

But Eron had been questioning his ghoul and was primed for an answer—there is no better state of general awareness than a zenoli pause—and what he saw from the corner of his eyes put him on instant danger alert. Under the iron mask and unkempt hair of Kikaju Jama's mathist was Nejirt Kambu. Fams are good but it was Eron's wetware which specialized in faces, jaw lines, gestures, gait, the first things a famless baby learns. How many hundreds of times had he and Kambu crossed? A workshop filled with ancient aeroship design. Sneaking through the bat-infested caves of antiquity's storehouse of radioactivity. Debating in a Lyceum seminar. Why was Konn's right-hand man here? A quick fam check of the planted sensors detected a suspicious pattern of movements outside the caucus chamber. A police raid?

"I'll have to set up a holo demo," Eron said quickly. Then to Otaria: "Help me." He took her into the holobeam booth behind the podium, closed the soundproof entrance, activated their shields, and detonated the "spare door" behind him with the device he had already planted there. With his peripheral vision he saw the police enter through all four portals. An usher raised a forbidden blaster. The police reacted.

At the sudden death of the usher, Kikaju Jama dropped his disguise as a fop and disappeared. All present, including the police, thought him true to form and assumed he was running. It was a tactical mistake by the raiders. An instant later the Hyperlord appeared on one of the tiny balconies and, in a flying leap, dropped on the policeman who had murdered his usher, yodeling the terrifying Hyperlord battle cry which hadn't been heard in millennia. As the man collapsed under the falling impact, Kikaju's mask radiated Kabuki anger, his left elbow locking around the man's neck while his right lace-wristed hand grabbed the flying blaster. By the time they hit the floor, Jama was in command, issuing orders from behind the shield of his hostage. Chaos was his element. He was a Hyperlord in fact as well as in name.

The raid came to a standstill. Policemen are reluctant to attack one of their own.

But the mathist in the iron mask had no such scruples. With the reaction time of an experienced psychohistorian field agent he blasted both hostage and the Hyperlord behind him. Too much was at stake.

Under cover of the disturbance Eron and Otaria staggered their way through the imploded wall and were gone, following the optimal escape path that Eron's fam was spawning with graphic overlays. They reached the doctored pod and were two kilometers along their way to freedom before a police dragnet grabbed them in a vice that killed their power. Eron made a quick assessment. "We surrender," he said to Otaria. "No choice. But not right now. Don't make a move till they settle down."

Otaria saw the hidden men, blasters drawn. "They'll kill your fam again. And mine, too."

"That's the optimistic scenario." Eron tuned the pod's frequency to the police band and spoke loudly and clearly. "Truce. We will consider surrender. We are armed and shield protected." He wanted them to know about the shields. "We do not intend to use our weapons unless provoked." While he was calming and cautioning the police, he relayed a quick briefing for Scogil, minus the apology he would give when he had the time.

Scogil replied by ordering Eron to order Petunia off planet immediately. No chance of that. She would stay until she knew her daddy's ghoul was dead—or free. Her location readings on his fam must have already given her the cue that they wouldn't be home for supper. At this moment she was probably fabricating wild media releases about the Orelian affair.

The pod's speaker blared with a police response. "Truce confirmed. Weapons on safety. We have a negotiator on the way. The esteemed Third Rank Nejirt Kambu. Please maintain open communications. Over."

"Who is Kambu?" Otaria whispered.

"Hahukum Konn's man. That's *much* better than being cornered by Hanis. Kambu was at the masquerade *posing* as the Hyperlord's mathist. Actually, he's an old friend, so we may get in some real negotiating." He briefed Scogil.

The reply scrolled across Eron's visual cortex in purple script. . . . *the trouble I have taken to escape interrogation by Konn. Death is preferable. I must tell you that I have a bomb in me and I will use it. I have no intention of being the first prisoner taken by my nemesis.*

"Sorry," said Eron aloud so that Otaria could hear, "Rigone has already nixed your bomb." Abruptly he abandoned Scogil to his dungeon because . . .

Nejirt Kambu was arriving on the scene, well guarded. He and Eron spoke to each other from a respectful distance via their pod's quantronics, Kambu first. "I have already noted that our famless psychohistorian is wearing the fam of the late agent Hiranimus Scogil. I have deduced the remarkable fact that you are in communication with the man's ghost since your discussion this evening went beyond the scope of your original dissertation, rambling into recent galactic history—about which a Seventh Rank would know nothing. You possess certain facts which you could have obtained only from an enemy of the Second Empire."

"I'm being accused of treason by an old friend?"

"No. You may be a traitor, but you're being offered a deal by your old teacher—protection from Jars Hanis and a new top-of-the-pick fam in exchange for the one you are wearing."

"Point one: How am I and my companion to be protected from Jars Hanis?"

"A natural sore point with you. Admiral Konn arrested Hanis about an hour ago in a general sweep-up. The situation is fluid. At the moment Konn is Rector of the Lyceum."

"And king of the Galaxy?"

"If you say so."

"Point two: My fam is wired with a suicide bomb over which I have no control." Eron lied.

"Ah. You are his hostage?"

"No," said Eron vehemently, "but he has veto power over my actions."

"You offer stalemate? We both sit here until we starve?"

"No. I'm dealing. You want to interrogate Scogil. I can talk to him. We talk; I keep Scogil. We talk with Hahukum Konn present. That's the deal. My Frightfulfriend comes with me and she stays with me. You get our weapons as a gesture of good faith."

"A reasonable man. I'm glad our honorable friendship still stands. Thank you for the weapons. As a reciprocal gesture of good faith I will allow you to keep your shields. They are not a threat to us. You may be interested to know that our mad Admiral has obtained a copy of your dissertation. He still thinks it is full of crap but you have his attention."

# FINALE, 14,810 GE

*TAMIC SMYTHOS: . . . born 351 Founder's Era . . . no childhood record until 366 FE when he was brought to the Splendid Lyceum by his Scav godfather with a self-taught mathematics talent . . . not an outstanding student . . . volunteered for the group of fifty martyrs, 374 FE, during the rectorship of . . . transported to . . . captured in 377 FE at the end of the Lakganian War during the deception arranged by . . . escaped massacre of the seven at . . . sterilized and interned on Zurnl with the surviving 43 martyrs by the edict of . . . Tamic Smythos spent his prison years on Zurnl, where the stars were thin and the hyperships infrequent, reconstructing in secret the Founder's Prime Radiant as an act of defiance . . . false death certificate in 386 FE . . . smuggled off Zurnl for predictive work by corrupt Chancellor Linus, 386 FE, who sought advantages in owning the only psychohistorian . . . disappeared . . . no record until 406 FE when he settled on Horan of the Thousand Suns Beyond the Helmar Rift to take up mechanical engineering . . . In later life he joined (or founded) the colony at . . . had no children or family or close friends . . . refused to teach . . . morbid recluse . . . His extensive hoard of psychohistorical memorabilia and personal writings, including a diatribe against the organizers of the martyrdom, was only discovered long after his death in a tailor's warehouse . . .*

—Quick File of Galactic Biographies, 1898th Revised Edition

The eight-chambered apartment that the new Lord and Rector of the Galaxy provided for the house arrest of Osa-Scogil and his Frightfulperson was a paradigm of luxury. In one of those touches of irony that the Admiral loved, it was the ex-residence of First Rank Jars Hanis. As his lieutenant Nejirt Kambu wryly put it, "This was the only prison we could find on short notice that had all the proper security features required to hold recidivist criminals."

DONALD KINGSBURY

The apartment might well have served as the tomb for a 784th Dynasty Rithian pharaoh, excepting perhaps the improbable dispozoria decorated with a goldsmith's abstract Foawan birds and equipped with such items as a penis holder and shaker for urination. Every article needed for a comfortable afterlife had been provided, including toy-size artificial servants fit for a pharaoh. Hanis' private mnemonifiers dominated their own special room, the machines paneled in bas-relief scenes depicting marshland reeds and grass done in gold foil and platinum and ceramic alloy, replete with extinct Rithian ducks and herons and geese and pterosaurs and various other flying beasts whose galactic origin Osa-Scogil could not identify. All devices were disconnected from the world of the living.

They were not being allowed either news of, or contact with, the mortal sphere.

Eron cased the mansion room by room for possible escape scenes, even the domed roof of the spiral staircase, while Scogil advised caution and grumbled that their predicament was the price Eron was paying for incomplete planning and let's not have more of the same. Communication between ghoul and host improved hourly as a mutual mathematical ingenuity invented more efficient protocols. There was no way around using words, but they had managed to up the word rate to a hundred times normal verbal speed. It made heated arguing easier.

With Eron's help Scogil had learned to see at about the level of a five-month-old child and, keen for more meaning in his images, kept insisting that Eron touch everything he saw and hinting that putting things in his mouth would add to the useful data. With Scogil's help, Eron's limited (de-fammed) vocabulary was being added to at about the rate of ten thousand words per watch.

"This wall is hollow," said Eron, after slapping the location where the air-conditioning ducts must be passing through.

*Forget it! We'll have to con our way out of this one.*

Under such conditions of isolation it was a major event when Magda arrived with a porter and a package of Eron's old possessions which the Admiral had slyly salvaged from the general destruction of Osa's records during the time of his trial. Included was his carved and inlaid Rithian skull. "Ah, my friend Yorick." He was strongly touched by Hahukum's thoughtfulness. *He's fattening us up for the slaughter* was Scogil's cautionary comment.

"When is the Admiral coming for dinner?"

Magda merely smiled and went off to prepare her best supper. Eron hadn't seen her since leaving Konn to work with Hanis, and he was saddened to note that she now wore stylish inertial bracelets around her wrists which had the function of actively damping the tremor in her hands. She could no longer play the violin. Probably she would only last a few more years—the victim of a fatalistic Rithian culture that accepted as natural a random assassination lottery for ridding its gene pool of accumulated mutations, believing, perhaps, that it was Destiny's will to let kind atheists pick up the pieces. The Admiral was, as always, a contradiction.

Otaria, starved for company and news, invited Magda to stay for supper, but she gracefully declined. It was against orders. When they tried to steal tidbits of news from her, she confined herself to small talk. "Will you let me see the rest of your apartment? It's fabulous." Then she shook her head. "But it's too full for me." When asked again about the Admiral, Magda offered only an incomprehensible Rithian idiom about men who danced with horses. Then she was gone. The Rector's personal search agent supplied unhelpful translations of her oblique idiom: (1) cavalry, (2) the circus, (3) when horses dance the polka under a blue moon, (4) good time partying by bovine farmhands.

All the while Scogil's ghoul kept up a worried dialogue about his daughter. Had she safely escaped Splendid Wisdom? What might have gone wrong? Eron didn't have heart to tell him that she was certainly still here, probably writing and distributing mischief to underground rumor mills claiming inside knowledge of multiple (and mythical) groups of psychohistorians plotting against the government. It had been her idea of what to do in case her father failed to return from the masked ball; Eron had humored her by working out a psychomathematical diffusion estimate for the spread of such colorful stories, showing her the design parameters needed if they were to be passed by word of mouth with a high mutation factor and a ridiculous longevity. He hadn't known then that Jars Hanis would be arrested in a coup d'état. That by itself would amplify the diffusion rate of such rumors by a factor of ten.

Specialists from the office of Cal Barna came to question, but these polite interrogators pressed no topic the two did not wish to pursue. In counterpoint Nejirt Kambu arrived late in every third or sixth watch but did not question. He always began his visit by offered Konn's apology for not making an appearance due to the press of "political events." Philosophical probing seemed to be Kambu's main pursuit. He was witty, if conservative, and Otaria took pleasure in needling him. Eron was frustrated by their discussions. Nejirt was one of these men of great integrity who believed firmly in his duty as a member of the elite to give good government but a blockhead on the subject of the right of vassals of the Empire to negotiate their own future. He genuinely believed that a man untrained in psychohistory was a danger to himself and needed benevolent guidance à la Galileo.

These debates left no doubt that Nejirt Kambu was a brilliant Pscholar of the breed who knew how to modify futures to fit a plan. When on the theme of directed change, he lost his conservative veneer and became a wild player who had mastered all the tricks of discreet historical manipulation. It was also obvious that he had been shaken by the appearance of astrological galactaria with a seventh layer that contained an unauthorized compendium of the Founder's lifework. At one point he tried to draw out Scogil's comment by mentioning that a task force, escorted by the navy, had been sent to investigate the Coron's Wisp Pentad.

*It does not matter,* Scogil briefed Eron. *The Eggs with the final Predictor's seventh level are not being released in the Wisp and are not being manufactured there. There are no plans to upgrade the Coronese from astrologer to psychohistorian. They are being used only as an astrological infection vector. Others of the Oversee are in charge of elevating talented members of the target population to advanced status. Konn's task force will find in the Wisp only astrologers.* Scogil was a game player with psychohistory as the rule book and futures as the winnings.

Even though Eron had reworked predictive mathematics to eliminate its main contradiction, he had been brought up within a worldview where psychohistory meant a single benign future determined by a single monolithic organization, i.e., history from the Founder's necessarily Imperial point of view. A trap. He was becoming very fond of Scogil's mind as well as exasperated by his angry ghoul. He remembered his tutor as a mellower man, almost too mellow. Perhaps the old Murek had achieved that mellowness only by burying his anger in his fam.

Otaria balanced the three male views of Osa-Scogil and Kambu with a lighter touch more interested in the inner energy that motivated mortal man over the vast span of galaxies and time. She knew her history. When she judged one of Eron's moral monologs to be pretentious she offered a funny historical anecdote to blunt his sharpness. Scogil she teased because she had known him as a man. And for every point that Nejirt made, she had a mischievous counterexample, delighting in being contrary.

Nejirt threw her only once. Without disputing a particularly cutting barb, he brought out a black card. "May I contradict you with a simple gift?"

She took the card with a puzzled distrust.

"The encryption codes to Hanis' personal archives." He read the incredulity in Eron's face. "No, the Admiral shouldn't have those in his possession, but then"—he shrugged—"he's been tracking Hanis for a long time."

"You can't be suggesting unlimited access?"

"Yes."

"Why?"

"I'm not privy to the Admiral's mind. He wants you to have full recourse to the past."

"But not the present?"

"The pace of present events would distract you."

As a result Eron-Hiranimus spent hours rooting about with Otaria in Hanis' old study. The deposed Rector's files consisted mainly of annotated pointers to the restricted library of the Pscholars. He was an organizer more than an original thinker. Otaria loved this kind of wallow with the relish of a gossip and a historian who has lucked into a musty store of documents unseen by man for ages. Eron, on the other hand, took the opportunity to roam over the full range of the official future history. As a Seventh Rank student he had worked with only a tiny part of it of which he remembered little. Scogil had a special interest in the plans Hanis had made for certain regions of the Galaxy, his mind almost automatically working up counter-predictions to futures he found disagreeable, some aspects of which he shared with Eron. A program whose inevitable result would be the hybridizing of Helmarian culture with it neighbors brought out the most indignation.

The renaissance Jars had intended to impose upon the Empire was awesome in its scope. Eron was reminded of a book he had once seen, a collection of sketches of architectural marvels which had never been built. He felt a stab of sympathy for the old codger—how else could a man of such lofty dreams have reacted to Eron's dissertation outlining in the clearest mathematical terms why his life's work was doomed?

With trepidation Eron decided to attempt activation of his own personal student files. In all likelihood they were wiped. They had once resided as a symbiotic subroutine of the Great Galactic Model. Though he had never been of high enough rank himself to revise that vast model, a student was allowed to test modifications from within a walled domain. He couldn't remember his entrance code, but it seemed that foresight had inserted it as a riddle in the index of his dissertation based on the poetry of Emperor Arum-the-Patient.

Otaria peered over his shoulder. Instead of receiving a notification of erasure, his call triggered a secondary startling security check: "Authority level uncertain. Additional information requested. What city was bombed on the 53rd watch of Parsley, 14,798?"

Konn must have blocked erasure at the time of Eron's trial! What a strange man!

His befuddled organic brain was going to have to find an answer to that question. Scogil might contain libraries but not that bit of information. Was it "B"? What began with "B"? Recklessly he input the name "Bremen" and—miraculously—opened up access to the currently defined state function of the galactic civilization. He tested. His own tools were still intact. That took a big strain off his brain; he knew he could *use* his old tools, but he didn't know if he had enough left of his mind, even with Scogil's assistance, to *re-create* them. Immediately he began to demonstrate to his ghoul why the Oversee would fail to achieve their goals. They, too, were using classical mathematics to predict their way through a peculiar psychohistorical crisis for which the mathematics of the Founder did not apply.

He got the same reaction from Scogil as he had first from Konn and then from Hanis. He shrugged; every century had its cardinals.

Eron calculated that it was just about time for the Admiral to make his grand entrance. Keeping the people who were important to him waiting and sweating a little was his style. He wanted to make sure that Eron Osa knew that Konn had power and that Konn chose to exercise his power via a very different mode than had First Rank Jars Hanis. There was to be no relentless bullying, no ultimatum, no conflagration of fams, no draconian solutions. That was the method by which the Admiral got his way.

When the curmudgeon finally came to dinner (on schedule), he appeared in the uniform of Ultimate Sam's Amazing Air Fangs: gold-braided knee-length blue-coat with the tricorn headpiece of a thirteen-star general. He held under his arm a box of Eron's favorite biscuits from the commissary near the Lyceum study carrels—as well as a heavy briefcase, which meant a long work session after the wine. It was so like Konn to remember the little details which were much more powerful than logic. Eron smiled and sneaked open the biscuits. Vanilla bunny rabbits with cherry eyes. But he still felt merciless. It was all a serious military campaign to this crusty old Admiral. Konn wasn't going to enjoy defeat. But he had never, to Eron's knowledge, burned anybody at the stake for disagreeing with orthodox reasoning.

"Good that you found time to see us, sir."

"That has to wait! First my bladder urges me to see the facilities. Pissing with Hanis has always been an extraordinary affair." When the Admiral returned from the dispozoria he picked up the conversation with Eron. "You've made an astonishing recovery for a young man shot down in flames without a parachute. For the sake of the rest of us, I was hoping you'd remain in a semicoma for a few more years."

Magda emerged from the dining room. "No fights! It will collapse my soufflé."

"How can I not fight? In dire emergencies, that's what cunning Admirals do." He turned to Eron. "Can that *thing* in your head hear me?"

"He's still sorting out the babble."

"Good. Then I can insult him, and you can diplomatically soften my remarks since you've been acting more like an ambassador for the heathen enemy than as my humble prisoner of war," admonished Konn.

"I *am* an ambassador." The crazy Admiral always tickled the sass in Eron. "I've come here to the Prime Residence of Splendid Wisdom to accept the surrender of the Second Empire." Scogil would blanch at that, if he still had a body. It was the kind of cheek that had caused Eron to be thrown out of all of Agander's best schools, forcing his father to hire a tutor—and, finally, to be de-fammed and thrown out of Splendid Wisdom's Lyceum in disgrace.

A startled Konn blinked for a moment before recovering. "Surrender, is it? Unfortunately I've not brought my sword." He grinned and grumbled. "I believe there will be another hundred years of hard war before we get to the point of a surrender. Youth equals impatience." By war Eron knew he meant psychohistorical corrective action. Though Konn built intricate scale models of the immense First Empire dreadnoughts of the old Grand Fleet, to win battles he never ordered into combat even the lightest of the Second Empire's hypercruisers. He wielded more power than any First Empire admiral could have hoped to amass. And now, as Rector, he also commanded all of Hanis' legions.

"You're planning a hundred years of war?" In Rithian history the Hundred Year War was the name for that awful period of seesaw conflict where every death or assassination of a nobleman gave rise to a claim on his land by various distant relatives who had at their disposal an army willing to travel and loot. Female generals were burned at the stake when captured. "You'll lose that way," said Eron. "Sometimes it is better to begin polite talks a century before a major defeat. But you have to be able to see that far."

Konn appraised Eron's face. "You're serious. You would actually negotiate with renegade psychohistorians! You know the equations! There has to be a central predictor. All else is chaos. Civilization will collapse."

"Only when your strategy is governed by inferior mathematics," rejoined Eron.

"Ha! Irresponsible youth! Arrogant! Driving without an autopilot! Sniffing the vacuum because papa said it was dangerous!" The Admiral reached into his briefcase and pulled out a heavy volume, printed on cellomet with a utility cover that was an active index, which he then slammed on the table. "I suppose you mean this! Your dissertation! Copies of it are appearing everywhere, not so erasable as virtual copies in the archives. I've scanned it. Studied it even. Slick math. You've cleaned up your sleight-of-hand since I last saw your act until you now look like a genuine magician, but it is still fraudulent deception! You pull an endless handkerchief out of your nose claiming you have a solution to all of mankind's problems." He turned to Otaria in her floating recliner. "You've thrown in with a mind-crippled madman!" He turned back to Eron. "I'll have you on the rack till you're a skinny giant! I'll squeeze what I want out of that homunculus on your back!" He sat down and ate a bunny biscuit. "Eron, my son, be serious. You know that fighting a hundred years down the line—and winning—is something we do all the time."

"Against a hidden enemy who ripostes with his own psychohistorical ploys?" countered Eron.

"That's why we *have* to interrogate this Scogil of yours. He's the first enemy psychohistorian we've ever captured. You promised to cooperate." His voice became quietly ominous. "Have you changed your mind?"

"No. What better way to interrogate him than to play a psychohistorical war game? Your confrères have long been the Galaxy's special experts on deviations from the Fellowship's planned future history. A modern Inquisition. Osa-Scogil hereby challenges you and your whole staff to a hundred year war game. You can't win, sir." Scogil was vigorously protesting this speech at his highest rate of word composition.

The Admiral brought his tricorn to his lap out of respect for the future dead. "I do believe Hanis *did* succeed in taking away your mind."

"Scogil thinks so, too, but he's stuck with me. And I'm stuck with you. Recall that I was valiantly attempting to avoid you when apprehended. You accept my challenge then? What you get out of it is to see Scogil in action."

"And you think you and your homunculus and your paramour are a match for my whole staff?" Konn had weakened. His voice and his expression said that he was willing to accept the challenge. But he was incredulous. "*I* couldn't get along with a staff of three."

"Great. So you intend to play fair? Assign me thirty of your best Lyceum students and I'll train them up in my methods. If I'm remembering correctly, I'm sure you can find thirty students willing to take a crack at the Admiral!"

Konn was beginning to be intrigued by Eron's boldness. "Your criteria of victory?"

"The immutable laws of psychohistory." Eron deadpanned the cliché.

"You young scupper rat! I've been applying the laws of psychohistory successfully since before you were born!"

"No," said Eron, enjoying himself. "You've been using blasters and neutron grenades against bows and arrows, exotic math against the ignorant masses. Your army doesn't have to know much strategy. Remember, *your* army is the one which executes the fam of any man who is willing to sell blasters to the warriors with the bows and arrows. Now I have to take off a few inamins to consult with Hiranimus. You'll excuse me." He left the room muttering and gesturing wildly to himself.

Otaria shifted herself to Eron's seat. "He's an unusual man."

Konn grumbled. "He was always like that, even when he was sane. Totally impossible. Best copilot I ever had, but impossible. I thought a new fam might rattle his bones a bit. He actually talks to the ghoul of this Scogil?"

"To me it looks like he's talking to himself. It's a ponderous chat they share."

"Do you think what remains of Scogil can actually play at psychohistory? Is this proposal of Osa for real?"

Otaria looked at her long hands wistfully. "Eron thinks highly of the abilities of Scogil's ghoul, more so than the ghoul does of himself. I don't know. The ghost seems to be missing much of Scogil's judgment and fire–I knew him before he was killed–but I don't talk to him directly. Have you ever met an engineer turned salesman of a technical product line? Do you *really* think you've caught a major psychohistorian? Scogil was a *salesman*! That's what he did best. He knew more about my organization, the one you raided, than I did myself–because he was selling to it. You *think* you got us all." There was malice in her voice. "I even thought, for a while, that you did have us all!" She smiled and said no more, and Konn knew he would get no more short of torture.

"Sorry about the accident with Hyperlord Jama."

"Your clumsy people seem to be accident prone. He was crazy as a coot–but there were times when I loved him. He would have been furious about the blood on his lace–which you may not be able to wash away so easily."

Konn brought out a jade ovoid as a gesture of reconciliation. "He would have wanted you to have this." He handed the Egg to Otaria. "We've seized forty of them already."

Otaria fumbled with the ovoid. Stars burst forth that melted into charts, the sky of Imperialis.

"How do you do that?"

"You still can't play it? Would you like your fortune read?" Glibly she made up his fortune on the spot. "Compromise with your enemies before stubbornness brings you disaster. That's your reading for the present position of the stars."

Konn leaned over, fascinated. "I've seen Nejirt do something similar. But it was what Cingal Svene did with it that chilled my old bones."

She ignored him. "I recently asked Hiranimus, through Eron, why he hid behind astrology. He said it was a simple way of giving people permission to hope that they can control their lives. You Pscholars have destroyed our willingness to predict and to choose which of our predicted futures we want to live. We have become fatalists. You choose for us!"

"We run good government. Our methodology doesn't speak to individuals," he admonished.

"If either of those statements were true," she flared, "I wouldn't be here in your comfortable prison and you wouldn't be the *illegitimate* Rector of the Galaxy!"

"And when the astrology doesn't work?"

"What's then to stop a failed astrologer from moving on to psychohistory? You? With your secret hoard of knowledge in your guarded Lyceum archives?"

Magda called them to dinner. She was always a calming influence. Osa-Scogil arrived at the table in a good mood, seeming to have settled his internal dissension. There were no further discussions of politics or psychohistory. Magda's rule.

Later, over sips of Armazin in the study suite, the Admiral confided in Eron the real reason for his visit. "Hanis goes on trial on the 38th watch of Salt. That's a bit early, too soon to get all of the evidence together properly, a bit of a kangaroo court, but the hard-core Hanis faction is beginning to react and reorganize, and I can't afford that. Press the attack while the enemy is in disarray. From the view up here at the top I can see that I have nowhere to go but down, fast. I must dispose of Hanis quickly. I need you as my prime witness."

"Oh?"

The Admiral thumped Eron's dissertation. "The charge is treason. As good as any other trumped-up charge. He has been willfully—and for personal gain—suppressing from his colleagues all knowledge of a coming psychohistorical crisis. That's as deadly a sin as we can scrape up from the bottom of the bin. You are to testify that you warned him."

"I think he panicked," said Eron.

To that the Admiral replied with spoofing humor. "You take pride in yourself as an alarming scarecrow, do you, straw brains and all?" He shrugged. "It doesn't matter. No one will believe he panicked. Hanis is seen to be a charming man with a calculated purpose behind his every action. All you have to do is testify that when you warned him of crisis, his response was to erase the messenger. We have the proof." He thumped the thesis again. "And Hyperlord Jama's group is in irons. We've had to manufacture evidence that Hanis knew about them. Since I'm making the rules, I don't have to be fair. And we have this." He produced another Coron's Egg from his bluecoat. "Every juror will be taken to a secret room to see the Founder's equations scrolling across the heavens. That will make them shit in their pants, like I did in mine. Then we tell them that a million such Eggs have already been scattered to Star's End. After which they can complete their evacuation by pissing in their pants, like I did in mine. What do you say? I'm calculating here. I suspect that you don't harbor any love for Hanis but—more than that—you want an audience for your thesis. I'll give you a roomful of audience. I want to nail Hanis in the upside-down position, Roman style. An old grudge. You pass me the nails. Is it a deal?"

"You'll back me up? You'll say there's a real crisis?"

"Of course."

"So you've finally come to believe what I've written?"

This time the Admiral *banged* on the dissertation angrily. "That? Are you asking me to sign my name to the bottom of that rubbish paper of yours? It is utter nonsense. I told you that years ago. But if it helps me to cut Hanis' throat, I'll swear the situation is ten times worse than you say it is and with candles on top—while my fingers are crossed."

"You want me to lie to a court of law?" Eron's sense of moral outrage was growing.

"No, no. *You* won't be lying. You believe every word you've written. I want your sincerity to shine through in the courtroom. I want tears in their eyes when they hear your story. I'll be the one who is lying to save my skin."

"What will you do with Hanis if he is convicted?"

"Boil him in oil. But I think you've earned first priority on that. What would you do with him?"

"He has interesting dreams. I remember being caught up in his dreams. He won't give them up easily."

"Tell that to your fam." The Admiral touched his own; had Hanis' methods scared him to act?

Eron had a suggestion. "Ship him off to a distant cluster he has picked out as one of his renaissance foci. He could teach the laymen there psychohistory and if they liked his dream they'd then have the power to make it real without asking permission of Splendid Wisdom—and Hanis could die happy."

"Have you lost your fam? Teach laymen psychohistory? Never. You know the equations for that scene. I'd rather boil Hanis in oil! Have some more Armazin." He took Osa-Scogil's delicate goblet and poured a refill. "Well. Are you going to testify? We have to make a deal right now. I won't force you. I can forge fake witnesses if I have to."

Eron stared at the blue light dancing over the etched scene on his goblet while he twisted it in his fingers, conversing in silence with Scogil. A thousand mock battles played themselves out in the goblet's shimmering while the argument raged between man and ghoul, ending finally in accord. "We agree to testify—if afterward we get to play two versions of this hundred-year simulated war, the initial conditions those of the Galaxy as they stand today as determined by the Fellowship—but some of the initial conditions, by necessity, must be arbitrary, since we have already crossed the topozone and psychohistory will be unable to predict when and where the Eggs are first used. We can roll dice on that, so to speak. The first war is to be governed by the Founder's classical rules, the second war by my Arekean modifications."

"The first is enough. A future viewed by your strange rules is a fantasy spun by a youthful dreamer of the impossible."

"I must insist on *both* simulations. It is necessary that these two possible futures be contrasted."

"The flaws in your method will be exposed."

"All the better. I must have your word of honor."

"Two wars then. Conceded."

"As well, Scogil would like to point out that, since he is not a command center and never was, errors will be introduced."

The Admiral was grumbling. "Error resolution can drag out the calculations interminably. May I suggest that each simulated year be limited to three or four watches? That should give us acceptable accuracy. At the end of that time we assume the outcomes with the highest probability and move on to the next year. If a hundred-year war were to last more than three or four months, my patience would be tried."

Eron nodded. "Scogil has asked me to remind you that in an enterprise of this complexity, we will need at least thirty of your best students as staff for our side if the game is to have any meaning at all. The galactic model handles predictions well, but with the introduction of so many new prediction nodes . . ."

Konn did not let him finish. "Obviously you will need help. Thirty won't save you. Conceded." Eron did not mention that this would give him thirty students to train in the Arekean methodology of distributed iteration, thirty more than he had right now. The Admiral smiled, anticipating victory in all galactic theaters as a foregone conclusion of any such "war"—as if his opposition were mere rowdy deckhands to be brought to order by a little fatherly discipline. He called on Magda to bring out another decanter of Armazin. It was a deal.

Eron also smiled softly. There was no way he could *tell* the Admiral what a predicament he faced. Hahukum Konn was brazen enough to think that he was a superior strategist even against an army of amateur psychohistorians. That was true. At present, the main tactic of Scogil's mysterious people was to pump, from as many spigots as they could, the technical literature of psychohistory. That wasn't enough. Neither Scogil nor the Admiral understood the long-term implications. The Founder *had* understood. Which was why he so adamantly insisted on secrecy.

The trial of the ex-Rector went slowly. The Admiral used it adroitly to induce the supporters of Jars Hanis to attack where the Admiral was strongest. Being accustomed to following a martinet, and now deprived of that leadership, they fell into disagreeing factions. Konn's smaller coterie decimated each faction, one at a time, counter-predicting their every move. In the old Imperial Navy, Hahukum would have risen to legendary status.

In the meantime, while the Admiral was occupied with his own personal vendetta, Eron prepared for the decisive event. He picked his thirty warriors from among the younger students who were most intrigued by the challenge of psycho-historian versus psychohistorian, prediction versus counter-prediction. Testifying at the trial had been an interesting place to spread the seeds of heresy, but the soil was poor. His thirty students were a different matter. In training them, he relied on Scogil's expertise as a tutor, giving them small conflicts to manage in which two sides, both wielding classical tools, converged to stalemate. Then Eron would join the team and show them how to use Arekean iteration to resolve the stalemate. He was only a step ahead of his students, since he was having to relearn his own methods as he went along as well as teach them to Scogil.

The First Hundred Year War began only when the Admiral was ready to give it his full attention—after First Rank Jars Hanis had been tried, found guilty by his peers (carefully picked by Hahukum), and sentenced. Eron knew the time had come when he saw the Admiral's beatific grin.

"What have you done with him?" Meaning the ex-Rector.

"Not what I wanted. I had to make deals. That's politics. No boiling in oil. Execution would have created lingering problems. And much as I would have enjoyed it, shredding his fam was not an option; it is one of the unwritten rules of psycho-history that you do not do to an enemy what he has so heinously done to you. Bad form. You have to think of something worse."

*Anything* could be expected from a man who would willingly defossilize a Flying Fortress and pilot it. "Is that wise?" asked Eron cautiously.

"Wisdom is for old men. I'm still young at heart! First we start with solitary confinement. For a social gadfly like Hanis, that's a good beginning. I've found an unused lab in which the life-support system for the Andromeda expedition was designed, with its entertainment module already stripped out—but the bare facilities lack in imagination. Anything so grim would drive Hanis to such despair that he would wither away and die. We don't want that to happen to *our* enemy. To prolong the torture, one has to provide hope where there is no hope. I have discovered an exemplary way of giving Hanis hope. Hence my good mood." It was not the Admiral's way to finish a story while he had an attentive audience. He enjoyed winning battles and prolonging his victory; he merely grinned and changed the subject. He was ready for the next big battle and eager to start. "So, Lord General Osa-Scogil, are your troops well trained and their boots polished?"

"As much as a ragtag army of volunteers can be."

"Good. How do we begin this silly gentleman's war of yours? Do we cut the Deck of Fate and high card gets to shoot first, or what?"

Opening positions were strategically important, so they spent several watches haggling over initial conditions. Both sides agreed that realism was important, but they didn't always agree on what was real. The Admiral was to begin with control of the entire bureaucracy of the Second Empire. That was a given. But who was receiving the Eggs? Who could use them? Where were they coming from? Scogil wouldn't have told if he had known, and the Admiral understood and accepted that constraint.

It was a matter of estimating probabilities, and from those probabilities allocating resources and attributes. The teams didn't always concur. Eron insisted that there were more insects in the woodwork than the Admiral wanted to acknowledge or were known to Scogil, estimating that there were at least seven hundred independent precritical psychohistorical nodes about to emerge, all of which would go critical very quickly once they learned about (and found a source of) Coron's Eggs. Scogil didn't believe his mate, but the Admiral had been sobered by Eron's prediction of a psychohistorical crisis that hadn't even shown up on the Standard Model—and thus was willing to concede the point. The Hundred Year War began quietly as these things do, its basic strategies evident from the beginning.

As the defender of the Second Empire, the Admiral was concerned with the total control of the Galaxy, the balanced and fair-minded control of a long tradition. Trade was regulated so that one region didn't grow wealthy at the expense of another. Of thirty million inhabited systems, only seven were undergoing population crisis. Only three systems showed signs of a political crisis that might escalate out of hand within the century. Culture and cultural exchange were thriving. Galactic standards were regulated in a way that encouraged commerce. The scene was nothing like the desperate affair that the Founder had inherited while he was inventing psychohistory.

The countervailing strategy emerged as different nodes began to develop their own centers of psychohistoric expertise. Local regions began to optimize their own futures with less and less regard for their neighbors. The level of conflict rose, most of it unintentional. What was very good for one star system might not be so good for the next. To compete, the less endowed systems made stronger alliances than normal with Splendid Wisdom or began to aggressively develop their own ability to counter-predict their neighbors.

The Admiral's staff valiantly tried to rebalance the Empire but normal corrective measures became less and less effective. Some systems acquiesced for the good of all, others counter-predicted the corrections on the theory that their psychohistorians could do a better job. The Admiral tried to bring all psychohistorians into the fold of the Fellowship—and failed. He tried to build alliances with the emerging states with only spotty success.

The disintegration of the Fellowship's monopoly brought swifter change than anyone had supposed possible. Osa-Scogil wasn't at all sure of how the Admiral was taking the grinding down of all that he believed in and began to worry when he received a disturbing but cautiously worded message from his mother (Eron's). She was quietly alarmed by an investigative team which had arrived on Agander and was methodically digging into Eron's first twelve years.

It took less than three months and only eighty-two simulated years on the most powerful historical computer in existence to predict a total alteration in the political face of the Galaxy. Over five hundred simulated interstellar wars, major and minor, were raging, confined only by the constraints of psychohistory. Arms production was up by three orders of magnitude. Eight billion youths were being drafted every year to study psychohistory in an effort by each faction to outmaneuver the others. Psychohistory had *not* become irrelevant; it was *essential* to the multitude of war efforts. Accurate prediction in conflict situations was just more difficult. There were 112 major centers of psychohistoric prediction and thousands of minor ones. The formidable stability of the Second Galactic Empire had long been reduced to shambles.

At this advanced stage of the game the criminal conspirators of the Regulation were no longer under house arrest by a stunned Konn. Hanis' old apartment was an open command center. Admiral Konn had assigned ten of his aides to work liaison with Osa-Scogil's group. It made no sense anymore to break the game into a contest between two opponents—Konn's staff, Eron, Scogil, Otaria all had to work together just to keep track of what was going on as the math churned out the changing constraints.

Petunia had been picked up by Barna's men and had been co-opted by a relieved Scogil to act as Osa-Scogil's chief of staff and general gopher to beef up their undermanned group. She ran reconnaissance into enemy territory and flirted with their resolute rivals. Otaria of the Calmer Sea frantically plotted historical trends. Hiranimus worked overtime in his dungeon at full capacity. Eron, amazed by his ghoul, was now fully cognizant of why the living Scogil had made such heroic efforts to keep his fam out of enemy hands—its psychohistorical utilities alone were the equivalent of the brain power of ten men like the Founder.

On the eighty-seventh simulated year Splendid Wisdom was sacked (virtually) by a vengeful alliance of enemies. Admiral Konn, ever the dramatist, brought a real sword, a genuine fake he had picked up on Rith, for the surrender ceremony.

And his exhausted staff, which had grown over the campaign to include almost every available student of the Lyceum not working for Osa-Scogil, broke apart. With Splendid Wisdom sacked no one had the courage or wit or energy to continue. It was generally understood that errors had accumulated to the point where the game could only be describing a low-probability, if sobering, future.

Instead of continuing the simulation to the hundredth year as originally planned, a spontaneous party began to happen in Konn's main command center overlooking the simulacrum of the Galaxy, now half washed in blue. Desks were overturned. Decorations festooned the equipment. Dignified Pscholars could be found asleep on the floor. Others yelled and rioted and threw hard bread rolls in mock warfare. The Lyceum became, for a span of watches, a genteel madhouse, the final fling at life of a doomed bunker just before the enemy troops break through. With his game, Eron had pushed the whole Lyceum across the no-man's-land of the mental topozones that represented familiar reality and into the chaotic neural activity of strange viewpoints and impossible stimuli. The results were so unsettling that no one involved had to be on drugs to behave outlandishly.

What were the lessons of the *surprising* mathematical collapse of the Second Empire? The outcome was debated everywhere in an orgy of learning. The unexpected nature of the game had agitated the mind of each participant: to reject the collapse as "unreal" was to reject the underlying mathematics, but the rejection of the underlying mathematics was a rejection of the foundation stone of the Second Empire which . . .

Osa-Scogil slipped among the groups, listening, dropping hints. He knew what had happened. He wanted his "students" to figure it out for themselves.

Hadn't the Pscholars persisted in the *fatalistic* mind-set of the final hopeless centuries of the First Empire in spite of the *fact* that the math of psychohistory contained a plethora of *alternate* futures? Over the millennial Interregnum, hadn't their Plan atrophied into a kind of supervised determinism? Wasn't it true that the Plan was no longer seen as a vigorous alternate future that led away from the chaos of Imperial collapse but as the *only* true future–with the Fellowship as its guardian?

A casual remark by Eron about Scogil's Smythosian connection immoderately grew into a quicky discussion. This ad hoc seminar already knew *how* groups like the Smythosians could destroy the Second Empire with only a millionth of the Second Empire's resources at their command. But no one knew who they were or where they had come from or why the Egg hadn't been predicted.

Scogil, through Eron, would say nothing about his homeworlds or his education, but he didn't mind telling the story of Tamic Smythos, who had, after all, been trained at the Lyceum when it was a besieged fortress set in the shambled chaos of what was now called the "First" Sack.

Nothing was known of the life and wanderings of Smythos for the twenty years between his escape from Zurnl and his appearance on Horan, not even the secret work he did for Faraway's Chancellor Linus. On Horan Smythos took up mechanical engineering, then fell into an invisible life as a self-imposed recluse, appearing in public only to earn money, spending most of his time alone writing long rambling documents for his own edification, rants, philosophical musings, incomplete psychomathematical treatments of odd problems, all stuffed in boxes when he lost interest or found a new interest. He died a recluse. His boxes, in storage, remained unread. The warehouse changed hands. A foreman, in charge of cleaning out the warehouse . . . As a late product of the chaos surrounding the False Revival, an amorphous cult grew up very gradually in the region of the Thousand Suns Beyond the Helmar Rift around these astonishing relics of the embittered

Tamic Smythos. Among the papers, developed in detail, were some of the seed ideas of psychohistory.

Scogil related the tale as cautionary advice to anyone who was thinking of building his destiny upon a foundation of secrecy. Secrets have a way of slipping through the finest mesh. (But Scogil kept his own secret; he told no one how the Helmarian Oversee had stumbled upon a Smythosian cell and what they did with what they found.)

When the lessons of the game were well on their way to assimilation within the Lyceum, Eron Osa gave his first speech to a quiet audience, his theme the failures of the Pscholars and the failures of groups like the Smythosians.

The Pscholars had failed from too much power. They had ceased to mine psychohistory for low-probability futures worth exploring. The Plan was, after all, a low-probability future discovered by the Founder. As an elite they had *deliberately* failed to explore the high probability that they would not be able to hold on to their monopoly of psychohistoric expertise. It was that decision which had produced the present crisis.

Worse, they had neglected psychohistory as a tool to explore undesirable futures (such as the high probability that Splendid Wisdom would be resacked within the century). Back some time in the Interregnum, psychohistorians had forgotten that one of the main uses of prediction was to position the savant to falsify the prediction. They had used their power only to avoid deviations from the Plan. Mankind's brain had evolved as a tool to predict undesirable futures in time to avoid them, not to predict highly probable futures that needed no intervention.

Other emerging groups—like the Smythosians, like the Regulation—had fallen into the trap of opposition. For centuries they remained small, content to oppose the Fellowship locally in invisible ways, afraid to operate in the open because of the Pscholars' known fiercely guarded monopoly. The more they tested the Plan, the more the Fellowship reacted—until the Lyceum had evolved a whole unit whose sole purpose was to oppose the actions of the diffuse counter-Fellowships—the survivors being those groups who were best at counterevolving a *secret* mathematics of prediction of their own, and, inured to the role of opposition, eventually were driven to use their ultimate weapon against the Second Empire. The Pscholars had no defense against a populace who could now visit their local archive and find all they might want to know about psychohistory. Long before the present crisis, the goal had become the destruction of the Pscholar's power rather than the implementation of a more flexible Plan.

In his rounds and talks Eron was preparing the ground for the Second Hundred Year War in which he intended to teach the Lyceum a second lesson. He already had thirty students pretrained in his Arekean methodology, tools he had deliberately withheld from use in the First War, a purely classical event. During the Second Hundred Year War he hoped to sweep the entire simulated Galaxy; he could envisage no defense against a mathematics able to force conflict resolution. Arekean iteration did not contain within itself a lethal vulnerability like the need for secrecy built so integrally into the classical mathematics of the Founder. Even Scogil should be impressed enough to make his final break with the Oversee, and then . . .

The Osa-Scogil being was evolving. The mere fact that ghoul and man had developed a language contact seemed to have catalyzed a process in which they were beginning to develop shared coding at a more machine-language level. The ghoul would eventually see through Eron's eyes, and Eron would feel the emotions of Hiranimus, perhaps already doing so if loyalty to a family back in the Thousand Suns meant anything: when he was reunited with his wife(?), he was going to demand that she deactivate that damned tuned compulsion to love and protect Petunia. Their daughter(?) was reaching the age when girls resent being overprotected.

The extended party was winding down. There was less revelry, less debate, and, more important, less hysteria. People were still asleep in chairs and zonked out in corners against the wall, or quietly chatting in groups of two. Some had even retreated to their own beds. Eron was too exhausted for that; he commandeered an empty divan and went to sleep.

And that was where the Admiral found Eron hours later, hidden away and asleep. He made enough space for himself to sit down where Eron's knees had been and shook his prodigy until he saw an open eye. "How can you sleep with your Second Hundred Year War coming up so close on the heels of the First?"

"Aren't you glad we can set the clock back eighty-seven years?" said Eron sleepily.

"No. I've lost my enthusiasm. I'm too old for this game. I'm more comfortable living peacefully in real time with my dog. Are you really serious about this second war? Can't I just buy you out? Another three months of this nonsense?"

"A contract is a contract. War it is. I don't want to have to slap your face with my glove. The Reformation isn't over yet."

"I'll have to bring Hanis in to help me. I need his brains."

"Inquisitor Hanis? You're not serious?" Eron sat upright, then rose to his full height.

"I might be."

"You never told me where you sequestered him."

"I did. He's toughing it out in an old experimental life-support module, all alone."

"Mitigating his torture with hope?" Eron was still curious. Enough time had passed for the Admiral to relent and relieve the suspense. "Come on. Tell us! What kind of hope did you devise?"

The mood of the Rector of the Galaxy rose to good cheer again, remembering his last and greatest victory. "I promised him a parole hearing once he finishes, to my satisfaction, a penitence task I have assigned him. It's a life sentence, a Sisyphus sort of task; once he gets the rock to the top of the hill, I've promised to review his case and *maybe* grant him freedom."

"And the rock?" asked Eron impatiently.

"Oh, that. I've set him to writing your biography. He raged at first, refusing. But hope has a way of seducing the soul. He hopes to finish your biography soon, but he's never been *my* student and isn't aware that I constantly raise my standards of excellence to ever more impossible heights."

"Writing about me is his penitence?"

"Writing up your childhood is the easy part. I keep supplying him with new material; Agander seems to be a place addicted to the creation of poetic myths, and your childhood seems to have achieved mythical status. You're going to be surprised at all the things you did as a boy that you've forgotten about. As I said, that's the easy part. The torture part is studying your dissertation, your *Early Disturbed Event Location by Forced Arekean Canonical Pre-posturing*." The Admiral, for the moment, had become his old teasing self.

"I thought my dissertation was elegantly beautiful, a masterpiece of clarity."

"Eron, I've tried to read it. I can't get through it. I assure you it qualifies as the *worst* sort of torture! So I've assigned Hanis the task of rewriting it until it is crystal clear to an old fossilized man like me who is probably getting older faster than Hanis can improve his style." The Admiral was now smiling diabolically. "Hope for Hanis rests on his ability to understand you, a sufficiently Sisyphean task since he did do his best to destroy all records of your existence short of burning you at the stake."

"So when can we start our next war?"

The Admiral lay down on the now-empty divan and invited Eron to sit on the cushion above his head. Uniform rumpled, his body flopped out in dejection, he confided, "Eron, I don't think I can go through another war like the last one. It's too much. First you present me with a galactic psychohistorical crisis that arrives unexpectedly like a spaceship out of a black hole. Then some damn Protestant steals the Founder's Bible from my burglarproof safe and invents the printing press. Theory says all that can't happen, but it did—and so the theory is wrong in that aspect. I tried to adapt. I thought I could handle your little war with *strategy*. My mature math is better than your inexperienced math. It didn't work. I might as well have tried walking on the sun in my bare feet. So here we are. I have awakened from a bad dream, a *nightmare* that never happened, surrounded by hysterical revelry. But what lies ahead? Must I live that nightmare in the real world, playing it out *again* exactly as it happened in the dream but at a painfully slow pace?"

Eron had never seen the Admiral in such a tragic mood. "Predicting is only half of the game; counter-predicting nightmares is the other half. You forget what the Founder said: Psychohistory is all about choosing your future."

"No it isn't!" snarled the old man. "Did I choose the Second Sack of Splendid Wisdom? Damn right I didn't, I fought it off with all the resources I had." His voice was that of a proud man in chains. *"I wasn't in control of anybody's willy-nilly destiny!"*

Normally brain activity flips back and forth across the boundaries twixt stability and chaos in the mind's ever active war between knowing and the need to learn—this outpost ridge temporarily chaotic, that beachhead stable for the moment, the front flowing in battle flux across the neural net.

On quiet days the mind stays stable by using old solutions. On other days some internal field marshal calls for an offensive and drives his troops against chaos. To conquer chaos one must *learn*. To maintain stability one must *know*. The dual struggle can be exhausting.

The Admiral was exhausted mentally, but Eron was sure he could goad him back to life again—in the months to come. He took the old man's head onto his lap and ran his fingers through hair he had never before dared touch. "Hey, you've been a father to me, a strange one, and I ran away from home, but I'm still your copilot and we're on the way home and we're going to come in for a smooth landing. Just another hundred years of war to go. We'll make it. I can see what you'll be doing five years from now. You won't believe this, but I'm good at predicting. You'll be sending out your students to teach psychohistory to the unwashed. Maybe, if Hanis learns his Arekean lessons up to your high standards, you'll be able to send him out with them. You'll be the author of a renaissance that Hanis could never dream of. And best of all—you'll be free from the burden of carrying around a deadly secret." He wet his finger wiping a tear from the Admiral's cheek.

"You and your starry-eyed astrological predictions. Son."

Later Eron's lover Otaria found them, brought in tow by Scogil's Petunia. "Is he all right?" Otaria asked.

"He's asleep."

Osa-Scogil felt very peculiar about having a wife and a Frightfulperson. And a daughter standing behind him with her arms wrapped affectionately around his neck. And an Admiral's head in his lap who was also a madman and a father. "Life isn't very predictable," he said.

"I know," replied the Mermaid of the Calmer Sea.

# Appendix A

# GALACTIC STANDARD TIME

One jiff is 3,066,899 cycles of light from cesium 133
One second is 9,192,631,770 cycles of light from cesium 133

Velocity of light is 100 million meters/jiff

Light year = 9,460.471452 trillion meters
League = 10,000 trillion meters

---

A Galactic Standard Year:
> = the time it takes light to travel 10,000 trillion meters
> = 12.87 months
> = 386.067 days

A Galactic Standard Month:
> = the time it takes light to travel 1000 trillion meters
> = 1/10 GST year
> = 1.29 months
> = 38.31 days
> = 926.57 hours

A Galactic Standard Watch:
> = the time it takes light to travel ten trillion meters
> = 1/100 GST month
> = 0.38 days
> = 9.26 hours
> = 555.94 minutes

A Galactic Standard Hour:
> = the time it takes light to travel a trillion meters
> = 1/10 GST watch
> = .93 hours
> = 55.59 minutes
> = 3,335.64 seconds

## A Galactic Standard Inamin:
= the time it takes light to travel ten billion meters
= 1/100 GST hour
= 33.356 seconds
= 0.556 minutes

## A Galactic Standard Jiff:
= the time it takes light to travel 100 million meters
= 1/100 GST inamin
= 0.33356 seconds

---

## An Archaic Year:
= the time it takes Rith to orbit Sol
= 0.946 GST years
= 94,604,714.58 jiffs

## An Archaic Month Varied at the Whim of Despots:
7,252,579 jiffs = 28 days
7,648,305 jiffs = 29.52 days, the time it takes the Moon to orbit Rith
7,770,620 jiffs = 30 days = 77.71 watches
8,029,641 jiffs = 31 days

## An Archaic Day:
= the time it takes Rith to complete one rotation around Sol
= 2.59 GST watches
= 25.90 GST hours
= 259,020.68 GST jiffs

## An Archaic Hour:
= 1/24 archaic day
= 1.08 GST hours
= 107.93 GST inamins
= 10,793 GST jiffs

## An Archaic Minute:
= 1/60 archaic hour
= 1.80 inamins
= 179.87 jiffs

## An Archaic Second
= 1/60 minute
= 2.998 jiffs

# Appendix B

# Timeline of Galactic History

Year Galactic Era: time it takes light to travel $1.0000000000 \times 10^{16}$ meters
Year Anno Domini: time it takes light to travel $0.9460471452 \times 10^{16}$

Conversion Equations: yearGE $= (\text{yearAD} \times 0.946047) - 61{,}248$
year AD $= (\text{yearGE} + 61{,}248) \times 1.05703$
year FE $= \text{yearGE} - 12{,}068$ [FE stands for "Founder's Era."]

---

### 64th Millennium BGE
Construction of the Great Pyramid (Rith), 63,591 BGE; 2478 BC

### 62nd Millennium BGE
Emperor Huangdi-of-Qin (Rith), 61,493–61,447 BGE; b259;
reign 247–210 BC
Emperor Augustus Caesar of Rome (Rith), 61,273–61,233 BGE; reign 27 BC
to 14 AD
Missing year catastrophe, 61,247 BGE; 0 AD
Jesus Christ born, saving mankind from sin, 61,247 BGE; 1 AD

### 61st Millennium BGE
Conquest of England (Rith) by Norman barbarians, 60,240 BGE; 1066 AD
Pope Innocent III (of Rith) exterminates Christian rivals in Zara, Constantino-
ple, and France, 60,114–60,097 BGE; 1198–1216 AD

### 60th Millennium BGE
Voyages of Discovery by sea (Rith), 59,929–59,808 BGE; 1394–1522 AD
Renewed religious dissent, Luther, 59,813 BGE; 1517 AD
Index of Forbidden Books, 59,773 BGE; 1559 AD
Astronomical mathematics, Johann Kepler, 59,762–59,706 BGE; 1571–1630 AD
Rediscovery of pendulum clocks, 59,700 BGE; 1636 AD
Begin 20th century AD, extreme population ramp-up, 59,451 BGE; 1900 AD
Max Planck's Nobel Address, 59,433 BGE; 1918 AD
Intercourse Of Commingled Bodies legalizes metric-meter for Americ colonies,
59,424 BGE; 1928 AD

First Venteen Flying Fortress built, 59,417 BGE; c. 1935 AD
Nuclear fission discovered (Rith), 59,414 BGE; 1939 AD
Begin 21st century AD, population ramp-up continues, 59,356 BGE; 2000 AD
Great Die-off (Rith) c. 59,250–59,000 BGE (undocumented)

## 59th Millennium BGE

First Rithian Interstellar Wanderer (sublight), 58,912 BGE; 2469 AD
Last Rithian interstellar expedition, 58,056 BGE; 3374 AD

## 57–49th Millennia BGE

Sublight colonization radius reaches 1000 leagues.
Hyperdrive discovered at Eta Cuminga, 48,211 BGE; 13,780 AD
Galactic colonization explosion

## 48–47th Millennia BGE

Eta Cumingan Empire
Cathusians of Rith begin to recollect old starship libraries

## 46–28th Millennia BGE

First expansion era, only minor conflict
Eta Cuminga gradually loses control
Era of 100 empires, 1000 states

## 27–4th Millennia BGE

Continuation of rapid colonization
Beginning of Time of Troubles
Core settled, Splendid Wisdom, 18,370 BGE; 45,323 AD
First Settlers in the Ulmat Constellation, 16,554 BGE; 47,243 AD

## 3–1st Millennia BGE

Era dominated by Sotama traders and mercenaries, 2435–812 BGE
Rise of Machan Confederacy from 812 BGE onward
    General decline of Sotama influence
Theory of multi-poled Hyperdrive invented, 777 BGE; 63,920 AD
    Galactic center spawning ground of experiments for next hundred years.
Amateur engineers of Splendid Wisdom first to perfect design of the new
        Hyperdrive in 603 BGE; 64,104 AD
Splendid Wisdom Traders competing with Machan, 500 BGE; 64,212 AD

## 1st Millennium GE

Kambal-the-First born, 0 GE; 64,741 AD
The army of Kambal-the-First takes over Splendid Wisdom's trading confeder-
    ation and crowns him Emperor, 32–62; 64,775–64,806 AD
Defeat of Machan attack on Splendid Wisdom, 400; 65,163 AD
Viceroy of Santar suppresses rebellion within Empire, annexes Machan,
    millions die, 567 GE; 65,340 AD
Civil War, 783; 65,569 AD

2nd Millennium GE: Splendid Wisdom controls 90,000 star systems, 65,798 AD
> Water ecology Splendid Wisdom nearing collapse, 1300
> Kambal-the-Eighth, 1346–1378, coregent 1378–1382
> Frightfulpeople infiltrate and dominate Splendid Wisdom and apparatus of
> fledgling empire.
> Tanis-the-First, often Tanis One-eye, 1378–1495, declared emperor during War
> of Two Emperors
>> Six Billion on Splendid Wisdom die.
> Kambal-the-Eighth captured and murdered, 1382, end of Kambal Dynasty
> Tanis-the-First dies at age 171 years, 1495

3rd Millennium GE: Splendid Wisdom controls a million star systems, 66,855 AD

4th Millennium GE: Splendid Wisdom controls 1,500,000 systems, 67,912 AD
> Emperor Ojaisun-the-Adroit, 3231–3245
>> defeated and executed by daughter, 3245, at Lalaw II.

5th Millennium GE: Splendid Wisdom controls two million systems, 68,969 AD
> Emperor Harkon-the-Traveller, disappears while on tour, 4327–4357
> Rise of Pupian Dynasty by election, 4512
> Admiral Peurifoy's preemptive campaigns, 4780–4822

6th Millennium GE: Splendid Wisdom controls four million star systems, 70,026 AD
> Pupian Dynasty ended by Etalun Military Family, 5220
>> Etalun Cotoya Court established to promote arts and refinement
> Composer Saramantin of Rith at his height, 5390; 70,438 AD
> Orr-of-Etalun, third Emperor Etalun Dynasty, 5395–5406
> Orion Arm Regionate subjugated, 5397
> Etalun Dynasty destroyed by internal conflict, 5413; 70,463 AD
> First Horezkor class battleship commissioned, warship of Middle Empire, 5517
> Emperor Daigin-the-Jaw, b. 5561, ascends throne 5578, d. 5632; 70,637 AD
> Emperor Daigin-the-Mild, second son of the Jaw
>> born during father's Persean-Cara campaign, 5597
>> coronation, 5632
>> castrated, exiled by Arum-the-Patient, 5641
>> died 5671
> Emperor Arum-the-Patient, first son of the Jaw
>> born 5591
>> conquered the Ulmat, 5634–5637
>> takes throne by military coup, 5641
>> poisoned by mother, 5662
> Time of 17 emperors, 5663–5678
> Establishment of Som Dynasty; end of confusion, 5678

7th Millennium GE: Splendid Wisdom controls fourteen million systems, 71,083 AD
> Establishment of the class of Hyperlords, 6654
> Dashian Dynasty replaces Som Dynasty, administrative coup, 6987

8th Millennium GE: Splendid Wisdom controls eighteen million systems, 72,140 AD
Composer Aiasin, 7028
Emperor Kassam-the-Farsighted, 7763–7775
Runs affairs by Mysteries of the Navigators
Empire strengthens Ragmuk in preparation for war, 7770
Wars Across the Marche begin, 7774
Battle of Thirty Suns, 7775
Execution of Kassam's confidant Cundy Munn
Execution of Emperor Kassam
Admiralty has mystical Navigators tortured, 7776
Treaty of Sanahadra with 1000 Suns of Helmar Rift
ends Wars Across the Marche, 7981 GE
Oversee founded to pursue hostility to Empire by covert means.
Count Ism Notkin rules on Treaty of Sanahadra, 7992

9th Millennium GE: Splendid Wisdom controls twenty-one million systems, 73,197 AD
Beginning of Time of Troubles: Oversee works from hidden bases
Stars&Ship Navy becomes supreme arm of Emperor
Emperor Krang-the-Blind, 8025–8036
Emperor Takeia the Happy, 8625–8653, orgies, deposed by Navy

10th Millennium GE: Splendid Wisdom controls twenty-four million systems, 74,254 AD
Emperor Stanis-the-Careful, 9103–9110, deposed by Navy
Emperor Ammenetik-the-Great, 9456–9504
End of Time of Troubles
Helmarian Oversee survives in hiding
Emperor Maximoy the Polite, 9700–9725
tradition of the Valodian Lament
Pax Imperialis; 9892
Splendid Wisdom declares suzerainty over Galaxy complete

11th Millennium GE: Splendid Wisdom controls twenty-five million systems, 75,311 AD
Emperor Hagwith-the-Ingenious, 10,232–10,268
invents robot Danny-Boy

12th Millennium GE: Splendid Wisdom consolidates power, 76,368 AD
Emperor Manwell-the-Bloody, 11,134–11,144
Emperor Zankatal-the-Pious, "the Noose," 11,907–11,925
Emperor Sarin-the-Gross, assassinated by bodyguards, 11,926–11,931
Stannelle-the-Peaceful, assassinated by bodyguards, 11,985–12,010
Founder born on Licon in Nora's Toes, 11,988
Future Emperor Cleopon-the-First born

13th Millennium GE: Splendid Wisdom cultural and organizational decline, 77,425 AD

Emperor Cleopon-the-First, assassinated, 12,010–12,052
    benefactor of psychohistorical research
Emperor Agile-the-Quintessence, 12,052–12,066
    impotent tool of feuding clans
Founder gives 8th Speech to Group of Forty-six, 12,061
    plots Faraway project
Emperor Dalubbar-the-Pliant, 12,066–12,100
    coronation when four years old, tool of deceptive advisors
Fellowship set up on Faraway, 12,068; 0 FE
Founder dies, 12,069; 1 FE
Precinct of Nacreome revolts successfully on Periphery, 12,116
    beginning of Interregnum collapse
First Psychohistorical Crisis, 12,118; 50 FE
    Faraway balances local power vacuum
Second Psychohistorical Crisis, 12,148; 80 FE
    Ambitions of local warlords constrained by religion based on technical
        magic
Oversee takes on hidden task of protecting the Thousand Suns, 12,170
Regent of Emperor Tien-the-Young seizes power through boy, 12,216
Viceroy Wisard of distant Sewinna plots usurpation of throne, 12,217
Loyalist local rebellion against Wisard, 12,219
    Tien crushes Wisard and revenges himself cruelly on Sewinnese.
    Massacre of Sewinnese by new Admiral-Viceroy
Tien-the-Young, his Regent, advisors, and concubines assassinated, 12,222
Exiled father of Cleopon II seizes throne, 12,222–12,238
Third Psychohistorical Crisis, 12,223; 155 FE
    Religion vs Trade; Merchant Princes of Faraway dominate
    Faraway begins economic conquests independent of religious power.
Splendid Wisdom accepts with relief strong Emperor Cleopon II, 12,238
Fourth Psychohistorical Crisis, 12,263; 195 FE
    War organized by banished general against Faraway
Successful general recalled to Splendid Wisdom and
    executed by Cleopon-the-Second, 12,264
Revolt against Firm hand of Cleopon II; he is murdered, 12,278
    General time of troubles and retreat for Splendid Wisdom
Sack of Splendid Wisdom, Cainali Invasions begin, 12,338
    Era of warlords
Cloun-the-Stubborn born, 12,351
Tuned-probes built by Helmarians for Lakgan pleasure houses, 12,370
    Cloun begins rise to power within Lakgan, using probe, 12,371
    Technique not covered by psychohistorical parameters
Cloun takes over Lakgan as First Citizen by mental coercion, 12,378
Fifth Psychohistorical Crisis, 12,379; 311 FE
    Civil War between Faraway and Traders, mispredicted
    Cloun Conquers Faraway

Emergency action by Pscholars restabilizes Founder's Plan, 12,383; 315 FE

Cloun dies, last years as enlightened despot, 12,388

Faraway breaks Lakgan rule, reestablishes economic sphere, 12,389

The Pscholars, having revealed themselves to Faraway during the Cloun crisis, make long range plans to go into hiding by pretending they have been destroyed, sacrificing 50 martyrs, 12,419–12,446; 351–378 FE

Pscholars provoke a six month Lakgan and Faraway war, which they know Faraway will win, to restore Faraway confidence in their destiny, 12,445; 377 FE

"Violence is the last refuge of the competent."

Tamic Smythos and forty-nine others are captured at the end Lakganian War to deceive their Faraway hosts into believing that the capture of fifty psychohistorians based on Faraway is a clean sweep. Exiled to barren Zurnl, 12,446; 378 FE

Tamic Smythos is smuggled off Zurnl by corrupt Chancellor Linus, 12,454

Period of Coalescence, 12,820–13,000

Slow but general acceptance of quantronic familiar

## 14th Millennium GE: Second Empire comprises twenty million systems, 78,482 AD

Formal establishment of Second Empire, Pax Pscholaris, 13,157; 1089 FE

Rebuilding of Splendid Wisdom begun

Pscholars induce power shift from the Periphery back to galactic core

## 15th Millennium GE: Splendid Wisdom controls twenty-eight million systems, 79,539 AD

Kargin Linmax born, 14,650

Jars Hanis born, 14,703

Hahukum Kon born, 14,707

Kikaju Jama born, 14,726

Rigone born, 14,762

Nejirt Kambu and Hiranimus Scogil born, 14,765

Eron Osa born, 14,778 GE, watch 328, hour 7; 80,362 AD, 3rd februan, 2nd hour

Frightfulperson Otaria of the Calmer Sea born, 14,784

Petunia Scogil born, 14,797

Story begins 14,790 GE; 80,374 AD; 2722 FE

# Ancient Rithian Measures

From the Cathusian Excalifate's Compendium of Ancient Metric Documents:
Surviving Fragment of an Article on Ancient Metrics by Donald Kingsbury, (probably written before the Great Die-off).

---

## [Basic Instrument:]

. . . commonly acknowledged that we use the time-reckoning devised by ancient astronomers of the Mediterranean. But few of us are aware that the foundation of the linear measures and weights that drove this ancient economy also rests upon that same time framework, the length of the pendulum that completes a full cycle in one sidereal-second, moving to-and-fro 86,400 times while the stars rotate back to the same position in the sky that they held the previous evening.

The ancients might have developed an escapement to keep their pendulums powered but we can't make such an assumption without evidence—however, it is plausible that the priestly team which counted swings either by tossing pebbles in a pot or by flipping beads on an abacus could also be imposed upon to man a small bellows. Puffing at the bob would not compromise the timekeeping as long as the swing angle of the pendulum was controlled.

The one second pendulum is not of constant length, primarily because our planet is a flattened sphere and gravity becomes stronger as we move toward the poles. Pendulum length decreases as the latitude decreases from pole to equator, decreases with increasing altitude, decreases as the swing angle increases, and will depend upon how much air and rock lies below the pendulum. We can expect a normal value well inside the range 0.246 to 0.248 meters. In spite of its variability, the length of the pendulum was the most stable of the lengths available to the ancient geometers.

Since these metricians derived their weight standards by variously dividing a carefully measured cubic foot of water, and since we have reasonable data on these ancient weights, we can calculate from such fossil artifacts the standard length of the pendulum used in ancient times. Livio Stecchini determined that the standard Roman libra was 324 grams and that there were 80 of them to the Roman talent comprising a cubic Roman foot, giving us a Roman talent of 25,920 grams. If we make the assumption—to be justified later—that the Roman foot is 6/5ths of the sidereal-second pendulum we can calculate a standard pendulum length equal to the cube root of 15,000 cc.

Stecchini did all of his work on Roman weights in the metric system, thus we can suspect that rounding error played a part, however, we can also make a similar derivation from the venerable English avoirdupois ounce which is not dependent upon the meter. The avoirdupois ounce (modern value) is 28.34952313 grams, the avoirdupois pound is 453.5923701 grams. The conversion between pound and libra was always via an English pound of 7000 grains and a Roman libra of 5000 grains. Therefore the Roman talent derived from English units is 80 x 323.9945501 grams = 25,919.56401 grams, giving the standard pendulum length as the cube root of 14,999.75 cc.

The cube root of 15,000 cc gives a pendulum of 24.6621 cm or 0.246621 meters.

Can we place a pendulum of this length and period at any reasonable ancient site? Keith P. Johnson has made a very plausible case for the niche in the Queen's Room of the Great Pyramid as housing for one such pendulum. Assuming that the Great Pyramid is on the 30th parallel and located 100 meters above sea level, at a gravity of 9.7930417 m/sec$^2$, we get the following values for the length of the pendulum that beats exactly 86,400 times in one sidereal day:

L = 0.246708 m, for a swing angle of 0 degrees
L = 0.246621 m, for a swing angle of 3.0374 degrees
L = 0.246482 m, for a swing angle of 4.9 degrees
L = 0.246370 m, for a swing angle of 6 degrees

(Do not make the mistake of assuming that gravity measured in meters per second squared is the same as gravity measured in meters per sidereal-second squared.)

Other sites should be investigated. Persian measures are a tad short and suggest that their calibration was done in the mountains around Persepolis, at an altitude of 1890 meters.

### Back Derivation of the Standard Foot

The Roman talent of 25,920 grams was divided into 80 libras of 324 grams, the libra broken into 12 unciae of 27 grams, the uncia broken into 3 shekels of 9 grams. For fine work in precious metals the libra was shaved into 5000 grains.

More conventionally, the sides of this cubic talent of water could be divided integrally to give a variety of weights:

(1) 12 by 12 by 12 = 1728 cubes of 15 grams
(2) 6 by 6 by 6 = 216 cubes of 120 grams
(3) 4 by 4 by 4 = 64 cubes of 405 grams*
(4) 3 by 3 by 3 = 27 cubes of 960 grams
(5) 2 by 2 by 2 = 8 cubes of 3240 grams, ten libra

These kinds of divisions were convenient for a civilization that computed in fractions with an arithmetic so clumsy that they had been forced to invent a calculation-free

---

*This weight, called the mina of the Heraion, is equal to a water filled cube whose sides are three tenths the length of a one sidereal-second pendulum (three Roman inches), or is equal to the wheat filled standard pint ration of 486 cc. It occurs repeatedly in ancient measures—64 in the Roman talent, 70 in the English talent where it is 404.9931876 grams, 72 in the Egyptian artaba of 29,160 grams (1000 ounces Tower), et cetera.

geometry just to get their surveying and geography done in reasonable time. Note that 1000 cubes of 15 grams pile up to make a cube whose side is the one sidereal-second pendulum length at the Great Pyramid.

Thus the Roman foot can be calculated at 6/5ths of the standard one sidereal-second pendulum.

### The Calibration Latitude and the Reference Latitude

It is known from many documents that the ancient navigators calculated 75 Roman miles to a degree of latitude. Since there are 5000 Roman feet in a mile and 360 degrees in a circumference, there are 135 million Roman feet in the circumference of the Earth*, and 375,000 Roman feet in a degree, 6250 in a minute of arc. Multiply these numbers by 6/5 and we get 162 million sidereal-second lengths in the Earth's circumference, 450,000 sidereal-second lengths to the degree, and 7500 sidereal-second lengths to the minute of arc.

What kind of numbers does this give us? Multiplying the pendulum length of 0.246621 meters by 450,000 gives us 110,979.5 meters, which is the number of meters to a degree in the notorious Stecchini latitude at 37°36', which Stecchini claimed was the reference latitude by which the ancients measured the circumference of the Earth. (There are 110,572 meters in a degree of latitude at the equator, 111,697 meters per degree of latitude at the pole, and 111,322 meters per degree of longitude at the equator.) Stecchini, himself, did not believe that the ancients used pendulums, extracting his numbers from old weights and measures, ancient building surveys, and by reading widely among old economic documents, as well as by reading Aristotle, Herodotus, Sumerian inscriptions, Egyptian tomb walls, et cetera.

Note here that the number 1.62 is an approximation to the golden section, 1.61803398. . . . If we were to send out surveyors to measure the length of the degree at 30 degrees of latitude in terms of a standard foot of 0.246621 meters we would get, not 450,000 sidereal-second lengths per degree but 449,454 lengths, which, when multiplied by 360, gives us 161,803,400 such lengths for the circumference (of a sphere tangent to the oblate spheroid) of the Earth at the Great Pyramid. This might be coincidence. Or it might be that the Egyptian astronomer-priests chose the very strange number, 86,400 seconds, to *make* the circumference divisible by the golden section. The Fibonacci numbers, which Fibonacci learned while his father worked as a diplomat in the Middle East, were known in antiquity and provide a very easy tool for computing the golden section if you are limited to an arithmetic heavily dependent upon fractions.

Two critical latitudes emerge once the sidereal clock is set at 86,400 seconds and the circumference at 162 million pendulum lengths.

The Calibration Latitude: To define the length of the pendulum whose period is one sidereal-second we must specify at which latitude our apparatus functions and at what altitude (usually ground level)—while at the same time being careful to confine the pendulum to a predetermined swing angle. At the Great Pyramid the sidereal-second foot cannot be greater than 0.2467 meters, corresponding to a swing angle of zero. At a swing angle of 5 degrees its length would decrease to 0.24647 meters. The evidence is good that in the later period it was calibrated close to 0.246621 meters using a swing

---

*Earth: one of the ancient names that the early Solurthians gave to the planet Rith.

angle of 3.04 degrees. The Egyptian Royal cubit of the King's Chamber of the Great Pyramid, as measured by Petrie, would have been calculated at a swing angle of 4.9 degrees as the 7/6th part of a pendulum with a sidereal cycle of 64,000.

**The Reference Latitude:** Once calibrated, the sidereal-second foot defines a mythical *reference* latitude at which a sphere with a circumference of 162 million feet will be tangent to the inside surface of our flattened planet.

**Example 1:** For a calibration latitude of 30 degrees, altitude 100 meters, and a 3.04 degree swing angle, we get a foot of 0.246621 meters and a reference latitude of 37°36'.

**Example 2:** Other regimes are possible. For instance, a pendulum set up just north of the Black Sea at a calibration latitude of 45°24', altitude of 100 meters, with a normal swing angle of 3.04 degrees will have a length of 0.246956 meters and a reference latitude of 45°24'–this being the *one* latitude at which the calibration and reference latitudes are identical. Stecchini, without invoking pendulums, claims that there is evidence of a very early Egyptian survey team that worked at this latitude from the mouth of the Danube, cutting across the Crimea, and ending at the foot of the Caucasus.

**Example 3:** If we go farther north, say to a calibration latitude 4/7ths of the way from the equator to the pole, a sacred latitude to the Egyptians, we will be setting up our pendulum near the Neolithic site of Avebury in England at 51°25', or even Greenwich in London at 51°28'. In this case our sidereal-second foot is 0.247092 meters and our reference latitude is to the *south* at 48°30'. Probably there was such a pendulum station at this latitude in England because the English foot can be derived from this foot, and, for very good reasons, the standard reference latitude of the British Navy was 48°30'.

## Circles

The ancients used different circle templates depending upon which estimate of pi they employed.

(a) Using $3+1/6 = 3.16667$ for pi and a diameter of 24 we get a circumference of 76. This is the template used for the English foot. Eighty times 76 equals 6080 (8 stadia of 760 feet) which is the number of English feet in a minute of arc, which gives us 131,328,000 English feet in the circumference at the reference latitude of 48°30'.

(b) Using $3+1/8 = 3.125$ for pi and a diameter of 24 we get a circumference of 75. This is the template used for the Nautical foot. Eighty times 75 equals 6000 (10 stadia of 600 feet) which is the number of nautical feet in a minute of arc, which gives us 129,600,000 Nautical feet in the circumference at the specified reference latitude.

The Roman foot also uses this template: $75 \times 1,800,000 = 135$ million, since it is based on a diameter of 43,200,000 feet at its reference latitude.

(c) Using $3+1/7 = 22/7$ for pi and a diameter of 21 we get a circumference of 66. This is the template used for the foot which divides the minute of arc into 5280 feet, since 80 times $66 = 5280$ (8 stadia of 660 feet). This foot is exactly 76/66 times the English foot in length and 75/66 times the Nautical foot in length. The value of 5280 English feet in a mile is probably an error introduced into the English metric system by an error in the translation of Ptolemy's writings from the Arabic which led the unsophisticated Europeans to believe that their planet was smaller than it really was. Early eighteenth century English texts such as *Cocker's Arithmetick* still assumed that there were 5280 English feet in the minute of arc because of this transcription error.

## The Circumference of the Earth

Aristotle's mathematikoi quoted 400,000 stadia as the circumference of the Earth. This is a stadium of 300 feet of a very common Mesopotamian foot, computed as the 60th part of a nine sidereal-second pendulum that divides the Earth's circumference into 120 million parts. It is 27/20ths of the standard sidereal-second pendulum calibrated at the 30th degree of latitude, a foot of 0.33294 meters, and was the commonest foot used in Greece at the time according to Stecchini.

Archimedes quoted 300,000 stadia for the circumference. This is a stadium of 300 Roman cubits. The Roman cubit divides the Earth's circumference into 90 million parts and is 9/5ths of the standard sidereal-second pendulum, 0.44392 meters. It is the 20th part of a six sidereal-second pendulum. The Roman foot is the 30th part of the same pendulum.

Eratosthenes never had to leave his library. All he had to do was dust off a scroll that Alexander had looted from an Egyptian school. He didn't even bother to get the latitude of Alexandria right. His quote of 250,000 stadia in the Earth's circumference is a reference to a stadium of 300 cubits of the standard Great Cubit which divides the Earth's circumference into 75 million parts. It is the 24th part of a pendulum that beats out 12,000 cycles per sidereal day, 2.16 times the sidereal-second length, 0.53270 meters, and was the standard cubit of Egypt in his day.

The Arabic or Black Cubit, which dates to a time much earlier than the Moslem conquests, divides Earth's circumference into 81 million cubits, with 3750 to the minute of arc. At 0.49324 meters it is exactly twice the length of the one sidereal-second foot and was probably computed as the eighth part of a four sidereal-second pendulum.

The Nautical foot which divides the Earth's circumference into 129,600,000 parts, 6000 to the minutes of arc, 100 to the second of arc, is 5/4ths of the one sidereal-second foot. When measured at the sacred latitude of 51°25'43" it is exactly 76/75ths of the English foot, the same ratio used by the British Admiralty.

The Egyptian Royal Cubit . . .

—End of fragment